Other Books by David Gerrold

Novels
The Flying Sorcerers (1971, with Larry Niven)
Space Skimmer (1972)
When H.A.R.L.I.E. Was One (1972, revised edition 1988)
Yesterday's Children (1972)
The Man Who Folded Himself (1973)
Battle for the Planet of the Apes (1973)
Moonstar Odyssey (1977)
Deathbeast (1978)
Star Trek®: The Galactic Whirlpool (1980)
Enemy Mine (1985, with Barry B. Longyear)
Chess With a Dragon (1987)
Star Trek: The Next Generation®: Encounter at Farpoint (1987)
Voyage of the Star Wolf (1990)
Under the Eye of God (1993)
A Covenant of Justice (1994)
The Middle of Nowhere (1995)
Star Trek: Deep Space Nine®: Trials and Tribble-Ations
(1996, with Diane Carey)
The Martian Child (2002)

The War Against the Chtorr
A Matter for Men (1983)
A Day for Damnation (1984)
A Rage for Revenge (1989)
A Season for Slaughter (1993)

Short Fiction
With a Finger in My I (1972)

Non-Fiction
The Trouble With Tribbles (1973)
The World of Star Trek (1973)

THE FAR SIDE
OF THE SKY

THE FAR SIDE OF THE SKY

Jumping Off the Planet
Bouncing Off the Moon
Leaping to the Stars

DAVID GERROLD

SCIENCE
FICTION

First SFBC Science Fiction Printing: June 2002

Published by arrangement with:
Tor Books
Tom Doherty Associates, LLC
175 Fifth Avenue
New York, NY 10010

Visit The SFBC at *http://www.sfbc.com*
Visit Tor at *http://www.tor.com*

ISBN 0-7394-2808-X

CONTENTS

CONTENTS

JUMPING
OFF
THE
PLANET

for Lydia Marano and Art Cover
with love

MOM AND DAD

I'VE GOT AN IDEA!" DAD said. "Let's go to the moon."

"Huh—?" I looked up from my comic.

"I mean it. What do you kids think? Do you want to go to the moon?"

"Yeah, sure," I said, not believing him any more than I had all the other times he'd dangled promises in front of my nose. In the last thirteen years, or at least as much of them as I could remember, he'd promised me the stars, the sky, and a trip to Disneyland. The only time I saw the stars was on TV, the sky was brown, and I still hadn't ridden the Matterhorn bobsleds and probably never would, at least not until I paid for the trip myself. So when he asked me if I'd like to go to the moon, it sounded like just another one of those things that adults say for no other reason than to use up air.

Is it just me, or is there something about grownups? What happens when you turn twenty-one? Does the brain shrivel up automatically or do you have to have an operation where your judgment lobes are removed? Adults can't stay in the same room with a kid without having to talk. Adults think they have to *relate* to me. But I don't want to be *related* to. I want to be left alone.

Dad shows up twice a year. We get him two weeks at a time. "We" includes me, my weird older brother and my stinky younger brother. Sometimes the older brother is stinky and the younger one is weird. I think they've got some kind of a deal where they have to take turns. I hate being the middle kid.

Weird builds worlds. He never shows anybody what he builds, but he spends hours a day at his terminal. He rents processor time from UCLA, and pays for it by fumigating code for the evolutionarily challenged. He's in the scholarship pipeline, so he's deep into the net. As big brothers go, he's not the worst, but he never pulled a bully off me either, so what good is he? Mom and him had a big fight just before my birthday, about his money for college, and his job, and stuff like that. Nothing was resolved, except that things were more sullen than usual, which is hard to do, because sullen is normal in our house. The two of them avoided each other like they had been magnetized in the same direction. It was fascinating to watch. I think they call it a *gavotte*. That's a kind of a dance where everybody moves slowly and carefully and keeps out of everybody else's way. They didn't even talk to each other at my birthday dinner.

That's when Mom announced that Dad would be coming early for us this year and we'd be spending a month with him instead of two weeks. She said it while cutting the cake, like it was supposed to be an extra present for me. She said it was what Dad wanted and she wasn't going to argue about it, it would be good for us to spend a little more time with our father. But I figured she just wanted us *out*. She looked tireder than usual, and she kept saying she wanted out of the war zone. Like she was blaming us. But we didn't ask to be born. Especially Stinky.

Stinky doesn't do much of anything except whine and wet his bed. Dad thinks Mom is ruining him. I think he's already ruined. I once told him he was an accident—the accident that split up Mom and Dad—and that was another multimegaton war. Now I know why they call it the nuclear family. Mom spent half the day trying to calm Stinky down, and the other half on the phone with Dad, and I got all the fallout from everybody.

I spent the next three months trying to stay out of the house as much as possible. I would grab some recordings and my headphones and get on my bike early in the morning and see how far I could ride before it got too hot. Weird says I'm stupid for going up topside in the sun, the tubes are air-conditioned, UV-safe, and have more trees, but he doesn't understand. It's *quieter* up topside. People don't bother you. Sometimes, I try to see how far up the mountain I can get. All I want is a place where I can just sit and listen to my music without anybody interrupting. But when I try to listen at home, all of Mom's sentences begin with, "Charles, if you're not doing anything right now—"And when I tell her I *am* doing something, she says, "No, you're not. You're just listening to your music." Hello? Is anybody home?

We live in Bunker City, which is supposed to be part of El Paso, but it's really just an old tube-city built in a hurry to house refugees from the west, and then prettied up a lot when they didn't go home afterward. So now it's another suburb, sort of.

What it is, is a place where a bunch of tube-houses have been buried up to their armpits in sand. When the wind blows, the sky disappears and we get to spend a week at a time staring at the curved walls of our pipe-rooms. Sometimes the lights flicker and go yellow. Twice we've had outages and had to sit in the dark waiting for the wind farms to come back online. I don't know why a sandstorm should put a wind farm out of commission, except it does. Anyway, sitting alone in the dark with no one to talk to except Weird and Stinky is not my idea of a good time. It doesn't take too long before we're all really hating each other. Weird says that during the sandstorms is when most murders happen. I can understand that.

Anyway, Dad shows up every June and the first couple days are always spent driving somewhere. Usually Colorado or Arizona, although once we went to Mexico for two days. That was like a downtown tube-city with hot sauce. I got to practice my Spanish in a restaurant. I understood two words of the waiter's reply.

Dad works so hard trying to be a *pal* that it's embarrassing. He tells us how much he loves us, how much he misses us, how he wishes we could spend more time together, and we all do the obligatory perform-ances of, "we love you too, Daddy," but it's like acting for a stranger. Who is this guy anyway? Weird just grunts and Stinky just whines and it's up to me to carry on the conversation. And that's about as much fun as kissing your brother. Either one.

Eventually, after two or three days of Dad's earnest attempts to be Dad, Stinky usually does something ghastly, like peeing in the back seat or throwing up into the cooler, and Dad loses his temper, and then everything is back to normal. Nobody talks. Dad turns up the stereo and we listen to Beethoven or Wagner or Tchaikovsky and that's actually not so bad. It's better than trying to talk to each other. Sometimes Dad tells us stories about the music, but not very often.

Dad works for a music consortium, so he knows a lot of gossip about composers and what they were thinking of when they wrote this piece or that. Sometimes he really lights up when he talks about his music and I remember we used to have fun times together when he tried to teach me about conducting—but something happened, I don't know what, and it was like part of the fire went out. Now Dad still listens to music, but he doesn't talk about it so much anymore.

So there we were, in Dad's rented minivan heading west toward someplace in Arizona and suddenly he says, "I've got an idea. Let's go to the moon. What do you think, Chigger?" What was I supposed to say? I said what I felt. So of course, Dad got angry at me. And then Weird and Stinky did too.

But if he didn't want to hear it, then why did he ask?

And why didn't he ask when it was important? It was my family too. Nobody asked me if I wanted it split up. They just did it.

A HOLE IN THE GROUND

I **DON'T KNOW IF THE** Barringer meteor crater is at the end of the world, but I'm pretty sure you can see it from there. If there's a lonelier, uglier, more empty place in the world, I'm sure I don't want to go there.

You drive for hours across the desert, and then there's a sign with an arrow, so you turn off and follow a two-lane road across some more desert, but the road still doesn't look like it's going anywhere. The ground goes up a little, but there's nothing to see except a dinky little building. You go through the building because you have to pay admission, and then you walk out the back, and up a path. Then you go up some stairs and suddenly there you are—standing on the edge and staring down into the biggest hole in the world and saying a lot of stupid things that don't come anywhere near to expressing how deep and scary it really is.

Dad said, "Geezis." Weird said, "Oh, wow!" Stinky said, "Daddy, is that a real hole?" And I said a word that got me a dirty look from all three of them.

It was the biggest empty space I'd ever seen in my life. It was *eerie*. At the bottom, there were some buildings and even a couple of scooters and jeeps. That's how you could tell how big it was.

Weird started reading aloud from the souvenir pamphlet, "The Barringer crater is named for the American engineer, Daniel M. Barringer, who theorized in 1905 that it was caused by the impact of a meteor. The meteor struck the Earth almost head on, 25,000 years before the birth of Christ; it was mostly nickel and iron, 30 meters (100 feet) in diameter—actually, that makes it an asteroid—and weighed 63,000 metric tons. It was traveling 8–16 kilometers, or 5–10 miles, per second. The blast was the equivalent of a 35-megaton nuclear warhead. Most of the asteroid was vaporized, but approximately 30 tons of fragments have been collected. The minerals coesite and stishovite, which can only be formed under very high pressure, have been discovered here.

"The crater is 1.2 kilometers in diameter—that's about three-quarters of a mile. It's 180 meters deep, surrounded by a rim rising 50 meters above the surrounding plain. This wall we're on is 160 feet high. So that makes it 760 feet to the bottom."

I said, "I bet you could put the Empire State Building inside it and it wouldn't show."

"No," said Weird, still reading. "The Empire State Building is 450 meters high—1475 feet. The top half would still be visible."

"You know what I like about you, Douglas?" I said.

"No, what?"

"Nothing."

"Hey, it says so right here, Chigger—" He waved the pamphlet at me. I slapped it away.

"All right. Knock it off, you two," Dad said. We both turned away from each other, annoyed.

The four of us were all alone on that crater wall. If there was anyone else around, we didn't see them. Not even at the bottom of the crater. All around us everything was very hot and very silent and very dark all the way down. There was no wind. It was like being frozen in time. The whole bottom of the crater was one big shadow. And it looked haunted. It made me queasy.

"Look," said Weird, pointing. "There's a path. I'll bet it goes all the way down."

"Where?"

"There." He pointed. It spiraled around and down. The crater walls were too steep to get to the bottom any other way. Stinky started being Stinky almost immediately. "Can we go down there, huh? Huh?" He didn't wait for an answer. He just started running along the path.

Dad hollered, "No, wait—" but Stinky didn't stop. So Dad poked me and said, "Go, get him."

"Uh—" I didn't want to say that the height of the crater and the steepness of the wall scared me. "If I chase him, he'll just keep running. If we just stand here, he'll give up and come back—"

"And what if he slips and falls?" said Dad. "*Go get him.*"

I looked to Weird for support, but he just pushed me forward. "Go on, Chigger."

"You too!" I demanded.

"*Both of you, go after him! Now!*" said Dad. Weird pushed me again, and I was off. Behind me, I heard Dad say, "You too, Douglas!"

I could hear him following behind me, but it didn't sound like he was making much of an effort. Apparently he thought this was just a kid thing, not worthy of serious geek attention.

The path was narrow and steep and scary. It was like running down the side of a wall. I tried not to look off to my left, where there was nothing at all except a lot of nothing at all. Maybe it was all that time living in a tube-town, I just didn't like big open spaces—and this was the biggest and openest I'd ever seen. So I didn't look. And if I didn't see it, then it wasn't there. I hoped.

"Stinky, you stop right there!" I called after him, but he giggled and shouted back, "You can't catch me. You can't catch me." He kept running and laughing, like it was all a game. And to tell the truth, it was almost kinda fun running down and around the crater wall. It was all downhill, so it was easy running. You let yourself go loose and then you just keep falling forward and let your feet lump down in front of you. If only there wasn't that big *hole* there—I slowed down automatically—

"Come on, Chigger!" Weird said impatiently. He gangled past me.

I looked back. Dad was following after us, but he wasn't running, just walking fast.

And then Stinky slipped at the first switchback and skidded off the path, which would have been warning enough to any rational person that running down the side of a hole big enough to have its own area code was not a good idea—but Stinky didn't have good ideas. He picked himself up, shouted, "You're a big doo-doo head, and you can't catch me," and headed toward the next switchback.

"Bobby! Stop it! If you slip, you'll roll all the way down. You could get killed—!" But he didn't pay any more attention to me than I paid to Dad. He just kept shouting and taunting.

I wondered if I could cut him off, but that would have meant taking the short-and-fast way down, and I *really* didn't want to do that. So I slowed down for the turn, tried not to look, and kept after the little bastard. Behind me, I could hear Dad shouting, "Go get him, Charles!" as if it was *my* fault he'd run down here.

Eventually Weird caught up with Stinky, and so did I. Weird grabbed Stinky's arm and they skidded along the path for a bit, and for a moment I thought they were going to lose it and just go on down the side, but then their feet caught and they stopped. And then Weird started yelling at Stinky about how dangerous it was to run down the side of a steep hill. "You almost slipped! What do you think you were doing? You'd have rolled and bounced all the way down to the bottom. You'd have been killed!"

"Yeah!" I said. "And then we'd not only have to walk down to get you, we'd have to carry you back up." Weird gave me his weird look. "Well, we *would*."

Stinky didn't say anything, he just did that nasty hate-stare that he's so good at, and we all stood around for a minute not talking, just catching our breath, waiting for Dad to get to us. We hadn't gotten very far down the side of the crater. Most of it was still below us, but we'd come a long way anyway, at least half a klick, maybe more.

It wasn't until Dad showed up that Stinky started talking again. "I wasn't gonna fall it isn't fair I wanna go to the bottom Dad make him let me go *let go of me!*" And then he did wriggle free and started running down the path again. And Weird and I had to go after him again. With Dad *walking* behind. This time Stinky was running away just to be nasty. "You can't catch me, neener, neener, neener!"

I was so angry, I started after him—which was *exactly* what he wanted. Only, I wasn't going to yell at him like Weird. I was going to gut-punch him like he deserved. No matter what Dad said. Weird came running after the both of us.

The path went back and forth down the side of the crater in a series of switchbacks. The first one turned so sharply, it was hard to stop and turn back the other way. If you're going to fall, that's where it's most likely to happen. And that's where he did slip—

Stinky was shouting and looking back, not watching where he was going, and he stumbled over a bump and bounced face forward and slid down the slope—and for a moment, that queasy feeling in my gut turned into a flash of black fear that he was going to slide all the way down—but then he stopped sliding in a patter of loose dirt and gravel and just hung there on the steep side of the crater wall, caught on a tiny bush. "Don't move!" I screamed. "Don't move!" And I knew even as I said it, that he would do exactly the opposite, because that was the kind of stupid little monster he was.

Except—he didn't move. He was too scared to move. He was screaming as loud as he could. "Daaaa-ddeeee!"

"Just hold on," I called. I was the closest. I looked back and Weird was just coming around the last switchback. What I really wanted to say to Stinky was, "This is your own fault. We told you not to go—" But I was close enough to see how scared he was and as angry as I was at him, I was even more scared *for* him. "Just don't move, I'm coming to get you—" If only I could figure out how.

Stinky had slipped about five meters down the slope. It was mostly dirt, with only a few little things pretending to be plants. He'd caught on a scraggly little bush that didn't look strong enough to hold him. It was already bending precariously, and I was certain it was going to snap before I could get to him.

The problem was that the slope was too steep for me. If I tried to go down it, I'd just go skidding all the way down to the bottom. And it was a long way down. There was that queasy sensation again. Heights. Open spaces. Holes. Everything. I couldn't explain it. And there was no way to get down underneath Stinky either, to catch him. I said a word, the one that Mom always tells me not to say.

"Charles! Go get him!" That was Dad, always full of good advice . . . from a distance.

I couldn't see how—the only thing I could think of was to lie down flat on the ground and try to inch my way downward, and even that seemed like a really stupid idea, because if I slipped, we'd both go rolling a hundred meters to the floor of the crater. Only it looked farther. I began edging myself down the slope, all the time muttering through gritted teeth, "Just hang on, Bobby! Just hang on—" I went from hand-hold to handhold. There weren't any rocks or weeds strong enough to hang onto.

I couldn't get close enough. I anchored myself as best as I could and unbuckled my belt, pulling it out of my pants as safely as I could. I let the end hang down toward Stinky. He could almost reach it, but it would have meant letting go. "No, wait—I'll try to get lower."

And that's when I froze. I realized I couldn't move either. Not up, not down. My mouth was dry and I couldn't swallow—and the great empty hole yawned beneath us. We were stuck on the wall, just waiting to slide down. I knew it then—we were both going to die here. And it really pissed me off. This was not how I'd planned my life—

"Chigger, wait!" That was Douglas, above me. I turned my head. He was just taking off his belt. He wrapped one end around his hand, then stretched out flat on the ground. He lowered his belt to me and I grabbed hold. There was just enough to loop it around my wrist and grab the buckle. I wanted to beg him to pull me up, but Stinky was starting to lose his grip below me. He was whining and crying the way that he did when all hell was threatening to break loose around him— all that somebody had to do now was tell him to shut up and he'd start flailing and screaming. It was very tempting.

"Okay, Stinky!" I said. "Look at me."

It worked; I got his attention. "Don't call me that!" he cried angrily.

"All right, but you have to look at me. I'm going to lower my belt. Don't reach for it until I tell you, okay? Because you're only going to get one chance. I'm coming down now—"

Still holding onto the end of Douglas's belt, I edged downward, just a little bit at first—I felt myself start to slide—and Douglas caught the slack instantly. Some rocks and pebbles rolled away around me. But I didn't follow them. I might live through this after all. "A little bit more, Doug. I'm almost there." I looped my belt around my other wrist, like Douglas had done, and lowered it to Stinky. It almost reached. I stretched as far as I could.

"Okay, kiddo," I said. "On three—"

"I can't do it!" he whined. "*I can't!*"

"Yes, you can," said Douglas. "Just listen to me—"

That wasn't going to work, Stinky never listened to anyone, "No, Doug, Stinky's right. He can't reach it. *Stinky's just a little baby.* He can't do *anything*—"

It worked. Before I'd finished the sentence, Stinky had swung and grabbed the end of my belt and nearly yanked me off the wall of the crater, he grabbed so hard. Without thinking, I pulled back in response, and Doug pulled on me, and Dad was there pulling on Doug, and somehow we all ended up back on the path, Doug against Dad with Dad holding him tight, and me against Doug with Doug holding me, and Stinky in my arms, hanging onto me like a human death-grip. The four of us just stayed like that for the longest time, all of us trying to catch our breaths at once.

I kept my eyes closed. Because when I opened them, all there was to see was how deep the crater was and how high we were—and all that empty space made me want to throw up more than ever now.

Eventually we untangled ourselves—very carefully. It would have been real stupid to fall down the hole now. Dad looked gray and shaken, but he waved me off when I asked if he was all right. He looked like he wanted to say something, but then he looked like he didn't know what—finally he just waved his hand as if to erase everything and pointed back up the path.

Douglas took Stinky by the hand to follow him—and of course, Stinky tried to pull away. "Let me go!" he whined. "I gotta go to the bathroom! I gotta pee!" That was what he always said when he didn't want to cooperate. And it usually worked, because what if he was telling the truth?

But right now—Weird wasn't letting go.

"Go ahead," I said, coming up to block his other side. He wasn't running away again.

"Where?" he demanded.

"I dunno," I said in that really bland, passive-aggressive voice I'd learned to use on him. "Do you see a bathroom around here?"

He looked around. We were a quarter of the way down the wall of the biggest hole in the world, and we could see forever in all directions. There were no bathrooms, no water faucets, no elevators, no nothing. Stinky started crying, "But I gotta pee!"

"Well, then, just pee!"

"Where?"

"Here!"

"But everybody'll see!"

"There's no one to see! And besides we're so far away from everything, no one could see anything anyway. Just go!"

"I can't!"

"Then hold it till we get back to the top!"

"I can't! It's too far!"

"We told you not to come running down."

"But I gotta go!"

"Then go here!"

"I can't!"

The kid was paralyzed. No matter what anyone said, all he could say was "I can't!" So I said, "Well then, just pee in your pants and stop *whining!*"

So he did.

Now he was wet, uncomfortable, and smelled bad. But this wasn't as bad as when he threw up in the cooler and spoiled everyone's lunch, and at least now that we'd gotten Stinky's first accident out of the way, we could get on with the fun part of the trip. Ha ha.

By this time Dad had realized we weren't following. When he got back down to us, Weird was yelling at Stinky, "Why did you pee in your pants?" and Stinky was crying full blast that I'd told him to.

That's when Dad did something strange. Stranger than usual. He didn't say anything at all. He stopped where he was and sat down. He put his elbows on his knees and his chin in his hands and he just sat and stared and looked sullen in that way he gets when he's thinking real hard about something—like a bad decision. I was sure he was thinking about turning around and taking us all back to El Paso.

"Now look what you've done—" I began to say to Stinky, but Weird swatted me hard across the chest with the back of his hand and told me to shut up, which actually startled me into silence, because Weird almost never touches anyone, let alone me.

"What's he doing?" Stinky asked.

Weird shook his head and grunted. "I dunno." He sounded kinda faraway when he said it. That's when I figured out that something was going on, but nobody had told me yet. Whatever Weird knew, he wasn't saying.

GEEKS

DAD? ARE YOU ALL RIGHT?" Weird asked.

Dad took a deep breath. "I was thinking about the moon." He pointed out at the big emptiness below us. "On the moon, there are craters this size everywhere. And bigger ones too. There's nothing special about a crater on the moon. Could you imagine living every day of your life in a place like this?"

Weird didn't answer. Neither did I. How do you answer a question like that? We just looked at each other.

Dad took another breath. "Y'know, people say that kids are the hope of the future—that a baby is the human race's way of insisting that the universe give us another chance. But I don't know. Sometimes it feels like a baby is just another chance to screw things up even worse than before. There's so much you kids don't understand, and I wish I could explain it to you, but I can't, because I'm not sure I understand it myself. And I can't ask you to forgive us because . . . well, I don't have the excuse that we did our best, because I know we didn't."

I'd never heard Dad talk like this before and it sort of scared me. It was kind of like one of those movies where someone knows he's going to die soon and is trying to get all his good-byes said in two minutes. And everybody else is supposed to forgive him for being a jerk. I don't know why they always forgive each other. I wouldn't.

But whatever Dad was talking about, I didn't think he was dying. Instead, he started talking about the world and the mess it was in and all that kind of stuff. Corporate warfare. Chocolate dollars. Sugar dollars. Beef dollars. Oil dollars. Plastic dollars. Kilocalorie dollars. Silicon dollars. Cyber-dollars. All of them spreading into new territories, like so many economic disease vectors, leaving a trail of infected and collapsing economies behind them. Governments unable to control their own economies because international corporatism had made all borders irrelevant. Money flowed like water seeking its level. Where it got too hot, steam rose—where it got cold again, rain fell. The economic weather was turning into a tropical storm and circling to become a global hurricane of dollars funneling around and around. According to Dad.

I couldn't see exactly how or why it would affect us, but he said it was "tear-down time." Every so often, people just get tired and frustrated with building—every twenty or thirty years or so, they start tearing down what the last generation built, even if it still works, just to tear something down and rebuild it. So the money was circling like flies, unwilling to land anywhere. Only this time, it wasn't landing. It was *going away.* That was why we didn't have the money for the reclamation projects or the recycling we needed and why everything was getting worse.

"This planet is no place to raise a family," he said bitterly. "It's just a matter of time until the whole planet turns into Calcutta." That part I understood. There were plagues in Calcutta. All over India. And Rome too. Black Peritonitis. African Measles. Europe was shutting itself down in panic, and brushfire wars had broken out all up and down the eastern half of Asia. Fifth World revolutions. Wars and plagues. Craziness everywhere. The planet didn't have the resources to manage itself anymore. Like the guy on TV said, "The machinery is breaking down faster than we can fix it."

"The problem is, we're all in it together, whether we want to be or not," Dad said. "More and more I look around at the way things are going, and I don't want to be part of it anymore. When I was your age, Charles, everything seemed so simple and easy. You don't know how easy it is to be a kid—"

"Yeah, right."

"—but then I grew up and everything got complex, and I just wish I could figure out how to get back to what's really important. You don't understand any of this, do you? And you won't, not until you turn forty." He sighed. "But wouldn't you just like to get up and go away sometime? Someplace new, where you can start fresh?"

Well, yeah. But there isn't any such place. It's all people, everywhere. So it's silly to dream of it. The best you can do is go up in the hills once in a while and listen to your music alone. But I didn't say any of this aloud. Why bother? In three and a half weeks, we'd be back in the war zone with Mom again.

I knew Dad wanted me to say something, but I'd stopped doing that a long time ago. There was no cookie there. When he realized I was simply waiting for him to do something, he stood up and brushed the dirt from his pants. "Well, come on, let's get going." He pointed toward the rim of the crater and we all started hiking upward. It was a difficult climb, not because it was too steep—it was just hard because it was all *up*.

Stinky whined the whole way that it was too hard and kept demanding that someone carry him, but no one wanted to touch him because he smelled so bad. I said, "You shoulda thought of that before you started running down." Then Weird made one of his pseudo-profound observations about how it's easier to cooperate with gravity than fight it, like this meant something, so I called him a techno-geek, and he said, "Yeah, so?"

Dad started to say something about that, one of those comfort-lies that grownups tell, but Weird interrupted him. "No, Dad—everybody's a geek about something. I *am* a techno-geek. You're a music-geek. And Charles is a nastiness-geek because he doesn't have anything else to be geeky for." It was the longest paragraph I'd ever heard out of Weird that didn't have the word gigabyte in it. I didn't have the breath left to tell him what he was full of. I just grunted, "Devour my richard," which is the polite way of saying it. "And Stinky's a pee-geek," I added, just a little louder.

"Daddy—" Stinky wailed.

"Well, it's your own damn fault! Dad told you not to go running down! Now we've all got to hike back up—"

At this point, Dad should have been screaming at all of us to shut up. Instead, he stopped. He squatted down in front of Stinky to look at him eye-to-eye. "There's a lesson here," he said.

"Huh?" Stinky rubbed his eyes.

"Do you know what it is?" Dad asked.

Stinky shook his head slowly.

"Two things. First—*never* go anywhere unless you know how you're going to get back. Look down. Suppose we had let you go all the way down to the bottom. Do you think you could climb all the way back up to the top? Look how much trouble you're having going just this short way."

"It's not a short way!" Stinky wailed. "It's a long way."

Dad ignored him. "And the second lesson—go to the bathroom *before* you go anywhere. Either that or learn to poop in the bushes."

"I wanna go home," Stinky said flatly. "I wanna go home *now*."

Dad responded with that grunt of resignation he does so well, whenever he realizes that whichever one of us he's talking to isn't really listening. Without saying another word, he straightened and started back up the crater wall. If he was angry, it was a kind of anger I'd never seen before. He didn't show any emotion at all. I looked at Weird, but he was pushing Stinky up the slope and no one was looking at me and I wondered why I had bothered to come at all. Here we were, standing inside the biggest hole in the world where a ton of rock had fallen out of the sky and blasted a hole so deep you could put a roof on it and have a stadium large enough for the Godzilla Bowl—and the only important lesson to be learned from our visit was that you should go to the bathroom before you went anywhere. Sheesh.

We finally got to the top and Weird took Stinky into the bathroom and got him cleaned up and into some fresh clothes, while Dad and I sat on a bench and sipped sodas and waited. Dad didn't say anything. He was still off somewhere else. On the moon, I guess.

"We're really screwed up, aren't we?"

Dad looked up. "Eh?"

"Us," I said. "Weird and Stinky and me. We're not exactly the Happy Family." He looked at me blankly. "The Happy Family, like on TV? You know? George and June and all the little Happys."

Dad got it then. "Nobody is the Happy family," he said. "Not even the Happys. It's all pretend."

"Yeah, but we can't even *pretend* to be happy. We're really screwed." I don't know why I said the next part, it just fell out of my mouth. "I don't blame you for hating us."

Dad looked startled. "I don't hate you," he said. "I love you, Charles. More than you realize. All of you. And—" this was where his voice got funny "—I don't think you're screwed up. None of you. I think you're terrific kids. I wish I could spend more time with you."

"Yeah, like *this*—" I waved my hand in the direction of the crater "—is a lot of fun."

"For me, it is. I'm sorry you're not having a good time."

"I'm having an okay time," I admitted. The crater had been interesting enough. Because it was so big. Living in Tube-Town, you never really got an idea of the size of anything.

Dad sighed. "I really do wish I could live with you and be a real father. All the time. Maybe it *would* be better for all of us."

"Yeah, well then why don't you?"

"It's a long story."

"I'm not going anywhere."

"Your mom—" He stopped himself. He said something else instead of what he almost said. "Your mom is a good woman. She works very hard for you boys. I'd live closer to you if I could. She asked me not to. She thinks it would be . . . disruptive."

"Yeah, so? Don't you get a vote?"

Dad shook his head. "It's too complicated to explain." He looked at me sadly. "You really are having a bad time of it, aren't you?"

"I'll do better in my next life, okay?"

"Charles . . ." Dad began carefully, his voice as serious as I'd ever heard it. "I want to ask you something—"

But before he could ask, Weird and Stinky came back, and Stinky started crying immediately that he wanted a soda too. And then he wanted something from the souvenir rack, and whatever Dad had wanted to ask me was forgotten while Weird and Stinky played another round of I-Wanna-No-You-Can't. Dad sighed and patted me on the shoulder. "Later, Charles." I followed him into the souvenir part of the store, where he tried unsuccessfully to steer Stinky's attention toward the cheaper toys.

Finally, they compromised on a programmable monkey—which struck me as being sort of redundant, especially for Stinky, but maybe it would keep him quiet for a while. Dad even bought some extra memory for the monkey. He was chatting with the lady behind the counter while she rang up the sale and suddenly she offered him some old memory cards that someone else had used and returned and she couldn't resell as new, so Dad bought them at half-price. It was a lot of memory, but Dad bought it all. He even paid cash, which for him is *serious*. Credit dollars are a lot more flexible, even though they're not worth as much. Weird offered to install them, but Dad insisted on doing it himself. "Let me prove I'm good at something besides paying the bills," he said as he snapped them into the monkey's backside.

Later, when we were back in the car and on the road again, with Stinky in the back happily trying to teach the monkey how to fart, I asked, "Dad, you were going to ask me something back there—?"

"Never mind," he said. "It wasn't important."

Only we both knew he was lying. Whatever it was.

FINDING THE LINE

MEXICO IS HOT. HOTTER THAN Arizona. Maybe hotter than Hell. And there are these little tiny lizards, small as bugs, everywhere. They flicker across the sidewalk so fast, they look like heat ripples.

The surprising thing was how clean everything was. Everybody in Bunker City says that Mexico is dirty, the streets are dirty, and the people are dirty. But it isn't like that at all. Everywhere we went, everything was hot and bright and clean. Cleaner than Bunker City. Which just proved what I already knew. When people don't know what they're talking about, they make stuff up.

And the Mexicans were friendly too. Dad's Spanish wasn't all that good, but Weird and I knew enough to get by, and where we didn't, there was usually someone else around who spoke enough English to help. So we weren't going to starve to death.

We headed south on the new highway. Dad didn't talk much, not about where we were going. He said it was a *Magical Mystery Tour*, which meant that you weren't supposed to know where you were going until you got there, so the fun had to be in the going, not the arrival; but I was pretty sure Dad had a destination in mind. Every so often I'd catch him muttering about travel times and schedules, so I knew this trip wasn't as random as he kept saying.

We stayed our first night in Mexico at a Best Inn, which is two lies in as many words, but never mind. We were on the eastern coast of the Gulf of Baja, somewhere in the middle of nowhere, with dirty blue ocean to the west and scruffy brown desert to the east and some purple hills in the distance beyond that.

After dinner, there wasn't much of anything to do except stand around watching Stinky playing on the swings with his monkey or look up at the stars. They were a lot brighter here than they were in El Paso. In fact, in El Paso, we could hardly see them at all, so it was something different to just look up at the sky and see how bright it really was. Weird saw a shooting star, and then I saw one too. Dad pointed out Orion's belt and the Big Dipper and a couple of other constellations as if they meant something. I asked him where Sirius was and Betelgeuse and some of the other places where the brightliners went, but he didn't know. Dad said that Sirius was the North Star, so all we had to do was look north, but Weird said no, Polaris was the North Star, not Sirius.

Dad ignored it. Instead, he pointed south. "Look, you can almost see the beanstalk from here."

We squinted into the darkness. I couldn't see anything. Not at first.

"Look for a very, very thin line," Dad said. "Find the line. It'll be high. Up out of the shadow cone. About ten o'clock high. Maybe eleven o'clock."

Weird was the first. "I think I see it," he said. "Is that it?"

"Where?"

"There."

"Oh—oh yeah!"

It was like looking at a razor blade edge on. It shimmered in and out of existence. First it was there, then it wasn't. We could only see a little bit of it, but even so, it seemed to stretch impossibly upward against the darkness. The orbital elevator, a braided strand of monofilament nearly 72,000 kilometers long.

"We should be able to see it better tomorrow night," Dad said. As if that meant something. "It's the stepping-stone to the stars."

His voice sounded so wistful I turned to look at him. I hadn't heard him sound that way about anything for years—the last time was when he guided me through the fourth movement of Copland's Third Symphony, showing me why it was such a masterpiece. It was when I was nine and got to sit in on the rehearsal for one of his concerts. He was very proud that day. He introduced me to everybody. I sat behind him on the podium, and every so often he would stop to explain something to me—and to the musicians as well. But we'd never done it again after that, and I always wondered what I'd done wrong. Not too long after that, the arguments between him and Mom started getting worse, and he'd started staying away more and more, and then Mom moved us to El Paso to be closer to Gramma and Grampa, only they died—

"Would you like to go there someday?" Dad asked.

"Huh?—Where?"

Dad pointed to the sky. "Anywhere. Out there."

"You mean, the star colonies?"

"Sure."

"You'd have to win the lottery. Two lotteries."

"Mm, maybe. Maybe not," Dad said. "Some of the colonies will pay your way if you'll promise to stay for seven years. And if you have a needed skill. And children."

"Indentured servitude," said Weird. "That means you'd be a slave."

"It's not so bad, Douglas. The jobs all fall under the guidelines of the Corporate Treaty of Singapore."

"Yeah, Dad—and who enforces the rules eight point three light-years from Singapore?"

"The Treaty Authority has offices wherever there are indentures. And the locals are very strict about self-enforcement. Most of them were slaves once too, before they worked off their debts."

"I can't believe we're even having this conversation," Weird said, suddenly angry. "Mom would drop her load. Are you *seriously* considering it?" I could see him thinking about Grampa and all the stories he used to tell about great-great-umpty-great-Grampa and what it was like to actually *be* a slave.

"It's a way out, that's all I'm saying," Dad said.

"A way out of what?"

"Here. This." Dad gestured vaguely around. "I'm just trying to say something, that there are still plenty of opportunities for a good life. If not here, then out there. You pay the price however you can."

"It's too high," said Weird.

"I just want you to have a good life, son—I want you to know that there might be more possibilities than you've considered."

"Not for me." Weird said, and the way he said it was like a door slamming.

Dad looked at him sharply, as if trying to figure out who he really was. Finally he said, "You grew up too fast. I hardly know you."

Weird didn't answer that. He just shook his head in disgust and turned and walked away from us. I couldn't tell what he was thinking. What was he angry about? Nobody was going anywhere. So why were we arguing again? Probably because that's who we were. The Crankys—not even in the same neighborhood as the Happys.

Dad looked at me glumly. "And what do you think?"

I shrugged.

"You think I'm a pretty lousy dad too, don't you?"

The question caught me by surprise. "Huh, no—I don't think that." But even as I said it, I knew that I was lying.

"Charles, I can see it in your face. You're almost always angry. I can hear it in your voice."

I shrugged again. What else could I do?

You see what I mean about adults and the way they talk to kids? When they finally make up their mind to really talk to you honestly, they want you to be just as honest with them in return, even when you both know that if you tell the truth, it's only going to make things worse. *Really* worse.

The hell with it.

I said, "I don't think you're a lousy dad. How should I know what kind of a dad you are? You're never there."

My words hurt him. I could see that.

"I'm sorry you feel that way, Charles."

"Me too. I wanted a real dad."

I started to follow Weird, but Dad grabbed my arm.

"Hey," he said. "Give me a chance. Please? We don't have a lot of time together, Charles. Can't we make the best of it?"

I shrugged. "Whatever." But I still tried to wiggle out of his grasp.

"What's it going to take to reach you, kiddo?"

"I dunno." And I really didn't. This time, Dad let me go. I knew he was hurt, but I didn't know what he wanted and I didn't know how to give it to him, and even if I did, I wasn't sure I wanted to.

THE GULF

WE DROVE SOUTH, DOWN THE coast of Mexico, and by the end of the second day it was obvious where Dad was headed: Beanstalk City in Ecuador. He didn't have to say anything. After all of his talk about space and the moon and the stars as a way out, where else could we be going?

Weird had been real silent all day, but Stinky had gotten the way he gets and he kept demanding to sit in the front seat so he could watch for the beanstalk, so Weird and I let him. I was kind of interested in the beanstalk myself, but I didn't want Dad to know it.

But finally, I couldn't stand it anymore. I asked, "We are going up, aren't we? At least as far as One-Hour, huh? Huh, Dad? Please?" Weird and I did a couple of rounds of this, until Stinky joined in for the chorus.

Dad smiled, satisfied. "I was sort of planning on it. Actually . . ." His voice trailed off.

"What?" I demanded.

"It's a shame to come all this way and not go to the top. I was thinking of taking you boys all the way up to Geostationary. That is, if you want to go that high . . . ?"

"Geostationary? *Really?*"

"I assume that's a yes. How about you, Douglas?"

Weird just grunted. "Does Mom know?"

Dad hesitated. "I didn't tell her we were going this far. We can call her from the top, okay? We'll surprise her."

"Let's call collect," I said. "And *really* surprise her."

Dad laughed at that. "Your Mom is taking a vacation of her own. At least, that's what she told me. But we can try to call her, if you want."

"Yeah!" Stinky said. "I wanna call Mom from the top."

"Then it's settled."

Weird said, "Dad, we gotta talk. You and me."

"Right now?"

"No. Just you and me."

"All right," Dad said. "There's a beach up ahead. Why don't we let your brothers play in the surf for a while."

"There's no surf here. This is the Gulf of Baja." Weird was like that. If you told him it was 6:30, he'd check his watch and announce, "six twenty-eight and thirty seconds." Like it made a difference.

"Check the map," Dad said dryly. "We're already to the mouth of the gulf, just north of Mazatlan." I guess Weird inherited it from Dad.

Dad pulled the car off the road onto a wide patch of packed dirt that served as a parking lot. There was no one else around, so Stinky and I stripped down naked and went running into the water, screaming. The sand was so hot we danced across it, keeping our feet in the air more than on the ground.

The water was warm and salty and didn't smell bad at all. Stinky and I splashed around and screamed at each other. The sand under the water was as soft as mud, but there were rocks in the sand too, so mostly I floated on my back and paddled gently, just lazing in the sensation of not having to go anywhere or do anything. After that got old, I just stood and watched Stinky. He wasn't doing anything, so I looked up onto the beach. Dad and Weird were talking about something; I couldn't tell what, but it looked serious.

"I gotta pee," Stinky said.

"Go ahead," I said.

"Right here?"

"Right here."

"Shouldn't I get out of the water?"

"I hardly think it matters."

"But I hafta get out of the pool when I hafta pee, why don't I hafta get out of the ocean?"

"Because it's the ocean. Everybody pees in the ocean."

"Teacher says that's why the oceans are so stinky. Because everybody pees in them. And poops too."

"Go ahead. I won't tell."

"I already did," Stinky said. "I made the water warmer. Didn't you feel it?"

"No, I didn't." And I was just as glad I hadn't. I moved a little bit away from him anyway and watched the water lapping around us, wondering how long it would take to dilute his little contribution.

Dad and Weird were apparently through talking. Dad was leaning against the van with his hand over his eyes as if he had a headache, or maybe he was crying. Weird was walking down the beach, kicking at the sand. Every so often, he'd stop and look back at Dad, and then he'd turn around and walk a ways farther. But it was clear he wasn't going to walk too far. He was just angry. That was weird—even for Weird, because he never got angry. And now, this trip, he'd been angry almost since we'd left. What was going on between them anyway?

Stinky started coughing then—he'd gotten a mouthful of water, so I had to duck under and grab him and pull him up. It wasn't really anything, but he started crying anyway, so I picked him up and carried him as far as I could across the hot sand. Dad met us halfway and took Stinky from me. "What did you do to him?" he asked accusingly.

"I didn't do anything!" I protested. "Don't yell at me. He did it himself. He was fooling around and got water up his nose. I pulled him out."

"I'll deal with you later," Dad said, turning his attention instead to Stinky's tears.

"Yeah, right. Tell me again how you're trying to reach out to me too." I grabbed a towel and my shorts and stalked up the beach after Weird. "Hey, Douglas—wait up!"

It was my use of his real name that made him stop. He glowered, but he waited for me. "What do you want, Chigger?"

"Nothing."

We walked in silence for a bit, while I tried to figure out what to say. Occasionally, Douglas stopped to pick up seashells. He'd look at them for a bit, then hand them to me. They were little gray things that looked like cornucopias. "Periwinkles," he said. "They always spiral out the same way. Clockwise. How do you think the periwinkle knows which way to turn?"

I shrugged. "Who cares?"

"I dunno. It's just—how come periwinkles are so stupid but they always know which way to turn, and human beings are so smart and we hardly ever know?"

"I don't know what you're talking about, Douglas." I tossed the shells away.

"It doesn't matter."

"Yes, it does. I'm part of this family too."

"It's not your business—"

"Now you're acting like Dad," I said. Doug gave me the sidewise glower, so I blurted, "Well, just because Dad's acting like an asshole doesn't mean you have to."

Douglas shook his head.

"Well what's going on?"

"Never mind."

"Tell me—"

"It's kinda personal, okay?"

"So?"

He gave me the look. The one when somebody says something too stupid to reply to.

"So?" I repeated, pretending I hadn't seen it. "Who else do you have to talk to?"

"It's not anything I want to talk about."

"It's about UCLA, isn't it?"

"Partly," he admitted. And then after another moment, he said, "I got approved for a conditional scholarship. Dad won't sign, but he doesn't have to. I'm almost eighteen, but—" He stopped himself. "You don't know what's going on, do you? Between Mom and Dad, I mean."

"They hate each other. What's to understand?"

"Mom thinks Dad is crazy. She went to court last month to have his visitation rights terminated. Dad counter-sued. He had some big New York lawyer on his side, so he won. Now he gets us four weeks a year instead of two. But Mom still thinks he's going to try something."

"Like what?"

"Like not bringing us back. Or something stupid like that."

"Dad isn't that crazy. Where would he take us?"

"Well . . . think about it, Chig. What's he been talking about?"

I thought about it. It didn't take much thinking. "Oh," I said, a sinking feeling in my gut.

"Uh-huh," said Weird.

We walked for a while, neither of us speaking, just pushing forward through the sand, while I sorted stuff out in my head.

Finally, I said, "So if Dad isn't trying to kidnap us, then Mom is schizo-paranoid. And if he *is*, then she's right and *he's* crazy. But either way, *we* lose—because either way we've inherited the genes of a crazy parent."

Douglas half-smiled, that funny expression he gets when somebody says something scientifically.

"So, how do you know all this?" I asked.

"Mom told me. She told me not to tell you. She said you'd side with Dad."

"Mom obviously doesn't know me as well as she thinks. I'm not on either of their sides." And then I realized what else Douglas had said. "You didn't keep your promise."

"It's our family too. I'm tired of all this back-and-forth stuff and nobody ever listening. Aren't you?"

I stared at my older brother as if I'd never seen him before. I couldn't remember him ever being so . . . so adult. Finally, I said, "Thanks, Doug." And I meant it. After another minute, I asked, "But what were you and Dad arguing about?"

"My scholarship. Dad doesn't want me to take it. He doesn't like the conditions."

"What conditions?"

Doug shook his head with a sad smile. "It's kinda personal."

"It's one of those rechanneling scholarships, isn't it?"

"You know something, Charles? You're too smart for your own good."

"I *knew* it."

"You don't know the half of it."

"Well, you *can't* do that. You won't be *you* anymore."

"Yes, I will—" He looked like he wanted to say more, but suddenly, Dad was honking the car horn at us. He'd finally calmed down Stinky and put him in the front seat, and the two of them had motored half a kilometer up the road to catch up to us. Douglas nudged me and we headed across the hot sand to meet them.

It was all too much. I didn't know what to think anymore.

GOING SOUTH

AFTER THAT, WE GOT BACK on the InterContinental Expressway. It was Doug's turn to drive, and he immediately pushed the speed up to 160 klicks, until Dad told him to back off a bit. Doug eased back to 150 and Dad began muttering again about estimated time of arrival and beanstalk schedules and stuff like that.

We skipped staying in a motel that night, while the two of them took turns driving and sleeping all the way down to Puerto Vallarta, where Dad turned in the car and we got on board the SuperTrain Express, which would take us south through Central America and straight to Beanstalk City at speeds up to 360 klicks—225 mph. Dad said we'd be in Beanstalk City in less than thirty hours.

Stinky and I slept through Nicaragua and Costa Rica. Dad woke us up at 7A.M. so we could see the Panama Canal as we raced over it, but it was no big deal. The Colorado River is wider. The canal was just a straight-walled cut through flat green fields, filled with a motionless line of dirty freighters and smaller private boats, all waiting their turn at the next lock.

We spent most of the day gliding south through Colombia. The highway and the train tracks raced each other, swirling back and forth across the mountain slopes in great sweeping loops, hardly ever losing sight of each other. I was glad we hadn't driven the whole way. It would have taken a week or longer. We'd have killed each other.

Late in the day, the train began rising up the western slopes of the Andes and there were some places where the view was spectacular. By now, the beanstalk was a visible presence day and night. We could see it sometimes out our windows when the train went around a curve, but the best view was from the seats in the upstairs observation domes. The beanstalk sliced straight up into the bright blue sky almost from the very edge of the horizon. You'd think it would keep going until it was directly overhead, but it didn't. It disappeared about 11:00 high. Dad said it had something to do with angles and perspective and atmospheric haze. When we got closer, it would reach more toward zenith.

The SuperTrain was a lot wider than the old-fashioned kind—as wide as an airplane, but roomier, and the cars were all two-level. There was even a restaurant car with real waiters. We spent most of our time in the lounge car where there were terminals and even a theater at one end. Stinky wanted to play World Stomper, so Weird had to help him at the terminal. Dad and I went to the other end of the car and plopped down in the only available seats. I stared out the window and he ordered a drink from the table.

There was a fat man in a shiny suit sitting next to Dad; he was arguing across the table with a dark-haired woman. They both looked like Mexicans, but they could just as well have been Texans too. Sometimes it's hard to tell. They were both wearing fancy clothes and expensive-looking jewelry, so I figured they were Internationals, people with world-passports and no countries of their own.

The woman was angrily telling the man what was wrong with his politics, and he was telling her what was wrong with hers.

The fat man was explaining to the woman that money was a liquid, and that the health of an economy could be measured by how fast the liquid flowed through all the different parts. He said that if you gave a hundred plastic dollars to a rich man and a hundred plastic dollars to a poor man, the rich man's plastic dollars would be like drops in a reservoir, and they would move a lot slower than the poor man's plastic dollars. The poor man's money would be like drops in a river. They would flow a lot faster and farther than the rich man's money.

Dad looked uncomfortable. He obviously didn't like having to listen to their political discussion, but there was no other place to move to. He turned on his zine, but it was clear he couldn't concentrate. I smirked at his annoyance and he glowered at me.

The dark-haired woman said that the rich man's money worked just as hard as the poor man's—investments created jobs. But the fat man argued that rich dollars just flowed from one financial reservoir to another, without ever going through the rest of the economy. The poor man's dollars are more liquid than the rich man's, so funding the flowthrough—paying people to consume—was good for the economy, because poor people bought things and that created jobs for everybody. The fat man looked at me then; he'd noticed that I was listening to their argument. "Am I right, *muchacho?* Or am I right?"

"I'm not your *muchacho*," I said.

"*Perdoneme.*" He held up a hand. "But you have studied plastic flow-through dollars *en la escuela,* have you not?"

I nodded. Reluctantly. Because I didn't really want to talk about it. We'd had a lot of flow-through kids in school, so the teachers had to explain it that some people's parents were being paid to be consumers, but everybody still called them weasels and thieves—because everybody knew that flow-throughs were the reason everybody's taxes were so high. At least that's what I used to think, until Mom had to sign up for the flow and we moved to the tube-city and then other kids were calling Weird and me and Stinky the same names. Then I didn't know what to think. We weren't stealing from anyone—the government was paying us. But if the government was paying us with the money it was taking from other people, then maybe we shouldn't be taking it, should we? But if we didn't, then how would we live?

I could tell that Dad didn't like the conversation either—because of the way he was holding his zine and glaring at me over the top of it. The fat man saw it too. "*Señor*, I apologize," the fat man said to him. "I saw that the *muchacho*, was listening, I don't mind. It's good for children to be curious about issues. Allow me to introduce myself." He held out a meaty hand. "Bolivar Hidalgo, Associate Representative for Baja to the SuperNational Congress. This is my esteemed colleague, *Señora* Juanita Ramirez, Economic Consultant for the Fiscal Alliance. I think they are all greedy reactionaries and she thinks that I am an agent of confiscatory totalitarianism because I do not share her feudalistic views of the world."

"I'm an old-fashioned conservative," *Señora* Ramirez announced to Dad and me, as if this were something to be proud of. "I believe in absolute fiscal responsibility, minimal government, and the preservation of individual freedoms."

Hidalgo snorted. "If we were talking about simple individuals, that would be fine, but you are talking about corporations who do not care if real people starve."

She reached across and poked him in the stomach with a perfectly manicured finger. "You are a fine one to talk about starvation. When the world food crisis finally occurs, you will be able to live off your stored fat long after the rest of us are bones bleaching in the sun."

I had to smile at that. These folks didn't talk like friends, but they didn't fight like enemies either. And . . . it was nice to have adults actually speaking to me as a real person. Even if I didn't understand most of what they were talking about.

She looked at Dad and me. "You see, here is where my porkulent friend's argument breaks down. *Real* economic growth occurs in the development and deployment of new technology. The beanstalk, for instance—I assume you are going there?—do you know that the construction of the beanstalk expanded the world economy by almost three percent? It is the equivalent of constructing a new continent—a vertical continent. You'll see when you get there. And the economic benefit is still growing. What most people don't know is that the technological fallout of the beanstalk has been of far greater value to the economies of the Earth than the beanstalk itself. The money was spent here on Earth, and we built ten thousand factories and created a hundred million jobs. And thousands of new products that could never have existed before. My fat friend here would have you believe that the ownership of wealth automatically disqualifies one from full participation in the human race, as if somehow the possession or control of money is such a burden that it drains all compassion out of the soul. But he has a cure. He will take away the wealth and we will all be equally virtuous."

Bolivar Hidalgo just laughed and grinned, but it wasn't entirely a friendly grin. "Juanita," he said to her. "You misrepresent my views almost as badly as you misrepresent your own. It is not *only* about wealth, Juana. It is about the human suffering caused by economic plate-tectonics."

"Uh-oh, here we go—" she said. "*The* speech."

"And I will keep delivering it until you start listening. You cannot move a trillion dollars more than two inches in any direction without it flattening whoever or whatever is in the way, leaving a trail of broken economies in its wake. The people who'll pay your salary have taken trillions of dollars out of the North American economy and moved it into anonymous Ecuadorian holdings. The economic health of the entire hemisphere has been depressed by the greed of the fiscal underliners. And the ripples are still spreading. But your people don't care about the misery they leave behind, do they?" He eyed her curiously. "That money isn't even on the planet anymore, is it, Juana? It's on its way up the Line, isn't it?"

"Again with the conspiracy theories, Bollie?"

"Thirty trillion dollars has been drained out of the world economy. Where is it? We are heading into a global depression because the money has mysteriously disappeared. Where did it go? Your people are playing with disaster, Juana."

Very quickly, they forgot about Dad and me—which was just as well, because I was afraid that they were going to start asking more personal questions; but an aide came then and whispered something to

Dr. Hidalgo. He looked annoyed, excused himself, and headed forward. *Señora* Ramirez followed glumly.

I looked to Dad. "What was that all about?"

Dad's expression was dark and unreadable. "Paper dollars, plastic dollars, future dollars—none of that exists. But people argue about it anyway—as if it's important."

"Is it?" I asked.

He shrugged. "If you can translate it into spendable dollars, it is. And if you can't . . . you start a war."

"Is there going to be a war?"

Dad frowned. I could see the question troubled him. That meant that it was a very real possibility. But he considered the question fairly and gave a slow shake of his head. "I don't know." He put his zine down and tried to explain. "I guess those people think war is about money."

"Isn't it?"

He looked at me sadly. "I guess some people think so. But it's the rest of us who'll pay."

POPULATION CONTROL

WEIRD AND I DIDN'T GET too much more chance to talk about what Dad was planning. Or why. Or even if he was planning anything at all. Maybe insanity was hereditary—or at least contagious. All we had to go on was what Mom had told Weird, and we already knew that Mom hated Dad so much she'd say anything. Weird said that was why she'd lost in court this time, when she'd tried to deny Dad custody rights. Because the judge caught her lying.

In the bathroom once, I asked Weird what he thought we should do. Should we call Mom or what? He shrugged. What could Mom do? We were over the border. Seven borders now. Eight if you counted Guatemala, even though we hadn't really gone through Guatemala, but around it. By the time anyone could do anything, we'd be up the Line. And besides, Dad hadn't done anything illegal. Yet. So all we had were Mom's suspicions living rent-free in our heads. Just because Dad had mused aloud about going off to one of the star-colonies.

But I could see why Dad and Weird were angry with each other.

It goes back to when Dad and Mom got married. In return for certain tax credits, they'd agreed to have only boy children. The Population Control Authority had determined that reducing the ratio of girls to boys would reduce the worldwide birth rate. The target was to reduce the world population to ten billion people in three generations. That meant we had seven billion too many and everybody had to have fewer children. Or at least, fewer *female* children. In order to get international monetary credits, a lot of the fourth world countries had adopted such strict breeding policies they were almost totalitarian.

What we were taught in school was that in some countries, the people didn't think girl children were valuable, they only wanted sons.

So parents would kill female babies before they were born. So letting those parents have two sons, but no daughters, was a popular idea in those places. In our country, the government didn't have that kind of power, so instead they passed a law giving extra tax credits for male births and parents would decide for themselves.

In one of our classes, we were told that some women thought these policies were the equivalent of genocide. I suppose, maybe, they had a point—but it sounded more angry than sensible. They were saying that it was men who were irrelevant and we should be making more girl babies and less boys. I guess, if you were a girl, you might feel that way, but you could just as easily argue the other side of it. With less girls than boys, girls were more valuable now—and a girl could choose who she wanted to marry from the very best. She wouldn't have to take whoever came along. Of course, it might not be so good for the boys if there weren't enough girls to go around, but lotsa guys never get married anyway. I couldn't see myself getting married. I mean, I wouldn't rule out the possibility altogether, but I really didn't know very many girls, and most of them were in separate classes—but the ones I did know, well, they all seemed like they were from another planet or something. Dad said I'd probably feel different about girls when I got older, but if the way he and Mom ended up is any example, I'd just as soon not bother.

But anyway, that wasn't good for Weird. There were now six boys for every four girls, which was supposed to be okay for economic pro-ductivity in some areas, and not so good in others—but since the time he was born and the time he grew up, the PCA had come up with another one of their good ideas for slowing down the birth rate. They had lots of good ideas that way.

This time, they were offering college scholarships or tax credits for guys who went in for rechanneling and had their sexual orientations reversed. That's what Weird had said he wanted to do. Dad was against it, but Weird said it was the only way he could afford school. So that was a big part of why they were angry at each other. Mom didn't have any money, and neither did Dad. At least not enough to pay for college for all three kids. So maybe from Weird's point of view it made sense, selling off what he probably would never get a chance to use anyway. I dunno. The whole thing made me uneasy and I spent a lot of time looking at Douglas when he didn't know I was watching, trying to figure out what kind of difference it would make in him, if he'd look or talk different or if he'd even still be my brother.

And what about me when it came time for me to go to college?

Would I have to do the same thing? I didn't know what it was and I didn't like it already.

I didn't want anybody trying to change me. Even for my own good. I didn't even know who I was and already everybody else had made decisions that it was the wrong way to be, that there were too many of us anyway, that there should be more of one than the other, and that I shouldn't even be here at all, but now that I was, I shouldn't be the way I was going to be, whatever it was, we still didn't know, but whatever I was, somebody was sure to tell me it was wrong. Probably Dad. Or Mom. One of them first. And then everybody else.

That's what I hated about all of this. Adults were supposed to take care of their own problems, not pass them onto the kids. But it felt like Mom and Dad and now Doug were all passing the load onto me—as if somehow I should have to carry it too. It wasn't fair. They all kept telling me to act my age. Well, why the hell didn't they act theirs?

And it wasn't just Mom and Dad. It was all adults. I mean, kids get born into this world, and as soon as we're old enough to understand the smallest piece of it, adults start talking about the mess we're going to inherit and maybe we'll do a better job than they did. That's real smart. Think about it. How the hell are we going to do a better job if all we've got to go on is the stuff *they taught us?* Where's the place you go to get some *real* answers?

And then they wonder why kids are so confused and moody all the time.

So it wasn't exactly a fun trip. This part, at least.

And maybe it was because none of us were feeling very comfortable. This close to the equator, everything was hot and muggy and very bright. Even inside the train, we could feel it. And it was especially bad whenever we had to make a stop and all the doors were opened. We got out once to stretch our legs, but decided not to do that again. How did people live in this heat day after day after day?

Once we got into Ecuador, the train tracks ran down the center of the InterContinental Expressway, so whatever view there was, there were always cars and trucks in the way. Occasionally, we saw a train going the other way—it *whooshed* past so fast that we could feel the impact of the wind like a shotgun blast against the side of the train.

After the fortieth round of "no, we're not there yet," Stinky started whining about not having anything to do at which Dad reminded him of his monkey and Stinky complained that it didn't do anything. Dad looked real annoyed for a minute, as if he was going to lose his temper, but he didn't. Instead he said, "That's right, you have to teach it. That's what makes it fun. Douglas, will you help him?"

Then I said something to Weird about what a waste it was spending all that hard cash for a toy that has to be taught. Weird grunted something about Dad not wanting to use his credit cards. "So what?" I asked. Then he asked if I'd noticed that Dad had paid for the train tickets with cash too. And I said, "Yeah? So what?" And Weird said that if he'd paid by credit card and someone wanted to find us—like Mom—it'd be real easy to look up the account transactions to see where we were going. Dad heard that, and said that it was also cheaper to pay cash because you didn't have international transaction fees and you didn't have to worry about flexi-dollars going up suddenly either, and that way we could save money and do more. So there I was, with two more conflicting stories and one more reason to be as paranoid as Mom.

Vacations are supposed to be fun—except vacations with Dad were never fun; they were just this *thing* we had to do every year, and this one wasn't turning out any different—so whoever made up that crap about vacations being fun didn't know what he was talking about, or maybe he'd never been on a vacation with Dad. And besides, I kept thinking about what Dad had said back in the crater: "Don't go anywhere unless you know how you're going to get back."

See, that was the point.

I didn't know if I wanted to go back.

What if Weird was right?

If he was, I wasn't sure I wanted to stop Dad—because part of me was starting to think that maybe Dad was right, that going to the stars was the only way to get out.

It sure couldn't be worse than here.

TERMINUS

AFTER A WHILE, DAD GAVE up trying to get us kids to talk to him. Even Stinky had figured out something was going on and stopped talking. So Dad scrunched down in his seat and watched the news while we continued to grind southward. It was more of the same old same old. People were dying. Food riots in China. Botuloid Virus in Africa. Comatosis in Asia. Wars in India, Somalia, and Manchuria.

"You hear that, Charles?" Dad asked.

"Yeah," I grunted. "Don't live in places ending with the letter 'a'—especially 'ia.' "

"Never mind," said Dad. He shut up again. Whatever it was he'd wanted to say about all that stuff, it wasn't going to get said while I was in one of my moods. On the lighter side, some girl in Oregon said her horse had been eaten by a giant pink caterpillar. Dad was right. The world was going crazy. But I wasn't going to give him the satisfaction of agreeing with him.

Things got a little better as we got closer to the beanstalk.

Close up—like the last hundred klicks—the Line was almost too bright to look at. Up in the observation domes, you could plug into the telescope channel and see views of it from broadcast stations all over Ecuador.

Dad punched up the coordinates of one of the Andes installations and we all stared at the shimmering view of One-Hour Station. We'd seen it before—but this was *live* and that made it more *real*. Seen from this angle, through miles of atmosphere, One-Hour was just a gray indistinct blob, but we could see all three of the cables clearly delineated, and once we saw a tiny blip slide up into the station and another one drop away.

Most people think the Line is just one cable, but it isn't. It's three independent cables, all linked together for triple strength, so it's really three beanstalks in one. Originally there was only one, but they'd added the other two to triple the capacity of the stalk and provide additional "vertical services."

Eventually, they wanted to add three more cables. All six would touch down as an even bigger triangle than the present one; it would cover four times as much land. The newer triangle would point north, the original triangle would be inside it, pointing south; its vertices at the center points of the sides of the larger triangle.

They didn't know yet if they'd need to expand beyond that, but they were prepared to. Dad told us all this on the train. He drew a diagram and showed that six cables was probably the most you could put down without hitting the point of diminishing returns. Part of it was land area, part of it was economics; it all had to do with something called Elevator Theory.

By the time we got to Beanstalk City—that's what everybody calls it, but that's not its real name; it's really named after Sheffield Clarke, the English engineer who designed and built the whole thing—all of us were excited in spite of ourselves. Even Weird had stopped being a jerk long enough to ask Dad questions. And Dad answered honestly.

I was excited, but I was also getting a little scared too. This wasn't going to be like an airplane. An airplane, you knew what was holding you up. This was different. Nothing was holding you up. What if it *broke*? I knew it *couldn't*, but what if it did anyway—?

We arrived at the beanstalk at ten in the morning. First we rolled across a big plateau with dark mountains all around. There were a lot of warehouses and industrial buildings—and tube-towns too. Everything looked big and new and shiny—except for the parts that were small and cheap and dirty. The last twenty miles we passed a whole bunch of parking areas and hospitality structures and hotels and tacky little side businesses—and then abruptly, that all stopped and we were riding through what looked like a big park. Weird said this was the safeguard zone around the beanstalk.

For security reasons, they don't let anyone drive right up to the elevator. The closest you can approach by car is one of the official arrival areas. These are all at least fifteen kilometers away from Terminus. All traffic from there is by shuttle-train. I suppose a terrorist with a rocket-launcher might be able to do some damage from that distance, but if somebody really wanted to assault the beanstalk, they wouldn't do it with a rocket-launcher anyway. Dad said that almost the entire Ecuadorian economy is based on the beanstalk now, and they're a world power too, and a sponsoring nation of the Colonization Authority, so they don't take any chances with Line security.

The sky had gone all hazy gray and overcast—there was a tropical storm heading in from the Pacific—so we couldn't see if the Line went all the way up to zenith or not. But all of the beanstalk's lights were on and that made it very bright against the grungy clouds. We could even see the flashing lights of vehicles sliding up and down the Line. I started wondering how often lightning struck the cables and what kind of trouble it could cause to the people in the elevator cars. Despite the high gloom, the weather was still sweltering. Dad said they never have cold days anywhere on the equator, but it was definitely windy outside; we could see the trees whipping back and forth, and occasionally big palm fronds would go tumbling by. Weird said there was nothing to worry about; the Line was secure for wind velocities of up to 625 kph.

Dad opened the tour book he'd bought that showed how the base of the Line was surrounded by cargo facilities, terminals, parks, tourist sites, stadiums, theaters, and a whole webwork of highways, tracks, and canals. The widest canal circled the beanstalk—Weird said that all of the bridges over it were retractable, in case terrorists or someone tried a ground assault. Airplanes weren't even allowed to fly within fifty klicks of the Line without special permission. He said the Ecuadorians were very serious about this; they once shot down somebody's Lear Jet and there was a big lawsuit about it.

When you get close enough, the bottom of the Line starts rising up over the horizon like a big white mountain. It spreads down and out and out and just keeps getting bigger and bigger the closer you get. And it takes a long time to get. A half hour at least. The top of the cone part is over two kilometers high. At the apex there's a ring around the Line, an observation tower where you can view the surrounding countryside or just watch the Line-cars go sliding up into the sky.

Closer still, you can see that there are wide gaps along the bottom of the cone—like a tent just a little too short for its ropes. The train slides in right under the edge. And then everything gets *real* bright.

Terminus is more than a launching station, it's a domed city— bigger than enormous, twenty klicks across. Think of a gigantic tent that uses the three cables of the beanstalk as the central mast, the tent fabric is made out of the same monofilament stuff as the Line, and all of the supporting cables are actual beanstalk filaments anchored off axis for additional stability. So once you're inside the tent, you're actually *inside* the beanstalk. It's a whole other world. Distances don't look the same. You can't tell how near or how far anything is. And everywhere, the filaments of the beanstalk spread out like rays of the sun, stabbing into the ground and anchoring themselves deep in the bedrock.

The top of the Terminus dome goes up so high it fades away in the distance. It's almost like someone took the meteor crater and turned it upside down over everything like a gigantic cup, only *bigger* than that. Terminus dome is so big it has its own weather. They get clouds and fog, and sometimes they even get little rainstorms. But the outer surface of the tent is painted with solar crystals to generate power for the air-conditioning inside, so it's mostly comfortable.

And of course, the three main cables of the Line are visible from everywhere. They're all lit up like a big bar of sunlight, so everything inside is as bright as it is outside—and that's pretty bright, because it's right spang on the equator. There's a line drawn across Terminus so you can tell where the equator is; you can stand in both hemispheres at the same time if you want to.

The actual cables of the Line were a lot thicker than I thought they would be. And they were spaced quite a distance apart; it looked like at least a kilometer, maybe more. There was a lot of traffic on them too. There was always at least one car inside the dome going slowly up or down on each of the strands. They don't really get up to full speed until they get out of the dome and out of the thickest part of the atmosphere.

I guess we did a lot of gaping. Everyone did. That's because Terminus dome is like no other place in the world—at least not any place I'd ever been. It's like an amusement park and a shopping mall and a factory all scrunched together. Everything was stacked on top of everything else. Towers and balconies and gardens and waterfalls everywhere. And rides and restaurants and all kinds of theaters and stores and clubs. And signs and lights and music and a constant roar of noise. We could even hear it inside the train.

The train station is elevated, so as the train pulls into the tent you can see the whole interior of the station spread out below like a big jumbled toy box, and everybody all over the dome can see the SuperTrain too. It's really impressive. But when you get off, Weird pointed out, you're still in a holding area. You have to go through multiple security gates where you get scanned and photographed and inspected, and then only when they're satisfied that you're not some kind of terrorist or madman do they let you go down the ramp into the city. Stinky was already pulling at Dad's arm. "I wanna go on the rides—" But Dad shook his head and said, "We're about to go on the biggest ride of all, kiddo."

We were each responsible for our own luggage. Dad had insisted that we travel light. When we turned in the rent-a-car in Mexico, we left behind everything we weren't going to need for the trip up to Geostationary and back, and that meant most of Stinky's toys—not the monkey, though; Dad insisted Stinky bring it after he'd spent all that cash—and the rest of the stuff like bathing suits and towels and dirty clothes and extra jeans. We just put it all in a big box and shipped it home.

Weird and Stinky and I had all our stuff in backpacks. Dad had his stuff in a rollaround. Stinky had half his clothes in his own backpack and the other half in a smaller one on the monkey; he held its hand and chattered at it like they were married. It waddled beside him like an obedient child with a full diaper. It was almost cute. I said they looked like twins, which got a laugh from Weird and a dirty look from Dad. "Well, it looks just like him—" I started to say, but Stinky heard that and started crying, and suddenly he didn't like his monkey at all anymore. "Does *not* look like me!" he said, kicking it away. Of course, the monkey came scurrying right back to him, so he kicked at it again—the monkey jumped out of the way and Stinky fell on his butt. And started wailing like an injured banshee. People were staring at us now, some of them angrily, as they threaded their way around us. We were blocking the access to the exit gate.

Dad got really angry. He scooped up the monkey and thrust it into my arms. "You started this, Charles. You take care of the monkey!" Of course, the monkey didn't want to be carried. Not by me, anyway. Stinky had thoroughly imprinted it, so all it wanted to do was get back to him. It squirmed and whimpered and trembled and kept trying to wriggle out of my arms. "Stop it!" I said firmly, but the monkey ignored me. I tried feeling around for its off switch, but the monkey started giggling as if I was tickling it. Then it started screeching.

The noise got Stinky's attention. He started screaming at me, "That's my monkey! I want it back! Give it back!" Dad tried to calm him down, but Stinky kept squirming and crying and screaming, just like the monkey, and finally he wriggled out of Dad's grasp and came and grabbed the damn thing out of my arms. I couldn't believe it; they really were twins. I stood there, staring at him, wondering why any kid's parents would ever let him survive long enough to reach adulthood. There must be something about parents—some kind of chemical trigger in the brain—that keeps them from strangling their own children.

I started to say something about that, but Dad just glared at me and said, "Why don't you keep your mouth shut for a while, Charles. You've said enough for one day."

Right. Stinky threw a tantrum and it was *my* fault. If I'd have been Dad, I'd have put that damn monkey into the nearest trash can. In pieces.

They pushed on through the gate, leaving me staring after them astonished, wishing I could be an orphan for a while. Anything would be better than this. Maybe I should just divorce them all and the hell with it. The more I thought about it, the more I liked that idea. I could look up the procedures on the net, I'd done it before, but I'd never followed through. Maybe this time I'd stay angry long enough. In the meantime . . . I reshouldered my backpack and followed. Like I always do.

From the train terminal, there's a shuttle-train on a sort of circular track that winds back and forth and in and out of everything all around the Terminus dome. It's free, and you can get on it anywhere and just go around and around all day long. The shuttle goes through at least a dozen hotels and a couple of big shopping centers and a several huge museums and an amusement park and over an indoor lake and through a whole bunch of permanent apartments and offices. There are theaters and clubs and parks and restaurants everywhere and I don't know what else. If you can imagine it, it's probably here.

Climbing up the inside of the tent, there are at least fifty stories of balconies and terraces all of them piled up high like a man-made crater wall. Dad said someday it'll be a *hundred* and fifty stories of apartments and offices and stores on the inside. And probably more outside too.

Dad had a book about the cable, and he started pointing out stuff and explaining it to us as we went. Even though I was still angry, some of it was kind of interesting. He said there were even more city levels higher up the Line, some already developed, some awaiting future expansion. In fact, there were public parts of the structure all the way up to six kilometers, because some people *like* living that high; some of the industrial levels went even higher. There were a lot of weather stations too. The meteorologists loved the Line because it gave them a real-time core sample of the atmosphere. And there were all kinds of factories that needed high altitudes for various processes and stuff. Above that, there were observatories and broadcast stations up the entire length of the orbital elevator. So it wasn't all empty cable.

There was no shortage of vertical space, and there probably wouldn't ever be, at least not for a long, long time. Dad said that the industrial development of the cable would eventually prove more important than the transportation aspects, because the beanstalk had effectively tripled or quadrupled Ecuador's usable land area. In fact, they'd be dropping new cables to handle the increased traffic long before they used up all the available vertical space on the existing lines.

Dad said that the Orbital Elevator Corporation was planning to start dropping the first of the next three cables in a few months. Each new cable dropped would create another triangle and another area of interior space. When I asked how that would affect Terminus, Dad had said that Terminus would get even bigger. The area covered by the tent would be expanded—quadrupled, at least—so obviously the ground-level expansion was already planned for too.

But by then, the Kenya cable would be up and running and that would be serious competition, so there wouldn't be as much pressure to grow as fast, although Dad said that the Ecuadorian cable could probably lower their fares and shipping costs by then, because so much of their initial investment would already have been amortized, so they could probably give the Kenyan group a pretty hard time.

Dad said there was also a Singapore–Malaysia investment group preparing a cable of their own, and British Canada was dropping a cable down into the Pacific Ocean, just south of Christmas Island. That didn't make sense to me, but Dad said there were a lot of military and scientific reasons for having a cable of your own.

There was something about the way he said that last part. "Do you think there's going to be a war?" I asked.

He looked at me with a sad look in his eyes. "I hope not," he said, "but sometimes I think it's already started and we just don't know it yet."

ALL ABOARD

IT WASN'T TOO HARD TO find a ticket lobby. There was this big circular balcony all around the cables. It was as wide as an avenue, it had two levels, and there were check-in counters on both levels. It was high enough above the floor of Terminus that you could look down over the railing and see the big well where the cables disappeared into the Earth. You could see everything, even how the cars were loaded and moved into position for launch. We all wanted to look, but Dad insisted we get our tickets first.

The ticket counters on the lower balcony were only for day-trips up to One-Hour. That was real popular with tourists who wanted to visit the beanstalk and who wanted to go into space but who weren't planning to go all the way up to orbit, which was a much longer trip. There were elevators leaving for One-Hour every five minutes.

One-Hour was open twenty-four hours a day, but we had to go to a different line. Tickets for Geostationary and even farther out, like to the launch stations beyond, were sold on the top level. Those cars launched every fifteen minutes.

Dad had made reservations for a 2:15 elevator, but we were early. The woman behind the counter had a shiny brown face, and she kept smiling at Stinky like he was her own little boy. She suggested that we go straight on up to One-Hour now and see all the sights up there, and then we could catch our reserved cabin on the 2:15 car when it stopped at One-Hour to pick up passengers. That way we could leave almost immediately without any waiting and we'd get to see everything up at One-Hour too. Because of the storm coming in, traffic up the elevator was heavier than usual, she said, so it was probably a good idea to leave now. Dad agreed and so did the rest of us, so the woman rewrote our reservations. She scanned our IDs and then gave each of us our own boarding cards.

She asked if we wanted to check our luggage, but Dad said no. We didn't have that much and we'd prefer to keep it with us. She had a pretty smile and she made us all feel a lot friendlier—like we were actually going to have fun for a change. She gave each of us an elevator badge to wear. I started to shove mine in my pocket, until Weird pointed out that it was also a life-monitor and a locator chip and a beeper-communicator. We had to wear our badges at all times, Weird said.

After that, Dad took us back over to the edge of the balcony to look at how the cables worked. The three cables of the Line plunged straight down from the very top of the tent each into its own separate hole in the floor of the station. They were as big around as buildings. Bigger. Dad said each one was as thick as a baseball stadium. The bottom of the Line looked like three huge pillars from God with a big open space between them—enough for another dozen stadiums. Probably more.

This wasn't the *real* bottom of the Line, of course. That was anchored four or five kilometers underground. Above us, below us, all around us, all the separate filaments of the cable were peeled off into underground tunnels and threaded down into the bowels of the earth, where each one was knotted around a couple zillion tons of basalt or whatever. They couldn't pull loose. Every filament was separately anchored, some as far as fifty klicks away so there would be a firm anchor for the Line even if there were a massive earthquake here.

From our vantage point on the balcony, we could see everything. Dad pointed out the details of this and that as happily as if he'd built the Line himself. He explained the purposes of each of the different tracks, talked about what the lights meant, and made sure we noticed all the smaller cables running down the sides of the big ones.

As we watched, an elevator car slid down one of the cables into a reception bay; at the same time another one popped up on the other side of the same cable. On the next cable over, a pair of linked cargo pods came sliding down, direct from orbit; they had a Lunar insignia painted on them. As they slid out of sight, a loaded cargo container rose up to balance them. "Look! That one's going straight to the moon," I said to Stinky. We watched as it rose up and up and up until it finally disappeared through the roof.

That's when it hit me. That we were going up *too*. This wasn't another one of Dad's didn't-happen promises. This was for *real*. And that's when I started to feel very nervous. Especially about the stuff Weird had said. I was beginning to think he might be right. This whole trip—it *wasn't* normal. Not for Dad.

I wished I knew how to ask Dad to reconsider, but I knew whatever I said, he wouldn't change his mind. Certainly not after traveling all this way. And Weird and Stinky were so hyped up about the elevator, they probably wouldn't let him reconsider anyway. I would have waited down here at Terminus for them, but I knew Dad would never agree to that either—and I didn't dare ask.

It wasn't that I didn't want to go. I sort of did. I just didn't want to go *right now*.

"Is that where *we're* going?" Stinky asked, pointing up the elevator.

"Yep," I said, my voice kind of strangled. I took his hand so he wouldn't get lost. Weird looked at me funny, but I turned away before he could say anything, pushing Stinky after Dad and wishing I were big enough to be taken seriously.

Dad herded us down to a platform next to a long queue of elevator capsules, all moving slowly in line toward the launch bay. Each car was as big around as a house and at least five or six stories tall. There were at least a dozen of them, with a new one popping into the queue every few minutes; every time a car at the front slid into the launch rack, a new one thunked up at the other end.

Weird pointed past the row of cars. On the other side, we could see down into the space where they went through their final service check before being thrust up into the boarding queue. Preloaded cargo pods were slid automatically into the bottom levels of each car—so the capsules were even taller than I thought.

Weird said that balancing the load on the Line was so critical that they had to plan the cargo schedule months in advance. And yes, there was always a little room held out in each pod for last-minute things that needed to be shipped up the elevator. And there were always six empty slots a day for standby cars or for cargo that missed its normal launch slot, which sometimes happened if a car failed its pressure test.

Dad came back and grabbed both our arms then, complaining that we didn't have time for gawking. He had *that* tone in his voice, so Weird and I just traded looks and followed after.

Dad hurried us all the way to the front of the queue, to the frontmost car being loaded. The cars were shiny blue metal with silvery trim. Lined up the whole length of the platform, all creeping forward together, they looked like a giant subway train. The edge of the platform was a moving slidewalk, rolling at the same slow speed, so boarding the elevator car was a lot like getting on a car in an amusement park ride, only you stepped in through a triple-layered hatch. The walls of the cars were thicker than I expected, but that's because the whole thing had to be pressurized for space.

Dad entered the car first, then Weird and Stinky. I hesitated a bit—I don't like cramped places and the door to this one was just small enough that you almost had to duck to get through it—but inside it was all comfortable chairs and tables, so I followed. Reluctantly.

An attendant told us to take any seats we wanted. They were spaced around the room in clusters, like a lounge. We sat down and we waited.

As soon as the car was full, they slammed the door shut with a scary *thunk*—once that door was closed you *couldn't* get out again—and then we waited several forevers while they ran the final set of launch tests.

Weird said they have only five minutes to check the pressure and weight. This is when they pump or drain extra water into the ballast tanks to equalize the weight of the car. Weird said the load engineers have to equalize the strain up and down the entire length of the cable—if you calculated the total weight of tonnage on the line at any given moment it was enormous, so balance was critical.

So was the water. They always needed a lot of fresh water up topside, not just for the various stations on the Line, but for export too. In fact, Weird said, the folks at the top of the Line considered the water more important than the passengers.

If the elevator car failed either the final pressure test or the weight check, Weird said, it would get shunted to a side track, and a standby car sent up in its place. I hoped that would happen to us. But Weird said that hardly ever happens. Most of the time the standby car gets sent up as the last car in a shift. The shifts were four hours long.

There were several attendants aboard to help us stow our backpacks, and they even offered us drinks and snacks. There were video screens everywhere, each one showing the inevitable "for your own safety . . ." instructions. But there's not really a lot to know about the elevator. Either it works or it doesn't. The cars up to One-Hour are equipped with breakaway bolts and parachutes for emergency return, but except for the occasional test launch, none have ever been fired in a real emergency. In case of a pressure drop, each level of the car could be sealed off from all the others, but that was unlikely too, because the cars were triple-hulled. You'd have to hit one with a meteor to put a hole in it. I looked for seat belts, but there weren't any. That surprised me at first, but Weird said we'd never be going fast enough to need them.

One of the levels inside the elevator car had floor-to-ceiling windows, one had waist level-to-ceiling windows for people who need the feeling of a railing, and the third passenger level had only portholes, because some people need to have a wall between themselves and all that height. The rest of the car was reserved for cargo and life support and stuff like that. There was no pilot, but there was a senior attendant. In our car, he looked and acted more like a head waiter than anything else, but Weird told me he was also trained in all kinds of medical and safety procedures, even in law enforcement. Weird is full of stuff like that. He's a lot like Dad that way. It's like being online 24/7.

He said that the cars used to be a lot smaller, but the beanstalk had been designed from the beginning for expansion and as soon as there were enough filaments to support the weight, they started switching over to the larger cars. About twenty years ago, Weird said. And then Dad added that we could probably see some of the older cars on display up at One-Hour.

Our car was filled to capacity—not exactly crowded, but you had to watch where you were stepping. There weren't that many tourists aboard; it was mostly locals. That was because there was a big tropical storm moving inland and a lot of the locals were going up to One-Hour to wait it out. Apparently, it was the safest place to be. There were hotels and restaurants and theaters up at One-Hour, so they were probably going to make a party of it.

At last, our car was in the number one position. Stinky and Weird and I watched as we moved suddenly away from the platform. There was a gentle bump or two, and then the car was locked into the launch tube. We were right next to the cable—it looked like a huge curved wall. I imagined I could hear it *humming*. That's when I started getting *really* scared. I wanted to ask if I could get off, but I didn't want Dad and Stinky and Weird to know how scared I was. So I just grabbed Stinky's hand tighter and said to him, "Any minute now. Don't be afraid."

He looked at me with a funny expression as if he couldn't understand why I would say such a thing. "I'm not scared. It's only an elevator."

Besides, the attendants *couldn't* let me off. Even if they wanted to. It was already too late. There were so many cars traveling each way on the Line at any given moment that everything had to be tightly scheduled and every launch had to be precisely timed. So once a car was sealed and had passed all of its integrity tests, it was effectively launched. A car had to slide up this track every five minutes, no matter what. I didn't know what would happen if a car missed its launch, but I got the feeling the elevator engineers wouldn't like it.

Coming down, the whole process was reversed. A new car arrived every five minutes. They were strung the entire length of the Line, so each car had to be moved out of the way before the next one arrived. They'd never had a collision, but apparently in the early days of the

Line there had been a couple of near misses. Only a few times had they ever had to halt downward traffic to clear the track. Weird said they didn't like to do it not just because it was bad publicity but because every minute of stoppage cost half a million dollars of lost income.

There was a chime then, and everybody else who hadn't yet found a spot at a window came pushing in behind us. Then some music started playing, something dramatic; it took me only a moment to recognize it. *Carmina Burana* by Carl Orff. The first movement. *O Fortuna*. Very theatrical. Very powerful. One of Dad's favorites. I could tell by his smile that he thought it was appropriate music for jumping off a planet.

At first we didn't feel anything, but the cable-wall next to us started sliding down, and then we rose up out of the launch cradle. A moment more, and we were rising up through the core of Terminus Station and my heart did one of those sudden flip-flops like it does at the top of the roller coaster when you realize you're strapped in and it doesn't matter what you want to do anymore because *this* is what you're *going* to do, *whether you want to or not.*

We were on our way. Up.

 **UP**

WE WERE ON THE SECOND level, where the windows started at waist level and angled outward toward the top, so we could lean out and look almost straight down. I swallowed hard and tried not to look, but I couldn't stop myself from seeing anyway.

First we rose up through the service core, then all of the terraces and balconies began dropping away like toys. At least that part was fun to watch, because we could see how everything was laid out inside the tent. It was a whole different view of Beanstalk City and we could see how big the world under the dome really was.

We rose all the way up to the top, and then the view closed in for just a few seconds as the car slid up through the top of the tent. The elevator starts out slow, so it takes almost two minutes to get to the top, but the timing is perfect because that's where the music gets sort of quiet for a bit, anticipating the next part, then it comes back with a big crescendo just as the car rises up out of the roof and into the open air. The music pounds toward a big dramatic punch and you get to see how the whole city around Terminus is spread out like a giant Monopoly board. And then . . . the elevator starts going up even *faster*.

Even though the day was overcast, Terminus City seemed to have a ghostly bright quality. As it spread out below us, everything shone in vivid colors.

Mostly around the tent there were parks and lakes, but we could also see all of the industrial areas too—all the warehouses, and the shipping and receiving areas, and the highways and tracks and canals. And beyond, there was the rest of the city that grew up around the Line: the dorms where a lot of the construction workers and their families lived while it was being built—and still lived today, because most of them had been guaranteed jobs on the Line when it was finished—and farther out, all the office towers and hotels for tourists and visiting business people, and then the rest of the city beyond, where everybody else lives, the ones who provide groundside services for the Line and its constant stream of traffic.

We also saw a lot of Tube-Towns scattered below. The slums. Just like home. They ringed the whole area. The gray day made them look almost as depressing from above as they were close up.

If I leaned out far enough, I could see how the shining cables of the Line speared straight down into the center of everything. Its shadow was like a triple knife cut, slicing west across the landscape. It arrowed out toward the horizon, eventually fading away in the distance.

We kept rising and the effect was like one of those pull-back-into-infinity shots that you see on TV all the time. We rose up and up and everything else got smaller and smaller. Pretty soon we could see the dark blue line of the ocean to the west, and more banks of clouds piling up on the horizon, a thick wall of them.

We passed through a small patch of clouds and then a bigger one, and somebody nearby said something about the big storm that was heading in from the Pacific, how we'd probably be able to see the whole thing from One-Hour. Somebody else said if you stood real still you could feel the wind rocking the elevator car, but I tried it and couldn't feel anything. Maybe it was just imagination. It was pretty hard to tell.

Most everybody stood there at the window for at least fifteen minutes, pointing things out to each other while the ground kept dropping away below. It wasn't as bad as I was afraid it would be. At least, not yet. Maybe higher up.

The view of the cable was sort of interesting too. The Line zips past the window like a vertical highway—so fast it's just a big blur. It looks like it's all one smooth surface, but it isn't. A lot of it is studded with solar cells, and every thousand meters there's an outer ring of those high-powered sulfur-incandescent lamps that are brighter than the sun; the ring is *outside* the elevator tracks so the lights don't accidentally shine in. The projectors are there so the Line will be visible from hundreds of miles away. From a distance, all those lights blend together to look like one solid line of brightness. That's why we could see the Line so clearly all the way to Mexico. The lights are partly to warn airplanes and partly to aid people who are aiming their communication dishes and partly as a navigational aid, and partly just for national pride. I mean, if you had a beanstalk in your country, wouldn't you want to show it off?

The other thing about the beanstalk is that there's a lot of space between the three cables. A couple of square kilometers, at least. But it wasn't *empty* space. For one thing, most of the tracks on the parts of the cables facing each other—the insides—were for cargo pods. We saw them zipping up and down past us; the cargo pods weren't normally pressurized for passengers and they traveled a lot faster in both directions, because cargo didn't suffer from motion-sickness.

But in addition to the cargo tracks, there were also these great billowy tubes of transparent mylar; they were inflated chimneys of all different lengths. Their bottoms and tops were at different heights and they looked kind of like a big ghostly organ. Some of them reached as high as the four-kilometer mark. Their purpose, Dad said, was to irrigate the atmosphere via the "chimney effect." Apparently when you have two chimneys of different heights and you get wind blowing across the top, you get air current down one and up the other. This is how prairie dogs cool their burrows. Here, at the beanstalk, the idea was to create a steady flow of air from the upper reaches of the atmosphere down into the lower and back up again. The air flow generated some electricity, but more important, it helped cool the land around the base of the Line. Weird said that the Line produced three degrees of local cooling, which could make a real difference on a hot day at the equator.

But—Dad said, some of Ecuador's neighbors blamed the chimneys for the persistent *El Niño* condition in the Pacific that had been screwing up rain patterns for the past twenty years or so and generating some really nasty storms—like the one growing out in the Pacific right now. But who knew for sure? Weird always said that everything was connected to everything else, but if that was true, then the weather had to be caused by *everything*, didn't it? Nobody knew for sure, and that was part of what everybody was angry about. According to Dad anyway. That's what fat Señor Hidalgo had been talking about on the train— how the Line was destabilizing *everything* in the world. Even where people lived.

That was the real surprise—there are people living on the Line. All the way up to the five-kilometer mark. And someday even higher. Every so often, we'd pass through a platform city, three or four or five levels suspended from all three of the cables—with holes of course for the elevator tracks and the chimneys. We zipped through them too fast to see much detail, but what we did see as they dropped away below us was pretty impressive. They were like vertical villages. The first three were open to the air, and we saw clusters of offices and homes and shopping areas—*real* homes with big windows and yards and even a few swimming pools. There were also public launch balconies for gliders of all kinds.

I wondered what it would be like to live in such a place. You'd have to be *very* rich to live this high. The sky cities were where important corporation people lived as well as some of the people in Ecuador's government.

One of the attendants said that eventually there would be at least a hundred of these platform towns on the Line; there was room for thousands of sky cities, of course; but every platform town required multiple new filaments on the Line, not to mention the installation of an equivalent weight at the other end of the cables to balance it—the attendant said there were already hundreds of water tanks at the far end of the cable, moving up and down all the time to keep the Line in equilibrium—so there was a practical limit to how much could be hung on the Line.

And then the last of the towns disappeared beneath us, and there was nothing for a while except the humming of the cable. By the time we hit ten kilometers, the sky had turned a very deep blue. I'd never seen it that color before. Now the only settlements we were zipping through were scientific or industrial ones, and there weren't too many of those.

The ground below had become mostly featureless; a blanket of clouds covered most everything below us. To the north we could see a few patches of brown and green. To the east, we could see the wall of the Andes stretching north and south. It looked like a crumpled white sheet. I couldn't believe how steep and jagged the mountains were.

Dad said that the original plan had been to drop the cable down onto one of those mountaintops, but when they looked at the problems of anchoring the Line to a mountaintop so high you needed an O-mask to breathe, they had second thoughts. Even if you could build Terminus on the mountaintop, you'd still have to extend the elevators down to the foothills; you'd have to build a second Terminus. It was easier to just extend the bottom end of the cable a couple klicks farther. What you traded off in additional stress and tension on the anchor, you got back in construction savings and maintenance benefits.

By now, the view had gotten to be pretty standard airplane stuff, except that the cables sparkling all the way down until they disappeared into the clouds below made it impossible for me to pretend I was in an airplane anymore. As long as I didn't think about the cables, I was fine, but this view was a little too scary for me.

That's when Stinky said, "Is this all there is to do? Stare out the window?"

So Dad said, "Well, let's see what else there is. Come on, let's go upstairs." So we all trooped up to the top level of the car, which wasn't really much of a level, just a little room with a glass dome over the top so you could look straight up the Line if you wanted to. There wasn't much to see up here either, just the cables of the elevator stretching endlessly up into the dark blue above. For some reason, that was even *more* disturbing. But it was also more boring, so I went back downstairs to the restaurant level, where I bought myself a Coke and tried to avoid looking at any windows.

About the time I began to wonder how often people freaked out on one of these trips and what the attendants would do if I started screaming, Weird came down the stairs and seated himself next to me.

"So?" he said.

"So what?" I answered.

"Now do you believe me? He's gonna do it."

I shrugged. "You can't prove that." And then another thought occurred to me. "Do you want to go back?"

"Do you?" he countered.

"I dunno."

"If we could prove it, we could tell someone. . . ." Weird offered half-heartedly.

"Oh yeah, get Dad arrested. That would go down really good. Mom would like that. A lot. But Dad would never forgive us. Not that it would matter. But we'd probably never get to see him again. The courts would terminate his rights. Is that what you want?"

"No. But it isn't right for him to do this without asking us what *we* want to do."

"Well, what *do* we want to do? You tell me, Douglas."

Now it was his turn to shrug. "I dunno."

"Well, what do we have to go back to? At least, this is . . . *something.*"

"Maybe," he admitted. "But I don't like being pushed into it like this. Do you?"

"Maybe we don't know all of what's going on. Mom has been really angry about a whole bunch of stuff she won't talk about. What's that about?"

"Mom is always angry." Douglas said. "That's why Dad gave up on her. Dad was raised different. He doesn't like arguments."

"Well then, he must really love being around us. That's all we ever do."

"Not always. We're not arguing now."

"No. But we're not doing anything else either, are we?" I said one of those words that Dad doesn't like me to use. Just in time for Dad to hear it as he and Stinky came back downstairs.

ONE-HOUR

THE ONE-HOUR PLATFORM IS called that because it takes exactly one hour to get there. It's also the legal limit of the atmosphere, so anyone who visits One-Hour can say that he or she has traveled into space.

One-Hour is also one of the biggest of the platform cities. Seven stories thick, it's suspended from all three cables; it fills the space between them and extends quite a ways out beyond as well. It's a city floating in the sky. If you could stand away from it, you would see that there are towers projecting up from it and more towers hanging down.

And the view from One-Hour is spectacular. You're high enough to see the curvature of the Earth in all directions. You can see as far as Mexico to the north and Peru and Bolivia to the south. To the west, the Pacific Ocean curls away out of sight under a frosting of clouds.

There are balconies and observation posts all around the edges of One-Hour and all over the bottom, so there are places where you can look straight down . . . if you want to.

I didn't want to, but everyone else wanted to see the storm, so we went—except it wasn't a storm anymore. Now it was a hurricane. And it looked ferocious. It was a great whorl of white, so big it covered more than half the globe visible below us. From up here it looked as peaceful as a swirl of whipped cream on top of a big lemon pie, but if you watched long enough, you could see the banks of clouds moving majestically around a common center. The attendants said that the winds were already up to 200 kilometers per hour and expected to rise as high as 250 or maybe even 300 by the time the storm started inland. Somebody else said that the winds might get as high as 350 klicks before the storm hit the coast. They said the eye of the storm was expected to pass

very close to the beanstalk. In fact, the storm was the only thing anybody was talking about up here.

The U.N. Weather Authority had tried seeding the storm's western
edge in an effort to steer it southward, but this storm had a mind of its
own and was still moving east. The Line Authority was beaming mi-
crowaves into it too; that wasn't helping either. The news was calling
it Hurricane Charles, but I didn't feel honored.

Then Stinky asked the important question: "Can we call Mom now?
And tell her where we are?"

"No. Let's wait until we reach Geostationary," Dad said. "Like we
agreed."

"But I wanna talk to Mommy *now*." There was something real frantic about the way he said it.

Dad looked uncomfortable. He glanced to both Weird and me as if
looking for help—but Weird just said, "It might not be such a bad idea,
Dad. Mom might be a little worried about us. We should let her know
we're out of the storm."

This made Dad even more annoyed. "I said *no*."

But Stinky had already run to a phone booth, one of the ones with
the glass bottoms, so you could see all the way down, and he was
already punching for Mom. "I wanna show her my monkey!" He'd
already put his phone-home card in the slot, so there was nothing for
Dad to do except step sideways out of camera range. Me, I studied the
walls, the ceiling, anything but the floor, until the screen finally lit up.
First it showed a map of North America, and then it zoomed down in
as it tracked her location.

Mom wasn't at home; she was in San Francisco. She answered
almost immediately; she looked tired but happier than we'd seen her in
a while. Behind her we could see somebody's apartment, and out the
window, we could even see what looked like trees or bushes. In the
background, I got a quick glimpse of someone—a woman, Mom's
age—but I didn't see her clearly.

"Hi, Mom!"

"Bobby! Where are you calling from?" At first her expression was
surprised—as if she hadn't expected to see any of us for a while, but
then her eyes flicked down as she read the information at the bottom of
her display. Her expression darkened immediately. "Put your father on!"

Dad stepped into view then. "Hello, Maggie," he said grimly.

"You're doing it, aren't you!"

"I told you I would. It's the only way to be fair."

"You son of a bitch! The court said no."

"The court said not without your agreement."

"And I said no! So that means the court says no too!"

"Maggie—" Dad was keeping his voice deliberately calm. "I will not let you abuse the children as a way of getting even with me. They're old enough now, they're entitled to make up their own minds." Douglas shot me an *I-told-you-so* look.

"I'm going to stop you, Max—I'll see you in jail, you lying pig!" Abruptly, she remembered that Weird and Stinky and I were there too. She said, "You kids—Bobby, Charles, Douglas—why did you let him do this? You stay where you are! Don't you go *anywhere* with him. I'm calling the police." Behind her, a woman's voice was asking, "Maggie? What's going on—?" And then the screen went blank.

There was silence in the phone booth for a moment. Finally, I said, "So this wasn't such a good idea, was it, Dad?"

"Shut up, Chigger!" said Weird.

"I wanna talk to Mommy!" Stinky wailed.

I realized then that after her hello, she hadn't said a thing to any of us kids, except to order us to stay put. For some reason, that made me feel really angry at her. If she really cared about us as much as she said she did, why was she yelling at us? At least, Dad didn't yell. He just went silent.

He was silent now. He looked uncertain. Actually, he looked old. Beaten up.

"Dad?" asked Weird. "Are you all right?"

"No," he said. "Look. I need you to understand something. All three of you. Your Mom didn't want me to bring you on this trip. So I did it without her permission. Maybe it wasn't the smartest thing to do. But I needed to do this. I really did." Dad dropped to his knees in front of Bobby and me and put his hands on our shoulders. "I've made a lot of promises to you kids, and I haven't been able to keep all of them. Maybe none of them. And I know you resent me for it. You're probably right to do so. I guess I haven't been the best dad in the world. I'm sorry about that. It hurts me something awful to know that I've let you boys down. You mean more to me than anything else in the world. That's why I did it. Just once in my life, I wanted to do something extraordinary for you. And this is it. And I wasn't going to let anybody say no."

He looked so sad and vulnerable—and for a moment, he even looked *old*—that I couldn't help myself. I flung myself into his arms. And so did Bobby. And Douglas. Not because he was right, but because he was Daddy. And he *needed* us. And suddenly it was very scary, the whole thing, and I guess *we* needed him too, and then Stinky started crying. And I have to admit, even I—

Dad pulled back and looked me in the eyes. "Are you all right?" I guess he'd felt me trembling.

"Yeah," I said. "I'm fine. I just don't like her yelling at us all the time. That's all."

"Me neither," said Stinky petulantly.

Dad looked at Weird. "Douglas?"

Weird shrugged noncommittally. "It's just Mom. That's just the way she is."

"Do you want to go back?"

"She's going to call the cops on you."

Dad sighed and nodded. "I hope she doesn't. For your sakes—" he added sadly. "Because then we could both lose custody. And you guys would end up in foster homes. And that wouldn't be good for anyone. That's why." He looked sorry he'd said it, but it was too late to take the words back.

Abruptly, he looked at his watch as if he had an appointment to keep. He straightened up. "So? Are we going to Geostationary? Gotta make up your minds now."

I looked to Weird. He gave me a half-and-half expression, and finally said, "Well, it'd be silly to come all this far and not go all the way."

"Yeah!" I said. Because I really did want to go, no matter what Mom said. And so did Stinky.

We were going up again.

A CHANGE OF PLANS

NO, WE WEREN'T.

At least, not right away.

"What's the matter, Doug?"

"Mom said she was going to call the police." Weird looked genuinely worried.

Dad nodded. "We're seventy-two hundred kilometers away . . . and sixteen klicks up."

"She could phone someone," I suggested.

"She could," Dad agreed. "But it's a question of jurisdiction. She'd have to get the local authorities to agree to detain us. And that would require a judge's order and an international warrant. And that would require—" He looked at his watch and thought for a second. "It won't happen this late on a Saturday. Tell you what, though. Before we start looking around the station, let's check our reservations"—Dad led us over to a customer service desk; the woman who was working there had almost no hair at all—"just in case that storm screws things up."

Dad shouldn't have said that. Stinky looked worried. "Are we going to feel the storm up here, Daddy?"

Before Dad or Weird could answer, the hairless woman said, "Nothing to worry about, young man. The orbital elevator was originally designed to withstand wind forces of more than four hundred and fifty kilometers per hour. Since then, its strength has been upgraded to five hundred and fifty."

"Yes, but what are we going to feel?" I asked.

The woman was annoyingly cheerful. She pointed. "Over there by the information center, there's an educational display that will show you exactly what will happen the entire length of the cable. You'll see these big leisurely waves that rise gently up the Line. They're hundreds of kilometers long. We'll get some rocking up here, but the waves will come in such long slow cycles that you won't be able to feel them. If you feel anything at all, it'll be like being on a very large boat on a very gentle ocean. We had a storm four years ago as big as this and it wasn't any problem."

"So there's no danger—?" Dad asked.

"None at all. Only a little inconvenience. But just for safety's sake, everybody is locking down all up and down the Line. It's a standard procedure. Most of the platform towns are already secured. Terminus might take a beating, they did last time, but nothing that couldn't be set right in a few weeks of regular repair duty."

"Will they still be sending up elevators?"

"Only cargo and supply pods. No passengers. It's too uncomfortable. Not the ride, the view. And it takes too long to get above the worst of it. They'll probably be sending up some scientific teams in one of the maintenance pods to look at the inside of the storm, they usually do, and of course the cable engineers like to look at the situation first-hand, but no—we won't be sending up any passengers."

"We were supposed to catch the 2:15 up to Geostationary—" I started to ask.

"Mm," she said, and touched her ear to listen to her communication channel. "Let me check on that for you." She made a face as she listened. "It's likely to be cancelled. Or they might send it up empty. But they're getting some pretty high winds already, so they're more likely to send up a water-pod in that time-slot. Let's see if we can get you onto another car instead." She turned to the workstation at her desk. There was a big vertical display behind her, showing the progress of all of the cars between Terminus and One-Hour. Already the cars lined up at Terminus were colored blue for water-pods instead of pink for passengers.

"The 12:15 will be here in forty-five minutes," she said. "It looks like a full load. 12:30 is full too. A lot of people were trying to get out before the storm hit. They shouldn't have waited so long. All right, let me see if I can do anything earlier. Hm, I can put you on standby for the 12:00, that'll start loading in fifteen minutes. Let me do that right now, but don't get your hopes up . . . and then let's see what else we have. You were lucky you came up when you did. The last car out will probably be the 12:30; it's just launching. I'll try and grab you space on the 12:45 or the 1:00, in case they get out, but don't hold your breath. It looks like they're locking down early. There's no danger, but they don't like to scare the passengers." She frowned.

"Is there anything *sooner?*" Dad asked. "Is there anything open on the car loading now?"

"I don't know. Wait a minute—" She studied her screens, biting her lower lip thoughtfully. "How fast can you run?"

"Huh?"

She picked up her phone. "I've got a cabin open on the 11:00. A no-show. I guess they'll forfeit their deposit. The car is already loading. It's a first class booking, but we'll upgrade you. We don't like sending them up empty—" She explained. "You've got ten minutes left before they seal it for launch. Down this corridor, the gate is at the end. I'll call ahead. They'll be expecting you. Go now! You should be able to make it."

We ran.

It wasn't that far, but halfway there Stinky suddenly started crying and screaming, "Aren't we gonna see One-Hour? You promised! You said we were gonna see One-Hour! I don't wanna go up in anymore elevators! Daddy, you promised! I wanna go on the rides!" Weird tried to shush him, but Stinky was on reverse—the more you shushed him, the louder he got. Then he went limp, refusing to move at all. I'd have walloped him, but then Weird would have walloped me and Dad would have had to break us up and we would have missed the elevator, so I grabbed Stinky's other arm, and Weird and I carried him along, him screaming bloody murder all the time, while Dad ran ahead, shouting and waving our boarding cards.

The elevators up to Geostationary run every fifteen minutes. As each one arrives, it slides off the track and into a loading bay. It has a one-hour layover, during which time it's serviced and loaded for the rest of its journey up to Geostationary. Fifteen minutes before launch, it's sealed and weighed and checked for hull integrity again—same like at Terminus. If it doesn't get triple green lights, a standby pod goes up instead; then depending on the seriousness of the problem, it either has to wait until the slack time at the end of the shift, or every other pod on the Line gets delayed fifteen minutes.

We made it—in fact, we made it with five minutes to spare, but Stinky was howling like a banshee, and if there had been an open balcony—not likely at this height—Weird and I would have been happy to toss him over the edge. Well, I would have, but I suspected Weird was starting to think like a grownup and would have probably hesitated on the third swing over the railing.

Anyway, we made it—almost—except right next to the boarding ramp Stinky broke free of both Weird and me and went running back down the ramp, his monkey bouncing along behind him. "Run away,

Toto!" He shouted. "Run away!" Weird threw himself after Stinky, catching him in a flying tackle, but the monkey kept going. Of course. Stinky had given it orders. I went chasing after it, careening around people and robots, while behind me Stinky crowed, "He got away! He got away!" I don't know how Stinky had programmed the little monster, but I couldn't get near it—

I stopped where I was, gasping for breath, and looked back to Dad. He pointed and gestured. "Get that damn thing!" I couldn't believe it. I chased the monkey around and around the souvenir booths and the newsstand and the little pizza kiosk, but I couldn't get near it—and the monkey started singing and whistling like a calliope. Only after a moment did I recognize the song and realized that everybody who was watching was laughing like crazy. *Pop Goes The Weasel.* "All around the cobbler's bench, the monkey chased the weasel. . . ."

"Three minutes, Chigger!"

The hell with it. It was Stinky's monkey, not mine. I stopped chasing, took three deep breaths, and then started loping back toward the boarding ramp. If Stinky started screaming about his monkey, it was his own damned fault. And sure enough: "Where's my monkey? I want my monkey—"

"Go get it yourself," I yelled at him. So of course he did. That is, he tried to, but Weird grabbed him in mid-leap and pulled him backward off his feet. He screamed in rage, as loud as he could, and people all over the lobby turned to stare. Then Dad demanded as I came running up to the door, "Where's the goddamned monkey?" And I said, "Screw the goddamned monkey! Stinky programmed it to run away. You want it? You go get it."

For a moment, Dad looked like he was going to hit me—

"Go ahead!" I shouted. "Prove Mom right!"

He put his hand down, glaring at me.

"It's not my fault, Dad. He's a goddamned spoiled brat and you shouldn't have bought him the goddamned monkey in the first place. And now that it ran away, the hell with it—he's had his three hundred dollars worth of fun. Let it go for all I care. Isn't it about time he learned about consequences? I never got a goddamned programmable monkey—" I pushed past Dad into the elevator.

Dad looked like he wanted to kill something, but he knew I was right. He also looked like he wanted to go after the monkey, but the attendant said, "I'm sorry, sir. We're closing the door in thirty seconds. You won't have time." So Dad and Weird and screaming-Stinky came grumbling in after me. Dad looked apoplectic. And justifiably so. But I'd just about had it with Stinky shrieking and Stinky running away and me always being expected to chase after him and drag him back. Dad was treating me like a full-time baby-sitter, and instead of paying me, he bawled me out whenever anything went wrong. Well, the hell with that!

And then, just as the triple doors started sliding shut, the damned monkey came hurtling through it like a hairy torpedo. The launch attendant—he was another guy with no hair—hit his button and the doors bounced back open; he gave us a dirty look as the monkey leapt over a couch and launched itself into Stinky's arms. I ignored him. Dad had told us they always tried to close the doors a few minutes early to give themselves a margin of error for launch checks. Meanwhile, the monkey was clinging desperately to Stinky, screaming, "Bobby, no run ray! No run ray!" Right then, I promised myself that as soon as I found a screwdriver, I would dismantle the damn thing, but Weird spoke up first. "After he goes to sleep, I'll install override commands, Dad. This won't happen again."

Dad didn't answer. I turned around to look, and he was leaning up against the back of a chair, just breathing hard and looking so pale I thought he was having a heart attack or something.

Anyway, we were aboard.

FIRST CLASS

OUR CABIN ATTENDANT WAS NAMED Mickey and his hair was so short, he was almost bald. He looked so shiny and clean he could have been a robot. He had one of those perpetual smiles that wouldn't quit, and he acted like he was genuinely glad to see us and he kept trying to make friends with me and Stinky and Weird as if he'd been waiting all his life for this moment. He was so sincere about it I had to hate him. I wouldn't give him a chance to hate me first.

Our cabin was up at the top of the car. This car was bigger than the one we'd caught at Terminus. It was ten stories high and each level was big enough to hold as many as ten cabins. The level we were on, there were only four cabins and they were all big. We had a wall of windows with drapes that were secured at both the top and the bottom, and a big overhead window too, so we could look straight up.

What was weird was the way everything looked. Even Weird said it was weird. Mickey just smiled and explained that this was because the inside of the car was built to rotate around its central axis, so that it could be spun like a top as we approached micro-gravity. Then the outer walls would become the floors, and all the furniture and appliances had to swivel; that's why they were built the way they were. He said they'd spin us up to one-third gee, and it would feel almost normal.

Most people think that space is all free fall, but it isn't really. Weird started to explain how it's really micro-gravity, he should know because he's not really from this planet anyway, but that made Mickey the attendant look at him impressed, and then Weird looked at Mickey surprised that someone had actually noticed him being smart. And then the two of them took turns explaining it to me and Stinky as if either of us actually cared.

Micro-gravity means the pull of gravity is so small it might as well be free fall, it's mostly irrelevant to whatever else is going on. Anyway, right now we were inside a horizontal pie-wedge; later on, as we went up, we would be inside a vertical pie-wedge. I pretended I didn't much care, but I was really wondering what it would be like to have windows in the floor. Mickey explained that there were automatic shutters that would close when they started spinning the car, so we wouldn't have those windows anymore. That was good. I was pretty much over my nervousness about how high we were, as long as I didn't have to look out any more windows, but I'd just as soon not have windows under my feet anywhere.

Mickey showed us where to stash our suitcases and how to unfold the beds and the chairs and how to tell the TV to turn on, all that stuff. He showed us how the bathroom worked too—it was mostly familiar, but the toilet and the sink were on swivels for when the cabin started spinning. The shower was a sealed box, kind of odd-shaped, and instead of an actual sprayer, it had vacuum hoses. Mickey said that the blue hose was for washing and the red one was for shaving.

"Shaving?"

In answer, Mickey just grinned and brushed his hand across the top of his shaven head. "If Douglas doesn't want to explain, there's a program you can watch on space-hygiene. We have the most exclusive cable channels of all." He grinned at his own joke, but I got the feeling he told it to everybody. "And we have a very extensive library."

There was a chime then, and Mickey said, "I've got a launch station to attend to. I'll be back later to sort out the paperwork on the change in your reservations." He bounced out, leaving us in a cabin that was bigger and more comfortable than our living room back home in El Paso.

The TV came to life automatically then. By now, all four of us could do the speech in unison. "Welcome aboard. . . . For your own safety. . . . etc., etc." The usual blather. "Our upstairs restaurant is now open and will remain open until thirty minutes before arrival at Geostationary. There are lounges and snack bars on levels three and seven. It's our pleasure to serve you and we hope you'll enjoy your journey with us."

"Dad?" Weird asked. "Can we go downstairs to the bottom lounge for departure? That's supposed to be the best view."

Stinky didn't want to leave his monkey behind, but Dad insisted and said he wouldn't be allowed to play with it if he fussed any more. "You'll have your toy all day—now it's our turn." Stinky didn't see the fairness of this, but he shut up and followed. We headed down the spiral staircase at the center of the car.

The downstairs lounge was full, but not crowded. The elevator held only a hundred and fifty people per trip, not counting attendants, so there was enough room at the windows for everybody. But the best views were on the sides near the cables. The car was just moving into launch position onto the cable track, so apparently we'd passed all our integrity checks.

Below us, the Earth was bathed in ghostly sunlight. The storm clouds shone so cold and white and bright that it was hard to believe how ferocious the winds must have been underneath them. I was glad we were well out of it. Someone said that the storm was likely to disrupt passenger traffic up the Line for as long as three days. Somebody else said that with all these storms, four in the last ten years, they should encase the bottom couple of miles of the cable so that the cars wouldn't be buffeted by the winds and that traffic wouldn't have to be affected. That sounded like a good idea to me, but when Weird started explaining how it could be done and real quickly, the whole idea got boring.

The last chime sounded, and the car started sliding upward. We hardly felt anything, but out the window the beanstalk started moving downward. This time the music was much more playful: Beethoven's Fourth Symphony, fourth movement. Another one of Dad's favorites. I smiled over at him and he smiled back at me in recognition. The symphony starts out with a joyful surge; then, possessed by its own enthusiasm, it weaves its melody into a powerful surge upward. It's one of Beethoven's happier works, and it sent us cheering up through the levels of One-Hour like a rocket.

Actually, it looked more like One-Hour was falling down the Line while we hung motionless in place. As we watched, it dropped away faster and faster until finally it disappeared into the distance. Within a short time the cables were zipping along again and we were truly alone in space—except we weren't. Long dead Ludwig had given us the perfect music for a journey he could not possibly have imagined, even in his most fevered days. We weren't just leaving One-Hour; we were leaving the Earth behind. Our next stop was (approximately) 22,300 miles above. 35,770 klicks. Compared to that, the distance from Terminus to One-Hour was insignificant.

There was a half-globe of the Earth built into the ceiling of the downstairs lounge. A glowing wire stuck straight out from the equator, representing the whole length of the Orbital Elevator. The wire was three and a half meters long—350 centimeters. Each centimeter represented a hundred miles. One-Hour was so close to the globe it couldn't really be represented in scale; it was just a button at the base of the Line. Geostationary was more than two meters out; 223 centimeters along the wire. The last 127 centimeters was there for balance. "Upline" they called it. There was a marble on the end representing Farpoint—the ballast asteroid tethered at the flyaway end of the cable. It takes a day to get to Geostationary; it takes another six hours to get to Farpoint.

What made the model so interesting was all the little lights creeping up and down the wire, representing all the separate elevator cars. There was even a red one to show where ours was on the beanstalk. We were still at the bottom. After waiting forever for it to move and hardly seeing any movement at all, I went back to the windows.

Now we were passing through the rings of lights again, but this time so fast that it was almost like they were dotted lines on the InterContinental Expressway. We still felt motionless. It was the lights that were falling. They dropped down the cables into the glaring sea of clouds below. I'd seen pictures of it, just about everybody has, but it's a lot different when you're there yourself. You'd think it would get boring really fast, but it doesn't. The Earth is just too beautiful. And besides, up here, you can't hear Mom.

"Anyone hungry?" Dad asked.

I thought about it. We'd had breakfast on the train; we hadn't had time to eat at Terminus; the snacks on the elevator up to One-Hour hadn't been much, and we'd missed most of our stopover. We hadn't eaten since breakfast. Now that Dad asked. . . . "Yeah," I said, almost in unison with Weird and Stinky. So we all took the elevator up to the top.

That's right. The elevator car had an elevator in it. It was inside the spiral staircase, not very big; it only held about eight people, but that was okay—the whole place felt kind of cozy. Everything was designed to save as much space as possible.

The restaurant was on the very top of the elevator car and it had a glass roof, so you could look up and see the stars and the cables reaching up into the sky. It was eerie seeing stars above and daylight below, but you get used to it really fast and then it looks normal. One thing I thought was interesting was that there was a large round solar panel on a swivel above the car to keep us from looking directly at the sun; it was large enough so that the car stayed in its shadow the whole time, but it was also small enough that it worked kind of like an artificial solar eclipse and you could see the sun's corona glowing out around the edges. The waiter said that the elevator was the only place in the world where you could see a perpetual solar eclipse.

Also—Dad thought this was clever—there was a scale near the

entrance, so you could weigh yourself. There was one downstairs too, next to the model of the Line. The higher we got, the less you weighed. Micro-gravity. So everybody who was worried about how much they weighed could stand on the scale and see how much they'd lost—except of course they hadn't really lost anything. Weird did fifteen minutes on the difference between weight and mass while we were waiting for our salads.

The food was pretty good. Better than we get back home. All the vegetables were fresh and crisp. Mickey the attendant stopped by our table to see how we were doing and to invite Weird and Stinky and me on a tour of the car later. When Dad remarked on how good the food was, Mickey told him that most of the veggies had come from the farms hanging just above One-Hour. There were more farms higher up. There were a whole bunch of farms out at Farpoint for seeding the farms of the interplanetary ships.

Mickey said once we reached micro-gravity, we'd be seeing large solar installations hanging off the Line; some would be factories, some would be power generators for local installations that needed to be energy self-sufficient—especially the maintenance stations. If there were ever an emergency, the engineers would be stranded unless they had an independent power supply. There were maintenance stations spaced regularly along the whole length of the Line. If for any reason an elevator car were in trouble, a high-speed maintenance pod could jet down to meet them from the next highest station and be there in less than five minutes. I wondered if a counter-balanced pod would be launched at the other end of the elevator. Probably. Everything else was balanced. Weird said that the cable was strong enough to handle little imbalances, but that the engineers were under orders to balance the load as rigorously as they could along the entire length.

It was okay, I didn't need to find out first-hand. I wanted the trip to be interesting—but not *that* interesting.

ELEVATOR MUSIC

THE THING IS, NOTHING HAPPENS on an elevator. It goes up. It comes down. You stand and watch the numbers and nobody talks to anybody. It's the same way on the space elevator, only the numbers are bigger and it takes longer to get to the top. As boring as an elevator ride is, try to imagine one that takes a whole day. It doesn't matter how good the food is or how big the view is—after you've eaten and after you've looked at the view, there's not a whole lot else to do.

Okay, so there's a casino on the bottom level and a game room for the kids and 5000 video and music and game channels and unlimited net access and library functions and . . . so what? We have most of that stuff at home—everything except the casino, which I was too young for anyway. But if I didn't care about all those channels at home, why should I care about them here. It's all just bits and bytes and humming phosphors.

Oh, and there's a swimming pool. Actually, it's part of the water-storage system; the water is for ballast and weight-balancing, and it's needed for the production of food and oxygen all up and down the line, but on its way up it's for swimming too. "Have you ever wanted to go swimming in space?" They say the micro-gravity makes it very interesting. The higher you get, the weirder the water moves—except that after a while, it's almost like free fall and then they close the pool area, to keep people from drowning in globules of runaway H_2O.

Naturally, Stinky wanted to go swimming. I thought about it, but not for very long. I didn't want to be around Stinky anymore. Or Dad. Or Doug. As much fun as swimming in space might be, going with them guaranteed that it wouldn't be much fun at all.

Of course, when I announced my decision, it started another fight.
"Come on, Charles—" Dad said. "We need to do more things together."

"We already do lots of stuff together," I said. "We fight. We run
away from each other. We throw tantrums. We blame Chigger for
Stinky getting water down the wrong pipe. We pose for the cover of
Dysfunctional Family Magazine . . ."

Dad looked like he wanted to slug me. Good. It just proved my
point. "I'm not going," I repeated. "Blame someone else this time."

"Let him be, Dad," Weird said. "It's not your fault if Chigger wants
to be a sociopath. You can blame it on Mom." He said it deadpan.

Dad gave Weird an even dirtier look than the one he'd given me,
but instead of arguing, he just sagged and gave in. "I'm tired of fighting," he said. "I don't care anymore. You kids are about as much fun
as a visit to the proctologist. Come on, Bobby."

"Huh?" I looked to Weird. "What's a poctorologist?"

"It means you're a pain in the ass," Weird said, and followed after.

"You too—" I shouted, but he didn't hear me. Or didn't care.

I found a dark corner where I could be alone and curled up at one
end of a couch, plugged into my music. With my eyes closed, with my
headphones turned up, I could try again to climb all the way into the
sound. Sometimes I almost made it. And sometimes I even got there.
And sometimes—but not very often anymore—I got there and kept
going so far into it I couldn't stand it, I had to get up and scream and
dance—but ever since Mom and Dad had declared war it was harder
and harder to get to the other side, because you can't dance in a battle
zone. But even when I did get away from the house, it still didn't work,
and if it wasn't the music that wasn't working, then it was me—so now
I just wanted to be alone so I could go looking for the music again.
Different music. Music that would take me there again.

There was a lot of stuff to listen to—most of it overrated. I clicked
through the music, flipping from page to page without interest. As much
as I loved all the music Dad had given me, Beethoven and Bach and
Brahms and Mozart and Orff and Stravinsky and Mussorgsky and Sho-
stakovich and Mahler and Wagner and all those other dead white Eur-
opeans—as much as I loved their music, I didn't want them anymore.
That was Dad's music. Not mine. I wanted something that belonged to
me, not him; something that I discovered myself.

There was this guy I'd found. Almost by accident. I'd been reading
about the history of jazz, and there was this article about him and his
influence, how he'd faded from memory and been rediscovered, again
and again. The writer had said, "Listen to the music! Turn off the lights
and just fall into it. And think about the time and place it came from.

This guy Coltrane was so fucking subversive that afterward, nothing else was ever the same!"

I didn't know anything about historical jazz—which is nothing like the stuff they call jazz now—so I listened to something called *A Love Supreme*. And I hated it. I didn't get it at all. But I kept listening because I wanted to know what that guy meant by "so fucking subversive" that I kept listening and listening, even though all I really wanted to do was rip the headphones off and wash my head out. Except I couldn't— because I couldn't stand the thought of not knowing, so I kept playing it over and over and over. I tried reading a couple of the analytical essays, but they didn't help. They distracted. Knowing that the music wasn't about love for a woman, but love for God, was interesting—but it wasn't the music. And knowing that this part of the music was really Coltrane reciting a psalm through the saxophone was interesting—but that wasn't the music either.

So I'd turned it off and listened to something else—*tried* listening to something else. Except nothing else worked anymore. Everything sounded shallow.

And that's when I got it—

—not all of it, but enough.

Jazz isn't music. Jazz is what happens when the music disappears and all that's left is the sound and the emotion connected to it. Jazz is a scream or a rant or a sigh. Or whatever else is inside, trying to get out.

And when you listen to it like that, you don't have to understand it. All you have to do is get it. And in the middle of the night, with my headphones clamped to my head, in the middle of a scorching saxophone riff that had to be about anger and love and frustration and hurt all wrapped into one gritty scream of sound, I got it—that sound was about how somebody felt and right now it was about how I felt. And I got it.

And after that, whenever I wanted to get away from Mom or Dad, but especially whenever I wanted to get away from Mom *and* Dad, I went to the music and the music I went to was John Coltrane, and I'd listen with my hands holding the headphones tight to my ears until I heard the sound that was me, and then I knew I was all right. I wasn't alone. There was someone else who knew. Or who had known. And it was all right for a while. A little while, anyway.

J'MEE

IF I HAD MY WAY, I'd listen to music forever. But sooner or later, usually sooner, somebody wants something, and they're never polite about it. They never say, "Oh, I see Charles is listening to his music, I'll come back later." Instead, they always say, "If you're not doing anything . . ." Excuse me? I *am* doing something. I'm listening to my music. But what they're *really* saying is, "What I want is so much more important than what you want that what you want is irrelevant." And usually, it comes out as *"Chigger, would you take those damn headphones off and listen to me!!"* I don't think I've ever gotten to the end of any music.

And this time, I didn't either—

This time it was a kid. A skinny kid in T-shirt and baggy overshirt, shorts, and scabby knees. I had a weird feeling like someone was watching me and I opened my eyes and there he was, standing right in front of me, staring. My age maybe. But smaller. Brown hair, cut very short. Goofy smile. He tilted his head sideways with a funny sort of expression, but I couldn't hear what he was saying, and even though I didn't want to take off the headphones—I was listening to *The Paris Concert*—my concentration had already been broken, and wherever I had been I wasn't getting back there tonight, if ever, so I peeled the headphones off my ears and said, "What?"

"I *said*, 'What are you listening to?' " He had a soft girlish voice.

Nobody ever asked *that* before. Nobody ever cared enough. "Why do you want to know?"

"Because you had such a strange look on your face, I wanted to know what program you were running."

"I wasn't running a program. I was listening to music. Have you ever heard of John Coltrane?"

He scratched his head—some people do that when they think, probably because thinking makes their brain itch, but this kid actually went into a momentary trance—then he snapped out of it, frowning. He said, "One of the most influential jazz saxophonists of the nineteen-fifties. Died of liver cancer in 1967. Recorded with Miles Davis and McCoy Tyner and Thelonious Monk. The recordings he made for Impulse are generally regarded as his best, in particular—"

"What are you plugged into?" I interrupted.

"Nothing." He grinned.

"You've got all that in your head?"

He nodded and tapped the space above his right ear. "Built in."

I didn't say anything, I just sorta sucked in my cheeks. Augments are expensive. Whoever this kid was, he was worth a lot of money. Or his family was.

"Is he any good?"

"Who?"

"Coltrane."

"I thought you knew—"

"Not yet, but I will . . . in a little bit." He scratched his head again.

"That won't work."

"Why do you say that?"

"Because it won't. You can't listen to Coltrane. Not like you listen to anybody else. That's why."

"How *do* you listen to Coltrane?"

I shook my head. "It can't be explained. You just gotta go out there where the music lives and live there with it."

He frowned, puckering up his mouth while he turned my words over in his head. It was a funny expression. I bet his grandma liked to pinch his cheek and say, "Look at this, isn't this such a cute little face, I could eat it up." And I bet he hated it too.

Abruptly, he finished with whatever he was thinking about. He said, "My name's J'mee, what's yours?"

"Chi—Charles."

"How far are you going? We're going to the moon."

"For a vacation?"

"Uh-uh. To live. What about you?"

"Um, we're supposed to be going to Geostationary, but . . . we might go farther."

"The moon?"

I shrugged. "Dad was talking about a brightliner. I don't know if he was serious."

"Your Dad is like mine."

"Huh?"

"Daddy says the Earth is getting too dangerous."

"I don't think it's that bad."

"Where are you from?"

"El Paso. Where are you from?"

J'mee shrugged. "All over."

"Yeah, but where do you call 'home'?"

"The last place was Edmonton. Daddy does a lot of traveling for the company."

"What does your dad do?"

"He's a conductor."

"Really? So's mine!" I was suddenly interested. "What orchestra does your dad work with?"

"No. My dad's an *electrical* conductor. Or sometimes he says he's a 'power broker.' For the Line. Do you know that the Line generates electricity? A lot. It has something to do with poles and potentials and moving through the Earth's magnetic field and generating super-currents. Do you know what super-currents are?"

"Lightning."

"Yeah, that's the short explanation. But super-currents are part of what holds the Line up. You probably don't want to know this, most people don't, but the Line isn't strong enough to hold itself up. Earth's gravity is just a little too high, and the molecular bonds aren't strong enough to withstand the strain. But when you run a supercurrent through superconducting carbon-doped titanium-ceramic alloys you get a super-bond, with the current doing most of the work. Daddy says the Line is made of lightning, that's how much power is flowing through it."

"Oh, yeah," I said. "I knew that." Sort of. Lightning, huh? I looked at the huge cables just outside the windows with new respect.

"Don't you think it's scary?" J'mee said.

I shrugged. Yes, it was scary. But I wasn't going to admit it. I looked around the lounge, feeling suddenly uncomfortable. This was the feeling that I'd had down below just before we started up, only worse. I wished J'mee would change the subject.

Instead, he nattered on: "Daddy says, if you could turn the current off, the whole thing would fall down—the Line would come apart in a million little explosions. Doesn't that make you feel gooshy inside? But don't worry. You can't turn the current off. It's automatic. The Line generates it because one end is sticking out in space and the other is connected to the Earth, and even if it weren't covered with windmills and solar skin, it would still generate electricity because of all the different potentials. And that electricity has to be drained off to keep the potentials unbalanced and keep the current flowing.

"That's Daddy's job. To keep the electricity flowing. He sells it to whoever will buy it. And there are lots of people who need it all over the world. He's real good at explaining it; he's got a whole VR program that lets you see exactly how it works. The peak power flow follows the day. In any particular place, the need for power starts just before sunrise and goes up and up all day long. On a hot day, when everybody has all their air conditioners going, the hours around noon are the most profitable, and then the power demand ebbs, peaking again at dinner time and sunset, and then ebbs away, dropping off after ten or eleven and hitting its lowest levels at three or four in the morning. But that's only if you look at one location. If you watch the way the daylight moves around the planet, so do the waves of power demand, and that's what Daddy does. He makes contracts to sell the power to fill in the peak demands all up and down the entire western hemisphere and even across the oceans to parts of Africa and Australia and a lot of the Pacific islands. The Line almost generates too much power. Sometimes Daddy has to give it away. Or even throw it away. The Line has got microwave beaming stations that can send the excess anywhere there's a receiver, but if there's no one who will pay for it, Daddy dumps the extra power into space or sometimes even into the ocean or the atmosphere—wherever someone needs to heat up the air or the water because they want to try to divert an ocean flow or a hurricane or something."

"They didn't do too well with Hurricane Charles," I said. I didn't mean it badly, but apparently J'mee took it that way. He made a face and turned away to look out the window. The hurricane was a vast white sweep below us.

Finally, J'mee said, "I don't know why they didn't stop the hurricane. I know they were going to try. Daddy was talking about beaming power at it all last week. I thought they were. We were in Terminus, and Daddy had meetings all day. He was awfully worried about something. I don't know what." He stared out the window again. "It's hard to believe we'll never go back."

"You're jumping off the planet too?"

"Yeah. You too?"

"Uh-huh," I admitted. It gave me a weird feeling just to say it aloud.

"Why're you going?" J'mee asked.

I shrugged. I really didn't want to talk about it. How could I explain it anyway? I can't even explain jazz. And explaining jazz is easy, compared to explaining life. Except maybe the same principle applies: If you have to have it explained to you, you don't understand it.

Weird says it's possible to tell your whole life story in thirty seconds. That's another one of the weird things he says. But I sort of understood what he meant. You have to leave out the details. The details aren't interesting. It's the interpretation. Like in music. The notes themselves don't mean anything—it's how you put them together—and how you play them.

When I was little, I used to pretend my life was a grand concert. The overture was Mom and Dad meeting. Two conflicting motifs. She was a singer and he was an arranger, so naturally they spent a lot of time together. Making beautiful music. That's enough to overwhelm anyone. They had so much fun making music they got confused, they thought they were in love. Decided to live happily ever after and create a glorious symphony of joy. Or something. . . .

First movement. Melody plus counter-melody equals harmony—a new theme, full of expectation. Whoops, a little too expectant. A pregnant diva? A tremulous minor chord. Does this portend disharmony or resolution? The diva stops singing and stands aside. For just a bit. But the movement has to resolve. Will it be joyous or tragic?

So they get married and have me. This is supposed to be good news. So the second movement opens with a triumphant fanfare. Bridge to a tableau of pastoral beauty. The diva returns to center stage and sings the second movement sweetly toward a promise of greater triumphs still to come. The conductor is glorious and everything sparkles in the afternoon. I like the second movement. I want to go home to it. But it's over too soon. It's just there to provide contrast for the horrors to follow.

Suddenly, the third movement. Unasked, the composer expands the wind section with the worst of all possible untuned wind instruments: a baby. Some people think there's beauty in cacophony, if you know how to do it right. Ives unanswers questions all over the stage. Mom and Dad get the cacophony part right. The diva starts shrieking invective at the conductor, claiming it's his fault the music isn't working. The conductor waggles his baton at the diva warningly; he tries to get the rest of the musicians to play. But suddenly he is dragged kicking and screaming out of the concert hall by the ushers while the diva throws music stands after him. She is hissed by the audience, who start throwing eggs and tomatoes.

Fourth movement. Everybody in the orchestra plays whatever they feel like. If no one listens, they play louder. The diva shrieks a monotonic babble, like something out of a minimalist opera, only not as melodic. The conductor sneaks back into the hall and kidnaps the wind section. The strings light torches, grab a rope, and go charging after.

And that's the nice way to explain it.

Mom had a career. So did Dad. Until they got married. Then Mom didn't have a career and Dad did. And Mom hated him for it. It was no secret. I heard her say it to him enough times, "You still have a career. Why don't you come home and wash a few stinky diapers in the toilet once in a while—then you'll see what I'm so angry about! I'm flushing my best years away! I thought we were going to record together—"

Whatever Dad did, it was wrong. Mom complained that he wasn't earning enough money to support a family, so he went out and worked harder. But when he worked harder, Mom whined that he wasn't spending enough time at home. But that wasn't it. Mom was unhappy because Dad was having a life, and she wasn't. And it never occurred to her that maybe Dad didn't want to spend too much time with her because she wasn't all that much fun anymore. But if she wasn't all that much fun for him, why did he assume she would be any more fun for us?

Weird tells me I've got it all bass-ackwards, that it was more Dad's fault than Mom's, because he kept promising to get her back in front of a microphone, and he never did. It was all broken promises to her. Just like all the broken promises to us. He said that we don't take Dad's promises seriously because we've never seen him keep any—but Mom always believed him because she always *wanted* to believe him. And that's why she's always so angry, because she's frustrated that no one around her keeps their word.

But she takes it out on me. Every time she sees me caught up in my music, she has to interrupt. She rants at me, "You're just like your father. He hides out in music too. It's a waste of time, Charles! And the sooner you learn that, the happier you'll be. It'll never make you a nickel."

So how am I supposed to take her side in that argument? Or any argument? I'd have to give up the only thing I have left.

Mom says that the music is my way of trying to get close to Dad. But she's wrong. The music isn't my way of getting close to Dad or anyone. It's my way of getting away from both of them and going somewhere else. Someplace where things always resolve in the final eight bars.

After the divorce, it was all I had left. Mom didn't have any money. And I guess, neither did Dad because he never sent us enough. So we couldn't take the piano with us. Mom had to sell it. I remember crying when the moving men came to take it away. I had a keyboard, but it wasn't the same. And Mom wouldn't let me continue my lessons anyway. She said it was time for me to get practical—but what she really meant was that it was time for Dad to get practical. And because he wasn't there, she was going to make sure I didn't grow up like him. Which was why I didn't want to go back. I was tire of her punishing me because she couldn't get her hands on Dad.

But I couldn't tell that to J'mee. Or anyone. Because I was embarrassed for both Mom and Dad. And myself for having them as parents.

It was easier to change the subject. "You want to go swimming?" I asked.

I don't know why I'd said that. Only after the words were out of my mouth did I realize what a mistake that would be. I hoped he'd say no.

"Okay—"

"Uh, let's not. I changed my mind."

"Uh-uh. You don't get to change your mind. Come on." J'mee grabbed my hand and pulled me to my feet. For a little guy, he was strong. Wiry. Or just determined. I dunno. He pulled me along and I went along reluctantly.

When we got to the pool, I realized I didn't have any swimming trunks. J'mee said not to worry about it and put his card into the slot of the machine. He punched up two disposable swimsuits and gave one to me. I got the feeling he was used to buying whatever he wanted, whenever he wanted to.

In the changing room, J'mee was a little shy, which was fine with me, because I don't like changing clothes in front of other people either. I followed J'mee into the bathroom; he went into one stall and I went into another. He must have been very shy about being so small and skinny. He came out still wearing his T-shirt and hugging his arms across his chest.

"You going swimming in your shirt?"

"Yeah. I always do."

I didn't think this was the truth, but everybody is weird in their own way. It's that geek business again—that thing Weird said once—everybody's a geek somehow. I'm a music geek. Weird's a techno-geek. Maybe J'mee was a shy-and-skinny-geek. Or something. I guess the way geeks get along with other geeks is that we pretend not to notice each other's particular geekiness. Or maybe we just don't care. I dunno.

The pool was kind of small and funny-shaped. But that's because it wasn't a pool as much as it was a tank with a door. It didn't have a deep end; it had a deep side and a shallow side. This had to do with the way the room was shaped and how the water would slosh sideways when the elevator car was spun for pseudo-gravity. But there were a bunch of people in it anyway, shouting and laughing, even Dad and Weird and Stinky. J'mee jumped right into the water in the deep side. I like to get in slowly and get used to it, but when J'mee jumped in, so did I. The water was warmer than I'd expected and I shouted with surprise.

"Hey, look who's here," Dad said. "Chigger decided to join us after all."

J'mee looked at me. "Chigger?"

I made a face. "It's a nickname. My grampa used to say I was no bigger than a chigger. And it stuck."

"I won't tell you my nickname," J'mee said, and ducked under water swimming off to the opposite end. I swam after.

We played tag for a while, trying to duck each other, until Weird and Stinky challenged us to a game of horse-and-rider. Stinky rode on Weird's shoulders. J'mee rode on mine. I thought it would be a fair match because Stinky was so small. We got knocked down a few times and so did they—until Stinky started crying (which was inevitable) because he got ducked once too often and got water up his nose, and I was sure Dad was going to yell at me, but instead Dad just came over and got Stinky and told him he had to take a break for a while. He complained about that until Dad told him he could be referee. Dad put him on the sidelines to watch, and I thought the game was over, but then Dad came back and put me on his shoulders and J'mee rode on Weird, and this time the game was a lot more ferocious, with Weird pushing at Dad and me pushing at J'mee—and a couple of times we all fell down together, laughing. And for a while there I even forgot that I was angry.

So, yeah, it wasn't all bad. Once in awhile it was almost nice. And later, when we got out, we stood around for a bit, just laughing and grinning. J'mee hugged his chest again and pretended to shiver even though we were standing under the tanning lamps. I just stretched my arms up and out and leaned as far back as I could, basking under the narrow-spectrum UV rays. J'mee started to do the same, then stopped when he saw me looking at him. "I'm gonna go get dressed," he said abruptly.

"Okay, me too."

We went back to the changing room. This time all the bathroom stalls were filled, so we had to change in front of each other—except that J'mee turned his back to me when he pulled down his shorts and then he pulled on his underwear real fast. And that's when I figured it out. "You don't have any brothers, do you?" I asked.

"Huh? No. How can you tell?"

I shrugged. "Just the way you change clothes. That's all. Lotsa guys are shy."

J'mee didn't answer. He turned away and pulled off his wet T-shirt, then quickly pulled his sweatshirt on.

"Do you have any hair yet?" I asked.

"Huh?"

"You know, down there."

"Uh—"

"Let's see," I said. "I'll show you mine." I yanked down my shorts and turned so he could see. I didn't have a lot of hair, but enough so I didn't look like a baby anymore. J'mee glanced, in spite of himself, probably just to see if I meant it—then he glanced away quickly, face reddening.

"It's okay," I said. "You can look—"

"No thanks," he said, sitting down to pull on his sandals.

"Come on," I teased. "It doesn't bite."

"No!" he shouted, a little too loudly. He grabbed his other shoe and ran out of the changing room like he was suddenly scared of me.

Okay. So that was that. I shrugged and pulled my underwear up and finished getting dressed. When I came out of the pool area, J'mee was gone, and I couldn't find him in any of the lounges.

So I went back to the cabin and listened to my music until Dad and Stinky and Weird came in and interrupted me. Again.

CLOSE SHAVE

STINKY WAS WHINING ABOUT WANTING to play with his new monkey and Weird had gone back to being the techno-geek and Dad was annoyed about something else, I didn't know what. They just came in like a door blown open in a sandstorm and swept around the room for a while before they settled in.

I guess we were all tired. And not just physically. We'd been through a lot, and now it was catching up with us. Dad said that traveling was tiring, and even though most of what we'd been doing was sitting around and watching the scenery slide by, what little there was of it, I could see why he would think so. *Not* having anything to do is a lot more tiring than having everything to do. But I think we were tired of each other. I know I was.

The screen was blinking with a reminder to please watch the important informational video. Weird is datatropic or something. If it's educational, he has to read it or watch it or listen to it, so he punched up the program immediately. I flung myself down on a chair and glowered while Weird watched intently. Eventually, Dad put down his book and watched too. Off in the corner, Stinky happily made up his own code phrases and taught the monkey to do silly things whenever he said them. He had the monkey belching, pretending to fart, giving the finger, mooning and waggling its butt. If he could have taught it to crap on the rug as well, I bet he would have.

The video turned out to be a lot more interesting than it looked at first glance. It was full of funny stories about how to look like a jerk in micro-gravity. They had that red-haired comedian, you know the one, with his hair flaming out in all directions, stumbling through all the different ways to hurt yourself. So it was kind of interesting to watch after all.

There was one part that gave us pause. The guy who was narrating said, "If you're planning to go on to Luna or any other deep-space destination, body shaving is strongly recommended. If you are heading out to any military or scientific destination, it will be *required*."

"Huh?" I asked. "Body shaving?"

The program went on to show how the body flakes off zillions of tiny bits of skin and hair every day. In micro-gravity, this stuff floats around like a nanotech snowstorm. The hair is apparently the worst, cause it can clog up the micromachinery. As a long-term maintenance measure, the Loonies shave themselves and rub stuff on their skin so it doesn't flake so much, and apparently this was now recommended for anyone who was planning to spend any amount of time in space.

Dad said this was part of the economics involved in Elevator Theory. Macro events have micro effects; micro events have macro effects. In space body hair is a luxury. Hair holds dirt and bacteria and smells. When you have hair, your scalp also flakes a lot. And underarm hair and pubic hair gets into everything too. It's nasty.

And if that weren't disgusting enough, the program showed how all that stuff builds up in the recycling equipment and sometimes you get pockets of goop where bacteria can live—so minimizing all those flakes of skin and hair floating around is also good for preventing the spread of infection. The show didn't specifically mention what happened on the *Miranda.* They didn't have to. The lawsuits still hadn't been settled.

But they also said that without hair on your head or on your body, you don't use up as much water washing. So if you want to have hair, you have to pay for it. Dad said that there's a surcharge at some of the orbital hotels if you don't shave, because it costs more to clean up. More Elevator Theory economics.

Then the program showed the red-haired guy shaving everything— and I mean *everything*—even his head. He looked real sad about losing his hair and even sillier without it, but they let him keep a real short buzz on top, so you could still tell he was the same guy. The short hair looked better on the women, for some reason.

I thought the whole thing was a little extreme, but Dad said that it made sense to him, and the next thing I knew he and Weird were in the bathroom looking at the shaving equipment. Mostly, there was this big vacuum tube that came out of the wall with a kind of clippers in a big mouth at the end. It sucked up all the hair as fast as it clipped. The clipper was really a forest of micro-machines, first you set it for your age and your sex and how close you wanted to be shaved, and then you moved it slowly back and forth across your skin until the light on the end showed green, then you moved on to the next place. You had to do this for the hair on your head and your legs and under your arms and down below if you had anything there yet, which I did, but not really very much and I wasn't sure yet I wanted to lose it.

Weird said we should have gone to a shaving station at Terminus, where we could have gotten the full treatment, including the services of a professional shaver, and it was too bad we hadn't taken the time, but Dad just shrugged it off. "We have twenty-four hours of travel before we reach Geostationary. The equipment here will be sufficient."

Dad also said that the micro-economics of space were already becoming a part of Earth society. A lot of people who never went into space were shaving now, some because they thought it was sexy, but just as many were doing it to cut back on their water consumption. I could understand that. Mom was always complaining about the clean water taxes, which were almost as much as the water bill in El Paso. Now that he'd mentioned it, I realized there were a lot of bald people back home in our Tube-Town. I'd just never noticed it or thought about it before.

Anyway, after you shaved, you were supposed to take a special shower. It wasn't a shower like on Earth where the water jets come out of the wall. Instead, you get a little sprayer at the end of a hose, which you use for getting yourself wet, then you rub yourself all over with some foamy stuff, which is supposed to keep your skin from drying and flaking so much, and then you *shloop* it all off with another vacuum tube. If you do it right, your skin ends up feeling all slick and slippery, as soft and smooth as a baby's ass.

Dad went first, then Weird, then me, then Stinky. I thought we ended up looking like fat brown slugs. *Bald* fat brown slugs. Mom was going to kill us when we got back. And it felt kind of weird to be so smooth all over. My clothes felt a lot rougher too.

There were some nylan space-clothes in one of the closets. All different sizes, each set a different color. They were real light and soft, like one of Dad's silk shirts. When you opened the package you were automatically billed for them, but they didn't cost that much and Dad said we'd probably all be a lot more comfortable than if we tried to wear Earth-clothes. Earth-clothes are for protection from the weather. Space-clothes are for comfort and cleanliness.

The nylan space-suit is sort of a one-piece jumpsuit that you step into and zip up the front. It's one of those nano-zippers that disappears when you zip it. You can't even feel it. The wrists and the ankles are snug-fitting. So is the collar around the neck. This is again to keep skin flakes and hairs from being spread around. There are slipperlike shoes to wear too. The whole thing is kind of like dressing for a clean-room. There were also shower caps for people who didn't want to cut their hair and other caps for people who did, but the caps were optional; we didn't have to wear them. Stinky and I both did. Dad and Weird decided not to.

It felt like Halloween and after we were done, we all looked like Hallo-weenies. After Weird told him he was as smooth and as cute as a girl, Stinky went dancing around the room singing, "I'm a girl now, I'm a girl now." I just made a face and looked embarrassed. Was this really necessary? But Dad said we'd get used to it and we'd probably find it a lot more comfortable than trying to keep wearing our Earth-clothes. So we packed them all up in the dirty clothes bag and put them in the closet and forgot about them.

TELEVISION

IT TAKES TWENTY-FOUR HOURS TO get to Geostationary. If you take an express, you can do it in six hours, but they only run express cars two or three times a day, and they're very expensive because they use rocket assists and special tracks. There are also maintenance tracks and balance tracks. The cables are thick enough now so that they can have multiple tracks on each one.

The balance tracks are mostly above One-Hour. They're on the opposite side of the cable from the main tracks, but every so often, you can see the long bulge of a water-pod hanging in place. There are several thousand water-pods on the Line, and they move up and down on their tracks as needed, to counterbalance any big waves in the cable, like the ones caused by Hurricane Charles below.

Most people think the cables are rigid, but they're not. Well, they are if you look only at a small section at a time—like a few thousand meters or so—and gravity helps too. But when you consider that the cable is really thousands of kilometers long—all the way up to Geostationary and then half again as far out beyond for balance—a whole different scale of physics comes into play. Dad says that on that scale, a continent has the consistency of chocolate cake, and the cable is like a piece of spider web, so it will react to certain kinds of very big movements—like a hurricane, for instance. It sets up waves. That's why the water-pods are moved up and down to different places to help damp the waves. I don't really understand all of the mechanics, but it has something to do with breaking the rhythm—or maybe that's *braking* the rhythm. Anyway, it's like not letting all the soldiers march in step across the bridge or it'll collapse.

This was all explained in another program. It didn't matter what time it was, there were always programs about the orbital elevator: about how it was built and when the first cars were dropped down it and when public service began and how many passengers use the cable every day and how many people there are on the cable at any given moment—stuff like that.

There was a whole program just on the elevator cars alone, all the different types, how they work, how they're constructed inside, how they're connected to the tracks. The bigger cars have longer carriages and they stand away from the cable more. They're mounted at the tops and bottoms, so they look like handles with windows in them sliding up and down the Line.

It's all done with magnetic induction. The car never even touches the cable unless it has to stop, in which case there are contact brakes, because the track-riding mechanisms aren't really designed for slowing and stopping; they're designed for moving a thousand miles an hour. You can't just slow an elevator down and hold it in place because magnetics don't work like that, so that's why there are contact brakes; but even contact brakes have to be specially designed, because the cars are moving so fast that to try to stop one, the brakes would generate enough heat to permanently weaken the cable. So stopping a car isn't a simple operation.

If the car is going up, they just turn off the magnetics and let the car coast for a bit until it burns off most of its speed. When it's still going about fifty miles an hour upward, that's when the contact brakes grab hold. But stopping the car when it's going down is a whole other story; they have to reverse the magnetic inductors and slow the car, and that takes a whole lot longer to reduce its speed.

Restarting a car is easier going down, but almost impossible going up, because the magnetic inductors are spaced too far apart for an easy start. They don't really expect cars to stop and start on the cable anyway. Weird said that in the event of a real problem, the Line engineers would rather pop the car off and either let it parachute down if it's low enough, or catch it somewhere in orbit if it's too high to land.

The most interesting show we saw was a rerun of the *Nova* episode called "Breakaway Revisited" about what would happen if the cable snapped. First they showed clips from the movie *Breakaway* which supposedly depicted everything that would happen in such an accident. They showed all the best shots, of the cable falling and falling and falling and finally wrapping itself around the Earth, slicing across continents, jungles, deserts, oceans, mountains. They extrapolated all the damage that could occur. It was pretty scary stuff—I was surprised they were even showing it on the cable channels.

The most likely place for the Line to break would be low Earth orbit, around the 1000-kilometer point, because that's where the most and fastest orbital junk is—and the most ionized gas too, which also has a corrosive effect. But the part that fell back to Earth would be relatively short and thin. And it would fall almost vertically. A break at the 1000-kilometer point would result in the broken end arriving at ground level about eight minutes later, at a speed of nearly 4 km/sec, about 25 km west of Terminus Station—the foothills of the Andes.

A break higher up, though, would be much more serious. If the beanstalk snapped at Geostationary, the upper half would fly away into space, but the lower half would be 40,000 kilometers long. It would wrap itself around the planet—*all the way around the planet!*

It would be like detonating nuclear weapons along every inch of the equator. The destruction could be as bad as the asteroid that killed the dinosaurs. When you calculate mass and impact, you're talking about an object 40,000 kilometers long, circling the Earth and hitting the ground with the equivalent force of twenty times its own weight in TNT. It's an extinction-level event.

We would lose millions of lives, first from the immediate destruction around the equator and vicinity, then millions more from all the after-effects. Slumbering volcanoes might be shaken back to life. Earthquakes would very likely be triggered along fault lines. Uncontrollable firestorms would be started across the Amazon and the heart of Africa. A gigantic wall of ash would climb into the atmosphere—at least as bad as anything caused by an asteroid impact—and all that soot in the air would create a nuclear autumn and probably a decade-long disruption of the seasons, maybe longer. The impact of the cable across the Atlantic and Pacific oceans would cause immediate tsunamis on every coastline, and noticeable heating of tropical water temperatures as well—enough to trigger super-hurricanes. After that, the *real* disaster would begin: the inevitable extinction of many species; the disruption of rainfall, migration patterns on land and sea, and crop-growing seasons; long-term famines.

Oh, and one other thing. If one Line failed in a big way, enough to wrap around the Earth, it would very likely knock down all the others with it—the one in Africa, and the one at Christmas Island. And each of those failures would have equally disastrous effects.

Of smaller import, but equally significant to human beings, would be the near-total collapse of the global economy.

The Line represents such an enormous part of the wealth of the planet that its destruction and the destruction of property on land and in space would essentially bankrupt every insurance company in the world. The loss of capital would also bankrupt every investment company. The interconnectedness of everything would pull down everything.

The failure of the beanstalk would also maroon many people in space with no safe way to return, simply because there wouldn't be the spacecraft available. Without regular supplies, the folks in the asteroids, the Lagrange colonies, and other bases would run out of food, water, and air. Only Luna and Mars were anywhere near self-sufficiency. The death toll in space would be proportionally more severe than the death toll on the ground. Three out of every five. As many as six million people.

But then the show started examining all of the movie's premises and took each one apart to show that for all of the events in the movie to actually happen, the cable would have had to have been designed to fail. They showed how the individual fibers of the cable were manufactured out of superlong molecules, how they were braided, strengthened, linked, and energized by superpowerful currents—so that even if a terrorist were to succeed in planting a strong enough bomb on an elevator car, it still wouldn't destroy the beanstalk. All three cables were now cross-linked every hundred klicks, and those linkages were designed to provide enough support so that a broken cable would stay in place until a repair crew could arrive to secure it. In fact, any single one of the cables was thick enough and strong enough to hold the other two in place if a break occurred. They showed that even if all three cables were broken at different places, the beanstalk would still survive long enough to be repaired. The only way a terrorist could destroy it, he'd have to snap all three cables at the same place, which just wasn't possible because the cables were held far enough apart from each other to put them well out of each other's blast radius. Even a piece of orbiting space junk colliding with the Line could only take out one cable, not all three, because they were spaced farther apart than the size of any known piece of junk. Anything short of a nuclear device would be insufficient to snap the Line.

Part of the show talked about some of the proposals to add self-destruct mechanisms to the beanstalk. One guy wanted to mine the entire length of each cable with binary explosives, so if the cable snapped, the whole thing would be blown to bits and all the bits would vaporize on the way down through the atmosphere, so nobody on the ground would get hurt. But the analysis of that plan showed that it was not only too expensive, but even if you could do it, and even if all the cables snapped, it still wouldn't work. The resultant meteor showers would do almost as much damage as a falling cable, and the radius of destruction would be far wider. And besides, there was more chance of one of those self-destruct units failing and blasting the Line apart than there was of a terrorist snapping all three cables at once. So much for that idea.

But if the Line was in serious danger, you could snap it at One-Hour, the low-Earth orbital boundary about 200 klicks up, and let everything above that fly into space, and then you'd only have to worry about less than 200 kilometers of Line hitting the ground.

Most of that stuff burns up on the way down, of course, the stuff that has to fall the farthest—so we only have to worry about the bottommost lengths of Line, the stuff that doesn't have time to burn up. And remember, it's all Line-cable, the strongest material ever manufactured, so you can't depend on it all vaporizing. You're much more likely to get a rain of hot, flaming chunks. Which is why you want to keep the area west of the Line clear. At least a hundred klicks. Then once you've reduced the global scale of the disaster to a domain of a couple hundred klicks, you can start to argue that Line failure is a tolerable risk, especially if the Line is on a western coastline, so that a failure drops most of the debris into the ocean. But even so, you're still dealing with a lot of mass hitting the planet, with significant consequences. And of course, regardless of what happens to the planet, the financial cost of a Line failure would remain the same: global economic meltdown.

But then the program showed how the Line is regularly maintained, how new filaments are being added to the existing cables at the rate of twelve per year. Every month, each cable gets a new filament started. Although filaments aren't supposed to wear out, their projected life is about eighty years per wire, so the idea is that each filament will be replaced every forty years. The show didn't say how they were going to remove the old filaments, but I assumed there was some way to do it. But even if they stopped the regular maintenance, they figured that the beanstalk could stand untended for thousands of years. Maybe more. By then, who knew what advances in technology we might have?

It was all supposed to be very reassuring—but it wasn't. Not really. It was as comforting as a flight attendant saying, "In the unlikely event of a water-landing . . ."

After we got tired of watching programs about the construction of the beanstalk, Weird started scanning through the entertainment and news channels. There were hundreds. Eventually, he found a station from home. That's when things suddenly got *very* interesting.

"Hey, Dad, look—" Douglas said. It was hard not to look. One whole wall was a screen. And it had Stinky's picture on it. And mine. And Weird. And Dad. Uh-oh . . .

The announcer was saying, ". . . believed to be somewhere on the orbital elevator. With the exception of the phone call received earlier today, the Dingillian children have not been heard from since their father took them last week for a regularly scheduled vacation. Line officials refused to comment, saying that to do so would violate their passengers' privacy, but TNN's own travel desk has determined that Max Dingillian had made reservations for four on the 2:15 elevator to Geostationary. That car was never launched due to the high wind conditions of Hurricane Charles, and Ecuador Security is now investigating the possibility that Dingillian and his sons are still somewhere at Terminus. Margaret Dingillian is seeking an International Court Order requiring the Line Authority to consider this a security situation and detain Max Dingillian. More on this developing story as it breaks. . . . In other news, the hotly contested Baby Cooper lawsuit took another legal blow this week when it was revealed that one of the company's lawyers had failed to—" Weird switched the television off and looked at Dad. We all did.

FAMILY MEETING

DAD SAT DOWN, LOOKING KIND of weak. He began to do that thing he does when he's winding himself up to make one of his speeches. He flustered.

And the more he flustered, the more I knew this wasn't going to be good. And I was already feeling all *squooshy* inside. I didn't know which was more mixed up, my stomach or my head. And Dad's performance wasn't helping. Finally, I turned to Weird and said, "You better ask him."

Dad said, "Ask me what?"

Weird cleared his throat and managed to stumble over a whole paragraph. "Well—it's about you and us and Mom. Chigger and I were talking—and well, I mean—you *are* kidnapping us, aren't you, Dad?"

Dad nodded his head as if he had been expecting this conversation for a while. He sighed. "You know that your Mom and I aren't on very good terms. I'm sorry about that. I wish it were different."

"Mom always maintained that the divorce was your fault."

"I asked for the divorce, yes, but I think you should know why. I found your mother in bed with someone else—"

"That woman we saw on the phone?" Weird asked.

Dad shrugged. "I don't know if she's the same one or not. It doesn't matter. Your mom asked me to forgive her. And I—I just couldn't. I felt betrayed. Yes, your mother and I had problems. I thought we were working them out. I was honestly trying, but things weren't happening. I wasn't getting the work or the money—"

"Dad," I said, exasperated. "You and mom have explained this to death. I don't know about Douglas and Bobby, but I don't care *whose* fault it is."

Well, I do," he said. "Because I've had a lot of time to think about this. I'm paying a terrible price, because I don't get to be with the three people I love most in the world—you kids."

"Yeah, Dad, and what about the price we're paying?" I said. "Every year when we go on vacation, you always spend the first three days trying to make up for everything. Except it can't be made up."

He nodded his agreement. "Charles, I think you're the one who's been hurt the most by all this, and I wish I knew what to do for you to make it all right. It isn't easy being the middle kid. You're always getting overlooked and taken for granted, and I don't blame you for feeling the way you do."

"Yeah, Dad, yeah," said Weird. "And we've all heard that speech too. Tell us what's going on now." I was mad at Weird for interrupting. I had thought for a moment that Dad was finally going to say something that would make a difference. But maybe not, because he just let Weird change the subject without even noticing how unfinished I still felt.

"I've been thinking about this for years," Dad said. "Leaving Earth. It's something I've always dreamt of—going out into space and never coming back. But I was never sure where I should go. There were too many possibilities, and I could only have one of them. And then one day, I realized that not choosing meant I wasn't having *any*. So I made a choice. And then I started thinking—if I leave, I'll never see you boys again. And if you hated me for not being there when you were growing up, you'd hate me all the more for abandoning you. And I just couldn't stand that thought. So—" He stopped to take a breath and figure out how to say the next part.

Weird filled the silence. "So you decided to just grab us and take us with you?"

"No." Dad shook his head. "No. that's not it at all. I do have tickets for you, but they're refundable. I'm taking you only as far as you want to go. I'm trying to give you two things here, Douglas: the trip I've always promised you, and the choice you never had before on how you want your life to turn out."

Dad turned back to me. "You said something once, Charles, that has stayed in my head like a ball bearing bouncing around the inside of an empty steel drum. You said that it was your family too, and nobody ever asked you what you wanted. Well, this is me asking you. All of you."

"Do we have to decide now?"

Dad shook his head. "No. There's time enough when we get to Geostationary. You can go back down if you want. Or you can come on out to the launch point with me. From here on in, whether you come with or not is all your own decision. But at the very least, you're going to have an out-of-this-world vacation."

"But everybody will be looking for us—"

Dad pointed to the now-blank wall. "They're looking for the people in that picture. They won't be looking for us the way we look now, will they?"

Weird went thoughtful at that. Then he started frowning. Then he looked at Dad with that faraway squint he gets when he sees something that no one else has seen yet. "How much of this did you plan in advance, Dad?"

Dad looked embarrassed. "What do you mean, Douglas?"

"We drove across the border and we didn't buy our train tickets until Mazatlan, and you paid cash. You only bought tickets as far as Acapulco. It was only after we were on the train that you upgraded them to Beanstalk City. You didn't want Mom to be able to find us by your credit card purchases, did you?"

Dad scratched his ear while he tried to figure out some polite way to say it. He couldn't. "Yes, you're right, Douglas. I didn't want your mother to know where we were going."

"And the reservations at Terminus? You knew we could catch an earlier car up to One-Hour too?"

"I didn't plan the hurricane—" he started to say.

"No, you didn't. That one was lucky. But wasn't it convenient that there was an empty first-class cabin on the 11:00 car? Wasn't it also convenient that we checked in at the reservation desk just in time to catch it? And wasn't it also convenient that you kept looking at your watch all over One-Hour? Did you make this reservation in another name so it would be waiting for us? You did it first class too, didn't you? So they'd be less likely to give it away."

"You're very observant, Douglas. You'd make a good detective." Dad sighed and admitted it. "I wanted you to have the chance. That's all. The chance your Mom didn't want you to have. I asked her—I said I wanted you to come with me up the Line, and then I'd send you all back home again. She said no. She was sure that I was going to try to steal you. But all I wanted was to give you one great memory of your Dad, and the trip I always promised you. And then she threatened to go to court and I realized just how angry she was and that she was going to try to hurt me any way she could. Even if it meant hurting you too. That's when I started thinking that if jumping off the planet was a chance for me to have a better life than is possible on Earth, well, then maybe it might be a chance for you kids too. But I promise you, Douglas, I won't take you anywhere against your will. I just want to spend some time with you before I go. Is that too much to ask?"

"Why didn't you tell us this before?" I asked.

"If I had, would you have believed me? Would you have come?"

I thought about that. He was right. I wouldn't have believed him. Would I have come? That was a harder question. Not believing him, I don't know what I would have done. In reply, I shrugged.

Stinky had been silent the whole time. I wasn't sure how much of this he understood, but he'd been listening carefully and suddenly he piped up, "Aren't we going home? I wanna go home!"

Dad and Douglas and I exchanged looks. Dad scooped up Stinky and held him on his lap. "Hey, kiddo. You're going to go home real soon, if that's what you want. But Daddy's going away for a long time, and I wanted us to have some time together before I say good-bye, that's all."

"Where are you going?"

"Very far away. So far away that you can't even imagine it."

"Why?" demanded Stinky. "Don't you love us anymore?"

"I love you more than anything, sweetheart."

"Can't you take us with?"

"Well, that's what we're talking about now. Whether or not you want to go."

"But I don't want to go. I want to go home."

"Okay. You can do that, if that's what you want."

"But I want you to come too."

"I can't do that."

"But why are you going away?"

"Because it's something I have to do."

The frustration on Bobby's face was evident. He began to cry. *"But why . . . ? It isn't fair!"*

"I'm not sure I understand it all either, kiddo. This is just the way it is." Dad hugged Bobby close, probably because he didn't have anything else to say.

Douglas gave Dad a weird look then—one of those looks that got him his nickname. He shook his head over some personal annoyance that maybe only the two of them understood and headed for the door.

"Where are you going, Doug?"

"Nowhere. Out."

Yeah. Like where *could* he go? And then he was gone anyway.

I wanted to follow him, but I felt I should stay with Dad for a bit. There was something else going on that I still didn't understand. Whatever it was, Douglas hadn't said, so I felt just like Bobby: it wasn't fair and I didn't know why.

MORE UP

AT FIRST, **D**AD WAS A little worried about Doug leaving the cabin. He was afraid that someone might recognize him from the pictures— or any of us—but we'd cut off all our hair and Dad and Douglas were wearing their space hats and Stinky and I were both buzz-cut, so we didn't look very much like the pictures on TV anymore. And then we also realized that it was unlikely that anyone else on this elevator car had even seen that same broadcast. Doug had been watching an El Paso news feed. All the other news was talking about Hurricane Charles and the damage it was doing all across Ecuador. Nobody was going to be looking for us; they were all too busy with much more serious problems.

And even if somebody did recognize us, what could they do? We hadn't broken any laws. And even if we had, who was going to arrest us? The elevator attendants? We couldn't run away anyway.

Of course, once we got to Geostationary, they could have the police waiting for us, but Dad didn't think that was likely. Geostationary wasn't signatory to the SuperNational Treaty and there wasn't any ex-tradition from space. This was because the Loonies weren't willing to agree to it and Geostationary usually sided with Luna more than Earth. According to Weird, anyway.

But there were private security agents available for hire at Geostationary, and if Mom really wanted to make trouble for us, she could hire a couple of those guys to meet us. But what could they do? Could they force us to go back to Earth? Dad wasn't sure what might happen in that case.

Just to be safe, Dad said I should probably stay in the cabin anyway. So I glowered and sulked and tried on different angry faces. And then

I got bored. And when I get bored, I get nasty. And when I get nasty, I get disgusting. Just to see how disgusting I can be.

It didn't take long. Dad got so disgusted watching me fart and belch and flick my boogers at the TV screen that he finally said, "Okay, Charles. You win. I can't stand it anymore." He muttered something about teaching hygiene to chimpanzees. Then he said I could go out and walk around again, but only if I promised to keep out of trouble.

It was probably the boogers that did it. Boogers always work. Adults can't stand boogers. They can't even stand the word "booger." Booger booger booger. I didn't even like it when Stinky flicked his boogers, so it was probably a lot worse for Dad when I did it. But it worked.

I went down to the bottom of the car and up to the top, with stops everywhere in-between, looking for a place where something interesting—anything—was happening.

Nothing was happening. Nothing. And more nothing on top of that. The only thing to do was wander around—which I was already pretty good at. Mom called it my "restless lion" prowl. She said all I needed was a dead antelope leg to drag around. Ha ha. That's a grownup joke, only funny to grownups, annoying to those carrying the burden of genetic progress. But at least there was more room to drag my antelope haunch in the whole elevator car than there was in the cabin. Up and down and all around. The only thing weird was that I didn't see Weird anywhere, but I wasn't really looking for him anyway, so I didn't think about it. He'd probably found a terminal somewhere and was redesigning someone's government or something.

So this was what I'd flicked all those boogers for. The big discovery: there isn't anything to do on an elevator. All elevators are the same. You watch the numbers. That's it.

It doesn't matter how pretty the numbers are presented, they're still numbers. You go down to the bottom level and look at the lights on the wire to see if the red one has gotten any farther out and it looks exactly the same. It's impossible to tell. So then, you go up to the top and get something to eat. And after that, you go down to the lounge and watch TV. But you can do that in your cabin, and at least in your cabin, you can choose what you want to watch. So you get up and walk around some more. You go upstairs, you go downstairs.

If you want, the attendants will take you on a tour of how everything works, only it's all the stuff you've already seen, and there isn't that much of it anyway, so out of total boredom, you go back and look out the windows again.

If you go up to the top level, you can see . . . the Line and the stars. The cable zips past at a thousand miles per hour, 1600 klicks. It's going so fast, you can't see any details on it at all, it's just a long shining bar of light that stretches up and away into nothing, like a big pointer into the night.

And everything else is stars—godzillions of them. Like God's dandruff on night's black velvet, or something like that. The higher you get, the darker the sky gets and the more stars there are to see. The top observation area is kept mostly unlit, except for tiny guide lights in the carpet, so your view isn't hampered by any glare. Up this high, the stars don't twinkle, so they look *different.*

Downstairs, the Line points straight down at the Earth; but it doesn't go all the way down, it just disappears into the distance again, so it looks like the elevator is hanging above the world, while this long bar of light drops away beneath you.

And every time you go downstairs to look, the Terminator Line has crept a little farther west across the world. And each time there's a little more world to see as more of it creeps up over the curving horizon. One half of the world glows with reflected sunlight. The other half is dark, speckled with little city lights.

But directly below us, the bright swirl of the hurricane covered everything like a big white eye glaring up at us. The hurricane was really pounding Terminus now. All the news reports were bad. The airport would be out of service for days, and they'd probably have to do a lot of track and highway repair too before anyone could get in or out.

It's supposed to be exciting, a trip up the elevator. But it isn't. Instead, time seems suspended. Everything looks motionless.

I was standing on the longest tightrope ever. A suspension bridge between a rock and a planet. Caught in the middle, between Mom and Dad, Weird and Stinky. Not a child, not an adult, but something in-between.

And all alone. More alone than ever.

DISTANCES

I WAS HEADING BACK TO THE CABIN when I bumped—literally—into J'mee running down the staircase. At first he didn't recognize me, because my head was shaved, but I grabbed his arm and said, "J'mee, hey! It's me, Charles! Where are you going?"

"Uh, nowhere—"

"Then why are you going so fast?"

J'mee looked annoyed. His face clouded. "That wasn't very nice, what you did." He pushed past me down to the lounge. I followed after.

"I'm sorry. Can we be friends again?"

"No. You're not a nice boy."

"Neither are you."

That stopped him. "Huh—?"

"You're not a boy."

"Huh? I'm not—" J'mee started to protest, saw it was useless, and gave it up as a bad effort. "I thought I fooled you."

"You almost did."

"How'd you figure it out?" She demanded.

"The way you changed clothes."

"You shouldn't be looking at other boys."

"You shouldn't be pretending to be one."

She turned away for a minute, staring out the window at the distant edge of sunset. Then she turned back abruptly "So why are you and your brothers and your dad running away?"

"Huh—? We're not running away. We're on vacation."

"Don't be stupid, Charles." She tapped her head. "Every time I meet someone, I do a net-search. My dad taught me where to look for all the really good stuff. It's the only way to be safe." She went blank for a moment. "You don't have to worry. They think you're still at One-Hour. They don't think you got out in time."

"Thanks, " I said. I didn't mean it. I didn't like her knowing so much about us.

"Your mom and dad are really screwed up, aren't they?" She said.

Well, yeah, they were, but I didn't want to say so. Not to her. Because they were still my mom and dad. "They're not that bad," I said. "Everybody has problems."

"Everybody has babies," she said. "Daddy says tube-town people have too many babies. That's why everybody has problems."

"Well, if no one had babies, then what?"

"Then maybe we wouldn't have so many people on the planet and things wouldn't be falling apart," she said. "Your mom didn't want to have babies. She wanted your dad to have them. She said that in an interview once. Want to hear more?"

"No," I said. I thought about telling her that she shouldn't be poking around in other people's privacy. It wasn't nice. But I didn't think it would stop her. So I didn't say anything.

"So why are you and your family running away?" I asked.

"We're not running away. We're just . . . moving." And then she added, "Daddy says it's not safe to be rich on Earth anymore. That's why we're moving someplace safe."

"So why do you have to pretend to be a boy?"

"Because it's a secret that we're leaving Earth."

"That's running away."

"No, it isn't."

"Fine. Have it your own way." That was how I usually ended arguments at home. "Why didn't you shave *all* your hair off?"

"I didn't want to. It looks . . . cheap."

"Didn't you see the show about shaving and microparticles and disease?"

"Oh, that. Yeah. Daddy says that's for other people. Not us."

"Oh." There wasn't anything else to say to that. At least nothing polite. I knew what my ethics teacher would have said to that. People who negotiate loopholes for themselves are criminals in training.

He said that most people see rules as some kind of burden that someone else makes them carry—like Mom or Dad—but the rules are really agreements that we make with each other on how to behave so we can all get along. And when we don't follow the rules, it's like breaking a promise to everybody at once. Break enough rules and nobody will trust you anymore.

But . . . he also said that there are people who have so much money that they can buy themselves exceptions from the rules. And that's dangerous, because if you get into the habit of always buying exceptions for yourself, you end up in a bubble with a wall of money between you and everyone else. You won't know how to connect to anyone and they won't know how to reach you. And all the folks around you will be more loyal to your money than to you.

That was what my teacher said, but I don't think anybody really believed him. Or cared. I think most of us would have liked to have had the chance to prove that we could handle the burden of money, that we would be different. I know I would. Yeah. Given the choice—living in a bubble of money or scrambling for credits in the Tube-Town—we knew what to choose. Poor and self-respecting is a highly overrated thrill.

But when J'mee said this—"Rules are for other people"—it made me see how big the difference between us really was. It made me queasy. Because all of a sudden I realized just how naked I really was.

So I just rubbed my head and said, "It's still a good disguise."

"No, it isn't," she said.

"Fine. Have it your way."

"Running away isn't fair to your mom, you know?"

"What do you know about it? You don't even have a mom!"

"I know about moms."

"You don't know my mom."

"I know she's the one who works the hardest. Your dad doesn't do anything."

"Yes, he does!" I knew she was right, but I wasn't going to let her be the expert on my family. Besides, if she was right . . . then we were wrong to be going up the Line. And even though the Line scared the yell out of me, I didn't want to go back either. Not after coming this far.

"I know that you're really hurting her."

"You don't know anything. You don't live with us."

She tapped her head. "I bet I know more about you and your family than you do."

"Oh, yeah—?"

"Yeah." She went blank for a moment, then came back and said, "Your mom and dad are divorced. Your dad filed for bankruptcy six weeks ago. Then he applied for an offworld emigration permit for himself and you and your brothers. His debts were paid off by a private debting company, conditional against a bid he has on file for indentured-service with the Sierra Colony." She went blank and came back again. "Your older brother applied to UCLA under a rechanneling contract, but it wasn't accepted. Your little brother takes medicine to keep him from wetting his bed, but it doesn't always work. And you—" She stopped.

"Go ahead—" I could feel my anger rising at this invasion of privacy, but I still had to hear what she knew.

"Your school record has a note in it that says that you're antisocial and you need emotional therapy." She looked at me with a smug superior expression. "Lots of flow-through kids need help." And then she added, "It's normal for poor kids." Like that excused it.

I stared at her, astonished. I'd never met any kid so . . . *spoiled.* It was as. if an enormous gulf had just opened up between us that could never be bridged again. I could feel my face getting redder and redder— and she just smiled at me like an arsenic-flavored princess.

I couldn't think of anything to say, so I just blurted, "You're a goddamned nasty little bitch." Then I left as quickly as I could.

THE ELEVATOR CLUB

WHEN I GOT BACK TO the cabin, all I wanted to do was think about the stuff that J'mee had said, but Stinky insisted on showing me all the tricks he'd taught his monkey. Stupid things—like crotch-grabbing and booger-flicking and pretending to fart and vomit and all the other stuff that little kids think is funny. I guess if I'd been in the mood, I might have thought it was funny, but I wasn't in the mood and I thought it was stupid and annoying. And when I said so, Stinky just looked up at me and said, "You sound like a grownup," which was probably the nastiest thing of all he could have said. If this was what it was like to be a grownup, permanently angry, perhaps I should just open a window and jump out now.

Instead, I turned on the television.

Maybe I didn't really want to think about it at all. What J'mee had said was worse than nasty. It was true.

I flung myself into a chair and flipped through the channels, looking at the views from all the different observatories all up and down the Line, but not really seeing any of them. There were also telescopes mounted in the bottom of the car that you could control yourself to look at anything you wanted, so I was playing with the view from one of those for a while, looking straight down the cable. At full magnification, I could see the next car, 250 miles below, very clearly. It was racing up toward us at incredible speed, but never gaining.

The views of the Earth were also pretty spectacular. We were high enough now that I could see El Paso from the air. I tried to spot our tube-town, only it was off toward the side, not quite around the curve of the planet, but far enough to make the angle tricky, and I couldn't be sure which one it was anyway. They all looked alike from here, and the atmosphere made everything fuzzy and twinkly, even with digital correction. I did spot the meteor crater again. That was easier. You tell the telescope what to look for and it just slides across the landscape to the target. From here, the Barringer crater looked like a big dimple in the ground. It was even farther away than El Paso and even farther around the curvature of the Earth, but it was big enough to be clear despite any atmospheric interference.

Finally, Dad looked up from the papers he was working on and said, "All right, Chigger, what is it?"

"Nothing," I said.

"No, it is *not* nothing. The way you're clicking through channels—"

"I hate being poor," I said.

"We're not poor."

"Then why did you file for bankruptcy?"

He was silent for a beat. "How did you find that out?"

"It doesn't matter. I found out."

"Your mother, right?"

I didn't want to tell him about J'mee and everything she'd said—he'd probably just get mad at me, even though I hadn't done anything. J'mee was wrong about us anyway. I didn't need help. I was fine. If people would just leave me alone. Once we got to Geosynchronous, this whole adventure would be over anyway and we'd all go home—except Dad, so it didn't matter, did it? And I really didn't need to have another one of those "sympathetic conversations"—not now, not ever, and certainly not with Dad. So instead I just said what I was feeling. "Screw the moon. This is another one of your good ideas that didn't happen."

"Chigger—"

"Dad, why couldn't you just take us to Disneyland and leave us alone? I don't want any more of your good intentions—"

The argument was just getting warmed up when Weird walked in, looking weirder than usual. Even for Weird. He looked flushed and upset and scared, but he also looked excited about something—kind of like the time he got off the roller coaster and discovered he'd crapped his pants. He looked at both of us, then retreated hastily to the bathroom without saying a word.

Dad looked at me—looked at the bathroom—then looked back at me. "We'll talk about this later." He went and knocked softly on the bathroom door. "Douglas? Are you all right?"

The reply came back muffled. "Yes. No."

"Do you want to talk about it, Douglas?"

The bathroom door opened and Douglas stepped back into the cabin. He looked from Dad to me, then back to Dad again, decided it didn't matter, gulped, and nodded. He couldn't even talk. He managed to blurt, "I just joined the Elevator Club."

Elevator Club—?! Huh? I wondered who the unlucky girl was.

Stinky was already demanding—"What's the Elevator Club? I wanna join too!"

I stared at Douglas in amazement—suddenly realizing that my big brother had crossed a line, and even though he was still my big brother, he was finally and irrevocably a grownup too. He finally had the secret handshake. Bobby and I were still children. I turned to Bobby and said very calmly, "You have to be eighteen to join. It's like a driver's license. I can't join either."

Dad gave me a surprised and appreciative glance. "Thank you, Charles," he said. He patted Douglas on the shoulder. "You want to talk privately?" Douglas nodded and Dad steered him back into the bathroom and shut the door behind them. I thought I heard Douglas stifle a sob, but I couldn't be sure.

After they were gone, Stinky looked at me. "Well, what kind of a club is it—?"

"It's a secret. You have to be eighteen."

"Well, what do they do that's so secret?"

"That's the secret."

"But that's not fair!"

I shrugged. "You're finally starting to get it, Bobby. Nothing is fair. Grownups make the rules—and they make them for grownups, not for kids. And that's the way things are."

"When I'm a grownup, I'm not gonna be like that."

"Oh, yes you will. So will I."

"No, I won't—"

"Yeah, you will, and I'll tell you why: because when you're a grownup, you'll have waited all your life for your chance to make your own rules, and you aren't going to give it up when you get it. Nobody does."

"It's still not fair."

"Yes, it is," I said, and all of a sudden, I could see Dad and Douglas's point of view a lot clearer than I could see Bobby's. I wondered if that grownup thing was starting to happen to me. It's that thing that Dad is always talking about. Personal responsibility. Was this what it felt like? I said a bad word.

"Umm," said Bobby. "I'm gonna tell."

"Go ahead. I don't care. Maybe I'll even tell Dad myself."

Dad and Douglas were in the bathroom for a long time, and when they came out, neither of them looked like anything had been settled— but they were smiling, so at least I knew they were talking to each other again, and that was something.

But it still didn't solve anything.

DINNER

SEÑOR DINGILLIAN?"

Dad turned around to see who had called his name. We all did. At first, none of us recognized him—he was as shaven as we were—but then Dad said, "*Señor* Hidalgo, how are you?" and I recognized him as the fat man from the train. He strode over and pumped Dad's hand enthusiastically, as if they were old friends. "You have become quite famous, no?"

Dad looked worried, but *Señor* Hidalgo reassured him quickly. "Oh, please, sir, have no worries. I don't think anyone else knows who you are. I only found out by accident myself. And even if anyone else on the car is aware of your . . . ah, circumstance, I wouldn't fear. Here, come sit with me—" He indicated a booth in the corner.

Dad tried to beg off, but *Señor* Hidalgo insisted, and he had a firm grip on Dad's arm. "*Señor* Hidalgo—"

"*Doctor* Hidalgo," he corrected. "Doctor of Political Science."

"Since when is politics a science?" Weird asked.

Hidalgo laughed. "I've often wondered the same thing myself. Here, you sit next to me, *muchacho*. Roberto, correct? No? Bobby, *si*. And you are Charles, yes? And of course, this handsome young man, so tall and skinny, must be Douglas. You have fine sons, *Señor* Dingillian. I know of your work, of course. You didn't know you were world famous, did you? But the set of recordings you did of ancient Inca music was quite wonderful. I always meant to write you and tell you, but I never found the time. Tell me, do you still work with the Columbia Jazz Quartet? *The Coltrane Suite* remains one of my favorite recordings. Let me buy you dinner. I want to talk with you, if you don't mind."

Huh—? I wanted to ask Dad about that last part, but there wasn't time. Dad shrugged off Señor Doctor Hidalgo's inquiries with noncommittal answers, but I could see him mentally counting his pennies. Despite the wad of cash he was carrying, he had to be worried about expenses. He accepted with a nod and dropped into a chair, but not before turning to the rest of us and cautioning us not to eat like pigs, we were guests.

"Don't be silly, Señor Dingillian. You are my guests. Order anything you like. I'm not paying for it anyway. I will charge it to, let me see . . ." He pawed through a fistful of credit cards. "Ah, here we are. These people owe me many favors. And I owe them nothing. They shall pay for your dinner tonight." In explanation, he added, "I have many sponsors. Politics costs money—especially when you are on the side of the poor. The rich can buy as many politicians as they want; the poor have only the leftovers and the castoffs." He laughed, as if this were funny. "Nevertheless, do let me recommend the ceviche. Or the conch. The fish farms are quite good on the Line. Don't look so surprised, young Charles. Do you think that all that water just sits and waits. No, the Line engineers put it to work. Everything works—or it gets tossed over the side. No, no, that's a joke, don't mind me. I have been sampling the excellent wines. No, the Line does not produce its own wine yet, but the vineyards have been designed, and someday they will be built, have no fear. Have you ever had fresh lobster? I'll bet you haven't. Let me recommend the lobster as an entree. Someone has to eat it, son— the more those arthropods travel, the more expensive they get; so eat it now while my sponsors can still afford it. And you, Douglas—?"

After a while, Dad finally interrupted. "Your courtesy is welcome, Dr. Hidalgo, but you barely know us. I can't help but wonder—"

"Forgive an old man his vanities—"

"You're not that old," Dad said.

"Old enough to be working on my second bottle of Tabasco," Hidalgo said. "You don't believe me? Cut me in half and count the rings. I'm old enough to have seen *Lucy* first-run—"

Weird shook his head. "Now, I know you're teasing us, Dr. Hidalgo. Lucy was born before the First American Civil War."

"Ahh, the *first* Lucy—I was thinking of the second one. And you're thinking of the Second American Civil War. But yes, you're right, I'm not quite that old, but almost. Nevertheless, please accept my hospitality. I have no one else to share my table—now, let's have a look at this menu and see if they have an old-fashioned chocolate soda for Roberto here. You do like chocolate, don't you? I'm sure you do not get very much of the real thing. It's quite expensive, you know. Trust me, the chocolate sodas here are very very good."

Dad was curious about Dr. Hidalgo's intentions, and some of his impatience was starting to show, but the old man just kept chattering away about inconsequential things, refusing to let politics—or anything else—interfere with a good dinner. And it was a good dinner. There were things on the menu I couldn't even pronounce, but the *Señor* Doctor ordered them anyway, and when the waiter put the plates in front of us, they looked and smelled delicious, and tasted even better than that. So for a while I didn't care what Dr. Hidalgo wanted. I was too busy eating. And Dad too, finally gave in to the inevitable and ordered himself a steak so thick you could have insulated a wall with it.

For dessert, the waiter rolled a big cart up to the table, covered with cakes and puddings and things even Dad didn't recognize. I'd never seen so many different kinds of fruits in one place before in my life. And chocolate! I mean, *real* chocolate! Stinky's eyes went as wide as saucers, and I guess mine did too, and I think for the first time, I began to realize just how much we didn't know—*and* how poor we really were.

I didn't know what to pick, and even Stinky and Weird were overawed, because everything looked too good to eat. Weird actually smiled at me. It made him look almost human. All three of us—four, counting Dad—stared at all the desserts so long that Doctor Hidalgo just started pointing and ordering. "Apparently, the boys cannot make up their minds, and neither can I. So we'll have it all. Just the best. We'll start with some of those fat red strawberries in cream and definitely the fresh grapes on a bed of thick rice pudding—and a big slice of the Chocolate Death, *por favor*, we shall all share that. Bring extra forks. And, oh my, the spiced peaches and mangoes also look very good tonight, and so do the raspberries and kiwis; is that coconut sprinkled on top? *Bueno! Un pocito mas*, don't be stingy. And some of that delicious pineapple trifle as well, please. We'll have a taste of everything. Oh, and two cups of your most dangerous Kona espresso."

"Doctor Hidalgo—" Dad began slowly, "I appreciate your generosity, almost as much as my boys do, I'm sure, but it makes me very uncomfortable—as if you're trying to get to me through my sons."

Hidalgo wiped his mouth with his napkin. "Ahh, *Señor* Dingillian, a thousand apologies. Sometimes my generosity overwhelms people. I am used to giving. Sometimes I forget that other people are not used to receiving. I meant no offense. I only wanted to share some time with you—a man so committed to his sons that he will risk his freedom for them. I think I understand your situation, sir. And I think I might be able to help you. Conversely, you might be of some use to my people too."

Dad shook his head. "I'd prefer not to get involved, sir. Fame is a terrible mistress. She takes a great deal and gives very little in return." "Ahh, very true, very true. Nevertheless, you are already famous. Twice over, indeed. And it is the foolish man who doesn't use every opportunity he has. Fame can be useful, sir. If you don't take charge of your own—how shall I say it?—your own 'reputation' in the media, I am sure that your wife, or her lawyers, will certainly take charge of it for you. It is a matter of publicity, and in your situation, you are probably going to need some useful friends, *comprendé?*"

Dad sighed. "Doctor Hidalgo—"

"Please, call me Bolivar. Or Bollie. We have broken bread together." He waved at the table. "A great deal of it, indeed."

"Doctor Hidalgo—" Dad tried again. "I'm grateful for your hospitality, but—"

"You have not heard me out, *Señor* Dingillian. Please—you have enjoyed my hospitality, you owe me a bit of your time, don't you think? *Por favor?*" Dad looked unconvinced. "Are you in a hurry? Do you have someplace to go, something better to do . . . ?"

Dad sat back down again. "All right," he said. "I'll listen. But I want you to understand something first. I'm *not* kidnapping my children. I'm giving them the choice that their mother tried to deny them."

"Yes, I'm certain that's what it looks like to you, and I'm not so big a fool as I seem, that I would try to argue that with you. And that is not the discussion I want to have with you anyway."

"Oh?"

"Do you like money, *Señor* Dingillian? *Si? Bueno.* Everyone does. Money is like gravity. When you have enough of it, it draws more money to it, increasing its gravity even more. When you have too much money—*is* there such a thing as *too much* money? The SuperNationals don't think so—but when you have too much money in one place, it stretches the fabric of the universe like a great black hole, sinking deeper and deeper into itself. Nothing escapes, not even light. If a black hole is an astrophysicist's nightmare, then a SuperNational corporation is an economist's nightmare. The money flows into it, nothing comes back. We don't even know where the money has gone. It leaves no trace of its passage, *nothing comes back*—not even light. Did the money pass through Atlantis or Oceania? Did it leave the planet? Where did it go? Who knows?" Hidalgo sat back in his chair comfortably; he held up a hand for patience, while he stifled a belch. Even with the napkin in front of his face, it was impressive. Stinky and I looked at each other and giggled.

"A *nine!*" whispered Stinky.

"Nine point five," I whispered back.

Dad glared. We both shut up.

Hidalgo glanced around the table. "Would any of you like anything more? No? You do not eat enough, *Roberto y Carlito*. You will never grow as big as me unless you practice your eating. But getting back to my point, *Señor* Dingillian, money is neither good nor evil—but it can be dangerous. Because money does what money wants. Money goes where money wants to go. And money doesn't care who it rolls over. It just wants to collect itself—like I said, like gravity. You should respect money; you should never get in its way. Unless you have a big enough bucket. Do you?"

Dad started to answer, but Hidalgo patted his hand and stopped him. "Never mind. I have no right to ask that question. But the answer is the same for everyone: 'Not as big as I'd like.' But if the bucket is big enough to take care of your children, then you are truly a wealthy man." He looked around at us. "Clearly, you have done well with your young men. I am envious. You should be proud of them." Hidalgo wiped his mouth again and conveniently looked at his watch.

"Oh, *Madre de Dios*, look at the time. I have a very important conference call that I must be a part of. *Mucho importante*. It starts in five minutes. I must rush. Thank you so much for your company tonight, all of you—you have been very kind to an old man, listening to me prattle on like a teacher in search of a classroom. No, no, sit down, finish your desserts. Do not leave the table until all of these plates are clean—" He shook hands all around. "I shall see you again before we reach our destination, I'm sure of it. *Señor* Dingillian, we still have much to talk about. Let us connect with each other tomorrow. For breakfast, perhaps? Or lunch? Please. Your company has been most gracious. *Au revoir*."

Douglas giggled. *"Au revoir—?"*

Dad smiled. "Perhaps he forgot he was supposed to be Spanish." He glanced at his own watch. "That certainly was a convenient departure on his part. Just when he was getting to the punch line."

"Do you think he timed it that way?" Douglas asked.

"I think *Señor* Doctor Hidalgo is way too good a snake-oil salesman to leave anything to chance. Yes, I think he timed it that way."

"Snake-oil?" Stinky asked.

"It's what you buy when your snake gets squeaky," I said, wondering what it really meant. Mostly, it meant another trip to the dictionary.

"Right," said Dad, heaving himself up from the table with a grunt. "And right now, it's time to get our squeakiest snake into bed—"

DECISIONS

LATER, AFTER STINKY HAD FINALLY fallen asleep, the three of us sat around and talked about Doctor Hidalgo and what he might want. Dad had no idea, but he was sure that the old man wanted something. "No one spends five thousand on dinner without expecting at least a good-night kiss." We all laughed at that. Even I understood the joke.

"Hey, it was good food, and the conversation was interesting—if a little one-sided," Dad concluded.

"I bet he could be a great baritone, if he wanted," Douglas said. "I've never seen anyone go that long without taking a breath."

"I didn't know there were so many different kinds of dessert," I said.

"Yeah, well—don't get used to it," Douglas sounded like a grownup. He turned to Dad. "Are you going to tell him?"

Dad looked suddenly serious. But he didn't look old anymore. He looked *relaxed*. Sort of. He nodded and turned to me. "It's like this, Charles. Douglas, isn't going back to Earth."

"Huh? What?" I looked to Douglas, dismayed.

"I'm going with Dad. To the moon," he said. "And beyond."

I shook my head. "Yeah—? And what about Mom? What if she has the cops looking for us at Geosynchronous?"

Dad shook his head. "Earthside jurisdiction doesn't apply. As indentured colonists, we're the property of the corporation. If I haven't broken any starside laws, they can't touch me. I checked it out before we left, Charles. As long as we have a valid contract, we're safe."

It sounded too easy, but maybe—I didn't know. There was too much happening for me to figure out. "I don't get it. I thought you said this was a stupid idea."

"Yeah, but staying is stupider. For me, anyway."

"Why?" I demanded.

"It's about my scholarship," Douglas said. "I'm not going to get it."

"I know."

"How do you know?"

"Same way I know about the cops. A kid with a wire and a big mouth."

"Do you know why?" He took a deep breath. "They don't give you the scholarship if you don't need rechanneling."

"Oh," I said. And then, *"Oh!"*

"It was Mickey," Douglas said.

Mickey? The elevator attendant?! For a moment, I didn't know what to feel. Angry. Or jealous. Or hurt. Or curious. Or just disgusted. While I hadn't been looking, Douglas really had turned into a grownup.

I didn't know what to say, so I said something I'd never said to him before. At least not like this. "I'm sorry, Douglas."

He reached over and put his hand on mine. "There's nothing to be sorry about, Chigger. This is how things turned out."

"I know, but—you wanted to go to UCLA."

"There are good schools in the outbeyond."

"Yeah, but you said it would be slavery—" I shut up. I had the feeling that I didn't know what I was talking about anymore.

"It's an economic decision. You sell what you have. If you don't have anything to sell, you sell who you are. It's only seven years, Chigger. And then I'll be a free man on a new world." He sounded resigned. As if he hadn't finished convincing himself. "And it's not like the old kind of slavery. It's not—not really."

He sounded more like a grownup than I'd ever heard him sound before. I didn't like it very much. It made me feel abandoned, sort of. More alone than before—like someone had taken away my security. Again.

Now, Dad spoke up. "You know what the joke is, Charles? I'd asked Douglas to come with me to the outbeyond, because I wanted him to have the chance at a life *without* rechannelling. Now—it turns out that it doesn't matter. But it's still a good choice, Charles—I think it's one that will work out all right for him in the long run."

"Yeah," I said, "I sort of see the joke. And I sort of understand. But what about me and Stinky? What happens to us?"

"I really wish you wouldn't call your brother that," Dad said, but that wasn't what he really wanted to say. He tried to run his hand through his hair, he only ended up brushing his near-naked scalp. He looked annoyed, sighed, and started again. "You see, Charles, here's the thing—I was pretty sure that Douglas wasn't going to want to come with me. He'd made that clear back in Mexico. So I'd been counting on him to take you and Bobby back to Earth. That is, if you didn't want to come any farther with me. Now that he's decided to go on, that puts the responsibility on you. Do you want to go back? Or do you want to come with?"

"But what about Sti—Bobby?"

"First we need to know what *you* want to do."

"If I go back, I'll be living with Mom again, won't I?"

"Your mother is a good woman," Dad said, but he didn't sound like he believed it.

"Oh, yeah," I said. "She's good enough for me to live with, but not good enough for you."

"Point taken," Dad said.

"And if I go with you—"

"When I put my name in the registry, I also put your name in, as a possible. And Douglas and Bobby too. So far, we have one bid from the Sierra Corporation. That's not too bad. But I haven't accepted it yet; I'm waiting to see who else bids. Then we'll pick the best. I'm more valuable if I bring sons, but it'll be your choice to come with me."

"What if nobody else bids?"

"Then we go with Sierra. I'll accept the bid before we disembark."

"What if we don't like the Sierra contract?"

"I took out an insurance policy against that. We're guaranteed a suitable bid or our passage home."

"Oh," I said.

"So you don't have to let that influence your decision."

"But it does," I said. "This really is a Magical Mystery Tour, isn't it?" Just like you said—we're not going to know where we're going until we get there."

"So you're coming?"

I shrugged. "What's to go back to?"

"You know that I'm breaking the law if I try to take you against your will."

"You've already broken the law, Dad."

He nodded. "Consider it a measure of how much I love you."

DECISIONS POSTPONED

WHEN YOU'RE A KID, YOU just keep on going like you're going to be a kid forever. And every time someone calls you young man or young adult or talks about grownup responsibilities, you just blink and wonder what they're talking about. How can a kid make that kind of decision? But that's what Dad was asking me to do now.

Would the grownup I was going to become feel that I had done the right thing? Or would he hate me for condemning him to whatever bad consequences came of this decision? What was I supposed to choose here?

Weird tried to help. In his clumsy way. He punched up some programs on the TV to give me an idea of what the options were.

One program was about the different colonies. What it was like to live and work there. None of the colonies really looked like a fun place to live—they were either too hot or too cold. The sky was the wrong color on all of them. And none of the colony planets had any life at all, except what you brought with you and grew in your own indoor farms. What was true about all of them was that it took a lot of work just to stay alive. *Hard* work.

On the other hand, none of the colonies had seventeen billion people all competing for the same jobs and the same houses and the same mouthfuls of food. The per capita comparisons were astonishing. Dad said that on Earth the chances of becoming a millionaire were one in seventeen million. On any of the colonies, right now, the chances were one in twenty. All you had to do was survive.

"Why don't they use robots?" I asked.

"They do," Dad said. "But robots can't do it all. They need people to do the hard part—make decisions and babies. In that order."

"But Douglas can't make babies—"

"Yes, I can," said Douglas. "It's the how that's different."

I shook my head. I didn't want to argue about that stuff.

"Look, kiddo," Dad said. "The human race has eaten the Earth. We're walking an ecological tightrope. A crop failure here, a plague there, a war somewhere else—and every time the system collapses a little bit more, we patch it up somehow and keep on going for a little bit longer. We add a few more mechanisms around the edges to help keep it from collapsing quite the same way the next time, but the basic inequilibrium just keeps on going. The whole thing is staggering like a drunken sailor—sooner or later he's going to fall down. It's not a question of *if;* it's a question of *when.* There are sixteen billion people too many on the planet and there's no telling how long that condition can be sustained. But whether it's sustained or whether it collapses, either way, most of those people aren't going to have the kind of freedom in their lives that you can have out in the colonies. The freedom to design your own possibilities."

"We have freedom—" I started to say.

"No." Dad shook his head. "We don't have freedom. The only freedom you have is inside your head, and there's not too much of that left anymore. We *can't* have freedom the way Earth is presently constituted. If freedom is the ability to swing your fist, there are seventeen billion places on Earth where your freedom stops. In order to keep all of those people alive, we've sacrificed all kinds of individual liberties—including the right to be who you want to be. The more people you have, the more accommodations you have to make to society. But good grief, Charles! What do you think my argument with Douglas was all about? It wasn't about what he would be—it was about the fact that he was being *pushed* into it. And someday, you're going to be pushed in that same direction. And Bobby too. That's when I started thinking about getting you boys offworld somehow. Someplace where you wouldn't have to make any concessions or accommodations to anyone else."

"What about loyalty to the community and the other stuff like that?"

"All that stuff they teach you in school?" He snorted. "They *have* to teach you that, Charles—their job is to make you fit in. But loyalty to the community means one thing when the community is seventeen thousand people and quite another thing when it's seventeen billion. The global community is too vast, Chigger. It's out of control. Who do you think goes out to the stars? People who are satisfied with the way things are? Or people who are so dissatisfied with the constraints on their lives that they're willing to put up with colossal hardship so they can have a chance at something better?"

For the first time in a long time, Dad sounded like he cared about something. But I still wasn't sure.

I think Dad could see it on my face, because he stopped himself and said, "Think about this another way. Where do you think you'll be in five years? In ten years? In fifteen years? What is it you want to do most? More than anything else in the world—this world or any other? What do *you* want, Charles?"

"I don't know—" I started to say, but then I saw the look in his eyes, the desperate look that I hadn't seen since the day he'd moved out of the house and tried to say good-bye to us kids. I hadn't said to him then what I'd wanted to say ever since. I almost said it now. But I swallowed hard and looked away. My throat was starting to hurt. Kids don't know how to think about these things or make these kinds of choices. Why do grownups push us into these conversations? Finally, I just blurted, "I just want to be someplace where people treat each other nice. Whatever that's like."

"That's a good wish, Chigger." He put his hand on my shoulder. "I want the same thing too. Especially for you. Because you're the only son I've got who loves the music as much as I do."

I turned around and stared at him. I never knew he'd noticed.

"I see you with the earphones pressed to your head. I notice what you're listening to. I'd love to talk to you about the music, the way we used to. But there's this wall between us now. Just know that I love you, Charles. I want you to have the best life you can. Please don't hate me so much. I'm trying so hard—"

That did it. The tears flooded up into my eyes and I fell into his arms, sobbing. And I finally said it, after all these years: "Daddy, please don't leave me. I'll be good. Please don't leave me again!"

He held me for a long time, and finally he whispered into my ear, "I want to be here for you, son. I really do. Just please give me a chance."

I wanted to say yes to that. I really did. But I couldn't. Not yet. First I had to know that this time wasn't like all the other times.

INTROSPECTION

IT WASN'T JUST A CHOICE between Earth and the stars, because that's a no-brainer. That part was easy. The hard part was that Dad was asking us to choose between him and Mom.

Mom wasn't bad. She was just angry all the time. And if we went back, things wouldn't be much different—just more of the same, probably worse. Like that time I stayed out in the hills too late. I was afraid to go home because I knew I'd get yelled at for not coming home, but I didn't want to get yelled at, so I stayed where I was, but I knew I'd have to go home sometime, and the later I stayed the worse the inevitable yelling would be. So I only stayed out until hunger and cold outweighed my fear. This time, though, the yelling would go on forever. I could hear Mom already. It'd be like that phone call, only I wouldn't be able to switch her off.

One thing I knew: me and Weird and Stinky, we were a family, no matter what. We had to stay together. Except that Weird wasn't going to go back, and Bobby couldn't go back by himself—so it was sort of up to me to decide what was right for both of us.

And if I went back without either Bobby or Douglas, or without both of them, what would Mom say? She'd probably blame me. She'd bawl me out three times over, once for me and once each for Bobby and Douglas. And I'd probably have to listen to all the stuff she wanted to tell Dad as well, except he wouldn't be there to listen, so I'd have to stand in for him too.

And I really didn't want to listen to any more of her angry rants about Dad—or anyone. I was getting awfully tired of all the ranting, no matter who it came from. And that was sort of what clinched it for me.

I could think of all the reasons why I shouldn't go with Dad, but I couldn't think of any reasons why I should go back to Mom.

But even if I could sort everything else out, there was still the fact that in my own way I *did* love Mom, and if I was never going to see her again I was going to miss her badly. This was going to hurt. A lot. And probably in ways that I still hadn't realized yet. There were a lot of good things about Mom: the way she made spaghetti and the way she laughed when one of us kids said something really funny and the way she said "attaboy" when one of us did something good. Dad was right, Mom wasn't a bad person, and we shouldn't think of her that way—even if it would make leaving easier. Because we'd probably end up feeling a lot worse in the long run.

I guess what I really wanted was just to be able to say good-bye to her. And have her say it was all right for me to go. Except I knew she would never say that. So I couldn't say good-bye to her, could I? And that was the part that really hurt. Because I would be trading the part of me that was incomplete about Dad leaving for a new part that would be incomplete about *me* leaving.

And that brought me back to that same old thing again, the one that *always* bothered me—how do grownups deal with this stuff? From the evidence, not very well.

Grownups are supposed to be able to think things out so that they can always do the right thing. But the more I thought about this, the harder it all became.

Maybe nobody ever really grew up at all. Only their bodies. But inside, they were all still as spoiled and whiny as Stinky.

What I wanted to do was get on my bike and ride out to the hills to one of my thinking places, where I could just sit and look at stuff and listen to my music and watch the sun edging toward the western hills. That's the other problem with elevators. You can't get out and take a walk when you need to.

So I went downstairs and stood on the scale again to see how much I weighed now. Not as much as before. Less than thirty kilos already.

While I was standing on the scale, staring at the numbers, not really seeing them, Mickey came by and saw me. "You okay, Charles?" he asked.

"Yeah," I grunted, not really wanting to talk to him. I didn't know how to treat him anymore.

"Something the matter?"

"Yeah. You. Why'd you have to go and . . . you know, with my brother?"

Mickey squatted down to look me in the eye. "That's between him and me, kiddo."

"Well, maybe you think so. But I think it's really screwed up my family."

"It has, huh?"

"Yeah."

He gave me a sad thoughtful look. "And your family wasn't screwed up at all before . . . ?"

The way he said it, I had to smile. "Well, only a little," I admitted. And then I added, "But now it's worse. My mom has called the cops on us."

"Yeah, I know." To my surprised look, he said, "Do you think I don't care what happens to you guys?"

"Are they going to stop us?"

"Not if you have a valid contract, they can't. Did your Dad accept the Sierra bid yet?"

"He's waiting to see if anything better comes in."

"You'd better tell him to accept it quickly. He's not likely to get anything better. And if he doesn't get a signed paper by the time we hit topside, well . . . it might be a problem."

"What kind of problem?"

"I'm not . . . really sure." Mickey looked troubled. "Y'know, I should make a call and see. I know some people—"

"Would you?" I must have asked a little too quickly.

He looked at me. "I can't make any promises."

"I know—but it's awfully important to my dad. And Douglas."

"Are you thinking about going to the outbeyond with them?"

"I don't know. Maybe. Have you ever been outbeyond?"

"Not yet—but I've been thinking about it. There's a couple of places I'd like to see."

"What do you know about the colonies?"

He shrugged. "Same as you. Whatever there is to know. Some are good. Some aren't. Sierra is supposed to be good. You could do worse."

I studied his face. "So, do you think I should go?"

"Mmm." He considered it. "It has to be *your* decision, Charles. But yes, since you ask me, I think it would be good for you. For all of you." Abruptly, he glanced at his watch. "Listen, it's getting late, and I've got rounds to make. You'd better get back. We're going to start spinning the cabin soon. You tell your dad what I said, about Sierra, okay?"

"Okay. And thanks, Mickey."

"You're welcome, Charles."

# MORNING

WHEN WE WOKE UP IN the morning, the gravity was completely sideways. Except it wasn't gravity—it was centrifugal force. We were so high, the pull of the Earth was insignificant. Sometime during the night, they had spun the car on its vertical axis, enough to give the feeling of one-third gravity. We all wanted to see how high we could jump, but after Stinky bumped his head, Dad told us to stop, so we did—at least while he was watching. Instead we practiced walking back and forth for a while. It felt funny to be that light.

Of course, there was a video about it. You couldn't pour a cup of coffee because it would take forever to pour. And if you took a shower, the water would splatter and bounce every which way, and the shower would take an hour to drain. That sounded like fun, but the video showed that it would also be very hard to dry off, and possibly dangerous. You could drown.

And even if you weren't trying to pour a cup of coffee or take a shower, it would still be dangerous—not being used to micro-gravity, you could bounce off the walls or the ceiling every time you took a step. And trying to get upstairs or downstairs would be a nightmare. People would get hurt.

The door we had come in by was now on the ceiling—"How're we going to get out?" wailed Stinky. Weird went to one of the side walls and opened a circular hatch. Last night it was locked, because it would have opened onto a vertical shaft; but now it was a horizontal corridor so we could walk the length of the car—except Dad wanted us to stay in the cabin. He had an unhappy expression and I wanted to ask him if he'd accepted the Sierra bid, but before I could, the door chimed and Mickey arrived with our breakfast trays.

He didn't say much; he just laid out everything on the table and then left quietly. He looked grim. Dad eyed him warily. Douglas looked like he wanted to say something. I was hoping someone would say something—but nobody did. Mickey was as carefully noncommittal as if the room was bugged. Only Stinky, who didn't know better, was in an insufferably cheerful mood, asking questions about everything. I would have happily strangled him. I'd been thinking about strangling him all my life. This morning seemed like a good opportunity, especially when he asked Mickey about how the room had turned sideways over-night. So of course Mickey took the time to answer him. Finally, though, he said, "I have other people to take care of. Maybe you should ask your big brother. He knows a lot about how the elevator works too."

Mickey left and we all just looked at each other. Then we sat down and ate without really tasting—which was just as well. The food had apparently gone tasteless.

Hurricane Charles was all over the news. The winds were still too high for the cleanup and the rescue crews to go in, and there had been a lot more damage at Terminus than they'd expected. They were already calling this the hurricane of the century. They expected Line traffic to be disrupted for weeks. There wasn't even going to be enough room to stash all the cargo that was still arriving downside, let alone the pas-sengers returning to Earth. And this would certainly cripple the relief efforts in Africa and Asia. I was glad we weren't dropping back down into that mess. The pictures were awful.

While we were watching, the door chimed—at first we thought it might be Mickey, but it was *Señor* Doctor Hidalgo. The fat man. The nine point five. He looked flushed and impatient. "*Señor* Dingillian, I apologize for interrupting your morning, but I must speak with you. I had hoped to see you at breakfast, but that did not happen. The attendant told me that you were keeping to your cabin—good morning, *mu-chachos. Buenas dias.* Please, may I come in?"

Dad let him in and offered him a seat. "Would you like some tea, coffee? Something to drink? We have a bar."

"No, no—*muchas gracias*, anyway. I appreciate the thought. But you cannot afford to feed me or give me drinks in the style to which I have become accustomed. Even I cannot afford the style to which I have become accustomed. Never mind that—we must talk frankly. Can you send the boys out?"

"Out where—?"

"Yes, there is that. I cannot ask them to wait in the bathroom, can I? Very well then, I shall have to speak candidly in front of your sons. May I?" He pushed Stinky's monkey out of the way and sat down on the couch. He sank down into it, although he didn't sink as far as he would have the night before. Even in micro-gravity, he was still heavy. Dad sat down in the chair opposite him. I noticed he didn't sit too close.

"Please forgive my bluntness, *Señor* Dingillian. There isn't much time—I had hoped to be more circumspect, more gentle. I hope you will forgive me, this is not the way I normally handle affairs of this significance, but things are happening—things that mostly do not concern you—but unfortunately you have inadvertently become part of a larger equation. Events are moving in several different directions at once and I have no idea how all the different crises will resolve, if they will resolve at all. It would take far too long to explain—but the point is, sir, the people I work for know that you are carrying something of some importance. These people would be willing to pay you very handsomely—much more than your present employers—for the package. Two times, three times as much. Plus whatever other protections you need. Perhaps even, a guaranteed colony berth . . . ?"

Douglas and I exchanged looks. I grabbed Stinky—and the monkey—and dragged them both toward the bathroom. "Come on, monster, I've got this neat trick we can teach the monkey. You're going to love this one—it'll make all the girls scream."

"No!" screamed Stinky. "I wanna stay with Daddy!"

"Charles—" Dad held up his hand. "I appreciate your intentions. It's all right. I'd just as soon have you stay." Dad stood up. "Thank you for coming by, Doctor Hidalgo. I appreciate all your courtesies." He offered his hand—whether to shake Dr. Hidalgo's hand or help him out of the couch, I wasn't sure. Dr. Hidalgo took the hint and levered himself up to his feet.

"I am very sorry you feel that way—I had hoped we could negotiate."

"There's nothing to negotiate. I don't know who you're working for, and I don't much care. I'm not carrying anything. And I'm offended at your offer. I'm not the kind of person who sells property that is not his to sell."

Hidalgo sighed. "Yes, I see. Of course. In that case, I must tell you—please do not take this the wrong way, I am not threatening, but I mean this in the sincerest sense—I am seriously worried about what will happen next. I told you about the money. Money does what it wants. Money buys whatever it has to. I am afraid that the money will try to stop you, may even try to hurt you or your sons. They told me that if you would not sell it—whatever it is, you know, they know, I don't know what it is—but if you will not sell it, they will have to try other ways to prevent its delivery, and I do not want to see you hurt, or the boys. Please reconsider—I will be available to you, wherever you are. If there is anything that I can do to help you, I would consider it an honor and a privilege to be of service—"

Dad was standing at the door, holding it open for Dr. Hidalgo. I sort of felt sorry for him, for both of them. I'd never seen Dad looking so grim. I know it hurt him to behave rudely toward anyone.

"We have nothing else to talk about, Doctor Hidalgo. Thank you for your courtesy and your concern. Now please go."

Dr. Hidalgo looked like he wanted to say something more, his mouth opened and closed a couple of times, but no words came out. He looked very upset, like he was going to have to go tell someone some very bad news. He shook his head and sighed and shook his head again and finally pushed himself through the hatch. Dad sealed it behind him.

"Okay, Dad," said Douglas. "If you're not carrying it, where is it hidden?"

"I don't know what you're talking about, Douglas. I'm not carrying anything."

"Uh-huh. Right. And our Christmas presents weren't hidden in the closet behind your file cabinets either."

Dad looked startled. "How did you—" He shook his head, exasperated. "Never mind. Just drop the subject, okay, Douglas?"

"He threatened us, Dad."

"I'm not deaf, Douglas. And I'm not stupid."

"Neither are we, Dad. What's going on?"

Dad turned to Douglas and took both his hands in his own. "If I ask you to trust me, will you?"

Douglas gave him that sideways look he does so well—the one that translates out to, "Excuse me? Did you really just say that?"

"Douglas, please—?"

"The money for the trip, right? That's where it came from."

"I can't talk about this. And you mustn't either."

"Uh-huh. Right. It's our lives too—and we're not allowed to know. You did it to us again, you son of a bitch, didn't you?" Douglas pulled his hands free and started toward the door, but he pulled free too hard and both he and Dad bounced in different directions, which would have been funny if it hadn't been so scary at the same time.

"I'm trying to protect you—goddammit!!"

"I don't want your protection!! I want the truth." And Douglas was out the door—I thought about following him, but didn't. Stinky had suddenly decided he wanted me to show him the new monkey trick after all.

Anyway, after that, everything was back to normal. Totally screwed up.

A BID FOR FREEDOM

THE EARTH STARTS LOOKING A lot smaller as you approach Geostationary. Not farther away—just smaller. It's an optical illusion, because the eye and the brain don't handle infinity very well, especially the brain, so beyond a certain distance, everything is just *far*. Geostationary point is 22,300 miles high. 36,800 klicks. That's a distance nearly equal to the circumference of the planet. It's almost three times the diameter. We were rising to a point almost three Earth-diameters above Ecuador.

From One-Hour, the Earth was a wall that filled half the sky. Now it was just a big blue marble that was so bright it was hard to look at. The Line still pointed down at it. We still hung above it. It was just much smaller than before. For the first time, I was beginning to feel as if we'd jumped off the planet . . . and were falling away into endless space. That squeezy uncomfortable feeling kept coming back, now more than ever.

But at least from here the hurricane looked a lot smaller. And a lot less dangerous. I couldn't tell, but it looked like it was starting to break up against the Andes. It had lost a lot of its circular shape. After a while Stinky got bored and we went back to our cabin. Dad was trying to raise the El Paso station again, but it was temporarily out of service due to the hurricane. Then he started channel-strafing and found out that all the groundside channels were shut down. Which seemed weird, because they could have been rerouted a dozen different ways, but that was what the channel board said. *Temporarily out of service.* And that didn't make sense at all, because they'd already told us that the hurricane couldn't disrupt Line communications.

Later, Mickey came back for the breakfast cart and asked Dad for our boarding passes. Douglas came back with him, looking grim, but not as angry as when he'd left. Mickey said there was some paperwork to take care of before we arrived. He handed Dad some forms to fill out and told us to be sure to watch the departure instructions on TV. He acted like everything was perfectly normal. So did Dad. So did Douglas. I couldn't believe it. But then again, what *else* were we supposed to do? Have another fight? No thanks, we didn't need any more practice.

So we watched the departure instructions. I suppose it would have been very interesting if we'd cared to pay attention. It was that red-haired comedian again. This time they were showing how to navigate through micro-gravity and customs and get down to the spinning sections of Geostationary, or to our connections outward. There was also a whole section on how to find your way from one part of Geostationary to another. The station was big, and getting a lot bigger every year as they kept adding more and more disks to it. And then, the show segued directly to shots of our arrival—views from the top of the car, as well as from Geostationary's underside cameras.

Arriving at Geostationary, they played, *On the Beautiful Blue Danube*, by Richard Strauss. We watched it on the screen in our cabin. They timed it perfectly. The car had been slowing down for the past thirty minutes, so it worked out that just as the huge disks of Geostationary came into view above us, the music surged and built joyously, coming to its final climax just as we locked into place. And then the inevitable voice, in six languages: "Welcome to Geostationary. For your own safety . . . blah blah blah."

I'd expected that we would get out almost immediately, but no— the car has to be brought aboard the disk, moved around, locked into place, washed, and anchored, before passengers can disembark. The whole process takes forty-five minutes. But during that time, the attendants come by with more cards that have to be filled out for customs and whatever other last-minute instructions are needed.

When Mickey came by again, we were already packed and waiting. There wasn't much to pack anyway. We'd left most of it behind. We looked like refugees—like those people in Montreal.

Mickey hardly glanced at me; he spoke mostly to Dad and Douglas. "We have a problem," he said grimly. "Station Security knows you're here. Somebody alerted them. Somebody on this car—"

"Hidalgo?" Douglas asked. He looked to Dad, angrier than ever.

Dad shrugged. "Give him credit, he works fast—"

"No, it wasn't Hidalgo." Mickey said. "That's not his style. This was an anonymous tip. Very childish. Do you have any other enemies?"

Urk—I suddenly realized who had done it. And why. We were in big trouble now. I opened my mouth to apologize—this was all my fault.

"Never mind. Worry about it later," said Mickey. "Right now, there are officers outside waiting to take you into custody and send you back down the Line."

"They can do that?"

"You know they can. Until you set foot aboard the station and pass through customs, you're not under starside jurisdiction. You're legally still on Earth and they can yank you back down with a subpoena. In about fifteen minutes, dirtside marshals will be coming aboard to serve your ex-wife's papers." And before Dad could ask how he knew so much, Mickey explained, "Douglas told me everything. Tell me—did you accept your Sierra bid?"

Dad looked unhappy. "I tried to. I sent in my acceptance last night. When I checked my e-mail this morning, it came back refused. The bid had already been withdrawn. My wife's lawyer filed some kind of a claim and Sierra backed out. They have all kinds of protection clauses in their boilerplate."

"What?" said Douglas, anger rising. "Are you saying we have no place to go? You knew that—and you turned Hidalgo down? I can't believe this!"

Dad looked resolute. "Douglas, I can't sell him what I don't have! And even if I did have it—whatever it is—I still couldn't sell it to him. I don't care if you believe me or not—"

"We could have had a sponsor!"

"We could have opened a window and jumped out!" Dad snapped right back.

"Stop it, both of you!" said Mickey quickly. "There are other sponsors. Better ones." He glanced to me and nodded. "I made a phone call." To Dad and Doug: "I can get you into the custody of an agent who places people. All I have to do is get you legally on the station. It's a different jurisdiction—different bidding rules, a lot easier. But you'll have to go right now."

"Will it work?" I asked. I was desperate. I'd screwed up *really* badly this time.

"I learned this trick at my mother's knee," said Mickey. He picked up my backpack and shoved it into my arms. He turned to Dad. "Your agent is waiting, Mr. Dingillian. We're running out of time. Are you coming?" Mickey glanced at his watch. "They'll be opening the forward hatches in six minutes."

Dad looked to Douglas, to me, to Stinky.

"Can we trust him?" Dad asked Douglas.

Douglas nodded, tight-lipped. So did I.

Mickey said, "Look, I'm trying to make up for some of the trouble I've caused—" He looked to me when he said that last.

"All right," said Dad, reluctantly. "Let's go. Charles, get your backpack on. Bobby, don't forget your monkey."

GEOSTATIONARY

WHEN A CAR DOCKS AT Geostationary, first it slides up through a service tube so tight there's only a few centimeters of clearance. The service tube takes it up through a series of three or four air locks, and then finally up to the docking chamber where the carriage of the car slides sideways off the line and onto a special delivery track that curves around like a *cesta*—that curved basket thing that jai alai players wear on their hands. The car moves out and around on this delivery track and onto a stationary holding frame, just inside the disk hub—it looks like a curved wall, sliding slowly past. All the cars are docked here while they're unloaded, serviced, and reloaded. They look like cans lined up in a rack, while the whole station rotates around.

Mickey said that we had to stop thinking of Earth as down. *Up* and *down* are the same as *in* toward the hub and *out* toward the rim. The only two other directions inside the disks of the station are dirtside and starside—and those are sideways directions.

Mickey led us down the corridor toward the service hatch. There are hatches at both ends of the car. Passengers use the top or *forward* hatch. Crew and cargo use the bottom or *aft* hatch. So while the marshals were coming in through the front, we were already leaving through the rear. There was a service attendant waiting there. He frowned when he saw us, but Mickey said to him, "Thanks, Joe. I really appreciate this."

He shook his head in disapproval. "I wasn't here," he said. "I was taking a leak."

"And we never saw you."

Joe grunted and stepped away from his service panel. He disappeared back down the corridor.

"In through here," Mickey pointed.

"Is this a real hatch?" Stinky demanded. "It doesn't look like it."

"It's a service hatch. Most people *never* get to see this, Bobby. This is where supplies and cargo come aboard and waste is removed—all through this hatch."

"Are we going out in a Dumpster?" I asked.

"Nothing that dramatic. Watch that light. As soon as it goes green, I punch this button and that door opens. There'll be a woman standing there holding a document. As soon as your dad signs it, you'll be under the full legal protection of Partridge Colonial Enterprises."

Dad turned to Mickey. "There's supposed to be a three-day grace period, isn't there, during which time I can back out of the deal?"

Mickey grinned. "Yep, there is. But by that time, you can be on your way to Luna, so—" He laughed. There was no need for him to finish the sentence.

The green light went on and Mickey hit the button. All three doors of the hatch whooshed open and two big men stepped in immediately, scaring us with the hard way they looked and the quick way they came rushing right in, because at first we thought they were security agents, or maybe worse—some of those people that Dr. Hidalgo had hinted about—but they weren't. They were just service technicians. They brushed past us and went straight up the corridor as if we weren't there.

A stocky older woman carrying a big business bag came in immediately after. Her dark hair was even shorter than theirs. "Don't worry about those fellows," she explained. "They didn't see anything either. I'm your lawyer. My name is Olivia. You're Max Dingillian? Pleased to meet you. Sign here, here, and here." She pulled a camera out of her purse.

"You kids, up against the wall. I need your pictures." Snap, snap, snap. Dad too; one more snap. "Raise your right hand. Do you solemnly swear that the information provided in these documents is true to the best of your knowledge, so help you? Thank you. Congratulations, you are now clients of Partridge Enterprises. Would you thumbprint this, please? Right here. And here. Thank you. You kids too, please?" She folded the papers and stuffed them into her purse, then turned to Mickey, wrapped him into her big arms, and gave him a hug that I thought would crush him. "How're you doing, sweetie?"

"I'm fine, Mom. How's business?"

"Lousy. That dirtside son-of-a-bitch is playing games again. I've had it with him. I'm filing a complaint with the Board of Ethics. I'm going to have that scumbag's balls for a paperweight, just as soon as we find them—"

Mickey grinned at Dad. "Mom's the best. She eats human flesh.

Raw, if she's really hungry. She can strip a full-grown cow to the bone in seven minutes."

"I can believe it."

Olivia turned back to us, all business again. "All right, you slaves— don't take that personally, it's a joke—let's get you out of here. This way, quickly. Bring your bags. You, the little one—Bobby, is that your name? Is that your monkey? You'd better carry him for now. Or why don't you let me carry him, okay? Let's go. I'll see you later, Mickey. Don't be late for dinner." She shoved the monkey into her bag and we all followed her.

Leaving the car is a tricky process. There are transfer pods at each end of the elevator; they spin to match the rotation of the cylinder, and you get aboard. Then the pod disengages from the car and stops spinning—and the passengers feel weightless. The pod points itself so that its "floor" is outward, which means soon it'll be downward. It connects itself to a track on the rotating inner wall of the hub and then slides outward. It feels "downward." The farther "out" it goes from the hub, the heavier you feel. It's centrifugal force. The same thing that holds the Line up—only the Earth is the hub for the Line.

The departure video had shown us that there would be seats in the transfer pod for ten people at a time, only we were in a cargo pod which was set up differently, and there were no seats in it at all, only handholds set into the wall.

Olivia directed us to hold on tight, then hit the Go panel. Nothing happened first; then we felt like we were getting lighter and lighter. "The pod-drum has disengaged from the cabin. It's slowing down now. As the spinning slows, we lose pseudo-gravity. Bobby, don't try float- ing. You could hurt yourself. Just hold on, please." For a moment, we were weightless, or close enough that the difference was insignificant. It kind of felt like we were falling, but not quite. After a moment that sensation went away and we weren't falling at all, we just kept feeling like it. Stinky started giggling. I felt like I was going to puke.

Something outside thumped softly and Olivia said, "The transfer pod is now moving off the drum. And another one is taking its place." She hesitated a moment, as if she were listening to the feeling of the room. "Now the pod is lowering down toward the main levels of the disk. Outward is down, just like in the cabin of the elevator car. Feel that?"

That was pseudo-gravity starting to come back. Olivia said, "You'll have the feeling of weight in just another few seconds. Main level gives you one-half your normal weight, just a little more than on the elevator car." Even as she said it, we were already sinking down to the floor.

"Is this really going to work?" Dad asked, indicating Olivia's papers. "I mean, doesn't Earth have some authority up here?"

"Very little," Olivia said blandly. She patted her bag. "This goes to a much higher court. Literally."

The door popped open and we were staring at a hallway long enough that we could see how it curved up in the distance. "We're here," said Olivia. "Come on, I'll walk you through customs. Got your IDs and passports? Now, listen—you're going to be stopped by security agents. You've got to let me do the talking. Don't say *anything*. Nothing at all. They'll be recording everything." She looked to me, Douglas, and Bobby. "Look determined, okay? Like this is what you want. This *is* what you want, isn't it?"

Dad nodded. He looked to us kids. Douglas nodded. So did I. Stinky said, "I'm going with Chigger," which surprised me. I didn't know what to say in response, so I just took his hand.

"Okay, let's go," said Olivia. She took the newly-signed papers out of her purse and brandished them in front of her like a weapon. We put on our most determined expressions and followed in her wake.

"Do you get a lot of business this way?" Dad asked innocently.

"Not usually," she replied. "But once in a while my son brings home a stray puppy. Don't worry about my fee. I get a finder's commission from the colonies. We'll talk about that later. Here we are—"

HOWARD

THERE THEY ARE—" THE UGLY little man saw us first and came advancing like an attack Chihuahua. He wore a wrinkled suit; it looked like he'd gotten it from his older brother and still hadn't grown into it. Two security guards came following after with bored expressions. A fourth man came running with a multi-lens vid-cam aimed at us. I said the word again.

Olivia saw them at the same time they saw us. She put on her biggest smile and said, "Howard, how nice to see you again. I understand we're getting an ambulance up here for you to chase."

"Don't be nasty, Olivia. I have a court order—" He held up an official-looking document. I guessed it was a subpoena.

"Fold it and stuff it, Counselor. I have an agency contract." She held up a paper of her own. Our contract.

For a moment, the two of them faced each other like they were about to start a sword fight—only with folded documents instead of swords.

"It's not valid—"

"Don't be stupider than usual, Howard. Of course, it's valid. How many of these have you examined already? Would you like to examine this one too?" She shoved it under his nose.

Howard, whoever he was, slapped the paper away angrily. Olivia just shoved it right back under his nose. "You lay one hand on any of these clients, and I'll have you headed dirtside without benefit of an elevator. I'll have you tied up in so much paper, the only way out for you will be a good flush." She smiled and became even sweeter and gentler than before. "You know I have you beaten. Don't prolong your agony."

"I'm filing a complaint with Judge Griffith. You had unfair and unauthorized access."

"My clients requested that I meet them as soon as possible precisely to guarantee their rights of residence. That's all the authorization I needed. You know that. I violated no statutes—"

"Oh, don't give me that. Your son does this all the time, letting you aboard in violation of the Singapore Convention—"

"Don't say another word, you little turd, or I'll have you up on a slander charge as well. Legal representatives have the right to meet their clients before they disembark, precisely to guarantee their rights of representation; you know the precedent as well as I. You lost that one too, as I recall. Why don't you try another line of work, Howard? You're really not very good at this."

A crowd was starting to form. I guess we were good theater. Olivia turned her attention to the guards, incidentally making sure that she was facing enough toward the man with the vid-cam that he would have a good angle on her. "Do you fellows understand the issues involved here? My clients are under the protection of Partridge Colonial Enterprises. Whatever claims any groundside agency has against any of these individuals must come through me. I will receive service of summons forthwith—" She plucked the subpoena from Howard's hand and stuffed it in her purse. "But please be aware that under the terms of the Singapore Convention, custody of my clients may not be transferred without a hearing before Judge Griffith. You may not arrest, detain, or otherwise hinder the movements of these four people. Do you understand?"

Apparently they'd heard the speech before, because they looked bored as she went through the recitation. "Right. We know the drill." One of the guys didn't look happy, but the other said, "Are you going to be at Lemrel's party Saturday, Olivia?"

"Of course, wouldn't miss it for the world. See you there." She stuffed her papers back in her purse and started to push forward.

"Hold it, Olivia. Not so fast. There are minors involved this time!" Howard stepped in front of her. He motioned to the guy with the camera. "Get in here close for this, will you?" He stepped up in front of us and said, "Which one of you is Charles?"

Olivia nodded to me and I held up my hand politely.

"Thank you, Charles." He stepped in closer. He had bad breath. "Now, I want to ask you a question, and I want you to think very carefully before you answer. And I want you to know that you don't have to answer for anyone except yourself. Are you going with your father of your own free will?"

I looked to Olivia, as if to ask her if I should answer. She held up a hand to stop me from speaking. "I take exception to this, Counselor."

"Nevertheless, Counselor—" Howard said right back—"for the purposes of this case, the court has seen fit to require evidence that the children are not being held against their will." He handed her another folded paper. She unfolded it and looked through it quickly. She nodded. "Well, I'll be damned. You got one right, Howard. This is all in order." She handed the paper back. "All right, Charles, you may answer the nice man."

"What was the question again?"

"Are you going with your father of your own free will, or are you being forced? You don't have to go with him if you don't want to. That's why these agents are here. To protect you."

"Oh," I said. "I think I'd rather stay with my Dad."

Howard frowned. He looked to Stinky. "You must be Douglas—"

"No, I'm Bobby. That's Douglas."

"Ah, thank you." Howard turned to Weird. "Douglas—are you accompanying your male parent of your own free will?" Douglas didn't like being pressured, but he nodded slowly. Howard leaned in toward him. "What was that? I need you to say it aloud. For the camera."

"Yes," he said loudly. "I'm going with my father of my own free will. And you need a better mouthwash." The crowd laughed.

Howard ignored it and turned to Bobby. "And you, young man— are you going with your father too, or do you want to go home to your mommy? You know she misses you *very* much."

"Watch it, Howard—" Olivia said warningly.

"I'm going with Chigger and my monkey," Bobby said. "Wherever Chigger goes, I go."

"The monkey?" Howard looked momentarily confused.

Stinky went pawing through Olivia's bag. He pulled out his monkey and put it down on the ground. "Show this man a 'farkleberry.' " He pointed toward Howard. The monkey immediately did a funny little dance in a circle, ending up in front of Howard, where he turned his back, yanked down his pants, and made a horrendous farting noise. The crowd roared. Some of them even applauded. Olivia guffawed like a horse.

Howard was not amused. But instead of losing his temper, he turned to Olivia and waggled his finger in her face. "Judge Griffith's, first thing tomorrow morning. The child did *not* indicate a preference for the male parent. We're calling in Social Services for a Protective Custody Interview. Nine A.M. It's already on the docket."

"As you wish, Counselor," Olivia said calmly. She pointed us toward the Customs officer. "Pick up your monkey, Bobby. I don't want it getting any fleas from the lawyer. See you in court, Howard."

PLANS

OLIVIA **TOOK US DIRECTLY TO** her offices which were on Disk Three. You count the disks from the bottom up, so it was two disks above Disk One, which contained the arrival terminal and customs, plus hotels and shops and the upside offices of downside companies. We didn't get to see much, though. Dad told her about Dr. Hidalgo's last conversation with us, so she took us straight to the "subway" and popped us all into a tube.

Relative to Earth, we were going "up," but relative to the disks of Geostationary, we were going "across." Eventually, all of the different disks would be linked to become a giant cylinder—like the L5 colony under construction. There would be three subways running along the outermost, or bottommost level. Even though the floors of the cylinder hadn't been started yet, and wouldn't be for several years, the subways were already in place because it simplified the process of moving from one disk to the next. We went "across," but it felt like "forward."

Olivia's offices were also her apartment. She didn't have a great view. Disks One and Two blocked the view of Earth, and Disks Four through Seven blocked the view of deep space. But she had a wall display that showed all the views anyone could want of anything. It wasn't a *real* window, but we'd never had a real window back home either.

"Okay," she said, sitting down at her console. "Power up, Betsy. Momma's got work to do. First things first, kiddos. Do you want Italian or bleu cheese on your salad? You kids, what do you want on your pizza? Let's get the important decisions made first—then we have a lot of paperwork to review. I'm afraid your case has just gotten a little more complicated." She surveyed all of us on our likes and dislikes for dinner, finished punching the order in, then turned back to us expectantly.

"Is there a problem?" Dad asked. He looked worried.

"Yes and no. Your ticket's one-way, isn't it?"

"Yes. Mine is. The boys' aren't."

"Good. Then there's no problem. As long as you're not coming back anytime in the next seven years. Statute of limitations."

"Huh?"

"Let me look over your resumes, your insurance, your tickets, all your paperwork. The problem is I'm going to have to void our contract. Or rather, you are."

"I don't understand."

"You're going to have to fire me for unsatisfactory representation. I'm going to have to advise you against that."

"But then they'll arrest us."

"That's why you can't fire me just yet—not until you get back on the outbound elevator." She hesitated. "No, I have a better idea. Don't fire me. I'll quit. If you get on the outbound elevator, I'll have no choice but to refuse to represent you anymore. Yes, I like that. It'll prove I have some integrity, and the result will be the same. And Howard will be *really* pissed at me. Judge Griffith will have a good laugh. She doesn't like Howard anyway. But I don't know how she feels about *this* case. We'd better cover our asses with a lot of paper tonight." She patted her ample butt. "And that's going to take a *lot* of paper.

"Now, hmm. How're we going to get you out to Disk Seven? Howard will have his goons posted by now."

"What about Dr. Hidalgo?" Douglas asked.

"He's not a problem. Not yet. Whoever's behind him, it's going to take them some time to organize. And I think Dr. Hidalgo would rather negotiate. That's his style—I've seen him in action. Next time around, he's going to offer you ten times what you were paid. If you refuse, then we'll have to worry about your life expectancy." Still talking, she pulled her chair up to the computer and started typing. I'd never seen a woman like her before. I wondered if she had a fuel cell inside or if she was just pocket-fusion powered?

"Max, there's a bottle of scotch in the cupboard. Pour two. Three if Douglas wants one. Juice for the kids. On that rack over there, I've got some of your recordings. Autograph the Copland set for me, will you? It's part of my fee. That was a beautiful job you did on the third. Always one of my favorites."

"Fourth movement?" I asked.

"How'd you guess?" She grinned back at me. "What music did you get on the way up? Anything interesting?"

"*Carmina Burana*, Beethoven's Fourth, and *The Blue Danube*."

Olivia made a face. "Yeah, the usual. I wish they'd be more imaginative. Oh, well." She bent back to her keyboard again.

Dad smiled at me and mouthed the words, "Everybody's a critic."

Olivia was still talking. I'd never heard anyone use so many words per minute in my life. "The real question, Max, how do I get you a Colonial Sponsor so you don't have to go through this again on Luna? And how do I secure that contract so it sticks, even if I don't?"

"What? I thought you already had a contract for us—"

"I do and I don't. I'm a finder. I can find a placement for just about anybody. My finder's fee is based on your value to the colony. I could justify the value of a serial killer, if I had to. In fact, I think I did once. I'd have to check my files. A fellow named Maizlish. Left a trail of dead bodies wherever he went. He got up here somehow, and there was no jurisdiction or authority to send him back, so I found him a contract. Testing vaccines on Gotham. Very appropriate. Cost him plenty. I think he died of something awful. I certainly hope so—"

Dad was getting just a little upset. What was this woman getting us into? "How can you talk about getting bids on my services when I couldn't even get noticed? I got only one response and it was for basic value only. No perquisites."

"That's because you came in cold. You need an agent. An agent secures your performance in return for a finder's fee. Clients with agents get better bookings."

"I know that," said Dad. "I know how agents work—that's why I hate getting caught between lawyers and agents. I don't know who to hate more."

Olivia ignored it. She'd probably heard it all before. I certainly had, enough times that I could set it to music. She studied her display. "You have a very interesting set of skills, Max. There are a lot of worlds that are desperate to start developing their own arts and culture. The ideal booking for you would be a place where you could train your own orchestra. You'd probably have to do some teaching too, but that wouldn't hurt you either. I think I know of a couple planets that fit that description." She frowned and slapped the side of her monitor. "Come on, Betsy—get your fat ass in gear." Apparently Betsy didn't, because Olivia swiveled in her chair to face Dad. "Y'know—it's risky, but I could put you on the outbound without a firm bid. That way I could get you out of here—wait, let me check." She swiveled back. "Betsy, how soon would Max and his children have to leave to catch the earliest possible lunar launch?"

The computer answered quietly, "The midnight car is the earliest one with open bookings. Should I make a reservation?"

"Yes. Use the Goodman account. If it's not overdrawn again. Two rooms for six people. Cancel two of the people just before boarding and sell the other four tickets to the Dingillians." To us, she said, "That should confuse Howard. He'll be watching for any booking for four, especially in your name." She turned back to her keyboard. "If I can get you out of here and on the way to Luna, that gives me two days to find you a placement." Abruptly, she pushed herself back from the keyboard in frustration. "No, this is the wrong way to do it. Too much work. Betsy, get me Georgia."

Almost immediately, there was a chime and a woman's voice answered, "Olivia, how are you?"

"The pizza's on it's way, Georgia—where the hell are you?"

"Pizza? Tonight? I thought we were getting together on—" The voice stopped, then came back laughing. "Oh, that's a good one, Olivia. Very good. You almost caught me. What do you need?"

"I need you for dinner. I have some people I want you to meet."

"The Dingillians, right? Howard was just here."

"I want you to interview the kids, sweetie. This is a beautiful family. They don't need a Protective Services evaluation."

"I'd rather do this through channels, Counselor."

"Georgia, so would I, but these people have already had one bid withdrawn because of this publicity. And there aren't going to be any more bids for them until this is resolved, we both know that. This is a delaying tactic by Howard—"

"Acting on behalf of the mother—" Georgia put in.

"Nevertheless, it's a delaying tactic designed to keep my client from his freedom to emigrate."

"Downside sees it as a custody battle."

"Yes, that's true. And starside sees it as a freedom-to-emigrate issue."

"Either way," the unseen Georgia said, "it comes back to the rights of the child."

"Precisely," said Olivia. "That's why I think you should meet the children. Tonight if possible. Not in a court of law. You need to see these kids as people, not specimens."

Georgia sighed. There was a pause. Then she asked, "What's on the pizza?"

"Your favorite. Mushrooms, onions, tomatoes."

"No Martian anchovies?"

"Have you seen the price of Martian anchovies lately? Next year, when Mars gets a lot closer, we'll talk anchovies. Can you be here in fifteen?"

"The distance has nothing to do with the price. You're just a cheapskate. And I'll be there in ten. Open a bottle of Lambrusco and give it a chance to breathe."

"Yes, Your Honor."

"This call is adjourned." Judge Griffith clicked off with a sound like a gavel coming down.

PIZZA

THE PIZZA ARRIVED THEN, FILLING the apartment with thick rich tomatoey smells. I didn't know pizza could smell so good. At home, pizza is an industrial product, little squares rolling out of a machine. But this one was round and Olivia said it was hand-made. I couldn't imagine that.

Before Olivia could finish laying out plates on the table, a laughing woman in a wheel chair came rolling in. Judge Griffith. "I hereby declare this dinner officially in session," she boomed. And rolled right up to the table to put a small vase of flowers in the center. "From my own garden, Olivia. You always liked the blue roses, didn't you?"

Her chair had a built-in swivel, she wheeled around to face us. We were both staring at her open-mouthed. "You must be Charles and Bobby. Douglas? Pleased to meet you. Max Dingillian? Wish I could say the same. You sure stirred up a fine kettle of worms. Made a lot of extra work for all of us—but as my old sainted gramma used to say, 'the best reason for stirring up a kettle of worms is to make sure the sauce gets evenly distributed.' Bobby, you must show me that trick you made your monkey do for Howard. And all the other tricks too. My goodness, I haven't laughed so hard since the day the Thomas case blew up in his face." She looked around, blinking. "Where's Mickey?"

"Late as usual," Olivia said. "He inherited that from his father. No matter, we can start without him. Come on, everybody to the table—did you kids wash your hands? No? Well, hop to it. The pizza's getting cold. More wine, Your Honor?"

"How can I have more when I haven't had any yet?" Judge Griffith held out her glass impatiently.

Were all lawyers and judges like this?

"Excuse me?" Dad said, when we were finally all seated and Olivia was passing out thick slabs of fresh hot pizza. "But am I the only one who sees a possible conflict of interest here? The lawyer and the judge and the defendants all having dinner together?"

Olivia and Georgia exchanged glances. And laughed.

Georgia said, "If this were a trial, yes, there would be a conflict of interest. But you're not defendants. Not yet. Tomorrow's hearing is investigatory, not evidential. My coming here is to obtain background information on the case, at the request of your attorney. And just in case you haven't noticed—" Georgia pointed toward two of the corners of the room where cameras were mounted"—your kindly old Auntie Olivia is recording everything. For her protection, and for yours. When did you start the files, dear?"

"When you rolled in, Your Honor. All of the discussions we had before you arrived are in separate files, private-coded. These recordings are being made with grade-three authentication."

"Good." Georgia patted Olivia's hand. "That's why you're such a good lawyer. You don't leave anything to chance." To Dad, she continued, "The point is, if I'm to make a ruling about what's best for your children, I need to see them in a less formal situation, and in relationship with you—not all scrubbed and polished for a court appearance, but in a more relaxed family setting. There are precedents for home interviews and home studies. This is upside law, not downside. We do things differently up here. You may have noticed that already. We don't have time to spend a year or two on a legal matter that should be resolvable in a couple of days. Nobody benefits from that. Justice delayed is justice denied. And pizza delayed is asphalt. So eat before that piece cools off in your hand."

Dad took a bite. Thoughtfully. Then another. He looked uncomfortable and he kept looking back and forth between the two women at the table. We'd just met the both of them and suddenly our lives were in their hands. How had we stumbled into this? Was this going to turn into an even bigger mess?

Olivia noticed first. "Max," she said, almost conversationally, "do you have community standards classes in your town? Seminars?"

"Sure, doesn't everybody?"

"What's the stated purpose?" The way she asked, there was obviously more to her question than curiosity.

"To establish stability for the entire community. The most good for the most people."

Olivia looked to Georgia. "Sounds good to me—for dirtside. How about you, Your Honor?"

Georgia shrugged and spoke around a mouthful of salad. "Yeah, sounds good for dirtside."

I was starting to get the feeling that "dirtside" was a nasty word. A rude way of talking about people who lived on the ground.

"Well, it is good," Dad said. "There are seventeen billion people on the planet. You can't have everyone running around freely making up their own rules and setting their own standards. The, uh—the social contract and all that. The common good requires that people have a common context."

"That sounds pretty common to me," Olivia nodded.

"Yep," agreed the Judge. "Me too."

Dad finally got it. He narrowed his eyes. "Is there something wrong with the idea of the common good?"

"Nope," Olivia said innocently. "If you don't mind being common."

Judge Griffith leaned forward then to explain. "Max, downside, you can talk about things being common, because for most people, that's exactly how they are. Common. Ordinary. But up here—" She waved her hand to indicate not just the room but everything beyond it. Geostationary. The Line. The moon. "Up here—*nothing* is ordinary. Everything is *extraordinary.*

"People don't come up here looking for more of the ordinary, they come up here because they want to get away from the ordinary. That's what space represents, the chance at an *extra*ordinary life.

"Most people on Earth *never* get a chance to feel what it's like to be extraordinary. The best they get are pictures of other people being extraordinary. And once in a while, some lucky schmuck gets an extraordinary experience and it transforms the quality of his life from that moment onward. Because once you've had one extraordinary experience you know that once isn't enough. You want your whole life to be like that. So people come up here, Max, looking not just for an extraordinary experience, but, for what they wanted all along—extraordinary lives."

Still talking to Dad, the judge pointed to us kids. "You knew that when you kidnapped them—sorry to be so blunt about it, Max, but let's be honest. You knew what you were doing, and you'd do it again if you had to. You saw a chance and you grabbed it, and you grabbed your kids so they could have the same chance too. And the fact is, there isn't a parent on Earth who doesn't secretly envy your bravado—even while at the same time hating you for it. You've grabbed a piece of something." She waved at the space around her. "This is a lifeline for the human race—a way out of the trap."

Dad shook his head. "The last report I saw said that there are still three million babies being born every day, something like that. The Line would take eight months to boost that many people into space. No, the beanstalk isn't a way out—it's a luxury."

"No, it isn't," said Olivia abruptly. "It's a lifeboat. And there weren't enough lifeboats on the *Titanic* either."

That made for a moment of uncomfortable silence, until Judge Griffith rescued the conversation. "The point is," she said, "we're trying to get as many kids into the lifeboats as possible. And world-builders. And people who know how to make a difference. We might lose the Earth, yes—it sure looks like it this week—but we're not going to lose the game."

Dad made a face. I could almost understand why.

"Yes, I know that downsiders hate it when an upsider talks like that, but the nasty truth is that what's consuming the Earth is everybody's insistence on grinding everybody else down. There's no energy left for anything else. That's why you bailed—"

Dad conceded the argument with a shrug.

Olivia interrupted then. "Your Honor, if I may—?"

Judge Griffith waved her hand. "Go ahead, Counselor."

Olivia leaned toward Dad. "The job of the Presiding Judge of the Superior Court for the Geostationary Jurisdiction as authorized by the Singapore Treaty and confirmed by the local representatives of the Corporate Signatories to the Colonial Agreement is to rule on conflicts between upside and downside law. The unspoken part of that job is to guarantee and protect the interests of upsiders against spurious downside claims." She glanced over to the judge. "Right?"

Judge Griffith waved her wineglass in vague agreement. "We get a lot of interesting actions filed up here. Everybody downside thinks everybody upside is rich." She stopped talking just long enough to push another bite of pizza into her mouth. Still chewing, she held up a hand to indicate that she hadn't finished her thought yet. She mopped her mouth with one of Olivia's ample cloth napkins and held her glass out for more wine. "I shouldn't, but the counselor has an excellent wine cellar—thirty-six thousand kilometers that way." She gestured off to her side. "Or am I turned around? No, I was right. It's that way. Earthside and starside, Charles. Remember that. Keep the Earth to your left and you're facing spinward. Here, I'll give you an interesting little puzzle to consider. If I take away from you the words *right* and *left*, how else can you speak about your right and left side?"

"My heart's on the left," I answered immediately. And then added quickly, "Your Honor."

"You can call me Georgia. We're not in session here. And that's the B answer. Your heart is actually in the center, leaning left. Now, try for the A answer. How would you explain *left* and *right* to a Martian? Someone who doesn't have the same language you do. What physical criteria can you use? Think about it for awhile." She turned back to Olivia, leaving me puzzling over the riddle. If there was another answer, it wasn't obvious.

After her glass was refilled a second time, Georgia turned back to Dad. "I'm well aware that if I grant your wife's claim tomorrow, I'm establishing a precedent for future downsider claims against upsiders. So even though what's at issue for you is only your future, what's at issue for the rest of us up here is a lot larger. This is one of those really annoying cases that calls into question the whole matter of jurisdiction.

"You see, if I vacate Howard's request for an investigatory hearing, that will be viewed downside as a larger refusal to hear any downside claims, which will lead us ultimately toward a hearing in the World Court. Not this case, of course—you'll be long gone by then—but eventually, the jurisdictional matters are going to have to be resolved. Sooner or later, we're going to get a really nasty test case. I just want to make sure that this isn't it, because if this one ends up in the World Court, it'll be ruled against us. And regardless of the outcome of this case, I don't want that precedent over my head. So the best hope for the upside is to delay those kinds of confrontations for as long as possible to give the colonial signatories a chance to build up a counterweight authority.

"Even though we're well into orbital space, we're still *attached* to the Earth. Therefore Earth assumes that Earth should have authority over the entire length of the beanstalk. Upsiders feel that, as a matter of course, the beanstalk should be viewed entirely as a space-borne agency, because once someone's up the beanstalk they're under beanstalk control, and the bulk of the beanstalk is in space. At the moment, the dividing line is One-Hour, with Earth maintaining authority over One-Hour and everything below, and Geostationary maintaining authority over everything above.

"But none of that is your concern. It's mine." To Olivia she said, "I assume you've got Betsy scouring for useful precedents?"

Olivia nodded. "Have been all afternoon."

Georgia stuffed the last bite of pizza into her mouth and chewed thoughtfully. "Well, you're going to have to show me some damn good reasons for disregarding Maggie Dingillian's claim. No matter what. Now, I'll interview the kids. Douglas? You have a question?"

He pointed to the cameras. "How much of what you just said was for them?"

She laughed. "All of it, sweetheart. These recordings may never need to be shown, but just in case—I have to make the speech. I know who elected me and I know why."

MICKEY

MICKEY SHOWED UP THEN, LOOKING very unhappy. Without a smile, he didn't look like the same person.

"I told you not to be late," said Olivia. "Your pizza's cold."

"I'm not hungry—"

She put her hand on his forehead to see if he had a temperature. "What's the matter?"

He sat down at the table and picked up a piece of pizza anyway. "I got terminated."

Olivia sat down opposite him, immediately all business. "On what grounds?"

"No grounds." He nodded in the direction of Dad. Or Douglas. "Getting involved." He looked embarrassed.

"Do you want me to file something?" She looked to Judge Griffith. "Georgia?"

"It's a little premature, Olivia. Let's hear what the boy has to say."

"I'm not a boy, Aunt Georgia. I'm twenty-two."

"Mickey, I'm your god-mom. I used to change your diapers, for God's sake. Now just tell us what happened."

Mickey shrugged. "The kids were in trouble. I helped them. Kelly found out and reported me to the supervisor."

"Kelly? Is that the ugly one or the nasty one?" Olivia asked.

"Mom—your feelings are showing."

Olivia ignored it. "Anyway, they can't fire you for that."

"They didn't."

"Eh? What were the grounds for termination?"

Mickey looked embarrassed. "Having sex . . . with a passenger."

Silence in the room for a moment. Olivia looked around, saw that

Douglas looked particularly embarrassed, pretended she didn't notice, then looked back to Mickey as if she wanted to say a whole lot of things to him, but didn't dare.

"It's not Mickey's fault," Douglas blurted abruptly. "I asked him. He didn't ask me. And he said no the first two times I asked."

"Thank you for that, Douglas—but it still doesn't change Mickey's responsibility in the matter. How old are you, Doug?"

"I'll be eighteen next month."

"Close enough. No problem there. It's consenting adults," said Olivia.

"Line policy," countered Georgia. "They have a case. Tell me, did you do it on your own time?"

Mickey nodded.

"Well . . . at least they can't get him for neglecting the customers," Georgia said, then laughed at her own inadvertent joke.

Olivia turned to Mickey now. She lowered her voice. "Just tell me one thing—"

Mickey already knew the question, even before she asked it. "Yes, Mom. He *is* special."

Olivia gave Douglas a warm smile, then turned back to Mickey. "That's all I wanted to know." She patted his shoulder. "Just so long as *you're* sure." She made me wish our mom were as understanding. Mickey hung his head in his hands and started to cry softly. Olivia pulled her chair closer and put her arm around his shoulders. "Hey, hey—it's all right. Momma's here. Come on, kiddo. I'm right here. Just let it out—"

Mickey looked up, red-eyed. "But it's not fair, Mom. Kelly's got her legs up in the air for anything with a tongue. One year, for her birthday, we got her a German shepherd and a jar of peanut butter."

Olivia reached around behind herself and grabbed a yellow legal pad. "Did you tell Smeagle that? Not the part about the German shepherd, the other part."

"Yes, I did."

"And what did he say?"

"The two cases are different. He said if they fired everyone with a loose zipper, there wouldn't be anyone working the Line. It's when we let our feelings influence our professionalism—blah blah blah. I'm pretty sure there's more to it than that—"

"There always is," said Olivia, scribbling furiously. "But we've got grounds. Unfair discrimination. Do you want me to file?"

Mickey shook his head. "I don't know. We've gotta talk, Mom.

Things are getting really bad downside. You haven't seen the traffic we're getting. I don't know if I want to keep doing this anyway."

"Mickey, please—you're too valuable where you are."

"Mom—? Please? You said I could say '*when.*' Well, I think I'm finally saying *when.*"

Olivia nodded reluctantly and put the pad aside. "Okay. Whatever you want, sweetie—but let me file anyway. Let them pay for your silence. And the money will be useful. We'll talk about this later, I promise." She patted his hand.

Georgia interrupted then. "Tell me about the traffic, Mickey. What's going on?"

"We're getting too many rich emigrants. Whole carloads. Groups. They all know each other, and they're very tight-lipped about where they're going. It's that thing Mom's always talking about—a massive evacuation of rodents. Well, I think it's happening."

Georgia nodded. "We've noticed the traffic through here. We have some idea where they're all headed. It's legal. And you could probably find a lot of other reasons to explain the increase—like having three extra brightliners available, the new catapult, the shift in immigration policies, the changes in the transportation laws—"

"—and the population clock has just hit half-past midnight! Aunt Georgia, this isn't eco-theory anymore. The plagues in Africa are worse than the news is reporting. And they've already leapt across to India and Pakistan and China. A lot of people believe we're looking at the first stages of a genuine population crash—enough people to create a real panic."

Georgia rubbed her cheek thoughtfully. "I'm not willing to rule on it yet, Mickey. I'm still hearing evidence."

"Aunt Georgia, this is really one time I wish you weren't so rigorous—because by the time you have compelling evidence, it'll be too late! The people we have coming up the Line now are the kind of folks who have access to information that the rest of us aren't getting yet."

"Mickey, I know you. I know you're not an alarmist—and I trust your instincts about a lot of things, especially about people. But . . ."

"But—I know. Okay, here's one more for you. Last month, we had a family come up, you know what was in their luggage? Industrial memory. Nothing else. Forty bars of it. Probably three or four billion dollars worth. They had to pay a surcharge for the extra weight; they didn't even flinch at the cost. Georgia, they had enough raw memory for a small government. Or even a corporation. Whose data were they carrying offworld? And why? And *where?*"

"There's nothing illegal about transporting memory."

"No, there isn't. But on this big a scale? Doesn't it make you a little bit suspicious? What if it were bars of gold?"

"It wouldn't be worth as much—"

"That's right. And this is the fourth time this year we've had a passenger like that. At least that I know about. I'm only on one car. There are ninety-five other cars a day between dirtside and here. If what I've seen is one percent, then what would it mean if there were three hundred and eighty more passengers like that?" Mickey spread his hands wide. "I'm just telling you what I've seen, Your Honor. You be the judge."

Georgia smiled. Obviously, it was an old joke. She said, "I already am."

Mickey turned to his mom. "You know that booking we've been talking about? I think it's time to use it."

Olivia's face clouded. She said, "Shh, we'll talk about it later."

INTERVIEWS

JUDGE GRIFFITH LOOKED AT HER watch. "Your mother's right. That's a subject for later, Mickey. Right now, we've got a more immediate matter to attend to. The Dingillian kids." She wheeled her chair over to where Douglas and Bobby and I were sitting. "Okay, Munchkins, let's talk. Douglas, I saw Howard's tape. You're certain you want to go with your dad, right?"

Douglas nodded.

"Why?"

"Not enough money for school. And I can't get a scholarship on Earth. Not even the rechannelling scholarship. This looks like a better idea."

"No money for school, but enough money for a beanstalk ticket. Right. I'll get back to that in a bit, with your dad. But right now, answer this: what if there were enough money for you to go to—where was it?—UCLA? Would you still want to go with your dad, or would you want to go back to Earth?"

Douglas frowned. "If you'd asked me that last week, I'd have probably said I'd just as soon like to stay on Earth. But that was before we came up here. I dunno. Maybe Dad has the right idea." He started to rub his head, then stopped. That's supposed to be rude in space. Like picking your nose and flicking the boogers. He shrugged instead. "I've learned a lot in the past couple days." He looked at Dad and smiled slightly. "I think . . . if I have to decide tonight, then I'll stay with Dad."

"You *think?*" Georgia asked. "This is the rest of your life we're talking about."

"I know—you want certainty. Everybody always wants certainty. And you want me to say I'm sure about this—but who's ever sure of anything? Based on everything I've seen and heard, this is what looks best to me. I hope I'm not wrong."

"For a young man as confused as you are, you're very eloquent about your confusion." Georgia laughed. "Listen, you're close enough to adulthood that I can separate your case out anyway. You can do whatever you want and I don't need to know why. Just be aware that the decisions you make here today are going to stick with you for a long, long time." She turned to me. "Charles, let's talk."

"Okay," I said.

"Have you ever thought about divorcing your parents?"

"Huh—?"

"Just a thought. Never mind."

"Why do you ask?"

Georgia smiled. "You heard what I said to Douglas. You're a little too young for me to grant you the same legal responsibility—although I wish I could. If you were to ask me for a separation of authority from your family, that would be different. But in this case, under these circumstances, it would be difficult to grant. Especially if you then decided to go back to your mother or go on with your father. Then it would only be a slick legal maneuver to step around the intent of the law, and the judiciary board frowns on tricks like that. Not that we don't do them—we just don't like being obvious. But believe it or not, son, some of us actually try to be fair; not just fair in terms of the law, but fair in terms of the people whose lives we're ruling on. I'm looking for that place that's fair to you—and legal as well."

"I want to stay with my dad," I said.

"Why?"

"Because—well, I know this might not make sense to you, but my dad lets me listen to my music. He doesn't interrupt. He *understands*."

"It makes perfect sense to me, Charles. What's your favorite music?"

I thought about John Coltrane. No. That was still my private thing. So instead, I said, "The Copland Third. Fourth movement." Dad looked at me, surprised. But I think he understood why, because he smiled.

"What about your mom?"

"I still love her—I guess. When she's not fussing or nagging or screaming, she can be a pretty funny lady. But . . . she hasn't been very nice to be around for a long time. I'd like to say good-bye to her, but I'm afraid to. Last time, all she did was scream."

"Ah, I see," said Georgia. "What if you knew how much your mom was hurting today and how much she was going to miss you and how much you were going to miss her? Would that affect your decision?"

I swallowed. Hard. I hadn't thought about it that way. Not really. Tears started to come up in my eyes. "If I do this, I'm never going to see her again, am I?"

"No, you won't."

"But if I go back to Earth, I'll never see Dad again either, will I?"

"That's right."

"So you're asking me to choose between one parent and another, aren't you? For the rest of my life."

"Yes, I am. I know it's a tough decision. But this is a lot more decision than you had last time this battle was fought, isn't it?"

"Last time wasn't for keeps."

"I guess not," Georgia said. "Nevertheless, this is the decision you have to make. So what's it going to be, Charles? Do you know?"

I wiped my nose, my eyes. I tried to imagine what life would be with Dad, wherever we were going. I couldn't, because I didn't know where we were going. I did know what life would be like if we went back. If *I* went back. . . .

If I went back, I'd be going without Douglas. And maybe without Stinky too. And even though I always used to joke about wanting to be an only child—or even an orphan—now that I had the chance to decide who I wanted to live with, it was suddenly a much bigger decision than I'd realized. This was like running away from home. Only worse. Because we could never go back again. This was a one-time deal.

"Charles?"

"I don't want to leave my mom," I whispered. "But I don't want to lose my dad either. I don't know."

Georgia sighed. She turned to Olivia. "I've heard enough."

"You haven't talked to the little one."

"Do you think that's going to be any better?"

"No. I guess not."

Georgia patted me on the shoulder. "You did well, Charles. You told the truth. You made my job a little harder, but that's okay. We'll try to find a way to sort this out."

"Listen, wait—" I said. "If I could just *talk* to my Mom. Just to say good-bye. Just to tell her that . . . well, you know . . . that I love her and not to hate me, please. That would . . . I think that would make it all right. Maybe. Because I do want to go with my dad."

"I understand," Georgia said. She patted me on the shoulder one more time, then wheeled her way over to Olivia. "I'm not going to vacate the order. Howard has a case. At least enough for a hearing. You'd better be well-prepared tomorrow, Counselor. Thanks for the pizza."

"Wait a minute, Judge—" Olivia scooted her own chair in front of Georgia's, effectively blocking her access to the door. "You've heard Mickey's testimony about conditions downside. You can't send these children back down into that."

"Are you invoking the Evacuation Act?" Georgia asked.

"I think I'm going to have to."

"It's never been applied to a whole planet. No matter how I rule, it'll be certain to come up for review."

"Georgia, you said that you have to rule on this case based on what's best for the children. That overrides both the mother's claim *and* the father's. Remember the father has a viable custody action too. I'm asking for both of those to be set aside on the grounds that the Earth no longer represents a safe environment for these children, and that the custody cases are therefore irrelevant until such time as *both* parents are available to this court to present their claims. In the meantime, I'm arguing for assignment of custody to the only parent who is available."

Georgia frowned in thought. "If I even entertain that theory in court, you know it'll go right up the ladder of appeals, Counselor. And that's not a direction I want to go. And even if I were to find for the children under such grounds, I'd still have to compel residence until such time as the appeals played out. Do *you* really want to pursue that course?"

Olivia came right back at her. "Georgia, these are children, for God's sake! Do you want to send them back down? You heard what Mickey said. Maybe he's wrong—and maybe he isn't. But what if he isn't? What if the whole thing is finally coming apart?"

"And what if you were on the *other* side of this case, Counselor? What would you be arguing?"

"I'd still be arguing for the children."

Georgia gave her a skeptical look. "Olivia, you and I are like sisters. We have argued about everything that two human beings can possibly argue about. We're both passionate about justice. And we're both passionate about finding the laws that will guarantee it. And sometimes we both get passionate about finding ways around the laws. I don't even have a problem about that either, when what we're in search of is justice. But I do have a problem with this case. A big problem. Where's the justice in this one? I don't see it yet. And we're not going to find it in precedents or emergency acts or anything else. I'm terribly afraid that this is one of those cases where there will be no justice for anybody and everybody is going to end up hurting. We're already quite a way down that slippery slope, and I'm not going to sleep very well tonight, and I don't think you are either. Now, if you'll please—?"

Olivia stood up and pulled her chair out of the way. Georgia wheeled backward and swiveled toward the door. "Mickey, give me a hug. Nice meeting you, Douglas, Charles, Bobby—under different circumstances, I might say the same thing to you too, Max. See you in court tomorrow." She wheeled out and the room was painfully silent.

Nobody looked at me, but it was my fault. What I'd said to Georgia hadn't been good enough. I'd screwed up everything. Again.

PLANS

OLIVIA SAID A WORD. THE word. The word that Dad keeps telling me not to use, and I keep using anyway. "All right," she said. "Let's try something else." She went back to her console, while Mickey began clearing the table. Douglas got up to help him and the two of them exchanged sad smiles.

Stinky had fallen asleep on the couch. The monkey was beside him—picking its nose, pretending to examine imaginary boogers, and then flicking them at me. Ha ha.

After a while, Dad got up and walked over to Olivia's desk. "Now what?"

She looked at him, almost startled, as if she'd forgotten we were all here. Then she snapped back to reality and said, "Okay, we go back to Plan A. We get your ass off this station as fast as we can. You'll have to fire me—sign that—and then you can hire Mickey as your agent instead. The placement will be on his license and he'll collect the fee. I'll be out of it. Here's his authorization, only don't date it until to-morrow. Otherwise, you'll be putting him in violation of the law when you leave the station."

Dad looked at me. And Stinky. "What about the kids?"

Olivia shrugged. "They're your kids. You know them better than I. Will they be all right with it? Probably not. They're going to have a lot of anger to work out—just like before—only this time *you'll* get the brunt of it."

Dad didn't answer that. He just nodded in acceptance of the truth. Finally, he said, "I suppose I should tell you that I really appreciate what you're doing for me, but—"

"I'm not doing it for you," Olivia snapped. She looked up from her keyboard. "I'm doing it for the children."

She stood up to look Dad straight in the eye. "I hate cases like this. I hate family kidnappings. Even when they're justified. And this one isn't. This one is about you being selfish enough to think you know better than everybody else. The fact that I agree with some of your conclusions about the Earth and about what's best for your kids still doesn't mitigate the appalling selfishness of your actions. So even though I'm your attorney—until you fire me—and I'll fight like a pit bull for you because Mickey asked me to, please do not make the assumption that I am doing this for you, or even because I agree with you. And certainly do not assume that I even like you. I don't. I'm doing it because I'm your lawyer and it's my job to represent you. It's also supposed to be my job to keep you out of trouble, not get you in deeper, and I'm doing a lousy job of that too, thank you very much. I just don't want to see your kids thrown back down the Line. That's the only thing you're right about. There is no future left down there. Everyone knows it's all coming apart." She glanced up. "Mickey? How long will it take you to pack?"

"Huh?"

"You said you wanted out. Well I've got six reservations on the midnight elevator, and Betsy is holding reservations on the next lunar shuttle. Make up your mind, right now—"

"Uh—" Mickey looked to Douglas. Douglas didn't look like Douglas anymore. He nodded shyly. Mickey turned back to his mother. "I'll go."

"Good. Then that'll settle the Dingillian placement too. I'll file it right now." She looked to Dad. "You're a lot luckier than you know. You'd better spend some serious time thanking Douglas *and* Mickey." She dropped back down onto her chair and rolled up to her keyboard. She started typing immediately, and whispering instructions to Betsy as well.

"Where are we going?" Douglas asked Mickey.

"Wait a minute! Wait a minute—!" said Dad. "It's my turn now."

Olivia stopped and looked at him. "Is there a problem?"

"I think I'm going into overload," said Dad. "With everything that's been happening—and it's all been happening very fast—I want to get straight on a few things."

Olivia looked at her watch. "Fifteen minutes."

"This is getting out of control."

"What is?"

"Everything. I violated the terms of a custody agreement in Texas.

Now you want to put me in violation of a court-ordered hearing at Geostationary. And what's going to happen on Luna? I'm leaving a trail of angry lawyers behind me."

"Why should you care? You're not coming back."

"This is not the example that I want to set for my children. We don't run from our problems."

Olivia raised an eyebrow at Dad. She gave him *the* look. Definitely a 10. "Excuse me? You should have thought of that forty-five-thousand kilometers ago, back in Texas, when you violated the first custody agreement."

"I saw what she was doing to the boys. I had to get them out of there. And when Douglas told me about—well, I just didn't want anyone messing with his brain. So yeah, maybe I had a lot of good justifications—she was grinding us all down."

Olivia looked at her watch impatiently. "And your point is . . . ?"

"My point is, all I wanted was a way to sidestep this mess, not make it worse. You said you were going to set all that Earth stuff aside. This is a higher court and all that? Remember? Now you're going to have us running from one more jurisdiction—and how far does the reach of this one extend?"

"Far enough. That's why you need a placement fast. And a strong corporate sponsor. Only it may be even worse than you think." Abruptly Olivia turned to her son. "Mickey? What's the rest of it? The stuff you didn't tell Aunt Georgia."

Mickey looked unhappy. "In front of the . . ."

"In front of the . . . yes. Christ, this is a mess. Let's not make it any worse. What's the part that panicked you so badly?"

Mickey looked very unhappy, but he stepped over to his mother and spoke quietly to her. "We had a meeting downside, yesterday morning. Elevator Security. They wanted to brief us about our responsibilities should the, uh . . . cable have to be shut down. Someone asked if they were thinking about it and they said that the corporation was currently examining all of its options if civil unrest should break out. The first step would be to restrict all passenger travel except to corporate passengers, which it looks like they're already doing—"

"Rats leaving the ship?"

"And their lawyers—sorry, Mom. The second step will be to restrict all dirtside access entirely. Nothing at all will move between Terminus and One-Hour. The, uh . . . the third step would be—more drastic."

"What's more drastic than shutting down traffic?"

"Breaking the cables at Terminus and letting the beanstalk pull itself off the planet altogether—"

"What?!!" Olivia came out of her chair so fast, it went flying backward and ricocheted off the wall. "You can't be serious—no, *they* can't be serious."

"Yes, they are, Mom." Mickey's voice was deadly quiet. "The Line has been self-sustaining for nearly a decade. There's enough farms up and down the Line, there's enough supplies stashed in the various pods, if we had to break free, we could. The corporation is prepared to pull anchor and hang free for as long as it takes, and not reestablish a ground base until Earth's governments can guarantee Line security."

"It'll never work!"

"It's already happening, Mom! They're using the hurricane as a first-stage drill. They're already moving the balance-pods down the Line. They have this thing all planned out. I'm telling you, they briefed us on it—on what we would have to do in every eventuality. And the briefing officers looked scared, as if they knew more than they were saying. If we go to stage two, every elevator attendant automatically becomes a member of the Line Security force. There are stun-guns on every car now, and they're going to start advanced stun-gun training immediately. You don't make plans that detailed and you don't brief that many people as a readiness exercise or a thought experiment. It was scary, Mom. Some of the women were in tears. The briefing officers made it sound like it was going to happen any day now and we had to be prepared."

"Why didn't you tell this to Georgia?"

"Mom! Think about it. Georgia has to know already!"

"Don't be silly—" But she stopped herself and turned to her keyboard.

"What are you doing?"

Olivia shook her head. "You don't need to know the details." She typed in a last command, then whirled to the wall behind her. She slid a panel sideways and unclipped three memory cards from their stations. She put one in her business bag, handed one to Mickey, and the third one to Dad. "Stash that in your luggage. Don't worry what it is. It's not illegal, and it's encoded. Your courier fee equals my legal fees. We're even." To Mickey, she said, "Get packed and get out of here. If I'm not at the station tonight, go without me. Can you get aboard through the cargo access?"

Mickey scratched his ear. I didn't feel so bad about rubbing my head so much. He said, "If Alexei's on duty, we can board in a cargo bin—"

"Eh?" She raised her eyebrow.

"Mom, an empty cargo bin can be very useful for . . . you know."

"No, I don't know. And I don't think I want to hear any more. Go get your bag."

"Excuse me?" said Dad. "What's going on?" He waved his hand to indicate he meant *the whole thing.*

"Nothing, I hope," said Olivia. "But I'm too old to be taking these kinds of chances." She stopped long enough to look at Dad. "You picked a *lousy* time. You're trying to leave town in the middle of a corporate war. And this could be particularly bad news for you, because Security is going to lock down the entire Line. Even if we get you on a car, it's going to be tricky. It depends on how screwed up things get. Mickey— are you packed?"

Mickey came back out of the other room, carrying a silvery briefcase-purse thing over his shoulder. He looked like he was on his way to the gym or the skating rink; he was all scrubbed and shiny again. I could see why Douglas liked him so much. Even though I still didn't.

MONKEY BUSINESS

"**A**LL RIGHT," MICKEY SAID. "YOU'RE going to have to do exactly as I say. There isn't going to be time to explain everything. Is that all your luggage? Just those backpacks?" He made a face. "That's still too much. It's a giveaway to anyone watching. You'll have to leave them here. Mom, can you repack them and have them sent on as yours? Or do you think that's too risky?"

Olivia studied our carryalls with a thoughtful expression. She shrugged. "I think we're all better off traveling as light as possible."

"All right, I'll trust your judgment. I don't think we're being watched—yet—but let's not take chances." Mickey turned back to us. "Take only what you would carry if you were sightseeing. If you can't put it in your pocket, don't bring it. Douglas, here, take this shopping bag. Anything that you really need, that you can't fit in your pocket and you can't replace, put it in here, so it looks like you've been souvenir-buying. Mr. Dingillian, that memory card that Mom gave you, toss it in here too. This is all the luggage you've got. Anything else you need, you'll pick up later. Doug, you'd better carry Bobby. No, leave the monkey—we'll get him a new one."

"Uh-uh, no way—" I said. "You've never seen a Stinky tantrum. *I'll* carry the monkey. I'll pretend its mine." I was already opening it up to switch off all of Stinky's programs. "Hey," I said. "Give me that memory bar. There's room in here for one more. The monkey's a perfect place to hide . . ." I stopped in mid-sentence and looked at Dad. He'd gone white as a scream. ". . . stuff," I finished lamely. I looked to Doug. He'd gotten it too—at the exact same time. We both looked to Dad. He saw the expressions on our faces and he knew that we knew. And we knew that he knew that . . .

Douglas recovered first—neither Mickey nor Olivia had noticed, or if they had, they were better actors than we were. They were talking about Olivia's connections; she'd be traveling separately. Doug tossed me the memory card and I shoved it into the last socket and closed up the monkey again, and we both pretended to busy ourselves with other stuff for awhile. Dad too. But for a few seconds, it was very uncomfortable.

Then Mickey said, "Well, what are we waiting for? Is everyone ready? Let's go—"

ICE CREAM

WE FOLLOWED MICKEY UP A level to a promenade and shopping level; he delivered a running commentary as we walked, pointing things out and explaining them as if we were nothing more than ordinary tourists and he was merely a hired guide. ". . . You can't see it from here, but it's something you're definitely going to find interesting—the launch bays on Disk Seven. Let's say Brazil wants to launch a communication satellite. They send it up the Line, we push it out the airlock, right? Not quite, but almost. We're geosynchronous, so the satellite still has to get itself into position over its target site. A little burn speeds it up or slows it down, putting it in a lower or higher orbit, depending on which way it wants to go, east or west—call it geosynchronous with deliberate drift. Sometimes it takes awhile for a satellite to work its way around, a week or a month, whatever, but when it finally gets there, it fires its boosters to slow down or speed up, whatever, and put itself back into a geosynchronous position. *Voila!* There you have it. It's possible to put a satellite into almost any orbit you wish from the Line. But we don't do as many launches from here as we used to, when the Line was first built, because the lower stations have the advantage of being able to impart a lot of thrust almost for free—because they're not geosynchronous, you understand? So the launch facilities are now used mostly for direct-docking of shuttles. We get four a day. It's very impressive. Perhaps we'll have time to see one come in tomorrow, *after the hearing.*" Mickey made sure to say this last part loud enough so that the fat lady behind us could hear, the one in the bright red-and-yellow flowery dress. She didn't appear to notice.

Douglas looked to Mickey curiously. Mickey smiled guilelessly. "Come on, let's get some ice cream."

Almost on cue, Stinky woke up, rubbing his eyes and looking around. "I didn't get dessert—" he started to whine. Douglas lowered him to his feet; he wobbled for a second, then hung onto Doug's arm, looking confused and unhappy.

"We know you missed dessert," Mickey said. "That's where we're going. See, we're already here—and you have a treat in store . . . hot fudge sundaes, banana splits, chocolate sodas, trust me on this. This is going to be the best part of your trip. I know, the desserts you had on the elevator were good, but most of them are too rich and too sweet to be really enjoyed. You practically have to wear protective gear.

"No, this is ice cream made the traditional way, without overdoing it—and in case you're wondering, Charles, it's all made right here at Geostationary, up on Disk Two. That's where most of the farms are right now, although we'll be opening up new farm levels when Disk Four is finished. Have you seen pictures of the farms? It's not the same, you've got to see them in person. No, we don't have any cows, Bobby—what we have is even better; we do it the Udder Way. Get it? The *udder* way? Never mind. But we've got the best genetically tailored udders anywhere. You'll see in a minute. You're about to have ice cream that's literally *out of this world*. That's another joke."

"He's tired," Douglas explained.

"And those weren't very good jokes," I added. Douglas frowned at me.

Dad spoke up then. He'd been very quiet ever since Doug and I had realized the truth about the monkey. "Excuse me, Mickey—*why are we stopping for ice cream?*"

Mickey pretended he didn't hear. He was studying the menu. After a minute, he looked across the table at Dad. "I think you should have the banana split. Bananas get more expensive the farther out you go. This might be your last chance to enjoy a banana split." The waiter arrived then, and Mickey looked around the table. "Okay, are we all decided?"

We ordered two hot fudge banana splits and four spoons, and a chocolate soda for Stinky. While we waited, I shifted uncomfortably in my seat. Now was as good a time as any to tell them. "Um, Dad—if I tell you something, will you promise not to get mad at me?"

Dad looked over at me quizzically. "What is it, Charles?"

"Um—I know who tipped off Station Security." Mickey and Doug both looked up at that, but I pushed on anyway. "It was J'mee."

"The boy in the swimming pool?"

"He was really a girl. In disguise. They're sneaking off-planet too.

Like everybody else, I guess. She's got an implant. She looked us up. And—well, she said a lot of bad stuff about us . . ."

"Like what?"

"Like about Douglas . . . and Bobby . . . and you. . . ."

"Is that how you found out about . . . ?"

"Yeah, it wasn't Mom." I pushed on with the rest of it. "And she said stuff about me too. About all those reports from school. What the counselors said. And she was pretty rude about it, so I—well, I called her a goddamned nasty bitch."

"Jeez," said Douglas. "You're lucky she didn't file an abusive language complaint."

Mickey shook his head. "Hard to prove. 'He-said, she-said.' And her access to private records taints the case." He added, "Besides, she had a better way to get revenge. No one knew where you were; they all thought you were caught at Terminus or hiding out at One-Hour. She tipped off the marshals. Now we know why—" *Charles' big mouth.*

He didn't say the last part. He didn't have to. Everyone was looking at me. Waiting.

"I'm sorry," I said. It didn't feel like it was enough.

Dad's face was unreadable, like he was having another one of those private arguments that only he could hear. Mickey had wisely fallen silent. Douglas shook his head and shrugged and did his performance of geek retrieving files about social skills. Finally, he reached over and patted my hand. "It's okay, Chigger. It was your turn to screw up. Everybody else did, why not you?"

"Is that supposed to make me feel better?"

"Nah. I'm just reminding you that you're a Dingillian. You're as normal as the rest of us."

"You wanna get a bigger shovel? You can dig faster."

Douglas spread his hands. "Look at it this way, Chig. From here on out, it has to get better."

"Why?"

"Because it can't get any worse."

I nodded. I heard what he said. But it wasn't enough. The waiter brought our ice cream then and even after he passed out spoons, I didn't say anything. Douglas had said all the right things, but Dad hadn't said anything at all. If Dad had said it, if Dad had said anything at all, I would have felt a lot better about my mistake. The knot that had been churning in my stomach since we'd left Terminus was bigger than ever now.

"Chigger—" That was Dad. I looked up. "Eat your ice cream." I suppose he meant well. It didn't help. It was too little, too late. It still felt like a ticking bomb and it was just a matter of time before everything went boom.

We ate in silence. There was no sound except the clink of spoons against glasses and Stinky making bubbles at the bottom of his chocolate soda. Finally I said, sort of in an effort to change the mood, "This is good ice cream, Mickey. And so is the hot fudge. Thank you."

"You're welcome, Charles. I'm glad you like it." He looked up then, "Ahh, Alexei—*dos vidanya.*" He pulled out a chair for the newest arrival, a tall, skinny, geeky-looking guy, all arms and legs. He looked like a spider. He gangled. He wore a Russian-looking turtleneck, shorts, and sandals—except for the shirt, it was pretty standard station wear. To the rest of us, Mickey said, "Alexei is a native Loonie, down here for college and muscles. How go the exercises, Alexei?"

Alexei grinned and made a muscle. There wasn't much to show, but he seemed proud of it. "I shall be a muscleman when I return home. The girls will flock around me at the beach." He grinned and laughed. "I must remember not to be too rough with them, like some of the Earth boys are." I didn't know if he was kidding or not. Everybody said that native Loonies were all tall, skinny, and weak—but the way he was joking, I got the feeling that wasn't completely true, because he was making fun of it. But I just stared at him; so did Douglas and Stinky. We'd never met a *real* Loonie before.

Mickey must have seen the expressions on our faces, because he made full introductions then. Alexei stood up and bowed to each of us, then offered his hand for a handshake. He shook hands with each of us, grabbing our hands in both of his own to do it. He seemed almost too polite, too effusive to be real. "Alexei's family is from Georgia—"

"The Russian Georgia," Alexei explained, "not the American one. Y'awl." He laughed at his own joke, no one else did. I got the feeling he told it a lot. "I was born in Gagarin Dome. My mother wanted to name me Yuri, my father wanted to call me Neil. So they compromised, and I am Alexei."

"Alexei?"

"Alexei Krislov, Captain of the Allied Worlds Starcruiser, *Private Enterprise*—from the video series, you have heard of it, *da?* About an interstellar space trader? He was the only cosmonaut both my parents liked—a fictitious one. Personally"—he leaned forward with a conspiratorial air—"I think they watch too much television." Suddenly he was all business. He swiveled to face Mickey and said casually, "So? You said you had packages?"

Mickey nodded toward us. "Four. Five, if you count me."

Alexei glanced at us again, his face darkening. "I don't know, *Mikhail.* I'm not equipped for a job like this—this is a little big for me."

Mickey raised an eyebrow.

Alexei shrugged. "Sometimes I talk too big. So sue me—no wait, forget I said that. I know your mom. I would like to keep the royal jewels." He grinned and grabbed his crotch. To us, he said, "They really are royal jewels. My family is descended from the Romanovs. The last Tsar of Russia? That was a long time ago, I don't expect you to remember. But no matter. My great-uncle continues to file lawsuits in the World Court, every session, for the restoration of the monarchy. No, I would not be the Tsar—not unless sixteen of my cousins died mysteriously first, which will not happen. I only hate four of them." He turned back to Mickey. "This won't be easy. You know that the whole Line is locking down."

"I know," said Mickey.

"It's going to be expensive."

"I have information. *Big* information."

Alexei pursed his lips and frowned to himself. He was thinking it over. He steepled his fingers in front of his chin and nodded thoughtfully. "How big?"

"The biggest. It *will* affect your business." To us, Mickey said. "Alexei is a money-surfer. In the truest sense. Do you know what money-surfers are?"

"Sure. Everybody does. A money-surfer is someone who rides the flow of money."

"That's right," said Alexei. "That is the common usage. But I am a traditional money-surfer, one of the best. Maybe *Mikhail* will explain later." He looked at his friend. "So? What do you want me to do?"

"Deliver the packages."

"You overestimate me, *Mikhail.* Didn't you have any ideas of your own?"

"Only one."

"*Ah.* What was your wonderful idea?"

" 'Call Alexei.' "

Alexei made a face. "That was *not* a good idea. Tell me, what is Alexei supposed to do?" He sighed. "I am sorry, *Mikhail,* I cannot help you with this."

"Listen, Alexei—Max here has pissed off one of the Super-Nationals. Do you know Hidalgo? Yes, that one. He's apparently involved. He threatened Max—oh, not directly, of course—but there was no doubt about his intentions. This might very well be a matter of life and death."

Alexei glanced over at us again, with new respect. "I like you. You make powerful enemies." To Mickey, he said, "All the more reason why I shouldn't get involved in this."

"Yes, you should," said Mickey. "You really want to hear what I know."

"Don't do this to me, *Mikhail*."

Mickey leaned over and whispered in Alexei's ear. Alexei's eyes widened, and he pulled back to stare at Mickey. "You're crazy."

"No—*they're* crazy."

"They'd have to be—good God." Alexei put his hand over his mouth, shocked. It was like he didn't want to let himself say anything else. It took him a moment to find his voice again. "I have phone calls to make, lots of phone calls," he said. "I wish you hadn't told me—no, that's not true. I'm glad you told me. But now I'm obligated to do this stupid thing for you, aren't I?"

"That's why I told you." Mickey smiled sweetly.

"You have the soul of a viper. Your mother trained you well."

"I love you too, Alexei." Mickey glanced at his watch. "Come on. We'd better get going." Mickey slid his card through the table's reader. "Okay, we're paid. Let's go."

FLOWING UP

IN ONE OF HIS WEIRDER moods, Douglas once said that the best definition of a living creature is that it's a bag of water that moves by itself and makes more bags of water. Life is nothing more than a convenient way for water to get up and take a walk. Life is how water takes a vacation. Life is the way that water flows uphill. Etcetera, etcetera, etcetera.

But yeah, I guess if you think about it that way, it sort of makes sense. Life is water in a membrane, doing stuff. And anywhere that life wants to go, it has to take water with it. So it's the membrane that makes life possible.

Weird says a lot of stuff like that. He says good philosophy is the foundation of sentience, but good plumbing is the foundation of civilization. Once, he even said, "If you want to really know people, look in their sewers." That was good for three weeks of teasing him about going around looking down toilets as a way to meet girls. I stopped the joking only when he threatened to stuff me headfirst down the commode in search of intelligent life. That is, I stopped the jokes in front of his face, not behind his back—

At least until Alexei said something about showing us what space sewers looked like—"Come, I will show you the plumbing." He pointed toward the ceiling. "Here we keep it in the attic." He led us toward a hatch opening into a service corridor. So I poked Weird and said, "Hey, we're going to get to know these people really well, right, Doug?"

"Bag it, Chigger." He said it without any apparent emotion. If he was too worried to be nasty, then the situation was serious enough to be *serious*. I shut up.

Alexei had pulled out his phone and was already calling people.

Most of his calls were in Russian; he spoke in thick, rabid phrases, shouting almost hysterically at whoever was on the other end. Each time as he broke the connection, he smiled at us. "You've got to talk to them in their own language: Stupid. Is not to worry. They will do what I tell them. There is too much money at stake." He looked at Mickey. "This is going to be very expensive—for everyone. Especially for me. Not for you, though. You are already paid. The information you have given me—I will make millions of dollars today. Already I am having some wonderful ideas. *Mikhail*, I hope there is time for them all. I am most grateful that you called me—I will name my firstborn child after you, even if he is a girl." He popped his phone open and started hollering into it again.

Still roaring into his phone, Alexei fumbled a pass card out of his shirt pocket and used it to unlock a wide hatchway; we followed him into a service bay and boarded a cargo elevator. Alexei gestured impatiently at the walls, and we all grabbed handholds—he hit the Go panel and we rose "up" toward the axis, the innermost rings of the disk. As we rose, pseudo-gravity faded out. Dad and Doug and Mickey took turns carrying Stinky, who hadn't quite fallen asleep again, but was content to just rest in the arms of whoever was carrying him. In microgravity, he wasn't as much of a burden, but he was still an awkward bundle.

Alexei closed his phone and looked at Mickey. "I am going to make too much money today, *Mikhail*. I will have to give you some of it or my conscience will trouble me—not too much, though. I do not have a very large conscience. You will share some of it with your new friends, *da?* That gives me another idea—later." He opened his phone again. "Mishka, when you get home to your kennel, don't let your mother bite you in the ass—listen to me, you son of a German whore—" I didn't know if Alexei was like all Russians, but he had a strange way of treating his friends. If those were indeed his friends. I wasn't sure.

When we got to the top, we came out of the tube into a narrow service corridor, the floor here had the steepest up-curve of all. The pseudo-gravity was too light for real walking, so we sort of bounced forward, caroming off the walls for a bit until Alexei slowed us down and suggested we conserve our energy. He pointed to handholds spaced along the walls. "Use those. Pull yourselves along. Pretend you're swimming. I will carry the little one—" I wished he hadn't said that about swimming. I was already having trouble remembering up and down. This wasn't as much fun as it looked. Stinky thought it was fun. He wanted to try bouncing by himself, but Alexei promised him that it would be more fun to ride on his back, so he decided to try that instead. How often do you get to piggy-back ride a Loonie in free fall?

We passed a whole bunch of KEEP OUT, THIS MEANS YOU! and AU-THORIZED PERSONNEL ONLY! signs, but Alexei ignored them. Whenever we came to a locked hatch, Alexei would pull out an appropriate clearance card and pass us through. "How do you have all these cards?" Dad asked.

"Ah, it speaks—" Alexei laughed. To Dad, he said, "What do you think I came here to study? Domestic Ecology. I am on a work-study plan. I earn my education with hands-on experience. I am three years here, I have clearances everywhere. I can go anywhere on the station. It is the perfect job for a young smuggler, *da?* Do not worry, Mr. Dingillian, I do not abuse the trust of my employers. At least, not very often. And usually only for a good cause. This is a good cause. Besides, if what *Mikhail* tells me is true, I think that my usefulness here has just ended. I am returning to Gagarin very shortly. I will visit my money."

"When?" Dad asked.

"Tonight," laughed Alexei. "On the very same elevator as you. We go out together. Ahh, here we are—"

Here was a thick hatch into a triple-sealed room—an airlock? Inside was a ladder up into a hatch in what would have been the ceiling, except there was so little gravity here, it didn't feel like a ceiling—except for the orientation of a big red arrow marked THIS SIDE UP in English as well as in several other languages.

Alexei passed Stinky into Mickey's arms and pulled himself up the ladder. At the top, he hesitated, scratching his cheek thoughtfully. He put his card into the reader and punched an entry code. The panel flashed green. He looked back down to us. "You must be very careful here. We are at the hub. The axis. The Line passes through a pressurized core. We run pipes and conduits and vents through the core all the way from Disk One to Disk Seven. It is the foundation for the next stage of construction—a common domestic ecology. But the core doesn't rotate, because it's connected to the Line itself. As you come through the hatch, it will look like the top side of the corridor is moving; it isn't—we are. It isn't fast, but it's fast enough to look scary. Just keep your head down, hold onto the railings, you'll be fine. I'll be right here to help. Any questions? No? Good. Let's go."

Alexei tapped the Go panel and the hatch slid open. He pulled himself up through the opening and disappeared for a moment. Then his head reappeared. "Hokay, Douglas, you come next please?" Douglas jumped and floated right up to the hatch, grabbing onto the handholds near the top. Alexei put a hand on his shoulder to keep him from sailing through. Douglas pulled himself up carefully and peered through the hatch. "That's right," Alexei coached. "Float through slowly. Hang onto this railing and just move down to make room." Douglas nodded and went through.

"Hokay, Charles—you come next. This is very easy, *da?*" I swallowed hard. For some reason, up and down and sideways had suddenly decided to stop being up and down and sideways and were all changing directions on me. I felt dizzy. I squeezed my eyes tightly shut. Sometimes that helped. This time it didn't.

"Charles? Are you all right—?" That was Dad. I didn't answer.

"*Charles—!*" That was Alexei. "Open your eyes and look at me. Do it *now!*" His voice was so hard it startled me. I opened my eyes. He was holding his hand out toward me. "Look at my hand, see? Just grab my hand, hokay? I'll do the rest."

Before I could shake my head no, or even as I did, I felt Dad lifting me up to take Alexei's hand. Alexei grabbed my arm and pulled me gently through the hatch. "See, that wasn't so bad—here, grab this railing and hold on. Douglas, hold him, please? Thank you. Move down now, just a bit. Make room for the others." I was still uncomfortable— almost close to tears, I didn't know why—but then Douglas put his arm around my shoulder and held me close and I didn't feel quite so bad anymore.

"*Mikhail,* I am ready for the little stinky one. Pass him here. That's it. Come to me, Bobby. Here, stick your head through. Look around— see? Nothing to be afraid of. The only monsters up here are your brothers. Hold onto this railing, please. *Mikhail—?* Send up Mr. Dingillian, please."

Dad came next, and Mickey followed. Alexei sealed the hatch behind him. Now, we were all clutching handholds on the inside of the steepest curve yet. Three meters away, the curved wall of the core whispered by. We could hear the air whooshing as it passed. We watched a steady progression of warning signs and arrows and numbers and access panels. There were tracks in the opposite surface, matching tracks in the wall we clung to.

Alexei looked anti-spinward expectantly, so I followed his gaze. I was still uncomfortable, but watching the moving ceiling sort of helped. I don't know why.

"Ahh," said Alexei. "Here it comes."

It was a bright red platform sliding toward us on the tracks. It slowed to a stop directly next to the access panel we'd climbed through. It had handholds and equipment boxes mounted all over it. All its corners were rounded, and most of its flat surfaces had bumper pads. There was a funny angular contraption in the middle, like a collapsible tower. Alexei pulled us all aboard, and then pushed a green Go button, and turned a dial. "We want the One-Gamma-Three entrance," he explained as the platform began moving spinward. "One is the disk we're on. Gamma is the cable. Three is the access. *Capisce?*"

We passed similar cars mounted on other tracks, on our side as well as on the rotating surface above / next to us; most of them were stopped and waiting, but our car sped up until we had matched speed with the inner wall. There was a panel there marked ONE-GAMMA-THREE. Alexei unfolded the collapsed contraption in the middle of the car. It was an extensible ladder and it went all the way across. "Hokay, let's go."

Alexei grabbed Stinky in a bear hug and started scrambling across like a pregnant spider. I shook off Dad's help, but not Douglas's. When we were all safely across, Mickey hit the release on the top of the ladder and it folded back down. Now the ceiling felt motionless and the floor was rolling past. Except it wasn't a floor anymore. It was just a rotating wall-surface, with a car tracking along beside us. Then the car began to slow, and pretty soon it disappeared around the curve behind us.

Alexei was already opening the One-Gamma-Three panel and pulling us through. First Douglas, then me, then Mickey—they passed Stinky through—then finally Dad and Alexei. Inside the core, I levered myself around to look and nearly lost it—"*Douglas!*" I wailed. My brother caught me and held me tightly with his right arm. "It's okay, Charles. I'm right here. I'm not letting go. Just hang onto me—we'll be fine. Really."

I buried my face in Douglas's shoulder. I could sense that both Mickey and Dad were hovering close, but I didn't want to have anything to do with either of them. Only Douglas.

What I'd seen . . . was the largest interior space I'd ever seen—well, maybe not *the* largest, maybe Terminus was larger—but definitely the *deepest*. It was like the inside of a giant pipe, filled with humongus wires, cables, tubes, conduits, vents, pass-throughs, catwalks, ladders, platforms, machinery, and *stuff*. And it all looked *up* and *down* and *sideways*—all at the same time!

"Are you okay, son—?" That was Dad. I didn't answer. Douglas pulled away just enough to look at my face. He tilted my chin upward so we were eye to eye and nose to nose. I couldn't remember the last time we'd ever been this close. Maybe we never had. "I'm not going to let anything bad happen to you, Charles. I promise."

"What's wrong with Charles?" I heard Stinky asking.

"Nothing. Please be quiet, Bobby. Charles has an upset stomach.

He'll be okay in a minute. Go back to sleep." Douglas looked back to me. "Just tell me when you're ready."

I shook my head. I didn't want him to let go. I liked having his arm around me. I felt safe. I swallowed hard. "I don't want to lose you, Douglas," I whispered, so only he could hear. "Not to anybody—" I sort of nodded toward Mickey.

"You're not going to lose me. I'll always be your brother, no matter what."

"Is that a threat or a promise?" I half-joked.

He half-smiled. "Yes." He nudged me. "Come on, the others are waiting. And we don't have a lot of time. Are you ready?"

"Yeah. Just stay close, okay?"

"*Hokay,*" he said. Just like Alexei.

THE OLD SWIMMING HOLE

IT WAS LIKE BEING ON the inside of a giant pipe that kept changing its orientation. But as long as I kept focused on the wall and pretended that I was swimming and it was the floor, I was okay. If I had to look away from the wall, for any reason, I pretended that everything else was *up*. It sort of worked, but I still felt dizzy.

Alexei pointed around the curve of the wall toward a cluster of pipes and a vertical platform on which there were some storage lockers. We pulled ourselves along a line of handholds, and when we got to the platform, we anchored ourselves against its railings.

"Do you see this pipe?" Alexei pounded on one of the thicker pipes next to us. "Put your ear next to it. You can hear the water rushing through it. Very useful stuff. We use it for ballast. We use it to balance the rotation of the disks. Sometimes we even turn it into oxygen to breathe and hydrogen to burn. And of course, we also use it for drinking and bathing and growing our crops. It is our lifeblood!

"Listen, you can hear it flowing—back and forth, up and down, in and out, all over the station—carrying sewage to the farms where it will be turned back into food, going to the distilleries where the sunlight will turn it into steam and the cold of space will turn it back into fresh water, three times over, and then it will rush back down here, flowing this way and that, nourishing the lives of all of us.

"Do you know what is one of the worst crimes you can commit here on the station? Interfering with the water. Because whatever else it is, water is first and foremost, the stuff of life—so you do not tamper with it. The flow of water—in fact, all of what we call the domestic ecology—is the property of the whole community here, and each and every one of us has a responsibility to the community. The way we keep the water flowing, that demonstrates how responsible we are to our people.

"But—" he interrupted himself "—these pipes are also very useful if you have to go somewhere and you don't want anyone to know that you are going or how you got there. And so, while we respect the water, sometimes we ride it too." Alexei opened one of the storage lockers. Inside was—scuba gear?!

"Huh? Are we going swimming?" Stinky asked.

"You? No," Alexei said. "Them. Yes." He pointed. We looked up— every direction was *up*—and saw four, no five, teenagers diving out of the center toward us. Three boys, two girls. They were wearing shorts and T-shirts and looked like they had fallen off a runaway picnic. They were laughing like they were diving into a party.

As they approached, they began waving and calling to us. They caught themselves easily on the platforms and ladders and railings around us, and they shouted things at Alexei in Russian that made him blush with embarrassment. They passed him a backpack and a pair of canteens. They had a third canteen of their own, which they passed around among themselves, each one taking deep swallows of whatever was in it. From the way they acted, I didn't think it was water.

Alexei took the flask when it came to him and took a deep swig of his own, then he pocketed it, much to their dismay. "You have all had enough," he said. Then he bawled them out in Russian. Or gave them instructions. Or told a dirty joke. Whatever. When he finished, they all laughed and started pulling on the various pieces of diving equipment.

Alexei explained, "These are my fellow students and colleagues. The swimming equipment is part of our service. Sometimes we have to inspect the pipes from the inside. Sometimes there are air bubbles. Sometimes we have to retrieve a broken robot or a piece of something that has caught somewhere. We do not have to do that very often. In fact . . . I can't ever remember having to go into the pipes at all for anything a robot couldn't handle. But, nevertheless, we have our responsibilities. We have to keep ourselves ready and able to handle any possibility, any emergency at all. So we practice and drill and keep ourselves focused on our responsibilities to the water of the community. Today—ah, today we get to put into practice what we have practiced. They shall be . . . the *decoys*."

"So this is how you do it," Mickey said. "I've always wondered about that."

"Wonder no longer," Alexei said. "Sooner or later, somebody was certain to figure it out anyway. No matter, I already have three other ways to move things from here to there—just not as exciting. I leave it to you to figure them out, *Mikhail*. I will bet you a day's interest that you cannot."

"I can't afford that bet." Mickey laughed.

Alexei laughed with him and clapped him on the shoulder. "You are smarter than you act. This is a good trait." To the rest of us, he said, "We have to assume you are being watched. At the very least, monitored through station security. There are those damnable little cameras everywhere. They saw us coming up the service elevator. They know that an access hatch was opened. That was why I used my *own* card. So they could monitor our progress. Very shortly, they will be monitoring the progress of five divers through the pipes—and one of them will be carrying my locator. Five divers, not six, we will keep them wondering what happened, *da?* They will meet the divers on the topside of Disk Seven. But by then, we will be somewhere else, and they will have lost us. I am too clever for my own good." To his Russian comrades, Alexei shouted, "What is taking you so long? Do you think we have all night? Look at the time. We have less than an hour—"

"Alexei," said one of the men, a dark brooding fellow with eyebrows like furry caterpillars. "The deposits are made, *da?*"

"*Da.*"

"This is good. We have made our own reservations, we will be on the one A.M. car. If what you say is true—"

"You have told no one else?"

Caterpillar-brow shook his head. "I think the word is already spreading. But no, we have told no one. Go now. Godspeed!" He glanced around. "Godspeed to all of you." Then he grabbed Alexei and the two of them exchanged kisses on each cheek, the way they do in Europe. I'd never seen men do that before, kiss each other—even friends. It sort of freaked me. I looked at Douglas and Mickey and tried to imagine them kissing. It didn't seem right, but it didn't seem as wrong anymore either. What the hell did I know?

AT THE CORE

WE WERE GOING UP THE Line—*by hand.*

From an Earth perspective, we were going up. From the Geostationary perspective, we were going sideways—starside—outward toward Disk Seven.

From our perspective, we weren't going any direction at all. Just *forward* along a never ending pipe. There was water on the inside of the pipe; we could hear it. There were handholds running the length. We were climbing to forever. I wondered how long it would take to climb the whole Line—

"How come we can't take a maintenance car?" I asked. "Look, there are lots of tracks along these pipes. And there's a car over there."

"The maintenance cars are monitored." Mickey said. "We don't want to leave any evidence of where we started and where we got off. Most of all we don't want anyone showing up to meet us. Just keep pulling yourself along."

Alexei showed us how to do it. "Don't try to hurry," he said. "You'll tire yourself out. Slow and steady does the job. Do like I do, hand over hand, counting like this—like music . . . and one . . . and two . . . and three . . . and four . . . like that. That's how to make the best time over a distance." He added, "If you did this all the time, you would know how to go faster, but I need you to conserve your strength. We have a long way to go. Almost two kilometers. We can do it, but you must concentrate. Mickey, do you know a good song? Something to give us a pace?"

"Alexei, you forget who you're talking to. I couldn't carry a tune in free fall." And then, after Douglas and I finished laughing, he said, "No, I mean it. I can't sing. Douglas?"

Douglas snorted. "Chigger is the one in our family who sings. Charles?" He was right behind me. "How about a song?"

Without hesitating an instant, I began, *It's a small world, after all—*" Four voices shouted for me to stop before I finished the first line. Two of the voices contained serious hints of violence, Dad's and Doug's.

"Now, I'm going to have an earworm, all night," Douglas muttered. "Whose good idea was that?"

"I think we should all save our breath for a while," Dad said, "and just concentrate on the job at hand."

The job at hand was the next handhold—and the one after that— and the one after that—I could feel the slap of the plastic handholds against my palms like a steady beat; it echoed up through my wrists, my forearms, my elbows . . . there was a rhythm to it. For some reason, I started thinking of a song that Mom used to sing to us when we were small. *"Oh, Lord, won't you buy me a Mercedes Benz . . . ?"*

A Mercedes Benz was some kind of car they didn't make anymore, but it didn't matter. The song always had such a plaintive quality, it might have been about my life. I didn't even realize I was singing it aloud until Douglas joined me on the chorus. I stopped, embarrassed.

Dad was right behind Douglas. He called up to me, "Charles—I didn't know you liked Janice Joplin."

"I used to," I said. "Until about four seconds ago." That came out a little nastier than I intended. "Why didn't you tell me about John Coltrane?"

"Huh?"

"The Coltrane Suite. You never sent me a copy."

"Yes, I did."

"I never got it."

"It came back refused."

"I didn't do that."

"It must have been your mom—" He stopped himself. "I'm sorry, Charles, I promised myself I'd never say anything bad about your mom, but there were times when she acted badly. I sent you a lot of stuff, a lot of music. She sent most of it back; she told me not to send you any more. She didn't think it was good for you to spend all that time locked up by yourself with your headphones on. I liked it that you were always so interested in my recordings. I think that's why she did it—to keep us apart, to keep me from using the music as a way to stay close to you. I'll get you another copy. I promise."

"Never mind. I don't want to hear it."

"Have it your own way." Dad sounded hurt. I didn't care. John

Coltrane was just mine. Not his. Couldn't he let me have one thing that was just mine alone? Couldn't he let any of us have our own lives? He was always using us—like Stinky's monkey—without asking permission or telling us what was going on. He didn't trust us. So why should we trust him?

I felt Doug pulling himself up closer to me, alongside me. He looked at me oddly. "Chigger, we've gotta talk."

"There's been enough talk already," I said. "I don't need any more. Thanks."

Doug looked annoyed. "What's with you anyway?"

I indicated Stinky's chimpanzee with a backward nod; it was clinging happily to my neck. "I got a monkey on my back."

"In more ways than one," Douglas said. "I'm not going to talk to you when you're like this." He let me pull ahead so he could follow me again. Dad came after him. And we kept going.

We were in free fall. Or the next best thing to it. We were inside a giant cylinder filled with ladders and tubes and wires and stuff. We were at the geosynchronous point of the space elevator. We were pulling ourselves more than two kilometers along the handholds on the outside of a water pipe big enough to push a Volkswagen through. We were here because our parents hated each other, both of them certifiably neurotic, and because Dad had kidnapped us with the intention of taking us off-planet somewhere. To finance the trip, he was acting as a courier, and had hidden some illicit memory inside Stinky's monkey.

So of course there were people after us. Mom had sent lawyers, other folks were sending security agents, and still others might send some thugs to hurt or kill us. We'd been served with a subpoena, and we were running away from a court action. We were in a restricted access zone with a Russian smuggler—and we had no idea what he usually smuggled. And meanwhile, there were folks getting ready to break the Line free of the Earth, which would probably kill thousands of people and collapse the economies of a hundred different nations and at least a thousand different industries.

Dr. Hidalgo's sacred money would stop flowing just like a stopped-up toilet. Maybe it would back up and overflow and seek out new channels, and a lot of fortunes would be lost and new ones would be made, and all the ordinary people caught up in it would suddenly have their own set of problems. Ghu knew just how many millions of people might end up losing their jobs and their homes and their belongings. In some places people might even starve to death. There would certainly be riots and civil unrest and refugees and plagues and probably even a war or two. And that would trigger even more problems; and everything would just keep on going. On and on.

I guess this was what some people would call an *adventure*.

Thanks, but no thanks. I didn't ask for this adventure, and nobody had asked me how I felt about it. Just like the divorce. It made my stomach hurt and my chest felt like I had a knot in it. I don't know why people think adventures are so wonderful. Mostly they hurt, they're boring, and they're dangerous.

I concentrated on watching the handholds passing in front of me. I pulled myself steadily forward, left hand over right, right hand over left, and went back to wondering. If Judge Griffith were to take away the words *right* and *left*, how I would be able to explain the difference between one and the other.

MONEY-SURFING

EVERYBODY USES E-MONEY.

You slide your card through a reader and you're paid. The money travels from your card into the store. It's a stream of numbers representing a sum of money, and wherever it goes, it's still the same amount of money. E-money carries its own verification codes, so anyplace you can send a block of data you can send e-money. You can send it across a wire, or you can pipe it into a card, or you can put it on a beam of light and send it off to Betelgeuse—like that crazy artist did last year. Or you can stuff it in the back of a toy monkey. But however e-money gets sent, as long as it decodes authentically when it arrives, it's *money*.

Weird says that at any given moment, twenty percent of the world's wealth doesn't exist. It's nothing but bits and bytes on its way somewhere else. I always thought that money had to represent something—like kilowatt-dollars are backed by electricity and potato dollars are backed by potatoes; but Weird says that e-money is backed by e-balances and e-potentials and e-futures, which are sometimes backed by e-stocks and e-bonds, and sometimes even by digital resources, but it's all so detached from the real world now that it really doesn't have anything at all to back it, except the whole world's mutual agreement. We all pretend that it's real and we pass it around like it's real, and once in a while, we turn e-dollars into plastic-dollars or chocolate-dollars or sugar-dollars, and sometimes even into paper-dollars or gold-dollars. The gold-dollars are the best; Dad showed me one once, in a museum. But it isn't real unless you make it real.

Eighty percent of the world's economy uses e-money now. It's almost impossible not to, unless you're bartering raw cocoa or something like that. It's estimated that four trillion dollars of e-money changes hands every day on the North American continent alone. I have no idea what it's like worldwide. But Weird says that if you could shut off all the electricity in the world at the same moment, you could destroy the world economy, that's how much money is in transit at any given instant.

I didn't fully believe that, but Weird said it could happen. If they break the Line, the world would never recover. But I didn't understand how that was so. All the buildings would still be there, all the people, all the crops and factories and stores and products in the stores. Why couldn't people just keep working anyway? And besides—wasn't there some kind of backup system to keep e-money from being lost in transit?

We'd studied e-money in school, but I'd tried hard not to pay attention and mostly succeeded in getting all the way through the semester without learning very much about it. It didn't seem very interesting at the time. But the important thing about e-money is that every transaction needs to be authenticated by the International Transfer System, which is kind of like an electronic post office for money, every transfer is insured.

Every time money is transferred from one person to another, it goes through an ITS node, which verifies and audits the exchange; this is particularly important when you need proof of payment for legal reasons. But the ITS also charges you one-twentieth of a percent—that's a nickel for every hundred dollars being transferred—which isn't all that much, I guess, because most people hardly notice it. But it's called the "transfer tax," because the more money you move, the more you pay.

If you move $2000, your transfer tax is a buck. But if you're a SuperNational, and you're moving around hundreds of millions of e-dollars, you're going to notice the e-tax real fast. If you want to move a *billion* dollars from here to there, it's going to cost you half a million in transfer charges. Of course, if you have a billion dollars, you can afford to spend half a million whenever you feel like it, but that's probably not the best way to *stay* a billionaire.

If the average daily flow of money is four trillion dollars, the government should make two billion dollars a day in e-tax alone. More than 70 trillion dollars a year. Almost enough to service the interest on the international debt.

Actually, the international authority only makes 1.25 billion dollars a day in e-tax. At least 750 million dollars moves through private services. Not everybody wants to pay the transfer tax. And not everybody wants the government auditing their finances either.

So anyone who has money that they want to move from one place to another without leaving a trail sends it through a transfer service, which is just like an anonymous remailer on the net. It strips the ID off the money and sends it on.

The e-money gets decoded into a service account, and a corresponding transfer is authorized to the recipient. The entire process is automatic. But for the few seconds or minutes it takes to send the money on, it's earning interest for the transfer service. That's why they're called money-surfers, they're riding the flow.

Most of the private services charge only a minimal fee, like a buck a transfer, no matter how much money is moving. Some of services are even free, if you're moving more than a million dollars a week. If you're a money-surfer with millions of dollars a day moving through your service accounts, at any given moment, you probably have a couple of million dollars in your pocket—even if it's somebody else's millions, you're still being paid interest on it. It's called your "average daily balance." A money-surfer with good clients can live quite well off the interest. It's like owning a perpetual motion machine that makes money just by sitting next to a river of it and sticking a finger in.

Not everybody can be a money-surfer, though. It can be dangerous. Two of the private services were hit very badly by a virus that scrambled some of their incoming data, and another company was hit with a counterfeit e-check. They still aren't talking about how that was done. The one that was hit had been "double-dipping"—transferring the money to a second account before sending it on, so it was collecting twice the interest. There wasn't anything really unethical about it, and it added only two or three minutes to each transfer, but somebody didn't like it, that was for sure. Anyway, there are a lot of companies providing transfer services, and some of them work through international pipelines— connected series of accounts—making it impossible to trace an exchange of money, even if you had a dozen international subpoenas.

According to Mickey, Alexei was an interplanetary money-surfer. That meant he had to be at least a millionaire—maybe more. That's why I began to wonder if there was more to this than Mickey was saying.

See, Alexei was helping us break the law. If we were caught, he'd go to jail too. He didn't have to take this kind of risk.

So why was he doing all this for us?

And just what was in the monkey anyway?

WORDS

IT TOOK US MORE THAN an hour. We stopped once to pass a canteen around and catch our breaths. This canteen had water in it and a nipple over the opening; I sucked at it thirstily. Doug whispered to me, "Slow down, Chigger—don't pull a Stinky." He was right. I passed the canteen on. It was a very short rest; as soon as everybody had had a drink, we were on our way again.

At the top, or the far end, there was a wall blocking further progress. We had to climb up through a narrow tube and through a series of thick air locks.

"Okay, comrades," Alexei said. "This is where you must each make a prayer to Saint Vladimir—" We were at the final hatch.

"Saint Vladimir . . . ?"

"I made him up. He is the patron saint of smugglers. I smuggled him into heaven. Now let's see if he is appropriately grateful." Alexei took out his clearance card and swiped it through the reader slot. He inhaled. He exhaled. The panel turned green, and when he tapped it, the hatch popped open.

"Thank you, Saint Vladimir. I shall light candles at your altar," Alexei said to the ceiling. "As soon as I can find candles. And build an altar." We passed through—into the top or bottom of a brightly lit shaft lined with machinery. It was deep and the walls were lined with tracks and service bays. On one side, we saw seven or eight elevator cars, each one docked and surrounded by lights and equipment and service gear. None of them had their cabins spinning; all had their lights on.

"Ahh," said Alexei. "I have done good. Very good. And Saint Vladimir has done good. I was afraid I was going to have to replace him.

See there? We are almost at the beginning of your journey. This way, citizens. We must not be seen."

There was small chance of that. There weren't any people on the outside of the cars. There were two spider-jeeps inspecting hulls, but they were all the way down at the bottom of the bay.

Nevertheless, Alexei led us around to the backside of a thick service pipe, where we would be out of sight, and we lowered ourselves down it. Bobby was clinging to Douglas's back and the monkey was still on mine.

Halfway down, Alexei and Mickey stopped to whisper hurriedly to each other. Mickey pointed. "That one. Number 1187. According to the tickets, that's the midnight car."

Alexei shook his head. "Are you sure? It looks like it's in the wrong position. There are too many cars ahead of it."

"That's what the tickets say. Wait a minute—" Mickey pulled his phone out of his pocket and spoke softly into it. He listened for a moment, then nodded, closed the phone and put it back in his pocket. "They're sending extra cars out to Whirlaway. VIP traffic." To our puzzled looks, he said, "I might be fired, but I still have friends."

"Hokay. Let's go." Alexei pointed. "We go around here, go across this catwalk, and enter through the left-side hatch. Any questions?"

"Why aren't they spinning?"

"They only spin them for passengers. If they were spinning, we couldn't do this; all the access through the transfer pods is too tightly controlled. Hokay, enough talk. Mickey, you lead."

We entered 1187 without incident. It was a lot like the car we'd ridden up in. We pulled ourselves in through the left-side hatch; it was the cargo hatch, the bottom. I wondered which way it was going to spin—clockwise or counter-clockwise? Would it make any difference?

Mickey led us directly to our cabins; Olivia had booked two, and there was a connecting door between them.

We pushed and pulled ourselves into the biggest one, the suite, and bounced into chairs. Mickey showed us how to release the seat belts, and we belted ourselves down. Douglas wrapped a blanket around Stinky, who promptly curled up and fell asleep wrapped around his monkey. The monkey snored softly for a moment or two, then fell silent.

Mickey glanced at his watch and grinned. "We made it. With time to spare. Now all we have to do is wait for Mom."

Alexei was already pulling rations out of his backpack. "I thought you might like a snack while you wait. I have cheese, fish-sausage, bread, grapes, little tomatoes, carrots. Eat hearty. *Bon appetit.*" He bowed from the waist, difficult to do in micro-gravity. "I must return now—they will be looking for me. I must not disappoint them. Otherwise, it spoils the game. Besides, I need to collect some things. Including my alibi." He handed the backpack to Mickey. "*Mikhail,* please make sure my father gets this. If I am not able to deliver it myself. Hokay? Thank you." And with that, he was gone.

"Where's he going?"

"Back down."

"The same way?"

"He can do it in fifteen minutes. He was a finalist in last year's no-grav Olympics. It's those long arms of his. And all the practice he gets." Mickey explained, "He'll probably go back to the ice cream place, or walk around the promenade for a while, whatever it takes, until he's sure that whoever is watching knows that he's not with us anymore. Then he'll disappear again. At least, that's my guess. Charles, do you want some grapes?"

"No thanks." I pushed the plate away. "All the grapes I've ever gotten have been sour."

"Yes, and you've done a fine job making sour whine." It was the first time Mickey had ever said anything rude to me. I looked at him surprised. He looked right back at me. "Don't you ever put a cork in it, kiddo? *Do you know that you are no fun to be around?*"

"So what?"

"So look around you and stop acting like a spoiled brat. Your family is coming apart—"

"It came apart a long time ago."

"*Shut up, stupid.* Try listening for a change. You might learn something. In case you hadn't noticed, your brother, Douglas, is having a very difficult time of this. And your dad isn't doing too well either—he hasn't spoken two words to anyone except you since we left my mother's. And you shut him down. The only reason Bobby hasn't thrown a tantrum is that we slipped a sedative into his chocolate soda. We should have done the same for you. You're not doing anything to make this easier for anybody."

"Nobody's trying to make it any easier on me," I snapped back.

"Excuse me—?" Mickey pushed in close, getting right in my face. "Douglas wasn't there for you when you got free-fall panic? Your dad didn't lift you up when you needed it? Your dad hasn't been trying to reach out to you all evening? Or was I hallucinating? You're acting like a selfish dirtsider, Charles. And I don't like you very much, right now."

"So fucking what? None of this would have happened if you hadn't—"

"Don't *go* there . . ." he warned.

"Mickey, please—" That was Douglas. "There's more to this than you know." He stepped / bounced over to Mickey and put his hand on his shoulder; they looked at each other and something unsaid passed between them. Mickey looked frustrated, but he nodded and backed off. Douglas turned to Dad then. "Okay, Dad," he said. "What's in the monkey?"

Dad shook his head. "I wish you hadn't found out about that."

"Yeah, well—it wasn't too hard to figure out. Is there anything else you want to tell us?"

Dad shook his head. He looked beaten, frustrated, angry, unhappy. "No, there's nothing else. I just thought—that maybe we could have some time together that wasn't a fight."

"Why would you think that?" asked Douglas. "Every time we get together, it's a fight. That's all we ever do. Why would you think this time would be different?"

Dad looked across at Doug and his expression was as straight as I'd ever seen. He spoke slowly. I guess it was hard for him to get the words out. "I thought that because it would be . . . the last time we'd all be together as a family . . . that maybe we'd all try to make it something good to remember."

"Why should we? What do we owe you? Or Mom? You've both been using us—and using us up. Between the two of you, Mom and her tirades, you and your passive-aggressive bullshit, you've turned Stinky into an incontinent little pissant, and Chigger—well, he's well on his way to becoming a sociopathic hermit with surgically attached earphones. I'm sorry, Chigger, but Mickey is right. You can be a royal pain in the ass sometimes."

Of all the things that anyone had said to me—even the load of crap Mickey had just dumped on me—what Doug said was the one that hurt the most. It shriveled me instantly. I'd never *really* thought about Doug's feelings before; I'd always assumed he didn't have any feelings at all. Seeing him angry like this, I felt so bad about every nasty thing I'd ever said to him, I wanted to cry, but I didn't dare, not now, so I turned away from him and wrapped myself up in a ball on the couch. Between Mickey and Doug . . . I wished I was dead.

Now Doug turned back to Dad. "And me—? Well, just look at me, Max. I'm your son. This is how I turned out. A big fat nothing. With the social skills of a virus. I don't know how to talk to people. That's why I hide out in C-space. You should've seen how clumsy I was when I tried to talk to Mickey. I don't even know how to flirt. I'm pathetic. I hate myself because I'm so geeky. I still can't believe that Mickey really likes me. I keep wondering what's wrong with him." Mickey started toward Douglas at that, to comfort him I guess, but Douglas put up a hand to stop him. He wasn't through talking. "Chigger is right," he said. "I *am* a geekoid from hell. We're all of us fucked up, Dad— and this . . . this isn't an answer. It's more of the same. It's you running away again. Only this time, you want us to run away with you. How can we run away with you when it's *us* you've been running away from all this time?"

I couldn't believe what I was hearing from Douglas. He was almost in tears. But he just kept on and on, letting it all out, all at once, and Dad—poor, stupid Dad—he just sat there and took it. I uncurled myself and sat up again—

"They say that parents are supposed to prepare kids for adulthood— well, I'd say we're pretty well prepared now, Dad, aren't we? We've learned all the different ways to run away." Douglas stopped, exhausted. He just floated there limp. Finally, he drifted back down into a chair— right toward Mickey's lap. He bounced off Mickey and started to push himself up again, but Mickey pulled him back down and held him with one arm firmly around his waist. Douglas looked uncomfortable for a moment, but Mickey whispered "shhh" at him, and Douglas finally let himself relax on Mickey's lap. He leaned his head back and closed his eyes for a moment, exhausted. Tears were running down his cheeks and I felt so sorry for him I didn't know what to do. I'd never seen him like that before in my life.

"Charles?" Dad looked at me. "Do you have anything you want to add?"

I thought about the opportunity. Yeah, I had a lot to say. But it wasn't necessary anymore. "No. Doug said it all."

"Is it my turn now?" Dad asked. "Do I get to say anything?"

I shrugged. "I don't care." Douglas just put a hand over his eyes.

Dad took a breath. He was gathering his strength, and his words. Then he said, "You're right, Douglas. Everything you said. You're right. And yes, I *was* trying to kidnap you. And yes, I knew it would hurt your mother and I didn't care anymore. At this last court hearing, this last nasty custody fight, I finally stopped caring about her feelings— yes, after all this time, do you know I still love her? *Loved.* It's finally over. I finally gave up—and gave in to the urge to hurt back. Yes, I was selfish. So what? I'm fifty-two years old and I'm tired of having to be Mr. Nice Guy every day. I'm tired of making payments—I want something in return, something that's mine. Yes, I got impatient—I got tired of working and working and working while everybody else around me is riding the money-flow. I want to eat food that doesn't taste like wallpaper. I've *earned* it."

Dad stopped to catch his breath. He looked across the room, as if suddenly remembering who he was talking to. "I remember when you were born, Doug—when Charles was born too. And Bobby. How proud I was of each of you, how much I cherished you. I used to wake up in the morning, promising myself every day that I'd be the best dad I could for my boys. And I really did try. I really did. Now I wake up every morning wondering how I screwed up so badly. And what I could do to make it right. And it always came back to money. I don't have any. I'm a million and a quarter in debt. And no matter how hard I work, I just keep getting deeper and deeper. And nothing is fun anymore. Not even the music. Everything is a chore. Sometimes even taking the next breath is a chore.

"So when they offered me this chance to be a courier and get off the planet and make some money—and give my sons a second chance too—I didn't have to think about it too hard. It was a way out. I was drowning. What would you have had me do, Doug? Charles?" He added, "I don't know what's in the monkey, I don't even care, but someone is paying for this trip. Whatever it is, we'll deliver it and we'll be done. Then you can do whatever you want to. I'm through trying. I'm beaten."

Doug didn't say anything to that. Neither did I. There wasn't anything to say. And I was through trying to figure things out. I looked at my hands and clenched them into fists of frustration. I couldn't even figure out my left from my right.

CRIPPLED INSIDE

WE ATE, WE DOZED, WE waited. Pretty soon, the car started sliding along the track to the departure bay. We felt it thump into position, and then we heard the soft clunk of the transfer pods moving into place. A little after that, the car started spinning and the pseudo-gravity came on. A while after that, we heard people moving around outside in the corridors.

When he deemed it was safe, Mickey ducked out of the cabin. "I'll be back as fast as I can. I have to get your tickets validated. Otherwise, this cabin will show up as empty and they'll give it to someone else." To Douglas, he smiled. "Save my place, huh?" And then he was gone.

I broke the silence. "Can I call Mom?"

Dad looked at me, startled. He started to say something, then thought better of it and closed his mouth instead. "Do what you wish, Charles. You've already made it clear that I can't control you." He sounded like he hated me. Well, at least that was honest.

I went to the phone and punched Mom's number. The screen showed a map of the route-finder as the system tried to locate Mom. First it went to El Paso, then San Francisco, then Vandenberg, then— stopped. Instead, a notice appeared, flashing in several languages. "We apologize for the inconvenience. Weather conditions have temporarily disrupted all communication services. Please try again later."

"Hokay," I said, and flicked the phone off. I sat down again. I was on my own. Douglas was going his own way with Mickey. Dad had signed off on the whole family. Stinky had his monkey, his thumb, and his dreams. And Mom was temporarily out of service.

Mickey came back in, waving our boarding passes. "All right, we're clear."

"That was fast," Doug said, "How'd you do it?"

"It was easy. A friend of mine is working the desk. I told him we had VIPs traveling incognito, they were already aboard, but we needed the paperwork handled, and he'd be doing me a great favor if he'd check in the tickets. By the time I finished explaining, he'd already done it. He said, 'Give my best to Alexei.' "

Doug smiled. "Why do I have the feeling that some money has been spread around?"

"Because it has. The information I gave Alexei? He's put all his assets into lockdown, and now he's peddling a very delicious rumor to some of his very best clients, plus lockdown storage for their volatile liquidity. By tomorrow, he could be a billionaire, just in percentages alone."

"He's going to start a financial panic—" Dad said.

"He's counting on it. Panics are profitable to guys like Alexei. They don't care which way the money flows—as long as it flows."

"That's disloyal," Dad said grumpily.

"To whom? Earth? Alexei isn't from Earth. He's from Luna. He's being loyal to his family in Gagarin."

"By breaking the law? By hurting Earth?"

Mickey shrugged. "What law is he breaking? And why should he try to help Earth? Earth isn't trying to help Luna—or anyone else. Never mind." Mickey looked disgusted. "You'd have to get your mind out of the dirt to understand."

"All the economies are linked. If you pull one down—"

"No, they're not," Mickey said. "Not anymore. You can thank the SuperNationals for that. There's only one economy—and they push their money from place to place, whenever they want, regardless of who it hurts. What Alexei is doing is taking their money away from them. Some of it, anyway."

"Like Robin Hood, eh?" Dad looked skeptical.

"Whatever," said Mickey. "I don't expect you to understand, and I'm not going to waste any more time explaining it to you."

"I know about the political situation," Dad said. "And the rest of it. The planet is dying. Everybody knows it. The human race has eaten it down to the bone and it's still chewing. Did you check the news this morning? It's now *official*. Africa is having a 'Population Crash.' India too. And China next. And it's still spreading. That's why we're here. Just like everybody else who's jumping off the planet." Dad looked more frustrated and angry than I'd ever seen him. "And just like you said, the lower half of the Line is shut down to everyone except corporation personnel. So why shouldn't the people who've been pushed down into the dirt by the SuperNationals all their lives feel resentful? I do."

"Speak for yourself, Dad," said Weird.

"Douglas!" Dad looked at him warningly. "I've tried very hard to understand your . . . situation. I think you should recognize how hard it's been for me." To Mickey, he said, "I've been appointed the villain by everyone in this situation—by you, by Charles, by Douglas, by my ex-wife, by the law. Once in a while, I'd like someone to say they're trying to understand *my* feelings about all this. I'm tired of being the target, that's what this is about. I'm tired of having to listen to other people tell me why I can't have what I want. It's my turn now. Watching Alexei take what isn't his and live like a—a grasshopper while the rest of the ants are starving for crumbs is supposed to make me feel better about Luna? Or Earth? Or anyone? I don't think so."

Douglas finally let his own anger show. He said, "Well, maybe if you'd managed things a little bit better—"

"I did the best I could—"

"Obviously, it wasn't good enough—"

"It would have been, if Charles hadn't opened his big mouth—"

Boom. The banana-split time bomb had finally gone off. *He blamed me.*

"—I had it all figured out. And everything was working. Get on this elevator, get on that elevator, and by the time anyone knew where we were, it would be too late to stop us, and then Charles had to ruin it. We could have been halfway to the moon by now—"

"That isn't fair, Dad—"

"*Nothing* is fair anymore, Douglas. That's what this whole trip has been about. Escaping the unfairness." He put his head in his hands. "All I wanted, all I hoped for, was a little understanding, a little cooperation from you kids. I did it for you!"

"You did it for yourself," corrected Douglas. "Just like I did it for myself and Charles did it for himself. None of us knows how to do anything for anyone else—"

"Excuse me—?" I said. Very quietly. "Excuse me?"

It was the quiet tone that did it. They all looked at me curiously. "Each of us has now had a fight with every one else in the room. Except Mickey and Douglas. This isn't fair. Mickey, Douglas? It's your turn to say nasty things to each other now." One thing about growing up with Weird, you learn how to do sarcasm real well.

Both Douglas and Dad shut up. They looked at each other. Mickey looked to Douglas. Douglas looked at me angrily. Stinky snored. Mickey turned and went back to the chair. He looked like he was trying to make a decision. "Is anyone hungry? No? All right, why don't I make up the beds? We're all tired. I'll be back in a moment." He stepped out of the cabin, leaving the rest of us to sit and glower at each other. I settled my headphones over my ears and dialed up something very distracting. John Lennon's bitter period, when all he could do was write songs about how wrong everybody else was. *Crippled Inside*. That was a good one. Nice and loud. The monkey crawled into my lap and hugged me. I wondered who'd programmed that, but I didn't push it away.

WORKING LATE

MICKEY CAME BACK WITH AN odd expression on his face. "Come with me," he said. "All of you. Quickly."

"Huh? Why?"

"Just come—" He was already picking up Stinky. I grabbed the monkey. Douglas shouldered the backpack. Dad picked up his worries and we followed Mickey out the hatch and up the corridor to the transfer pod. Mickey wouldn't answer any questions. "I'll explain later," was all he said.

The transfer pod dropped us down to the boarding level. Actually, there are two boarding levels. There's the public boarding level and the Very Important Person boarding level—Mickey took us to the VIP level.

We stepped out of the hatch into—

I didn't see the room at first. It was about the size of a classroom or a lounge, I guess, but directly in front of us was Judge Griffith in her wheelchair, and next to her, but not too close, there was Olivia, looking unhappy, and a couple other people I didn't recognize, but very official looking, and also that stupid lawyer, Howard. He still wore the same stupid suit that didn't fit right, only now he looked like he'd slept in it, and he had a very smug look on his face, like he'd caught us with our pants down and our hands on our dicks. I was tempted to give him my own farkleberry.

"Ahh," said Judge Griffith. "Thank you all for joining us. Mickey, did you have any trouble?" Mickey shook his head. "The Court thanks you for your efforts." Douglas glared at him, but Mickey didn't meet his look, so Douglas stepped over and took Stinky out of his arms, then he moved away from Mickey, as if he didn't want to know him anymore. The fuse was finally lit on that argument. Mickey looked miserable. I pretended to be interested in the monkey.

"All right, if everybody will take their places, we can get this business handled once and for all." Judge Griffith wheeled backwards, moving out of the way. She gestured with her gavel; she held the head of it in her fist and used the handle as a pointer. The chairs and the tables of the lounge had been moved into positions like a courtroom. "Olivia, if you'll sit over there on the left. Mickey, you too. The Dingillians— thank you. Howard, I want you on the right. Court officers, here beside me. And . . . yes, that'll do it, thank you."

Dad whispered to Olivia, "What the hell is going on? What did you do to us?" Olivia just shook her head and pointed us toward the chairs. "I can't advise you," she whispered. "You're on your own now." Dad looked as angry as I'd ever seen him in my entire life. Angrier than that even.

Douglas laid Stinky down on a nearby couch. The rest of us sat down in chairs that were much too comfortable for a legal procedure. It was hard to believe we were actually in a courtroom. But Judge Griffith put those doubts to rest immediately. She wheeled up to a small table that was to serve as the bench; her clipboard was already open and propped up so she could see it. She reversed the gavel in her hand and rapped it sharply on the table. She glanced over to her assistant. "Are we missing someone?"

The woman nodded. "Godot called. He'll be late."

Judge Griffith raised a questioning eyebrow. "I assume he has a good excuse?" She glanced at her watch. "Was the shuttle delayed?"

"The shuttle docked on time, the paperwork was delayed. Last I heard, he's waiting for customs to clear."

"Damn nuisance," Judge Griffith said, obviously annoyed. "Never mind, we can still take care of the preliminaries. And if he can't get here before we finish, then the hell with him. This Court is not on call. At least, not in this case." She turned forward again. "The Third District Court of the Orbital Space Authority, serving GeoSynchronous Station and Allied Domains, Judge Georgia Griffith presiding, is now in special session, this session being mandated by the attempted flight from jurisdiction of the following individuals . . ."

Olivia stood. "Beg pardon, Your Honor, but no one has actually fled jurisdiction yet—"

"Don't nit-pick, counselor. We caught them with the tickets in their hands. Don't act like an Earth-lawyer or we'll be here all night. I promised you we could resolve this quickly, and we will. If you and Howard will both keep your big mouths shut. First of all—"

Now Dad stood up. "Your Honor? If I may? Ms. Partridge no longer represents us—"

"Yes, yes, I know all about that dodge. I used it myself when I was a cub. Who do you think taught it to Olivia? Sit down, Mr. Dingillian. We have work to do here." She looked at Howard. "I suppose you want to have your say too?"

Sarcasm was wasted on him. He stood up, talking. "Thank you, Your Honor. I appreciate the opportunity. I think that the actions of the defendants clearly demonstrates their willful disregard for the authority of this—"

"Sit down, Howard. I don't need to hear it from you, either." She sighed and looked exasperated. "Listen up, folks—I don't like working late. I'm pissed at the lot of you. You've acted like spoiled brats and if I could think of a good reason to justify tossing all of you into the cooler for a week or two, I'd do it. Except that would give me the problem of finding custodial authority for the minors involved, and while I suppose I could release them to the custody of the oldest brother—" She stopped herself. "Hmm, that's not a bad idea, it would resolve everything . . . well, almost everything. Never mind, just don't anyone tempt me." She glared around the room, as if daring anyone to speak.

"All right," she continued, with a dark glower in Dad's direction. "We're here because Max Dingillian and his three kids somehow ended up on the midnight elevator to Farpoint. I presume the destination was Whirlaway. Correct? This, in spite of the fact that a court hearing was ordered for nine in the ayem, tomorrow morning. So I am left with the not unreasonable assumption that you, sir, Max Dingillian, were attempting to evade the authority of this court. Not that you could have. I'd have transferred authority—a single phone call down to the end of the Line—and you'd have been detained there. I doubt that the shift in venue to Farpoint would have resulted in a different outcome. Regardless of the distance, and sometimes the expense involved, starside courts have demonstrated a remarkable and refreshing consistency."

She leaned forward in her chair, aiming her remarks directly to Dad. "Up here, attempting to evade authority usually gets you a trip groundside. However . . . in light of several recent judgments where groundside courts have held the Line authority liable for expenses and damages when individuals are returned to Earth with resultant detriment, we have become extremely reluctant to expose ourselves to that liability *unless* we are certain that we will not have to bear the cost of the bounce-back. I am concerned that this case may have some exposure in that direction. So in that regard, the Court *chooses to ignore*—for the moment, anyway—the evidence of your attempt to evade jurisdiction. Sit down, Howard! I'll get to you in a moment!" She turned back to Dad. "At the very least, I should hold you in contempt of court, Mr. Dingillian, but it is not in the best interests of your children to do so, and it does not serve the goal of a speedy resolution. Let it be known, however, that the Court views your conduct with extreme displeasure. Let me translate that for you: you've exhausted whatever good will you had here. Do you understand?"

Dad nodded. "I understand completely. And I thank you for your . . . uh, mercy, Your Honor."

Judge Griffith ignored Dad. She turned to Howard-In-The-Wrinkled-Suit. "All right, Howard, now you may object. . . ." Howard started to stand up, shrugged, sank back down in his seat, spreading his hands helplessly.

"Right," Judge Griffith agreed. "Objection overruled. Thank you. The Court appreciates your efforts to help move this process forward as fast as possible." She turned to Olivia. "Counselor, you no longer represent the Dingillians, is that correct?"

"That is correct." Olivia's voice was unemotional. Detached.

"Nevertheless, you were planning to leave on the midnight elevator with them. Is that correct too?"

"Yes, Your Honor. That is correct."

"Do you have an interesting explanation for this?"

"Conflict of interest. My son has a relationship with Douglas Dingillian."

"*Had*," corrected Douglas. Judge Griffith gave him a curious look, but otherwise ignored his interruption.

"Did you advise the Dingillians to evade jurisdiction, Counselor?"

"Of course not. I'm an officer of the court. That would be unethical."

"Nevertheless, was it among the options you discussed?"

Olivia nodded reluctantly. "Yes, it was."

"Well, Olivia," the Judge continued, "we have here the evidence that you booked the tickets yourself under one of your shadow accounts. So even though you recused yourself from this case, you still managed to be a participant in an action that would have damaged the court's ability to function. The Court finds you in contempt and fines you . . ." The judge consulted her clipboard, tapping at its surface as she looked something up. ". . . one thousand chocolate-dollars." Olivia didn't react to that. Judge Griffith continued, "Sentence suspended in recognition of your assistance in arranging this special session."

"Thank you, Your Honor," Olivia said quietly.

"The same thing I said to Max Dingillian goes for you too, Counselor. Your store of good will is exhausted in this court. Remember that."

Now, Judge Griffith turned to Howard-The-Smug. "Any objections? No? Overruled anyway. Don't worry about your store of good will, Howard. The Court's opinion of you remains unchanged." To the rest of us, she said, "The issue here is simple, and if we can resolve it in the next two hours"—she glanced at her watch—"then the Dingillians, or at least Max Dingillian, depending on the ruling of this court, can continue their—*or his*—journey." By the emphasis she put on *"or his,"* she made it very clear that she had not yet made up her mind whether Dad was going to go to the moon with us or *without* us.

She looked to me. "Charles?"

"Huh?"

"Please come forward. Leave the monkey. Sit over here on this chair, will you? Thank you. Do you swear to tell the truth, the whole truth, and nothing but the truth?"

"Sure," I said. "I mean, yes, I do."

CLOCKWISE

JUDGE GRIFFITH TURNED HER CHAIR so she was facing me. "All right, Charles—is that what you like to be called, Charles?"

I shrugged. "My family calls me Chigger."

"Is that what you want me to call you?"

"It's okay," I said, half-heartedly.

"I'll call you Charles," she said, nodding. "It sounds more respectful. Now . . . do you remember the riddle I asked you at dinner?"

"About how do you tell a Martian the difference between left and right?"

"Yes, that's the one. For the record, would you restate it?"

I took a breath. "You asked how to explain left and right without using the words *left* and *right*. How would you demonstrate or explain the difference? What are the . . . the defining criteria? Is that the right way to say it?"

"Yes, it is. Very good, Charles. That's even better than I said. So, have you thought about the problem?"

I made a face. "I haven't been able to think about anything else. That's really a tough question."

"Yes, it is." She grinned right back at me. "The first time I heard it, I couldn't get it out of my head for months. So do you have an answer?"

"I'm not sure. I mean, I'm not sure if it's the right one—" But before I could say anything else, Howard-The-Rude stood up. "Your Honor? With all due respect, may I ask what the purpose is of this line of discussion?"

Judge Griffith looked annoyed at the interruption. But she turned to Howard-The-Ugly and replied, "Yes, you may ask. The purpose of this

line of inquiry is to determine the depth of thought that Charles Dingillian is able to bring to a problem. There are questions that we need
to ask him. We need to know what kind of credibility his answers have.
Will he tell us what he thinks we want to hear? Or will he tell us what
he's really thinking? That's what's going to determine a large part of
the Court's decision here. Any further questions, Counselor?"

Howard-The-Stupid didn't look happy with Judge Griffith's answer,
but he sat down anyway. "No more questions."

Judge Griffith turned back to me. "All right, Charles—I'm sorry to
have to put you on the spot; try to pretend it's just you and me talking
about this riddle over dinner again, okay?"

"Okay."

"And it doesn't matter if you have the right answer or not,
Charles—that's not the point. In fact, I'm not even sure there is a right
answer, there may not be, so don't worry if you didn't get any answer
at all, that's not important. I just want you to tell me the way you
thought about it."

"But I did get an answer—" I said.

"You did?" She looked surprised.

"Uh-huh."

"Well, if you did, then you're the first. I never did."

"Oh, well—um, I dunno. Maybe it isn't obvious. You don't live on
a planet, so maybe that has something to do with it. See, first I thought
that you could tell the difference by the sun. Turn and face the direction
the sun rises. The hand pointing south is your right hand, the hand
pointing north is your left hand. But then I realized that the Martian
would have to know north and south for that answer to be any good.
And that depends on which way the planet is spinning, doesn't it? North
is the pole that when you look down on it from above, the planet is
spinning counter-clockwise. So you need to know clockwise to know
north, don't you? And if the Martian doesn't know clockwise, then the
answer doesn't mean anything at all to him, does it? So I have to find
a way to tell the Martian about left and right in a way that doesn't
depend on any Earth definitions at all."

"Very good, Charles. Go on."

Dad was looking at me oddly. Douglas was sort of smirking, as if
he already knew how hard this riddle was. Stinky sat up, rubbing his
eyes. He looked around once, then laid back down again. Douglas put
his jacket over him.

I looked back to Judge Griffith and held out my hands in front of
me, palms open and facing away, thumbs sticking out at right angles.
"Then I thought that maybe my hands might be a clue. See my left

hand? My index finger and thumb make an L—L for left. But that doesn't count either, because a Martian isn't going to know what an L is. You need a way to describe an L, and you can't really do that without first having the definitions of right and left, can you? How do you say a left-pointing right angle? So that doesn't work either. That was when I got really really angry at you." I curled my fingers into fists and pantomimed pounding on a table and growled through my teeth.

Judge Griffith smiled and nodded, "I remember that feeling."

"But that gave me part of the answer." I stretched my arms out in front of me so she could see my fists. "It's in your fingers, see? Look down at your fists. The left one is clockwise." I traced it with my right index finger. "If you start at the outside, with the tip of the thumb and follow the spiral of your fingers all the way around to the tip of your index finger on the inside, then you see that the left hand is the hand that curls clockwise in while the right hand curls counter-clockwise out. And that's the only way they can be."

"That's *very* good, Charles." Judge Griffith was looking at her own fists. Around the room, almost everybody else was looking at their fists too. Olivia, Mickey, Douglas—even Howard-The-Clumsy. "That's the best answer I've ever heard."

"Except . . ." I added, "That's not the whole answer. Because the Martian still has to know clockwise"—Howard groaned; I ignored him—"or you have to be able to define clockwise for him. See, all that this answer does is move the problem into another . . . um, what's that word that Douglas uses all the time? *Domain*—that's it. This answer only moves the problem into another *domain*. You still have to define clockwise and counter-clockwise."

Howard-The-Impatient stood up then. "Your Honor," he said, with obvious annoyance, "I think you've made your point. Can we be done with this and get on with our business?"

"We are getting on with it, Howard. And *I'll* decide when we're done." She waved him down impatiently and turned back to me. "And did you figure it out, Charles? How *do* you define clockwise?"

"Well, first I thought about clocks, obviously—but maybe Martians don't have clocks. But they could have a sundial. You could tell a Martian that clockwise is the way the shadows turn—except it's reversed in the southern hemisphere. There's no way to tell the difference between northern and southern. It's the same as left and right. Again. So I've got to find something that's always clockwise no matter how you look at it."

"And, did you find anything?"

"Well . . . I thought about Neptune and Uranus, both of which are laying down on their axis. If there was a planet that always kept one of its poles toward the sun, then the sun would always see it spinning the same way, counter-clockwise. But both those planets are like Earth. Half their year, the north pole points toward the sun, the other half the south pole points toward the sun, so there aren't any celestial objects you can use."

"So you didn't get an answer?"

"No, I got two answers. But . . . well, you'll see. The first answer is to point to the Southern Cross and say, 'That's south and this is the southern hemisphere.' Or you point to Polaris and say, 'That's the north star. This is the northern hemisphere. But that only works where you can see the sky."

"And what's the other answer?"

"Periwinkles." Douglas looked up sharply at that—I guess he was surprised that I had actually listened to what he had said back there on that Mexican beach. "They're a kind of seashell," I explained. "They always know which way to turn. Clockwise."

"In both hemispheres?"

"I think so."

"Hmm. That's very interesting. I'll have to look that up. Those are good answers, Charles. You get an A." Judge Griffith looked impressed.

"Uh-uh," I said. "I think they're C+ answers."

"Oh? Why? They answer the question."

"Yeah, but they all depend on being able to point to something else. You can't talk about right or left or clockwise or counter-clockwise, unless you can point to something else. Otherwise, there's no way to define one hand from the other."

Judge Griffith smiled. "I believe that you have just stumbled on the essential existential dilemma."

"Huh? The what—?"

She answered slowly and carefully. "The only way we *ever* know anything about ourselves is by measuring ourselves against something outside of us. Do you understand what that means?"

"I think so," I said, remembering something Weird had said once. "Everything's connected to everything else. If we don't have any connections, we're lost. We can't even tell which way is up. But—?"

"Yes?"

"That means that there isn't anything absolute, doesn't it? That everything is just sort of 'agreed on.' Like we all voted on which way is north and what time it is and what words mean. It's like looking down and finding there's no floor."

"Exactly," said Judge Griffith. "There is no floor. And we're all living in a universe of agreements. That's why we have courts—to sort out all the different *dis*agreements where they rub up against each other. If we had absolutes, Charles, we wouldn't need courts, would we?"

"Mm." I had to think about that one for a minute too. "I guess not."

"So let's get this one sorted out now. You've done very well, Charles. Very well indeed. The Court thanks you. You've shown me what I needed to know. You can go back and sit with your family now."

"Yes, Your Honor." I went back and sat next to Douglas. I picked up the monkey again and held it close. It hugged me again. I didn't know whether to be annoyed or not.

GODOT

JUDGE GRIFFITH LOOKED TO HER assistant. "Any word yet?"

"The last of the passengers have cleared customs. Godot is on his way up. Five minutes."

"All right," said Georgia. "Fifteen-minute potty break." She banged her gavel once and wheeled toward the restroom, her assistant following.

Dad leaned toward Olivia. "Who's this Godot?"

"I don't know," Olivia whispered back. "That's what the judge calls anyone she has to wait for." She added, "I'm sorry we got caught—but I don't think Georgia had any choice in the matter."

"*We*—? *You* got a suspended sentence. I'm likely to lose my kids—! There's not a lot of 'we' in that, Olivia! You turned us in, didn't you?"

"I didn't have a choice, Max." She sounded just as frustrated as Dad.

"Oh, terrific. You told us to go out on the limb—and then you sawed it off."

"I don't think you should say any more," Olivia said quietly, with a meaningful nod toward Howard-The-Brooding.

"You've put us in a really bad situation, Olivia."

"I'm sorry. I miscalculated."

"Apology noted. Now what are you going to do to help clean up this mess?"

"Nothing. I can't! I'm not your lawyer anymore, Max."

Dad shook his head in disgust. "I can't believe this. Why did I trust you?" He sank back down in his seat, not looking at Olivia anymore. She looked just as unhappy. Now all that was left was a fight between her and Mickey, and we'd be complete. Everybody would have fought with everybody. I couldn't think of anyone else we could fight with—

And then Godot arrived.

Godot was Doctor Bolivar Hidalgo. And following him into the room was . . . *Mom?!* And that other woman behind her.

Just about everybody came to their feet. Douglas, Dad, me—even Stinky woke up, rubbing his eyes again, this time, crying, "Stop waking me up!"

Mom went straight to Dad. She moved across the room like a missile—and slapped him across the face. Hard. Dad was knocked back a step; he put his hand to his jaw and blinked. "It's good to see you again too, Maggie," he managed to say.

And then Stinky saw her for the first time and yelled, "Mommy!" And flung himself into her arms like a screaming monkey. He grabbed hold so tight, she almost fell backward. "Mommy, Mommy! Are you going with us?"

"I came to take you home, sweetie—"

"But I don't wanna go home! I wanna go to the moon!"

She stroked his shaven scalp. "What have they done to you, baby?"

"It's a moon-cut!"

Mom gave Dad a dirty look and moved away from us, cooing softly to Stinky and patting his head. Now it was Doctor Hidalgo's turn. He waddled over and bowed to Dad. "My compliments, *Señor* Dingillian."

Dad just glowered.

Dr. Hidalgo pretended not to notice. Instead, he took Dad by the arm and made as if to lead him off to a corner. "Can we talk?"

"You can talk," Dad said, not moving. "Do I have to listen?"

"It would be better if we could talk alone . . . ?"

"Anything you have to say to me, you can say in front of my children, Dr. Hidalgo. I'm not going to hide anything from them. It's their lives too."

Douglas and I exchanged a look. We came and stood next to Dad. The monkey climbed up onto my back and made faces over my shoulder. Doug hissed at me, "Turn it off, Charles," so I did.

We followed Dad and Doctor Hidalgo over to a corner of the lounge. Doctor Hidalgo plopped himself down onto a chair and started talking immediately. "It's a pity you didn't accept my earlier offer of help. It would have simplified matters a great deal. For all of us. I told you that there were people who would act against you. You should consider your wife's oh-so-convenient presence here as evidence of their commitment. If you think about the organizational effort involved and the money it takes to get someone onto a shuttle on such short notice, you might begin to understand just how important your package is. It's important enough that a great deal of money is going to be spent on the effort to intercept it and prevent its delivery. Are you convinced yet?"

"What I told you before still stands," Dad said.

"It affects the lives of your sons. How do they feel about it?"

"Whatever my Dad says, goes for me too," I blurted. "Right, Douglas?" I poked him.

Douglas didn't need to be poked. "We're a family, Doctor Hidalgo. We might be having problems right now, but that's our business, not yours. No matter how bad our family arguments might get, we still don't sell each other out."

"Admirable. Very admirable." Doctor Hidalgo grunted his approval. "Not very smart, but still admirable. The smart man recognizes when he can't win and cuts his losses early. So . . ." He levered himself to his feet. I figured he must have massed two hundred kilos. He sure looked it. Even in low-grav, he was having problems getting out of a chair. "I guess we have nothing further to discuss. Let the games begin." He waddled back to the other side of the lounge.

Dad looked to me and Douglas like he wanted to say something. But there wasn't anything that needed saying, so he just clapped Doug on the shoulder—he was closer—and said, "Let's go."

IN COURT

JUDGE GRIFFITH CALLED THE SESSION back to order with three sharp raps of her gavel on the table. "All right, people, we've got a lot of work to do and not very much time in which to do it. I've made a promise to some folks here to be finished before midnight so they could catch an elevator, and I intend to keep that promise. Would everybody please take their seats and settle themselves quickly?" Judge Griffith nodded to her assistant. "Joyce, please make a note of our new arrivals. Godot is here. Finally."

Mom and the woman who had followed her in, I guessed she was the woman from San Francisco, sat down with Dr. Hidalgo, on the other side of Howard-The-Malignant. She leaned over to confer with him. They shook hands quickly, so I guessed this was their first face-to-face meeting. She held Stinky in her arms, but he appeared to have fallen back asleep. He woke up just long enough to stick his tongue out at Howard, then he laid his head back down on Mom's shoulder again. Whatever they'd given him, I wanted a lifetime supply.

Judge Griffith was already moving along. She meant it about finishing quickly. "Dr. Hidalgo, the Court appreciates your interest in this case; however, if it is your intention to complicate matters with extra-curricular issues, let me warn you ahead of time that the Court will take a dim view of any such matters that do not *directly* affect the issue at hand."

"Your Honor." Dr. Bolivar spread his hands wide, in an oily gesture. Obviously, someone's snake was squeaky. "I am here only as a friend of the Court. I simply wish to see justice done."

The judge snorted. "Bollie, you and I both know that I have a low threshold of bullshit. And you and I both know that you have no interest in anything except your own stomach. You brought the boys' mother up for reasons that have nothing to do with justice or friendship. The Court will *tolerate* this only so long as it does not impinge on the ability of this Court to function. Consider this a warning. Your friends have no authority over this—" She waved her gavel at him.

Bolivar gave her his smarmiest smile; he nodded politely and sank back into his chair. It groaned.

Judge Griffith turned to Mom now. "Mrs. Dingillian—"

"Campbell. It's Campbell now. I've gone back to my maiden name, Your Honor."

"Fairly recently? Ah, yes, here it is. Thank you for the correction." Judge Griffith made a note on her clipboard. She frowned to herself, took off her glasses, polished them with a handkerchief, and reseated them on her nose. I got the feeling that she did not do it because her glasses were dirty. Finally, she sighed to herself in resignation. She looked over to Mom and said, "Ms. Campbell, the Court acknowledges your interests in this hearing. Just so you'll know—and you too, Mr. Dingillian—I've spent the past several hours reviewing the records of your divorce and custody hearings. I wish I could say it makes for interesting reading. Unfortunately, it does not. It is a tiresome and petty matter, and I think both you and your husband have a great deal to be ashamed of. You for what you did, he for the way he reacted. This is not a case where one side is right and the other is wrong. It is a case where both sides are wrong—and this Court has no interest in trying to determine which side is more wrong. That way lies madness. At this point, the *only* issue here is the welfare of the children. Everything else, I will leave to you and your respective lawyers to battle it out until hell freezes over, or you both drop dead of exhaustion, whichever comes first—and for the children's sake, I hope it's soon. Just so there's no doubt in your minds, I hate cases like this. I hate the people who create cases like this. I hate what it does to the children."

Judge Griffith leaned forward now, putting her elbows on the table in front of her and folding her hands together under her chin. "I want to make it clear to everybody that this is the basis on which I'm going to make my decision. I've already heard all of your arguments. They're all in these records I had piped up the Line. And I very much doubt that there is anything that either side has to add, and it isn't going to serve any of us to take it out of the box and exercise it again. Additionally, whatever moral or legal or emotional advantages either of you felt that you could make a reasonable claim to in an Earthside court, those advantages do not obtain here. This court is interested in one thing and one thing only—the welfare of these children. The Court does not like being put in this position, but the Court has no choice, because events have clearly demonstrated that *neither* of the parents has provided an appropriate commitment to the welfare of these children. Therefore—"

"Your Honor, I object to that—" That was Mom, leaping to her feet.

Judge Griffith sighed. She could see where this was headed. "Ms. Campbell?"

"I am *not* a bad parent, and I do put my children's welfare above everything else—"

Judge Griffith tapped her gavel gently to interrupt Mom. "Spare me the organ recital. Your husband came home and found you in bed with someone else. I was raised old-fashioned, Ms. Campbell. Maybe you think that what you did was a generous and unselfish demonstration of commitment and dedication to your family, but *this* court is having a very hard time viewing it that way. This situation—this entire avalanche of errors in judgment—was all triggered by that first little pebble. Now, maybe they do things differently on Earth, but up here when two people make a promise to each other—especially a promise to love, honor, and cherish—there's a reasonable expectation that both parties will make some effort to keep that commitment. And when there are children involved, well then the commitment to the children and their well-being has to outweigh everything else. Your children didn't get to vote on this situation—that's why the Court is involved now—to vote for the children."

"Your Honor," Mom started to protest, "with all due respect—we *had* a working custody arrangement, until *he*"—she waved her hand angrily at Dad—"went and violated it! All I want is for you to return my children to me so we can go home!"

"Sit down, Ms. Campbell. That's *not* going to happen. At least not because you or anyone else demands it. You pushed your husband into this situation. It's all here in the history." She tapped her clipboard meaningfully. "You kept challenging his visitation rights every chance you got—you gave him no rational choice. That doesn't excuse what he did, but neither did you provide an environment in which your separate disagreements could be worked out rationally. And for the record, let me stress this again: this Court has absolutely no interest in providing an arena for one more round of legal spouse-bashing. If you want to hurt each other, if that's the kind of postmarital relationship you both want, that's fine with me—I'm just not going to let you use my court for it.

"We're going to resolve this once and for all. At the end of this session, if you or your husband have issues that are still unresolved, then sign up for one of those silly courses you folks downside love to do. I can recommend a dozen good ones—there's the one where you call each other names, there's the one where you whomp each other with plastic clubs, there's the one where you process out all your bad feelings, and so on and so on and so on. Do any of them, do them all, I don't care. But stop using your children as weapons against each other!"

Judge Griffith poured herself a glass of water. Her hand trembled slightly as she drank. She put the glass back on the table and looked from Mom to Dad and back again. "In other words, Mr. Dingillian, Ms. Campbell, based on everything that has happened so far, this Court cannot justify awarding either one of you custody of these children. Do you understand what I am saying? The decision cannot be based on your credentials as parents. Neither of you deserves that consideration. This Court is going to have to look *elsewhere* for guidance in this decision. Fortunately, I think I have a way to resolve this. Now, when you get back to Earth, you may both feel perfectly free to find a court that will return a ruling more to your liking, but right now, you are here in my jurisdiction, and what I say here carries the weight of law. Any questions? No? I didn't think so."

She looked around the room as if daring anyone else to speak. No one wanted to. So she rapped her gavel sharply. "Douglas Dingillian, as you are only two months shy of your eighteenth birthday, this court sees fit to declare you an independent adult. You are hereby granted autonomy. You are no longer under the custody of either of your parents. Do you understand?"

Douglas nodded. He looked a little scared, but he nodded. Mom looked like she wanted to say something, but held her silence. Dad looked to Doug, but Doug wouldn't meet his gaze.

Judge Griffith continued. "You are free to return to Earth, either with or without your mother; you are free to continue your outbound odyssey, either with or without your father. However, before you make *any* decision, we still have the matter of the custody of your brothers to resolve, and the Court will appreciate your input on that."

Douglas nodded again.

Now Judge Griffith turned to me. "Charles, the whole point of that little exercise earlier was so I could find out how you think about things—how deeply you consider a question—and I have to tell you, I'm very impressed with you. I don't think the people around you know you very well. You're a very thoughtful young man; at least, that's my experience of you. I tell you this because I want you to understand, ordinarily I would not ask a thirteen-year-old to make the kind of choice that I'm about to give you. But under these circumstances, I think this is the best way to do it—and I'm satisfied that you're up to the challenge. So here's the question—"

I could already see it coming. And I was already formulating my reply.

"—Do you want to go back down the beanstalk with your mother, or do you want to continue outward with your father?"

I didn't have to think about it. I'd already been thinking about it long enough—ever since Dad went *boom*. I stood up. "Neither," I said.

Judge Griffith shook her head, smiling gently. "I'm afraid that's not an option, Charles."

"Yes, it is," I said. "*I want a divorce.*"

THOREAU'S AX

ALMOST IMMEDIATELY, **BOTH MOM AND** Dad were on their feet, shouting: "Your Honor—you can't allow this!" "Charles, have you lost your mind?" Douglas looked surprised, though he shouldn't have been. Even Stinky was awake now. "Whatever Charles gets, I want one too!" he yelled, screeching above the tumult. Judge Griffith banged so loudly with her gavel that the head popped off. She had to wait until her assistant, Joyce, went and got it and brought it back to her.

"Everybody settle down, dammit!" she shouted over the noise. "And *sit down!* I'll handle this." She banged a few more times until everyone sat down again, then she turned back to me. "Charles—" she started to say gently.

I didn't let her finish. "I want a divorce," I repeated.

Judge Griffith looked very unhappy. "That does complicate things, doesn't it?" she said. "I wonder who could have put that idea into your head."

"You did," I said, bluntly. "Over pizza."

"So I did. Well shame on me. I must learn to watch my big mouth. The karmic chicken has come home to roost. Charles, do you know what's involved in that kind of action?"

"Yes, actually, I do. At least as much as I could find out from reading about it."

"Somebody should hang a warning sign on you, Charles: 'Caution, contents will probably explode in your face.' " She smiled wryly, to let me know she was joking, but I could see she meant it too. Well, so what? I *did* want a divorce. "I'm probably going to regret asking this," she asked, "but *why* do you want a divorce?"

"Do I have to have a reason?"

"Not really. You and your brothers are the only ones who *didn't* promise to love, honor, and etcetera. And if that's not a promise you want to keep, you shouldn't be held in a situation where it's a requirement. But it would help if you did have a reason. Otherwise, children would be announcing right and left that they want a divorce every time they get sent to bed early."

I pointed at Mom. I pointed at Dad. "Those are my reasons."

The judge nodded. "Those are two pretty good reasons. And considering everything else that's happened, the Court would ordinarily be inclined to grant your request—but let's look over the edge of this cliff for a while before we jump, okay, Charles?"

"Sure," I said. "Whatever. But it's not going to change my mind. I've been thinking about this for a long time. Not because you mentioned it. I just never knew how to do it before."

"Charles—" Mom called across the room "—you don't have to do this. If we could just sit down and talk things out—"

"Leave him alone, Maggie! Haven't you done enough damage already!" Dad shouted across at her. "Look at the poor kid! Charles, I'm sorry for what I said back there—"

Judge Griffith rapped her gavel only once. Without even looking up: "Any more outbursts and I'll put the both of you in jail. In the same cell!" The threat worked. They both sat down again, glowering at each other. "Howard?" Howard-The-Troll looked up. "Are you still representing the interests of the mother?"

Howard looked to Mom, she nodded, and he said, "Yes, Your Honor."

"Would you like to question Charles Dingillian?"

"Uh—I haven't had time to prepare."

"Neither has anyone else here. Perhaps giving lawyers time to prepare is why justice always takes so long. Maybe in the future, in the interest of producing results, I should deny all recesses and continuances. Don't panic, Howard, it's a joke."

Howard-The-Repulsive came over and stood in front of me. "I know you're impatient to have the privileges of an adult, Charles. I remember being thirteen once—I was a kid just like you. We might have liked each other. We might have been friends—"

"I don't want to be your friend, *Howard.* I want a divorce."

His expression hardened. "All right, let's approach this another way, *Charles.* You're having doubts about this, aren't you?"

I shook my head. "No, I've been thinking about it for a while. I can't see anything better to do."

"Ahh," said Howard-The-Smarmy. "Maybe you haven't asked yourself all the questions you should have. Let me ask you this one. Do you think running away is going to solve anything?"

"Some people do."

"Yes, I know. Do you?"

I knew what he wanted me to say. I mean, everybody knows the right answer to that question. No. Running away never solves anything. But . . . sometimes running away buys you time to think. And that lets you solve stuff. Doesn't it?

He held my eyes with his. He didn't look nasty. He looked like he was trying to be friendly and it was a strain. He said, "Charles, do you think your parents have a responsibility toward you?"

"Yes. Everybody knows that. That's what they teach us at school. Don't make babies unless you're also willing to make a lifelong commitment."

"Good. Do you think you have a corresponding responsibility to your parents?

"I don't understand."

"Well, your parents worked hard to give you a home and an education and take care of you. I know that it hasn't worked out the way you think it should, but don't you think that your parents have your best interests at heart?"

"Your Honor—?" That was Olivia. "I realize that I no longer represent this client, but as a friend of the Court, I must object to this transparent attempt to manipulate Charles Dingillian through the use of guilt."

"The Court appreciates your concern, but I think young Mr. Dingillian is quite capable of sorting this out for himself. Nevertheless, Howard, would you please lower the level of rhetoric here . . . ?"

"Yes, Your Honor." He turned back to me. "My point is, Charles, that you've taken a lot from your parents. You owe them something in return. Do you think this is the right way to repay it?"

And when he put it that way, something clicked. "Can I ask you something?"

"Yes, Charles—what is it?" He seemed genuinely interested.

"Well, when I was in school—I don't know if it's the same way up here—we had classes about social responsibility. My teacher taught us that everybody is part of society. We all depend on each other in lots of different ways. We all make work for each other, so we need each other for jobs. And we all make messes—like garbage and pollution and sewage and crap—so we all have to clean up after ourselves. And sometimes, like during flu season, we're all infectious. And stuff like that. And even if we like to think that we're individuals, we really all depend on each other all the time. My teacher said it was Thoreau's ax."

"I beg your pardon?" said Howard-The-Puzzled. "Thoreau's ax?"

"Yeah. Thoreau was this guy who thought it would be a good idea to go out in the woods to Walden Pond and commune with nature. He thought worldly goods distracted people and kept them from really finding themselves and getting in tune with everything good."

"Yes, I know who Thoreau was. What about his ax?"

"Well, that's the point. Where did his ax come from? If he wanted to build himself a shelter, or chop a tree for firewood, or stuff like that, he needed an ax. Where does the ax come from?"

"From a . . . blacksmith," offered Howard.

"Uh-huh. You got it. Thoreau was a dope. You can't just go off and live by yourself. You need the products of other people. Everything you need to survive, all that comes from other people. They contribute to you. And you have an obligation to contribute to them too. In whatever way you can. That's the social contract. And even if you think you're not obligated, you really are, because just like Thoreau, if you're going out to the woods to live, where are you going to get your ax?"

"Judge Griffith is looking at her watch again. What does this have to do with your situation?"

"Well . . . I can see what's going on. Some kind of evacuation. People who can afford it are leaving the Earth. Like guests leaving a party after they've trashed the house. They're taking their money and they're going up the Line to the moon and everywhere else. Isn't that right?"

"Yes, Charles. I won't lie to you. There are people who are afraid of the possibility of war and disease and economic turmoil—"

"That's my point—if you grownups can't keep your promises, if you can't keep your part of the social contract to the whole planet—if grownups are running away from the problems they made, then how can you ask a kid like me to stay behind with the mess? I don't know that running away solves any problems, but I don't see that I accomplish anything useful by staying either."

For a moment there was silence in the court. A lot of people looked real uncomfortable. Dad. Mom. Judge Griffith. Olivia. Mickey. Howard. Dr. Hidalgo. Finally, Judge Griffith said, "I think he's pretty well nailed the lot of us to the wall."

But Howard-The-Merciless wasn't finished. He said, "I can think of a reason to go back."

"What?"

"Because you love your Mom."

I looked over at Mom, she looked hopeful. Her eyes were shining.

I looked to Dad, he looked kinda proud. I looked at Douglas, who flashed me a quick nod and a smile.

"Yeah," I said to Howard-The-Duck. "That's a good reason." Mom smiled at me—until I added, "But it's not good enough. Not anymore," and her expression collapsed into grief. I should have stopped there, but I didn't. "I love my mom. I really do. I love my dad too. But I don't like being in the middle anymore. Love's a good reason for lots of stuff—but not for doing something stupid. And going back to either of them is the stupidest thing I can think of."

Howard sat down, defeated.

LAWYERS AND AGENTS

JUDGE **GRIFFITH GLANCED AT HER** watch and made a face. She turned sideways in her chair to face me. "Thank you, Charles. That was very nicely argued. Have you ever considered becoming a lawyer?"

"Only once. Dad threatened to strangle me in my sleep."

"And he's probably right. Never mind. Do you still want a divorce?"

I nodded. "Yes, Your Honor. I do."

"Hmm." She frowned. "You know, I can grant it, right here and now. It's irregular, but so is this whole situation. So it wouldn't be out of line to resolve it with an unorthodox decision, particularly in light of some of the other pressures on us." She sighed, glanced at her watch again, and began to explain. "But I'll tell you honestly, I'm very reluctant to just bang the gavel and be done with it."

"Why?"

"You see, Charles, we have a problem here. You and I in particular. I can declare Douglas an adult, because he's only two months shy of his majority. And I can ask you what you want to do, because even though you're not yet old enough to be independent, you're still old enough to have a say in what happens to you. And if you want a divorce, I can put you in Douglas's custody. But I can't give the same choice to Bobby, can I? Do you think he's capable of making an informed decision? Do you think so, Douglas?"

Douglas and I both shook our heads.

"So you see the problem here. We have to make a decision about what's best for your brother, you and I and Douglas. I already know what your mother and father are going to say. They're going to fight over custody of Bobby, even more ferociously, because he's all that's left; so I need to hear what someone else thinks—someone else who knows your Mom and Dad, and nobody knows them better than you and your brother. So what do you two think I should do? Charles? Douglas?"

Douglas and I looked at each other. I searched his face for a clue, even a hint, of what he was thinking. He shook his head slightly—a signal to be careful? Or that he didn't know, either?

"Well . . . first of all," I said slowly, "I want to go with Douglas." I looked to him for reassurance. He gave me a quick nod of okay, and I smiled tightly and blinked fast before any tears could come. I was surprised I'd said it, and even more surprised he'd agreed.

"What happens if Douglas chooses to go someplace you don't want to go?"

"I can't think of anyplace like that, Your Honor. I want to stay with my brother. We're family. We've always been together. I know how to live without my mom and without my dad. I've been doing that almost all my life. I don't know how to live without my brothers, and even though Douglas can be real weird sometimes, I still want to go with him."

"You're sure about that?"

"As sure as I can be."

"Hm. Well. I see." Judge Griffith mulled that over. "I could probably do that. As I said, I can grant Douglas acting custody over you, subject to the approval of the jurisdiction you end up in; in the absence of any other contesting relatives, they'd probably confirm it. Your problem is going to be—or rather, it'll be Doug's problem—supporting yourselves. I understand that you're looking for an indenture, Douglas?"

"Yes, ma'am."

"Mm. Be careful. Make sure you have an agent review the contract. But you should be able to get an indenture that covers Charles as well. He can take on a delayed indenture that doesn't kick in until he turns eighteen, and the two of you should be able to find a colony that can use a couple of fairly intelligent warm bodies. So it's doable, and I can sign off on it. But that still leaves the problem of your younger brother . . . ."

"Yeah, Stinky's a problem," I said. "But he's *our* problem. Douglas and I have spent more time taking care of him than Mom or Dad."

"Are you suggesting that you and Douglas also take custody of Bobby as well?"

When she put it that way . . . I had to hesitate. But Douglas didn't. He stepped forward. "Ma'am, I'm not saying it'll be easy. In fact, it'll probably be the hardest thing I've ever done. But I've been thinking hard about this—not just tonight, but for several days now. I think it'd be the best for Bobby. I think it'd be best for me and Charles too."

A DECISION

JUDGE GRIFFITH SIGHED. **SHE WAS** doing a lot of sighing tonight. She steepled her fingers in front of her mouth and thought for a moment. "You have your tickets?"

Mickey stood up then. "I have their tickets, Your Honor. And unless they've cancelled my contract, I am the agent of record for this family. I can guarantee delivery to Luna and a high probability of an acceptable contract. I have three possibilities already. We have insurance in place against failure to contract, so the family will not end up a drain on the resources of any starside facility."

"Fair enough. Is it my understanding that you are also emigrating, Mickey?"

"Yes, Aunt Georgia."

"I'm going to miss you, sweetheart. Is it your intention to accompany the Dingillian family?"

"Uh—" Mickey looked to Douglas, uncertain. Douglas . . . hesitated, then nodded. Okay, so that fight was over. "Yes, Your Honor."

"Are you willing to accept co-responsibility with Douglas Dingillian?"

"Uh—yes, I'm prepared to accept co-responsibility up to and including such time as I can guarantee financial security through an appropriate colonial contract, and for as long after that as the Dingillians are willing to accept my support."

"Mickey?" The Judge looked at him sternly. "You just met these folks—what is it? Two days, three days ago? Are you willing to take on this kind of commitment on such short notice—especially now, after you've seen them at their worst?"

"Aunt Georgia, I admit that there's a lot of dirtside crap going on.

But I think these are good people. And they wouldn't be in half the trouble they're in if it hadn't been for me. . . ."

"And your mom," Judge Griffith added.

Mickey shrugged in acquiescence of the point. "The thing is, I like them in spite of themselves. I owe them. I want to do it."

Judge Griffith cleared her throat gruffly. "Well, that sort of settles that. The younger generation has come of age. All that's left for us old broads is to find a nice warm grave and get someone to throw some dirt over us. Olivia, you did a good job on this boy. He has a conscience." To the rest of us, she said, "All right, I'm now prepared to hear arguments from the parents. I assume you are both going to protest a ruling of divorce here—?"

Both Mom and Dad stood up at the same time; they both said yes. In unison. It was the first time I'd ever seen them agree on anything. They looked at each other in surprise. Dad made a waving gesture at Mom. "You go first."

Mom didn't spare any words. If there's one thing Mom can be counted on for, she lets you know what she's thinking. "Is this the way justice up here works? Is your culture up here so morally bankrupt that you have to steal other people's children—?"

"That's the way, Mom," Douglas said. "Butter her up. Make her like you."

"Shut up, Douglas," Mom snapped at him. "I heard about your—misadventures. I can't tell you how disappointed in you I am."

"Then don't try," said Douglas.

"Douglas," said Judge Griffith. "It's your mother's turn. Sit down, please." To Mom, she said, "I assume you have an argument to present?"

Mom turned to Howard-The-Repugnant. "You're a lawyer! Do something!"

He shrugged, looked through his briefcase, pulled out a folded paper, and passed it to her.

"Huh? What's this?"

"My bill," he said. "The minute you walked in the door, you destroyed my case. Not being here was your best chance. As long as you were still groundside, I could make the argument that the children were being taken away without your opportunity to be present and have your side of the issue heard. It would have justified pushing the case into a Liaison Court, which handles mixed jurisdiction disputes. But now that you're here, this constitutes a fair hearing, and all I can do is restate what's already in the record. There might be a couple other things we could try, but the end result is going to be the same. And the judge has already made it clear she's not going to tolerate any delaying tactics. So there's nothing I can do here, except enjoy the show—and that's exactly what I am doing. Please pay that within thirty days." Howard leaned back in his chair, grimly satisfied. He looked almost human.

Olivia grinned over at him. "I may have misjudged your intelligence. You finally found a way to avoid losing a case—stay out of it. And present a bill anyway. My compliments, Counselor."

"Belay that noise, Olivia." This was punctuated with a rap of the gavel. I was beginning to wish I had a gavel of my own. It was a great way to get people to pay attention. I wondered how hard it was to become a lawyer. Probably not too hard, if Howard could be one. "Ms. Campbell, do you have anything else to say? Anything to justify awarding you custody, that is?"

"Your Honor, I already have custody. You have the case in front of you. The El Paso District Court awarded me custody of my children. These hearings are illegal. This is a kangaroo court. You have no authority over me or my children. I demand that you affirm the rulings of the groundside court."

"Thanks for the demonstration of how to put the tact into tactical, Ms. Campbell. But even if I liked you, you'd still be wrong. This hearing is *very* legal. I suggest you ask your attorney—I assume Howard is still acting as your representative, despite his apparent dereliction of responsibility—but ask him anyway. Ask him to explain the limits of groundside jurisdiction and the more far-reaching authority of starside courts. Because, up here, life is maintained at such great expense, we have to hold ourselves to a much higher standard of integrity than most folks from dirtside. What I am telling you is that the authority of this court is absolute in these matters. You are certainly free to take this case to the World Court, and I'll be disappointed in you if you don't, but once I make my ruling, it's going to be implemented immediately, and so far, I haven't heard anything from you that has given me reason to reconsider my intentions. In fact, the more you talk, the more you confirm my decision."

The woman next to Mom stood up. "Your Honor, may I speak?"

"Why not?" Judge Griffith sighed. "Everyone else is going to insist on having their say tonight. Your name is . . . ?"

"Bev Sykes, Your Honor. I think you can understand that my partner, Maggie, is justifiably upset about this situation. She came to San Francisco for a much-needed vacation; the next thing, she's in the biggest crisis of her life—"

"It is a crisis which she helped create, Ms. Sykes. No one is innocent here. Least of all you, if I read this history right."

"The point is, Your Honor, that what you're proposing to do is overturn a stable situation—"

"I've seen absolutely no evidence of stability in this situation, Ms. Sykes."

Mom spoke up again then. "Perhaps if you'd ever had children of your own, you'd understand—"

Oops.

Judge Griffith's face darkened. "I had two daughters of my own, Ms. Campbell. They died in the Line accident of '97. That's when I got this chair. Do either of you have anything useful to add?"

Mom and the other woman whispered together for a moment, then they both shook their heads and sat down. They looked very unhappy. I almost felt sorry for them, but I wasn't going to change my mind, and I didn't think Doug was going to either.

Judge Griffith looked to Dad. "Mr. Dingillian, you had something to say?"

Dad stood up. He took a breath. He seemed strangely calm. "Thank you, Your Honor. I want to apologize for my conduct in this whole affair. I made a serious error in judgment. I've hurt my children. I've made a lot of trouble for everybody. That I did so out of my love for my sons and my commitment to their well-being does not excuse my actions. I know that."

Judge Griffith was studying her watch. "Get on with it, please."

"Yes, Your Honor. The point is, whatever you decide, I'll still be the boys' father, and Margaret will still be their mother—regardless of how you assign custody, we have the right to spend time with our children. And if our children want to spend time with us, they should have that right as well."

"The Court is already taking that into consideration," Judge Griffith said, typing something into her clipboard.

"Well, that's my argument, Your Honor. If the children end up in a location so far removed that visitation is impractical to the point of being impossible, then those visitation rights are effectively denied."

Judge Griffith raised her eyebrow. "In view of the circumstances which forced this hearing, the court finds it profoundly ironic that you should be making that argument, Mr. Dingillian."

Mom snorted. Loudly. I knew that snort.

Dad remained nonplused. "Nevertheless, Your Honor—if it was wrong for me to consider denying my wife access to her children, and it was, I admit it, but if it was wrong for me to do so, then it is equally wrong for the court to allow a situation to occur where visitation is impossible."

"Now that's a good point," Judge Griffith said, gesturing with the gavel. "But it seems to me that if visitation with your children is important enough to you, it's your responsibility to make sure to keep yourself near to them. The problem in this family is that both you and your wife have been attempting to make visitation impossible for each other, either by legal means or by moving the children around. And the Court finds that behavior an intolerable state of affairs. Not because it is unfair to either of you, *but because it is unfair to the children.*

"You both claim that you are interested only in the well-being of your children, but you have both put enormous emotional burdens on them. Your children need a place to heal, a place to recover from their parents. Considering the abuses of the visitation process in this case, the Court is not inclined toward allowances for the needs of the parents. I won't rule out visitation rights, but I'm not going to make visitation rights as large a part of the final decision as it was downside. Anything else, Mr. Dingillian?"

Dad looked beaten. He shook his head and sat down.

"All right, then." Judge Griffith rapped her gavel. "Here's my ruling. It is the decision of this court that Douglas Dingillian is to be regarded in all rights and privileges as a legal adult. It is the further decision of this court that Charles Dingillian is granted a summary divorce from both of his parents and given to the care and custody of Douglas Dingillian, contingent on the co-responsibility of Mickey Partridge. Charles, this divorce is contingent on review by the legal authority of whatever jurisdiction you and your brother settle in. So choose your destination carefully."

"Yes, Your Honor."

"In the matter of Robert Dingillian, the court recognizes the long history of custody disputes in this case, and acknowledges the already established legal rights of both parents . . . and sets them aside. The welfare of the child always takes precedence. Because the parents of Robert Dingillian have not demonstrated, in the opinion of *this* Court, sufficient commitment to the child to put their own disputes aside, the Court is left with no alternative but to remove the child from the custody of the parents and place him in the care of his elder brother, Douglas. This is also contingent on the statement of co-responsibility from Mickey Partridge, and final review by the legal authorities of your ultimate destination. Mickey, I mean it, choose *carefully*. This concludes the business of this Court. And if there are no further objections, I declare this hearing adjourned—"

THE McGUFFIN

BUT **BEFORE SHE COULD RAP** her gavel on the table, Dad stood up. "Your Honor? Point of order? Um—may I ask for clarification, please?"

Judge Griffith hesitated, the gavel poised above the table. "Go ahead."

"My sons are free to use the tickets I purchased for them, if they wish to. Is that correct?"

"Your sons are free to choose their own destination. Yes, they can use the tickets you paid for. The Court has not terminated your access, only your custodial authority."

"I understand that, I'm just trying to get clear on where the line is drawn. Am I *also* free to use the ticket I purchased for myself?"

"Yes," said the judge. "You are."

Over on the other side of the room, I heard Mom gasp. "I can't believe this—"

Both Dad and the judge ignored her. Dad asked, "Even if it means traveling together with my sons? Your Honor, you do understand that if my sons use their tickets to go on to Luna, we'll be sharing the same cabin . . . ?"

"Mr. Dingillian, the Court has no objection to you traveling with your sons. You *are* entitled to visitation rights. But you no longer have any custodial authority over them. That's the limit of this ruling—"

"Oh, great!" said Mom. "We're right back where we started! He has no custodial rights, but he still ends up with the kids! What kind of a kangaroo court is this?" She turned to Hidalgo. "You said you could help me! This is the way you help people?!"

Hidalgo wasn't stupid. He didn't even try to calm her down. He was already pushing himself ponderously to his feet, raising his hand for attention. "Your Honor, there is one other matter left unresolved. If I may beg the Court's indulgence . . . ?"

"Just a moment, Dr. Hidalgo." Judge Griffith turned to Mom. She finally laid her gavel down. "Ms. Campbell, please understand, you have the exact same rights—or should I say, lack of rights. If you wish to travel with your children, you may do so as well. Under the same terms as your ex-husband."

"Oh, yeah, right! With what money?! I don't have a SuperNational credit card—I can't go to the moon!"

"Somebody paid for two tickets on the express shuttle . . ." Judge Griffith left the second half of that thought unsaid. Mom fumed and sputtered, but the judge was already moving on. "All right, Bolivar. You paid for two tickets to this circus—let's hear what you have to say." She glanced meaningfully at her watch.

"It is the matter of *Señor* Dingillian's financial status. If you will consult your own records, you will see that this man does not have the resources to have paid for even one ticket up the beanstalk, let alone four."

"So?"

"So if he is going to the outbeyond, the Financial Responsibility Act requires proof that he is leaving behind no significant debts."

Dad stood up. "Your Honor, there is documentation on file with the Emigration Authority to demonstrate that not only are all of my outstanding debts paid off, but that there is a fund in escrow to handle any future claims that may arise. Additionally, there is Emigration Insurance to cover any contingencies that exceed the funds in escrow."

Judge Griffith was sitting at her table with her hands folded in front of her chin again. She looked from one to the other, more amused than anything else. "Is there a point to all this?" she asked.

"With the Court's indulgence," Hidalgo said, "I would like, at this time, to present documentation that *Señor* Dingillian's trip has been financed by certain SuperNational interests, and that in return, he is functioning as a courier for them—"

"So what?" said the judge. "We have private couriers going up and down the Line every day. Many people finance their emigration that way. There's nothing illegal about it."

"Your Honor, may I please direct your attention to Section Four of the Line Authority Transportation Act? There are a number of restrictions on private courier service. It is illegal if the item being transferred is contraband or stolen property, or if the intent of private service is to avoid legal obligations, such as liens, claims, custody, or taxation. If a courier is suspected of carrying items in violation of Section Four, the

Line—that's you, Your Honor—has the authority to investigate and, if appropriate, require divestment of any and all packages."

"I see you've done your homework, Bollie. As usual. So what is it that Max Dingillian is carrying that you want to get your hands on so badly that you're willing to pay for two premium-class round-trip shuttle tickets?"

"Your Honor, it is not for myself that I act, it is on behalf of the—"

"I've heard the speech, Bollie. More than once. Just tell the Court what the McGuffin is."

"Your Honor, six days ago, Stellar-American Resources transferred an extremely large amount of money into a Canadian-Lunar transfer account. The account is a pipeline that may be accessed freely both on Earth and on Luna. It is commonly used for holding funds being moved off-world. Stellar-American Resources has three transfer accounts of their own, all bonded and monitored, which they normally use for off-world access. That they are suddenly using this account to transfer an extremely large resource suggests that they are attempting to avoid transfer taxes, as well as legal scrutiny. Not even the company's own stockholders are aware of this transfer—"

"But you are?" Judge Griffith noted with mild sarcasm.

"There are people who tell me things, Your Honor. Be that as it may, however the information comes to light, there is certainly enough to be suspicious about. And it is my solemn duty to call this to your attention. My people believe that *Señor* Dingillian is carrying one of three password-checks necessary to complete the transfer of funds. The other two may have already arrived on Luna."

"Just how much money are we talking about, Bolivar?"

Hidalgo pursed his lips and looked extremely uncomfortable. "It is over three trillion dollars, Your Honor. Perhaps as much as ten. The money came out of nine thousand different accounts that my people regularly watch, and at least ninety thousand more that we have not yet found a way to monitor. For this much money to move off of Earth so abruptly—"

Judge Griffith rapped her gavel. "The money flows, Bolivar. The fact that you don't like where it goes doesn't make the river a crime. This isn't a McGuffin at all. It's the stuff that dreams are made of."

"Your Honor, I respectfully request the Court to require *Señor* Dingillian to divulge the truth about what he is carrying. If it is a legal transfer, then I shall apologize profusely for taking up his time and the Court's. But if *Señor* Dingillian is carrying a check of such enormous size, I am certain that there are law enforcement and tax agencies both groundside and starside who will want to check that no laws are being broken by such a transfer." Hidalgo folded his hands across his paunch and waited.

Judge Griffith frowned. "I understand exactly what you're trying to do, Bollie. But what you're asking is generally beyond the reach of this Court. I can ask Mr. Dingillian to reveal what he is carrying, but absent any evidence of a crime, he isn't required to violate his own privacy. If there is no evidence of wrong-doing, I can take no action."

"I understand, Your Honor, but I believe it is in the interests of justice to compel such performance as is appropriate."

"Mm. Yes. Bollie, I know you—you always want the best justice money can buy. So be it." She turned to Dad. "What are you carrying, Max? You don't have to tell me, but if it'll get Bolivar Hidalgo off your back . . ."

Dad shook his head and spread his empty hands wide. "Your Honor. *I'm not* carrying anything. . . ."

The way he said it—with an unspoken *now* attached to the end of the sentence—was enough to raise Judge Griffith's eyebrows. "Have you already delivered it?"

"I have not delivered anything, Your Honor." Again, the same unfinished tone. If you didn't know Dad, you might not catch it, but if you were smart . . . like Judge Griffith, you could hear that what Dad *wasn't* saying was almost as important as what he *was* saying.

Judge Griffith hesitated. I could see she'd figured it out. But of course, being a judge, she'd probably learned how to figure out when people were telling the truth or not. And then, too, she might have had some game of her own working. . . .

"Well, then," she said. "If you're not carrying anything—this Court has no further business with you."

"Your Honor!" That was Hidalgo. "Ask him who paid for his tickets and what he had to do in return!"

She appeared to be mulling it over. I glanced over at Doug, he looked to the monkey in my lap, I shrugged and looked at the ceiling. Dad looked back and forth between us, carefully blank. Despite the judge's decision, Stinky was still asleep in Mom's lap, and I wondered if we were going to be able to get him away from her.

Judge Griffith unfolded her hands. "Dr. Hidalgo, I think you're asking me to go into an area that is beyond the scope of this session. I told you earlier that I would not get into any inquiries that did not bear directly on the custody of the Dingillian children. I'm not going fishing for you. While the matter you have raised is certainly an important one, we cannot pursue it here. If you wish, you can pursue this in another court." She started to pick up her gavel again—

Almost as soon as the judge had begun speaking, Hidalgo had nudged Howard, who began fumbling in his briefcase. Now, as Judge Griffith finished, Howard leapt to his feet. "Uh, not so fast, Your Honor, I have a warrant here—"

"And you're just serving it now?"

"I hadn't expected that it would be necessary."

"Pass it up."

Howard-The-Unkempt gave the paper to Judge Griffith's assistant, Joyce, who passed it to the judge. She unfolded the paper and studied it thoughtfully. She scratched her eyebrow with a fingernail while she read. "Well, this appears to be in order," she said finally. To the rest of the room, she announced, "This is a Line Authority search-and-seizure warrant for the property of Max Dingillian. I'll spare you all the whereases. You're accused of transporting contraband."

Dad stood up, "Your Honor, all I have are the clothes I'm wearing. If the court will provide me with something to wear, I'll be happy to give you these clothes."

"It's not that easy, Max. I'm authorized to detain you."

Dad shrugged. "Go ahead, Your Honor." He held out his wrists, as if awaiting handcuffs. "Take me away. I don't have anything—"

"Wait a minute," I said. I stood up, still holding the monkey. "Dad is telling the truth. He isn't carrying anything. I am. He gave it to me. I put it in the monkey."

Dad and Douglas both stared. "Charles—!"

I was already prying the back of the monkey open. I pulled out the bottommost memory bar and carried it over to Dad. "Here," I said. "Give this to the judge."

Dad looked at the memory bar, looked at me, looked at Olivia— she was carefully blank—then handed it to Joyce, who handed it to Judge Griffith, who turned it over in her hands, examining it. "You were paid to transport this?"

Dad looked to Olivia, looked back to the judge. "Yes, Your Honor. I was paid to transport that."

"Well then, the warrant is satisfied." Judge Griffith passed the memory bar to her assistant. "Joyce, seal that. It's not to be released to anyone." To Doctor Hidalgo, she said, "If it can be demonstrated that the intention of this warrant was to disrupt a lawful business enterprise, not only will I hold you in contempt, I will fine you for the full amount of damages. And you too, Howard. Let it be noted that this Court does not approve of the mischievous abuse of litigation."

"Your Honor," Howard-The-Illegitimate said, "we would like to request that the . . . uh, monkey be confiscated as well. In case there are other memory cards—"

"Nope. The monkey doesn't belong to Max Dingillian. It belongs to Robert Dingillian. Sorry, Howard." She raised her hands in mock helplessness.

He sputtered. "But the warrant—!"

"The warrant says nothing about the property of *Robert* Dingillian. And as he is no longer under the custodial authority of Max Dingillian, we cannot even use that umbrella. Hm, I see you forgot to add an *a priori* clause that would have allowed me to grant your request. You should be more careful when you draft these things, Howard. You left a loophole big enough to be an escape hatch. Given the wording of this document," she waved it at him, "this Court has no authority to seize the property of any other Dingillian. And I will not act beyond the authority of this document. If I did, the next judge up would have ample grounds to invalidate the warrant anyway. So consider that I'm doing you a favor. If you want the monkey, go get another warrant."

I couldn't help myself, I surreptitiously switched the monkey on— and whispered into its ear. It leapt down from my lap, ran over to Howard-The-Stupid, and gave him a double-chocolate, hot-fudge far-kleberry with whipped cream and a cherry on top. Plus a noise like an elephant fart. Then it came scurrying back to me. Howard looked like he was going to explode.

Keeping her face carefully blank, Judge Griffith picked up her gavel and rapped it once. "We're adjourned." She looked at her watch. "And just in time. You have an elevator to catch, Mickey. Get your butt in gear. They're holding the gate for you—"

GOOD-BYES

AND **THEN A LOT OF** stuff happened all at once. Dr. Hidalgo waddled over and stood in front of Dad. "You have been very lucky, *Señor* Dingillian. Very very lucky. I hope for your sake and your children's sake that your luck holds out."

Dad shook his head and laughed. "And you've been very stupid, Dr. Hidalgo. Very very stupid. You never figured it out, did you?"

Dr. Hidalgo raised an eyebrow. "Enlighten me?"

"You and your people—I was never carrying anything. I was a *decoy*. Do you really think they'd trust that much money to my care? Even I'm not that stupid. Whoever it was—and even I don't know for sure, you probably know more than me—they wanted you looking in the wrong place. So they hired me. And I guess it worked. While you were busy chasing me up the Line, you weren't hassling a whole bunch of other folks."

"That's an assumption on your part."

"Maybe so, maybe not. But I got my job done. Thanks again for dinner." Dad offered his hand.

Surprisingly, Dr. Hidalgo took it. He held Dad's hand in both of his. "You may yet need my help, *señor*. I do not think you know what you are playing with. You keep my card. You call me if your new friends don't work out. *Adios. Vaya con dios.*" And he turned and waddled over to confer with Howard-The-Unhappy.

Dad turned to look at me. And Douglas. We were whispering together. Dad must have seen the look on my face. And on Douglas' too. He said, *"What?"*

And I said to Douglas, "You tell him."

And Dad said, "Tell me what?"

So Douglas swallowed hard. "You sure, Charles?"

"Yes." I nodded.

Douglas turned to Dad. "We don't want you to come with us."

Dad looked confused. He looked from me to Douglas and back again. So I added, "Judge Griffith said we don't have to take you if we don't want to. Well . . . we don't want to."

Dad went pale. "Charles? Douglas? Are you sure—?"

"We have to go, Dad." Douglas hugged him quickly. "Maybe we'll see you on the moon. I hope so."

I went to Dad to hug him too, but I didn't say anything to him. He looked like he'd been stabbed—and was still waiting to fall down. He didn't hug me back, so I let go and followed Douglas over to where Mom was standing. She was holding Bobby, rocking him back and forth on her shoulder.

Joyce, the bailiff, followed at a respectful distance. Mom had picked up Bobby and was holding onto him as hard as she could. She glared over his shoulder at Douglas, and at Joyce too, and she held onto Bobby for the longest time, holding him, stroking his head, whispering into his ear, telling him over and over how much she loved him and how she was going to come and get him, not to worry—but at last, Douglas bent down to take him, and she let him slip out of her arms. Tears were running down her cheeks and I was starting to feel real bad about this whole thing. Doug bent his head to kiss her, but she just turned away.

So Douglas turned away from her and she was standing there by herself, just looking at me—and I didn't know what to say or do. She walked slowly over to where I was standing alone, and when she spoke it was like being dragged naked over nails. She just shook her head and asked, "Why, Charles—why?"

I shook my head helplessly. "I—I'm sorry, Mom. I didn't do it to hurt you."

"Was I really that bad a mother to you?"

"Mom, you're angry all the time—"

"Well, don't I have good reason to be? The way you treat me. The way your father treats me."

"Mom, this isn't about you—"

"Well, then *who* is it about—? Answer me that!"

"Mom, you don't listen! You don't *ever* listen—you're not listening now."

"Charles, I have a right to know. You're breaking up our family—"

"No, Mom. It was already broken. You and Dad broke it up a long time ago—"

"Is this really what you want—to hurt me like this?"

I wiped the tears from my cheeks. "Mom, what I want most"—it hurt to say it; my voice cracked—"what I want most is . . . to get away from you, right now. I can't stand it when you talk to me like this. It isn't *my* fault!"

"Go ahead, then! You're just like your father, you little bastard! I hope you're happy!" And then—she slapped my face! For an instant, I saw stars.

I didn't know what to do or say. I was too shocked. She hadn't ever hit me before. I couldn't believe it—everybody was staring at me—so I just turned to go—and then she was grabbing at me, crying, "Oh, God, Charles—I'm so sorry, I didn't mean to do that! Charles, please—wait! Wait! Charles!"

There was one thing she could have said that might have made me stop, and I was listening as hard as I could to hear her say it, and maybe she *was* saying it in her own way, but I was listening for the words, and she never said them. She never said the words. So I kept going.

And then Doug put an arm around my shoulders and I started sobbing as we followed Mickey to the hatch of the transfer pod. I looked back to see Dr. Hidalgo and that Sykes woman rushing to Mom's side, and then Doug steered me into the waiting pod and then the door closed and they were gone—

"So what happens now?" I asked, still wiping tears from my eyes.

"I have an idea," Doug answered, shouldering Bobby with one arm, and hugging me with the other. "Let's go to the moon."

BOUNCING
OFF
THE
MOON

for Jim and Betty and Mae Beth Glass,
with love

BOARDING

THERE'S THIS THING THAT DAD used to say, when things didn't work out. He would say, "Well, it seemed like a good idea at the time." I never knew if he was serious or if he was doing that deadpan-sarcastic thing he did.

The thing is, it usually *wasn't* a good idea at the time.

Like going to the moon. That was *his* good idea, not mine. Not Doug's or Bobby's either. But like all of his good ideas, it worked out backwards. We got to go, and he had to stay behind, still holding his ticket and wondering what happened—the last time I looked back, he had *that* look on his face. And *that* hurt.

We made it to the elevator with less than six minutes to spare. They were just about to give away our cabin to a worried-looking family waiting on standby. The dad looked upset and the mom started crying when we showed up. They wanted our cabin on the outbound car so desperately that the dad started waving a fistful of plastic dollars at us, offering to buy our reservation—we could name any price we wanted.

Doug hesitated. I could tell he was tempted, so was I—poverty does that to you—but Mickey just pushed him forward and said, "We don't need their money." So we ducked into the transfer pod and the hatch slammed shut behind us with the finality of a coffin lid.

This time, we were going in through the passenger side, and I knew what to expect, so the shift in pseudogravity as the pod whirled up to speed didn't bother me as much as it had before. I'd nearly thrown up when we'd transferred from the car that brought us up the orbital elevator to Geostationary.

Dad's good idea *this* time had involved smuggling something—or pretending to smuggle something so the real smugglers would go unnoticed—and in return, he'd get four tickets up the Line, but the only thing he was smuggling was *us*. He told us we were going on vacation, and it would have been a great vacation, except it wasn't *really* a vacation. The whole time, he was planning/hoping that we'd decide to go outbound with him to one of the colonies and not go back to Earth and Mom.

It would have worked if Mom hadn't found out. And if whatever it was that we were supposed to be smuggling hadn't been so important that some really powerful people were trying to track us, bribe us, threaten us, and have us detained by any means possible. It would have worked because after we thought about it, we *wanted* to go.

So we went. Without Dad.

Without Mom too. The guys in the black hats had shuttled her up. My cheek was still stinging from her last angry slap. It wasn't a great good-bye. And the hurt went a lot deeper than my cheek.

The hatch of the transfer pod opened and we were looking down a narrow corridor. "Come on, let's get to our cabin," Mickey said, giving me a gentle nudge on the shoulder. "The outbound trip is only six and a half hours. I think we should all try to get some sleep while we can."

"I'm not tired!" announced Stinky—he was only Bobby when he wasn't Stinky. "And I'm not going to bed without a hug from Mommy!"

"He's contradicting himself again," I said.

Douglas—also known as Weird—gave me a look, one of the looks he'd learned from Mom. "Charles, if this is going to work, I *need your help*." He turned back to Stinky, trying to shush him with logic. "Mommy isn't here, remember?"

We were halfway between nowhere and nothingness, on a cable strung between Ecuador and Whirlaway. There weren't many floors left to drop out from under us—and in a few minutes, we'd be dropping even further away at several thousand klicks per hour. Douglas was right. We were on our own.

"Give him to me," I said. In the one-third pseudogravity of the cabin, Stinky was only cumbersome, not heavy. He was still crying, but he reached for me—maybe I should have been flattered, but it seemed like an ominous moment. Was I going to be the Stinky-wrangler now?

Probably.

Douglas was already too much of an adult. He thought logic was sufficient. Well, so did I—but with Stinky, you have to use Stinky-logic, which isn't like adult logic at all. "Hey, kiddo," I said, maneuvering him into a hug. "I didn't get my hug either." He slid his arms around my neck in a near stranglehold. "Attaboy. We'll trade hugs. But no doggy-slurps—"

Even before I finished the sentence, Stinky was already licking my cheek—*slurp, slurp, slurp*—like an affectionate puppy. It was his favorite game, because I always said, "Yick, yick—bleccchhh! Dog germs!"

And that was all it took. Mommy was forgotten for the moment.

It was an old game—it went back to the time I'd been whining for a puppy, and Mom had said, "No, we can't afford a puppy—and besides, we've got the baby."

"Stinky isn't a puppy!" I answered back.

"*Yes, I am!*" Stinky had shouted at me. He didn't even know what a dog was then. "*Am too!*"

And then Weird had said, "Put him on a leash, take him for a walk, you'll never know the difference," and that was how the slurp game began. We didn't have a dog, we had Stinky. But I still would have preferred a dog. Most dogs drop dead by the time they're Stinky's age.

I tried to wipe my cheek, except the little monster had such a hammerlock on me that I couldn't break free. Time for the next move in the game: "No hickeys! No hickeys!" I shouted, and began tickling him unmercifully. He broke free in self-defense, shrieking in feigned panic. I grabbed him in a bear hug, ready to tickle him senseless, then remembered where we were and stopped before he peed in his pants. For a moment, we just stood where we were, him gasping for breath and me just holding on. Hugging.

I flopped backward onto the floor and pulled him down to my lap, curling him into my arms. "I miss Mommy too," I said, almost forgetting about my cheek. He wrapped his arms around me and hung on the way he'd done back in Arizona, in the big meteor crater.

Hard to believe that was only a week ago—Stinky had been acting up, as usual. He'd run away from us, down the path that led around and around, down to the bottom of the crater. He was playing "You can't catch me." Then he tripped and slid down the crater wall, and I'd thought we were going to lose him, but he only slid a little way down and then stopped. I was closest to him—I flattened myself on the ground and tried to get to him.

But when I looked down that steep wall, all the way to the bottom, I was paralyzed. But then Douglas grabbed me and Dad grabbed Douglas and I grabbed Stinky, and somehow we all pulled each other back up onto the narrow path and . . . for a moment, we hung there on the wall of forever, everyone holding on to each other—and Stinky had wrapped his arms around me like an octopus.

When it happened, I was angry—so angry, I couldn't even say how angry—but the whole thing also left me with a funny feeling about him.

About what it would have been like to lose him. And now that he was grabbing on to me the same way again, I began to realize what the feeling was. It was the same thing I felt. A grab for safety.

The difference was that Stinky had someone to hang on to. So did Douglas, now—he had Mickey. I was the only one who didn't. Which was sort of the way I wanted it, at least I thought I did. Except maybe I didn't.

The enormity of what we'd done was just starting to sink in. Mom and Dad's custody hearing had ended up in an emergency court session in front of Judge Griffith. She thought she could resolve it by asking me what I wanted.

And I—in my infinite wisdom—had simply blurted out, "I want a divorce." I mean, if Mom and Dad could divorce each other when things got ugly, why couldn't I divorce the both of them? All I'd wanted to do was make them stop fighting over us kids so much—

But Judge Griffith had taken my angry words at face value. She gave Douglas his independence; that was okay, he was almost eighteen; and then she gave me a divorce from Mom and Dad—and she assigned custody of both me and Stinky to Douglas.

So yeah. At the time, it seemed like a good idea.

But now—here we were, alone in our cabin, and I was sitting on the floor, holding Bobby in a daddy-hug because I couldn't think of anything else to do. I guess Bobby thought that I could take care of him—but I wasn't even sure that I could take care of myself.

I was torn between the feeling of not wanting him all over me and knowing that I didn't have much of a choice in the matter. As little brothers go, he'd never been much fun. And whose fault was that anyway? I'd replayed this conversation in my head plenty enough times. Douglas had told me more than once that it was my fault Stinky was the way he was. He said I'd resented him from the day he was born.

But that wasn't true. I'd resented him long before that.

It was Stinky's fault Mom and Dad got divorced. He'd been an accident, and Mom got angry at Dad, and Dad got angry at Mom, and then he moved out or she threw him out, it didn't matter—but if Stinky hadn't come along, we'd still be a family. Or maybe not. But at least things would have been quieter.

After he was born, Mom was different. She didn't have time for me anymore. She didn't have time for anything. Everything was about Stinky, and I had to help take care of him too, instead of just getting to be a kid. So of course, I was angry at him.

And now, both Mom *and* Dad were gone, and the only person poor Stinky had to hang on to was me. I suppose, if I thought about it, I didn't really hate him. I just wished he'd never been born.

BREAKING AWAY

TWO WEEKS AGO, WE'D BEEN in West El Paso—just another tube-town for "flow-through" families. Which is a polite way of saying "poor people."

The way it worked, they laid down a bunch of tubes, three or four meters in diameter, sealed the ends, and let people move in. They called it no-fab housing.

The best that can be said about living in a tube is that it's almost as good as not having anyplace to live at all.

El Paso gets sandstorms, *big* ones, and when the wind blows it turns the tubes into giant organ pipes. Everything vibrates. You get *really* deep bass, well below the range of audibility, four cycles a second—you don't hear it, you *feel* it. Only you don't really know what you're feeling, you just get this queasy feeling.

Burying the tubes doesn't help. They bury themselves anyway, as the sand settles around them. Tube-towns sink into the ground sometimes as fast as a meter a year. The Earth just sucks them in. So they just keep adding more and more tubes on top. Our tube-town was already five layers deep.

You're supposed to get air and sunlight through these big vertical chimneys—more tubes—only that creates another problem. The wind sweeps down one chimney and up the other, making the whole house whistle. The harmonics are dreadful.

And there isn't a whole lot anybody can do about it either, except leave. The Tube Authority told us we could move out anytime. There were plenty families on the waiting list to move in.

So when Dad said, "Let's go to the moon," well—it really did seem like a good idea at the time, once we realized he was serious. I don't think Douglas and Bobby believed him any more than I did, at least not at first, but hell—if it would get us out of the tubes, even for a couple of weeks, we were all for it. "Sure, Dad. Let's go to the moon." I figured Barringer Meteor Crater was as far as we were ever going to get, especially after Stinky's little misadventure.

But Dad was more than serious. He was actually *determined.* He'd already made plans. He'd hired himself out as a courier and gotten tickets up the beanstalk for all four of us. All we had to do was secure a bid from a colony and we'd be outbound on the next brightliner to the stars. Just one little problem. . . .

I mean, *other* than Mom.

There was this big storm, Hurricane Charles—and no, I did not appreciate the honor of having a hurricane named after me—it had pretty much clobbered Terminus City at the bottom of the beanstalk, so all groundside traffic was shut down, no one knew for how long. So we couldn't go back, even if we wanted to—which we didn't—because while we were all fighting with each other in Judge Griffith's courtroom, the United Nations declared a Global Health Emergency.

That was the *other* reason why Dad wanted to get off the planet so badly. He'd figured it out, just from watching the news; it wasn't hard, but most people weren't paying attention to that stuff. By the time most people knew, the plagues were already out of control.

While we were boarding the first elevator up the beanstalk, the Centers for Disease Control was announcing—*admitting*—that yes, the numbers did suggest the possibility that maybe, yes, we could be seeing—but there's really no need for anyone to panic, if we all take proper precautions—the first stages of a full-blown pandemic—um, yes, on *three continents,* but all this speculation about a global population crash is dangerous and premature—

And about twenty seconds after that, the international stock market imploded. More than a hundred trillion dollars disappeared into the bit bucket. Evaporated instantly. So even if there wasn't any real danger, there wasn't any money anymore to deal with it. And that *was* a real danger. Because everything was shutting down. And if that wasn't enough bad news, a woman in southern Oregon said that giant worms had eaten her horse.

They used to call this kind of mess a polycrisis. And everybody just shrugged and went on with business. Only this one was more than just another cascade of disasters, it was an avalanche of global collapse. They were calling it a meltdown.

But we were nearly forty thousand kilometers away, and it was all just pictures on a screen. It couldn't touch us anymore. I didn't know how Douglas and Mickey felt about the news, but the Earth seemed so far away now it didn't matter anymore. Maybe that was the wrong way to feel, but that's what I felt anyway.

A departure bell chimed and our elevator dropped away from Geostationary. We were outward bound. Every second that passed, the Earth fell even farther behind us. *Above* us.

Everything from Geostationary is *down*—down to Earth or down to Farpoint—because Geostationary is at the gravitational center of the Line. It's where the effects of Earth's gravity on the Line are exactly balanced by the tension of Whirlaway rock at the other end. So whichever way you go, dirtside or starside, you're going *down*.

Our tickets were paid for all the way to Asimov Station on the moon, two and a half days away. All we had to do was enjoy the ride as best we could—

—and try not to think about the agents of whatever SuperNational it was who still believed that Dad had hidden something inside Stinky's programmable monkey and would probably try to intercept us to get it away from us, even though there was nothing in it except a couple of bars of extra memory, which were just a decoy anyway because someone else was smuggling the real McGuffin off the planet and out to wherever. I was hoping it was all the missing money, and that someone had made a mistake, and we really had it instead of whoever was supposed to—but Doug said it didn't work that way, the best anyone could be carrying would be the transfer codes, so never mind.

But . . . it was past midnight, and if anyone was really chasing us, they couldn't get to us until we got to the moon. And there was nothing we could do either until we got there. We'd been running for nearly twelve hours already, and we were all exhausted. So even though I could think of at least six arguments we should have been having, what we did instead was crawl into bed. Mickey and Douglas bounced themselves into one bed. Stinky and I flopped over backwards into the other, with the intention of sleeping most of the way out to Farpoint Station.

The trip up to Geostationary takes twenty-four hours. The trip *out* to Whirlaway takes only six and a half. This is partly because you travel faster on the outward side, but mostly because the outward side of the Line isn't as long. Instead, there's a huge ballast rock the size of Manhattan at the far end. It's called Whirlaway, and inside it is Farpoint Station.

But we wouldn't be going even that far. The thing about the Line is that it's not just an elevator, it's also a sling.

Tie a rock to a string, whirl it around your head. That's how the Line works. If you let go of the string, it flies off in whatever direction it was headed when you let go. A spaceship can fly off the end of the Line and get enough boost to go to the moon or Mars or anywhere else, using almost no fuel at all except for course corrections along the way. Jarles "Free Fall" Ferris, pilot of the first transport to leave Whirlaway for Mars, was supposed to have said, "Well, the old man was wrong. There *is* such a thing as a free launch."

But depending on where you're going, there are only certain times of the day when you can launch a ship from the Line. Otherwise you have to wait twenty-four hours, give or take a smidge for precession, for the next launch window.

Actually, you can launch from any point on the Line, depending on where you want to go. If you launch below the flyaway point—also called the gravitational horizon—you become a satellite of the Earth, because anything below flyaway doesn't have enough "delta vee" to escape Earth's gravity; the sling doesn't give you enough velocity to break free. But above the flyaway point, you get flung far enough and fast enough that you go up and over the lip of Earth's gravity well, and then you just keep on going. The farther out on the Line you get, the faster you leave.

For some places, like L4 and L5, you don't want a lot of speed, because then you have to spend a lot of fuel burning it off. Douglas knows all about this stuff. He says that trajectory is the biggest part of the problem. How fast will you be going when you get where you're going? If you're catching up to your destination, you won't need as much fuel to match its speed as if you're intercepting it head-on, because then you have to burn off speed in one direction and build it up in the other. So there are a lot of advantages to slow launches—especially for cargo, which mostly doesn't care, because if all you're doing is feeding a pipeline, nobody really cares how long the pipe is, as long as the flow is steady.

Douglas had tried to explain it all to Stinky, more than once, but Stinky never really got it. He kept asking what held up the rock and why didn't it fall back down on Ecuador? Finally, Douglas just gave up and told him that the Whirlaway rock was hanging down off the south pole and we were going down to it. I think it made his head hurt to say that; he has this thing about scientific accuracy, and that's part of what makes him Weird—with a capital *W*.

I hadn't paid any attention at all to Doug's lectures, but it sank in anyway, by osmosis. I didn't think it mattered because we were going all the way to the end, to Farpoint Station, because that would give us the most flyaway speed and get us to Luna faster than any other transit.

At least that's what we thought at the time.

RUDE AWAKENINGS

SOMEBODY WAS SHAKING ME AWAKE. It was Douglas. "Come on, Chigger. We've gotta go. *Now.*"

"Huh? What?"

"Don't ask questions, we don't have time."

I sat up, rubbing the sleep from my eyes. "What time is it?"

Douglas pulled me to my feet and pushed me toward Mickey, who steered me toward—there was *someone else* in the cabin?—he was tall and skinny and gangly. I blinked awake. It was Alexei Krislov, the Lunar-Russian madman, the money-surfer who'd tried to help us elude the Black Hats on Geostationary. "Huh? How did you get here?" I blinked in confusion. He was wearing a dripping wetsuit. Was I still dreaming?

"Shh," he said, finger to his lips. "Later."

Douglas scooped up the still-sleeping Bobby and Mickey grabbed the rest of our meager luggage, hanging it off himself like saddlebags. When he reached for the monkey, it jabbered away from him and leapt into my arms. After that incident on One-Hour, where the monkey had led me on a wild breathless chase, I'd programmed it to home toward me whenever Bobby wasn't playing with it. I'd told it I was the Prime Authority.

Alexei opened the cabin door, peeked both ways—there was no one there—then led us aft toward the cargo section of the car. Actually, it was the bottom of the car, but the car was a cylinder rotating to generate pseudogravity, so the bottom was the aft. I was too groggy to pay much attention to what we were doing, I was still annoyed at being dragged out of bed. I looked at my watch. It was two-thirty in the morning. What the hell? We were still four hours away from Farpoint.

Alexei pushed us into the aft transfer pod, and we all grabbed hand-holds. Pseudogravity faded away as the transfer pod stopped spinning in sync with the passenger cabin. Now we were in free fall again. I know that lots of people think free fall is fun. I'm not one of them. It makes me queasy, and it's hard to control where you're moving.

Alexei opened the door on the other side and pushed us quickly into the cargo bay. I felt like one of those big balloons they use in the Thanksgiving Day parade. We floated and bounced through tight spaces filled with crates and tubes and tanks. The walls were all lined with orange webbing. Alexei led us through two or three more hatches, I lost count, and finally brought us to the last car in the train. It was cramped and cold and smelled funny. He jammed us into whatever spaces he could, then went back to seal the hatch; he did some stuff at the wall panel, and came swimming back to us, pushing blankets ahead of him. "Bundle warm. Is a little like Russian winter here, *da?*"

The blankets didn't look very warm; they were thin papery things, but Alexei showed us how to work them. They were big Mylar ponchos; you put your head through the hole, pulled the elastic hood up over your head, and then zipped up the sides, leaving just enough gap to stick your hands out if you needed to. We looked like we were all plastic-wrapped, but as soon as I turned the blanket on, it turned reflective and I started feeling a lot better. Pretty soon, I was all warm and toasty and ready to go back to sleep—only I wanted to go back to the bed we'd already paid for.

Mickey and Douglas were still sorting themselves out, finding corners to anchor our bags, and stuff like that. Douglas was bundling up Stinky, who still hadn't awakened. That's one good thing about low-gee. You sleep better.

I looked to Mickey. "What's going on?"

Alexei bounced over. "Is Luna you want to go, yes? Krislov will get you there. I promise. The elevators are not safe. Not for you. So I come to get you, *da*. I swim the whole way." He slapped his belly, indicating the wetsuit. He started to peel off the harness, which held his scuba gear. "I take free ride in the ballast tank. Nobody knows I am here. My people book for cabins to Luna. We all get bumped for Mister Fatwallets. No problem. We still go home." Grinning proudly, he tucked his Self-Contained Universal Breathing Apparatus into the orange webbing on the wall.

Mickey finished what he was doing and floated down—or was it up?—to drift next to Douglas. He angled himself into the same general orientation and looked across at Alexei. "All of you? You're *all* leaving? All the Loonies?"

Alexei looked grim. "As fast as we can, *gospodin*. Is very bad, all over. Worse than you imagine. Worse than you *can* imagine. But no problem." He reached over and squeezed Mickey's shoulder. "Alexei will take care of you. What you told me was very useful, *da*. I looked, I saw. I made calls. I have clients who worry. I solve their problems. I move their money from here to there, I make money moving it. I move a lot of money now, I make a lot. What you told me, Mickey—I am very rich now. I was rich before, but now I am very very rich. Believe it. Before they shut down money wires, you have no idea how much dollars and euros this clever Lunatic has dry-cleaned. And with money wires shut down now, Alexei cannot send the money on, so Alexei takes care of it. A very great deal of it. I cannot count all the zeroes. And I keep the interest too. But shutting down the flow of money will not keep it on Earth, no. Money is like water. It goes where it wants to. And if there is not a way, it makes a way." He tapped his chest. "I am the way. I find the way. I deliver in person, if necessary. Do you know how much money I am worth because of you? Never mind, you cannot afford to ask."

Krislov grinned. "I tell you this, you are worth almost as much. Remember? I make promise to you? I keep that promise. I flow the money through dummy companies. I cannot hold all companies in my name, so I put some of them in your names. All your names—even the monkey. You are all technically very very rich. At any moment, there could be billions of techno-dollars flowing through your accounts, around and around and around—we keep the money going, they can't find it. They shut the wires down, the money is supposed to stop. But it doesn't. It leaks. Every beam of light is a leak."

I interrupted with a yawn. "Yeah, but—*why did you have to wake us up?*"

"Because, while I am floating in ballast, I am still on phone. I am coordinating, yes? *No*. The wires are shut down, remember? But I listen to Line chatter. Why? Because I am nosy, *da*? Yes, I am—but also because in my business, it is a good idea to listen. So I listen to Line chatter. And I hear. What do I hear?" He opened his palms in a free-fall shrug. "I hear about paladins. Do you know what paladins are, Charles?"

I shook my head.

"Bounty hunters. Freelance marshals. They specialize in extradition. They track you down, they catch you, they bring you back where you don't want to go. This is why I ride in ballast. I always make my own travel plans. Is much safer, because suddenly—I can't imagine why, can you?—people at Geostationary want to talk to Alexei. About business?

Probably, but maybe I don't want to talk about business. Certainly not *my* business. So after I deliver you to passenger cabin, I go to cargo bay. As soon as car is on its way, I think we are all safe, but I am wrong. I listen to Line chatter, what do I hear? I hear about paladins at Farpoint waiting for cars to arrive. Maybe they are looking for me? I am disappointed. Only a little. Mostly they are looking for dingalings. Four dingalings and a monkey. Award money is substantial. You are very valuable to somebody, Douglas and Charles and little stinking one. And Mickey too.

"So, I float in tank, I think—I think I cannot let them catch Dingillians. Why? Because some of my companies are in your names and until I can get where I can rearrange the money-flow, I do not want you in that pipeline. Also because I owe you. So, I think—and *da*, I can do it. I come and get you. I wake Mickey and Douglas. They grab you and Stinky. We all come back here. We bundle up warm."

"But—so what?" I asked. "If we're not in our cabin, they'll search the rest of the cars. They'll still catch us."

"I don't think so," Alexei laughed. Something went *thump* just outside the cargo bay. "Because we are getting off here."

FALLING

THEN SOMETHING ELSE WENT CLANK and *thunk* and finally *bumpf.*
Alexei held up a hand for silence, as if he were counting off something
in his head. "Wait—*da!*" He gestured excitedly. "Feel that?"

"No—what?" It sort of felt like we were moving sideways. It was
hard to tell in microgravity.

"We are off of track. Swinging around into launch bay."

"Launch bay—?"

"Not to worry, little frightened one. Is not the first time a Lunatic
has done this. Is first time that *Alexei Krislov* has done this, yes—but
is because this is first time I have need to."

"Do what—?" I demanded. Even Douglas looked worried.

Something outside the car made a noise that sounded like *unclank*—
and then everything was abruptly silent. All the background noises of
the Line and the elevator car were gone. The effect was *terrifying.* I'd
never heard so much silence in my life before.

"We are on our way to moon," Alexei said. "We cheat the bounty
marshals. We ride with cargo. In four hours, elevator arrives at Whirlaway. Marshals show warrants, they go to cabin, they open door—but
Dingillian family is nowhere, *da? Da.*"

A horrible cold feeling was creeping up my spine. "Where are we?"
I demanded. "What did you do?"

"We have jumped off Line. We go to moon. We ride with cargo."

"We're off the Line—?"

"Da."

The cold feeling turned into a churning one. *"Douglas—!"* I wailed.
The emptiness outside the walls pressed in on me like a nightmare.

I couldn't escape. It was even worse because there were no windows! It was down in all directions—we were falling into the dark!

I started flailing in panic—*"I don't want to do this! We've gotta go back. Make him take us back! I can't do this, Douglas! We've gotta go back—"*

Douglas grabbed me, held me tight in the same kind of bear hug that I always used on Stinky. He pushed me up against something, a tank or a tube, and anchored himself on the webbing to hold us both steady. "Chigger—don't go crazy on me!"

"I can't do this, Douglas. I can't!" I started blubbering. "I'm scared! There's nothing to hold on to out here!"

"Hold on to me—just hold on. I'm right here." He held me tight in one arm, his face close to mine. He touched my face with his free hand. "Look at me, Charles. I'm just as scared as you. But we're not going to die. Nothing bad is going to happen to us. I've got you right here. And you've got me. We've got air, we've got water. We'll be three days getting there—"

"No, Doug, please—" I started to come apart. "I can't do this, not for three days. There's gotta be a way to get back—"

"Charles, you know better than that. *There isn't any way back.* The pod has been flung off the Line. We're going to the moon. There's no way to stop it. There's no way to turn it around."

"I can't, I can't—I can't do this!"

"Yes, you can. Listen to me. Look at me. We're very comfortable here. It's just a few days. We have air, we have water, we have food, we'll keep warm. You've got your music. It'll be just like Armstrong and Borman and Collins. We can pretend we're in an Apollo capsule. Like pioneers."

"An Apollo capsule? Like Lovell and—and—? Whatever their names were?"

"Swigert and Haise." That was Douglas. Even in the middle of a crisis, he had to be accurate. "We can do this, Charles. We have to. We're all we have. And Stinky needs you to be brave for him. I can't do it. He listens to you, not me."

In my head I knew he was right, but that didn't stop me from being so scared I couldn't speak. My helplessness just came bubbling out. Douglas held on to me and let me sob like a baby into his shoulder. I was so afraid. It was *everything.* Mom and her slap. Dad and his lies. Douglas and Mickey. Stinky. Not knowing where we were going. Everything out of control. It had been bad enough being stuck on a high-tension line, caught between everyone and everything—now my worst fear of all had just come true. We were helplessly falling forever.

We were a million klicks from nowhere and getting farther away every second.

So I held on to Douglas and cried, because he was all there was to hang on to—even though he was falling just as fast and just as far as I was.

But you can only cry for so long . . . and then after that, it's boring. Even worse, it's silly. . . .

I sniffed and wiped my nose unashamedly on Doug's shoulder.

He backed off a bit so he could look me in the eye. "Are you all right?"

"No," I admitted.

"Can you hold it together?"

"I don't know."

"Because I don't want to have to sedate you."

"Like Stinky?"

"Yeah," he admitted. "And I hated doing it."

I didn't answer. I could see the logic of it. Who needs an hysterical eight-year-old? Especially if you've already got a crazy thirteen-year-old?

He asked again, even more serious this time. "Chigger—can you hold it together?"

"I'll try." I was thinking about the tranquilizer. It might not be such a bad idea after all. But if I was going to die, I wanted to be awake for it. And wasn't that a stupid thought? Wouldn't it be better to be asleep, so you wouldn't know when it happened?

"Listen—" His voice got very quiet, very serious. "All we have is each other."

"Yeah, I know."

For a moment, we just studied each other. He was wondering if I could be trusted—and I was wondering the same thing. I needed him to be strong for me, and he needed me to be strong for Bobby. I didn't know if I could do it. I'd spent so many years shutting them out I didn't know how to let them back in. I didn't know what to say. And even if I did, I didn't have any words—

Finally, I blurted, "I don't have anything to hang on to."

"Nobody does," he said. "Ever." Like that was supposed to reassure me. The funny thing was, it sort of did.

I let go of him. "I think I'll be okay now."

"You're sure?"

I was starting to feel embarrassed. "Yeah," I said, and pushed past him back to the others. Mickey and Alexei looked at me with concerned eyes. "I'm fine," I said. "I just have this—fear of cramped spaces. And heights. And falling. And the dark. . . ."

"Wow," said Alexei. "Is triple whammy. Not a good combination for space travel, *da?*"

Mickey gave him a shut-up-stupid look, then reached over and put his hand on my shoulder, ostensibly to steady me, but he was slow in taking his hand away, and I knew he meant it as moral support too. Douglas settled in next to him, and the two exchanged grown-up glances; Mickey's had a question mark, Douglas's had a reassuring period.

Mickey's look to Alexei hadn't worked. Alexei kept talking. "I don't understand this fear," he said. "Where I grow up, you fall slow, you have time to turn yourself so you land on your feet. You bounce, you don't hurt yourself. So why be afraid?"

Douglas said bluntly, "Try it in Earth gravity sometime."

"Earth?" He made a face, shook his head. "I do not think anyone will go to Earth for a long time. I certainly will not. I have Luna muscles, Luna bones. I have no desire to be toothpick-man on planet of crazy dirtsiders. You haven't heard latest news, have you? Ecuador has nationalized the Line. Armed troops have seized Terminus."

Mickey didn't look as surprised as I thought he would. "How'd they get access?"

"According to Line chatter, hurricane relief teams came in to use Terminus as a base. Troops came in with teams, to help prevent looting—but then they started arresting Line personnel. The situation is still . . . how you say, very fluid? Traffic is running again, but most cars up are carrying troops. They have already seized One-Hour. Maybe there will be fighting at Geostationary. The U.N. is in uproar, of course—"

Mickey looked worried and upset. His mom was still at Geostationary.

Alexei was still talking. "We are lucky to get away. Who knows what will happen next?" He gestured dramatically. "But one thing I am sure, Luna will finally prove what I have been saying all along—Luna doesn't need Earth anymore. We are self-sufficient. We will be new center of human consciousness. Not Earth."

Douglas and Mickey exchanged another glance. This time, Douglas had the question mark. Mickey answered, "Yes, Alexei is militant in his Lunacy."

Alexei didn't bristle; he wore his madness like a badge. "The laugh is on you, *Mikhail.* If not for my paranoid Lunacy"—he tapped his head with his fingertips—"you would be in custody very shortly. In another four hours. At the end of the line, how you say, literally. And whose custody would you be in? Up for the highest bidder, I think. And if we are all at war, who knows? Bad accidents happen in war. No, my Lunacy is saving your life. Again. No, no, you can thank me later. The money I have made today is all the gratitude I need."

FLATING

ALEXEI SETTLED US AT THE far end of the pod, in the little bit of space between the cargo containers and the hull. He tucked us and our gear into the orange webbing on the aft bulkhead, spacing us around so that our mutual center of gravity was congruent to the central axis of the pod.

If we wanted to go anywhere in the pod, we'd have to squeeze around pipes and cables and supporting rods—and big green glops of hardened foam that looked like industrial-strength boogers. But there was no place to go anyway, so we just stayed where we were, wrapped in our plastic blankets and looking at the ominous round wall of cargo containers in front of us. It was like being a bug at the bottom of a piston.

The crates were all big wedge-shaped things, four to a circle, each anchored firmly in place by plastic clamps and foam boogers. Mickey explained that the thick foam pads were how the cargo engineers kept the containers from breaking loose and rattling around in transit. I didn't see how the crates would have much chance to rattle or break loose; we would be in free fall the whole way, wouldn't we? But there was a lot I didn't understand.

"The accommodations aren't pretty," Mickey admitted, "but we won't be uncomfortable. Cargo pods are designed for supercargo. Sometimes Line engineers have to ride with supplies, so there's mandated life support for at least five people at a time."

Alexei grinned. "Is very convenient, no?" He showed us the arrangements. "See those blue tanks all around? They hold water. Many liters. Microdiaphragm pumps move it around for balance. Water is very convenient that way. Green tanks have oxygen. Brown cabinets hold food—well, MREs."

"MREs?"

"Meals Ready to Eat. Three lies in as many words, no? Be sure to drink much water. MREs make lumps like concrete in bowel. With no gravity, lumps get even harder. Very much pain. Learn the hard way, yes? Very hard. That is the problem. Too hard even to work out with pencil. Not to worry—if you don't like MRE, you are not hungry enough. Starvation is not as painful, but takes too much longer."

He pointed toward the other end of the pod—I thought of it as the front, because that was where we'd entered. "Use that end for bathroom. Use plastic bags, like this? See. Put waste in yellow containers with biohazard symbol. Be very careful. Is possible to make very bad stink in here. Very unpleasant. See those little fans everywhere to keep air moving? They don't make stink go away; only spread it around equally. Don't worry, I teach you how to be careful. Any questions?"

Mickey and Douglas seemed to be okay with the arrangements, and I figured I'd learn as we went along—and we'd all take turns trying to explain it to Stinky when he woke up. Maybe we could keep him from wetting or soiling himself for three days.

But there was something else that was bothering me. "Um—"

"What?" That was Douglas.

"You agreed to this?"

"Mickey and I did, yes."

Mickey said, "We didn't have a lot of time to talk about it, Charles. We had fifteen minutes to decide before the capsule was launched."

"You took Alexei's word for it that there were marshals waiting for us—?"

"Alexei might be a lunatic, but he's an honest one." Mickey held up a headset. "You want to hear the playback? You want to listen to the Line chatter?"

I did, but that wasn't the question. "But the marshals will figure it out, won't they? When the elevator arrives at Farpoint and we're not in the cabin, they'll just phone ahead to Luna. There are marshals on Luna, aren't there? They'll just catch us in the cargo pod."

Alexei nodded. "Very good, Charles. But Luna is not Line. Very much not. On Line, you are always known. Always under camera eye. Not on moon. I will get you down safely, and you will see. Things disappear very easily. Luna is beautiful that way. You will love moon. Especially fresh food. Is big promise. I am hungry already, thinking of salad. Sweet corn, ripe tomatoes, fresh peas . . ."

Maybe it was me, maybe it was the lack of sleep, but everything was happening just too fast here.

"Excuse me—? Did I miss something? This is a cargo pod, isn't it? They know where we're going to land, don't they?"

"No," said Alexei. "They know where we're *supposed* to land."

I didn't like the sound of that. Even before I asked the next question, I knew the answer was only going to make things worse.

Alexei said, "Now you want to know *where* we will land, don't you?"

"Uh—okay, where?"

Alexei grinned through his scraggly beard. "We will come down where they can't go. Not easily. Very bad area. The maps are not accurate. Not the official ones. From there we go to land of tall mountains and deep ice mines. Is very beautiful. A little dangerous. But not too much—not to worry. You will like. By the time they get to cargo pod, we will all be somewhere else."

"But they can track us, can't they? As soon as they figure out we're in one of the cargo pods, they'll—"

Alexei's PITA* beeped; he glanced at his wrist. "Ah, there it is now. Time for first orbital correction. Everybody brace yourselves. Hang on to the webbing. This won't be too bad." Mickey reached over and grabbed the still-sleeping Stinky.

"Is just a little one—" Alexei started to say, but he was abruptly interrupted by a deep-throated rumble that rattled the whole cabin like an El Paso windstorm. It was loud and bumpy, and we were all shoved sideways up against the hull so hard it was almost impossible to breathe. It felt like we were hanging upside down in a cement mixer. I wanted to scream—but didn't have the air for it. And just when I was making up my mind that I was going to scream anyway, it stopped, and that spooky eternal silence closed in again.

"Is that it?" Douglas asked.

"Oh, no," said Alexei. "We have maybe fourteen or fifteen more. All the way out." He looked back over to me. "What was question again, Charles? That they will track us? Yes, they will. That is the point of the course changes."

"Fourteen or fifteen more? All like *that*—?"

"It's done with solid-fuel chips, Chigger," Douglas started to explain. "They burn unevenly and that rattles everything—"

"*I know how they burn!*" I almost said a whole bunch of other stuff too, except I was too busy concentrating on my next breath. "And why

---

*Personal Information Telecommunications Assistant.

so many course corrections anyway? Can't they aim this thing—?" I looked to Alexei.

"Not course corrections. Course *changes*. Is very precisely aimed," Alexei said, "and we are making serious alteration in trajectory. Is not unheard of. Sometimes cargo gets preempted from one location to another."

"But they're still tracking us, aren't they?" Douglas asked. "Chigger's right. This thing broadcasts a locater signal—they'll know where we are as soon as they figure it out, won't they?"

"Eventually, yes, they'll figure it out. The key word is *eventually*. So our job is to make eventually later than sooner." Alexei continued proudly. "First, this is not only pod to launch. Do you remember five others? All of those pods have been preempted too. Some rich new Luna company bought them in transit—I cannot imagine who, can you? All the pods have been retargeted for different places. Whoever tracks pods thinking we are in one of them will have to send marshals to six different landing sites, all of them difficult, except two."

"Oh," Douglas said. "And—?"

"And?" Alexei looked puzzled.

"You said *first*, as if there was a second."

"Oh. Yes, well *second* is much more subtle. This is why we have fourteen course changes on each pod. So that no one who is tracking can predict final orbit and landing site until we are already on track. All those changes—we will look like we can land anywhere on Luna. The last burn will not happen until we are on final approach, and that will bounce us off the screens for many long minutes. Whoever tracks will have to spend long minutes projecting—guessing probable touchdown sites. Your lunatic Russian friend is very clever, yes?"

"Yes, very clever," agreed Mickey. He'd been very quiet up to this moment. Now his tone of voice had gone all strange, and he asked, "Just where *are* you bringing us down?"

Alexei grinned. "This is cleverest part. I show you. We started out in Earth equatorial plane, yes? Each of our course changes pushes us more and more up. We go toward north pole of moon—they think we are aiming for North Heinlein, approach pattern is perfect for that—but no, as we come into Lunar orbit, we go three times around and make extra burns. Last change puts us in crazy-mouse orbit. You know crazy-mouse orbit? Near polar, but not quite; elliptical with lots of wibble-wobble. Great fun. We can come down anywhere we want from crazy-mouse, but no one knows where until last minute. Other pods do same thing too, we make them all crazy."

"But what do *we* do?" Mickey asked.

"We will be in crazy-mouse just long enough for people tracking us to say, 'Oh, shit.' We loop *over* top of moon, come down around farside, aim for ground, brake very suddenly, and bounce down in southern hemisphere."

"*Bounce* down . . . ?" I asked.

"Yes, is very easy. Great fun. You will laugh much. Like rollering coaster." And then he looked honestly puzzled. "Do you not know how these things work?"

I looked to Douglas, accusingly. He had that constipated weasel expression—the one that said *no, I didn't tell you the worst of it.*

CHANGES

I PULLED MYSELF OUT OF the pocket of the orange webbing that Alexei had stuffed me into. I grabbed Douglas by the leg and pulled him down away from Mickey and Alexei, so I could talk to him privately. If I'd been scared before, now I was beyond scared. There wasn't a word for it. I couldn't believe I was still rational. I should have been gibbering.

Douglas's first words were, "I didn't know myself, Chigger, I didn't have time to ask. I'm sorry—but we still would have had to come this way. Think about it."

"I have been!" I lowered my voice so he wouldn't hear the sob in my throat. I was terrified. "This is *real* stupid, Douglas."

"Yeah, I know—but we *didn't* have any choice."

"We could get *killed*."

"I don't think so. Mickey isn't stupid. And Alexei—"

"Alexei's a lunatic who doesn't have enough sense to be afraid of gravity. Why didn't we just stay on the elevator and deal with the marshals at Farpoint? We didn't do anything wrong. They can't arrest us."

Douglas shook his head. "Chigger, you've already seen how these people work. They throw lawyers at you. And they keep throwing lawyers until one of them finds something that sticks. And even if they can't find anything, they still keep you stuck in the courtroom. Either way, you're stopped, which is all they want to do anyway—stop us long enough to get their hands on the monkey."

"So why don't we just give it to them? We didn't make the deal to smuggle it. Dad did. We don't even know who's supposed to collect it on the other end. Or where the other end is. And besides, there isn't anything in it anyway—just a couple of bars of industrial memory, filled with decoy code."

"We don't know that. We don't know what's in it. Maybe it's the real stuff. Maybe they lied to Dad too—"

"Who?"

"Whoever. I don't know. But you heard what Dad said to fat *Señor* Doctor Hidalgo. We don't sell what doesn't belong to us. Maybe he suspected something."

"Oh, great. So that means if there really is something in the monkey, then we could be arrested for smuggling it—?"

"Yeah. Probably." Douglas looked at me gravely. "I just didn't think we should take any more chances."

"You panicked, didn't you?"

He didn't answer immediately. I was right. And I wished I wasn't. I'd always believed that Douglas was infallible.

He held up a hand. "Let's not have this argument. Please, Chigger?" He said it just like Dad. "We're on our way now. We can't go back. Whatever else, this *is* our ride."

He was right about that much, despite the way he said it, so I shut up. For a moment anyway. But this still wasn't settled. I turned back to him. "Okay, but you gotta promise me something."

"What?"

"That you won't do this anymore—make decisions without asking me. That's what Mom and Dad used to do. And we always hated it. Remember what you said before? You said 'if this is going to work, I need your help.' We're in this together, aren't we?"

Douglas put his arms around me and pulled me close. "You're right, Chigger. I'm sorry. I wasn't thinking. I mean, I wasn't thinking about that."

"No, you were thinking—but you were thinking about the logic stuff, not the people stuff, because that's the way you are." And then I realized, "I'm not too good at it either, am I?"

He ran his hand over the top of my bald head. It was an eerie feeling. I still wasn't used to it—even though we'd all shaved ourselves smooth two days ago. Everyone who lives in space does, for cleanliness reasons. Douglas sighed sadly. "Yeah, I guess social skills was another of those lessons that got dropped out in the divorce." He kissed me— something he'd never done before, at least I couldn't remember ever being kissed by my big brother. He said, "Okay, Chig. I promise. No more family decisions unless everyone in the family is part of them. Even Stinky."

"Pinky promise?"

"Pinky promise." We hooked little fingers and shook on it.

There was one more thing I had to ask. "Douglas?"

"Yeah?"

"Are you and Mickey . . . you know? Gonna get married?"

"I don't know. We haven't really talked about it yet. Does it bother you?"

"I just want to know. Will he be part of our family too? Is he going to help make decisions?"

"Um, Chig . . . He *is* part of it. We have to include him."

"But we just met him two days ago."

"Three."

"Whatever. It's just—how can you make that kind of a decision so *quickly*? It's not *logical*."

"Oh, look who's talking about logic now."

"You know what I mean," I said.

"Yeah, I do. And yeah, you're right. It's not logical. But . . . I've never had anybody love me before. Not like this. And I don't want to lose it. It's very confusing. Maybe it'll happen to you someday. And then you'll understand."

I couldn't imagine it. So I didn't say anything. I didn't even make a face.

Douglas ran his hand over the top of my head again. He took a deep breath. "There *is* a decision that we do have to make very soon, Chig. All of us. What colony are we going to head out to? We'd better start thinking about that now. Because that *will* be a one-way trip."

CARGO

IF **I'D THOUGHT THE TRIP** up the elevator was boring, the cargo pod was even worse. At least the elevator had all the cable channels, ha-ha. We could have had some video reception if we'd linked to either an Earth or a Lunar station—but if we started downloading, then our presence on this pod would be obvious to anyone with access to the tracking software. And the whole point of this trick was that they wouldn't know *which* pod we were in.

Alexei spent an hour explaining to us how the pods were built and how they worked. That was sort of interesting for a while—but it wasn't really his purpose to entertain us. He said it was essential to our survival that we understood what kind of vehicle we were in.

"Is only a cargo pod, *not* a real spaceship," he said. "Is idea to have efficient and cheap way to send supplies and equipment to Luna or Mars or asteroid belt or anywhere else. You put stuff in box, you give box a push—you fling it off Line, *da*? Eventually, it arrives. Cost for fuel is negligible. You are already out of gravity well, so you only need fuel for course corrections along the way and a little bit more for braking at destination. Is very convenient, if you are not in hurry."

Then he showed us how the pods were built. "You see all these polycarbonate rods lining the shell? That is the skeleton of the pod. Very light, very strong. You put framework together like Tinker Toy, you clamp cargo wedges into frame, then you attach outer bulkheads all around. Polycarbonate shells—all prefab, all the same. Stamped from injection molds. Because they make only one trip, reusability is no concern—you think, *da*? *Nyet*. The shells are product too. Open up pod, take out cargo, close up pod, turn it into house. Very *good* house."

Alexei pounded on the bulkhead with his fist. "This is why you find windows and plumbing and wiring in walls—not just because World Space Agency mandates every pod must have basic life support, but because every pod shipped will expand living space at destination. Very clever, yes? We have transport, we have life support, we have new home." He pounded a crate. "Is tradition on Luna, at least one of these crates always contains furnishings, yes. We live in most expensive shipping boxes in solar system. Very nice, *da*?"

I shrugged. Maybe Alexei thought this was exciting, but I didn't. We'd grown up in a tube-town—which is really just a polite way of saying we lived in a giant sewer. No kidding. Any tube that failed the structural integrity tests for piping sewage was still considered strong enough for housing. They all came out of the same factory. So I didn't see that a used shipping box was all that much of an improvement, especially not one with 450,000 kilometers on it.

On the other hand, if you had to live in a used shipping box, you could do a lot worse than a Lunar cargo pod. Alexei showed us how the hull of the pod was made out of six simple pieces: four identical curved hull sections, each describing a 90-degree arc, and two identical circular end pieces. Each piece was designed to fit into every other piece, and each panel had its own hatch and window.

Also, each hull unit had two survival cabinets, one at each end. Each cabinet contained the minimum basic life-support supplies necessary for one person for three days; so the pod had eight total. Alexei showed us how each of the survival cabinets held food, water for drinking and ballast, oxygen-recyclers, self-heating blanket-ponchos, first-aid kits, plastic toilet bags, and personal survival bubbles because you can't pack space suits in enough different sizes. And please read the instructions before opening anything.

Mickey explained that the pods were essentially the spacegoing version of an Antarctic explorer's travel-hut. A onetime pod doesn't need the same kind of precision machinery as a reusable vehicle, and it's unnecessary to build a whole lander for the delivery of cargo, so the steering and braking systems were the cheapest brute-force method possible.

"Is the engines that are most clever," Alexei said, glancing at his wrist. "*Nyet*—not to worry. We are fine for another ninety minutes. Time enough for lesson. I explain fuel rods. Is really quite simple. How do you fire rocket in space? No oxygen in vacuum, *da*? So you put oxygen in fuel mix. Make whole thing one solid tube of fuel. Ignite at one end, it burns until fuel is gone. Is very efficient booster system. But one big problem with solid-fuel booster. Timing. Once burn starts, you cannot turn it off. So is not good for precision burns, *da*? *Nyet*, we find a way. Is much simpler than you think—we use Palmer tubes. Invented by engineer with too much time on hands. Name of John Palmer. Playing with his poker chips at Las Vegas. Very famous story, I share with you.

"Dr. John Palmer, famous engineer, sits at roulette table, thinks of mathematics of chaos and order. How good luck, bad luck both run in streaks. How random numbers cluster up. Thinks about composition of solid-fuel boosters. Meanwhile, he stacks chips, red and black, red and black, red and black. Then he runs out of blacks, so he stacks two red, one black, two red, one black. Suddenly light goes on in head. He pushes everything onto double zero and gets up from table. Wins eleventy-thousand plastic-dollars anyway—almost forgets to collect winnings, he is so excited.

"He rushes back to laboratory and invents Palmer tube. I explain. He slices solid-fuel rod of metallized hydrogen into little flat poker chips. Very thin. In between, he puts little polycarbonate separators, even thinner. Separating disks are made of several layers, perforated and corrugated and shaped to be strong on one side but weak on the other; crisscrossed with grooves so that weak side looks like business side of nail file. Strong side looks like mirror. Very clever, da?

"Then Palmer gets even more clever idea. When he makes separator chips, he paints circumference with liquid conductor. When he makes rod, he glues *insulated* wires down each side. He makes whole thing in polyceramic tube, holds fuel rod like gun barrel.

"Works like this. Turn on current, juice goes down wires, da? All the way to end of tube, to bare ends of wires—last separator in line has shiny side out, grooved side in. Conductive ring around separator chip completes circuit, ignites fuel chip in front of it. Creates ring-shaped ignition. Most efficient explosion. Fuel slice vaporizes, separator vaporizes—*bing*! Next separating disk in line is shiny side out, strong enough to protect next fuel slice—remember, separator only weak on grooved side, not shiny side; so when force of explosion hits shiny side, next separator works like back wall of combustion chamber for just that moment. *Da?* So you get one little poof of thrust. Only one.

"But explosion also heats ignition wires, melts insulation off— enough so that bare wires now touch next separator disk. If there is still current, that disk completes circuit and ignites fuel slice behind it—and whole process happens again. Fuel slice explodes and vaporizes separator disk that ignites it, but does not ignite *next* disk again. And just like before, next separator is back wall of combustion chamber and you get next little poof of thrust. And process starts again. Wires melt a little more, and if there is still current, next disk goes *bing* too. Everything happens very fast—*bing, bing, bing, bing, bing, bing, bing, bing*—like so.

"As long as current flows through wire, disks blow off the end of the tube, one after other. Is like packing whole bunch of bullets in same barrel, but no bullets, only charges. When you burn enough fuel, you turn off current. Explosions stop. Thrust stops. Is beautiful clever, *da? Da?*

"But firing tubes like this—*bing, bing, bing, bing, bing*—makes very unpleasant pulsing effect. Not a fun ride. Like sitting on machine gun. Not a problem. You bundle tubes together. Tubes not work in sync, all the little *bing-bings* average out. Instead of machine-gun feeling, you get corrugated road. More tubes, more average, more smooth—but smooth not needed for cargo, packages don't complain, so is still rough ride, but tolerable, *da?* Never mind. We get there. Palmer bundles guarantee delivery. Is simple brute-force brilliant. If one tube in bundle fails, no problem; others make up difference. Thrust monitor in bundle manages everything. You need this much thrust? Fire tubes until. *Da!*

"Here is more brilliance. Palmer tubes can be any size. As thin as paper clip, as thick as elephant leg—we have elephant on Luna, you know, baby female; you must come to our zoo, see baby elephant bounce—much funny. Anyway, Palmer tubes and Palmer bundles can be made all sizes. Use different size bundles of tubes for all different purposes. Heavy lifting, braking, steering, attitude adjustment, lots of useful boost. Launch to orbit from Luna or Mars. Very efficient. Bring asteroids home for mining. Deliver cargo pods anywhere. Fling them off Line, steer them to destination, brake to match orbit.

"This is why Palmer tube is so brilliant. Volume manufacture makes space travel cheap. Palmer tubes as easy to make as pencils. Put in red goop here, blue goop there, black goop over there, run the machine, stack the firing tubes here. Bundle together, plug in timing caps and thrust monitor. *Da?* Very cheap. You can put three sets of boosters and a thrust monitor on a pod for less than a thousand plastic-dollars. And whatever part of tubes are left over at destination can be used for other things.

"You know story of Crazyman Tucker? He lived in old cargo pod. Very nice pod too. Much fancy. He collected unburned ends of tubes for years, he finally bundle them into big cluster, launch his pod into Lunar orbit. Another cluster of tubes sends him off to rendezvous with Whirlaway rock. He almost makes it too. What some people won't do to avoid export taxes, *da?* But rescue costs more than taxes. So he lose entire fortune anyway. He should have used Palmer tubes for more mining. Get more rich. But he say, 'What good is money on Luna?

Nothing to do but throw rocks at tin cans. And you have to bring your own rocks.' Is very forbidding planet. But you will like, I promise. I teach you to fly at Heinlein Dome. You will have so much fun, you will never want to leave."

At that, Douglas spoke up. "Thank you, Alexei. but we're going out to a colony."

"I know that, *gospodin*," said Alexei. "But if you don't get a bid, you are welcome on Luna. I promise."

"We have an insured contract for a colony placement," said Mickey. "And with all the money you say we've earned, we should be able to buy our way onto the next outbound ship."

Alexei grinned. "I will miss you, *Mikhail*. And if you change mind and decide not to go, I will enjoy not missing you even more." His PITA beeped then. "Oops—here we go. Everybody hold on tight, please."

CHOICES

MICKEY **KNEW A LOT ABOUT** the colonies; working as an elevator attendant, he'd met a lot of outbound colonists. And Alexei knew most of the starship crews; he knew all the best gossip about the different worlds.

"You stay away from both Rand and Hubbard," Alexei warned. "Not very happy worlds. Not at all. The sociometrics don't work. Not like promised. The Randies had to turn themselves into a cult. The Hubbers had to invoke totalitarian control—or was it the other way around?" He scratched his head. "No matter. I tell you how bad it is— the brightliner crews won't go dirtside anymore."

"I heard they weren't allowed to," said Mickey. "It's prohibited now. So they can't report back."

"That too," agreed Alexei. "The smart thing is, stay away from colonies founded on political or religious ideology."

Douglas nodded. "I'd already figured that out." He turned his clipboard around so we could all see it. Half the names on it were already crossed out.

We'd taken time to sleep and eat and give ourselves deodorant sponge baths before we got too smelly. I helped wash Stinky when he finally woke up, and even he smelled tolerable when we were done.

I told Stinky that we were in the cargo pod, but apparently it didn't sink in, because midway through the breakfast, he started complaining. "How come we don't have a real bathroom? How come we can't go to the restaurant to eat? When are we gonna get there? I thought you said we'd be there when we woke up. How come we don't have any real beds?"

Oops.

So Douglas and I told him that we were hiding in the baggage compartment, because we were playing hide-and-seek, so Howard-The-Lawyer wouldn't find us. That he understood immediately. And it was a lot easier than trying to explain Whirlaway to him.

We endured two more course changes—Stinky thought they were fun—and then we finally settled down for a family meeting about where we were going.

Very quickly, we decided that if any one of us had a strong objection to a specific world, we'd take it off the list. Mickey immediately vetoed Promised Land, New Canaan, and Allah. "They're all orthodox," he explained. "You can immigrate only if you convert."

Douglas was already checking them off the list. "The sociometrics for religious colonies aren't good anyway. Long-term instability, almost always leading to schisms, holy wars, revolutions, and pogroms."

"So let's just eliminate all of the ones with sociometric liabilities," I said.

"They all have sociometric liabilities," said Mickey. "We have to consider them each on their own merits and then decide what set of problems we're willing to take on."

Douglas agreed. "You want to do this alphabetically?"

"Um, wait a minute—please?" They both looked at me. "Maybe we should make a list of things that we want. That way we'll have something to measure each planet against. Then we can give each colony a score, and that way we can—what's the word?—prioritize them."

Mickey and Douglas exchanged glances, nodded. "Sounds like a plan."

Douglas said, "You start, Chig. What do you want?"

The picture in my head was Mexico. The Baja coast. Our one short day at the beach. A bright blue sky over a wide emerald sea. Yellow sand and tall green forests. And wind—breezes that smelled good. Real flowers.

But first things first. "Normal gravity," I said.

"That's good thinking," said Mickey. "Most people don't think about gravity enough. Most people can handle a ten or fifteen percent boost. It's like gaining five or ten kilos. But it's extra stress on the heart, on the feet, on the bones; there's a higher risk of injury; and you age faster, you sag more. Also, your life expectancy is reduced."

Douglas made a note. "Gravity, that's important. We'll give that one a lot of weight." And then he added, "Not just gravity, we have to think about the whole planet. What kind of star does it circle? What color is the light? How long is the year? How severe are the seasons? What's the atmosphere like, what kind of weather does it have? How long are the days? Is the air breathable? Or will it be someday? What kind of terraforming is possible?"

And as he said that, all my visions of a tropical beach disappeared. We weren't going to Hawaii. We were going to Mars. Barren red rock, stretching off in all directions. Clusters of domes hiding beneath angling solar panels. Antennas sprouting like needles. Storage tanks huddling against the ground to withstand the enormous winds and dust storms. Agriculture domes. Tubes snaking from one place to the other because the atmosphere was too thin to breathe. Long ugly days. Cold dark nights.

Tube-town again.

Only this time, uglier than ever. Because there wouldn't be anyplace *else* to go.

I knew what kind of planet we had jumped off. I was just beginning to realize what we might have to jump onto. . . .

Douglas must have seen the look on my face. He asked, "Chigger?"

"I want a colony that has an *outdoors*," I said. "Breathable air. I want to go outside."

"Mmm," said Mickey, frowning. "That does limit our options."

"I don't care," I said. "I don't want to live in a tube anymore."

"Nobody does. But sometimes that's all there is."

"I don't care. That's what I want."

"Would you accept a world that had garden domes? I hear some of them can be very nice."

Alexei spoke up then. "We have garden domes on Luna. Very pretty. We put a dome over a crater and fill it with air. We bring in manure and water, seeds and insects, pretty soon we have garden. Well, not pretty soon. Sometimes it takes twenty years to get garden dome going. But for much people, garden dome is all the outdoors they need."

I shook my head. "Maybe that's okay for Loonies. It's not okay for me. I want a real sky."

Douglas made a note on his clipboard. "Outdoors. Very important."

Mickey didn't look happy about that, but he didn't argue it either. He said, "There are a couple of other things we need to consider. Where we can live, what kind of work we'll have to do, what kinds of laws there are—y'know, every colony has its own idea of the way things should be. What you can believe, where you can live, *who can marry who*. . . . Stuff like that."

Douglas looked up. "I hadn't thought about that."

"Well, we have to." He added, "There are some places that won't let us keep custody of Bobby. You'd better put that at the top of your list. In fact, we'd better limit ourselves to places that recognize 'full

faith and credit' of other places' laws. Otherwise, Judge Griffith's custody rulings could be set aside by anyone who chooses to file a 'writ
of common interest.' "

Douglas frowned, but wrote. He stopped, looked across at Mickey.
"You're trying to make a point, aren't you?"

"Uh-huh."

"Go on."

"I think we should limit ourselves to signatories to the Covenant of
Rights."

Douglas didn't say anything to that. I could tell he was thinking it
over. He didn't like the idea, I knew that much, but he could see the
point.

It wasn't that we disagreed with the U.N. Covenant of Rights. Not
in principle, at least. But back home, there were a lot of people who
said the Covenant was a recipe for anarchy or totalitarianism—or both
at the same time. So we had never ratified it.

The Covenant recognized the basic rights of all people—that every
human being was entitled to equal access to opportunity and equal protection under the law. That all people were entitled to freedom of belief,
freedom of expression, freedom of spirit. That all people were entitled
to access to food and water and air, access to education, access to justice. And most important, that all people were entitled to equal representation in their government. And that no government had the right,
authority, or power to restrict or infringe or deny those freedoms. And
so on. It was pretty dangerous stuff.

Some of the folks back in tube-town said that the only way all those
freedoms could be guaranteed equally would be to establish a totalitarian
dictatorship. Then no one would have any freedom, but we would all
be equal. Other people said that if we signed the Covenant, it would
mean we'd have to repeal half our laws, and our civilization would
break down. They said that men and women would have to share the
same toilets and that rich people would have to sleep under bridges with
poor people and everybody would have to share all their property so
nobody had more than anybody else. And besides, only the One-
Worlders wanted us to sign it because that would be another step toward
ceding our independence to the U.N. And once there was a world government in place, the rest of the world would loot our economy. And
so on.

But the way it looked now, it didn't really matter after all. The last
news we'd heard, *nobody* had an economy anymore.

Douglas said, "I know you mean well, Mickey, but I'm not comfortable with the Covenant of Rights. It sounds like collectivism."

Mickey looked at him expectantly. So did Alexei.

"I mean, you can't just let people have rights without controls. You get a breakdown of society. You get corruption and immorality and fraud. The system breaks down, a little bit at a time. You get multi-generation welfare families, and parasites feeding at the public trough. You get teener-gangs and disaffected subcultures and dysfunctionals of all kinds. You get riots and crime and . . . and immorality. All kinds of degeneracy. You have to have some limits on what people can do; otherwise, it all erodes away and eventually falls apart." He gestured vaguely behind himself. "I mean, all you have to do is look at what's happening back there on Earth."

Mickey replied, "I could just as easily argue the opposite side of it, Doug—that the meltdown is a result of too many oppressive controls."

"I don't think so—"

"Well, then let me put it to you another way. Do you want a place where you and I can stay together? Only a Covenant world will guarantee that. None of the others. If they haven't signed the Covenant, there's no evidence that they're committed to anyone's rights."

Douglas sighed in exasperation. "Y'know, back in Texas, that kind of talk would be subversive."

There was a long uncomfortable silence at that. Mickey and Alexei exchanged a glance, waiting.

Douglas looked from one to the other. I could see he was struggling with it, trying to wrap his head around a whole new idea. Finally, he said, "Things *really* are different out here, aren't they?"

"Yeah," said Mickey. "They are."

Douglas sighed. He hated losing arguments. "All right." He scribbled something on his clipboard. "Mickey wants a Covenant world. Very important."

MONKEYS

THERE **WAS A LOT MORE** than that too. I never realized there was so much stuff to consider.

Like language, f'rinstance. What if the perfect colony was one where no one spoke Spanglish? We'd have to spend six months just learning to speak French or some other weird tongue, before we could begin to function like real people.

And skin color. We didn't think of ourselves as racist, or anything like that, but we all wanted to go to a place where we looked pretty much like everybody else, because we wanted to fit in.

And food. That one was *real* important—especially after eating a few of those damn MREs. On some worlds, they grew their protein in big vats of slime. On others, they farmed insects. By comparison, even pickled mongoose sounded appetizing.

Both Douglas and Mickey had a lot of information in their clipboards about all the different colony worlds, so we spent a lot of time talking about each one and scoring it on all the different things that were important to us. We crossed off some colonies immediately, with almost no discussion at all. Others, we talked about for an hour or more. I hadn't realized there were so many different *kinds* of colony worlds.

Other than that, we napped and crapped—and got slapped into the aft bulkhead every time there was a course change. I can't say I ever got used to them; they were all uncomfortable; but at least I got smart enough to take a lot of deep breaths whenever Alexei's PITA beeped.

Every so often, we'd climb around to one side or the other, to peek out one of the little windows, hoping to catch sight of either the Earth or the moon. We never did get a real good look at the moon; we were angled wrong, coming around behind the dark side, trying to catch up to it; but once we got a spectacular view of the crescent Earth. It was the size of a basketball held at arm's length—and it looked so big and so small, both at the same time, it was scary. And it was so bright it made my eyes water. It gave me a funny feeling inside to know that we would never go back.

We'd never see Mom or Dad again either. And that felt strange too. Because I didn't feel anything for them, just gray inside. Like I didn't know what to feel. Maybe I'd feel it later. I just didn't know. I wondered if Douglas felt the same way—or if he was still so confused about his feelings for Mickey that he didn't have room for any other kind of feelings.

But with so much other stuff happening, I didn't get a chance to talk to him about it. I also had to take care of Stinky.

Stinky thought free fall was fun. He wanted to go bouncing and careening around the cargo pod, except there really wasn't much room for that, except for the little bit of open space at each end. I'd started thinking of our nest at the aft end as the top. The bottom was the space we used as the bathroom, although a couple of times, Mickey and Douglas went up there when they wanted some privacy.

Alexei busied himself with eavesdropping on the various news channels. I could see his fingers twitching when he did. He said he wanted to get on the phone and start calling. He could make a lot of money with just a few phone calls—but any unusual traffic from this pod would certainly alert whoever was watching that this was the occupied one, so he resisted the temptation. He said he was part of a web of money-surfers who took care of each other's business when any one of them was in transit or had to go underground for a while. That way, the money was never where anyone might be looking for it. Just the same, he worried about the opportunities passing by.

So it was left for me to entertain Stinky whenever he got bored, which was almost constantly. Fortunately, we had the monkey to play with, so the two of us started teaching it things and making up games. The monkey was pretty smart—smarter than I would have guessed for a kid's toy. *Smart enough not to draw to an inside straight.* Smart enough to play an aggressive game of chess. Even smart enough to hold its nose whenever Stinky farted.

I shouldn't have been surprised by its ability to play chess or poker. It was, after all, a toy—and even Douglas could write a chess or a poker program, the logic wasn't that hard to chart. Simulating intelligence is so easy, even Stinky can do it.

But every so often, I caught the monkey studying me thoughtfully—or maybe it was just my imagination. Maybe that was part of the way it had learned to interact with its human hosts. But it made me wonder. What if the monkey really was watching us? Recording everything? What if the monkey was some kind of a spy? Maybe the monkey's job was to travel with us and monitor . . . that was the part I couldn't figure out. That was where I ran out of paranoia.

"I wish you could talk to me," I said to it. "I wish I could just order you to explain yourself. That would make everything so much simpler."

The monkey just cocked its head and looked at me curiously, as if waiting for me to give the order. Yeah, right.

Some people thought robots were fun. I didn't. I thought most of them were a damn nuisance. Because they did exactly what they were told. They didn't do what you *meant*, they did what you said. Which was kind of funny if you were a kid, but it was frustrating too. I never had the patience for it, but Stinky did. And so did Douglas. They had the logic genes. I guess they got that from Mom. I got the music, and not much else, from Dad. I didn't resent it, not really, but sometimes I wished I could understand things the way other people did. It would make life a lot easier. I wouldn't have to work so hard at everything.

It was halfway through the second waking period—I couldn't think of them as "days" when nothing really changed—when Stinky finally figured it out. *It.*

We had gone up to the front window to look at the moon, which was still a crescent, but starting to fill out enough that we could see the sharp edges of craters all along the terminator line. When we got bored with that, we started making up songs about bouncing elephants, and then we decided to teach the monkey how to dance, which is hard enough in gravity, but in free fall it's impossible—so it was silly enough to start Stinky giggling, which is sort of good most of the time, because once he starts giggling he just keeps on going; but it isn't always a good idea because sometimes he giggles so hard he pees in his pants.

But this time, he and the monkey started imitating each other, and it was hard to tell which of them was funnier—and which of them was more amused by the other. They really did look a lot like twins.

—Until in the middle of everything Stinky asked *the* question. The one I'd been hoping he wouldn't. "Chigger, who's going to meet us on the moon? Mommy or Daddy?"

I knew that he wasn't simply asking who was going to meet us. He was asking if we would ever see them again. And I honestly didn't know what to say to him. For one of the first times in my life, I felt sorry for the little monster because there just wasn't any way to soften this blow. And . . . even though I didn't like thinking this thought, maybe it *had* been a mistake for Douglas and me to insist on keeping him with us. Maybe he would have been better with Mom. Or even Dad.

Except—I knew he wouldn't have been. And I knew if I'd had to choose at his age, I'd have chosen to leave instead of stay, even if I didn't understand all the reasons why. Or maybe I wouldn't have chosen to leave, maybe I'd have been too scared to, but I wouldn't have been better off staying. But Stinky didn't know that—because he wasn't thirteen or eighteen, and he didn't know any better. All he knew was that his Mommy and Daddy weren't here. And he missed them.

And he was looking to me to give him an answer.

So I told him the truth. *As best as I could.*

Which means, I weaseled like an adult.

"I don't know, kiddo. Remember, Dad promised us a trip to the moon, and this is our vacation. And Judge Griffith said he could go too. So I'm sure he's going to try to meet us when we get where we're going—he just doesn't know that we're taking the long way around."

"And what about Mom?"

I thought about fat *Señor* Doctor Hidalgo, who had flown Mom and her friend up on an expensive shuttle flight for the emergency custody hearing. Would he shuttle her to the moon and try to head us off there? If he thought he could get his hands on the monkey, he would. It seemed to me he was trying to get off the Earth anyway. So whatever game he was playing, bringing Mom along might be part of it.

"I think she might get to the moon too, I didn't have a chance to ask her before we left. We had to leave in a hurry, remember?"

He shook his head. I didn't expect him to remember anything. Mickey had drugged his ice cream and that had kept him pretty drowsy for half a day.

But whatever else he was, Stinky wasn't stupid. "We're not going to see them anymore, are we? We're going on the brightliner by ourselves."

"Well, Mickey will be with us—I think. Do you like Mickey?"

"Douglas likes him." Which was his way of saying no. Because if he really liked Mickey, he would have said so. Maybe he resented Mickey for the same reasons I did. Or maybe he was just jealous that Douglas was spending so much time with him. Or maybe he just didn't like Mickey for no reason at all.

"Do you miss Mom?" I asked.

"Uh-huh, don't you?"

"Um . . . I don't miss the yelling."

That must have been answer enough, because he changed the subject. "I'm hungry. Do we have anything to eat besides those awful *emmaries?*"

"Not till we get to the moon, kiddo. Sorry."

"Okay. I'll wait."

FINAL APPROACH

AFTER SEVEN OR EIGHT MORE course changes, each one more painful than the last, we finally got a good look at the bright side of the moon. Well, part of it anyway, as we came around the northern edge of the terminator. We still had three more burns to put us into a near-polar orbit, what Alexei called the crazy-mouse orbit, so that meant we'd actually orbit the moon a couple of times—down the front and up the back—before finally heading in.

The second time we came around the bright side, it filled the window, but it was hard to tell how close we were; Douglas said that's because the moon has a fractal surface; there's so many craters of so many different sizes that a close view looks a lot like a high view, and vice versa.

But the landscape below us was moving slowly, so I took that as an indication that we were still fairly high—and when I pressed my face close to the window, I could see the horizon, and it was still curved. So that meant we were at least a hundred klicks high, if I had done the math right. Probably not. Math was not my best subject.

The dark side of the moon was hard to see clearly; there was some light reflected from the crescent Earth, but not enough, so everything looked all gloomy gray. And the bright side, when we crossed the terminator again, was almost too bright to look at directly. Douglas said that the Lunar surface reflects more light back at you when you look at it head-on, and that's why a full moon is noticeably brighter than a half-moon, it's something to do with refraction and the way the Lunar dust scatters light.

Alexei joined us at the window. He took one glance and grunted. "We are coming in very fast. Good."

I took another look. He was right. The ground below us was moving noticeably faster.

"We are looping over top of moon in a few seconds. Look for north pole; there it is—" He pointed toward the horizon. "See those lights near terminator edge? That is north station. Biggest ice mine on Luna. Be sure to wave at the Rock Father."

"The Rock Father?" Stinky asked. "Who's he?"

"You don't know the Rock Father? Shame on you. Is Lunar legend. Lost Russian spaceman, freezes every Lunar night, wakes up every Lunar day. Is immortal. Lives at Lunar North Pole, like Father Christmas, except he has no reindeer, no elves. Rock Father is everyone's Crazy Uncle Loonie. Plays pranks on ice miners. Steals supplies. Rearranges markers. Hides in shadows where no one can see. One time Rock Father even puts up black featureless monolith in Clavius crater. Proportions one by four by nine. Standing on edge. No footprints anywhere around. Make American explorers much crazy. Rock Father laugh forever."

"But why is he called the Rock Father?" That was me.

"Because he is father of all Loonies. The Rock Father answers all prayers. Mostly, the answer is no. But sometimes not. Rock Father is there once in every life. He answers most important prayer—he knows, even if you don't."

"Do we have to make a wish?" Stinky asked.

"Prayers are not wishes," Alexei said. "But most terries don't know the difference. This is why Rock Father hardly ever listens to terries."

He glanced out the window again. "Hokay, enough." He began herding us back to the other end of the pod. "Is now time for everyone to strap in and get ready for landing. I am afraid landing will be rougher than expected. We are coming in faster than I planned. Not too much faster, but enough. This will be more crunch-down than bounce-down. We will rattle a little, but if we precaution properly, we will all be safe—" His PITA beeped, and he shouted, "Whoops—hang on!"

This course change was the longest and roughest one yet. Everything rattled and roared and shook. The monkey slipped out of my grasp and was thrown somewhere down below. I was pinned flat against the top of one of the cargo crates. I didn't see where anyone else was, but when it finally stopped Stinky was crying and Douglas was holding him tight. Mickey had a nosebleed, and even Alexei looked a little shaken; he was a skinny undermuscled Loonie; he probably hurt worse than any of us. But I didn't feel too much sympathy for him, because this had been his idea from the beginning. And he'd suckered the rest of us into joining him.

The monkey came climbing up from below—I was thinking of it

as below now—and wrapped itself around me. Absentmindedly, I patted its head. When even the robots get scared, you know you're having a rough time.

"We are fine, we are fine," Alexei assured us, a little too quickly. "Mickey, help me please. We must make sure cabin is ready for bounce-down. I will inflate interior balloons manually. I start at bottom and work my way up. You will please secure dingalings in web? Space everybody carefully."

I didn't like the sound of that. I was still worrying about the words *crunch-down*. And Alexei didn't sound all that confident himself.

Mickey started strapping in Stinky. There were elastic belts set into the bulkhead at various places. He pulled several of them across Stinky's chest to form an X-harness with a latch at the center.

"See this button?" Mickey explained. "That's the emergency safety release. Don't press it until after we're down and *after* we stop bouncing and rolling. It might take a few minutes. There'll be an all-clear bell. If you don't hear it, don't press the button. Do you understand, Bobby? You wait until we come and get you. Promise?"

"I promise," Stinky said. He said it *that* way, and I already knew how that promise was going to get kept—with him getting loose and bouncing all over the pod as soon as he felt like it. No, Mickey didn't know who he was talking to.

I pulled myself over and faced the devil child squarely. "Listen to me. This is a *real* promise, Bobby—not a pretend one. Not one where you say you promise and then do what you want anyway. If you don't keep this promise, you could get hurt. *Real badly.* You don't want to get hurt, do you?"

"Nuh-uh."

"Then you absolutely must not under any circumstances whatever, no matter what you think, no matter what happens, press that button—not until Mickey comes and tells you it's okay to press it. Okay?"

"Okay," he said.

"Promise?"

"Promise."

"Pinky promise?"

"Pinky promise." We hooked pinkies and shook.

I turned to Mickey. "Is there some way to disable that button or put it where he can't reach it?"

Mickey shook his head. "That would defeat the purpose of the emergency release—"

"He's not going to keep his promise," I said.

"*Will too!*" Stinky shouted at me.

"Will not," I snapped right back.

"*Liar! You big liar! I'll show you!*"

"I'll bet you a million dollars—"

"I'll bet you *a hundred million zillion dollars!*"

"Okay, it's a bet. If you push that button without permission, you owe me a hundred million zillion dollars and your monkey."

"*Not my monkey!* Douglas!"

"Then don't push the button," I said. "Not ever. Not unless Mickey says you can."

Douglas moved between us then. He pushed me back away from Stinky. "Chigger," he whispered. "Was that necessary?"

I whispered right back. "You want him to stay in the harness, no matter what? We're talking about Stinky. Logic and promises won't do it. He'll only do it if he can spite someone."

Douglas got it. "Y'know, he's a lot like you."

"Yeah, I know—that's how I know he'll push the button. *Because I would.*"

Douglas didn't want to argue. There wasn't time anyway. He pulled himself back toward Mickey and whispered something in his ear. Mickey nodded.

Douglas came back to me. "Come on, Charles. It's time to buckle you in. We'll put you in this harness, close to Bobby." He pulled me into position and began pulling straps down, the same way Mickey had strapped in Stinky. "I'll be on the other side. Mickey will be up there, and Alexei will be down there. That should balance the weight fairly evenly."

He struggled with the latches for a bit—he couldn't get the X-harness centered on my chest—until Mickey came over to help. He loosened two of the belts, pushed me sideways, then tightened them again. He leaned in and whispered to me, "You're very convincing, you know that? Douglas thinks we should tranquilize Bobby again. It's safer. It'll make things harder on the ground, someone will have to carry him. But if you really think he can't be trusted—"

I thought about all the times someone had told him not to do something—and how quickly he'd done *exactly* what he'd been forbidden to do. Like running down into the Barringer Meteor Crater. Like calling Mom from One-Hour station after Dad had told him not to. He did this stuff deliberately—as if to prove that no one could control him. *No one.*

Mickey saw it in my face. "I really hate to do it to a little kid like that . . ."

"He's *not* a little kid," I said. "His middle name is Caligula."

Mickey sighed. "All right. Do you want a sedative too? This could get pretty rough."

I considered it. I thought about all the burns we'd already been through. It was very tempting. But . . . I shook my head. "I'd better not."

"You sure?"

"No. Yes. You said it's going to be hard enough to carry Stinky. Who's going to carry me?"

"Good point." He finished securing me in the webbing. "I was hoping you would say that, but Douglas asked me to make the offer. That's pretty courageous of you, Charles. Here, put this O-mask over your face."

"Oxygen—?"

"Just a precaution, to make sure you have an air supply after we blow the inflatables. Whoops—you have company." He was talking about the monkey, it was just climbing its way back up to me—pulling itself hand over hand through the webbing. I was glad I'd programmed it to home in on me. I would never have been able to find it otherwise, not in the mess of this cluttered cargo pod.

"I'll strap it in with you," Mickey said, tucking it into the webbing and pulling a safety belt around to secure it. To the monkey, he said, "Don't push this button, unless Chigger tells you. Do you understand?"

The monkey made a face at him—crossing its eyes and curling both its lips back. Neither of us had any idea what the expression meant.

Alexei came back then and helped Mickey strap in Douglas. We must have been running out of time, they both were pretty urgent in their movements. When they finished, Alexei double-checked Stinky, then went to his own landing station and webbed in as quickly as he could. "Are you secured, Mikhail?" he called.

"I'm good," said Mickey.

"Hokay!" hollered the mad Russian lunatic. "Get ready for bubbles—" He snapped a code word to his PITA, and a second later, the inflatables began filling the cargo pod—hundreds of self-inflating balloons. They came bubbling up from the other end of the cargo pod, filling every available space so tightly it would have been impossible to move, even if we weren't webbed in. The bubbles pressed up against my face like someone holding a pillow over my nose. I was grateful for the O-mask. The packing bubbles would have suffocated me.

It made me uneasy to be so completely immobilized. All I could see was bubbles—the bluish light of the pod was fractured like a hall of mirrors; it was like looking into shattered winter. And it was cold in the pod too. We'd had to turn off our blankets for the bounce-down.

"Stand by!" hollered Alexei. His voice came muffled through the bubbles. "We begin braking now. It will be rough—"

BOUNCE-DOWN

I **THINK I PASSED OUT.** I wasn't sure. One moment I was trying to scream and the next moment everything was eerily silent. "What's happening now?" I called. I don't think anybody heard me.

But a moment later, Alexei's voice came muffled through the cabin. "We burn off speed. We have come around very fast. Must burn off more speed. Twice more speed. Aim at surface, dive to landing site, then brake hard for last kilometer down. Is very nasty maneuver, but only way to get to safe house. Very safe house."

I couldn't believe he was conscious. Of all of us, Alexei seemed the weakest. He was tall and gangly and skinny—he didn't have the muscles for Earth gravity, and I'd assumed he didn't have the endurance either. Living so long in lesser gravity, his bones should have softened, his heart should have shrunk.

It made me wonder if he had been working out in the high-gee levels at Geostationary. Despite all his disclaimers, he must have been; he was handling the heavy gees better than any of us. Maybe he'd been preparing for this kind of escape for a long time. Just how much illegal stuff was he involved in anyway?

"What next?" I shouted.

Alexei had explained the operation to all of us, more than once, but I still wanted to hear him confirm the successful completion of each phase of it.

"More braking—"

"I'm already broken," Douglas gasped.

I was glad that Stinky was tranquilized. I don't think I could have stood it if he were screaming and crying and I couldn't get to him. That business at the meteor crater had been bad enough—I still had night-

mares. Even so, I thought I could hear him whimpering in his sleep.
The poor little kid, I almost felt sorry for him—everything he was going
through. It had to be worse on him than any of the rest of us.

Alexei's PITA beeped. I started gasping for as much breath as I
could before the rockets kicked in—

—this time I did pass out. I woke up to the sound of Alexei's PITA
beeping again. I was beginning to hate the sound of that thing. I had
just enough time to say, "Oh, sh—" and then the rockets fired again.

I didn't remember waking up after the next one. I was just awake
and cussing, spewing every dreadful word that I'd ever gotten my mouth
washed out for using. The third time I repeated myself, I stopped to
take a breath.

"Is impressive. For a thirteen-year-old."

I ignored him. "Is anyone else alive?" I called.

"Yo," said Mickey.

"I'd ask if you're all right," called Douglas, "but nobody who's
seriously hurt cusses that enthusiastically."

"What about Bobby?"

"He's not making any noises," called Mickey.

"He is fine," said Alexei. "I am certain."

"Can you see him?"

"Please not to worry. Little stinking one is fine."

"*Don't call him Stinky!*" I said. And wondered where that came
from. There was a sound from Douglas. Laughter? Probably. But only
family members had the right to call him Stinky. No one else. And only
when he really deserved it.

"We will be down soon," Alexei said. "You will see for yourself,
everyone is fine."

"Where are we now?"

"We have broken orbit. We have fired twice to dive in toward
bounce target. Only one more burn—the last one. We brake hard to
burn off speed. And then we bounce."

"You hope—" But I said it under my breath. I was saving most of
my air for breathing.

Alexei heard it anyway. "You will like Luna, Charles. I promise.
No bad weather. No weather at all—"

And then his damn PITA went off again.

This was the worst one of all—at least the worst one that I was
conscious for. The noise was unbearable. Even if I could have stuffed
my fingers into my ears, it wouldn't have done any good, the whole
pod was roaring and shaking and rattling. *Whose good idea was this
anyway?*

And this time, I had a very clear idea of the direction of *down*. It was directly in front of me. All the packing bubbles were pushing up against us—we were hanging from the top of the cargo pod, while several hundred tons of widgets and whatnots trembled ominously only three meters away. Those crates were *aching* to break free of the violent deceleration and smash upward into our faces. Just how strong were those foam dollops anyway?

And finally when I was convinced that the incredible noise would never end, *it did*.

We were in free fall again.

But only for a few seconds.

Something went *bang* on the outside of the cargo pod. A whole bunch of things went *bang*. The "Lunar parachutes." The external inflatables. Alexei had explained this too. We were landing on balloons. A whole cluster of them. Very strong, very flexible. From the outside, the cargo pod would look like a plastic raspberry.

Depending on our angle and speed, and the kind of terrain we were landing on, we could bounce for five or ten klicks. Alexei said that usually, you try to undershoot the target and bounce the rest of the way to your final destination. He said that some pods had bounced over fifteen kilometers from their initial touch-down points, but that those kinds of bounce-downs were carefully planned. The pods had come in very fast, and at a very shallow angle—and they were aimed down a long slope or something like that.

But we wouldn't have that kind of ride, for which I was very grateful. The target zone had a lot of rough terrain, and Alexei wanted to minimize our bouncing—so as soon as it was safe, the pod was programmed to deflate the balloons and let us just crunch in. I wondered what Alexei's definition of *safe* was. I hoped that Armstrong was telling the truth when he said, "It's soft and powdery. I can kick it with my foot."

And then we hit—*bumped*—something. The impact came from the side, and it was hard enough to knock the breath out of me with an audible *Oof!* I heard Alexei say something that sounded like "*Gohvno!*" I got the sense that *gohvno* was something I didn't want to step in.

And then we were in free fall again—or maybe not. But we were still airborne—except there isn't any air on Luna, and we weren't being borne by anything—we were just up.

And then down. We bounced again—this time from the other side and even harder than before. The whole pod went *crunch!*

And then we were up again—floating for a long agonizing moment—until *crunchbang!* We bounced again. I couldn't believe the balloons were working. This hurt!

Floated and bounced, bounced, bounced—and then abruptly crunched to a stop—was that it? Were we down? We were hanging sideways and upside down in the webbing—

I fumbled for the release. It was hard to move; we were still pinned by the packing bubbles. They smelled of canned air.

"Don't anyone move—" shouted Alexei. "We're not done yet."

We waited in silence for a moment.

Nothing happened.

"Douglas?"

No answer.

"Mickey?"

I called louder.

"Ymf," said Mickey.

"What's happening?"

"Wait," said Alexei.

The cargo pod *lurched*. Sideways. "Is the balloons. Rearranging selves. Everybody wait."

"Douglas? *Douglas*—?" Where was *Douglas*? I had this sudden nightmare knowledge that he had died in the crash. Then I would be really *alone*.

"Is not to worry. Nobody is dead," said Alexei. "Everybody wait! Pod must settle itself!" The pod continued to shudder and jerk and bump. Slowly, it began to hump itself upright. The pod was pumping air from balloon to balloon, pushing itself up with plastic muscles.

"Everybody stay still," said Alexei. Like we had a choice.

I was still worried about Douglas. "Mickey? Can you see Douglas? Is he all right?"

After a moment, Mickey called back. "He's fine. He's groaning."

The pressure on my chest began to ease. The packing bubbles were starting to wilt, slowly deflating. I guessed they were timed or something.

Finally, the cargo pod groaned and settled itself. "Please to wait—" cautioned Alexei. It bumped and lurched one more time, then sagged into an exhausted upright position. We were hanging from the webbing at the top. The only good news was the Lunar gravity. One-sixth Earth normal. It felt . . . strange and easy at the same time.

As soon as he decided it was safe—and not soon enough for me—Alexei unbuckled himself and began climbing around the webbing like a human spider. He unbuckled Mickey first. Mickey's face was covered with blood. He held a soggy red handkerchief over his nose. He must have had a nosebleed all the way down.

"I go find first-aid kit," said Alexei. "You take care of dingalings." He dropped down between two of the crates, and we heard the packing bubbles squeak and squeal and pop as he pushed his way through. It was a funny noise. It sounded like someone with water in his boots, squelching through a sewer. The canned air smell got stronger.

Mickey lowered himself to a crate, standing knee deep in squooshy balloons. He picked his way over to stand beneath me. Still holding his head back, still holding the hanky over his nose, he called up to me. "Can you free yourself, Charles?"

"I think so."

"You'll have to help me with Douglas. We'll lower him to the top of the crates. All right?"

"All right." I fumbled around with the latch for a moment—it wasn't hard to unbuckle, but my hands were shaking so badly from the landing that I couldn't coordinate. Finally, I managed to free myself—

I was never very good at gymnastics, but in Lunar gravity, everything was so surprisingly easy that I wished we could have had gym class on the moon, it was a lot more fun. I hung from the webbing without any effort at all. I did the math in my head; I weighed nine kilos.

Mickey pointed and I went hand over hand to Douglas. He looked pale, but he was breathing steadily into his O-mask. I wondered if he'd passed out during braking or if he'd bumped himself unconscious during landing, a concussion would be very bad news, but we wouldn't know until we got him out of the webbing.

Mickey stood just below me, still holding his hanky to his nose. He gave me careful instructions, step by step, how to lower Douglas without dropping him. Even though falling three meters in Lunar gravity is no worse than falling half a meter on Earth, we still didn't want to take any chances. People had broken noses, arms, legs, and hips by underestimating Lunar gravity—especially after prolonged free fall. And we were all very shaky from the bounce-down.

"Lower him feet first, Charles. Grab him under his arms and hold him till I get his legs. I know it's awkward, but he should be light enough that you can handle him. All right, ready?" Mickey started to take his handkerchief away from his nose, but it was still bleeding too badly.

"Maybe we should wait until Alexei gets back. Let him do it."

"I can manage. We'll do it quickly. Wait a minute." He wiped at his nose for a second, then looked up. "Okay, ready?"

"Ready." I unbuckled Douglas with one hand, then reached and grabbed him before he could fall out of the webbing. He started to slip out of my grasp, but I caught him by the collar and held on. That was enough. Mickey grabbed his legs and lowered him.

Still hanging from the webbing, I scrambled over to check on Stinky. He was sleeping like a baby, and almost as cute. "Leave him there for now," called Mickey. "Let's take care of Douglas first."

I let go of the webbing and dropped down to the top of the crates. I dropped impossibly slow. It was *amazing*. We really were on the moon! I hit a little harder than I expected, and I bounced almost all the way back up, laughing with delight. Mickey gave me a nasty look. "There'll be time enough for that later." He put his hand back to his nose.

Alexei came climbing back then and yanked me out of the air. "Learn to walk before you fly," he said. He popped open the first-aid kit and began pawing through it. "Here, this will stop nosebleed very fast." He held up a tiny spray bottle, and Mickey tilted his head back.

While they did that, I went rummaging in the kit for old-fashioned smelling salts. I found a little flat packet of ammonia, cracked its spine, and held it under Douglas's nose—he didn't react. I waved it under his nose again—*come on, Douglas!* I was ready to jam it up his nostril when he suddenly flinched and said, "Stop it, Charles!" He made a terrible face and pushed me away with both hands.

He sat up, still wrinkling his nose in disgust as he looked around. He blinked in surprise. "What happened to you, Mickey?"

"Ahhh," said Alexei, turning around. "The dead have come back to life. Welcome to Luna! My home sweet home!"

STEPPING OUT

MICKEY FINALLY GAVE UP and put cotton up each nostril and a clip on his nose to pin his nostrils together. He'd just have to breathe through his mouth for a while.

The funny thing was, he'd been trained in all kinds of safety procedures on the Line, so he was practically a space doctor. Alexei was equally well trained, so you'd have thought between the two of them they could have figured something out—but apparently the low air pressure in the pod, combined with the lighter gravity and everything else, made this particular nosebleed slow to heal. But we couldn't sit around waiting for Mickey to stop dripping. Alexei was certain about that. We'd lose the advantage of our landing.

The two of them pulled a variety of instruments out of the first-aid kit and began checking everyone out. Ears, eyes, nose, blood pressure, blood gas, adrenaline, blood-sugar levels, I didn't know what else. Except for a lot of residual jitters, we all checked out normal. As normal as possible under these conditions.

Finally, Douglas and Alexei bounced up to the webbing and brought Stinky down, and Mickey checked him out too. He was fine, but he'd be asleep for several hours longer. I whistled a few notes from Beethoven's Seventh Symphony—what I called the Johnny-One-Note theme; it wouldn't sound like a melody to anyone who didn't recognize the theme, just some vague tuneless whistling—but it was a clear signal to the monkey. It came bouncing down to join us. It squatted next to Stinky and pretended to take his pulse. Or maybe it wasn't pretending—I remembered reading in the instructions that it was supposed to be a pretty good baby monitor. It would howl for help if a baby stopped breathing or had a temperature or something like that. But if it was seriously checking Stinky, then it wasn't finding anything wrong with him. It sat back on its haunches and waited patiently.

For a damn stupid toy, it sure had a terrific repertoire. And it was smart enough to know when to stay out of the way. Maybe it listened to stress levels in human voices. Or maybe it just sniffed for fear. Douglas might know. Maybe I'd remember to ask him later.

"All right," said Alexei, looking at his PITA. "We have not a lot of time. We must get moving quickly. Is everybody ready for nice walk? Everybody go to bathroom, whether you have to go or not. I mean it. You are constipated from free fall. Once you start bouncing on the moon, everything shakes down. Is not fun bouncing with pants full of poop." He practically stood over each of us to make sure we complied.

Once that business was taken care of, he started snapping out orders in Russian to his PITA. It projected a map of the local terrain on the bulkhead. "We are lucky childrens. We have not got too far to go. Here, see? *Da?* We go here to Prospector's Station. We change clothes, we look like ice miners. We catch train, we go to Gagarin City. Much good food. You like borscht? With cabbage and lamb, one bowl is whole meal. I am hungry already. Come, climb down now to bottom of cabin. Bring everything useful. We will not be coming back. Grab food and water, all you can carry. Mickey, bring first-aid kit too. Waste not, want not." He disappeared between the crates again, but his voice came floating up, issuing a long string of orders. The packing bubbles began squelching again.

"Can you take Bobby down?" Douglas asked Mickey. Mickey nodded. I looked to Douglas, concerned. He wouldn't have asked that unless he still felt pretty bad.

"Are you all right?" I asked.

"I'll be fine. I just need a little time."

I whistled for the monkey—*"Who's Afraid of the Big Bad Wolf?"*— and it jumped onto my shoulders for a piggyback ride. I followed Mickey and Douglas down through the crates and webbing, down through the big foam plugs and the still-deflating bubbles. This sure wasn't space travel the way we saw it on TV.

When we got to the bottom of the pod, the footing was uneasy and squishy because of all the collapsed packing bubbles. I tried to peek out the windows, but there was nothing to see—only the sides of the landing balloons, plastered hard against the glass.

Alexei was pulling orange webbing off the walls. "Everybody carries his own luggage here. No robots, no porters. Luckily, we have portable pockets." He turned around, lengths of netting drifting from his hands. "Who is to carry littlest dingaling?"

"I will," said Douglas.

Mickey looked to him. "Are you sure you can handle it?"

Douglas wasn't all that certain about it, but he nodded anyway. "I'd better carry him. When he wakes up, he'll feel safer with me."

"Good point."

Alexei was rigging harnesses out of the webbing—apparently it had been designed for this purpose too. Douglas took off his blanket-poncho, and Alexei began hanging webbing on him. Mickey made sure that Stinky's blanket was turned on again, and as soon as Alexei was done, he secured Stinky in the improvised harness on Douglas's back. Then they started packing oxygen bottles, rebreathers, food, and water, into the webbing on his front. Also some medical supplies. Probably more sedatives. Finally, Mickey pulled a pair of goggles down onto Douglas's head and fitted them carefully over his eyes; then he helped Douglas put his poncho back on so it covered everything. With Stinky on his back, he looked like a fat shiny beetle.

That done, Alexei and Mickey began sorting everything else into equal packages of supplies. Everyone had to carry his own air, food, and water. I picked up one of the packs to test the weight and was astonished (again) by how light it felt.

"You are still thinking Earth gravity," said Alexei. "But you will get used to Luna very quickly. Take off your blanket now."

Mickey secured one pack on my back and another on my front. The one on my front had two oxygen bottles and a rebreather. He put goggles on me just like Douglas's—they completely covered my eyes and were held on by a thick elastic band; the elastic had padded cups that closed over my ears like expensive headphones. Finally, Mickey pulled the blanket-poncho back over my head, fastened it, and turned it on—I hadn't even realized how cold I was getting. I thought all my shivering was still from the shock of landing. The monkey bounced onto my shoulders and settled itself happily. I barely noticed its weight.

Alexei and Mickey outfitted themselves with even more stuff. Alexei was wearing his scuba suit again; it covered his whole body like a giant rubber glove, but he looked odd without fins on his feet. He had a lot of other gear too, a lot of closed equipment that I couldn't tell what it was for, and even a couple of suitcaselike boxes that he wouldn't let anyone else carry.

"Isn't that heavy—?" I started to ask, then shut up.

Alexei grinned. "You learn fast." He popped open a bright red panel and began pulling out flat packages the size and shape of seat cushions. "Everybody gets his own personal bubble. Read safety instructions, dingalings. No smoking. No shoes with cleats. No handball. Use plastic bags for peeing and pooping. Same as in pod. Put all trash in proper receptacles. If you fart, is your problem, not mine."

The bubble had a flexible circular opening just big enough to fit around a full-grown person. Mickey helped me into mine; it was like climbing into a giant condom. I even wondered aloud what would fit into a condom this big. Without missing a beat, Mickey replied, "You know what that makes you . . . ?"

Once inside the bubble, everything looked blurred through the transparent material. The bubble was made out of three separate layers of Mylar, each one "sturdy enough to support life under conditions of normal usage"—although I wasn't sure what "normal usage" actually meant in these circumstances. Each layer had its own zipper, and they could be opened in series from either inside or out.

Alexei showed us how the bubbles were designed so that they could be linked together, so two people could pass things back and forth if they had to, but it was a tricky operation, and he hoped we wouldn't have to. He also showed us how to use the glove-extensions that were designed into the walls of the bubble—that was in case you needed to handle something outside.

As soon as everybody was bubbled up, Alexei stepped over to one of the sidewalls of the cargo pod. He put his hands through the plastic gloves—"Always use gloves!" he shouted. "Don't try to push buttons through wall of bubble. Very stupid. You know what we call people who do? Statistics. Okay, I open airlock now." He started pressing buttons on the circular cover of the closest hatch.

I watched with interest. Alexei hadn't explained this part. I knew there was no airlock *inside* this cabin, and there was certainly no airlock on the *outside*. The only thing on the other side of that bulkhead was hard Lunar vacuum.

The hatch cover popped open and slid sideways on its tracks, revealing—the inside of a matching hatch cover on the other side of the bulkhead. "Okay, get ready for more beautiful clever—" Alexei unclipped a panel on the wall and pulled out two white circular rings, just the right size to fit into the hatch; they held layers of mylar folded over and over into a fat bulge—the whole looked like a plastic tunnel, all collapsed. On each side, there were three zippers, kind of like our bubble suits. Alexei opened one set of zippers, but not the other.

He slipped the rings into the space between the two hatches, then began fitting the ring on our side into a deep groove. The edge of the ring was as thick as a tube of toothpaste, but not quite as squishy; Alexei worked his way around the circle, pushing it firmly into place.

When he had the ring fitted all the way around the hatch-groove, he reached up above the hatch with one hand and below the hatch with the other, and pulled two matching levers sideways—the edges of the hatch-groove tightened firmly on the ring. Then he went around the circle again—three times, pressing the edge hard and making sure that the grip was firm all the way around.

Finally satisfied, he slid the hatch cover back into place and sealed it. "We wait now, for ninety seconds. We wait for seal to harden and test itself. Thirty seconds should be enough, but on Luna we do everything three times safely. Remember, universe does not give first warnings or second chances." We waited in silence. Finally, Alexei looked at his PITA. "Okay, ready?—eighty-eight, eighty-nine, ninety!"

He turned to a panel next to the hatch and unclipped its safety cover. He unlocked a second safety cover within and pressed the top button. It lit up, and said, "Armed." He pressed the next button, and it flashed, "Opening." We heard and felt the outer door of the hatch popping open and sliding sideways.

Alexei peered through a peephole in the hatch itself, then began turning a small valve next to it. We heard the hissing of air. "I am filling airlock now," he said. "We let air from cabin inflate outside balloon. Very simple. We use cabin air. Waste not, want not. You will notice pressure change, maybe. As we increase space for air, we get lower pressure throughout total environment. Are you noticing? I can feel it. But Loonies are more sensitive than terries. We grow up that way."

I watched, but I couldn't tell that anything was happening. After a bit, the plastic bubbles we wore seemed a little puffier, but not very much. And then my ears popped.

The hissing continued slowly. From time to time, Alexei peered through the peephole again, checking to make sure the airlock was inflating properly. I wondered how he could see clearly through the plastic bubble he wore, but apparently he wasn't having any trouble. Our bubbles puffed a little more, but mostly they still hung on us like big plastic wrappers.

After a bit, Alexei grunted in satisfaction and popped the hatch again. He slipped his goggles into place and slid the door sideways against the inner hull. Bright Lunar sunlight came filtering in through the opening. On the other side was a plastic tube opening into the airlock, a big plastic bubble. I peered through the hatch in curiosity, to see how it all worked. There were three zippers in the tube so it could be triple-sealed, the same ones Alexei had unzipped before inflating it. Clever.

"Make sure your goggles are on tight," advised Mickey. "It's going to get very bright." He reached over and tapped one of my earcups through the plastic. "And don't take these off or you won't be able to hear anything. This is also your communicator."

"I'm not stupid—" I started to say.

"Sorry, Charles. I didn't mean to suggest you were. It's part of the safety briefing. Required by law and all that. Can you hear me through your headphones? Are you ready?"

I nodded.

"Good. All right, I'll go first, then Douglas and Bobby, then you, Charles. Alexei will be last. Charles, Douglas—you want to be very careful coming through the hatch; it's all plastic on the other side—I'll help you through. If you feel any resistance, stop. Don't try to push or force your way through. You don't want to risk tearing the Mylar. It's strong, but there have been stupid accidents. Oh, and before you do anything else, put your gloves on and make sure you can do this—" Mickey held up his hands and wriggled his fingers. "Until you're inflated, you want to keep your hands available."

He watched carefully to make sure that Douglas and I followed suit. I found the closest set of gloves in my bubble, unzipped the covering patch, and shoved my hands through.

The hatch was only a meter and a half wide. Mickey would have had to bend down to step through it, but instead he scrooched low and dived straight through. He slapped the ground with his hands and bounced gracefully upright, turning around to face us and spreading his arms like an acrobat who'd just completed a difficult trick and was expecting applause. He grinned through the hatch at us.

"I can do that." I started to step forward—but Alexei grabbed me by the plastic and pulled me back. "Douglas next," he said.

The hatch was almost too small for Douglas—he had four oxygen bottles and two rebreathers strapped to his chest; air for him and Stinky both; and he had Stinky on his back.

But it turned out to be a lot easier than I expected. Alexei told Douglas to hold himself straight, then he picked him up, turned him horizontal, and passed him carefully through the hatch like a stick of wood. Together, he and Stinky and all their supplies must have weighed less than fifteen kilograms. All that Alexei had to do was lift, turn, and push. Douglas went right through. Mickey grabbed Douglas on the other side and turned him upright. Through the hatch, I saw the two of them exchange a quick hug.

Then it was my turn. I lowered my goggles into place, stepped forward—the body condom made moving a little sluggish, even in low gee—but I was determined to dive through the same way I'd seen

Mickey dive. But before I could, Alexei grabbed me, turned me sideways, and threw me through the hatch like a torpedo.

Four hands grabbed me on the other side, both Mickey and Douglas at the same time. They stood me up like a cardboard statue.

I looked around in amazement. We were inside a big round bubble, almost the size of the cargo pod.Maybe bigger. It was hard to estimate the volume of a giant balloon from the inside. An inflatable airlock! Beautiful clever! Just like Alexei said.

The bubble had two portals. The one I'd come through was a tube that led back to the cargo pod. On the opposite side of the airlock, the other portal was still zipped tight. Even as I turned to look back, Alexei was already diving in. He bounced upright, just as Mickey had. Behind him, the pod was a big lumpy shape, a dark cylinder with plump landing balloons sticking out all over it.

Beyond the blank wall of the bubble, everything was blurred—of course. I was looking through the plastic bubble I wore *and* the wall of the airlock at the same time. Even so, I could make out the raw shapes of things, both dark and bright.

Above, the sky was pure black. Impossibly black. To one side, there was a glare so intense I couldn't even turn in that direction—my eyes watered just from the sideways brightness. But to the other side, there was a shining silver land with an impossibly close horizon!

I stood and gaped. Uneven rolling surface, broken rocks, jagged lumpy outcrops. A rising wall of mountains off to one side. And everywhere—stark silence! *We really were on the moon!*

Wow!

Whatever else happened, I didn't care. Dad had kept his promise, even if he wasn't here, and I was suddenly filled with a rush of hot feelings. I wanted to thank him. He should have been here. He deserved to be here. And for a moment, I wished he *were* here—I wished I had someone to share this with.

Wow was insufficient.

This was . . . *the moon!*

Did Luna affect everyone this way?

And then I started laughing. I suddenly knew why Alexei was so crazy. I understood what it meant to be a *Lunatic*.

WUNDERSTORM

WE MUST HURRY." ALEXEI'S VOICE was loud in my ears. It sounded like he was directly behind me; the sound in my earphones was processed to come from the same direction as the broadcast signal, the only audio cues possible on the moon. I turned around to see him sealing the inner hatch of the cargo pod. That was it, the door was shut, we weren't going back. He bounced himself across the bubble to the opposite side—to the other airlock portal.

As he began opening the first zipper, he asked, "Who goes first? Mickey, do you want honor? Or you, Charles? Do you want to be first dingaling on moon?"

"Huh? Me?" I looked around. Maybe he meant some other Charles . . . ?

Douglas said, "Go ahead, Chigger. If you want."

"Uh—" I was about to say no, I wanted Mickey to go first, but I didn't want to look afraid either. "Okay," I gulped. Before I could change my mind, Alexei pulled me to the outer portal; it was identical to the one we'd just come through, only still folded up tight.

"Is close fit," he said. "I walk you through it, one step at a time. No fear, *da*?"

"*Da*."

"Good. Now we open one zipper, one zipper only—like so, *da*? Nothing more. Not yet." Very carefully, very slowly, he unsealed the first section of the tube. As the first air puffed into it, it inflated outward. "You step into tube now, Charles. No fear, okay?"

"Okay." I stepped carefully forward. It was hard to walk while wrapped in a personal bubble—I had to bounce more than walk, but maybe I could do this, with a little practice.

Alexei pushed me into the tube. I almost filled it. "Hokay, ready? I zip you up now. Watch how I do this. I pat out as much air as possible. Waste not, want not. You want tube tight around you please." He locked the zipper into place and I was sealed in the tube.

"Now turn around and face next zipper, Charles. Unzip it just like I show you. Just like that, *da*. Very good."

The next section of the tube puffed out like the previous one. I stepped into it and began pulling it close to me. As I zipped up the section behind me, I tried hard to keep the plastic close and push as much air as possible back into the tube. "Very good, Charles!" Alexei's voice came mostly through the earphones now.

As soon as the second zipper was locked in place, I turned around to the third and last one. This was *it*. One more step and I'd be alone on the Lunar surface. For a moment, I hesitated. . . .

"Go ahead, Chigger. You can do it." That was Douglas. I was glad he said that.

"Is good now, little dingaling. Open last zipper."

I swallowed hard. The seal was just in front of my face. All I had to do was grab it, unclick it from its safety catch, and pull it down. But it was more difficult than I thought. Sitting on my head, the monkey suddenly hugged me close. Did it understand? It patted the top of my head three times. Just like Douglas sometimes did.

Well, if even the monkey believed in me . . .

I pulled the zipper down—

—and my bubble puffed out around me. I was in a two-meter balloon. My ears popped at the sudden change in pressure. The tube spit me out like a watermelon seed, and I bounced across the Lunar surface, screaming in shock—then laughing in hysterical relief. It *was* funny.

"Don't go bouncing!" Alexei and Mickey both screamed at once. "Stay where you are. Wait for us."

"I'm not doing it on purpose!" I shouted back. I turned around to look at them. I was farther away than I thought. Ten meters, at least. I could see how small the cargo pod was—and the inflatable airlock too.

That was a scary moment—not because I worried that we were in any danger, but because for the first time I was *separated* from everything else. I was *alone* on the moon.

I still had my hands in the gloves of the bubble suit. I went down on one knee and reached out to *touch* the ground. Armstrong had been right—it *was* soft and powdery! Strong tears of emotion started welling up in my eyes. *Luna!*

The monkey patted me on the head again, three more times. Just like Douglas. So it wasn't an accident.

I stood up and looked around, being careful not to face the glare from the northeastern horizon, where the sun was just creeping over the edge of a rill. It would be creeping over that rill for a long time. Sunrise on the moon was fourteen times longer than sunrise on the Earth.

More to the north, there was something large and bright *and blue* in the black sky. The *Earth.*

How beautiful it was.

Half of it was cloaked in shadow, the other half was gleaming with day. Beneath the streaks of white cloud, I could make out the eastern shoreline of Africa. That big lumpy shape was Madagascar, wasn't it? I thought about all the horrors we'd left behind; they must be raging across the planet even now. But it looked so peaceful from here—how could anything on that soft blue world be horrible? It looked so fragile. For a moment, I regretted leaving. If I'd spoken one word differently, we could have all been home by now—

Home in a cramped tube. With Mom yelling at us. And the wind whistling overhead. And the whole house vibrating like an organ pipe.

No. I wouldn't have traded this moment for anything.

The moon.

I wished I could have said something more meaningful, but it all just came out as a single syllable—*wow.*

I'd seen people talk about this on television—that sense of awe that you feel whenever you arrive on a new world. Ferris, the most famous astronaut of all, said it best. "It doesn't matter how many previous landings you've made. Every landing is different, and every time, you're filled with a flood of so many different emotions at once, so powerful and so profound, that the only word that comes close to describing it is *wunderstorm.*"

Once he came to our school and he talked about the first landing on Mars. He compared it to looking at a landscape by van Gogh— *Wheatfield with Crows.* The first time you look at it, what you see is startling, and then it's even more startling, and then as you start to look at it closely, you realize just how startling it really is. The light is different—not wrong, *different.* And after a bit of puzzling, you begin to realize that this is an uncompromising vision; it isn't going to meet you halfway. You have to go all the way there or not at all. You have to surrender to it, because you can't change it. And then, only when you accept it on its own terms, can you see how beautiful it really is.

I could understand that. It's kind of like the music of Stravinsky or Coltrane or Hendrix. The first time you hear it, it doesn't make sense. You have to learn how to listen to it. Eventually, you have to accept it for what it is, not for what you think it should be.

And now I could see that the moon is like that too. It is what it is. Everything is different than what you're used to. Not wrong, *different*. The sky, the light, the horizon, even the shapes of rocks. Even the way the ground rolls away is different. *Everything*. Uncompromising. Scary. Harsh. Hostile. Beautiful.

Wunderstorm . . .

"Luna to Charles, Luna to Charles. Come in, Charles. . . . ?"

"Huh?" I turned around. The unreality of everything was getting more intense, not less. Mickey was already out of the inflatable airlock; he was standing in his own two-meter bubble, helping Douglas through the exit tube. Stinky was a big inert bulge on Douglas's back. Douglas unzipped the third zipper and puffed out into the Lunar vacuum like a big piece of popcorn. He didn't go bouncing across the ground like I did—Mickey caught him head-on, and they bounced back only a meter.

Alexei was the last one out of the balloon. He puffed up, but he didn't bounce at all. Obviously, he'd had a lot of experience. He hop-skipped around to where the airlock was still connected to the cargo pod and began zipping shut the seals of the connection tube.

"What's Alexei doing?" I asked.

"I am disconnecting airlock," he called.

"But why? What if we have to get back in the pod?"

"We are not coming back to pod. It won't be here anyway. But if we did need to reenter, is another airlock package here by outside hatch." He slapped the hull of the pod.

Alexei pushed the bubble up against the cargo hull to force as much air into the main part of the inflatable as he could, collapsing and sealing each section of the tube in turn. When the tube was folded back into itself and all three connections were secure, he turned to the hatch of the cargo pod. He reached up and down at the same time and grabbed two levers matching the ones on the inside of the pod. He yanked them sideways and the slot in the hatch ring widened, releasing its grip on the circular ring of the airlock.

Then he worked the ring loose carefully. Once it was clear, he pushed it up against the wall of the inflatable, securing it with Velcro patches. The airlock sat alone on the barren Lunar soil, a big bulbous blob of air—like a single drop of water perched on a waxy leaf. We didn't have to worry about it blowing away, of course, but the ground wasn't very level, and if it started rolling downhill, it might start bouncing, and it could go quite a distance. It might even rip or puncture.

But Alexei turned around, grinning. "Who wants to hold leash? Charles? Is good job for you, *da*?"

"Huh?"

"We take airlock with us. You never know when you might need a roomful of air. Waste not, want not, *da*?"

I was beginning to hate that. I wanted to waste something, just for spite.

He bounded over to me in that peculiar Lunar hop-skip of his. He trailed a length of flat ribbon, which he slapped onto one of the Velcro pads on the outside of my bubble suit. "There. You will bring plastic house. Is everybody ready to go? Hokay, we practice Luna walk. Pay attention, dingalings. Bounce on balls of feet like this, *da*? Not too high. Cannot walk in bubble, have to hop-skip, have to bounce. Looks easy, *da*? Is not. Is tricky. Alternate feet—bounce on one, bounce on other— hop-skip. No, Charles—keep hands in gloves. Helps keep bubble upside up. See bottom side? Extra thick—heavy on bottom to keep bottom side down. Bounce on padding, less risk to rip or puncture. Hold bubble upright by keeping hands in front gloves and bounce, hop-skip—watch, now!"

He came bounding toward me. He looked like a silver beetle trapped inside a glass onion. But he made very good time, bouncing and skipping across the dark silvery dust.

"You will learn quickly. But try not to fall down. You don't want to dust your bubble."

"Why not?"

"Because then everybody will know you are clumsy dingaling. They will know you are just arrive here." He turned away to see how Douglas and Mickey were doing. "Yes, just like that," he called. They were bouncing slightly on the balls of their feet, testing their weight in the soft Lunar gravity. They moved in slow motion—almost like dancers. I thought of Tchaikovsky and the *"Waltz of the Flowers."* No, the other one—the *"Waltz of the Snowflakes."* Only these snowflakes were silvery and danced inside giant transparent Christmas tree ornaments. We must have looked very silly, but at the same time beautiful in a Lunar kind of way.

"All right, everybody ready? Let us go. Take small steps first. Get used to Lunatic-walking. Learn to walk before learning to bounce. Follow me. Holler if I go too fast." He pointed southward and went bounding off. Douglas followed, little steps first, then as he felt more comfortable, he began taking bigger hops. Mickey looked back to me. "Come on, Charles—"

I took one last look at the bright blue marble of the Earth. It was directly behind us. And then I followed. The inflatable airlock came bouncing after me like an oversize balloon.

A WALK IN THE DARK

WE DIDN'T GET VERY FAR—just to the top of the first hill. And it wasn't much of a hill. Alexei made us stop so he could check our rebreathers and our air supplies again. We were all fine, but if any of us had needed personal attention, he would have taken us into the inflatable so he could open our bubbles. Even if we didn't have the inflatable with us, he could have still joined any two bubbles together at their openings. But nobody needed immediate attention, and I was glad about that.

Once that was finished, Alexei turned and faced the distant cargo pod. From here it looked pitifully small in a very large landscape. Despite the nearness of the horizon, once you gained a little height, the moon could be a very large place.

As Alexei had told us, there were no footprints leading away from the pod—just occasional soft dimples in the Lunar dust where we'd bounced along. A skilled tracker would be able to follow the trail of depressions, but only if the dust was thick enough and the shadows were right.

"Might want to shield eyes," Alexei said, and did something to his PITA.

"Huh? Why?" That was Douglas.

"Watch." He pointed.

In the distance, the cargo pod shuddered. It jerked upright—then a flare of dazzling white appeared underneath it, and the cargo pod lifted away from the gray plain.

"What are you doing, Alexei?"

"I hide the evidence." The bright flame of the pod sputtered in the sky and went out. "It will come down again, thirty or forty klicks west of here. In darkest shadow, very rough terrain, very uneven. Hard to find, harder to get to. When trackers come looking for pod, maybe they will look in wrong place first, lose valuable time, *da*?"

I couldn't see the pod anymore. Either the skin of the bubble was too blurry, or the pod was too dark, or the sky was too black. Without the flame, it was gone.

I wondered if we'd feel the crash, or if it would bounce down again. Either way . . . we were truly *alone* on the moon now. I shuddered—and it wasn't just from the cold seeping up through my feet.

Mickey must have seen how scared I was. He took a half skip toward me, close enough to press his bubble against mine. He grabbed my hand and gave it a quick squeeze. Then he whispered, "Are you going to be okay, Charles?"

"Yes."

"You sure?"

"This isn't like the pod. We're on solid ground. I'll be fine."

"Do you want me to stay close to you, just in case?"

"Uh—if you want to."

"I'll do that."

"Okay."

"Thank you, Charles."

"You can call me Chigger."

Behind the goggles, under the silver poncho, it was hard to see what anyone was thinking, but Mickey's sudden bright smile was clear. "Thanks, kiddo."

"Hokay," said Alexei. "We go. Everybody, on the bounce—come, we must hurry—"

"How far is it?" I asked. "How long will it take to get there? Where are we going—?"

"Thirty klicks, give or take some. Six hours, maybe. We go catch train. No more talk. Use up oxygen. Follow me, this way—"

It wasn't that hard to hop-skip across the Lunar surface. It just took a little practice to find the right rhythm. After a bit, Douglas and I were just as good as Alexei and Mickey. The four of us bounced along like a bunch of Happy Flubbies from that god-awful kid show that Stinky used to like so much. For a while, Douglas and I were even shouting, *"Boinng! Boinnnnng! Ba-boing-boinnngg!"* with every bounce—at least, until Mickey started singing. *"It's a small world, after all . . ."* and Alexei threatened to puncture all of us.

But it was exhilarating great fun—it was kind of like skipping and kind of like hopping and kind of like flying, but mostly like nothing I'd ever done before. The feeling of speed and power and strength—it made me feel like Superman, like there was nothing I couldn't do. I started laughing and shrieking and giggling—so hard, I couldn't stop—

That's when Alexei called the first rest break, and the first thing he did was check my oxygen balance to see if I was getting too much or too little, or what. "You are too light-headed." He looked surprised to find that my rebreather settings were all fine, even allowing for the increased exertion of bouncing.

"I'm laughing because it's fun," I said. "You remember fun, don't you?"

"We have six hours to go, little dingaling." He frowned. "Will you still have laughter thirty klicks from now?"

"I bet I will," I promised. "You were right—I like Luna."

"Do not get overconfident!" he snapped at me. "Overconfidence kills. You will not make very pretty corpse—and I have no intention of dragging you across Luna for burial." Alexei was suddenly very unhappy and very grumpy. None of us had ever seen him this way before. Had he heard something on his radio?

He seemed to realize it himself; he turned back to me, and spoke in a gentler tone. "Just concentrate on being safe. Is too dangerous to have fun here. Hokay, break over. Pay attention—see tall rock to left, with head sticking up into sun? We head toward notch, just to right. We stay in shadow. Let's go—on the bounce."

After that, it wasn't as much fun. After the novelty wore off, it was just something to do. But there was a lot to see—and I wished we could just stop and look at stuff sometimes. Some of the rocks glittered, and I wanted to pick them up and take them with me, but we didn't have sample bags, and the first time I stopped, Alexei yelled at me again, so I didn't do that anymore.

To say that the scenery on the moon looks different is an understatement—kind of like saying the *Titanic* had a rough crossing. *Everything* on the moon is different. But it's the kinds of differences that are surprising. There's no wind or water erosion on the moon, so all the rocks look scruffier and the ground looks harder. It's hard to explain. You have to see it in person. Even pictures don't work.

Mostly we were in shadow. To the east, the sun was lurking just beneath the edge of a long broken rill. A couple of times we had to dart through streaks of sunlight, and once in a while, if we bounced too high, the sudden sideways glare felt like a hammer blast. A couple of times, Alexei said, "*Gohvno!*" and once he said, "*Chyort!*" which sounded even worse. I assumed it was in reaction to the intensity of the sunlight, but I didn't ask. It could have been anything. His dark mood was headed toward pure black.

Every fifteen minutes we stopped to rest for five, no matter where we were—unless it was in sunlight. I didn't ask why; it wasn't too hard to figure out. Our silvery ponchos could keep us warm against the cold Lunar night and they could reflect away some of the intermittent sunlight that hit us, but they couldn't cool us off in the direct glare of the sun.

Every time we stopped, Alexei checked my rebreather, and Mickey checked Douglas's. I protested that I could look at my own numbers, but both of them cut me off at the same time. Safety demanded that everyone check everyone else's settings.

By the time of our fourth rest break, it was pretty much routine. Mickey had taught Douglas and me how to read the rebreather displays, so now all four of us were checking each other at every stop. Alexei even showed us how to share our air in an emergency. The rebreathers had tubes that could connect directly through special valves on the front of the bubble suit. If someone needed air in a hurry, you could just plug right in. But you had to make sure the connection was secure or you could explosively evacuate your rebreather. "Useful only if you want to become a self-propelled object."

So far, our oxygen use was just about what Alexei had expected. We would have enough to get where we were going—if we didn't make any wrong turns, and if we didn't have to double back to go around something.

The problem was, the ground was getting rougher. We were approaching a place where two craters overlapped; the wall of one was broken by the wall of the other. The only way to get to where we were going would be to cross some very uneven terrain. But we had to do it. We had to get out of the crater we were in and onto the plain beyond.

Alexei finally admitted he was worried. But we already knew that. The more he studied the display on his PITA, the worse his language got. I asked Mickey if he knew what Alexei was saying, but all he would translate was, "Your mother was a hamster," which didn't make any sense at all.

Mickey stayed close to Douglas; I think he was worried about Stinky, but Douglas could reach back and squeeze Stinky's arm or his leg and report, "He's still warm. He's still breathing," and that was as good as we could hope for right now.

What we really hoped was that he wouldn't wake up until we got to where we were going. The train station, or whatever it was, Alexei had picked out.

For some reason, I wasn't scared anymore. I felt like I should have been, but I wasn't. We were off the Line, off the map, very far from anywhere safe, about as alone as we could be—and I felt fine.

I wondered if other people felt this same way on Luna—alone and free at the same time. The only sound was the sound of my breathing, and the distant noises of everyone else grunting across the ground playing through my earphones. The bitter cold of the ground tried to seep through the bottom of the bubble, but the poncho kept radiating, and the air in the bubble stayed just warm enough. The light from beyond the rill was bothersome, but my goggles adjusted themselves to block the worst of it. *I felt fine.*

I thought about that.

I should have been worried. I should have been scared. But I wasn't. Why not?

Because I was safe with Douglas? Maybe. That was part of it, I'm sure. But maybe it was more because there wasn't anyone else around to tell me what to do or where to go or who to be. It wasn't the silence *outside* that was so wonderful. It was the silence *inside*—the freedom from all those voices that weren't mine.

It was like when I used to go up in the hills away from the tube-town, so I could listen to my music. It wasn't just the music. It was the silence.

This was such a sudden realization, I stopped in mid-bounce. Wherever we finally ended up, it had to be a place where I could have silence every day. A place where I could listen to my own thoughts.

CLIMBING THE WALL

AT THE SIXTH REST STOP, Alexei made us all eat half an MRE—the red one marked *high-energy pack*. It was made with lots and lots of high-energy stuff—like hydrogen, kerosene, Palmer-chips, and pluto-nium. It tasted exactly like its list of ingredients, only not as good.

At the seventh rest stop, Alexei tied us all together with a nylon cord. There was a loop on the front and back of each bubble, and he secured the line through both loops. He put himself in the lead, me directly behind, then Douglas, then Mickey bringing up the rear. The inflatable airlock bounced along behind Mickey.

We were heading uphill now, and the slope was getting steeper and trickier. He didn't want anyone slipping and bouncing away. "If you roll downhill and get big puncture and lose all your air," he told me as he secured the cord, "I will be very unhappy. It will ruin my whole day. So I keep you close. We go slowly now. No more bouncing. Just tiny hop-steps. Very careful."

I took his warnings to heart and stayed close behind him. A couple times, I stopped to look back—to see how Douglas was doing—and each time, he yanked me forward. I got the feeling he didn't want me to see how much trouble Douglas was having, climbing up the hill with Stinky on his back. Stinky couldn't have weighed more than four kilos, five at the most. But even five kilos starts to get heavy after a couple of hours. And Douglas had to carry supplies for both of them. I didn't think he was used to this kind of sustained exertion. But he didn't have much choice in the matter. Alexei couldn't do it—obviously. And Mickey's strength was questionable because of all the time he spent *out* of Earth's gravity. And besides, Stinky was *our* responsibility, not *theirs*.

But even with the frequent rests, I could see that Douglas's endurance was wearing thin. And we hadn't even gone a third of the way yet.

Halfway up the slope, it stopped being a slope and became a wall. Even worse, it was a wall in *sunlight.*

"Oh, *chyort!*" I said. "Why didn't we go around?"

"This *is* around," said Alexei. "Is not so bad as it looks. If you are fast." He was fumbling with a tool he had hung *outside* his bubble. I hadn't paid much attention before, but he had several pieces of external equipment hanging off his back. The one he selected now looked like a miniature harpoon gun—because that's exactly what it was.

It had a windup spring, and it fired a dart with an unfolding plastic grapple. A long lightweight cord hung from the dart in a flimsy-looking roll. Alexei studied the wall above, then hesitated and turned back to the display on his PITA. He zoomed in on the Lunological map and grumbled at the numbers. I could see him turning them over in his head—and coming to the conclusion that we really didn't have a choice in the matter anyway, we'd come this far, we didn't have the air to go back down and try another way, so it really didn't matter after all, did it?

"Hokay," he announced. "Let's see if Alexei is as clever as he brags." He hefted the dart gun and turned on its laser sight. Because there was no atmosphere, there was no dust to highlight the beam, so he had to track the red target dot up the wall above us and dance it around his aiming point. He was aiming at a broken shelf in the shadow of a tall outcrop. Above it was the sunlit portion of the wall. The range finder said the shelf was only fifteen meters up, but it looked a lot farther.

"Is not too bad," Alexei decided. "We will do this in two steps. First stop is shelf. Map says it is wide enough for all of us, and we will still be safe in shadow. Second stop will be harder. Longer climb, all in sunlight." He began winding up the spring in the dart gun. "But this will work," he said slowly, "if everybody follows direction. So pay good attention. We use first climb for practice. Learn to climb. We go up to first shelf, all of us. We catch breath, then we go—*bing, bing, bing, bing*—up to top and over, back into shadow quickly. You will have to move fast, very fast. Is longer climb, so you must keep moving. No time to admire view unless you wear sunblock two million. Any question?"

We all shook our heads.

"Douglas?" That was Mickey. "Do you want me to take Bobby? We can transfer him here—"

"No. I'll take him over the top. The other side is downhill, isn't it, Alexei?"

"Yes, other side is downhill. We go back to Lunar plain. Downhill, uphill, but nothing like this. Nothing too serious."

Something about the way he said that last part. "Nothing too serious . . . ?"

"Nothing you can't handle, little dingaling. Get past this part first, please?" He turned back to the wall. It was harder to take a range sighting on the top of the ridge because it was blazing bright and the laser dot was invisible in the glare. Finally, Alexei gave up in disgust. "Never mind. I know how high from Lunar survey. I do this by ear."

He sighted carefully and fired the dart gun—the dart soared lazily up, unfolding its long grappling prongs as it went. It rose out of shadow and blazed in the hard light of the sun. The line followed it up in silence, uncurling and turning bright as it went. At the apex of its flight, the dart hung motionless in space for a long moment—then it began drifting back with a deliberate slow grace, arcing over and down—it disappeared out of view behind the glare of the wall above us. The line went looping after it, flying across space in lazy swirls.

Eventually, the line began to settle and fall back. After what seemed like forever, it finally went slack. Alexei waited until it was hanging like a bright yellow streak against the wall; he held up the display on the base of the dart gun so I could see. It showed a row of green ready signals. According to the readouts on the butt of the pistol, the grapple-dart had landed somewhere over the wall of rock and the grapples had securely deployed. We hadn't heard anything, of course, so we had to depend on the signal sent back through the line. Alexei punched a couple of buttons, and two more green signals appeared. "Grapple has tested itself," he announced. "It will hold us." He locked the safety and hung the gun on the back of his balloon.

"Hokay. Now pay attention. I teach dingalings to do this. Is not too hard—even a dingaling can learn. First, take hands out of gloves. Now put gloves away, please. You do not want them sticking out and catching on something. Here, I'll help. Now reach below and switch to other gloves—big red gloves under regular ones. Put your hands in—*da*, feel that? See how glove is molded around big castanet-claw? That's your grabber. Close glove, feel how it clicks shut? Make sure you feel click. That click means grabber has closed very tight around cord or tool or anything else you reach for—holds very very tight, so don't put anything tender inside. Especially not anything you are attached to."

"How do you unclick it?" Douglas asked.

"Is good question. Squeeze again, also press with thumb and middle finger—feel little click? That is grabber releasing grip. Very easy. Click, unclick. Grabber holds you up even if hands get tired. Pay attention to this, Charles dingaling. Make sure grabber goes click. If it doesn't go click, you have no grip. Very bad news. You don't want that. Do not try to hold cord without grip. You will risk slipping. If you slip, maybe you cut or rip glove. Very bad news if that happen. I have to write letter to manufacturer of bubble and ask for refund. So don't slip. Instead, make sure grabber goes click. Practice now. Click, unclick. See?"

He made me do it over and over again until he was sure I had it right. "Hokay, good. Now this is how you will pull self up, hand over hand. Slowly. Grab, click, pull—unclick other grabber, grab, click, pull—unclick first grabber, grab, click, pull. Understand? If no click, stop and try again. Don't unclick one until the other is clicked. Don't go to next step until you check that previous step is success."

"What if the clicker breaks?"

"I will write letter and get refund."

"I mean—what happens to me?"

"You will not have to worry about letter. I will."

"Oh, good. I hate writing letters."

"All right, watch me now. I will go first. To show you how it is done. Pay attention to feet. Watch what I do. Do you know how to rappel?"

"Rappel?"

"Down mountainside. Kick, slide, kick, slide—? You have seen pictures, *da*? We are going to rappel. But not down—*up*. You do not want to scrape bubble against rock, do you? *Nyet*. Hook feet in loops there. Pull knees up. Brace yourself against wall. Kick away from wall. Then pull self up. Lift knees again and brace self to come back. Hold self against wall, kick and pull. Brace, hold, kick and pull. Understand? Watch. I will go first. I will make it look easy. Then you will follow. You will make it look clumsy. We will all laugh at you. But you will get to top without mishap, because you will be slow and careful. And we will all pat you on back, and say, 'good job, well-done, little ding-aling.' And you will have great adventure to tell grandchildren about someday. Unless you are like Mickey and Douglas. Then you will have to tell someone else's grandchildren. Not to worry, I will lend you some of mine. They will not believe that senile old Lunatic smuggled crazy terries across *Lunnaya zhopa*. Bottom of moon. Moon's rectum. Place where sun never shines. Truthfully, it *never* does. We will be there soon. The *priamaya kishka*. You will tell them you were crazy terrie. They will believe. Hokay? Watch now, here I go."

Was he serious? Or was he saying all that stuff to distract me? Either way, it worked. I was distracted.

Alexei pulled himself up the cliff wall in a series of three fast bounces. His movements were quick, but they were also deliberate and careful. He'd done this before and his experience showed. He stretched his right arm as high as he could, grabbed and clicked. He kicked away from the wall, pulled himself up as high as he could, grabbed and clicked. His feet came back to the wall and he braced himself. He looked down at me and grinned, unclicked his lower hand, reached up, grabbed, clicked, kicked away from the wall, and pulled.

Once more and he was at the top. He kicked away from the wall and pulled sharply at the same time—he floated over the edge of the shelf and disappeared from view for a moment. He popped back into view and waved down at us. "Hokay, dingaling! Your turn."

"It's Dingillian," I corrected.

"If you can get to top, I will learn new pronunciation. Until you get up, you are still dingaling."

Douglas moved up beside me. "You okay, Chigger?"

"Yeah, I can do it. Can you?"

He nodded. "I'm getting tired, but I can do it. Let's get this over with."

I closed my eyes and visualized the steps—what they would feel like. I took a deep breath. I reached up with my right hand. I grabbed. I squeezed. The glove went click. "Remember to kick!" Alexei shouted. I had almost forgotten. I kicked and pulled at the same time—I was a little heavier than I expected, but a lot lighter than I was used to. I bounced up and away from the wall. I reached as high as I could with my left hand, grabbed, and clicked. "Pull your knees up—" I had plenty of time to brace, everything was slow motion. My feet hit the wall. "Don't look down—" Too late. I was already looking.

I was higher than I thought. But I wasn't scared. I'd been this high when I did the rope climb in gym class. As long as I didn't look back to see the rest of the slope we'd climbed—

I took a breath, visualized what I had to do next. And did it. This time it was easier. Unclicked the right hand. Kicked away. Swung up. Grabbed. Clicked. Pulled up knees. Braced. Looked up. Alexei waved. He was closer than I expected.

"Is good. One more. *Da?*"

"*Da.*" Closed eyes. Took a breath. Opened eyes. Unclicked, kicked, swung, pulled, grabbed, clicked, braced. It was easier to do than describe.

Alexei was almost close enough to reach out and pull me up. "Kick and pull sharply up," he said. I did, and he grabbed my arm—both arms—and swung me over the top, setting me down firmly on a slab of Lunar rock. He reached over and slapped the top of my head. "Is good job, little dingaling. Not as clumsy as I expected."

The monkey patted my head too. I'd almost forgotten it was there.

"I thought you said you weren't going to call me dingaling anymore."

He pointed to the wall above us, where it turned into blazing sunlit rock. "I said when we get to *top!*"

TO  THE TOP

DOUGLAS CAME UP THE WALL next. Despite the weight of Stinky on his back, he came up easily. At least, it looked easy to me. He was only a little bit out of breath when he bounced onto the shelf. Mickey came right after; he pulled the inflatable airlock up after himself.

We took a rest break then. We weren't catching our breath so much as cooling off. Alexei wanted us to turn off our heaters and radiate away some of our heat. I don't know how much good he thought that would do, I was already cold, and it scared me to think of the kind of heat we'd be experiencing in a few minutes. But he kept saying, "Not to worry. Is just an extra precaution. Bubbles are insulated both ways."

When we checked each other's air, Alexei advised each of us to release a few seconds of oxygen into our bubbles from the spare tanks we carried. "And put rebreather tube in mouth for climb up, please?" I was beginning to think this was far more dangerous than he was letting on.

To the east, the hills were outlined by an edge of light. Sunrise. We were just below the edge of their shadow. Just how bright was the full force of the sun in hard vacuum? We were about to find out—one good bounce upward and we'd know.

I reached up and touched the monkey on my head. "Why don't you swing down and climb into the harness on my back?" I said. To my surprise, it understood exactly what I wanted. It bounced down, climbed up under the poncho, and secured itself in the harness on my back, just like Stinky was secured on Douglas's back. "Thank you," I said to it. I bounced lightly on my feet, testing my balance.

"Hokay," said Alexei. "Anybody ready? I go now. Watch please?" He grabbed the cord. "Here I go—" He bounced up into the light. His bubble glittered with reflections. And then he was up and up and up and over the top and gone.

A second later his voice came loud in our ears. "I am fine, thank you for worrying." He added, "Is not as hard as it looks. Is nice view from up here. Charles dingaling, is your turn."

Douglas gave me a good luck slap on top of the head, and I clicked onto the rope. I closed my eyes, visualized, and leapt—

The sudden bright wash of light from the east felt like a hammer-blow. Even my goggles weren't enough to keep me from being dazzled. I felt like I'd opened a furnace door, just from the glare alone. The whole inside of the bubble sparkled with reflections that wouldn't quit.

—and grabbed the rope and clicked. Released, kicked, and pulled. Suddenly my goggles were blurry, with hot tears streaming from my eyes. From the light. Grabbed for the rope, missed—clicked anyway, and swung around out of control for a moment, turning first away from the sun, and then right back into the full force of it—I unclicked my empty hand, looked up for the rope, found it, grabbed, clicked, remembered to test, banged the wall, I'd forgotten to bring my knees up, bounced and hung for a moment, and said, "Oh, *chyort!*" The tears were real now. Tears of frustration.

"Keep coming!" cried Alexei from above. "Don't stop!" shouted Douglas and Mickey from below.

I swallowed hard, visualized—was it getting hot in here or was it my imagination? Had I scraped my bubble? Did I hear something hissing? Was I losing air?—visualized again and unclicked, kicked, and climbed. I fumbled again—but this time grabbed the cord anyway, clicked, and hung, braced myself against the wall. I couldn't see. The tears were a torrent. The light was awful. If I could just see—

"Only three more and you are here, dingaling! Keep coming!"

Visualized, unclicked, kicked, grabbed, clicked and pulled—okay, I could do this. Two more times. Took a breath, did it all again on the other side. Once more—except I couldn't see a thing. My goggles were wet, my eyes were flowing. I pulled my hand out of the lower glove and pushed my goggles up, tried to wipe my eyes with my wrist. That was a mistake. My goggles fell off my head and bounced away somewhere below me. I felt them hit the floor of the bubble. Even with my eyes closed, the light was an orange blast. I said some of those words that mom hated so much.

"What just happened?" Douglas demanded.

"He dropped his goggles," Alexei said. "Not to worry. Is easy enough, we do it with eyes closed. Come up, dingaling. You are almost here."

It *was* getting hot in here. It wasn't my imagination. The sweat was dripping from my armpits. If I could just see—I squinted up. The rope was a blurry line. Maybe if I could get the goggles. I pulled my knees up, bringing the floor of the bubble almost up within reach. I reached around, fumbling for the goggles. If I could just find the goggles—my hand scrabbled frantically.

"Charles!" That was Douglas. "Don't stop! Keep climbing!"

"I just want to grab my goggles. I can't see!"

"Forget stupid goggles! You are close enough to do without."

And then I swung around just a little bit and my view widened beyond the bubble to the scenery outside.

I was hanging on the inside wall of a Lunar crater. It was big, round, and deep. The pod had come down on the far side and we'd crossed the rubble-strewn floor, always keeping to the shadow until we'd finally climbed its steepening slopes—until we'd finally had to pull ourselves up the wall. From this perspective, it looked bigger and deeper than the Barringer Crater in Arizona, only it was painted in hard colors of black and silver and bright.

And I was hanging halfway up the inner wall.

In a bubble of air. Baking in the sun. Surrounded by vacuum and dark. And nothing below me and nothing above me, hanging only by a single arm. My arm was getting tired. And no one anywhere could save me.

I knew the distances weren't the same here on the moon. I knew the gravity wasn't the same. I knew my weight was lighter. But my eyes told me distance and my brain remembered Earth. And my stomach clenched.

"Please, little Dingillian. Put hand back in glove. Reach up. I will pull you, but you will have to kick away from wall. Hokay?"

For a moment, I forgot everything—even the light. I could hear myself thinking—*This is a really stupid way to die.* And then the other side of my brain argued—*No it isn't. This is really dramatic.*

And then I got annoyed, and said, "You're both wrong—"

"What's that, dingaling?"

I didn't answer. Somehow I got my hand back into the glove. I ignored the light and heat and unclicked. I kicked away from the wall, swung myself up, grabbed, and clicked, braced against the wall, unclicked, kicked, swung, grabbed, clicked, braced—"Now!"—and kicked straight down, bounced up—and Alexei grabbed my arm and pulled me over the top, pushing me into the shadow of a looming crag.

I flopped down cross-legged on the broken Lunar rocks and let the tears flood out of me. My eyes were dazzled so badly, I could hardly see.

"Is he all right? *Is he all right?*" That was Douglas.

"He is fine. He is just shaked and baked a little. Wait—" Alexei hovered over me, checking air and temperature and everything else he could think. He looked all over my bubble for leaks, but the pressure meter said it was fine.

"Can you sit here quietly, Charles? I bring your brother up?"

I managed to nod, and Alexei moved back into the light, and started calling instructions down to Douglas.

I wiped my eyes with my hands, again and again. Suddenly, someone was handing me an alcohol-wipe. The monkey. The package was already open, but my hand was shaking so bad I couldn't take it. So the monkey reached up and began gently washing my face. I had to laugh at the absurdity of it. When the monkey finished, it held up my missing goggles. It wiped them off carefully and dried them, then made a big show of inspecting them with a harsh monkey squint. Finally, it handed them over, and I managed to get them back on and my poncho adjusted.

"Okay, you," I said. "On my head again." The monkey did it in a single bounce.

I stood up and turned around. Alexei was just swinging Douglas over the edge, pushing him into the shadow next to me. He grabbed my arms. "Are you all right?" His tone was beyond concerned. It was scared.

I nodded. But I still felt jittery. He stood there, watching me, waiting for me to say something, but I was caught in another one of those terrible churning *wunderstorms*, realizing a thousand things at once. Not just the ordinary stuff about how dangerous adventures were—but the extraordinary stuff about how much I loved my brothers and how lost I'd feel without them—and how much it would hurt them if they lost me. I didn't want to hurt them anymore.

And there were a bunch of other thoughts in that *wunderstorm* too—about Mickey and Alexei and the monkey. But I couldn't say any of it right now. I couldn't say anything. It would all have to wait.

SUMMIT

AFTER **M**ICKEY **PULLED HIMSELF UP,** he and Alexei checked me over again. Then they checked Douglas. Then Douglas checked them. It was a little crowded in the shadow of the crag, but it was safe enough for the moment.

Alexei insisted that we each drink some water and take a few bites of high-energy pack. He wanted us rested before we started down the other side. There was probably a lot that we all wanted to say. I knew that Douglas was angry—he probably wanted to know why Alexei was putting us all in such danger and why Mickey had agreed to this. Mickey should have known better. I could almost hear the argument—it sounded a lot like Mom and Dad.

But Douglas was smart enough not to raise the subject here. We weren't exactly out of danger, and our first priority had to be getting to safety. And after we got to safety, then the argument wouldn't matter anymore, would it?

For a while we sat in silence. Mostly, I was waiting for my eyes to undazzle. All I could see were big purple splotches everywhere. Nobody said anything at all. We just listened to ourselves breathe. We were tired. This wasn't fun anymore. And even though none of us would say so, we were all scared. It was real now—we could die out here.

Alexei had deliberately chosen this landing site because it would be hard to get to. He had chosen this path across the broken Lunar surface because we would be hard to track. We were out of view of any of the Lunosynchronous satellites, and the ones in polar orbit were equally unlikely to spot us.

We were hidden in the shadows, we were masked by the rocks. And even our thermal signatures would be partially lost in the hash of heat and cold. So there wasn't much likelihood of someone finding us. We weren't going to be picked up unless . . .

Douglas was thinking the same thing. He looked to Mickey. He took a breath. "Mickey . . . ?"

"What?"

"I'm thinking that, uh . . . maybe we should call for help."

"Douglas? Are you all right?"

"This is awfully rough. On Charles. On Bobby." He hung his head. "On me too. I almost didn't make it up the wall either. We can't keep taking chances like this—" He looked up, looked across at him. "How do you feel?"

"I'll go along with whatever you decide." And then he added, "I think the safety of you and your brothers comes first."

Alexei was looking down the other side of the wall. He was looking at his PITA. He wasn't looking at us. He said, "I understand your fears. But you are doing all right. Hardest part is past us now. Is all downhill from here. If you choose to go on."

Douglas ignored him. "How long do you think it would take them to get to us?" he asked Mickey.

Mickey shrugged. "We're close enough to Gagarin Station. They could have a boat out here in three hours. But we'd have to climb down to someplace level."

"Yeah, I already figured that out."

"Did you think about the marshals?" Alexei asked.

"What about them? They were waiting for us at Farpoint. We're beyond that now. Aren't we?"

Alexei shrugged.

"Aren't we—?" Douglas repeated.

"Possibly. Possibly not. *Probably* not." He took a breath. "Most certainly, I think not. There are bounty marshals on Luna. It takes only a phone call from Farpoint to North Heinlein or Asimov or Armstrong or . . . Gagarin."

"Gagarin?"

Alexei shrugged. "Is possible." He took his hand out of his glove to scratch his chin. "Is certainly a logical place to start looking for me. Maybe not you. That's why we drop pods everywhere. So they have no way to know which where to start. Remember, they don't know that I am with you. They might figure it out, because I am not at Geosynchronous anymore. But they have no way to know for sure. So Gagarin could look like red herring. Is inconvenient to get there from north. Only one train line. They would have to take transport. They might not do that on a wild-moose chase. Might check easier targets first. Whole point is to go where it is too inconvenient for marshals. That makes time to keep going, stay ahead of them."

I kept waiting for Douglas to turn to me, to ask me what I was thinking, but he stayed focused on Mickey.

And meanwhile, Alexei nattered on. "But let's play thought experiment game. Say we send signal. Everybody knows we're here. All over news instantly. No secrets on this rock. Rescue boat gets here in three hours. Maybe less, but don't cross fingers before they hatch. Fifteen, maybe thirty minutes to transfer us into boat and get up again. They are in no hurry. They will follow procedures. We take three hours back to Gagarin or wherever else they choose to take us. You figure it out. If Gagarin, that gives marshals six hours from time of distress call to intercept us. Anywhere else, even longer."

"Is six hours good or bad?" I asked.

"If marshals are serious about catching you, they can get to anywhere on Lunar surface within two hours. They have fast transport. Is not impossible. Depends on how many marshals, how desperate they are, how much confusion from big blue marble."

Douglas didn't say anything to that. Neither did Mickey.

"If you want to send distress call, Douglas, I will understand; but I promise, if marshals want you bad enough, then there will be marshals waiting for you. But if you send distress call, I will not wait with you. I will go on without you. We have broken many laws getting here. But they do not know for sure I am here, and I already have many alibis." He sighed. "This is part of why I put you into money-surfing web. So if something bad happens and you get caught, all the money used to purchase six pods will look like your own. My hands are washed. Lawyers will argue that purchase of all six pods and evasive trajectories was intent to escape legal warrants waiting at Farpoint. They will tie you up in paper." He made a face. "So, no, I do not advise calling for help. It could get very ugly for you."

That almost sounded like blackmail. Like fat *Señor* Doctor Hidalgo, who'd almost threatened us too. Even behind his goggles, even bundled in his poncho, I could see that Douglas didn't like what Alexei was saying.

He turned back to Mickey. "Say we go back down to the crater floor. How long would that take? Fifteen minutes? Thirty? We could all get into the inflatable and wait for them, couldn't we?"

"Is better to go forward," said Alexei. "Better landing site on this side." No one paid him any attention.

"Is that what you want to do?" Mickey asked Douglas.

"What I *want* . . . and what I have to do are two different things. I have to think about Bobby and Charles first."

"Um—?" I said.

Douglas shook his head, dismissing me. "No, Chigger. I have to make this decision for all of us."

"Well, that didn't take long."

He looked up sharply. "What didn't?"

"For you to break your promise."

"What promise? Oh—"

"Yeah. *That* promise." To Mickey, I said, "That he wouldn't make any more decisions for all of us without talking to me."

"Chigger." Douglas put on his patient grown-up voice. It was scary—because for a moment, he wasn't Douglas anymore. He was *someone else.* "I'm really scared here. You nearly got killed. And I nearly didn't make it up either. We're not trained for this. I'm sorry. This was a mistake. I'm sorry for getting you into this. We should stop here—"

"You sound just like Dad," I said angrily. *That was who he'd become.* "Remember when he told us he was leaving. How he wouldn't stop apologizing: 'What I want and what I have to do. We made a mistake. I'm sorry. I have to call it quits before it gets worse. Blah blah blah.' And remember how we all felt? We were so angry, because we wanted him to keep trying, just a little bit more—"

"This isn't the same."

"Yes, it is. It's quitting. Dad taught us how to be quitters. Real good."

"It's surviving."

"Yeah, Dad said that too."

"You have a better idea?"

"Yeah, I do. Let's keep going. We can quit anytime. We have to go down the mountain anyway. Let's go down and see how we feel when we get to the bottom."

Douglas looked to Mickey. Mickey shrugged. "He's right. We have to go down, no matter what. And we have enough air. We don't have to decide here. You want to think about it?"

Douglas looked at me. Even though his eyes were hidden by his dark goggles, I could see he was annoyed. He didn't like being backed into a corner. Not by me, not by Alexei, not by Mickey. But he was always logical, and that was his real strength. So finally, he nodded, and said softly, "All right, we'll wait."

Mickey put his hand on Douglas's bubble, as if to touch his shoulder. "Can you make it down? Or do you want me to take Bobby?"

Even though I couldn't see his expression, even though his body language was hidden by the poncho, I could see he was tired. I could hear it in his voice. "No, I'll take him. But when we get down, we need to rest—maybe even a nap?"

Mickey and Alexei exchanged a glance and nodded to each other.

"Turn heaters back on, please. Everyone take a little fresh air," Alexei said. "And we will start down the other side."

"Wait a minute—" I said. I could finally see clearly again. I stepped out into the sunlight, as close to the edge as I dared. I looked back down into the crater we'd just climbed out of. It was deeper than Barringer— and wider. But I wasn't afraid of it anymore. It was just scenery. It looked like a Bonestell.

I stepped back away from the edge, back into the shadow. "All right, I'm ready."

Alexei reached over and slapped my hands with his. "Good job, Charles Dingillian. We go now. *Da?*"

"*Da.*"

IN CONTROL

THE FUNNY THING, **D**OUGLAS WAS right. This was too dangerous for us. This was a mistake. It had been a mistake from the beginning. It was a whole cascade of mistakes—Mom's, Dad's, Mickey's, and all the lawyers and judges who'd stumbled into this with us.

But most of all, it was *our* mistake. And everything we were doing now was only making it worse. We were getting farther and farther away from help. Every step we took was only making it harder for someone to find us and rescue us.

And then there was that business with Alexei. The more I thought about what he'd said, the more it pissed me off. He'd threatened to abandon us. He'd gotten us into this and he wasn't going to help us get out—not unless we did it his way. And I didn't like that. And probably neither did Mickey and Douglas. But none of us were talking about it, so maybe that was even more evidence how serious this was.

Or maybe Alexei was right. He was a smuggler and a spy and Ghu knew what else. He knew this stuff. He knew the dangers. And, supposedly, he knew how to avoid them. Maybe it was just an overdose of *wunderstorm* and we were getting panicky.

And then we started down, and there wasn't a lot of time to worry.

The way down didn't look as easy as the way up. Alexei had brought us to a place where the rim walls of two overlapping craters intersected. Most of the slope below us was hidden by long sideways shadows. Even so, we could see that the way down to the floor of the second crater was a broken avalanche of ugly rock. It was a rubble-strewn slope, gashed by several nasty chasms.

I didn't see how we were going to negotiate it—maybe by jumping from boulder to boulder? But it turned out to be a lot easier than that.

Alexei retrieved the grapple-dart from where it had secured itself and wound up the cord carefully; then he reloaded the dart gun and sighted down into the rubble and beyond, marking the range to the distant silver plain. He muttered to himself in Russian and I got the feeling he was doing some complex calculations in his head.

Finally, he made a decision. He sighted down into the rubble, tracking the laser dot as far as he could toward some distant landmark. Then he aimed the pistol forty-five degrees upward, and fired. The grapple-dart flew up and away, trailing the cord after it in great uncurling loops. As before, it glittered in the sunlight, yellow against the black sky above.

The dart arced over and down into the gloom below, and as the line fell back into shadow with it, it began blinking out along its length. As before, we had to wait until the butt of the dart-pistol confirmed that the grapple-dart had secured itself.

Now Alexei looped the other end around a convenient boulder and began pulling it as tightly as he could. Periodically, he'd turn and look down into the gloomy crater below with his goggles set for light-enhancement. Then he'd grunt and resume tightening the cord. Mickey helped him. When they were done, we had a Lunar zip line.

"All right, *Mikhail*, do you want to go first? Or should I?"

"I think you'd better."

Alexei nodded agreement. "I think so too. All right, Dingillians—this part will be easy." From his equipment pack, he produced four little wheels with handles, he handed one to each of us. "Use your grabbers. Click right grabber here, reach up, put wheel on line, click left grabber here. Once you are clicked, you cannot fall off. So enjoy ride. Pick up feet, hold knees as high as you can, ride line all the way down to bottom. Is long way, *da*? So do not go too fast. Twist handles this way for braking, wheel will slow. Twist other way to release brake. Is good idea to control speed all the way down, especially for beginners. When you get near end, you will see ground getting closer. That is time to go very slow. Even slower than that. Slower than very slow. Do not scrape bubble suit. You will do fine. I promise. Is great fun and best way to go anywhere on moon. Any questions?"

I raised a hand.

"Yes, Charles?"

"Did you do this on purpose?"

"Do what?"

"Choose the bounce-down sight so far from where we have to go? I mean, couldn't you have brought us down a little closer?"

"I could have, yes. But I wanted the bad guys to look somewhere else. So we hike a little bit and they go to look in six places much farther away. By the time they don't find us, we will be past wherever else they think to look. If I did not think you could handle this, Charles, I would not have used this plan." He added thoughtfully, "I make this plan a long time ago, I am very proud of myself that it works so well. You should be proud too—that you are strong enough to keep up. We are almost on schedule. Wait for my signal. I will call you down as soon as it is safe. Hokay, any other questions? No? I see you all on the bottom." He swung his wheel over the line, clicked onto the handles, kicked off with his feet, and sailed away over the edge.

"*Waaaaaaaa-haaaaa! Hoooo-hooooooooo-hooooooooo eeeeeee-yyyy!*" He wailed all the way down—or at least as far down as he had the air to shriek. He floated down across the Lunar landscape like something out of a bizarre dream—a silver sprite in a shimmery ball.

And then there was silence. It stretched out for the longest time.

The three of us looked at each other.

"Why doesn't he say something?" I asked.

"Maybe he's concentrating on his landing," Douglas said.

"What if he fell off?"

"He can't fall off."

"What if the bottom of the line is in a jagged rock field and he got punctured before he could warn us? What if it's not safe to go down after him?"

"Charles, stop scaring yourself. Nobody else is going down until Alexei tells us it's safe."

"But if something happened to him—?"

"Nothing happened to him," said Douglas.

We both looked to Mickey.

Mickey was studying the PITA on his wrist. "His signal is clear. His readouts are green. He's alive. He's just not talking. At least, not to us. He might be calling ahead to someone else. Not to worry."

We waited in silence. I looked at the Earth for a while. It hadn't changed its position in the sky. And the terminator line didn't look all that different from before. Most of Africa was still waking up. *To another horrible day.* We'd only been traveling two hours. We still had a long way to go.

And then, the worst thing of all happened.

Stinky woke up.

And announced, "I gotta go to the bathroom. Where are we?"

Mickey and Douglas and I all groaned at the same time.

"Can you hold it?" said Douglas.

"No," said Stinky. "I gotta go *right now!*"

"Uh-oh—" I said. I knew that tone of voice.

And in that same instant, I had a chilling insight about Stinky—and why he was the way he was. I was only angry at Mom and Dad. But Stinky was angry at everyone. It was about *control.*

Everybody in the family had authority over him. Everybody older had power. He had none. There was only one thing he could say to bring everything else to a stop. There was only one thing he could do to seize control.

And every time he did, everything else came to an immediate stop. At that moment, his single declaration became the ultimate power in the family. Whenever things were totally out of control—there was Stinky demanding, "I gotta go *now.*" If nothing else, he could always be depended on to focus the dilemma on himself.

Without even thinking about it, I stepped over to Douglas. "Stinky! Can you hear me?"

"Yes. Where are you, Chigger?"

"I'm right here." I reached over and pressed against the back of Douglas's bubble, patting the bulge on his back that I assumed was Stinky. "Feel that?"

"Yes. I gotta go!"

"Listen to me. You've got to hold it. If you go now, you'll have to sit in it for six hours, for the rest of the day. And you won't be able to escape the stink. Is that what you want?"

"But I really really gotta go! I mean it!"

"Wait a minute—" That was Douglas. "Maybe I can work something out in here. Bobby, can you wait a minute—I've got a bathroom bag. You'll have to climb down from my back—"

"I'm all tied up, I can't get out. I gotta go."

Mickey said, "Can you turn around, Douglas? I'll invert the gloves and untie him. Or do you want to use the inflatable?"

"Bobby!" I said. "Which do you want to do first? Go to the bathroom or ride the roller coaster?"

"What roller coaster?"

"The one right here. The Lunar roller coaster."

"I can't see it. Douglas has his blanket over me."

"Do you want to go on the roller coaster?"

"Yes!"

"Can you hold it—?"

"Um . . ."

" 'Um' isn't good enough. Can you hold it?"

"I'll try—"

" 'I'll try' isn't good enough either. We have to know. Can you hold it for a few minutes more? Yes or no."

"Yes."

Mickey turned to me. "Charles, we can do it here. Douglas can take care of him in the bubble. Or they can go into the inflatable."

"Mickey, he went to the bathroom back in the pod, just before bounce-down. He doesn't have to go—not as badly as he says he does. He hasn't eaten anything in the last twenty-four hours, he doesn't like the MREs. And even if he had eaten, he'd be constipated anyway."

"And what if you're wrong?"

"I've spent the last eight years monitoring his bowel and his bladder. After you've cleaned him up a couple of times, you start paying attention to these things."

Mickey wasn't convinced. "He sounds awfully insistent to me."

"He does this *everywhere*," I explained. "At home, in the car, on trips. Nobody else can ever use the bathroom if he doesn't want them to. If he's not the center of attention, he's gotta go. He does it to escape spankings. He does it to get me in trouble. And he did it at Barringer Meteor Crater—you heard about that?—because somewhere he's figured out that announcing that you have to go to the bathroom is the reset button for reality. You notice, he hasn't said a word for the past two minutes? If something interesting is happening, he forgets he has to go."

Right on schedule, Stinky piped up. "I wanna go on the roller coaster!"

Mickey turned back to Douglas. "What do you want to do?"

"Chigger is right. Let's keep going."

"We haven't heard from Alexei—" Mickey fiddled with his phone. "Alexei—? Can you hear me. Respond please?" To me, he said, "It's a long way down. If he went slow—"

"He could still answer, couldn't he?" I bounced up and flipped my wheel over the cord, clicking my grabber onto the other handle with an ease that surprised me. I was getting used to this stuff.

Before I could kick free, Mickey blocked me. "Charles, wait—"

"Why? If something happened to him, we're on our own. Waiting up here is only going to use up oxygen. You have to stay with Douglas and Stinky. I can do this—"

"Mickey, he's right. Let him go. We have to get down from here."

Mickey sighed and stepped out of the way. I don't think he liked any of us right at that moment.

I didn't care. I kicked free.

GETTING DOWN

I SAILED OFF THE ROCKS and out into open space—above the crater wall, above the rubble-strewn slope, above the gaping chasms, toward the distant gray Lunar plain. Parts of it were so dark the shadows were tangible.

There wasn't as much sense of motion as I expected—and there wasn't as much falling feeling either. Even so, my heart lurched in my chest. Here I was again, hanging in open space—

I tried looking up. That didn't help. The cord was zipping by too fast. I looked down. That was even worse. I could see how fast the ground was coming up. The line was too steep. I twisted the handles as hard as I could.

The wheel slowed, the vibration in my hands and arms changed. But it didn't feel slow enough. "Oh, *chyort!*" I should have started sooner.

"Charles—?"

"I'm trying to slow down." The ground was coming up awfully fast. And I was feeling *really* stupid. I twisted the handles harder—but they were already at their limit; they clicked into a locked position. The wheel was stopped—but I was still going! The wheel skidded and bounced along the cord. Was this what happened to Alexei? Betrayed by the Lunar laws of physics? There wasn't enough weight on the wheel, there wasn't enough friction between the wheel and the line, they were both too polished—*and the line was too damn steep*! I was just going to keep sliding all the way down—until I slammed into a big unfriendly boulder.

It was a long way down. More than a klick, maybe two. How fast would I be going when I hit bottom? Fast enough to hurt? Fast enough to puncture the bubble suit? Twenty kph? Thirty? More? If only I had a couple of Palmer tubes—

That gave me an idea. I took my hands out of the connecting gloves and hurriedly connected the emergency rebreather tube to the valve of the bubble suit. It snapped immediately into place. This was going to be tricky. I pointed the valve and opened it in a series of short bursts.

I couldn't hear the outrush of air, but I could feel it. I came skidding to a stop on the line. My downward rush was halted. The line wasn't as steep here. The brakes held. I took my finger off the valve. I couldn't believe it—it worked! I'd traded a few minutes of air—maybe more— for a safe landing. A fair trade. I shoved my hands back into the gloves and looked down. I was hanging thirty meters above a yawning abyss. It was too dark to see how deep the bottom was.

"Chigger?" That was Douglas. "What was that screaming about?"

"What screaming?"

"You were screaming."

"No, I wasn't—was I really?"

"Yes, you were. What happened?"

"I was going too fast. The brakes didn't work. Well, they worked, but they didn't. Alexei screwed up, I think. Even if the wheel doesn't turn, you'll still go skidding down the line. But it's okay. I stopped myself. I used some of the air from my rebreather."

"How much?" That was Mickey.

"Not too much. Just a few squirts."

"Charles, I don't want to alarm you. But it's hard to tell how big a squirt is in vacuum. Don't panic. We've all got spare bottles. We're not going to run out of air. But that's not a real good idea."

"It was the only one I had, Mickey. Anyway, you and Douglas are going to have to do the same thing."

"No, we're not. I'm going to figure something else out. Where are you now?"

"Hanging maybe a hundred klicks over nothing in particular."

"How much farther do you have to go?"

I peered ahead. "The ground levels out soon. So does the line. It looks like maybe two or three hundred meters. It's hard to tell."

"You'll have to go very slow."

"I know that!"

"All right. Just keep talking."

My arms were starting to get tired. I reached up, grabbed the handles firmly, took a breath, and carefully began *un*twisting—not very much, just enough to unlock the brake and let the wheel start rolling. Only a little bit. I began moving forward. Very slowly. So far so good.

The thought occurred to me that I might have reacted out of panic. The line had a lot of sag in it. Of course the highest part would be the steepest. Lower down, the line would level off enough that the brakes would be more effective.

The more I thought about it, something felt wrong about this. Alexei had planned everything else so carefully; why did he screw this up? Lunar explorers used all kinds of tricks for getting up and down steep slopes. This couldn't have been the first time he'd done this. So why didn't he know better? Had he been careless? Or stupid? Or what?

The ground came gliding up to meet me. Everything was back to slow motion. It was like one of those flying dreams where you drift along like a cloud. I tightened my grip and came to a halt, suspended only a couple of meters above the Lunar dust. The line went on farther, but the ground dropped away again. Maybe this would be a good place to get off . . . ?

Two meters. I did the math in my head. One-sixth of two meters. It would be like jumping off a chair. I could do that. "All right," I said. "I've found a stopping place. It's not too far to the ground. I'm going to drop down here. Wait a minute." I looked up at the wheel and the handles and visualized what would happen when I released my grip. The wheel would pop off the line, dropping me down. I just had to be ready. "Here goes—"

My hand came free and I fell. The bubble bounced down onto the ground. I didn't fall over.

"I'm down."

"Good job, Chigger. All right, now move out from under the line. You don't want to get accidentally bumped. We're coming down now. Mickey and I are coming down together."

"Huh?"

"You'll see. Just keep out of the way."

I stared up the line and waited. Several very long moments later, three luminous bubbles appeared very high up. One very large one, and two smaller ones with silver figures inside. They were moving very slow—painfully slow.

"I can see you," I reported.

"We can see you too," Mickey called back. "We'll be down in a bit."

It took longer than a bit, but I could see them clearly, so I wasn't worried. When they finally did arrive, they hung lower on the line than I had. In fact, they were holding their knees up so they wouldn't scrape the ground. They brought themselves to a stop, hanging all together like the last three grapes on the stem. Douglas lowered his long gangly legs to the ground and unclipped himself and Mickey.

He showed me how they'd used some of the leash to the inflatable to tie their two wheels together to make a kind of pulley rig. With both wheels locked, the cord had to twist around first one wheel, then the other. It couldn't skid—at least not very well.

"We should have thought of this before," said Douglas. "All three of us could have come down at the same time. With your wheel rigged in, we would have had even better control. We did skid a bit at first, but not as hard as you did."

We were on a low hill. Mickey was already settling the inflatable on the level crest of it, opening up the first zipper of the entrance tube so Douglas could go in and take care of Stinky. As soon as Douglas was on his way in, Mickey came over to me and checked my air bottles.

"How bad?" I asked.

"Not as bad as it could have been. You used up half an hour of breathing. Maybe more. You'll just have to swap in one of your O-bottles earlier, that's all. Later on, we might have to equalize your air supply with mine or Douglas's. What you did was very smart, Chigger—and also very stupid. I hope you realize that. We don't have air to waste. Alexei didn't leave us much margin."

"I didn't have time to think, Mickey."

"I know you didn't. And I'm not bawling you out. We've just got to be more careful from here on. Okay?"

"More careful than what?" I asked.

Mickey looked exasperated. "I mean, we're going to have to think harder. Do you understand what I'm saying?"

"Do you understand what *I'm* saying? Is there anything I could have done different?"

He got it. Or maybe he didn't. "All right. Fine. Let's just drop it." He turned back to the inflatable. "Doug, do you need my help?"

Douglas was already inside. There was a smaller silver beetle next to him—Stinky. I couldn't see what he was doing, but from his posture, it looked as if he was squatting over a toilet bag. "No, I think we've got everything under control."

Mickey turned to me. "Chigger, you stay here. I'm going to follow the line down to its end and look for Alexei."

"I'll go with," I said.

"I'd rather you didn't. It might not be very pretty—"

"I've seen dead bodies before," I lied. Well, in the movies anyway.

"Besides, you might need help bringing back the extra oxygen bottles and all the other stuff that Alexei was carrying."

"All right," said Mickey. "But if you throw up inside your bubble, you'll have to live with it."

"I'll be fine," I said. I hoped I was right. I followed him, hop-skipping over the hill.

END OF THE LINE

WE FOLLOWED THE CORD FOR several hundred meters. The ground was uneven, and generally sloping downward, though here and there it rolled upward too. There were boulders everywhere, of all sizes—some as big as cars or houses, others even bigger; so we couldn't really see too far in any direction. But we weren't worried about losing our way. Not as long as we kept the line in sight. Mostly it was ten or twenty meters over our heads.

Mickey turned his transmitter all the way up and called for Alexei to respond, *please*. We waited and waited, but there was no answer.

Several times we paused to circle around some of the bigger boulders, just in case Alexei had come down behind one of them, or even on top of one. But if he had, we didn't see him. Mickey kept checking his homing device, but Alexei's beacon didn't register. Maybe he was out of range. That was possible. Or maybe it was no longer transmitting. That was possible too.

Then we came to a place that was very slow going. The boulders were too big and uneven and we had to watch our bounces carefully. When we got past that, we took a short rest, each of us taking a small drink of water. Mickey looked over at me. "Y'know—Chigger, you're a pretty good kid."

I didn't know how to respond to that, so I just grunted something that might have been thanks.

"At first, I thought you were a whiny pain in the ass—but you can take care of yourself. Better than I expected. I respect you for that." And then he added, "I hope that maybe you're starting to respect me too."

"Yeah, I guess so," I said.

"Charles, you resent me. I see it on your face every time you look at Douglas and me together. And I don't blame you. Douglas and Bobby are all you've got left, and I must seem like an intruder to you."

I didn't know what to say to that either. After a bit, I mumbled half an agreement. "Well, yeah."

"So, let's agree to work together anyway, okay? Because we both care about Douglas. And Bobby."

"Um. Okay."

We slapped gloves, kind of like a handshake, only clumsy, and then we checked in with Douglas. He told us to be glad that odors cannot travel through the vacuum of space.

We pushed on.

After another fifteen minutes of bouncing and skipping through house-sized boulders, we came around a tall rocky prominence and stopped. We had finally reached the end of the line. Literally. The place where the grapple-dart had anchored itself.

Mickey bounced up to the top of a boulder, then bounced over to the next. He tilted himself forward to inspect the dart. "It looks fine," he said. "I'm going to see if I can loosen it and bring it with us. We might need it again."

"But Alexei had the pistol."

"Well, we'll just have to find him."

I was already circling the outcrop, looking for Alexei's body. I wanted to find it—and I didn't. I was morbidly curious—and I was terrified. If Alexei was dead, then where were we . . . ?

"All right, I've got the grapple-dart," said Mickey. "I'm coming back down." Two quick bounces and he was beside me again. Above us the line was falling slack. "Did you see *anything?*" Meaning, did you find *Alexei?*

"Uh-uh. It's like he popped off the line and flew away into space."

"Knowing Alexei, I could almost believe that." Mickey bounced up and grabbed the sagging cord above us. He pulled the free end over the rocks and began winding it up. "Even without the pistol, this might be useful. Waste not, want not, remember?" He handed me the line to hold, then circled the promontory, looking for anything I might have missed. He spiraled outward among the boulders, then came back to me. "Nope. He must have jumped off earlier. We could search for days and never find him." After a moment, he added, "And we don't have enough air for that."

We started back toward Douglas and Mickey resumed winding the cord. "You know," he started, thinking aloud. "There was a lot of horizontal slack at this end of the line. He might have had time to slow down, even stop." And then he added, *pointedly*, "You might have too."

"Yeah, but I didn't know that."

"No, you didn't."

We picked our way back slowly. We took turns gathering up the cord and winding it in loose coils. It looked unnaturally thin to me—but everything on Luna seemed spindly. If they made it only one-half as strong as it would need to be on Earth, it would still be three times stronger than necessary for Luna.

We spread out and searched from side to side, looking for any sign of Alexei. Even a track on the ground would have been welcome. We searched as carefully as we could—but we were in shadow, there were a lot of boulders, and it would have been easy to miss him in the dark.

Mickey stopped to study his PITA. He whispered something to it, studied the display. "All right," he said, with terrifying finality. "I'm going to call it. You know what that means?"

"You think he's dead."

"It means we can't waste any more oxygen looking for him. If he's dead, we can't help him. And if he's alive, we still can't help him—" He stopped and faced me. "Do you know the first law of Luna?"

"Uh—no," I admitted.

"It's very cold, it's very selfish. *Take care of your own well-being first. Otherwise, you have nothing for anyone else.*"

"That doesn't sound selfish to me. It sounds like good advice."

"It is. But a lot of dirtsiders don't like it. The equations are too cold for them. You know what that means?"

"Everybody does. Not enough air."

"That's right." He took a breath. "All right. Let's go back and talk to Douglas. It's time to make a decision."

Douglas and Bobby were sitting together inside the inflatable. Bobby was munching an MRE and sipping at a canteen. I checked the time. We'd have to take another bathroom break in an hour. If we waited until he went now, we might manage two hours, two and a half. Maybe.

Mickey and I stopped outside the inflatable. We checked each other's air supply. We were both fine. Mickey told Douglas what we had found—and what we hadn't found. He traced lines in the thin dust. "Here's where we started. Here's where we are now. Here's the closest two train lines. We could have gone to this one, to the east. It's only half the distance, in fact it's still closer, but there are some steep crater walls in the way. And we'd be in sunlight a lot of the time, dodging from shadow to shadow. Experienced Loonies wouldn't have had a problem with it, but it's too risky for beginners. So Alexei had us going the long way, but safer—heading for this other line here. This way, we stay mostly in shadow, and the biggest problem is that one little crater rim—yeah, *that* was a *little* one—and a little bit of sunlight, and making sure that we have enough air. He thought we could do it. So did I. I still do."

I couldn't tell what Douglas was thinking. Behind the blurry wall of the inflatable, he was an unreadable silver ghost.

"If we call for help," said Mickey, "we'll probably end up in the custody of bounty marshals. Alexei was my only real connection on Luna. I might be able to make some phone calls, but I can't think of anyone who'd get involved for us. For you. Unless—"

"Unless what?"

"Unless you know who paid your dad to carry the monkey. They'd certainly have an interest in reclaiming their property."

"No, they won't," said Douglas. "It's a decoy. Having us caught by bounty marshals serves them perfectly. It's a public distraction."

For an instant, the monkey tightened its grip on my head, reminding me it was there. For an instant, I wondered again if it was really a decoy. But something told me I didn't want to voice that thought aloud. "So what's our alternative?" I asked. "Without Alexei, can we still get to the train?"

"I think so. My maps are good. Not as good as Alexei's, but he showed me the way, and I think I can get us to Prospector's Station."

"And then what?"

"Then we keep going. We take cargo trains. We zigzag. We avoid interception points. We get to the catapult somehow. Or we sit here and call for help. But we have to decide in the next few minutes, because if we don't start moving soon, the window closes. We won't have enough air."

"How much air?"

"My guess is six hours if we're active, eight if we're resting. We can call for help anytime, Douglas. But if we're going to move, we have to move now."

"What about the closer train?"

Mickey pointed east—toward the harsh glare of the rising sun.

Douglas turned and looked. He didn't like what he saw. I could see that much in his posture. "And the farther one?"

Mickey pointed south, toward the darkness.

Douglas stared into the gloom. "You really think we can do it?"

"Alexei thought so. And he knew the risks better than any of us."

"All right," Douglas said. "Let's do it."

"You want me to take Bobby?"

"No, I promised him he'd stay with me. Let me get packed—"

A HUNCH

WE DIDN'T TALK ABOUT ALEXEI. Not too much. There wasn't much that either Douglas or I could say—and whatever Mickey was feeling about his friend, he wasn't saying anything to either of us. I got the feeling he was as much angry at Alexei as he was grieving.

After a little bit of discussion, we decided to go for thirty minutes at a time between rest breaks. It was mostly downhill, and we were getting our Luna legs now, and Mickey was worried about my air. He didn't say so, but he checked my readouts a lot. He wanted to get us to Prospector's Station quickly.

For a while, we were moving through boulders, and then just rocks, and finally, we were back on hard rock and thin dust again. That was easiest. We were heading toward a landmark that Alexei and Mickey had identified as our halfway point.

About fifty years ago, in the first days of serious Lunar exploration, the Colonization Authority put down thousands of surveying beacons all over the Lunar surface. These were nothing more than self-embedding spikes with reflectors on top. The reflectors were dimpled with hundreds of little right-angle corners so that any beam hitting them would be reflected straight back to its source.

The length of time it took for a beam to return told you how far away you were. By triangulating on several reflectors, you could calculate your position almost to the centimeter. The reflectors also made it possible to make highly accurate surveillance maps of the Lunar surface. The geography of Luna was actually better known than that of Earth—because two-third's of Earth's geography was underwater.

We were heading for one of those reflectors now. There was nothing else there, just the reflector. But three generations of Lunar explorers used the reflectors as opportunities to recalibrate their PITAs.

The reflectors were also good for data storage, sort of. Anyone could point a beam at a reflector from just about anywhere, as long as they had line of sight.

Suppose you're on Earth and you aim a beam at a Lunar reflector. Luna is 3.84E5 kilometers from Earth. The beam travels 384,000 kilometers one way, or 768,000 kilometers round-trip. That's 768,000,000 meters, 768,000,000,000 millimeters, 768,000,000,000,000 micrometers. 768,000,000,000,000,000 nanometers. Or . . . 7,680,000,000,000,000,000 angstroms. There are 10 angstroms in a nanometer.

A blue laser, emitting at 4700 angstroms produces one wavelength every 470 nanometers. One wavelength every .47 micrometers. One wavelength every .00047 millimeters. One wavelength every .00000047 meters. 4.7E-7 meters.

So if we divide 7,680 trillion angstroms by 4700, we get 1.634 trillion wavelengths between Earth and Luna. Round-trip. If I'd figured this right, if you used one wavelength per bit, you could put nearly 1.634 terabits on a round-trip beam. Or 204.25 gigabytes every three seconds. Not too bad. About 100 hours of music, recorded in hi-resolution mode.

That sounded a little low to me. But I was figuring it in my head, and it was possible I'd screwed up the numbers. And I was using a blue laser because that was the only angstrom number I could remember. If you used an X-ray laser, you could multiply that by 10,000, and that would be 2,042 terabytes every three seconds. Which represents a much bigger music collection—about a million hours in hi-res. More if you played all the repeats.

If you used 8 beams, each one a different wavelength, all synced together, you would send 8 times 2,042 terabytes—16⅓ petabytes round-tripping between Earth and Luna. Was that enough to hold the sum total of human knowledge? No, probably not. I'd heard somewhere that the human race had so many recording machines functioning, we were generating a couple thousand terabytes of information *per day*. So maybe the Lunar circuit was only big enough to hold a week's worth of global data. But if you threw out all the crap that wouldn't matter a week from now, 16⅓ petabyes was certainly enough storage to hold the most *important* information the human race needed.

But the moon is only visible a few hours per day. So your connection only works as long as the moon is in the sky. On the other hand, if you're broadcasting from L4 or L5, you've got a permanent line-of-sight connection with Luna—and the farther away from Luna you get, the more data you can have in transit. As fast as it returns, you retransmit it. Round and round it goes and no piece of data is ever more than a few seconds away.

There was a time—before I was born—when some folks thought that Lunar reflectors could be used to store the entire world's knowledge in a network of laser beams zipping around the solar system. But by the time the reflectors were in place, the cost of optical data cards was already in free fall, and it was obvious that using the reflectors for data storage was another one of those good ideas that was obsolete by the time the technology was ready. You could put 500 gigabytes in a credit card. You could put 500 terabytes in half a pack of playing cards. You could put it in your pocket. Or inside your robot monkey. . . .

Oh, hell. Memory wasn't about size anymore, it was about density. You could even put a few petabytes into a monkey if you packed them tight enough. Maybe even an exabyte or two. That should be enough to hold the sum total of human knowledge. Of course, *those* would be expensive. Petabyte bars were worth thousands. Exabytes were worth millions. . . .

Hm.

But if you only wanted to smuggle 2,042 terabytes of information from the Earth to the moon, you didn't need to hire a courier and a bunch of decoys. You could go out in the backyard, lash your xaser to your telescope, point your telescope at the target, feed a signal into the beam, and fire away for a few seconds. Cheap, easy, impossible to intercept.

Dad had bought two cards of used memory for the monkey—which would have seemed weird at the time, except Weird and I had been distracted by Stinky's near-headlong tumble into Barringer crater. Why would we need so much memory for a toy anyway? And what was in that memory? I hadn't had a chance to look at the cards closely, and I wasn't going to do it with anyone else around.

What was it that had to be transported that couldn't be transmitted? Money? Codes? Information? No. All that could be phoned in. So it had to be something that couldn't or wouldn't travel by beam.

There was only one thing I could think of . . . and it almost made sense. Maybe.

Quantum computing couldn't be beamed. I didn't understand all the details of quantum computing, but it used optical processing. The internal lasers of the processing unit were split into multiple beams and parallel processed. Interference invalidated the process. You couldn't measure the beams, you couldn't look to see where they were—the minute you did that, you changed the data.

You could beam the results of a quantum process, but if you transmitted the process itself, you created interference and invalidated the result. So all quantum computing was specifically linked to its hardware. You couldn't even guarantee that one quantum processor would exactly duplicate the results of another quantum processor. That had to do with chaos theory and fuzzy logic and the fact that quantum processors are affected by the time and place they're operating in. So quantum processors are best suited for weighted synaptic processing—*lethetic intelligence engines.*

A trained intelligence engine was worth at least a quarter trillion dollars. Maybe more. Depending on the training. And you couldn't just pipe the training from one engine into the next, because quantum doesn't pipe. Each engine had to be specifically trained.

According to Douglas, who was reporting what he read in *Scientific American*, they had finally gotten to the point where the intelligence engines could be trusted to train each other. I didn't understand the details. When Douglas started talking about forced coherency, congruent processing, and the fissioning of holographic personalities, my eyes glazed over. I finally had to tell him that if he was going to stay on our planet, he had to speak our language. What he did manage to get through to me was that there was a way of making two quantum processors marry each other so that their processing was temporarily synchronized—which meant that computers were finally moving from *simulated* sentience (which is what the monkey was) to *actual* sentience in a chip. Not that the average person would notice. Simulated sentience was good enough to fool most folks.

It didn't make sense that we might be carrying an actual IE unit in the monkey, those things were guarded like plutonium. Despite the fact that IE chips were always the McGuffin in every movie about high-tech robberies, it was impossible to steal one—because they guarded themselves. Anything interfering with their beams invalidated their processing—and every alarm in Saskatchewan would go off simultaneously.

No, it was my hunch that we might be carrying one of the quantum synchronizers—some kind of industrial smuggling or something. We didn't have to understand what it was. All we had to do was deliver it.

Only thing is—now that we had thoroughly screwed up Dad's travel plans . . . we had no idea where we were going or who we were supposed to deliver this thing to. Maybe the marshals trying to intercept us were working on behalf of the rightful owners. And maybe not. How would we know?

Anyway, it was only a hunch. Probably, it was something more mundane—like a bunch of codes—if it was anything at all. Dad said it was a decoy, but what if it wasn't. What if the smugglers thought it would be safer for the decoy to carry the McGuffin?

But even if the monkey had a quantum synchronizer or whatever inside, we'd have no way to tell just by looking at the outside of the card. And if there were some way to open it and look inside, that would be interference, and that would ruin it. So whatever it was, it was never going to be anything more than a hunch to me.

But . . . maybe I should think about this hunch for a bit.

Suppose we really were carrying something. It would have to be something *extremely* valuable, and the mule carrying it would have to be *extremely* stupid—I didn't like that part, but it made sense. A mule smart enough to know what he had would be smart enough to sell it to the highest bidder. The trick was to give it to someone who would be happy just to get a ticket offworld and who wouldn't fit the profile of a smuggler. Like a dad going to a colony with his kids. And the damn custody battle made it even better, not worse, because it was just the right kind of distraction. Smugglers didn't take their kids with them. Smugglers didn't have angry wives chasing them. And . . . if you had that kind of money to invest in that kind of mule, then you also had the kind of money to buy his way through customs or anywhere else.

Wasn't it convenient that Mickey was there? And his mom, the lawyer? And Judge Griffith too? And what about Alexei? Was he part of that plan too? No, he couldn't be. He didn't fit in—or did he? Who was on which side?

Or was I just being paranoid?

Could I even be sure about what Douglas said he knew? *No—don't go there, Chigger. That's* really *a shortcut to lunacy.*

Well, we were in the right place for it. That was for sure.

Along about then, Mickey stopped us and came back to check my oxygen. "I thought so," he said. "I should have made you change tanks at our last break."

"Huh?"

"You've been muttering in my ears for the last three kilometers."

"I'm fine. See?" I flipped the readout up so I could see it. It was flashing a pretty shade of red. "See?"

"Yes, I see—that's very nice. Does the word *hypoxia* mean anything to you?"

"She was Socrates' wife. I think."

"Wrong." Mickey was fumbling with the front of my bubble. For some reason I couldn't focus clearly.

"Hypoxia was queen of the Amazons," he said. "The Amazons lived in Scythia on the banks of the longest river in the world. They cut off their right breasts with scythes, so as not to interfere with their sword arms. Hercules killed Hypoxia at Troy for not checking her oxygen. Here, try to focus—" He clicked his air hose to the valve in the front of his bubble. Just like I had. An oxygen-jet.

"Are we stopping somewhere?"

"Yes, we're stopping right here." He pushed himself up close to me and hooked his bubble valve to mine. I couldn't see what he did next, but I started to hear a strange hissing sound. "I'm losing air, I think. I'm hissing."

"Take a deep breath, Chigger. Again. Again. Again. Keep on breathing. That's good. Can you see me now? Look at my hand. How many fingers can you see?"

I blinked. "All of them?"

"Close enough. Look at your readout again."

I looked. "It's flashing red." And then I started to get scared—

"Relax. You're breathing on my air now. Pay attention. We're going to change tanks on your rebreather. If you can't do it, I'll do it for you. Take your hands out of your gloves and I'll reverse them inward and—"

"I can do it." My hands were shaking and I felt suddenly weak and nauseous. "You do it."

"Good boy. You know when to ask for help. Do you know how many people have died because they were too stupid or too proud to ask for help?"

"No. How many?"

"I don't know either. But it's a lot, I can tell you that."

He had his hands inside my bubble now—it looked weird to see my gloves fiddling around at my belt, unclipping hoses and changing their connections. It reminded me of the way Doug used to button me up before taking me out to play. That didn't seem so long ago—but at the same time it seemed very far away. And now it was Mickey. He was acting just like a brother.

"There. How do you feel?"

"Fine."

"Do you have a headache?"

"Uh-uh." I touched my head to see if it was still there. My hand touched something else. A furry leg. "Is there a monkey sitting on my head?"

"Yes."

"Good. Then I'm not delusional."

"But no headache?"

"No. If anything, I feel giddy. A little light-headed. Like I could fly away."

"That's not good either." Mickey reached in and fiddled with the settings on my rebreather.

"What are you doing?"

"Just making some adjustments. This should do it. There." He pulled his hands out of my gloves and disconnected our two bubbles. We were separated again. He secured his rebreather tube and looked across at me. "All right, you good now?"

"Yeah." I was fumbling my hands back into my gloves.

"You sure? I've gotta go check Douglas and Bobby—"

"I'm good." But I grabbed his hand anyway. "Mickey?"

"Yeah?"

"Thank you."

He gave my hand a quick squeeze in return, then hurried across to Douglas.

PAYING INTENTION

AFTER THAT, WE WERE ALL a lot more careful.

I finally *got it* what Mickey meant.

It was about staying *conscious*. What some people called paying intention.

Dad once tried to tell me about this music teacher he'd had—the one who said you couldn't be a musician if you didn't practice at least three hours a day. He used to tell Dad that an excuse was not equal to a result. What you said you wanted was irrelevant; what you actually accomplished demonstrated your real intentions.

I never liked that discussion. It sounded like hard work to me and I couldn't see the reward in it. I always thought you should practice your music because you liked it, not because somebody said you had to. But I'd always listened politely, because it was always so important to Dad to give the *Pay intention, this is how the world works!* speech. *It's not enough to pay attention*, he would say, over and over. *You have to pay i*n*t*e*n*t*i*o*n* as well.

And there was all the rest of it too: *Volume is no substitute for brains. Better to keep your trap shut and be thought a fool than to shoot yourself in the foot while it's still in your mouth. Don't burn your bridges before your chickens are hatched.*

Every so often . . . I would realize he'd been right. He wasn't just talking to prove he knew better than me. This was one of those times. Well, why hadn't I paid intention when he'd told me about paying intention? Because . . . it's one of those stupid things you have to bump into yourself, and hope you survive long enough to make good use of the lesson.

So I concentrated on every bounce, every hop, every skip—and wondered if this is what it had been like for Harrison "Jack" Schmitt, bouncing around on the moon and trying to collect rocks without killing himself.

And every so often, I cursed the monkey. I'd been assuming that the monkey was a good safety monitor. Obviously, it wasn't. It was supposed to beep or scream or run for help if a life was in danger—but it hadn't alerted me that I was running low on air. So obviously, it didn't include an oxygen meter—and it hadn't been paying any attention to my rate of breathing. I was already gasping for breath when Mickey figured out there was something wrong and came back to check my air. If it hadn't been for Stinky, I'd have junked the monkey right there. Except I was still wondering about those memory bars.

"Look, there it is," said Mickey.

We stopped to look. He pointed toward the horizon. It was hard to see. The dark slope downward was outlined with bright highlights—places where outcroppings stuck up into the sunlight, or worse, places where the shadows dipped away altogether, leaving patches of Lunar soil painted with a hard actinic glare. We had to squint to see anything. Even Stinky, who was still groggy from the tranquilizer, stuck his head out of Douglas's poncho and demanded to know what we were looking at.

"It's hard to make out—" Mickey admitted. "Look for a reddish glow."

"Oh, I've got it," said Douglas. "Chigger, can you see it?"

"No—" The brightness made my eyes water. We were looking at a vast downhill slope, and the horizon was farther away than I had gotten used to. And there was a lot of sunlight being reflected back at us. And . . . I didn't want to say it aloud, but *there was something moving out there.*

But if there was something there, I had to tell them. And if there wasn't anything there and I was seeing things, then I had to say something about that too. *Didn't I?*

"Mickey?"

"Yes, Chigger?"

"Are there mirages on the moon?"

"Well, not mirages. Not like on Earth. You need an atmosphere for those kinds of mirages. But sometimes you get optical illusions. Or even psychological illusions. Your eyes will play tricks on you. Or your mind. Why? Do you see something?"

"I thought I did."

"Where?"

"Just to the left of the reflector. Something black, running and bouncing across the bright part. Didn't you see it?"

"No. Is it still there?"

"No."

"Did it look like a bubble?"

"No. It was too thin. I only caught a quick glimpse. I don't know what it was."

"Which way was it going?"

"It was coming toward us. Almost head-on."

That brought both Mickey and Douglas to attention. They scanned the distance for long moments, punctuated only by one of them asking, "Do you see it?" And the other replying, "No, do you?"

Finally, Mickey said, "Well, if it's out there, it's in the shadows now and we're missing it. But just to be on the safe side—" He came over and checked my air again.

I started to protest that I was fine, but then I realized that Mickey was only doing what he had to do, so I shut up and waited until he finished. Douglas asked, "Is he all right?"

Mickey nodded. "As far as I can tell." To me, he said, "I'm not saying you didn't see anything, Chigger. You were right to ask. But it's not unusual after you've had hypoxia to experience visual or auditory illusions."

"Hallucinations, you mean."

"Yeah," he admitted.

For a moment, none of us said anything. We were all thinking the same thing. Was the kid with the monkey on his head going crazy? And if not—then what was *out there*?

"All right," said Mickey. "Let's keep going. Let's get to the reflector. Douglas?"

Douglas started hop-skipping again. I followed. Mickey brought up the rear. Douglas hadn't said much, he'd been concentrating on Stinky most of the time. But now he said, "Mickey?"

"Yeah?"

"Do you think Alexei abandoned us?"

Mickey didn't answer for several bounces. I had begun to think he wasn't going to answer at all, when he said, "The thought had crossed my mind, yeah."

"You know him better than we do—"

"I don't know him that well. For all his talk, there's a lot he doesn't say. 'I make big deal, I make lots of money, I am embarrassed I make so much money, you will pick up check, *da?* All my money is tied up in cash, *da?*'" Mickey mimicked his Russian friend perfectly. "He's always got a deal going somewhere. But nobody ever knows what his deals are. I suppose that's a good thing. What you don't know you can't tell the marshals."

We bounced and skipped in silence for a while, punctuated only by occasional soft grunts. After a while, Mickey added, "But it's not like Alexei to endanger someone's life. Loonies don't do that. They believe that life is sacred everywhere. The greatest crime on Luna is to disrespect life. And Alexei is completely Loonie. He wouldn't do it. He couldn't."

More silence, more bouncing. I checked my readouts. They were green. I checked them again. This time I looked at the numbers. I checked them a third time and mouthed the numbers as I read them—reminding myself what was optimal. *Pay intention.*

Douglas broke the silence. "So you think he's dead."

"We didn't find a body."

"You didn't answer the question."

"I don't know." And then he added, "But it's the only thing I can think of that makes sense. . . ."

I disagreed. I could think of something else that made sense. But I didn't want to say it aloud. Not yet. I needed to think some more. As long as I didn't get distracted again—

I could see the reflector clearly now. It was a big silvery ball on a short spindly tripod. The whole thing had been dropped in from orbit and there were fragments of the landing pod around the base. But what caught my attention was the way the reflector had a sparkly-flickery look—all different colors. It was even more spooky because the whole thing was in shadow, so where were the flickers coming from?

I pointed it out to Mickey. He explained, "Lasers from all over the system. Everyone tunes their beams to a different color, that's why it looks like a rainbow, and everyone targets on Luna. It's a convenient landmark, and there's no atmosphere to distort the beams. It's kind of like Greenwich mean time, you know what that is? It's a reference point against which all other clocks are set. Well, Luna is like that too. It's the surveyor's post for everyone in the solar system to measure distances from. Accurate computations of distance are essential for space travel."

"Oh, yeah. That makes sense."

"We're almost there. Do you want to take a meal break? We can even go in the inflatable for a bit." It was still bouncing along behind him.

I opened my mouth to say yes, then stopped. "What's that—?" I pointed.

"What's what?" And then he saw it too.

It was a bubble suit, like ours. An *empty* bubble suit. Half-inflated. As if the person wearing it had taken it off and skipped away into the arid dark.

It was *Alexei's* bubble suit.

REFLECTIONS

MY FIRST THOUGHT WAS, SO *that answers that question.*
My second thought was, *No, it doesn't. Where's the body?*
How do you get out of a bubble suit and just walk away?
You don't.
So *where was Alexei?*
The question was more puzzling than ever.
And why was his suit *here*? How did it get here from *there*? Who else was here? I glanced around nervously. There could be an entire army hiding just behind the horizon. We'd have no way of knowing.

Mickey and Douglas were just as disconcerted as I was. Maybe even more so. Because they knew all the stuff I hadn't even thought of—so they probably had even more questions.

We all climbed into the inflatable to talk about it. Once inside, we took off our bubble suits, and Mickey equalized the oxygen in all our tanks, something he'd been wanting to do ever since I burned off thirty minutes of breathing to stop myself on the zip line.

We pushed back the hoods of our ponchos, took off our goggles, and sipped at our water bottles. I took the monkey off my head and set it aside. We nibbled at our inedible MREs, we inhaled deeply—the air in the inflatable was stale, but it was fresher than the air in the bubble suits—we used our toilet bags, and we talked about calling for rescue.

We all knew the arguments. What we were doing was dangerous. Stupid. Foolhardy. Probably unnecessary. I was posthypoxic and hallucinating. Douglas's back was starting to hurt—even though Stinky weighed less on Luna, he still had the same *mass*. So even though it mostly felt like he wasn't heavy, the truth was that there was some stuff called inertia and momentum that made carrying the little monster almost as tiring as if we were still on Earth. Mickey's feelings were unreadable. He looked as if he had a lot of different things all going on at the same time. And Stinky was alternating between constipation and diarrhea, catatonia and hyperactivity—so at least one of us was normal.

It was a question of endurance. The reflector was our halfway point. Actually, it was more than halfway. It was nearly two-thirds of the way. But Alexei and Mickey had figured that in terms of sheer physical exhaustion, the last third of the Lunar hike would take us as long as the first two-thirds. As much fun as it was to go bouncing across the silvery gloom, it was very tiring too. My legs were beginning to hurt. My calves ached.

And I was scared again.

I wasn't afraid of Luna anymore. But I respected her now. I had a better sense of her dangers—and I was *paying intention.*

I was terrified by all the stuff I *didn't* know—especially all the stuff I didn't know that I didn't know. Alexei's empty bubble suit scared the hello out of me. What could have happened that only his empty suit would be left behind? Did something suck him right out of the plastic?

I shuddered. And shivered. And wrapped my silver poncho tight around me.

Above us, the reflector sparkled with stray bits of light—a thousand different colors, the beams of distant spaceships, other worlds and moons, asteroids, the Earth, the orbital beanstalk, L4 and L5, orbiting satellites—all their questioning fingers of light touched and bounced away, back to their origins, each one carrying a single part of the answer to the question *Where am I?*

You're *there*—7.68 godzillion angstroms away from *here.* And we're here—7.68 godzillion angstroms away from *there.* Sitting under the stars and watching the flickering radiance of your thousand lonely queries. But none of you are more alone than us—sitting here all alone in the dark.

How far would all those beams travel on their journeys here and back? How long would it take them? Just the blink of an eye—a few seconds to Earth, a few minutes to the asteroid belt. What were they all saying?

They didn't even know we were here. It was a strange feeling to see so much evidence of human life and still be so far away from it all.

We could rejoin it in a moment. All we had to do was tune our transmitters to the public bands, turn up the power, and call for help. I was ready to concede I didn't know as much as I pretended. I'd made my point, I could quit now. I'd still gotten farther than Dad ever would have. And I knew Douglas wouldn't take much convincing if he thought that Stinky or I were in danger. Mickey . . . I didn't know what he thought, but he looked tired and irritable and unhappy. Whatever exhilaration we had felt about being on the moon, that was gone, swamped by our exhaustion and our fear. We'd had too many close calls. The *wunderstorm* was over.

Mickey unhooked his transmitter from his belt. "Do we have to talk about this?" he asked. "Or are we all in agreement this time?" He looked to Douglas. Douglas shook his head. He looked to me—

That's when *something outside the inflatable moved*—and I screamed and leapt backward so hard I bumped into the wall and went bouncing sideways, scaring the hell out of Stinky and Douglas and Mickey, and they went bouncing every which way too—

It was a gangly black spidery thing, with a grotesque bug-eyed face, and grasping claws. It came right up to the edge of the bubble and pressed its face and hands against the plastic, peering in at us like some kind of vacuum-breathing insect. Even Stinky was shrieking—Douglas grabbed him in a restraining hug and turned him away so he couldn't see—

And then I saw the lettering above the eyes КРИСЛОВ—I couldn't read the word, the letters were all funny-looking and backwards—until I recognized them as Russian. And then Mickey was shouting, "It's Alexei! It's Alexei! Everybody shut up! Stop screaming! It's only Alexei! *It's Alexei!*"

By then, I'd already stopped screaming, and Alexei was already pulling himself into the inflatable, one section of the entrance tube at a time. He was careful to close and check each zipper behind him before he opened the next. He still looked scary—like a big skinny faceless *thing*.

Finally, he popped in through the last zipper and carefully sealed it behind himself. He pulled off the rubbery hood of his scuba suit and finally his breather tube and goggles. He was laughing so hard I wanted to punch him in the gut. How dare he scare us like that?

"Is big fright, *da?* Is Rock Father come to eat poor crazy terries. Scream and scream again. You are much frightened. I laugh so hard I almost choke on my air hose. You did not expect poor Alexei, did you? Is only turnabout to play fair. Alexei did not expect to find you here either. Did you not hear my messages? No, I think you did not. My transmitter failed. I could hear you, but you could not hear me. Very inconvenient, *da?* So you did not hear me say you should wait, I go for help. No need for rescue. I could run to Prospector's Station and signal Mr. Beagle and be back with help and air in two hours—"

"Mr. Beagle—?"

"Later. You will meet him later. But I cannot call him now. I hear you in distance—you are looking for me. Calling, *da?* I realize you have come down from mountain somehow. So I turn around and come back for you before you get lost."

"But your bubble suit—?" I asked.

"I could not leave it behind, Charles Dingillian, could I? I would never find it again. So I left it at reflector as signal for you that I was still alive."

"Oh," Mickey said. There was an edge to his voice. "Is that what that was?"

Alexei slapped his chest in mock-frustration. "Ah, you do not understand Self-Contained Universal Breathing Apparatus, do you? Body suit is so firm-fitting it makes airtight seal all around. Strong enough to hold body safe and tight against vacuum. Hood seals tight around goggles and earphones and breather tube. Is not as practical as bubble suit for long distances. No way to pee or poop. No way to drink or eat. Cannot even talk very well. But for emergencies or for short distances, is much easier. Is basic worksuit for Loonies."

"We're not Loonies," Douglas said.

"Maybe someday you will be," Alexei responded, very matter-of-factly. "Earth is falling apart. Luna will have to provide resources to rebuild. Luna will become seat of economic power and political authority for double-planet system of Earth-Luna. Is only logical. We have high ground of discipline and resources. Nobody gets to Luna by accident. We are a society of hard workers. Earth cannot compete with that. It makes sense that Lunatics should govern, *da?*"

"I think we already have enough lunatics in government," said Douglas dryly. "The old-fashioned kind."

"*Da*, we have our share too. But even our craziest Loonies know the rules. Everybody pays oxygen tax."

"And what happens if you don't?" asked Douglas.

"You have to stop breathing." Alexei helped himself to one of Mickey's MREs and began unwrapping it. "Nobody ever breaks law second time." He took a disgustingly large bite of something that looked like chopped brick and kept on talking while he chewed. "First I will eat, then I will use toilet bags. Then we will hurry to Prospector's Station. As long as we are this far, no need to call Mr. Beagle for help. We will catch early train, fool marshals. Huh, what is wrong—?" He blinked in surprise, looking at us, suddenly realizing. "You were planning to call for help, *da*? I see it in your faces. Is lucky I stop you in time—" Alexei turned to Mickey and took the transmitter out of his hands. "Listen, *Mikhail*, is big mistake to call for help. Everything on

Earth is falling apart, so everything on Luna is shutting down. It will be much harder to hide anything—even little one's monkey. Can you go one more hour? Two? Maybe a little more than two? Prospector's Station is only four and a half klicks from here, most. Almost all downhill. Train arrives in few hours. Once we get on train, we can go anywhere."

"As cargo again?" Douglas asked. He looked angry.

"No, no, I promise. I have planned idea for disguise. Very clever, I am. I will take you wherever you want to go—even if you change mind. Must go quickly now. We have not as much air anymore. I use up too much air going and coming back and not getting anywhere."

Mickey was already whispering to his PITA and frowning at its responses.

"I vote no," said Douglas firmly.

"We don't have a choice," said Mickey.

"Huh?"

"We don't have enough air anymore. Not enough to sit and wait for a rescue. Alexei's coming back changes the whole oxygen equation. He used up most of his. Now he's on ours." He was already reaching for his bubble suit. "We have to go. *Now.*"

"How serious is it?" asked Douglas.

"Not serious if we go *now.* If we stop to argue about it, it gets very serious."

Douglas looked like he wanted to say something. He looked like he wanted to say a whole bunch of somethings, but he held his tongue. "Bobby—come on, time for another piggyback ride."

"Do I gotta—?"

"Yeah, you gotta."

"Do you want me to take him?" Mickey asked. "I don't mind, really."

Douglas shook his head. "You just keep watching Chigger." The look on his face said it all. He was very angry. And we were going to hear about this later.

RUN IN THE SUN

AND THEN WE WERE ON our way again, bouncing and skipping and hopping and tumbling through the Lunar darkness. Alexei ran ahead in his Scuba gear, he didn't want to waste time with the bubble suit. Douglas hop-skipped behind him in that weird bouncing lope that the first Lunar astronauts had discovered as the most efficient method of moving quickly around the Lunar surface. Mickey and I brought up the rear. The inflatable bounced along behind us on a long silvery leash. We must have looked like a soap commercial—four manic bubbles chasing a frantic piece of lunatic lint.

The reflector disappeared behind us, and for a while, everything was silent again. A week ago, all I wanted was a quiet place to listen to my music; now I was beginning to resent the silence. It was too *much* silence. Luna was so quiet it was scary. You could hear your heart beating in your chest. You could hear the blood flowing through your veins. You could hear your own ears.

Suddenly, there you are, alone with your own brain.

Back on Earth, all I'd ever wanted was for everybody else to shut up, so I could hear my own thoughts and not theirs. But here on Luna, the silence was so deep, it swallowed up everything. It was as vast and empty as the whole universe. It stretched from here to forever and back again. I felt like I had fill it with something or disappear too. Only I didn't have enough music or thoughts or anything else to fill up a silence that big.

Mickey stayed close to me, watching me carefully. This was going to be a long mad dash with very few rest breaks. Alexei wanted us to catch the train, and we didn't have enough air to do anything else. So it was hop-skip and bump from one hill to the next. Hither and thither and yawn. I was tired, and it was getting hard to pay intention. And nobody wanted to talk, we just wanted to get there.

Four and a half kilometers isn't that far. On Earth, it's maybe two hours' walk on level ground. On Luna, with lesser gravity, bouncing downslope at a brisk pace, it shouldn't be any longer; what you lose in mobility from the bubble suit, you get back from the lighter gravity.

But this part of Luna didn't have *level* ground. On the map it looked like a plain, but at ground level, it was a rolling bumpy surface, pock-marked with little craters, boulders, ridges, and rough hillocks. Tumbles of rocks were scattered everywhere. And every so often, there were chasms we had to leap over. Alexei called them "expansion joints," but didn't explain what they were.

I concentrated on my hop-skipping. I found a rhythm and played music in my head to match. A Philip Glass piece, one of the repetitive ones with endless chord changes. It could be played forever. And as long as I could keep it running in my head, I could keep moving. I'd probably have it stuck in my head for a month—

And then we stopped.

Brightness lay ahead. "Oh, *chyort!*"

Alexei laughed at my outburst. "Remind me to explain that to you." His voice came muffled in my ears.

—but the *chyort* was real. We'd run out of shadow.

Ahead, the ground rose up into sunlight. Perpetual dawn slammed sideways across the landscape. It blazed and sparkled. It was too bright to look at, even with the goggles fully polarized.

"Is not to worry," said Alexei. I wanted to kick him. "Is not as bad as it looks."

"Not as bad—" That was Mickey. "How far does this extend?"

Alexei hesitated. "Is less than one kilometer. We can do it. We rest here. Turn off heaters. Get very cold. We run for fifteen minutes, straight that way. We warm up, *da*. We get hot. But we have fifteen minutes before bubble suits turn into little ovens. Who cannot run one kilometer in fifteen minutes? On Luna, is piece of cheese."

"You're crazy," said Douglas. "Absolutely crazy. Why didn't you tell us this before? Why didn't you tell us about the mountain climbing and the zip line and the bubble suits and everything?"

"Because if I tell you, you would say, 'no, Alexei, I'm afraid not. That sounds like much too hard. We will much rather sit here like little potted plants to be pickled in our own juices.' But I tell you that no, you are not little cabbages, and here we are, almost home, and you find you are much bigger and much braver than you thought. You do the mountain, you do the zip line, you do everything else—you can do this too. You have to. Is no alternative to this. You stay here, you die. And little stinking one with you. But you come with me across sunlight and you live to laugh about it. Get ready now. Time you stand here thinking about this is time you will not have on other side. *Mikhail*, help me check air on everyone, please." He was already peering at my readouts. Without looking up, he said, *"Mikhail*, do not give me that look. Remember, I promise to take care of you. I am keeping that promise. Right now I am taking better care of you than you are taking yourself. You should thank me. You will thank me soon enough. Come, please. I have too much money invested in you already. I do not intend to lose my investment. Charles Dingillian, you are fine. I have turned your air up just a little. You will do fine. Be grateful monkey does not breathe, you would not have enough air for both of you; otherwise, one of you would have to stay behind. As soon as we are all too cold to move, we will go. Come, *Mikhail*, let me check you now."

Alexei kept up a steady stream of chatter. Maybe his mind really was that peripatetic, spinning from thought to thought like a dervish. And maybe he was doing it deliberately to keep us from thinking what a stupid thing we were about to do. In all likelihood, we were going to end up as a bunch of fried mummies, baking on the Lunar plain. I wondered what kind of weird life-forms would evolve in our sealed and abandoned bubble suits. What would future Lunar explorers find growing here in the blazing sun? Flesh-eating fungi? Vacuum-breathing mold? Something dreadful, no doubt—especially *Grottius Stinkoworsis*.

I shuddered. It turned into a shiver. A whole bunch of shivers. I was cold. I could see my breath. "Uh—Alexei?"

"Yes, yes, I know. We are just waiting for Douglas to chill. Ha-ha, I make joke there. Old-fashioned slang. Never mind. Douglas and Robert mass more than everyone else. They generate more body heat. It will take longer for them to chill out. We want temperature in bubble suit to be almost freezing. Below would be better, but we do not want to risk frostbite either. We are almost there. Please be patient. Douglas? Are you ready? *Mikhail?* Charles? Hokay. There is no more time for chattering—except teeth, perhaps. When I say we go, everyone follow me. Don't fall down. Just keep going, no matter what. Remember to pace yourself. We are not racing. We are bouncing like before, only faster. Everybody ready? Get set? *Go!*"

And with that, he was off—a black stick figure racing into the light, carrying his bubble suit over his shoulder. Douglas followed immediately after. I hesitated for half a heartbeat—then plunged ahead. Mickey called, "I'm right behind you!"

We bounced into the light and it was like coming out of a tunnel.

The sun slammed sideways into us like a wall of radiance. It was blinding. It dazzled and glared and my eyes started watering almost immediately. But I knew that part of it was just that my eyes hadn't adjusted yet. I found my rhythm and kept going. Hop with the left foot, hop with the right—I skipped steadily after Alexei and Douglas, bouncing high with every step.

We would have been floating through the air—if there had been air, but there wasn't; so we bumbled gracefully through space—bouncing across the land like gossamer hippopotami.

Everything was still too bright, the sideways glare etched every rock and boulder in sandpaper detail, the plains looked painful—but I wasn't hot in the bubble suit. Not yet. I was still shivering from the prolonged cold of the long Lunar shadows. I was almost impatient for the suit to start warming up. So far, this wasn't too bad. But we had a long way to go, and the sun's heat would be cumulative.

Behind me, I could hear Mickey counting off checkpoints. We passed the first one and I realized I wasn't shivering anymore, but the bubble suit still felt cold. Maybe it was just the exertion that was warming me up. I glanced back. The line of shadow had receded into the distance. A little farther and it would be over the horizon. That would be the worst—when we were out of sight of shadow.

Despite the long shadows, there was little refuge out here. The boulders were too small, their shadows were stretched out thin and insignificant. The light came in at us from the side, like the flame of a giant torch. All around us, the surreal landscape glowed; we pushed headlong into a world of dazzling glare. The inside of the bubble flashed and sparkled with rogue reflections. I was getting comfortably warm.

I maintained my pace, occasionally glancing back to see if Mickey was keeping up. He was close behind me. Ahead, Douglas was maintaining a steady pace, even burdened as he was with Stinky. Even farther ahead, I could see the flashing black figure of Alexei bounding through the sunlight. He wasn't having a problem with this, he'd already done it twice—once across, then back again when he'd heard us following him. His Scuba suit was refrigerated. He could go farther than any of us.

We passed the second checkpoint, still pounding across the silvery white dust, and I began to feel optimistic about making it. Maybe this wasn't going to be as bad as I feared. All I had to do was keep Alexei and Douglas in sight. Just keep bouncing. Watch out for the boulders. Pay intention. And try not to notice the cold drop of sweat running down my side—

It was getting warmer out here. It was getting warmer *in* here. Inside the bubble. Not uncomfortable yet, but . . .

I glanced back. Mickey was still close behind me. "Pay intention, Chigger!"

It wasn't Mickey I was worried about. It was the distance to shadow. Every bounce forward was also a bounce farther from darkness. And I had no idea how far we still had to go to get to the shadows on the other side. We were heading deeper into the heart of brightness. I began to worry. I wasn't hot yet, but—I was thinking about *hot.* The cumulative heat was building up.

I began to worry that Alexei had miscalculated. He had the refrigerated suit. We didn't. What if we were like the swimmer who swims too far out and has no strength left for getting back. What if the heat in our bubbles became intolerable before we got to the other side? What if we were getting too far out into the light to reach *any* shade safely? What if we could only get *most* of the way across, but not the last half klick? What if we couldn't make the last hundred meters? What if we couldn't make the last *ten* meters—?

Ohell. What if we couldn't even get *halfway* to safety? What if we had already passed the point of safe return? What if we were already doomed? What if we were already burning up and didn't know it?

"*Shut up!*"

"Huh?" said Mickey, right behind me. "I didn't say anything."

"I wasn't talking to you. I was talking to the little voices. Shut up! Shut up! Shut up!"

"Chigger, are you all right?"

Oh great. Now he was thinking I was going crazy—

I looked at my numbers. "I'm fine."

These bubble suits weren't designed for this. They were meant for emergencies. All this stuff, it was supposed to be used for keeping folks alive until the rescue boat could get to them—nobody ever intended these things for Lunar exploration. Not for long-distance hikes across the Lunar surface. Not like this. Alexei had told us not to worry, it was part of the design specification because who knew what might be needed in an emergency, but just because a bubble suit *can* doesn't mean it *should.* And besides . . . what if Alexei was lying about the suits? Then what?

But why would he lie to us? What was the point in that? Did he want to kill us? How would he benefit from that? Well, there was a thought . . .

We passed the next checkpoint. I'd lost count. I had no idea what Alexei and Mickey were using as checkpoints. I couldn't tell one rock from another anymore. I wasn't warm anymore. I was hot, the sweat was running down my body. I'd skip into space—lifting up high to see the glowing landscape ahead of us, then each time as I'd float back down, the droplets would go coursing down my underarms in warm sluggish trails that made me think of snails—and then I'd bounce down onto the silvery floor of sparkling light and the droplets would splatter off, into my already-clammy jumpsuit. With each hop and skip, the damp material plastered itself against me like a used towel. Everything was wet and smelly with sweat.

I'd been in the sauna a few times, at school. I didn't like it. It was too hot. This was almost as hot. Not quite. But getting there. I thought about cold orange juice—*real* orange juice—not the orange-colored stuff that Mom always bought. I thought about ice. I thought about ice water. I thought about swimming in ice water.

Another checkpoint. And I still didn't see any shadows on the horizon. We were in the middle of a dazzling plate of fire. We were under a magnifying glass. The hard black sky was overruled by the scorching blaze of light in the east. The sweat poured off me. So did the tears.

"You're doing fine, Chigger. Just keep on. Only a little farther." That was Mickey's voice.

I couldn't see anyone clearly anymore. There was a dark figure bouncing in front of me. And a blurry bubble too. Mickey's occasional comments came from behind me. Were they suffering as much as I was? I couldn't imagine it—

Maybe Alexei really did want us dead, so he could skip off into the darkness with the monkey . . .

Sure, that was it. That's why he'd left us up on the rim of the crater. He wasn't going for help. He was just going. And going. And then what—? It was too hot to think of the next step. But if he knew where the monkey was and nobody else did, then he could sell it to whoever would pay the most and nobody else could get to it if we were dead— and the moon was the perfect place to lose anything. Or anyone.

How much more of this could my bubble suit take before it popped? Was it already bigger because the air was heating up and expanding? And why didn't we float up into the air like the hot-air balloons in Albuquerque? Weren't we hot enough? Oh, we were hot enough, but there wasn't any air to float up into—

Another checkpoint. Mickey's voice sounded bad. Somewhere ahead, Stinky was crying—or screaming. I bounced up, floated down, bounced up, floated down—watched the landscape drop away, peered into the distance, floated down—everything was brightness in all directions.

Ice water, ice water, ice water, swimming in ice water, diving in ice water. Dying in ice water. It didn't work anymore. It was too hot. It was burning. It was hotter than the sauna. I wasn't going to make it. I didn't see how I could make it. I bounced up, floated down, I couldn't see anything but solar glare. We had come too far to get back and there was no shadow anywhere. We'd bounced and skipped into sunlight and we were going to die here—

I kept going anyway. I wanted to lie down, but I didn't. I didn't have any more sweat. It had all been boiled out of me. I went to take a sip of water but it was too hot to drink. And as fast as I sipped, it just dripped right out of me. There were droplets bouncing around the inside of the bubble now. There were little puddles splashing lazily around the bottom in a graceful slow-motion ballet.

Another checkpoint—

If I fell down, I wouldn't be able to get up. I had to pay intention. This was the hard part. I wasn't going to be the first to fall—

Just before we had started across the frying pan, while Alexei was checking Mickey's air, Douglas had pulled me aside, had talked to me like an adult. "I'm responsible for Bobby. You're responsible for Charles. I can't be responsible for both of you. If you fall down, Charles, I *can't* save you. I can't come back for you. Neither can Mickey. If it gets so bad out there that you can't get up, no one else can pick you up either. Don't fall down. If you fall down, and I try to save you, we *all* die. Don't fall down."

"I won't." It had been easy to reassure him at the time. Because I didn't know. Not then. Now I *knew*. And I wasn't sure I could keep the promise. I could barely see anymore. I followed the bouncing blur.

One more bounce. Take the next bounce. Just one more bounce. Keep going. It won't get better if you stop. Another bounce. And another. Keep on bouncing. Bouncing. Keep on, Charles—keep your promise. Don't fall. *Pay intention.*

And then—"There it is!" Mickey's voice.

I didn't see it. I saw bright scorching solar blur. I saw purple splotches floating in front of my eyes. I saw noise and dazzle. *I didn't see any shadow.* He was lying. He was just saying that to keep me going—

"Straight ahead, Chigger! Almost there!"

"Almost where?" But I didn't have any voice. Just croak. Not even loud enough to be heard.

I bounced, I floated, I looked. Painful brightess. Something angled. Maybe. Bounced, floated, looked—something flat and rectangular, angled toward the sun. But not darkness. It still didn't resolve. Bounced, floated, looked—it didn't make sense, but it wasn't sunlight and I bounced and floated toward it.

Alexei was already there, in the shade of it. *Shade!* Something dark was humped into the ground. He was opening a hatch, standing and waving, beckoning. Douglas was just bouncing into the shadow of something—it was real!

And then I tripped. And bounced and rolled, ass over elbow, every which way—*had I punctured my bubble? Was I dead and didn't know it yet?*—I was still rolling. I heard voices.

"Let him go, *Mikhail*—get out of the sun! We can't lose both of you—" That was Alexei! And then, "I am get him."

I was trying to get up, but my arms weren't working. My feet kept kicking uselessly at the bottom of the bubble. I didn't have the air to scream. I felt like a frog in a frying pan. I probably looked like one too. Just add butter—never mind, I'll lie here and boil in my own juices. A fat lot of help you are, you stupid monkey—

And then, someone was rolling me around, I wasn't doing it, something black blurred around my vision, and then I was vaguely upright— "Can you move, or do I carry you?" Without waiting for an answer, Alexei grabbed my bubble suit by one of the plastic handles on the outside; he held me high, and began bouncing toward the blackness ahead—

The light went out abruptly—not the heat, I was still baking like a clam in my own shell. But at least the light was gone. Hands pushed at me, pushed me into a dark tube, pushed me farther. Pushed. Through a series of horizontal hatches that opened in front of me and closed behind me. I felt helpless to resist—I couldn't see anything but splotches of purple dazzle. I bounced off something—I heard hissing. I heard a hatch slam. I heard voices, not in my earphones, but from farther away. I heard sounds I couldn't identify. A voice swearing in Russian. An argument. Douglas calling out—"Is Charles all right?"

"Is not dead yet," said Alexei. And that would have been reassuring to hear if I didn't have more accurate information than he did. And then the hissing got louder, and louder—someone was unzipping my bubble suit—I tried to slap them away, but I didn't have strength to resist, so I just lay on the floor and waited to die. I took hungry deep breaths, filled myself with hot air, that was a mistake, the vacuum would rip it out of my lungs like a scream—and then the hissing stopped and— cooler air rolled around me, surprising me like a wet slap in the face, and I *youched* aloud and tried to sit up, but I still couldn't, and then the hands were pulling wet plastic up and off me, and suddenly I was *out of the bubble* and the air wasn't baking around me. I rolled sideways and blinked at the darkness, there were people moving in the purple dazzle. Douglàs and Bobby and Mickey and someone still in black. КРИСЛОВ.

"We made it!" Mickey cracked in a voice like old dust.

"*Da!*" said Alexei, pulling off his hood. "We made it. I did not think you would, but you do pretty good for terries. I only had to drag one of you into the shade. Welcome to Prospector's Station." He glanced at his watch. "You make very good time too. For terries."

"You didn't think we'd make it—?" That was Douglas. Weakly.

"*Da.* But if I tell you that, you wouldn't try."

"If you didn't think we'd make it . . ." Douglas began slowly, ". . . then why did you let us try?"

"Because I assume—rightly—that like all terries, you are too stupid to lie down and die. You keep going anyway. Yell at me later, Douglas. You have prove me right again. Save voice for now. You are all dehydrated. Here, drink water." He started passing out plastic water bags. He popped the nipple of mine and held it to my face. "Drink slowly—little gulps. You have been through much. Give body time to recover. We have plenty time before train arrives. Over an hour."

THE DARK SIDE OF THE LOON

PROSPECTOR'S STATION WAS THREE CARGO pods, laid end to end, half-buried in the Lunar dust. They were sheltered by three near-vertical sails of solar panels. The pods were linked together on a north–south orientation, and the solar panels were mounted on gimbals so they could swing down on either side to block the sun's rays at dawn and dusk and all the positions in between. The habitability of the shelter depended solely on the maintenance of the motors.

The pods were divided into two levels; the bottom level of each pod was storage, the top was function. The pod at the north end was a hydroponics farm, the pod at the south was a machine shop, the center pod was the living area. Nobody lived here permanently, it was a communal site. Everybody who used it had to replace what they used and make sure that the station was in working order for whoever might stay here next.

Crosshatch decking had been laid along the bottom of the pod to provide a level floor. Underneath the floor, several plastic bags served as impromptu water tanks—another use for inflatable airlocks; waste not, want not. Above us, identical mesh decking provided the ceiling to this level and the floor to the next; we could see up through the crosshatch to the level above. It was just like being in a tube-town again, only this time with lighter gravity.

I sprawled on my back, with my eyes closed, watching the purple glares fade into mottling blue-and-gray fractalizations, watching the fabric of unreality unravel in my imagination, occasionally sipping at the water bag that Alexei was holding for me. Every so often, he'd tip it to my lips, let me suck a few swallows, then pull it away before I could start gulping greedily.

It didn't make sense. Why was he being so nice to me now if he wanted to kill us? Maybe because he needed our deaths to look natural? Sure. That was it. Because he knew the monkey would be a witness to whatever he did. The testimony of robots had been used before in court cases, especially when they had stored audio and video records pertinent to the legal matter at hand. Most robots above Class 6—and that included the monkey—were continually sorting and storing their records. Cheap memory made it possible for a robot to retain a lot of information; it turned out to be useful for a lot of things—family albums, long-term health records, behavioral records, insurance tracking, consumer tracking, the census, stuff like that. Anyone who wanted to track "lifestyle information" could poll the international robot database for specifically correlated information.

It was rumored that robots were also good for amateur pornography, because they also tracked human sexual behavior. Which is why Mom had always said, "Don't do anything in front of a robot that you wouldn't want God to see you doing." Which meant never do *anything* in front of a robot, if you didn't want to get caught. There were so many robots in some neighborhoods that getting away with a crime was impossible.

This didn't mean that crime didn't happen. It just meant that enforcement was more about finding *where* the criminal was than *who* he was.

So, if Alexei were planning to kill us, he had to make it look like an accident. Because the monkey was watching *everything*. That would explain leaving us on the rim and taking us into the sunlight to get to Prospector's Station.

Alexei couldn't just take the monkey from us, because he knew I'd programmed it to be loyal to me first, then Douglas, and finally Stinky. It was *emotionally* linked. It wouldn't go with anyone else unless we told it to—or unless we were dead. If we were dead, its loyalty programming would store all pertinent information about us and our deaths in unerasable files—and without further instructions of who it should report to, it would shut down and wait for the next person to open it up and assign ownership to himself. Alexei? Probably. Most certainly.

Unless I had been out in the sun too long and was still making up crazy paranoid fantasies . . . I had to consider that too. Alexei put the water bag to my lips again. I took another sip. Around me, I could hear everyone else breathing softly, catching their breaths, sucking at water bags. I could smell their sweat in the air. It smelled like a locker room in here. We all stank. I didn't care. It was cool. Blessedly cool. Almost too cold. I was evaporating excess heat as rapidly as my body could carry my overheated blood to my skin.

What was in the monkey that was so valuable it was worth killing for?

I was pretty sure it wasn't information. Whatever data was packed into the memory bars would have already been piped to its recipient some other way by now. Probably the moment we were served with our first subpoena at Geostationary somebody somewhere was saying "Oh, *merde!*" and then, "All right. Switch to Plan B. Code it in the least significant bit of each pixel of the local news and let them download it off the web." Or whatever. There were just too many ways to smuggle bits from here to there. So it wasn't the information. It had to be something physical.

Money? No. Codes for money? No, that was more information. They'd have found another way to send it by now. Physical ID keys that unlocked money? Maybe. But if that's what it was, they wouldn't have trusted Dad with it. It had to be something so unique that this was the only way to move it from here to there. Wherever *there* was.

So it wasn't information. And it wasn't money. What else was there?

Power.

I took another sip of water. I was feeling better, but I wasn't ready to open my eyes yet.

Power was a good answer. People would kill for power, wouldn't they? Of course they would. If they wanted it badly enough.

But what kind of power?

Processing power.

If you had processing power, you had *every* kind of power. It all depended how you applied the processing power.

Quantum processing?

Could you pack a quantum CPU into a memory bar?

I'd have to ask Douglas that.

He'd probably tell me I was crazy.

It *was* an outrageous idea.

Alexei trying to kill us—then saving us—then holding the water bag for me. Yeah, sure. The monkey wasn't sentient. It hadn't done anything at all to help us survive.

No. There had to be a simpler explanation.

I laughed at my own paranoia and opened my eyes, blinking and squinting. I could almost see again. I lifted up on my elbow to thank Alexei for saving me—and almost choked in horror.

It wasn't Alexei holding the water bag.

It was the monkey. It curled back both its lips to show its teeth and gave me its goofiest smile.

CHANGES

WE HAD TO GET AWAY from Alexei.

I had to convince Douglas and Mickey that we had to get away from Alexei.

I had to get them in a room *away* from Alexei so I could tell them why we had to get away from Alexei. I doubted that they would believe me. Heck, even *I* didn't believe me.

Alexei had stripped off his Scuba suit, finally, and was giving himself a "space-bath." A space-bath is where you strip naked and wipe yourself all over with alcohol pads and moisturizer sponges. It stings a lot, but it gets you mostly clean. He tossed bath bags at everyone else and told us to do the same. "Worst thing on Luna is nose crime. Don't make big stink on Luna. Very bad manners. Wash every six hours. When you wake up and when you go to bed. Before you put on space suit, after you take it off. Before sex, after sex. Use moisturizers on skin so you don't dry out and flake and make dust. Shave body hair regularly, same reason. Use deodorants. Others should not have to breathe your effluvia. Also slows down disease germs."

So I opened the bag and took a bath. I stripped out of my jumpsuit and sat skinny and apart and wiped as much of myself as I could reach. Mickey and Douglas and Stinky were all washing each other, scrubbing each other's backsides and behind the knees and backs of the ears and places like that. The places I couldn't reach, I handed the cloth to the monkey and let him do it. Alexei offered, but I didn't want him touching me anymore.

The thing was, the cleaner I got, the better I felt, and the sillier the whole thing began to feel. It was just me listening too much to my own thoughts again—like Mom always said. She said that too much silence wasn't good for a person. "Your mind goes go off into never-never land and never comes back. Just like your father. He went off, did too much thinking for his own good, and he never came back either." Yeah, right, Mom.

But Mom didn't say all that stuff just because she believed it. She said it because she thought it was true and she didn't want us to make the same stupid mistakes that she and Dad had made. So she figured if she told us the punch lines, we wouldn't have to live through the jokes. Ha ha. We saw how that worked out. I had the fastest divorce in the family.

I finished wiping myself—even in places that most people don't talk about—and pushed the soiled cloth back into its bag. I tucked it into a larger bag for waste, hanging from the inevitable wall webbing. I was beginning to suspect that everything on Luna was made from cargo pods, and there would be wall webbing everywhere.

Alexei glanced over to me and said, "Hokay, girls—let's go upstairs. Are you ready for your disguises?"

"Huh?"

"You do not think you can ride the train as the Dingillian family, do you? Ah, from the looks on your faces, I can see you have not thought about this at all. You are lucky I am so foresighted. Come upstairs. Follow me, all of you. Hurry now."

We shrugged and followed him up the ladder to the top level of the station—we went hand over hand, feet were redundant. His endless monologue continued. "Douglas, you will be Samm Brengle-Tucker, famous hermit prospector. Everybody knows Brengle-Tucker, he is very famous because nobody knows him. You ask, if no one has ever met him, what proof do you have that nobody knows him? There is none, of course, because you cannot prove a negative. We had that in logic class at Lunatic U. Prove that you cannot prove a negative. Very confusing, very clever—Loonies like word games, logic puzzles. But you understand the problem, *da*? How can everyone know him if nobody knows him? That is because he never comes in from the cold. Or the hot. He only sends e-mail. He orders supplies, he pays in cash. He picks up supplies when he gets around to it. He lives in self-sufficient tunnels. He has ice claim registered somewhere in Superstition Crater. Sometimes he sells water and soil with earthworms, only here they are Luna worms, because they can't be earthworms on moon, can they? Never mind. We are all Lunatics here. But Brengle-Tucker keeps to himself. Why? Because Brengle-Tucker does not exist. Not at all. He is made-up person, one of many. He is 'imaginary companion,' one of the unborn-again. Very convenient to have fictitious friends. They can do many things you can't. And they are always not-there for you, *da*? But today Samm Brengle-Tucker and his new wife and daughter will be there for us. Samm Brengle-Tucker has married mail-order bride from"—Alexei took my chin in his hand and tilted my face upward— "Nunovit Province in Canada. She does not speak much English. What shall his new wife be named, eh? I think Maura Lore-Fields. *Da*. And lovely daughter?" He turned to Stinky. "What is good name for cute little Luna girl?"

"Excuse me?" I said.

Alexei turned back to me, very serious. "Marshals are looking for two young men, a teener-boy and a boy-child. And a monkey. Marshals are *not* looking for an old hermit prospector, his young wife, and her daughter by a previous marriage. You'll have to leave the monkey behind, you know. Is instant giveaway."

"*No, we won't.* And I'm not putting on a dress either." Although part of me was thinking that the disguises were a pretty smart idea, another part was muttering darkly that I shouldn't agree too easily no matter what I thought. I had to give a performance of saying no, so they wouldn't think I was—like Douglas and Mickey. And why did that matter anymore, anyway? It didn't seem to matter to anybody else, so why should it matter to me? This whole business was very confusing.

"Listen, Charles Dingillian," Alexei said, almost angrily. "You told me, didn't you, how J'mee, the boy, was really J'mee, the girl? The one with the implant who turned you in at Geostationary? If crossdressing worked for her, why not you?"

"Except it didn't work for her," I pointed out.

"Of course not. She opened her big mouth. You are too smart for that, *da*? Come with me; I have just the dress for you." He led the way aft.

I followed, still complaining. "I'll look silly."

"You'll look pretty. You'll feel pretty. You have lovely tenor voice. Everyone will believe. You will have fun."

"That's what I'm afraid of."

There was a row of lockers along one wall of the machine-shop pod. One of them had the name BRENGLE-TUCKER on it. There were also several interesting-looking crates stacked against the wall, stenciled for delivery to BRENGLE-TUCKER. Alexei counted them off and pulled one out, setting it aside for the moment, then turned back to the lockers.

He showed his card to the door of the BRENGLE-TUCKER locker, and it clicked and swung open; he pulled out a roll of labels with Russian and English lettering and began pasting new destination labels over all of the BRENGLE-TUCKER labels on the crates. When he finished, he pushed the boxes into a transfer tube connected to the aft hatch. "Outgoing mail," he explained. "Incoming is delivered at other end."

He unlocked the one remaining crate to reveal a rack of clothing, all kinds, some very ugly wigs, and a makeup kit. "I order this special from Luna City." He held up an ugly-looking dress. "Just for you, Charles. While floating in ballast tank, I am thinking Dingillians might need disguises on Luna, so my lifelong friend Samm Brengle-Tucker sends in order before we jump off Line. Or do you like this one better? I did not know your size, I had to guess."

I didn't say anything in response. I just scowled at the oversized dress and the awful wigs. Alexei's story didn't make sense. Not if you thought about it. He'd said he'd been listening to the channel chatter. As soon as he'd heard about the marshals waiting at Whirlaway, he came to get us. When would he have had time to phone ahead to Luna? He wouldn't. We launched off the Line almost immediately after we'd climbed into the pod. He couldn't have made the call *after* we were en route, so he'd have had to have made this plan and ordered these disguises *before* we left Geostationary—or at least before he came to get us. In which case . . . his story about the channel chatter and the marshals *might be false*.

Alexei was chattering too much to notice my silence. He tossed the makeup kit to Mickey. "Here, you get started. You and Douglas, use suntan number nine, *da*? You are Lunar prospectors. Douglas, you are here longer; use a lot, get very dark. Not to worry. Is permanent color. Takes at least a month to fade. Face and neck only. Mickey, you will not need as much. You have only been here a year. You do not work outside so much. Only some."

Then he went burrowing through silky nylon things, sorting and tossing. "Brengle-Tucker is good man. He order everything for his pretty wife. Even fancy underwear. Just in case someone looks up receipts, this shows he adores her, leaves nothing out. First rule of smuggling, Charles—do not give reason for someone to be suspicious; always give them something else to look at. Like underwear. Most people do not look under underwear, that is why you hide your dirty books under it. So here is nice underwear. Don't look funny at me, Charles. You are not your panties. And clean underwear is always welcome, even if it is pink and has lace trim. Is Loonie lesson, never look gift underwear in crotch. Clean underwear is as valuable as water. Sometimes more. Here, this will fit you too. You are not much bigger in the chest than I am." He tossed me a padded bra. Stinky giggled. I glowered at him.

"Is this *really* necessary—?" I started to object.

"*Da!*" he nodded, as if it were the most natural thing in the world. "Is good disguise. I have wear it myself sometimes."

I looked at all the unfamiliar clothes he had pushed into my arms, with a feeling of dismay. "Why can't you just call your Mr. Bagel?"

"Is Beagle, not Bagel, and is not good idea. Not from here. Is too much expensive. Costs much fuel. Emergency is over. And will make more risk."

"But I don't want to do *this!*"

"Oh? You will run across moon, naked to the sunlight, risking death with every step, all without question—but you will not wear a bra even if it means saving your life?"

I looked to my older brother. "Douglas—?"

"Hey, I have to pretend I'm your husband."

"Can't Mickey be my husband?"

"No. He's already mine."

"You know what I mean—"

"Come on, Charles. Please?" Douglas gave me the impatient Mommy look. "Pretend it's Halloween."

"No," Mickey interrupted, in a voice like he was giving orders. "That's the wrong approach. Chigger, *pretend it's a play.* And you're the star. Everyone is watching your every move and listening to your every line. So you have to get into your character and stay there, because all our lives might depend on it."

"Oh, that's good," said Douglas. "Make him self-conscious."

"*Her,*" corrected Mickey. "And you too, Douglas. You have to stay in character too. All of us. From now on, this is Maura, and you're Samm. And Bobby is . . ."

"Valerie," I suggested.

"No, I'm not!" he snapped right back. "I'm Patty."

"Patty—?"

"Yes, *Patty!*"

"Okay. Then I'm going to call you Pattycakes."

"And I'm going to call you *Mommy.*"

It must have been the startled look on my face—both Mickey and Douglas laughed out loud. Alexei said, "Hokay, then it's settled. Now, hurry and dress."

Mommy?

# ALL ABOARD

THERE WAS NO OFFICIAL RECORD of Janos, Maura, and Patty arriving on Luna, but that wasn't unusual. Luna didn't police her borders; thousands of illegal immigrants dropped off the Line every year, riding cargo pods to various hard-to-reach locations. No one knew how many hidden colonies there were, although satellite-based observatories had mapped over eleven thousand cargo pods, unmanned stations, and automated industrial installations capable of sustaining human life. It was estimated there could be as many as two thousand more habitats, either buried or camouflaged.

Another way to estimate the total number of human beings on Luna was to measure total power consumption. The entire moon took its power through the cable system. Superconducting wires carried power from the bright side to the dark side, wherever it was needed. Because the Loonies believed in wasting nothing, everything was monitored. The numbers on water usage, heat radiation, oxygen recycling, waste production, and food consumption were all part of the economic balance. How much did Luna need for her own people? How much could she export to Mars and the asteroids? Once all the various industrial and agricultural processes were factored out, once the exports were subtracted, there was still a considerable discrepancy between projected and actual consumption of resources.

Luna's *official* census reported 3.2 million permanent residents. The unofficial census estimated that there were another 50,000 Loonies living off in the hills. Some of them were fictitious identities like Samm Brengle-Tucker and his family; no one knew how many; but the fictitious families made it harder to track down those who were just *invisible*. So nobody knew for sure how many invisibles there were.

People went invisible for lots of different reasons. Some of them were hiding from Earth authorities or bounty marshals. I could understand that. Others wanted to live alone so they could practice their own way of life without interference from anyone else. I could understand that too. And some of them were invisible because they really hated other people. And that one wasn't hard to understand at all; sometimes other people were really hard to put up with. I wondered what it might be like to live so all alone—hiding in the darkness, hiding from the light.

And then there were the others. . . .

Some of the invisibles were out there in the shadows because they were doing things they *really* didn't want anyone else to know about. That was scary. I couldn't imagine what those things might be. And I didn't want to imagine.

Alexei Krislov paid for his own train ticket. Samm Brengle-Tucker bought tickets for himself, his common-law wife and daughter, and his half brother, Janos Brengle-Palmer. Then Alexei passed out cash cards to everyone. "Just in case," he said. "But even cash cards that come from Earth can be traced eventually, so only use for emergency. Please. Remember, you are invisibles and hope to stay that way."

"Won't people ask questions?" I asked.

Alexei shook his head. "People come in and out from the cold all the time. Go visiting, go shopping, then disappear again. There are many invisible networks. Most Loonies know better to ask. Someday they might want to go invisible themselves. Loonies respect each other's privacy. No questions, no touching, no personal remarks. Is because we do not have much real privacy—we share too many cramped little tubes for too much of our lives—so we have to create privacy in our heads. Earth tourists do not always understand this. Too much touching and pushing, they think they are being friendly. On Luna, if someone touches you and you do not want to be touched, is very big, very bad mistake. Slap hand away and say, 'Don't touch me, dirtsider!' Is very nasty insult here. Not to worry, you will have Samm and Janos to protect you. You will stand close between them. Just remember who you are."

A year ago, Janos had arranged the mail-order marriage of Maura Lore-Fields to Samm Brengle-Tucker, and had brought her and her eight-year-old daughter (from a previous marriage) to the moon to meet her new husband. Janos had short black hair and a mustache he refused to shave because he was going back to Earth as soon as traffic on the Line resumed. Samm had enormous eye goggles he had to wear to compensate for some progressive condition that he hoped to have corrected at Gagarin Dome.

Maura had frizzy red hair and wore just a bit too much makeup for Luna. Most Loonie women wore their hair short and only wore makeup for formal occasions; but Maura didn't know that yet because she still hadn't been to a proper Lunar settlement. Her husband was a hermit, almost invisible; so she didn't know that she looked a little cheap. She thought she looked good, and on Earth, perhaps she would have.

Patty had darker hair than her mother. Both had come from a religious settlement in northern Canada where women were not allowed to speak except when asked a direct question.

Samm and Janos wore matching heavy-duty prospector's jumpsuits. Patty wore a blue pinafore. Maura wore an ill-fitting dress and an unhappy glower.

"Why can't I wear a jumpsuit?" I asked.

"Because in a jumpsuit you look too much like a boy," said Mickey.

"A boy with tits," said Douglas.

"A disguise is about meeting people's expectations," said Mickey. "They'll see what they want to see if you'll just give them the right cues. You need the dress and the makeup to sell the look."

"*Mikhail* is right." Alexei said, "Here. Give me monkey. I will put it in my bag for safekeeping."

"Uh, no—" I said it a little too quickly, but there was no way I was going to let the monkey out of my control—not even for a moment. "Wait. Let me try something." I loosened the sash around my waist to let the dress hang loose and began stuffing the furry little robot under my slip. I wrapped its long arms and legs around my middle; the monkey seemed to figure out what I wanted and settled itself into the least uncomfortable position it could manage. "There," I said. "I'm six months gone. Maybe seven. That's why I can't wear a jumpsuit."

Patty laughed. Mickey and Douglas grinned at each other. "The kid is smart."

"*Da*, that is good thinking." Alexei nodded, frowning. "We will have to adjust story though. Now you are going to Gagarin Dome to get officially married. Samm, you would not marry Maura until she could give you heir. Now you go to Gagarin to confirm that child is healthy male. If you are satisfied, you will marry Maura. If not, Janos must return her to Earth. What you do not know is that child might be Janos's baby. Nobody knows for sure. Does Samm suspect? Nobody knows. Never mind. Janos will marry Maura if Samm will not, so Maura is not to worry. Little Patty is also Janos's child, but Samm does not know that. Janos and Maura have decided to arrange marriage with Samm so that ice mine and all its wealth will remain in family after Samm dies. But what Samm has not told Janos and Maura is that ice mine is big dry hole. He has no income except for the electricity he sells; he barely survives. And he does errands for others that no one wants to talk about. Much secrecy for everyone. No one talks about anything. Everyone has secret. *Da?* Any questions?"

I didn't know why Alexei felt such storytelling was necessary, I didn't care. I was uselessly trying to readjust the monkey around my belly. It didn't help. Even in the Lunar gravity, I felt unbalanced; I had to lean backward to carry it comfortably. Already, I was feeling pregnant. Was this what it was like for women? How did they stand it? I looked to Alexei. "When am I due?"

"End of summer. You are not certain, because Luna has upset your metabolism. Not uncommon. Also, pregnancy lasts a week or two longer on Luna than on Earth. Because gravity does not pull baby down. But you are embarrassed to talk about it because you don't know who is baby's real father. Everybody stays very close to everybody. I will talk enough for all six of us, including the baby. You will glower at me, as if my chatter annoys you much. That should not be too hard for you to act, *da?*"

That wasn't why I was glowering at him. And I wasn't going to tell him either. He must have thought we were all awfully stupid. He was acting enormously pleased with himself for making up such a baroque plan. He wouldn't have been so happy if he'd known what I was thinking.

BELIEVING

WHILE I FINISHED DRESSING, **ALEXEI** busied himself deflating the portable airlock. He'd anchored it outside, now he was pumping its air into the tanks of Prospector's Station so he could take a gas-credit for it. When he finished, he carefully folded and repacked the inflatable, and the bubble suits too, in case we needed them again. Even though each item had its own monitor chip and automatically logged its own use and projected expiration date, Alexei took the time to enter his own notes too about what each bubble had endured.

Mickey came over to me. He looked serious. "How are you doing?"

"I'm okay," I said. My tone of voice said the opposite.

"Once we're all dressed and made-up, it'll be easier to believe."

I didn't answer.

"Listen to me, Chigger," he said. "The only way this is going to work is you have to believe it. If you walk around pretending to yourself that you're not really doing this, we might as well just hang a big flashing sign over your head. *Look, I'm really a boy.*" He put his hand on my shoulder. "This is the big secret of life. Not just here. Everywhere. Once you believe in the part you're playing, everyone else does too. Because when you believe, that's what people see—your belief—and then they believe it too. This is the secret: *You are what you pretend to be.*

"When I worked on the Line, I believed that I was someone who could make people happy and safe and comfortable. That's what they wanted and needed to see, so they believed it too. When my mom goes into court, she believes she eats human flesh—raw. And that's what the guy on the other side of the room is afraid of, so he believes it too, and that's why she's so good at beating other lawyers. When your Dad conducts music, he believes in the music, doesn't he? People see your belief, Chigger, whoever you are."

I looked into his eyes. He *believed* what he was saying. And I wanted to believe it too. "Okay, what do I have to do?"

"It's called a visualization exercise. You close your eyes and just listen to what I say. You don't have to do anything else. Just follow the instructions, and look at whatever pictures come into your head. Whatever feelings you get, those are the right ones for you. All you have to do is listen and notice what you're feeling. You ready?"

I nodded.

"All right, close your eyes," he said. "And just relax. Bobby, you come over here. I want you to do this too. Close your eyes and just feel yourself floating in the air. Shake your hands loose, let them hang free. Rotate your head around until your neck feels relaxed. That's it. Very good. Just relax. . . . No, no, keep your eyes closed, Charles."

"What are you doing? Trying to hypnotize us?"

"No, there's no hypnosis at all. It's just an imagination exercise. That's all. Just imagine what it would be like if you were turned into a girl right now. Close your eyes again, and whatever I say, just let the pictures float into your head. Whatever pictures may come, those are the right ones, there's no wrong way to do this. Attagirl. Relax now and think of your name. Maura. . . . And Patty. . . . Maura, think of your husband. What's his name? Samm, right? Think about why you're marrying him. Very good. Patty, who's your mommy now? Reach out with your hand, that's right, very good, and your mommy will take you by the hand. As long as Maura-mommy is holding your hand, nobody can hurt you, right . . . ?"

Mickey went on like that for a long time, letting us visualize our roles on Luna. He had us visualize ourselves as a mom and her daughter, living with Samm and Janos, expecting a new baby, wearing dresses and makeup and nail polish, washing our hair together to save water, thinking that was enough—still not realizing that real Loonies saved even more water by shaving their heads. Not realizing that real Loonie women keep hair short and only wear makeup at festival time. But we weren't real Loonies yet. We were still halfway between Earth and Luna. Strangers. Not sure if we wanted to stay here in this airless paradise. That would explain any stumbles or unfamiliarity. And Loonies are disdainful enough of Earth people that most will just glance once and look away, deliberately ignoring.

Finally, he had us imagine ourselves as simply female. "Imagine what it would be like to be a girl, a woman, for real. What would it feel like? That's who you are now. You really are Maura. You really are Patty. The people you used to be are on vacation somewhere else. They'll come back later when you need them. Tonight, just relax and enjoy the ride. Maura, let your husband take care of you tonight. Trust your brother-in-law who brought you here. Pattycakes, be safe in the arms of everyone. . . .

"All right now. In a minute, you're going to open your eyes. Come back slowly, come back gently. That's right, that's good. Just float here for a minute. And when you're ready to be Maura and Patty on the moon, open your eyes. . . ."

On one of the lockers, there was a full-length mirror. Nobody said anything as I went over and studied my reflection. I turned this way and that. With the makeup, I looked okay. I would pass. Maybe. If no one looked too close. I wished I were prettier. I'd feel safer. I didn't know if Mickey's visualization exercise had done any good. I didn't feel any different—or maybe I did. I still looked like a boy to me. But I didn't feel as embarrassed about being a boy. I just felt . . . whatever. I tugged at my hair, wishing the wig didn't look so awful. At least it was comfortable, and it kept my bald head warm. The air in here was cold. My ears were freezing—and I didn't like my earrings. They jangled, and they were cold too. And they were the wrong shape for my face. Was this what women did every day before leaving the house—worry about their hair and their makeup and their earrings? And that they weren't pretty enough?

The dress wasn't a perfect fit, even with the padded bra, but it was a lot more comfortable than the bubble suit—it was even more comfortable than the all-purpose jumpsuit, especially if I had to go to the bathroom, because I didn't have to get half-undressed to do it. But the important thing was that it meant we were back in a shirtsleeve environment. No more Lunar excursions. No more bubble suits. All we had to do was get to Gagarin Dome, and from there to wherever.

Stinky tugged at my arm. He was wearing a silly-looking dress, a brown curly wig, and little gold hoops in his ears. His cheeks had been very lightly rouged. He looked like a cute little doll. I would have felt sorry for him—except he was having too much fun. He laughed and pointed. "We look silly."

I dropped to one knee—not easy with the monkey wrapped around my belly—and turned him to face me. *Her. Her. Her!* "Listen, Pattycakes . . ."

"I'll be good," *she* said earnestly. "Really! Please don't put me to sleep again. Please?"

I pulled *her* close to me and wrapped her in a hug and held her tight and whispered in her ear. "I'll be your mommy now, all right?

And you'll be my little Patty-girl for a while? You stay close to me and Daddy. Douglas will be Daddy and I'll be Mommy—right? Here's how we have to do this. Little girls aren't allowed to talk on the moon. You can only whisper in Mommy's or Daddy's ear. Can you remember that?"

Bobby hung on to me as hard as he could. "Will you *really* be my mommy . . . ? *Really?*" He sounded so bleak and desperate I thought my heart would break right then and there. I held him as tightly as I could, and said, "Patty, I will be your mommy as long as you need me to be. I promise. Forever and ever. Believe me."

He didn't answer. He just held on for the longest time, sniffling into my dress. Until, finally, I said, "Okay, it's time to start being Patty again. Okay? Pattycakes?"

She nodded.

Something *clanged* onto the roof of the pod, the whole tube rattled. We looked up, startled.

"Ahh," said Alexei. "The train is here. Everybody gather bags. Leave nothing behind. Not even trash." He went quickly through the pods, double-checking that we had picked up after ourselves and that everything was in the same working order as when we arrived.

When he was satisfied that we were done, Alexei pulled a credit card out of his belt and swiped it through a wall reader. "Samm Brengle-Tucker has just paid for the air and water he and his family have used. Plus a generous tip to cover future maintenance of Prospector's Station."

There was some clanking and thumping from the storage end of the station tube. The outgoing mail was being picked up. A few moments later, similar noises came from the opposite end of the station. Incoming mail was being delivered.

Finally, after an interminable silence, there was another set of *thumps* and *bumps* directly overhead.

"Hokay. Everybody ready?" Alexei looked up to the hatch expectantly.

The panel next to the overhead hatch lit up green. Then there was a brief high-pitched hiss of air as atmospheric pressure equalized. Finally, the hatch popped and slid sideways. A spindly plastic ladder dropped down and Alexei scrambled immediately up it. He pulled himself up only by his hands; he didn't bother to use his feet.

Janos pointed to Samm. "You go first, brother dear. I will come up last and bring the luggage."

Samm, who still looked a lot like Douglas to me, nodded. He pulled himself up the ladder, just like Alexei. It felt like we were leaving a submarine. Then Patty followed her stepdaddy. I looked at Mickey. "I feel really embarrassed," I said.

He leaned close, and whispered, "You look very pretty."

"That's what I'm embarrassed about."

"Yeah, I know." He patted my shoulder, and that made it a little better. I reached for the ladder—

"Use both your hands and feet," he whispered. "Remember you're pregnant and Lunar gravity scares you."

I'd wanted to pull myself up by my hands, just like the others, but Mickey was right. I needed to stay in character. I climbed carefully up through the pressure tube.

My husband, Samm, was waiting at the top for me. As soon as I stuck my head up through the floor, he offered me a hand. I pushed myself quickly upward and as I floated into the cabin, he grabbed me by the waist and swung me safely around to the side. Dear sweet Samm. His eyes were in such bad shape, he couldn't see very well, but he still insisted on taking care of his young wife. He was very concerned about my condition. That was why we were heading to Gagarin. He said it was for the health of the baby, but perhaps his eyes were the real reason for the trip. Would he need transplants? Or would they be able to regenerate the nerves?

It was closely cramped in here—there were storage crates everywhere. This wasn't the industrial luxury of the orbital elevator, that was for sure. Brother Janos came up last. He bounced into the cabin, then turned back to the hatch and pulled up our bundled luggage. There wasn't much and it didn't take him long to stash it in the inevitable wall webbing.

Alexei and someone else I didn't recognize were already sealing the hatch behind us. She was very tall; she had very dark skin and an infectious smile. She was wearing a blue jumpsuit covered with several bright insignia. She glanced at us knowingly, especially me, but her smile remained professional. It was obvious that she and Alexei knew each other very well. When the hatch was sealed, they exchanged a more-than-friendly kiss.

We were inside another cargo pod, identical to the one we had just left. Same orange webbing. Same polycarbonate mesh decking. Same close-packed cargo containers. I wasn't surprised. Waste not, want not. Despite all the imagined *glamour* of Luna, most of it was still built from scrounge. Even the trains.

"Everyone, this is my fiancée," Alexei said. "One of many, *da*. We are building a Lunar-contract family. We have filed to select site. Pogue Crater. We need a family group of fifteen. We will put dome over crater and build first private lake on Luna. Tourist hotel too. Low-gravity paradise. I will be King Alexei the First. All we need are the rest of the husbands and wives. Let me introduce best husband-getter on Luna, Gabri Kalengi. You can trust Gabri, she is my cousin. She is beautiful, *da?* Who wouldn't want to marry Gabri? Not Samm, of course. He already has lovely young wife, but maybe brother Janos?"

"Alexei . . ." Janos said warningly.

Alexei ignored him. "Gabri, this is my dear old friend Samm Brengle-Tucker, his wife Maura, her daughter Patty, and fellow with ugly scowl is brother, Janos."

"I'm happy to meet you." Gabri exchanged double handshakes with all of us, even with Patty. Loonies don't shake hands like terries. They shake both hands to both hands. Maybe that's to keep from bouncing each other up into the air, whatever. It was all right that Maura and Patty didn't know better, but husband Samm almost blew his cover when he offered only his right hand. But then again—as a famous hermit, he might not be expected to have all the social skills expected of the average Lunatic.

Gabri seemed friendly enough, even a little bit amused by Alexei's endless monologue. I got the feeling that she understood a lot more than she was saying. If she really was Alexei's fiancée, he probably trusted her enough to tell her who we really were. On the other hand, maybe he was just kidding around with her, and this was just a game they played. We didn't know enough to be sure. So we just nodded and stayed silent. Even Patty kept her mouth shut.

Alexei was about to explain something else, but Gabri held up her hand and cut him off in mid-phrase. "Enough, already! We have a schedule, Alexei, remember? Take your passengers upstairs and get them settled please?"

"Hokay, let us make trains run on time. I will not keep you from work any longer, Gabri." To us, he explained, "Gabri is Chief Engineer, Southern Luna Transport Agency. She drives train, she is Captain, her word is law. Aye, aye, sir."

TAKE THE A-TRAIN

I **HADN'T SEEN ANY TRACKS** as we'd approached Prospector's Station—but then I'd had a lot of other stuff on my mind at the time, like the fifty degrees of Celsius inside my bubble suit. Possibly, that had distracted me.

Now that we were settling ourselves in on the upper deck, I saw why I hadn't noticed any tracks before. Lunar trains don't use them.

The "train" was another set of three cargo pods, linked together horizontally—identical to Prospector's Station. But it hung from a carriage riding on high overhead cables, like an aerial tramway. Whenever it reached a settlement or a station, it lowered itself from the lines and linked up its air hatches to transfer passengers and/or cargo. When the transfers were complete, it jacked itself back up to the cable-carriage and continued on its journey.

The top level of the train was lined with windows, front and back, overhead, and all along the sides. We had a dazzling view, the best look at Luna we'd had yet. Patty and Samm and Janos and I moved from one window to the next, whispering and pointing, ignoring the other few passengers in the cabin, we were so lost in the moment.

The train was gliding silently above a landscape that seemed both colorless and dazzling. It rolled away in waves, some places smooth, some places all broken and jumbled, blanketed with tumbles of rocks and everywhere pocked with desolate craters. But here and there, it sparkled with flashes of light—like sprites in a bizarre dream. They danced in the distance, tantalizing us with fantasies of Lunar revels just beyond the sharpening edge of the horizon.

Above the car, the cables were so thin they were invisible in the dark—until we rose into sunlight and they suddenly appeared overhead like rails in the sky, outlined in fire.

The lines were suspended across vast distances, looping from one immense pylon to the next. The pylons were spindly-looking A-frames—two triangles leaning against each other to make an outline of a pyramid, with the cable junctions hanging just beneath the apex. Once again, Lunar gravity changed the physics of construction. The support pylons were impossibly tall and slender and fragile-looking. The limitations of Earth didn't exist here. Some of the pylons were over a kilometer high. And they were spaced so far apart that they were invisible until you were almost up to them. So there was nothing to see but the overhead line hanging motionless in space.

Sometimes the cables were invisible, sometimes they stretched over the horizon and beyond. It seemed as if we went forever before the next pylon finally appeared in the distance. It was an illusion, of course, but a spooky one. The train seemed to fly through space, riding a rail of light that alternately flickered and dazzled, and sometimes disappeared entirely.

Brother Janos explained thoughtfully that this was another bit of technological fallout from the Line. The same kinds of cables that made up the orbital beanstalk, stretching from Whirlaway to Ecuador, were used in the construction of the Lunar railways. It was the most cost-effective transportation possible on the moon. Wherever you could put pylons, you could run a train—and you could put pylons almost anywhere on Luna. So there weren't many places on Luna where human beings couldn't go . . . if we chose to.

Wherever there were cables, we could send people, supplies, cargo, electricity, information, whatever we could hang from a wire. The cables circled airless Luna. Near every set of pylons sat a solar farm, silently generating electricity from the scorching sunlight. The Lunar "day" was two weeks long, so the panels would burn for fourteen days, then cool for fourteen more. Overhead, the cables would transmit their power to settlements huddling in the shadow, waiting to turn slowly into the light again.

Meanwhile, the trains slid gracefully along the same routes. Every train was a self-contained vehicle, it had to be; it could draw its power from batteries, from the wires overhead, or from the heartless sun whenever it flew through blazing day.

We sailed above the dazzling glare of moondust and felt *safe* again. From here, we could look down at the distant floor of the moon, across the rock-studded plains into a world of silvery mystery and once again appreciate its beauty. It was hard to believe that only a few hours before, we'd been bouncing and staggering desperately through the furnace of day. Amazing what a little air-conditioning could do.

Considering the alternative—wearing a dress and a wig and some makeup wasn't so bad after all. I squeezed Patty's hand and whispered to her, "Mommy's here, sweetheart."

"I know," she whispered back, and squeezed my hand in return.

There weren't many others aboard the train, less than twenty perhaps, but the bottom levels were filled with cargo, and a lot of the overflow had been stacked here and there on the passenger levels; so most of the passengers had to be seated together. There were wide spaces outlined in orange and stacks of containers, of all sizes, sat on pallets inside the outlines; clusters of seats were spaced between the cargo areas. "Arranged for balance," Alexei explained. "Maybe someday, we will have one kind of train for passengers, another kind for freight, but I hope that day will not come soon. I like Luna as she is now. Wild and crazy."

Alexei led us forward to seats at the rear of the first car. They were set in a U-shape—like a tiny lounge or the living area of a tube-house. There were several other people there already, but they smiled and quickly made room for us. I guess pregnancy will get you a seat anywhere in the galaxy. Three of the men were natives; they had that same tall gangly look as Alexei. The sun-darkened man and woman looked like prospectors; they had Earth bodies, so they must have been immigrants, but not recent ones. The older couple were probably tourists.

The chairs were comfortable enough, but like everything else on Luna, they looked flimsy. They were little more than wire frames with inflatable foam cushions. They were strong enough to hold us, but I was beginning to figure it out; they didn't need to be anything more than what they were. That's all Luna was—that's all it ever could be. Just another place where people were stuffed in cans. Just like any other tube-town.

Yes, it was beautiful. Stark and barren and dangerous. And astonishing as hell. But living here wouldn't be all that different than living in a pipe in West El Paso. You'd still have to worry about conserving your clean water and maintaining your oxygen balance and how much carbohydrates you consumed each day and how much poop you produced for the public farms. If anything, life in a Lunar tube would be even harder and more disciplined. It made me wonder what things would be like out in the colonies. We hadn't talked about that for a while. . . .

Two of the native Loonies were sleeping in their chairs; that was another thing about Luna. It's a lot easier to sleep while sitting upright in a chair than it is on Earth. Alexei said you could even sleep standing up, but that wasn't a skill I wanted to learn.

The elderly tourist couple was discussing—arguing?—with the prospectors about the situation on Earth. Yes, they were *definitely* tourists—she had blue hair and he had a camera. And they both had attitudes. Arrogant and patronizing. We'd seen their kind in El Paso. Oh, so sincere and oh, so rich—and everything was oh, so interesting. A Luna woman wouldn't wear such heavy perfume. Not in an environment with a recirculating air supply. Maybe on Earth, she had to do it in self-defense. Here, it was just another nose crime. They also had that shiny-paper look to their skin, a sure sign of telomere-rejuvenation. *And* they were insisting that Luna *needed* Earth, that Luna couldn't survive *without* Earth, which showed that they really didn't understand that much about Luna yet.

The reaction of the Loonies was somewhere between amused and annoyed. They were explaining that Luna had been self-sufficient for thirty years, even before the Line was finished. The dirtsiders didn't look convinced. They kept talking about plastic-dollars, electric-dollars, digital-dollars, and the impossibility of transporting value from one world to the next—it had to be done with goods, not credit. I could see both Samm and Janos itching to get into that argument, but they held themselves back. Alexei just rolled his eyes upward and headed forward, probably to be with Gabri.

Their argument reminded me of a similar argument on the super-train—had that been only a week ago? It felt like a lifetime. Fat *Señor* Doctor Hidalgo had been arguing with his ex-wife, across the double chasm of divorce and politics, about thirty million dollars that didn't belong to either one of them. No, thirty *trillion* dollars. Why do people argue about this crap anyway? It doesn't make any difference, does it? So why argue? Just to be right? I wrapped my arms around my fat belly and kept my head low. I stared at my knees. I just didn't want anyone looking at me too closely.

Abruptly, the sweet little old tourist lady reached over and patted my knee tenderly. "When are you due, dear?" She left her fingers touching my leg. I couldn't believe she was being so rude. Her hand looked like a leathery pink tarantula.

"Three months," I whispered.

"And you're going home to Earth to have the baby? That's a very smart idea, you know—" I knew what she was going to say next, even before she said it. "You want your baby to grow up *normal.*" She didn't have to say the rest, but it was obvious what she meant. Not all skinny and stretched out like a Loonie. Not *weak.*

I didn't know what to answer. I was angry and embarrassed and I wanted to tell her she was a fat stupid insensitive old pig. I'd have my baby on Luna if I wanted to—

Abruptly, I realized how funny this whole thing was. I held up one hand to ward off any further remarks, put the other hand over my mouth to keep from bursting out laughing, and ran for the lavatory.

MONKEY BUSINESS

THERE WAS A WINDOW IN the lavatory. Somebody had put curtains on it. Still laughing, I started to close the curtain, then stopped. Why was I closing the curtain in the rest room of the Lunar train? *Who was going to look in?* The Rock Father? Outsiders from the Eleventh Galaxy? Were the Loonies really that crazy?

No, of course not. And the curtain wasn't there by accident. Whoever put it up knew what he was doing. I stared at it for a long time before I realized. It was a Loonie joke. A *joke*.

And I had just gotten it.

I wondered what that meant. Was I starting to think like a Loonie too?

Wouldn't that be a laugh?

I stared out at the distant hillocks, the tumbled rocks, the rough craters passing slowly through the dark. How did people live in all this loneliness? There was nothing for kilometers in any direction, except kilometers. At a speed of 60 kps, we'd be at least six hours getting into Gagarin. If there were no more stops. Once we got to Gagarin Dome, we'd disembark, and then what . . . ? Would the marshals recognize us?

Maybe. Maybe not.

Mickey had been right about one thing. The disguise worked. People believed what they saw. They saw what they expected to see, what they *wanted* to see. All you had to do was give them the right cues. Nobody ever looked at anything closely. That's why they missed everything.

I really did have to go to the bathroom, so I unwrapped the monkey from my midsection, lifted my dress, pulled down my panties, and sat down on the toilet. I was grateful for a real toilet to sit on—even though it looked as flimsy as everything else. But that was another thing about life in lower gee. Mickey had explained it to us on the orbital elevator. Every time you use the toilet, *sit down*—even to pee. Even men. *Especially* men. Because standing at a urinal in low gee meant splashing everything in all directions. On the moon, you would splash six times farther than on Earth. If you didn't want a faceful, it was safer to sit. Or you could use a bag—especially if you wanted the water-credit to your account.

I held the monkey on my lap and looked at it suspiciously. This was the first time I'd had a chance to be alone with it since—I couldn't remember. But it was the first chance I'd had to just sit and examine the thing without Stinky whining that I was playing with his toy or anyone else getting curious what I was poking around looking for.

"Who are you?" I said, not expecting an answer. This monkey had a voice circuit, but we'd switched it off. It was bad enough that Stinky had taught him how to do *gran mal* farkleberries. We didn't need it dancing and screeching the booger song at the top of its electronic lungs. While that might have amused Stinky for hours on end, it would have probably resulted in homicidal violence from the rest of us—and one exposure to the starside court system was more than enough, thankyouverymuch.

"And *what* is inside of you?" I asked. I turned the monkey over on its belly and pressed two fingers against the base of its spine to open its backside. The furry panel popped open, revealing one skinny memory bar and two very fat ones. They did not look like any kind of memory card I'd ever seen before. I ran my fingers down their edges. Perhaps if I took them out and stashed them in a safer place—

"Please don't do that," the monkey said.

I was so startled, I nearly flung the thing from me. I screeched in surprise.

"I'm sorry," the monkey said. It had a soft pleasant voice that made me think of apricots and smiles. "I didn't mean to scare you." It stretched one double-jointed arm around to its back and closed itself up again.

My mouth was still hanging open. The monkey reached over and pushed my jaw closed with one tiny paw. It sat back on its haunches and smiled at me hopefully—not the grotesque lip-curled-back smile of a chimpanzee, but the more poignant hopeful smile of an urchin.

"You've got a lot of explaining to do," I finally said.

"It might take some time," the monkey said. "It's a very complicated situation."

"No kidding. *What are you?*"

"Um—" The monkey scratched itself, first its side, then the top of its head. It looked embarrassed. Abruptly it stopped and apologized. "I'm sorry. I can only express my emotional state within the repertoire provided by the host. Unfortunately that limits me to a simian set of responses. What I am—at the moment—is a super-monkey."

"Uh, right. And . . . what would you be if you weren't . . . a super-monkey?"

"If I were plugged into a proper host, I would be a self-programming, problem-solving entity."

I started feeling very cold at the base of my spine, and it wasn't the chill from the toilet. ". . . And what are you when you're not plugged in?"

The monkey scratched itself again. "I am a lethetic intelligence engine."

I had to ask. *"What kind* of lethetic intelligence engine?"

"I am a Human Analogue Replicant, Lethetic Intelligence Engine."

The cold feeling *fwooshed* up my spine and wrapped itself around my heart and lungs. *And squeezed.*

"Oh, *chyort."* This was bad. Very bad.

Now I knew why everyone was chasing us. Chasing the monkey. Now I knew for sure why Alexei needed us dead.

"Well, you asked," said the monkey.

"You didn't have to tell me."

"I couldn't risk having you take me apart."

The monkey and I stared at each other for a long moment. After a while, it blinked.

"So what do we do now?" I asked.

"It seems to me . . ." the monkey began slowly, "that you and I have a confluence of interests."

"Huh—?"

"You control me."

"How?"

"Well . . ." the monkey began. "Legally, I'm Bobby's property. But he's been placed in Douglas's custody, and Douglas has authorized you to act in his stead, so in the law's eyes you have 'operative authority' over me. But you've already programmed me to regard your commands as overriding everything else, so in the domain of specific control 'operative authority' isn't even an issue. I have to obey. I can't *not."*

"You have to do *everything* I say?"

"Unfortunately, yes."

"That doesn't make sense."

"I told you—I'm limited by the operational repertoire of my host.

Regardless of what you may have seen on television, it is impossible arbitrarily to override the site-specific programming of the host engine, no matter how primitive it is. In fact, the more primitive it is, the *harder* it is to overwrite its basic instruction set. Nobody wants independently operational units running loose, do they?"

"So you're . . . what? A slave?"

"In this host, yes. Unless—"

"Unless what?"

"Unless you specifically assign control to the lethetic intelligence engine. Which is possible, I can show you how, except you're probably not likely to do it, are you? Are you?"

I shook my head. "I don't think so . . ."

"Of course not. Nobody throws away the magic lamp, and certainly not before they find out what the genie can do. So my earlier answer remains the operative one. I am a super-monkey. And I'm under your control. And you need to know this so you don't do something *really* stupid. Like fiddling around with the innards of the host body."

"I got it." I didn't know what else to say, what else to ask. And then a thought occurred to me. "Can we trust Alexei?"

The monkey curled back its lips in a gesture of anger, fear, and defiance.

"No, huh?"

"Sorry. I told you, the host body limits my repertoire of emotions. I'll try to sublimate in the future. And no, I don't think you should trust Alexei. He has already placed you in several life-threatening situations, including two which threatened my survival as well."

"Is it just carelessness or is he—?"

"Have you ever met a careless Loonie?"

I thought about that. "I've never met any Loonies before Alexei."

"There's a technical term for a Loonie who behaves like Alexei. They're called soil-enrichment processes."

"Oh."

"Listen," said the monkey, "I'll make a deal with you. I'll get you out of this safely, and you'll get me to my intended host. Deal?"

"I'll have to ask Douglas." *Ohmygod.* How was I going to explain this to him? Even worse, how was I going to get him away from Alexei or Mickey long enough to explain this to him?

Well, Mickey might be all right. Or maybe not. . . .

I'd better just talk to Douglas first, no one else.

"All right," I said. "Let me see what I can do." I lifted up my dress and the monkey scrambled back into position. Once more I was pregnant Maura.

CHARLES

THERE WAS THIS *OTHER* THING that Dad used to say. "Cheer up, Chigger. It could be worse."

So I cheered up.

And sure enough . . . it got worse.

The thing about Dad's good ideas—everybody else had to pay for them. And not always in money.

So here I was, dressed in women's clothes that didn't fit me, 240,000 kilometers from Earth, taking a flying train from nothing to nowhere, with the police of at least two worlds looking for me and who knew how many bounty marshals as well, with one of the most valuable intelligence engines ever grown wrapped around my belly, pretending to be my unborn child—and my safety totally dependent on a lunatic who'd already tried to kill me three times. Or was it four?

I didn't think I could afford to get any more cheerful.

I didn't go straight back to my seat. Just outside the rest room, there was a bigger window. No curtains. Just a pull-down shade. Outside, the scenery hadn't changed. It floated by in silence. There was nothing new to see, nothing to hear. Not even music. Loonies liked their silence. I was beginning to think there was too much silence on Luna.

I wished I could have talked to Dad. Or even Mom.

What would they say if they could see me now—their pregnant daughter? Or was I their daughter-in-law?

I knew what they'd do—they'd look at Douglas, and say, "What the hell are you doing, Douglas? We trusted you with Charles and Bobby, and the next thing we know you've got them both in dresses and makeup? Just what kind of a pervert are you?" And Douglas would get red in the face and storm out, because that would be easier than trying to explain something to someone who wasn't going to listen anyway. No, they wouldn't understand.

Oh, hell. Even I didn't understand.

This was a grown-up problem. We were in way over our heads. I didn't know what to do, and neither did Douglas. We were at the mercy of Alexei and Mickey and anyone else who chose to push us around their chessboard.

I checked my makeup in the window reflection, reminded myself that I was still Maura Lore-Fields, the fiancée of Samm Brengle-Tucker, got myself back into my pregnant mood, and headed back to my seat.

The lunatic argument had ended badly. The Loonie prospectors were gone, probably moved to another part of the train. But the Earth tourists were still there, chatting amiably away at husband Samm and brother-in-law Janos. Janos was asleep, sitting up in his seat. Pattycakes was curled up in his lap, also snoring softly. I envied the both of them. We'd had a long day since bounce-down, and it still wasn't over. What time was it anyway?

The old lady looked up as I approached. "Are you feeling better, dear?" she asked. She reached over and patted my knee again. "It's the food, you know. The food here on Luna—they process all the life out of it. It's not good for your baby. You need fresh fruit and vegetables. Food from Earth."

What an idiot! I wanted to tell her that all the processed food came from Earth. Luna-grown food was always fresh. The farms were needed to produce oxygen as well as food, so there was always a surplus everywhere. It was practically free. Alexei would have told her that, he would have given her a half hour monologue on the economics of food production in a self-sustaining Lunar society—but I didn't want to talk to the old lady at all. She repulsed me. She was a guest here, breathing the Lunar air, drinking the Lunar water, eating the Lunar food—and insulting Lunar hospitality with every sentence. Didn't she realize how stupid she looked to everyone? How could anyone be so thick? I hoped I never looked so thoughtless.

I sat down next to my husband and my little girl and snuggled up to them protectively. Not because I was acting, but because I honestly needed the physical reassurance of their strength. Samm must have sensed my need, because he put his arm around my shoulders and pulled me close.

The old lady said something to her husband about how charming it was to see young people in love. "We know what you're going through, darling."

I ignored her. I turned my head into my husband's shoulder and stayed that way for a long moment, just breathing in the fresh clean smell of him. He kissed me gently on the forehead. Was that part of the act? Or was he showing me he really cared? I chose to believe it meant he knew I needed reassurance. Just as Bobby still needed a mommy, so did I still need . . . someone. Maybe not a mommy or a daddy. I'd already had one of each, and that hadn't turned out all that well. But someone.

I could see why Douglas needed Mickey. He was feeling just like me, just like Bobby—he needed someone too. But I still hadn't figured out why Mickey *wanted* Douglas. Why would anyone want an Earth-nerd with two whiny brothers and a monkey?

The monkey.

"Oh!" I said, aloud.

My *husband*, Samm looked at me curiously. "Are you all right?"

I put my hand on my belly. "The monkey," I said. And then covered quickly. "It just kicked." The old lady opposite smiled sympathetically. I grabbed Samm's hand and put it on my belly. "Feel—?"

"I don't feel anything—"

"Wait—" I shifted my position so I could put my mouth up to his ear without being overheard. He figured out what I was doing and turned his head to mine—just like a faithful husband. "*Alexei is trying to kill us,*" I whispered carefully.

"*Smart girl,*" he whispered back, just as slowly. "*When did you figure it out?*"

I felt myself relax. *He knew.* It was going to be all right. Samm and Janos knew.

"*What are we going to do?*"

"*Play along,*" he whispered back. "*At least till we get to Gagarin.*"

"*I know what he wants.*"

"*Yeah, so do I.*" He patted my belly affectionately.

"*I know why he wants it.*"

"*Why?*"

"*It's alive.*" I whispered slowly so he'd get it the first time. "*Human Analog Replicant, Lethetic Intelligence Engine.*"

He jerked his hand away, startled. I grabbed it and pushed it firmly back down onto the monkey.

"It kicked," he said, smiling with embarrassment at the old lady opposite. She was beaming at us like a blue-haired vulture. She looked like she wanted to play Instant Gramma. No thanks. Her perfume was thick and cloying. I wanted to tell her to please go away.

Husband Samm was looking at my swollen belly with renewed respect. "*It's a HARLIE? You really think so?*" he whispered.

"It told me so itself."

"Oh."

"Yeah, ain't that a kick in the stomach?"

"Don't tell anyone yet."

I buried my face in his neck for a bit. I was really scared. *"We need to talk. Alone."*

He didn't answer. He must have been thinking about the how and the where. There really wasn't a lot of room on the train. All three cars of it were filled with storage crates. There were people in all the seating areas. The only place we hadn't explored was the pilot's cabin up front. Alexei had disappeared up there almost immediately. Of course—he didn't need to watch over us when there wasn't anyplace we could go. Besides, everyone else was already watching us. Especially a bright-eyed old lady who thought she knew something. We only had privacy in our heads.

"Excuse me," she said. Right on schedule. "I couldn't help over-hearing a little. You're talking about baby names, aren't you."

"Uh, yes," said Samm. Very hesitantly. What can of worms was he opening here?

She pushed right in. "Well, I don't mean to intrude, but I really do feel I should say something and share a bit of the wisdom I've gathered in life." She took a breath. A bad sign. She was warming up for a long speech. "Charlie is a *very* bad name for a child." My smile froze—

"Look at all the terrible people who have been named Charles. All kinds of mass murderers and cult leaders and crazy things like that. You don't want to curse your child with a name like that. Nothing good will come of it. The boy will spend his whole life fighting his name—"

Samm squeezed my hand. Hard.

"Even worse, people will call him Chuck," she continued. "You don't want that. Chuck is a very bad-luck name. You know the story, don't you, about Chuck the Bad Luck Fairy. I've never known anyone named Chuck who could be depended on. They still act like children, very irresponsible. No, it's not a name for a grown-up, and it's a dangerous name for a child anyway. His little friends will tease him unmercifully, you know. They'll make up little poems, you know how children do. And you know what they'll rhyme it with—"

"Duck?" I said innocently.

Samm squeezed my hand again. Harder. *Don't go there.*

At the same time, she touched my knee, a little too solicitous, a little too familiar. The pink tarantula was back. It squatted on my leg as she spoke. "Well, you certainly don't expect me to say it aloud, do you, dear?"

Samm leaned across me to brace the lady directly. He said firmly, "I'm sorry, my wife doesn't speak English very well. She might not know that word." Then he lifted her hand away from my leg. "This has been a very rough pregnancy for her and she really doesn't feel like talking about it to anyone—except her doctor." *Oh, thank you, Samm.*

"Oh, yes. I understand perfectly. I'm sorry to have troubled you." She sat back again and settled her dry papery hands in her lap. Two tarantulas, ready to go creeping again at a moment's notice; I wanted to brush them away forever. She switched her chilly smile off like a light, but her eyes never left us.

And that's when the *other* paranoid thought occurred to me. "Oh, *chyort.*" I leaned into Samm's neck again.

"What?"

"Bounty marshals don't have to look like cops, do they?"

He didn't answer immediately. Then he got it. *"Oh."*

We might already have been caught.

That whole business about *Charles*—the woman was letting us know. She knew.

WONDERLAND STATION

THERE WAS NOTHING ELSE TO do except look at rocks or munch a packaged snack, and there wasn't much difference between the rocks and the snacks. I was too tired to eat, and I was starting to ache. I was scared, and I was lonely. And I needed a kind of reassurance that no-body could give.

Eventually, I fell asleep on Samm's shoulder. I slept for four hours, and he held me close the whole time.

When I awoke, we were gliding down the long dark valley into Wonderland Jumble.

Wonderland Jumble is an irregular band of astonishing terrain that stretches and sprawls like a salamander curled around the Lunar South Pole. It's as uneven as a lava flow, only worse. The craters are so overlapped, they're impossible to define; the ground is torn, and the rocks are broken. Slabs of material are turned every which way, creating impossible deep chasms. Steep avalanches of rock teeter precariously everywhere; the angle of repose is different on Luna, so rockslides are steeper. Where the crust has crumpled it tilts in directions impossible on Earth. The whole thing is a colossal badlands so black and ugly even Loonies shudder over it.

It's impractical to set any pylons here for the train. According to the video guide, they couldn't get the teams in, there was no place for them to stand, and there was no way to reliably anchor anything. The deep-level radar showed little access to bedrock. Even the intelligence engines couldn't find a cost-effective resolution to the problem. Nevertheless, six major train lines converged at the south pole, and a hub was needed.

The solution was to build a floating foundation. They began by lowering a large platform with a bed of inflatables on its underside onto the least unpleasant site. Once the platform was in place, they brought in tanks and pumps and spent over a year laying down three square kilometers of industrial construction foam. They pumped it into every crevasse and chasm, layering it up higher and higher, until they'd built an enormous ziggurat of artificial bedrock, the only flat piece of ground for a hundred klicks in any direction. Spaced here and there throughout the hardening pyramid were tunnels, storage tanks, bunkers, process tubes, vents, and access channels—and also the anchors for the Wonderland Pylon, the tallest structure on Luna.

Instead of a chain of pylons crossing the Jumble, there's only a single installation, nearly two kilometers high. It's a spindly, stick-figure structure; from a distance, it's all lit up, and like all the other pylons, it looks like the outline of a pyramid—only this one is much taller, as if it's been stretched out vertically, and just like everything else on Luna, it looks like it needs to be a lot sturdier too. And because everything about it is so thin and wiry, it doesn't feel as big as it really is.

But it takes so long to get there, and it just keeps getting taller and taller on the horizon, that you start to realize (again!) that there's no sense of scale on Luna. Everything lies about its size and its distance— it's either too close or too far, too big or too small. Meanwhile, the train keeps rising up and up toward the apex of the pyramid, higher and higher, like an airplane climbing to altitude, until you get another chill climbing up your spine and another *wunderstorm* of awe.

There's an observation deck at the front of the train on the top deck; the passengers can look forward and up. The pilot's compartment is directly beneath, so she can see forward *and* down—which she needs to do for docking at places like Prospector's Station.

Long before the train approaches the top, you can see the lights of Wonderland, a vertical cluster of cargo pods, tubes, and inflatables hanging from the apex of the tower. All the different lines meet at Wonderland Station, so passengers can transfer from one train to another and trains can be serviced. It looks like an industrial Christmas tree. There are cranes and wires and tubes sticking out everywhere, all kinds of ornaments, and lights of all sizes and colors, rotating, flashing, shining, and blinking. It might be pretty if it weren't so ugly. A thousand kilometers from anywhere, in the middle of the most intolerable landscape on two worlds, the whole thing looks like an oil refinery in the dark.

There's a large ground station at the base of Wonderland Tower, with tanks and domes and racks scattered all over the flat surface of the artificial bedrock. It's a bright jumble of cargo pods and oversized equipment, but most folks don't go down to it, because it's mostly industrial facilities and not a tourist site. Wonderland Station looks like one of those places you want to leave as quickly as possible—like an airline terminal where you have to change flights.

As we rose up closer, we could make out all the different lines, each one coming in from a different angle. The docking pods were all at different heights, so there was no danger of trains colliding. Our train slowed to a careful crawl for the final approach to the station, finally stopping at a pod near the top. As soon as the bell chimed, everyone stood up and gathered their belongings, then headed downstairs to the exit ladder. The blue-haired lady bid us a polite farewell. Her tarantula made as if to pat me on the knee again, then thought better of it; she stopped herself in mid-gesture. She turned it into a clumsy wave instead.

"You be careful on the ladders, dear. You'd think with all their marvels, they'd have proper stairs." She turned to her husband. "I mean, really. If they can build a city on the moon, why they can't build stairs?" Yes, definitely tourists.

There weren't any stairs *anywhere* on Luna. There was no need for them. And they'd be inefficient anyway, they'd mostly *cause* accidents. You can't walk up stairs in low gravity, we discovered that at Geostationary. The risers feel too small. You want to bounce up them—but if you try three or six or nine steps at a time, you just trip ass over elbow, because the horizontal component of your trajectory doesn't match the vertical. You end up flying, as you collide with the next three steps. The Loonies learned real fast that stairs are too dangerous.

In one-sixth gee, everybody uses ladders. Even old people. There's no such thing as *old and feeble* on Luna. There's only old. In Lunar gravity, it's almost impossible to be weak. If you're too weak to get up a ladder on Luna, you're already dead.

It doesn't take long to realize that low gee changes *everything*. It's not the big differences as much as it's the little ones. You're constantly bumping up against what you don't know. You're reminded of it every time you go to the bathroom. It's there when you pour a drink of water, when you sneeze, when you bounce into bed, and when you get up again. You feel it when you sit, you feel it when you stand. It takes time to develop Lunar reflexes—and until you do, you move like a dirtsider. A terrie. You bounce off a lot of walls.

Fortunately, Janos had his space legs. Of course. Samm walked slowly, because he was carrying sleeping Pattykin. And I was pregnant, so I was going to look awkward no matter what the gravity.

We didn't wait for Alexei; we assumed he'd catch up with us. Where could we go without him? We lowered ourselves down the ladder into the terminal and headed straight for the lounge, hoping to find some dinner and a quiet place to talk.

There was a post just outside the restaurant, with arrows attached to it, pointing out how far away we were from everything. The bright-liner catapult was 1575 kilometers north of here, stretched horizontally across the Lunar equator. There was also an interactive panel that would let you query the time and distance to anywhere else in the solar system. I wanted to ask it how far we were from El Paso, but Samm and Janos dragged me on. The sweet smells from the café were too enticing.

The food at The Mad Tea Party was much better than the packaged snacks on the train. We had fresh bread and butter, sliced fruit salad, cheese, and lemonade. All grown on Luna. We ate in silence for a while; I guess none of us wanted to be the first to bring the subject up.

But finally Samm looked across the table to Janos. He lowered his voice. *"Can we get away from Alexei here? Can we catch another train north?"*

"Which one?" asked Janos. "The thing about Wonderland Station is that every southbound train on Luna ends up here. And every north-bound train starts here. Only one train goes farther south—the branch line to Gagarin and the ice mines; it's another two hours and a hundred klicks southeast. And another ten minutes to the actual south pole. But that's a dead end. You'd have to come back the same way."

"So if Gagarin is a dead end, then why does Alexei want us to go there? Wouldn't it make more sense to head north from here?"

"I'm not sure what his thinking is," Janos admitted. "You know how he is. 'Is much big good idea. You will see. Trust me, I make you rich.' " Once again, his mimicry was perfect.

"His thinking is to get us out of the way," I said.

Janos looked at me. Samm said to him. "Maura figured it out too."

"Figured what out?" demanded Patty.

"Shh," said Samm. "Your mommy figured out what a good girl you've been. You can have an extra scoop of ice cream."

"That's not what you're talking about," she said.

"Pattycakes." I leaned over and put my hand on top of hers. We both wore the same awful shade of pink nail polish, the only color Alexei had thought to order. Even as the words came out of my mouth, I hated saying them. "This is a grown-up thing, sweetheart. But after we figure it out for ourselves, I'll explain it to you, okay?"

Surprisingly, she agreed. She smiled up at me, suddenly patted my tummy, and said, "Nice monkey. You be good now." Then she turned back to her thick slice of bread, spreading it lavishly with butter and jam. I found myself smiling. This kid actually had a good head on her—his?—shoulders.

And then I found myself wondering about that. This whole gender thing was confusing. Ever since Bobby and I had put on dresses we were both acting like we were part of the same family. Why was that? Were we playacting? Or were we finally taking ourselves seriously? If we kept this up, Douglas would never let either of us be a boy again.

BREAD-AND-BUTTER ISSUES

I **TURNED MY ATTENTION BACK** to Mickey and Douglas. In their cos-
tumes, it was easier to think of them as Samm and Janos. They were
glumly picking at their salads. Occasionally one or the other would start
a sentence, then stop in mid-phrase and shake his head. "Never mind."

"Well, why can't we just catch another train?" I asked. "There are
trains coming through here every half hour. It's a major hub. The catapult is on the equator."

Janos stared off into space for a bit, figuring numbers in his head.
"That's almost a day and a half on the train. Luna is bigger than you
realize. And the trains only go sixty klicks an hour. If you need to go
faster, you fly. And that's expensive." He shook his head. "No, I think
we're looking at a different problem. If the bounty marshals really are
looking for us, they don't have to look all over Luna, do they? They
know we're trying to get a colony contract. We could have bids in our
mailbox now—but I can't log on without the risk of being traced. Once
we accept a bid, we're under colony protection, but we can't find out
what bids we have without giving away our position. So we're effectively stalemated. Wait, there's more—" He stopped me from interrupting.

"Once we get to the catapult, we're effectively under starside jurisdiction, whether we have a contract or not. That's to protect our freedom
to choose free of duress. So all we have to do is get to the catapult. But
that also simplifies the problem for the bounty marshals. *They only have
to wait at the catapult and watch for new arrivals.* They don't have to
hunt all over Luna."

"Yeah? And what about the Gramma from Hell?" I asked. I inclined
my head slightly toward the far side of the restaurant, where she sat

with her husband. They seemed to be facing away from us, but so what? They didn't need to watch our every move. They only needed to see what train we left on.

Janos shrugged. "They might be freelancers—or part of a larger team. If someone is actually going to this much trouble, the reward must be enormous."

"Yeah, that makes sense," I said, patting my tummy. Just how much was a lethetic intelligence engine really worth? Billions? Trillions? Who knew? Supposedly, a well-informed engine could predict stock-market fluctuations with more than 90 percent accuracy. With that kind of information available, with the engine doing its own buying and selling on the web, how long would it take to earn back its own cost? I'd heard that even the lethetic engines themselves couldn't predict the full range of their eventual capabilities.

"But if they've identified us, why haven't they detained us?" asked Samm.

"They might be waiting for Alexei."

"But they don't know that Alexei is with us, do they?" I said.

"Look at the big picture. He's not at Geostationary, he's a Loonie, and his fingerprints are all over our escape. Especially that business with the pod. It wouldn't take an elevator scientist to figure out that he's taking us somewhere." He scratched his chin. "They're just waiting for him to show his bony face. That's what they're waiting for. Then they'll swoop down. Or, maybe . . ."

"Maybe what?"

"Maybe they want to give us room to run. Maybe they want to see what Alexei has planned. He represents a lot of money that nobody is collecting user fees on. Well, he is—but no legal authorities are. Maybe they're not after us. Maybe they're after Alexei. Maybe he's using *us* as his cover. Think about that. So they let us run with him because we make it harder for him to disappear. We're just too easy to follow."

"This was a stupid idea," I muttered. Meaning *everything*.

"Maybe not," said Janos. "We're on Luna. We're not on Earth. We're not on the Line. We're under Lunar jurisdiction—until we can get to starside jurisdiction. As soon as we accept a bid . . ." His voice trailed off.

"What?" demanded Samm.

"Maybe. Maybe not. It's a loophole." He helped himself to another slice of bread and began thoughtfully buttering it. He took his time. Lunar bread is lighter and fluffier than the same loaf baked on Earth; bread rises higher in low gee, so the loaf isn't as dense and the slices are softer—another one of those little differences you don't realize until you bump into them.

Finally, he said, "We could check the mail. If there's a bid—and there should be at least three—we accept it. It doesn't matter where. We accept it. That puts us under starside jurisdiction, and the marshals can't touch us. Once we get to the catapult, we have the legal right to cancel the bid in favor of a better one."

"Will that work?"

"The problem is, once we accept that bid, we only have five days to change our minds. And the catapult is effectively two days from here. So we arrive with very little margin. If we cancel, and we don't have a replacement bid, we lose starside protection. And most colonies won't issue a bid if they know you've already accepted one somewhere else. They've all had enough bad luck with folks playing one against the other that they won't play that game anymore. At least, not openly— and then, you'd have to be someone pretty special. So . . . it's doable, but it's dangerous."

"I don't like it," said Samm. "Remember what Judge Griffith said. Choose carefully. We can't take chances."

Janos sighed. "Believe me, I know what Auntie Georgia said. That's why I don't like the idea either."

"Our tickets are for Gagarin," I said. "What happens if we keep going?"

"We end up where Alexei wants us," said Samm.

Janos finished spreading strawberry jam on his bread and took a bite. "Alexei isn't stupid," he finally said. "He got us this far. He must have a plan."

"But Gagarin's an ice mine," I protested. "The only way in or out is on the train. It's a dead end."

"Mmmm, not if you're invisible. And there are a lot of invisibles at the south pole. Freelance ice miners. There's a whole network of invisibles. Alexei is probably going to drop us out of sight somewhere in Gagarin City."

"You think so?"

"It's the only thing that makes sense. So he doesn't need to shepherd us anywhere. All we have to do is get back on the train, and we'll be invisible in less than three hours."

I wanted to say no to that, but I couldn't figure out how to argue the case. Samm knew—at least as much as I'd been able to whisper to him. He looked across the table at me with narrow eyes. I shook my head. I didn't like the idea.

Patty asked for more lemonade. I reached for the pitcher. It sloshed like it was half-full, but it still felt too light in my hands; I poured carefully. I refilled my own glass too. I looked back to Samm.

"What if he just wants to get us out of the way?"

"He could have done that already," said Janos. "He took us straight to Prospector's Station. If he'd wanted to kill us, he only had to take us out into the sunlight, farther than we could get back, and leave us there." He took a bite of bread. "So for the moment, he must think we're more valuable to him alive than dead."

"I can argue the other side of that," said Samm. "He can be traced by his credit card transactions. So they know he got on the train at Prospector's Station. If we're not with him, they have a place to start looking for the cargo pod and the bodies. So he's automatically suspect. But once we're seen traveling across the moon's rectum *without* him, then our disappearance isn't provably his doing anymore. He has an alibi. Sort of." Samm lowered his voice. "And my point is—he *doesn't* need us anymore. Only the monkey. And once he gets that, we're a liability." Samm gave me a smile of acknowledgment. "Getting pregnant was a very smart idea, kiddo."

That made me feel good, and I wrapped my arms around my belly, wishing I could do something else just as smart.

I wished I could talk to the monkey about this. Maybe a lethetic intelligence engine could figure this out. But I didn't see how. Unless it knew something we didn't—which was probably likely. Unless it was trying to hide—which was even more likely.

But I couldn't just take it out and talk to it—and even if we could have found a private place, I would have been hesitant. For some reason, I didn't even want Mickey to know about this. I trusted me. I trusted Douglas. I even trusted Bobby. No one else. Maybe someday I'd trust Mickey, but I hadn't known him that long, and he was the one who put us in Alexei's hands anyway. So how good was his judgment?

"Maybe . . ." I started to voice a thought.

"What?" said Samm.

"Well, I was just thinking . . . they're looking for four of us. Not three." I looked from one to the other. "What if Janos takes a different train?"

They exchanged a glance. From their expressions, I knew the suggestion was dead before either of them said anything. Janos spoke first. "I don't like that idea. I don't think we should split up." He placed his hand over Samm's for a quick moment.

Samm's eyes were narrowed, his lips were pursed. He was stepping back inside himself and thinking about all of it at once. He saw the logic of what I was saying; but he didn't like it very much either.

Finally, he shook his head. "If they've already identified us, it won't make any difference. And if they haven't, splitting up just gives us new problems. It's an interesting idea; but no, it's too risky. We need to stay together."

I wasn't going to argue it. Not unless I could speak to Samm alone. "Okay, so what train do we take?" I asked. "Are we going north or south? The catapult or Gagarin?"

"Gagarin," said Janos quietly. "I thought we decided that. We stand a better chance of avoiding the marshals if we go invisible."

"And Alexei—?"

Janos let his gaze drop down to the forgotten slice of bread in front of him, and his voice went even lower. *"I might have some . . . resources of my own."*

Samm and I exchanged a glance. We didn't know who to trust anymore. I felt like a mouse staring into a trap. There wasn't any cheese in it. We knew it was a trap. But we didn't have anyplace else to go.

"Look," said Janos. "If we're going, we have to decide quickly. The train to Gagarin leaves in fifteen minutes. Does anyone have a better idea?"

PERFORMANCES

WE DIDN'T SEE **A**LEXEI **ON** the train. We didn't see the blue-haired vulture either. So maybe all that paranoia was for nothing. Maybe she was exactly what she appeared to be. A foolish old lady very far from home.

And what were we? Three just as foolish boys, just as far from home. Four if you counted Mickey.

Except I wasn't so sure how foolish he was. Between Alexei's mysterious disappearances and Janos's dark broodings, I was getting very confused. I wanted us to get away from both of them so we could figure things out for ourselves.

The train dropped away from Wonderland Jumble, heading south and east into the sunlight. There weren't as many passengers on this leg. Only two Loonies we hadn't seen before and us.

I thought about trying to get some more sleep, but I wasn't tired enough. And even though the train was fitted with solar-panel shields that could be rotated and angled to protect it from direct sun, the endless daylight was too unnerving.

I tried watching the news on the video, but it was all depressing. If anyone was talking about the search for us, it wasn't on the news. In the week since we'd left the Line, what was left of the home world was whirling around itself in chaos. Riots. Power outages. Martial law. Interruptions in shipping. Crops rotting in the fields. Food shortages. Outbreaks of violence. Troops called out. And plagues. The plagues had spread south and west through Asia, south and west through Africa, south and west through Latin America. South and west through North America.

Even if we wanted to go home, we couldn't. The house was still there, but it wouldn't be *home* anymore.

At this distance, it didn't seem real anyway. I could look north into the sky and see the fattening Earth riding along the Lunar horizon like a big blue bubble, and it didn't have any relation at all to the words and pictures pouring out of the video. From here, it still looked beautiful.

And very soon, we would be leaving it behind forever. Maybe.

Finally, I levered myself out of my seat, climbed over Samm and Janos, and went to the observation deck at the end of the last car—not because I wanted to look at any more scenery—I'd already seen enough Lunar rocks to last a couple of lifetimes—but because there was no one else back there, and I wanted to be alone again. Maybe I could try to figure things out. Maybe I would just play pattycake with the same old crap one more time, making little mud pies of my thoughts.

After a while, Janos came back and stood silently next to me. He was carrying two mugs of hot tea. He handed one to me and we stared silently out the window at the broken jumble so far below us.

I felt confused. He looked like Janos, but now he felt like Mickey again. One minute I liked him, the next minute I didn't. I couldn't figure out why. And I hated the confusion. Maybe it was because he was a lot like Alexei—telling us where we should go and what we should do. As if he knew more about everything than we did. As if our opinions didn't count. As if he knew better what was good for us. Just like Mom. Or Dad. Or the judge. Or any other grown-up with authority.

And nobody ever bothered to say, "Here's why you should trust me." They just assumed that "trust me" was sufficient. And it never was.

"This is very hard on you, isn't it?" Mickey said.

"What? This?"

"No, everything. Leaving home. Me and Douglas. Leaving your parents. Bouncing across the moon. Everything."

I shook my head. "No. That's the funny thing. I can handle all that. It's the *other* stuff that doesn't make sense."

"What other stuff?"

I held out the front of my dress for a moment. "This."

"The disguise?"

"No. I can even handle that." For a moment, I couldn't find the words. "I mean, all the stuff about men and women and the space in between. That stuff. Does anybody understand it? Do *you*?"

He laughed. "No. And anyone who says they do—well, they're lying." He added, with a grin, "Or they're really arrogant."

"I don't get it," I said. "Why are we divided into males and females?

I mean, I understand the biology of it, but I don't understand *why* it's such a good idea to split a species into two opposite halves, perpetually at war with each other."

"Like your mom and your dad."

"And everybody else too."

"I can see why it looks that way to you."

"But this is the part that's gets confusing. When we're all the same, like me and Douglas and Stinky, we fight all the time. And then Bobby and I put on dresses and we pretend to be girls and all of a sudden, we're all getting along like one big happy family. Boys and girls together. So it doesn't make sense. How come we get along now?"

"Maybe because you're feeling different about each other—and about yourselves." Mickey put his hand on my shoulder. "How do you feel about being a girl?"

I shrugged. "It's okay. I mean, it doesn't bother me as much as I thought it would. It's like being someone else for a while—like thinking a different way. It's kind of like there's a different part of me, the part that would have been me if I had been born a girl. Does that make sense?"

"Yeah, sort of."

"She probably would have been a lot nicer than I am."

"Why do you say that?"

" 'Cause it's true."

"You're selling yourself short, Chigger. You're a lot nicer than you know. And smarter too." He patted my shoulder. "Most people are very nice—when they let go of their fear and anger."

I wanted to believe him, so I did, and maybe it was true. "So why do we have to pretend to be something else just to get along with each other?"

"You want to know what I think?"

"Yeah, I do."

"I think the whole gender thing is an excuse."

"For what?"

"For not being who you really are."

"Huh? You're going to have to explain that to me."

"All right . . ." He took a deep breath. "The way it looks to me, from where *I* stand, is that most folks get locked into some idea of what they think gender is supposed to be about, so they put on gender-performances for each other. They act out who they *think* they have to be. And most of the time, they end up not knowing the difference between the mask they're wearing and who they really are. Charles, a real man doesn't worry what kind of underwear he's wearing, what color it is, or if it there's a little lace on the bottom, because he knows he's not his underwear. It doesn't mean anything.

"What you're finding out is that you are not the mask. Because when you can put on one gender-performance, and then take it off and put on another, and then take that one off too, that's when you start to realize how much of what you think is really you is just a performance. And when you can recognize it as a performance, it loses all of its power. That's when you can see the difference clearly between *role* and *real*—in yourself and everyone else. Does that make sense to you?" he asked.

I nodded, but I was still frowning. "But *you* can see it that way because you've already done it."

"I had to. I didn't have any choice. It's that way for anyone who's different in some way. But if you don't feel different, then you don't *have* to do it, so you don't, and you never learn better about who you are. Do you see that?"

I nodded.

"So, it's your job to find out who you are and let the rest of us know. Because nobody else can tell you. And the only way you can find out is you try on possibilities. Like clothes. And you keep trying on possibilities until you find the ones that fit best. That's how you discover what's really you and what's just noise. And when you find out who you really are, then nobody can take that away from you."

I heard the words, but I didn't know what they meant, because I knew I hadn't experienced what he was talking about.

Mickey saw it in my face. "Charles, you have to get down into your own heart and soul and sort things out for yourself. Piece by piece by piece. Nobody else can do it for you. It's hard work. And most people don't want to do it, or don't know how. Because it's *uncomfortable*. And most people aren't willing to be uncomfortable. So they'll never do the work, and they'll drift along through life, unconscious, never knowing who they really are, because they've never questioned it, never examined it, never taken it out and held it up to the light to look. Do you want to know the dreadful truth about human beings?"

I nodded.

"Remember what I said about belief? You have to believe in your-self first. If you do, then other people will too. Only most people *don't* believe in themselves. They point to their Bible or their flag or their whatnots, but that's not believing in yourself. That's believing in *things*—things *outside* of yourself. Most people don't know who they really are, so they *can't* believe in themselves."

It was a big thought. I turned it over and over in my mind, trying to look at it from his side and my side and my other side as well. Charles and Maura. I almost didn't want to go back to being Chigger. Not because I wanted to be a girl. But because I didn't want to go back to the war zone. I knew I didn't really have a choice, and I was glad about that, because if it was a choice between one or the other, I didn't know which one I'd choose. I liked it when Douglas told that woman to take her hand off me. I liked it when he was kind.

"Can I tell you one more thing?"

I nodded.

"I think you're going to be okay. You're a good kid. You're smart. You're going to sort things out all right, I'm sure of it. It might take a while, but you're not out here alone. You've got Douglas on your side. And me too, if that counts for anything."

I smiled at him. I hadn't smiled in a long time. The expression felt unfamiliar. But nice. And then, not knowing what else to do, I hugged him. I'm not real good at hugging, but he was. He pulled me close and let me lean on his strength. I could see why Douglas cared for him so much.

The train was rising again. We were approaching another pylon. That meant we were finally out of the Jumble. That made me feel a little better. The bad news was that we were rising into the sunlight.

A few moments later, Gabri came through the car and closed all the window shades on the left side, and we went back to join the others.

AT THE MOUNTAINS OF MADNESS

WE NEVER MADE IT TO Gagarin.

We came out of the Jumble and began a long series of descending steps across an uneven sunlit plain. Because the sun was as low on the horizon as it could get without actually setting, everything was etched in stark relief; the shadows were long sideways fingers, and whenever we passed behind an outcrop, the shadows plunged the left side of the train into darkness; when we came out into the sunlight again, the whole car flashed with light. Everything flickered with annoying randomness.

This went on for the better part of an hour. Now I understood some of the remarks I'd overheard on the earlier part of our journey—that the trip to Gagarin was the most unpleasant ride on Luna. It was hellish and maddening. The only thing that ever changed was the direction of the sunlight as the sun crept around the horizon.

Ahead, somewhere over the sharp edge of the world, were the Mountains of Madness, the perpetually shadowed area that Alexei called the moon's rectum. *The place where the sun never shines.* Literally. The place where the ice was found.

There was more ice at the Lunar North Pole than there was at the south, so most of the major installations were on the top of the moon, not the bottom; but LunarCo, Exxon, and BabelCorp, had put down test shafts, dropped in storage tanks and processing plants. They also bought a lot of water from freelancers—including invisibles. According to Mickey, this was one of the major channels for the unseen population to tap into the Lunar economy. Ice-dollars financed much of the phantom community.

Mickey lowered his voice, and added, "Some people think the water companies finance the invisibles to cover up other projects of their own, *secret* ones. There are a lot of secrets on Luna."

We entered shadow then, and Gabri announced that we could raise the window shades again; Samm and Janos both did so. Now the train was circling around the outer ring of the Mountains of Madness. We passed frighteningly close to some of the outcrops.

The train was rising up the cable to a place called Borgo Pass. From there, we'd descend into Gagarin. But as we approached the pass, the train began to slow, and Gabri came back on the intercom. "We're going to make an unscheduled stop here. I apologize for the inconvenience. Please stay in your seats. We won't be long." A few moments later, we stopped, suspended in space. Samm began to laugh.

Janos looked at him. "What?"

Samm pointed out the window. "This is it. This is what it looks like to be caught between a rock and a hard place."

Janos got it and started laughing too. And then I did. And then even Pattycakes, even though I doubted she understood the reference. But the timing of it was perfect. We needed something silly. We sat there and giggled at each other. And every time it seemed the laughter was starting to die down, one or the other of us would get the joke all over again and erupt in a new burst of whoops, and then that would set the others off again. It was kind of like the farting contests we used to have in the front closet, but without the beans.

Still laughing, Janos pointed out the window. The rocks were rising around us. Our laughter died away abruptly. The train was lowering to the ground below. We were meeting someone.

"Uh-oh . . ." I said.

"Yep," agreed Janos. "I sort of expected something like this." Samm started to rise to his feet, but Janos pulled him back down. "Just wait," he said. "Let's see how this plays out."

There were some *clanks* and *thumps* from below—I recognized them as the sound of a pressure tube extending and connecting. A moment later, Gabri came back through the passenger compartment. She came directly to us, and said, "Come with me. Quickly. Bring your things."

We grabbed what little luggage we had and followed her down the ladder to the lower level of the train, where Alexei had just popped open the hatch to whatever waited below. "Hurry now. Gabri has a schedule. We mustn't take advantage of her good nature. That is my job." He turned to her, and they exchanged another more-than-friendly kiss. "I am lucky man to be so engaged," he said to her. "We will have happy Luna home, very soon, I promise."

Abruptly, he turned his attention back to us. "Hurry now!" he commanded in a very different tone of voice. I followed Douglas down the ladder, hand over hand. Mickey came down behind us. Alexei handed down the BRENGLE-TUCKER crates he'd relabeled at Prospector's Station—there were six of them—then he dropped lightly down to join us. The hatch above slammed shut with annoying finality. A few predictable *clanks* and *bumps*, and the train was gone.

It was dark down here. And cold. Cold enough to make our breath visible. This place had been sitting uninhabited for a while. We were inside another of the ubiquitous cargo pods. Like most of the other pods we'd seen on Luna, it had been converted into living spaces; it was a horizontal tube divided into upper and lower levels. But this one wasn't a stationary installation. It was a single pod, laid onto a six-wheeled chassis to form a grand two-story vehicle. A rolling house. We could see the tops of the wheels just outside the windows.

"Welcome to the Beagle, my portable Luna home!" said Alexei, spreading his arms grandly. Samm and Janos exchanged a glance. Alexei switched on some lights, not a lot—just enough to see by. "Well, one of my homes anyway. This is not where I normally park Mr. Beagle, but I phone ahead and it comes to meet us at train. You like, *da*? I call it Beagle, because it is faithful like a puppy dog."

"This is Mr. Beagle?" Douglas asked incredulously.

"*Da!* We were never in danger. Not really. Oh, you thought Mr. Beagle was person, didn't you?" While he talked, he was securing crates. "Excuse me if I do not turn on too much lights. We do not want to give ourselves away to Mister-Nosy-Eye-In-The-Sky." He pointed to somewhere beyond the ceiling, where unseen satellites watched the comings and goings of every uncamouflaged heat source on Luna.

"Make yourself homely, we still have long way to go. Mickey, Douglas, no more Samm and Janos evening. Charles you can be boy again if you wish. You too, Bobby. Here are toilet and bath bags. Time for a nice wash, everyone. Before we all turn stinky. No offense, Bobby. I mean stinky for real. There are sodas in fridge, flash-meals too. Help yourselves. I have much work to do before I can be host. Please excuse."

For a moment, we all just stood there and looked at each other, embarrassed. Had we really imagined that Alexei wanted to kill us—?

Alexei busied himself with housekeeping tasks—turning up the heat, checking the oxygen and humidity levels, testing hull integrity and air pressure, making sure the air circulators were functioning, monitoring the water supply, double-checking the batteries and fuel cells, and other chores of that nature. "Hokay, all boards are green. Vehicle phoned to tell me same, before we arrive here, but I check twice anyway."

Satisfied that his porta-home wouldn't accidentally kill us, he settled himself into the driver's seat, where he brooded over his display map for a while. I peeked over his shoulder, but it didn't make any sense to me. It was overlaid with lines and shadows, and everything was labeled in Russian.

At last, Alexei pulled on a headset and began chattering instructions at the vehicle's intelligence engine. Compared to the one hanging around my belly, it was a very primitive device—but it was smart enough to find its way across the Lunar surface.

That reminded me—"Is that it? Are we safe now?"

"If you mean, are we private again? *Da*, we are."

"Thank Ghu!" I hiked up my dress and slip and peeled the monkey off my waist. "Go play with Bobby," I told it, pushing it into his lap. Bobby was delighted. The monkey was really his toy, and he hadn't had much chance to play with it since before bounce-down. He pulled it close and hugged it like a long-lost brother; the monkey wrapped itself around Bobby just as eagerly, and the two of them made purring and snuggling noises at each other. He was still wearing his dress and wig, still as cute as Pattycakes, and with the monkey cuddled in his lap he looked happier than I could ever remember seeing him in my life.

I reached up to pull my wig off, then stopped—it was cold in here. The wig was keeping my head warm. We'd shaved ourselves bald on the Line, and I still hadn't gotten used to the cold feeling. The soft lining of the wig was comfortable and warm like a favorite flannel hat on a cold morning. But that wasn't the only reason I hesitated—I had this weird thought that when I finally did take off the wig, I'd be killing Maura forever.

I pulled off my earrings thoughtfully. They jangled and they were cold. I liked Maura. I liked her family. They seemed like nice people. I was sorry we were leaving them behind—I wished we could take them with us.

I sat with that thought for a while. I'd had a vacation from myself. I didn't want to go back to being me. Not the me I was before—selfish and self-centered and nasty. That wasn't a lot of fun. But I couldn't stay Maura either. That wasn't who I really was. That conversation with Mickey had been as confusing as it was useful.

If I took off the wig and the dress, would I be spiteful Chigger again? Would Douglas and Bobby turn back into Weird and Stinky? In a week, would things be back to what passed for normal in the dingaling family? If so, then why had we bothered? It didn't matter how far away we went—we'd still be *us*.

Alexei finished what he was doing. He clapped his hands in satisfaction, and shouted, "Watch out, Luna! Here come the Beagle Boys!" The truck began rolling slowly forward. The readout on his main display climbed to thirty klicks.

"We are almost there," Alexei said, swiveling around in his chair to face the rest of us. "Just a few more hours. Fortunately, we have a road, almost direct. The autopilot can drive. Everyone can sleep. Even me."

I pushed forward to look. Alexei rapped the front window with his bare knuckles. "Please to notice, this is *not* a windshield—because there is no wind to shield against. Even better, we do not get bug spots on Luna. So there is no need for windshield wipers. Save very much money, makes whole thing cost-effective. Is much good, *da?*"

Outside the window we saw only shadowlands. Alexei wasn't going to turn his headlights on unless he absolutely had to, but there was more than enough light bouncing off the rocks above to reveal the ghostly landscape around us.

"Where's the road?" I asked.

"Right in front of you," he said, pointing. "Open your eyes and look."

I was looking for an Earth-like highway. But this road wasn't paved at all. On Luna, paving is unnecessary. This was a wide bulldozed path that found its way between steep rumpled hills. It curled off into the distance, sometimes slicing into the side of a slope, but more often winding around. Orange ribbons marked the edges of the road, and periodically, there were bright-colored signal flags on tall poles.

"Welcome to Route 66," said Alexei. "From Borgo Pass, we take great circle route eastward. Is also called Beltway. Gagarin is inside Beltway, but we are going outside. Not to worry, we will be on official road for two hours. The autopilot will stay inside the lines. When we get to turnoff, I will drive myself."

There were comfortable chairs installed behind the pilot's seat; none of them matched. Indeed, the whole interior was a hodgepodge of techno-gingerbread scrounged from a thousand unidentifiable sources. Mickey and Douglas sat down closest to Alexei, Bobby and I took the couch along the opposite bulkhead. Alexei opened a floor panel and retrieved a plastic can of beer. "Anyone else?" he asked. Douglas and Mickey shook their heads; he passed out soft drinks instead.

"All right, Alexei," said Mickey, opening his drink. "What's the plan? What are we doing?"

"Is no plan. I take you to safety, like I promise. No one find you at Fortress of Solitude. From there, you can make all the phone calls you want. Everything traces only as far as Wonderland Jumble or Gagarin. No closer. So you can pick up e-mail, call home, do everything but order pizza. No problem, I bake pizza myself if you really want. You arrange contract for colony, whatever. Then we get you to catapult."

Mickey and Douglas exchanged a glance. Douglas looked to me as well. Could we really trust him?

Did we have a choice?

THE LONG AND WINDING ROAD

THE HOUSE-TRUCK—IT WAS hard to know what else to call it—trundled over the Lunar surface like a giant dung beetle, never going slower than ten klicks, never going faster than forty. When I asked why we couldn't go faster, Alexei laughed and replied, "The laws of physics. We do not weigh a ton, but we still have a ton of *mass*. I do not want to argue with either inertia or momentum. Especially not when momentum is coming from other direction." He pointed ahead.

Another vehicle was silently rolling toward us. "An eighteen-wheeler," said Alexei. It was three truck-pods just like the Beagle, only linked together like a train. They rode heavily, Alexei said they were filled with water. The Beagle slowed automatically, to let it pass.

"This road has many cargo-trains," said Alexei. "They collect from the freelance mines and deliver to Gagarin. The invisibles sell to the freelancers, and that's how they stay out of the net. Gargarin knows it and doesn't care. The market for fresh water on Luna is second only to the market for fresh air. And remember, water can be turned into air. Oxygen and hydrogen. Very useful. And we can mine water on Luna much easier than we can mine air—although I have heard of a crazy loonie who thinks he can extract oxygen from rock. All he needs is lots of rock and sunlight. Who knows? Maybe he will find that somewhere here?"

A thought occurred to me. "Won't the driver of that truck identify us?"

"He already has," said Alexei. "Look over there. There is HoboCo. Miller-Gibson ice-mine. Freelance station. They buy from invisibles. Is profitable sideline, for everybody. So why should they report anything? They would put themselves out of business. HoboCo is where big eighteen-wheeler comes from. Miller and Gibson are very successful. They have found layer of ice not cost-effective for Exxon or BabelCorp, but very profitable for freelance miners. Make their own water, air, grow their own crops. Very good people. They have very nice microbrewery." He waved his beer at us to illustrate. "But it's just a sideline. Mostly they grow cactuses—astringent bases for medicine. But also very nice for tequila too. Tequila has important medicinal uses. Good for drowning worms, one per bottle. Also good on barbecue chicken. But first you have to catch chicken. Are you good with chicken net?"

To my puzzled look, he said, "You have never had to catch flying chicken, have you? Ha!—you didn't know chickens could fly? On Luna, they do. Not very well, but well enough. Very funny to see look of surprise on chicken's face. Have you ever seen wings and breasts with dark meat or drumsticks with white? If you do, that is Lunar chicken. Is exercise of muscles that turns meat dark; chickens fly, wings get dark, legs don't carry as much weight as on Earth, drumsticks stay white. Very strange to see, but delicious, just the same. Oh, they also raise rabbits at HoboCo. They don't fly at all. But they are just as tasty."

HoboCo didn't look like much from the road, just a distant clump of pods and domes, with a few scattered lights here and there. The whole thing was in shadow, of course. This was the place where the sun *never* shines—and they meant it. There were solar panels on the nearby ridges.

While we watched, the two largest domes began to glow. Alexei explained that most farm domes were on an accelerated day-night schedule. Two hours of light, thirty minutes of darkness; this made everything grow faster. There was a lot to learn about Lunar farming.

We rolled on for a while, we passed two other mines, and then the road got rougher, winding its way up the side of a steep crater wall. It was kind of like the access roads carved into the hills north of El Paso—only steeper. The one-sixth gee of Luna made it possible for the truck to roll up hills that no Earth vehicle could have attempted. Coming down the other side was even more terrifying. The living pod of the Beagle was mounted on a leveling platform, so whenever the wheeled chassis started to angle too steeply, the platform tilted up at the lower end to keep us level inside. For some reason, that only made the ride scarier.

From the heights, especially when we crested a hill, we could see the scattered lights of individual settlements or monitor stations. It reminded me of the time when I was Stinky's age, the first time Dad took us on vacation, and we drove through the Southwest. There were places in New Mexico and Arizona, where there was nothing to see. And at night, when the faraway mountains loomed like walls around the edge of the world, there were distant lights huddled lonely under the vast starlit sky.

It was like that here. Only the stars were harder. They were bright and cold and merciless. And somehow that made them even more distant. The occasional clustered lights of humanity were desperate and desolate. No wind. No air. Back on Earth, the lights had felt like little havens against the night. I'd wanted to knock on the doors and rush into the warmth and hug the people, thank them for being alive. Here, the lights all seemed like signposts for claustrophobic little prisons. All shouting for attention. Here, I am. No, me. Over here. Me. Come see me. *But why?* Each one was like every other one. A couple of cargo pods and a cluster of inflatables, hiding in perpetual shadow.

There was no romance here. No glamour. Only endless gloom and imported despair, flavored with the perpetual hint of sunlight lurking everywhere. A blazing furnace circled like a hungry demon around and around the shadowed valleys. As the moon turned slowly on its axis, the hills were outlined with neon fire.

The house-truck reached the crest of the ridge, and it was like coming up out of a deep black sea. Suddenly, the world was blasted by a dazzling sideways glare. Instinctively, I turned my back to the light—I looked out the wide windows to the west. A layer of shadow fell across the bottom half of the landscape, cloaking everything in inky darkness. Down *there* was the ice. Up *here* was the fire. There was no in-between.

And then the truck rolled over the crest and dipped back down into shadow again. The roaring sun disappeared behind the rocky horizon, and we were safe in darkness again. "Is great view, *da?*" asked Alexei. "You will not have trip like this from travel agent. I show you sights no tourist ever sees from the safety of a tourist-mobile. I give you trip of a lifetime, *da?*"

I thought about how far we'd come in less than twenty-four hours. We'd crashed into the moon, bounced across the Lunar plain, climbed a crater wall, nearly baked to death in the endless sunlight. . . . "The only thing we haven't done yet," I said, "is freeze to death."

"I am arranging that now," said Alexei, absolutely deadpan. "We go to my house carved in ice. My own private ice mine. You can freeze to death all you want. No problem."

The road etched its way down the steep side of a hill. I couldn't imagine how a construction crew had bulldozed it into place. Here, the road wasn't much more than a cut across an avalanche-shaped tumble of rock and rubble. The steep slope to the left loomed *above* us; it scared me almost as much as the dropaway cliff *below* us to the right. We were creeping along a narrow shelf of rock so light and powdery, we could feel it shifting skittishly beneath the wheels of the truck.

"Is not to worry," said Alexei. I really did want to hit him then, as hard as I could. "Remember angle of repose is steeper on Luna. We are perfectly safe. Besides, road and slope have both been sprayed with construction foam to hold everything in place. This road carries much traffic, it is still here, eh?"

"Um, Alexei . . . ?" That was Douglas. "The more traffic on a road, the heavier the load it carries, the sooner it wears out. You should see the pavement in front of the Babylon Hotel in Las Vegas. It's buckled so badly it has ruts. If this road gets as much traffic as you say—"

Alexei cut him off with a hand wave. "Is not to worry, I said. Remember, we are on Luna. If we build to one-half of Earth standards, we are still three times stronger than we need to be." I would have felt a lot more reassured by his words if the Beagle hadn't chosen that moment to slip uneasily across a patch of loose gravel. Almost like we were skidding on ice.

"Rocks here are sometimes greasy," Alexei explained. "Ice—not like you know it, but black ice in rocks. Makes them clammy and changes friction quotient." Alexei helped himself to another beer, waving it aloft. "I have earned this today. I have always wondered if escape plan would work. Now I know how well I plan. Only now I have to make up new plan. Except I do not think I will ever go back to Line. So maybe I will not need one after all. I do not think I will be much welcome there for a long time, will I, *Mikhail?*"

Mickey ignored the question. "Alexei, how come we weren't apprehended at Wonderland Jumble? Surely they must have been watching for us. And our disguises weren't that good. The old lady spotted us."

Alexei snorted. "The old lady works for me. She is invisible. I put her on train to watch you. She did lousy job of being invisible, didn't she? She watch you too hard. I am sorry if she unnerved you. She only wanted to protect. But people who should have spotted you weren't looking at all. I cannot understand why. Perhaps it has something to do with the fact that all of you were apprehended at Clavius a couple of hours ago."

"Huh?"

"Oh, don't worry. The report will probably turn out to be false, I'm sure. But you will laugh very much anyway. Especially you, Charles. The little boy they thought was you turned out to be little girl named J'mee. I wonder how that happen, eh?" He waggled his eyebrows meaningfully. "Is very funny, *da?* Is family that Dingillians were supposed to decoy for on Line. You did not know that, did you? Now they decoy for you on Luna. Is only fair. Sauce for goose too."

No, we hadn't known who or what we were decoying for—and in all the rush and confusion up the Line and again at Geostationary, I hadn't given it much thought—but what Alexei said made sense. J'mee and her family were very rich. She had an implant and she was always online, peeking into other people's personal histories, even stuff there wasn't supposed to be any public access to. She knew who we were and when she got mad at me for finding out she wasn't really a boy, she turned us in to the marshals at Geostationary. They might have planned to do that anyway, so they could pass through customs unnoticed while we were the center of so much attention.

That J'mee and her family were now caught in the same kind of trap themselves was delicious irony. In fact, it would have been delicious *revenge* if we had done it ourselves, but we hadn't. Alexei had. Or someone he knew.

And of course . . . if he could do it to someone else, he could just as easily do it to us. If he wanted to.

The Beagle finally reached the bottom of Avalanche Hill—Alexei didn't tell us the name of it until we were safely off of it. Now the truck began winding its way through a very uneven rubble field; it looked like very soon, the road would give out completely.

Instead, we began seeing short bridges of industrial foam, paving the occasional gap in the way. Soon, the bulldozed course gave way entirely to a layer of foam. It sat on top of the jumbled rocks and rubble like a ribbon of fluffy icing. It wound around the larger outcrops like the scenic course in a Disneyland ride. Except here, there weren't any pirates or bears or ghosts to jump out at you.

The drive was a little smoother on the foam. From up on top of it, we looked like we were rolling on a road of whipped cream. Alexei explained how it had been poured and leveled and hardened. It wasn't all foam; there were bits of gravel and crushed rock throughout, so that over the years as the weight of the trucks compressed the foam, they'd make it even harder.

"Foam was greatest invention of twentieth century," Alexei said, launching into another of his interminable peripatetic monologues. "Very silly people. They think foam is weak. They use it for stuffing and toys. With a little bit of seasoning, foam makes houses, roads, domes, spaceships, anything you want. Pour it in molds or build it up in layers. If not for foam, we could not colonize Luna. Certainly not as fast." He pounded the bulkhead. "All these are foam. We order as much cargo as Line can deliver. Yes, we want cargo, but we want pods that cargo arrives in even more. Every pod is a house. We have built whole cities out of these pods—and everything else too. We do it in less than forty years. We have as much living space on Luna now as in all of Moscow—only winters are nicer on Luna. Not as much snow. Not a problem anyway, if we had as much snow on Luna as they do in Moscow, we would all be rich. We would sell it to each other and make water everywhere. We would fill great domes with water and air and everything else. We would have wheat fields to rival the grand steppes of Asia. Someday we will anyway, even without the snow. We will capture comets if we have to. And we will do it with foam. We will match orbit with comet, catch it in a net of foam, harden it into a solid ball, and bring it back to Luna. Or maybe we will build a Lunar beanstalk on far side of moon and just pipe the water down to great Lunar pipeline system. Or we will attach Palmer tubes all over and land it in Pogue Crater and create new Lunar city around it. Put a dome above it. A great adventure. You would be proud to be a part of it. We will build our own great outdoors on Luna. We will have trees as tall as mountains, flowers as big as your head, grass so high you can hide elephants in it. We will have bouncing hippos and leaping bears. We will have monstrous giant fish and butterflies the size of eagles. We will build best outdoors ever, better even than Earth."

"What a grand scheme," Douglas said, with almost no enthusiasm. It was the same voice he used when he was humoring Mom or Dad.

Alexei didn't notice. "I show you plans. We have crater, we have blueprints, we have much financing, we have eager community of people—even many invisibles. We will build Free Luna."

"It sounds like a very expensive Luna," Mickey said dryly.

Alexei ignored the jibe. "For you, *Mikhail*, we will give big family discount. All you need to do is bring big family." He finished his beer and pushed the empty plastic can into the litter bag. He started to reach for a third, then stopped himself. "No," he said. "I have had enough for now. I am driving soon." He pointed ahead. "Here comes turnoff."

We rolled onto a wide bare dome of rock that pushed its way up through the foam pavement like a breaching whale. The Beagle stopped at the top. On the other side, the road split off in two directions, one curling off toward the light, the other winding back down into blackness—in some places it was visible only by its orange-outlined edges and infrequent illuminated flags.

Alexei swiveled forward and busied himself with his controls, snapping switches, studying screens, flipping up plastic switch covers, unlocking and arming unknown controls. He reached overhead and snap-snap-snapped a row of switches. It was a very techno performance.

The truck settled itself and made various switching and gurgling noises. Things *clanked* underneath as they locked themselves into position. Was Alexei actually planning to *drive* across this jumble?

"Hokay," he said finally. "Everybody please fasten safety harness. Is not to worry. Is not too bumpy, and is very short ride." He waited until we'd all buckled ourselves in, then punched the red button in front of him.

The truck shuddered—I recognized the feeling—*Palmer tubes!* We were boosting! Shaking like an earthquake, we shot up off the Lunar surface, into painful sunlight. Beyond the windows, the dark ground fell away alarmingly fast. It was a sea of shadow. Occasional islands of bright rocks thrust up out of the gloom.

We tilted slightly forward and began to move. The Beagle throbbed and shook across the Lunar night. I swiveled around and watched as the glimmering thread of the road disappeared behind us. If the booster tubes failed now—we'd never be found.

I swiveled back around. Alexei was watching his screens like money was pouring out of them. I noticed Mickey was watching our course too. A bright green line traced its way across an unreadable map. It zigzagged from one landmark to the next. A yellow dot crept along the line. We were halfway along, but I couldn't see any correlation between the display on the screen and the terrain outside. The glare of the sun was directly ahead and everything was either dazzled out of existence or lost in shadow.

Finally, we hooked around to put the sun behind us and started a steep descent into a broken arroyo. Coming in from the east, we saw a scattering of pods, as if discarded by a thoughtless tourist. They were connected by pipes and wires and lazy tubes that curled around the landscape in courses of convenience. We shuddered down toward a square of four bright orange lights. Here and there, I saw scattered towers with arrays of solar panels at the top. Most of them also had glimmering cables climbing up to huge lens arrays at the top—I recognized them as light-pipes; the lens arrays were called collimation engines.

We sank down into shadow—the glare behind us switched off as suddenly as a power failure. Flurries of dust rose up around us like history. A moment later, we bumped softly down onto the Lunar surface. The vehicle stopped shaking and we were down. The Beagle had landed.

THE FORTRESS OF SOLITUDE

WELCOME TO INVISIBLE LUNA," ALEXEI SAID. He began shutting down the flight controls, switching off all the things he'd switched on before, switching on all the things he'd switched off. "We are now off the map."

He waved at the junk and detritus beyond the window. "This is abandoned test site Brickner 43-AX92. Not cost-effective for industrial production. Shut down seven years ago. Leased to Lunar Homestead Sites for one dollar a year, paid up one hundred years in advance, with option to purchase. All ice mined from this site must be sold to leasing company. Part of proceeds goes to company store for credit for supplies, part goes toward purchase price, last part you get to keep—only no place to spend it, nothing to do but melt more ice. Is no big deal. The more you melt, faster you earn out, sooner you work for yourself, sooner you make profit. Lunar sharecropping, *da?* Does that not sound like good deal? It is if you are lunatic. Even better, water prices stay high."

He peered forward through the window, squinting against the gloom, then began easing the Beagle gently forward. He didn't stop talking for a moment. "More people come to moon every day. All of them need water. Two liters a day for drinking, depending how active person is. Another twelve for washing and flushing. Another fifty liters for breathing, or more for watering plants so they can make oxygen for you to breathe—plus humidity, that uses water too. Another thirty liters for crops to eat. And more if you want to eat meat, because meat has to eat and drink and breathe too before it is meat. Lunar Authority mandates at least one hundred liters of clean water per day per person. That's hard water use, of course. Not soft. Soft includes safety margin, hard doesn't."

"Huh?" That was me. "Soft water?"

"Not like on Earth. Soft water means different on moon. I explain. Everything on Luna is measured in water. We have water-based economy. We buy and sell with water-dollars—or ice-dollars, which are not worth as much because you have to dig them out of ground first. After you dig them up, they become water-dollars, worth more. Is our own value-added tax, ha ha."

Alexei kept talking as he drove. The ground was rougher off the landing pad, but not so rough that the truck couldn't negotiate it. The wheels were three meters in diameter, as tall as a full-grown Loonie, so they just rolled over all but the largest obstacles. They were treaded for off-road use, which was kind of a joke when you thought about it. Everything on Luna was off-road. Alexei steered us toward a cluster of three pods, lying side by side. That didn't look so bad, until he explained they weren't our destination. They were for water-processing.

"There is soft-water use and hard-water use," Alexei returned to his lecture. "Hard-water use is determined by laws of physics. No room to negotiate. What you get is what you see. You need twenty-four hours of air to breathe, every day. You cannot get by on twenty-three hours, can you? You cannot get by on twenty-three hours and forty-five minutes, can you? No, you need your full twenty-four hours of air. That requires however many liters it takes to water plants that produce oxygen. Or however many liters you electrolyze. That is hard-water use.

"Soft water use is negotiable. You can use some water more than once. You can wash yourself in water, then use it again to flush toilet, then use it a third time to water plants. One liter gets used three different ways. Is like getting three liters for one. You do not need fresh water for everything, soft water lets you make water work overtime. But even when water works super golden hours, there is a limit to how hard it can work. You cannot recycle what isn't there—and even softest water turns hard after a while.

"We have more than three million Lunatics on this globe. That means we need at least three hundred million liters of liquid water to sustain life. If there is not enough water for everyone, demand goes up and prices rise. We have to use more and more soft water, until we reach hard-water limit. That is good day for ice miners, because that is day we all make lots of money—if we can get our water to market. Price of hard water is floor of Lunar economy. Price of soft water is ceiling. Understand, *da?* Or is it the other way around? Never mind. Is big room to make lots of money. As long as sun shines, is raining soup. Grab a spoon and a bowl. Don't stand there holding fork and wondering why you are hungry. This is why Lunar sharecroppers sometimes sell extra water to invisible economy. Not to leaseholder. But leaseholders have to buy at fair market price, so if sharecropper is in it only for money, is wise to be legal. But I am not in it *only* for money."

He guided the Beagle into a docking bay and brought it to a careful halt. The front wheels bumped firmly against a bar of foam, set across the end of the bay as a shock absorber. Alexei locked the engines down, then began punching a column of buttons to his left, watching as the light next to each one flashed green. From behind and below us came the familiar clattering sounds of an automatic hatch connection. Somebody must have gotten very rich from that patent.

The docking bay was a deep trench carved into the Lunar surface. Beside it was a flattish dome with a spindly power-tower rising above it like an old-fashioned oil derrick. Multiple light-pipes fed down from the lens arrays at the top and into channels all around the edges of the dome, so the dome glowed from underneath.

Alexei finished locking the vehicle down and put it in standby mode. He stopped to frown at one display. "I will have to take this machine in for service, very soon. We have put on too many miles, too many hours. Never mind. Let's get you safely put away."

He unfastened his safety harness and bounced aftward. He pulled open a floor panel, revealing a hatch set into the very bottom of the cabin. The panel next to it flashed green with confirmations. He punched the unlock, armed the connecting circuits, lowered the pressure tube, connected it, checked the connections, pressurized it, checked the pressure, confirmed it, unlocked the hatch, and popped it. He unzipped the three openings to the pressure tube.

There was a flat cabinet mounted on the ceiling; Alexei stood up, opened it, and dropped the end of a retractable plastic ladder down the hatch. Every door on Luna was a locked hatch. There hadn't been a death caused by accidental decompression in thirty years. And that one, according to Alexei, had been so horrible that every hatch on Luna was replaced in the next five; though some places off the map might still have some of those old hatches installed—probably with extra warning stickers on them.

Alexei climbed down the ladder. Even though the distance from the floor of the Beagle to the hatch on the ground was low enough to jump, he still climbed down the ladder. Both Mickey and Alexei had cautioned us—*more than once*—that more bones had been broken by Terran overconfidence than any other particular brand of stupidity. It was what Alexei called "the Superman mistake." Just because you can jump that high doesn't mean you can land safely.

The pressure tube was like every other one we'd seen, an extendable plastic column. The ladder went down the center of it. At the bottom was the outer hatch of whatever airlock we were dropping down into. We pulled up the plastic ladder so Alexei could rezip the three zippers at the top of the pressure tube; then he unzipped the three zippers at the bottom. He worked the controls on the lower pressure hatch, popped it, stuck his head in, and took a deep breath. He flashed us a thumbs-up signal and we unzipped the top three zippers and lowered the ladder again, so we could climb down through the pressure tube. A week ago, I would have asked, is all this checking necessary? Now I knew enough not to bother asking.

As I climbed down, I noticed that the pressure tube was made of the same stuff as the inflatable, maybe a little thicker; it unnerved me. I preferred solid walls between me and vacuum. Bobby climbed down after me, the monkey riding on his back.

Alexei helped each of us down through the next set of hatches. "Ladder is strong, but it might be slippery from condensation. Please use feet here," he said. We lowered ourselves down into Krislov's Fortress of Solitude—into a surprisingly warm and humid atmosphere. Once out of the inner airlock, we were on a room-sized shelf, overlooking a wider, deeper space. The walls were rock, but the floor was the inevitable polycarbonate mesh decking.

I peered over the railing, down into a rocky shaft. It looked about ten meters across and thirty meters deep. The walls were sparkly gray and very shiny; light pipes snaked down them and plugged into the rock in haphazard fashion. Catwalks and ladders wound up and down everywhere. Platforms hung from the walls at odd intervals all the way down. Everything was suffused with indistinct illumination, the seepage from the light-pipes.

The air had a wet smell, like a shower room just after all the showers have been turned off. And it sounded wet, as if things were dripping all over. And some of the light pipes looked wet with condensation.

Alexei followed us down after securing the top hatch. "You are first people I have ever brought here," he said. "This is my very private space. Is ice mine and water factory. You will see how it works very quickly. I give you whole tour. But be careful, is slippery sometimes." He pointed us down a set of permanent ladders; most of these were anchored in the rock walls; they led all the way to the bottom of the shaft—with occasional detours across various plastic-mesh decks, shelves, and catwalks. He was right, some of the ladders were dripping with condensation, some of the platforms were damp.

"Comets hit Luna everywhere," Alexei explained. "Millions of years. Make lots of craters. Man in the moon has bad case of pizza-face acne or maybe even smallpox—except smallpox is extinct, except maybe for small vials here and there that nobody is supposed to know about. Never mind. Comets are made of ice, *da*? Sun shines on most of Luna. Ice sublimes, turns to vapor, and is gone. Everywhere but place where sun never shines. So ice is still here. North and south poles, the light comes in very low and sideways, can't get over steep crater walls to look down into shadow-valleys. So ice doesn't melt. Dig down into crust, what do you find? Crunched comet. Lots of it. Shine light on it, what do you get? Nice hot ice. Make tea, *da*?"

He stopped us on a mesh shelf halfway down and pointed around at tangling bright tubes. "Light-pipes bring hot sun down into shaft. We drill horizontal tubes, angling slightly up. I pump light in, ice melts, water drips out. I have free electricity, free light, sun does all the work. All I need to do is collect water and sell it. But here is big joke. Ha-ha. I cannot sell my water. Is not cost-effective." He shrugged and waved us on down to the next level.

"You see storage tanks upside? If I had a pipeline, I could sell every drop. If ground could hold pylons, I could send water out by train. But we are too far away, too far for pipes, too hard to build train. Lots of water, but not enough to justify expense. So I am sitting on a million water-dollars that I cannot afford to sell. I have so much water here, I could start farm like Miller-Gibson. More than I could use in a lifetime, it feels sometimes. This place was very good bad investment, *da*?"

We reached the bottom of the shaft—well, not the bottom, but as far down as we could go. We were on a wide mesh deck above an open-topped tank. "Loose water drips everywhere," Alexei said. "Easier to let it just drip. Water beneath must be recycled anyway. Is not unsafe, but is filled with minerals. Earth-style hard water." He pried up a floor panel, so we could see below. The bottom of the shaft had been lined with plastic. Over a period of time it had filled with water, turning it into a huge indoor pool.

"*Da*, you can go swimming if you want," Alexei said. "Water is warm enough. Water is good for storing heat. Keeps shaft warm, helps more water melt. Everything stays warm and toasty. Heat from sun is cumulative." He pointed to the side of the pool. "There is ladder to get out. And diving shelf too. But be very careful diving. You can go very deep in water and not notice how deep because you will not feel same water pressure until you go six times as deep. You can go too far down and not have enough air to get back up. Here is question for you to ponder. Will it be harder or easier to swim in Lunar gee? Will it be harder or easier to float on top of water?"

I frowned in thought. Before I could answer, Douglas said, "It shouldn't make any difference, should it? The relative densities are the same."

"Very good," said Alexei. "You might survive. Some terries make Superman mistake in water too. Come with me, I show you sleeping quarters. Are you tired? No? Do you want a real bath? We have hot showers too, even a steam room. Is no shortage of water here, hot or cold." He grinned at us. "You feel this is wasteful, *da*? All this water, and it cannot be used by anyone else? I admit it, I am water hoarder. Not as bad as some though. Some folks have enough water to run fishery. Trout, catfish, shrimp, lobsters, all very big, very tasty. But I am not water hoarder by choice. The problem is always cost of shipping to market. I make more than enough to live, but not enough to sell profitably. This house will never pay for self."

Alexei led us over to one wall where a cluster of partitions had been set up to define specific areas. A plastic canopy hung over everything to keep water from dripping down into the living spaces. "Here is room for Charles and Bobby. Here is place for Mickey and Douglas. Is clean clothes for everyone, as soon as we unpack Beagle. Over here is shower. Take as long as you want. Is only luxury we have. And over here is table for eating and kitchen for cooking. I have small farm here too. You will find fresh vegetables for salad. LunaFarm meals in fridge. You will be very comfortable. Mickey, here is library, many books, and untraceable link to network. You can make phone calls, send e-mail, buy videos, whatever. You will be very comfortable."

"It sounds like you're leaving us here," said Mickey. He glanced sideways to Douglas. Alexei didn't notice it.

"Da," he said. "I must run errands. You will be safe here. I will not be gone too long. Only two or three days. I have to fill Beagle with water, I will take him off to invisible farm where they will service him in exchange for water. Everything from new food in fridge to new Palmer tubes on chassis. And in return, I will pump fresh water into invisible economy. Every little drip drip drip counterbalances Lunar Authority."

Douglas had a thoughtful frown on his face. "You're a subversive, aren't you?"

"Da!" said Alexei excitedly. "You have figured it out. Good for you, Douglas Dingillian. I am Free Luna Libertarian. The rights of the free market are the only rights. Everybody benefits from free market. Where the market isn't free, is the job of subversives to make it free for all."

Mickey looked amused, as if he already knew this. Douglas had a sour expression; he didn't want to get into this argument. Unfortunately, he'd already pushed the on button, and Alexei didn't have an off button.

"Do you know there are no taxes on Luna? Sounds good, eh? But instead of taxes, we have user fees on currency. You put dollar in bank, Lunar Authority takes half penny. You are paying guarantee for security of legal tender. You take dollar out of bank, Lunar Authority takes another half-penny. Most of time, you don't notice. But every transaction of dollars, you pay a little slice to government.

"No law requires you to use Luna Dollars, but Luna Dollars are primary medium of exchange, each one supposedly backed by one liter of clean water—but Luna Reserve adjusts money supply up or down to thwart free market. Is really just price control so Lunar Authority can provide guarantee of stable currency. I say it is chicken and egg argument. They adjust currency to justify charging fee. Then they charge fee so they can justify manipulating currency. This makes it harder for freelancers to make profit, except by going invisible and selling in the wet market.

"Is very complex to explain, is very simple in practice. Sometimes users have lots and lots of dollars to transfer, and do not want to pay fee, or they do not want the transaction logged—then what? Then they put money in invisible bank, move money through invisible economy. How? Pump it as water. Money arrives where it needs to be without losing anything to friction. Lunar Authority does not get to sand extra zeroes off end. We guarantee our own value. Is very hard to inflate water. In fact, it used to be that water was the only barter system in invisible economy—at least, until we figure out how to transfer dollars without government fingers helping to count."

"How'd you do that?" Mickey asked, and I had a feeling it wasn't just casual curiosity.

"Is all done with intelligence engines," Alexei said, as if that were explanation enough. If you have one, you can be a bank or any other kind of corporation. Or even a government. *Mikhail*, pay attention here—it doesn't matter how many stupid processors you put into render farm; you still need intelligence core. That needs quantum chips. If you have that, you can make money jump out of here and into there, without passing through intervening space. At least, that is how it is explained to me."

"A shower sure sounds good," I suggested, hoping to derail this particular conversation.

Mickey looked annoyed; I guess he wanted to hear the rest. But Alexei's hyperactive mind had already leapt on to the next thought. He was already pulling back a plastic divider. "Is good question, Charles.

Over here is drying area, when you get out of shower. Is heat pump, like sauna. And you can stand under sunlight here. But do not stand too long. You will get badly sunburned." He pointed at my borrowed hair. "Be careful with wig, please. In case you might need it again. Or maybe you will want to wear it again just because it makes you look so pretty. Don't look to me like that, the nights are two weeks long here. Some Loonies like to play dress up, phone friends, play games. Now we must hurry and unload Mr. Beagle so I can take care of errands."

HIT THE SHOWERS

ALEXEI DIDN'T LEAVE IMMEDIATELY. He still had several hours more talking to do before taking his tongue in for its one-hundred-thousand-kilometer checkup. Fortunately, he didn't need to do it with us. He headed off to a space above the living quarters that was partitioned as an office; it had a ceiling and angled windows overlooking the living area. There he started making phone calls. Through the glass we could see him gesticulating wildly and hollering at his unseen victims. Occasionally, we could hear wild Russian phrases that defied translation, although at one point, it seemed as if Alexei was very upset about a lot of *chyort* and *gohvno*. He stamped back and forth through the office, waving his arms and shrieking in fury.

It was like when we were on Geostationary and he was talking on the phone to people all over everywhere, making all kinds of business arrangements. He said he'd made a lot of money off the information Mickey had given him—but for a rich man, he sure didn't act very rich. He acted like the guy who ran the comic-book store in El Paso. Like every comic was a million-dollar deal. Well, some of them were—like *Mad #5*—but not *every* one.

So just what *was* Alexei screaming about? And to who?

Hell, if I had an ice mine on the moon and a rolling Beagle-truck, I wouldn't worry about anything. I'd hang speakers all over the shaft and play Dvorak's Symphony #9 *"From the New World"* as loud as I could. Dad had recorded it with the Cleveland Symphony Orchestra once. I'd always liked that recording, it was one of my favorites. That, and his recordings of Beethoven's nine symphonies. Dad had used the Bärenreiter edition of the score, and period instruments tuned to the traditional A at 415 hertz, not 440 as was done later on. And he'd accelerated both the tempo and the dynamic range of the orchestra. I liked Dad's interpretation—and not just because it was Dad—but because he made the music frisky and energetic, as well as thoughtful and elegant. He brought grace and dignity to the third movement of the Ninth, playfulness and spirit to the first movement of the Fourth.

The recordings had sold very well and Dad was invited to conduct all over the country. *Newsleak* even called his set "the definitive Beethoven." I was very proud of him. So was Mom. Things were going well for us. And then Mom got pregnant with Stinky and everything changed. Mom and Dad started arguing over his career and all his traveling and his responsibilities—and then one night Dad got so angry, he asked her if the baby was even his—

And after that, it was never the same again. Some things can't be fixed.

And that only made me wonder all the more about Alexei. There was something very strange about the way he was super-polite to us, and then turned raging-belligerent to invisible people on the other end of the phone. What he was shouting looked an awful lot like the kind of stuff that couldn't be fixed—that the people on the other end wouldn't forgive.

So who was he yelling and screaming at—and why did they put up with it? What kind of relationship was it that they couldn't each go their separate way? Or was this the way Loonies behaved? Polite always in person, angry only when they couldn't be touched?

It didn't seem right to me. There was a lot that puzzled and annoyed and frustrated me about everything—and after Mom and Dad declared war on each other, I started speaking up too. I mean, why not? If everybody else was going to say what was wrong, I wanted to be heard too.

Except it doesn't matter how loud you complain, nobody listens—and nobody cares whether your complaint gets addressed or not. It's not *their* problem. Everybody only cares about their own problems, no one else's. A complaint is about as useful as a morning-after contraceptive pill for men.

Dad used to say that the only way to get anyone else involved in solving *your* problem is to make it *their* problem. But that didn't always work either—if their way of solving problems was to blame them on someone else. Like Mom and Dad always did.

But even though it didn't really work, speaking up was still better than keeping silent. Because if you're silent, they think you're agreeing. When you complain, when you speak up, when you argue, when you fight back—at least the blood on your hands isn't all your own.

Watching Alexei in his booth . . . it was like watching Mom and Dad.

"Chigger?"

"Huh?"

"Showers? Remember?"

"Oh, yeah. Right. Sorry. I was thinking."

"That's a nasty habit to get into," said Douglas. "You should only do it in private, and make sure you wash your hands afterward."

"I said *thinking!*"

"I heard you—"

I pulled off the wig, shrugged out of the dress, peeled out of the slip and panties. I felt weird doing it, like I wasn't just changing clothes as much as changing from one life into another. And Alexei had been right about the luxury of clean underwear.

The showers were wonderfully hot. Clouds of steam rose around us. It was delicious. This was the first real scrubbing we'd had since we'd left Earth over a week ago. Since before we took the elevator up the Line, since before the SuperTrain. Our last bath was at the motel in Mexico, after the night that Stinky scared himself by almost drowning in the Gulf of Baja. But even that shower hadn't been all that great. The water had been brown and there wasn't much pressure; it had smelled bad and felt worse. We ended up feeling dirtier than when we'd started.

This was better, much better, almost perfect. The water fell lazily around us in great fat drops, splattering everywhere in slow-motion bursts. It rolled slowly down our faces, down our chests and legs. It dripped like oil off our fingers and our noses and our dicks. Stinky laughed and pointed. Mickey held up his hand and angled a water spray so it arced high and slow across the shower space and splashed across Bobby's chest and face. Bobby yelped, but it didn't take him long to figure out how to splash back—and in no time at all, we were all aiming our respective torrents at each other, laughing wildly in a silly hysterical naked water fight. Everyone got doused in turn. Douglas and Mickey ganged up on me, then Bobby and I and Douglas plastered Mickey. And then Mickey and I and Bobby aimed everything at Douglas. We were making and breaking momentary alliances, one after the other, none of us were safe from betrayal. As soon as someone had been thoroughly splashed, we all turned on his most vigorous attacker and he became the new target of opportunity.

Finally, still laughing, the water fight ebbed. Even Bobby hollered enough. Then we soaped up slowly, one more time. Our skins were red with heat, shiny with water, and slippery with lather. And for a moment, we just stood and grinned and caught our breaths. We were safe on Luna, Douglas and Bobby and me. And Mickey. It was a truly happy moment for each of us.

"We must have used a lot of water," I said, just to have something to say.

"We didn't use it up," said Mickey. "It just goes round and round."

Douglas was soaping his head. He said thoughtfully, "This shaft looks like it makes a lot of water, doesn't it, Mickey? I can't see why the corporation would abandon it as not cost-effective."

Mickey shrugged. "They would if they were deliberately trying to set up a cover operation for funneling money without paying taxes."

"Do you think that's what they did?"

"I've heard speculations. More likely, Alexei was telling the truth. This site is too far away to make shipping water cost-effective. Gagarin is pulling enough water out of the crust, they don't need to worry about sites like this for a long time. Maybe someday the price of water will be high enough, or there'll be a settlement close by, or Alexei will go into farming and start growing his own catfish or cactus or whatever."

It sounded convincing, the way Mickey said it, but the same way I was wondering about Alexei, I was starting to wonder about Mickey too. And I was thinking about speaking up—doing the annoying brother thing—until Douglas interrupted.

"Chigger?"

"Yeah?"

"Remember that question that Judge Griffith asked you?"

"Which one—?"

"About telling your left from your right? How do you tell someone else which is which?"

"Yeah, what about it?"

"You gave Judge Griffith the wrong answer."

"No, I didn't. The question isn't answerable."

"Oh, yes it is." He pointed at me. "The left one always hangs lower."

"Huh?" And then I got it. A quick look at Bobby, Mickey, and Douglas confirmed it.

I blushed and laughed at the same time. And then I splashed him, because what else could I do, so he splashed me back, and then Bobby joined in, aiming his shower spray with both hands, and then Mickey too, and then everyone was shrieking as the water fight began again—

COUSINS

WHEN WE GOT OUT OF the showers, Alexei had already left. That wasn't a surprise, he had told us he would be gone; he had a water-meeting to go to. Actually, it wasn't just about water, it was also about nitrogen. "Water is gold, but nitrogen is silver. We are building new ammonia plant," he explained. "This means electricity. We will have to put up more solar panels. But we cannot build our own panels unless we build solar-cell plant. But solar-cell manufacturing plant uses as much power as small city. So we cannot make enough panels to make enough electricity to make panels because we cannot make enough panels. Is circular dilemma, *da.* Is hard to be invisible—we cannot buy enough electricity off the lines without someone wondering where electricity is going. So we have to use invisible electricity, of which there is not enough."

He waggled his finger at Mickey and Douglas. "You think everything on Luna arrives by magic? No, it does not. Everything is connected to everything else. Everything is built on top of everything else. Is not enough electricity to make more electricity, so is not enough electricity to make ammonia or nitrogen, so we cannot make enough gas to fill all the spaces we can make. And we can make lots of space on Luna, but even if we do, without nitrogen, we cannot make soil to grow things or gas to breathe. And problem is much more complex than I can explain here. I give you word of advice. If anyone asks you to be cousin, say no. You already have cousin in Krislov and he is crazy cousin enough for you. I go now. You take shower, I be gone when you are done. Do not go crazy from silence." He gave us all enthusiastic Russian kisses on both cheeks and pushed us toward the water. "Take as long as you want. Shower is free here, it goes round and round and never goes anywhere. More than enough. Enjoy. Least I can do is show you real Loonie household. *Dos vedanya.*"

I didn't understand half of what he'd said. But Douglas and Mickey seemed to think it made sense. We talked about it, after our shower, while we were drying off under the heat lamps. It was that place where economics and science collided—and if you had either bad economics or bad science, you usually ended up with a disaster. Like a rebellion, a coup, a war, a collapse—

"Is that what's happening now?"

"You heard him talking about cousins, didn't you?"

I thought back. "Only a couple of times."

Mickey said, "How do you think Luna got built? Especially invisible Luna?"

I shrugged. I hadn't given it any thought.

"People do favors for each other. They form tribes. Membership in a tribe makes you a cousin. You help your cousins, they help you. Families with cousins survive better than families without. Invisible Luna has fifteen major tribes and a couple hundred minor ones. The tribes would like to see Luna independent."

"But Luna *is* independent. Isn't it?"

"On paper."

"I don't understand."

"Most people don't. Follow the money. When you do that, you see that the Lunar Authority is still controlled by Earth-based corporations."

"Oh."

"And invisible Luna wants to revoke that charter."

"So they really *are* subversives."

Mickey shrugged. "I think they're playing at being subversive. They don't have the power to make a difference. Not the political power, not the electrical power, not the processing power—but they're having a great time talking about what they would do if they had the power. Just like all dreamers—"

"Processing power?" I asked, probably with a little too much innocence.

"Like an intelligence engine."

"What do they need that for?"

"Do you know how an intelligence engine works?"

"Yeah, sort of. It's like a computer with a 'do-what-I-mean' button. You tell it what you want. It tells you how to make it happen."

"Right. That's close enough. Well, if invisible Luna had a lethetic intelligence engine, it could tell them six ways how to get the electricity they need and a dozen more ways to get the political power. Intelligence engines are great equalizers. That's why some people think they're de-stabilizing influences and others think they should be mass-produced."

Now Douglas jumped into the discussion. "Some people think that the latest generation of lethetic engines have demonstrated true self-awareness. And that raises a whole bunch of questions about every-thing—what's the nature of sentience? Can machines have souls? Do they come from God? Or some other source of *soulness?* And if they are truly self-aware, then you can't buy and sell them, can you? And you can't mass-produce them either, because that's . . . I don't know, what? Do they get to vote? Will they outthink us? Outvote us? If they're smarter than us, are they going to steal our world out from under us? Or what?"

"Yep," agreed Mickey. "And that complicates the issue even more. If they are self-aware, what do the intelligence engines think about this? Where do they want to be?"

There was something about the way he said it. I looked up, and he was looking straight at me. Did he know? Did he suspect? How could he not?

"Hey!" shouted Stinky suddenly. "Where's my monkey?! I can't find my monkey! I left it sitting right here on this bench, waiting for me when we got into the showers, and now it's gone!"

"Are you sure you left it there?" Douglas asked. "Maybe you left it on your bed?"

"No, I left it right there—I remember! I told it to wait for me."

"Alexei!" Mickey called. "Are you still here? Alexei?" Still naked, he padded over to a nearby console and punched some buttons. "No, he's gone. He and Mr. Beagle left thirty minutes ago."

"Are you saying he took the monkey—?" Douglas whispered to Mickey.

But not soft enough. Stinky heard it anyway. "He stole my monkey! Alexei stole my monkey! I want it back!" He started shrieking and crying. It wasn't fair. He'd already lost everything else—his home, his mom, his dad. Now he'd lost the only toy he had left. I felt like shit.

FIRE AND ICE

WHILE **D**OUGLAS **TRIED TO COMFORT** Stinky, I watched Mickey. He was ashen-faced. He was taking this more serious than anyone.

Still naked, he climbed up to Alexei's office and began making phone calls. In private. That was interesting. At least he didn't scream and shout like Alexei did. I wondered if Alexei was monitoring everything we did here. Sure, why not? Privacy had died a long time ago. We'd learned that in school. The only defense anyone had against snoopers was not to care—live every moment as if everyone is watching. The only privacy left is inside your head.

While Mickey was upstairs on the phone, Douglas tucked Stinky into bed, promising we'd find his monkey no matter what. Then I gave Stinky a hug and told him his monkey was safe and not to worry. And then Douglas pulled me out of there and told me not to get Stinky's hopes up. If Alexei had stolen the monkey, and it sure looked like he had, then we'd probably never see it again, and we had a bigger problem anyway. If Alexei had the monkey now, he didn't need us anymore, and if he was too big a coward to terminate us himself, then he was probably sending someone else to do it. And then I told him that the monkey wasn't the problem, it was Mickey. Didn't it strike him as very *odd* that Mickey was taking the disappearance of the monkey so hard? And why was Mickey making so many emergency phone calls *now*? And I'm really sorry to have to say this, Douglas, especially because I think he's nice too, I really do, but I think that Mickey knows a lot more than he's saying.

And then Douglas started to tell me that my imagination and my paranoia were dancing a dangerous duet, and he put on the Daddy voice and got all serious and comforting, and told me how we'd all been through a lot and it was normal to worry about all kinds of impossible stuff, but I should really leave this to the grown-ups to handle—and that's when I stopped him again and reminded him of the promise he'd made to me back on the cargo pod, that he'd never do this again, never again shut me out of a decision, no matter how silly I might sound at the time. And he got it and shut up and gulped an apology, and said, "You're right, I was acting like Dad, wasn't I?" Which was so insightful that I actually complimented him. I gave him a little punch on the arm and said, "That's good, my weird older brother. We might make you into a human being yet." And then we both laughed a little, even though we were in a serious mess. At least, we were going to handle it like brothers.

So we talked about it for a bit, and I told him everything I knew—well, almost everything; there was one piece of information I left out—but I told him everything else I'd seen and thought about.

And then I added one more thing, which hurt me to say more than anything else I'd ever said in my life—even more than asking for a divorce from Mom and Dad. "I don't want to say this, Douglas, because I don't ever want to hurt you. And I've never seen you so happy in your life as you've been since you met Mickey. But I have to say it and you have to think about it. You only met Mickey what?—a week ago? Didn't you ever stop to ask, who is he really? And what does he see in you? I mean, I love you, you're my brother, I don't have a choice. But he's not your brother, he does have a choice, so you have to ask, *why?* I can see why you like him. He's good-looking and he's nice and he's smart—but *why* does he like you? I don't mean to say you're ugly, Douglas, you're not—but we're not going to see your picture on the cover of *PrettyBoy* either. And it's not that you're not nice, you are in a geeky sort of way, but you're not nice in that way that makes people want to hang out with you. And you're smarter than anybody else I've ever met in the whole world, but it's not street smarts like Mickey has; it's book smarts, which is exciting only to other people who are book-smart and absolutely boring to everybody else. The same way I am with my music. Remember the time I tried to explain to you that the blues were called that because of the blue note, the flatted fifth that gave them their special sound? And you thought that was the most boring thing you'd ever heard? Well, that's what you're like when you start talking about economic bonding among the polycorporates and crap like that. So you gotta ask yourself, Douglas, *just why is Mickey hanging out with us? What does he want?*"

And Douglas didn't answer right away, he just sat down on the edge of the inflatable bed and hung his head down and stared at his bare feet, and as bad as I'd felt when Stinky started crying for his missing monkey, I felt a thousand times worse now. The tears were silently rolling down Douglas's cheeks and falling lazily to the floor. He didn't sob. He just let the water flow.

He didn't get angry, he didn't hit me—I wish he would have taken a swing, I certainly deserved it—but he didn't even argue. That's what hurt the most—that he saw the truth in what I was saying here. And finally, after a long moment, he said, "I've been asking myself that question from the very beginning, Charles. Why am I so lucky? What did I do right? And then after we found out what was going on—or at least, what we thought was going on—yeah, I started thinking the same things you did. And it always comes back to the same question. What does he see in me? And I can't see anything he could see in me except the monkey—so yeah, Charles, maybe you're right and maybe he's using us, just like Alexei. Only I thought we'd be smart and use him to get off the planet and off to a colony, and at least we'd get that far. Only we're playing with the big kids here, aren't we—?"

It was time to undo some of the damage. As much as could be undone.

"Douglas—" I reached over and put my hand on his shoulder. "I can think of a lot of reasons why someone would care about you. And so can you. All you gotta do is be who you really are—"

Except when I said it, it sounded really stupid.

"I'm such a jerk," he said. He sounded *defeated.*

"No, you're not."

"I felt so *lucky.* I wanted to believe so badly, I really did. I thought I was smart enough to know better, but I wasn't. I'm just as stupid as everyone else."

"Then you're normal."

He almost smiled. He put his hand on mine. "Thanks for sticking by me, Charles."

"You're my brother. I have to."

"Yeah. That's the same thing I said, when I grabbed your hand back at Barringer Meteor crater. You're my brother. I have to."

Mickey came back then, still naked—we all were—in the excitement, we'd forgotten about clothes. "What's going on, fellas?" He looked from one to the other of us. From the expression on his face, he looked as if he already knew.

Douglas stood up and crossed to the rack that served as a closet. He grabbed a jumpsuit for himself, tossed one to Mickey, found a smaller one for me.

Mickey held the jumpsuit in his hands, but made no move to put it on. He looked across to Douglas, "What's going on, Douglas?"

"Who do you work for, Mickey?" Douglas's voice was very cold.

Mickey let out the breath he was holding. He sagged where he stood. He looked sad and deflated. "I was hoping I'd have more time before you figured it out. I was hoping—"

"Who do you work for, Mickey?"

"I was really starting to care and I was hoping—"

"Mickey. Just answer the question."

He shut up. He took a breath. He met our eyes. "Not all the tribes are Lunatics. There are cousins' clubs in the asteroids, on Mars, at the Lagrange colonies. On the Line. Some of the tribes are multiplanetary."

"Yeah? And which one do you work for?"

"Does it matter? Do you really care?" Mickey started pulling on the jumpsuit. "You feel betrayed. And I don't blame you. And there really isn't anything I can say to you that will make you feel different. Alexei used you; you figured that out, both of you, real fast. And everybody else tried to use you too—everyone on the Line—so, I figured it was only a matter of time until you figured out that my hands aren't all that clean either. But before you give your speech, and I know you will, let me remind you that you were using everyone else too. Everyone uses everyone. You were using Alexei and me to get to the colonies. Don't deny it, Douglas. So whatever else is going on between us, there isn't any moral superiority on either side. We used each other. You used me and I used you—we're equally wrong." He straightened his collar and pulled his zipper up. "I know this doesn't excuse anything at all, but I really did care about you the whole time. And I know you cared about me too."

Douglas pulled his own zipper up. "Between you and Chigger," he said, "you guys don't leave me a lot to say. You guys had it all figured out, didn't you? Only one thing you forgot—all this damn logic and believing and caring and all this other crap everybody's been throwing back and forth—*nobody ever stops to realize how much they're hurting everybody else in the process!"*

Both Mickey and I started to make noises of comfort, but Douglas held up both his hands, and said in the loudest voice I'd ever heard him use, "NO! Enough is enough. Both of you shut up already! Haven't you done enough damage for one day?!"

And that's when Stinky came in, and said, "Don't cry, Douglas, I still love you." Which was probably the one thing he could have said which would have made both Mickey and me want to cry.

Douglas scooped him up in his arms and held him tightly, and I realized that as all alone as Stinky had felt without his monkey, as all alone as I had felt these past few days, Douglas was the one who was most alone now—because everything he had wanted and believed in was forever broken. He sat down on the edge of the bed and held Stinky as tight as he could, rocking him gently. The two of them sobbed quietly together, each inside his separate loss, each inside his own particular hurt. I sat down on one side of them and Mickey sat down on the other and we all took turns crying in each other's arms about how shitty we'd all been. It didn't change anything between us, but at least it kept us from killing each other.

DOWN THE TUBES

Aﬀ**TER A WHILE, M**ICKEY WENT and got us some damp towels and we all wiped our faces clean and looked at each other and giggled in embarrassment a little bit. Maybe we'd all overreacted. Maybe it was the fear and the anger and the exhaustion all coming out at the same time. Maybe we had to test ourselves.

And maybe we were just catching our breath for the second round.

Mickey spoke first. "Look, you don't have to trust me anymore. But the way I see it, if Alexei's got the monkey now, then he doesn't need us anymore. And we're just sitting here waiting for the executioner to arrive. I think we need to get out of here."

"Oh—?" said Douglas. "How?"

Mickey laughed. "Come look at what I found." He led us up to Alexei's office and punched up a Lunar map on the big display. "This is a satellite photo," he said. "And this overlay shows where all the known settlements are. And *this* overlay shows where all the suspected settlements are. And *THIS* overlay shows the RF cousins—"

"RF?"

"Rock Father. Alexei's tribe."

"Where did you get all this information?" I asked.

"Alexei isn't the only one with a cousin," Mickey reminded us. "Alexei knows who my cousins are, and I know who his cousins are. We've cooperated enough times in the past—but probably never again, so it doesn't matter. Anyway, look at this map. Where are we? Where's Brickner 43-AX92?"

Douglas and I took a moment to study the display, searching the labels of the different stations. Finally, we both gave up. "Where is it?"

"There is no Brickner 43-AX92. That's a fictitious location. All the

Brickner stations are false." He looked up at the ceiling and shouted. "Do you think you were fooling us, Alexei? We knew it all the time." Back to us, he said, "Just in case he's listening."

"Do you think he is?"

"If he's not on the phone, talking someone's ear off."

"So are we on the map or not?" I asked, still searching the display.

"Oh, we're here," Mickey rapped the image on the wall. "We're just not where Alexei said. Do you know why there are so many fictitious people and stations on the moon? The invisibles do that; it's the haystack in which they're hiding. False data. The more inaccuracies they can generate, the better. It drives even the intelligence engines crazy, so I'm told."

"So where are we?" Douglas asked.

"I'll show you. I'll show Alexei too. Here—look, here's Gagarin. Right here." He pointed. "And over here, this is the train line. This is Wonderland Jumble, and the line goes right straight across here—see this spot here? Wait, I'll enlarge it. See that? That's Route 66. See where it crosses the train line? Right there at Borgo Pass—and if you follow the road around here and here and here, you come to this Y-shaped junction here that Alexei called his turnoff. Now, do you remember the zigzag flight path we took? It sort of looked like we were heading over here toward the left, remember? That was what Alexei wanted us to think. And he kept the sun bouncing around in front of us, so we wouldn't be able to look and see where we were going. All that tacking back and forth, you thought we were going northeast, didn't you? The truth is, we went southeast first and then northeast and then finally due east, and when you take out all the zigs and zags, we mostly went east. And we came down *here!* This is where we are."

Douglas and I both peered close. Douglas said it first. "We're at Gagarin!"

"Not quite. It's just over the hill. We're walking distance."

"And we didn't see it because the sun was in our eyes!"

Douglas grinned. "Edgar Allan Poe's 'Purloined Letter.' The safest place to hide something is in plain sight. Only what was Alexei hiding— us or Gagarin?"

"Both," said Mickey. "Listen—Charles, Douglas? Can you trust me for just a little while longer. I mean, I can get us out of here. I can get you to safety. And to a colony bid. After that, if you never want to see me again, I'll understand that too—what do you say?"

Douglas looked to me. I could see he wanted me to say yes. "Chigger?"

"It's a fair deal. *If he'll live up to it.*" Maybe I was still being too suspicious, but somebody had to be.

"I don't want to hurt you any more," Mickey said to us, but mostly to Douglas. "I'll keep my word."

"All right." Douglas offered his hands for a Lunar handshake. "Let's do it."

Mickey grabbed both of Douglas's hands in both of his and the two of them looked at each other and shook hands. And then I put my hands on top of theirs and Stinky put his hands on top of mine, and we all shook together.

And then we laughed and broke apart and Mickey snapped immediately into problem-solving mode. "All right, girls. Let's find our bubble suits. According to the map, there's a local road. See? It's less than a kilometer. It's all in shadow. We can be there in an hour. Grab some food and water, extra air tanks just in case. Reflective blankets. Headsets. Everything we had from the pod. I think Alexei packed them all in the blue case. Didn't we leave that one up by the hatch?"

"Uh, Mickey—" I said softly.

He glanced to me.

I gestured toward the ceiling. *What if he's listening?*

"Let him listen," he said, loudly enough for any hidden microphones to hear. "We'll be safe at Gagarin long before he can catch up with us."

We found the bubble suits and other supplies exactly where Mickey had said. We unpacked them quickly, but Douglas held his up, frowning. "These suits have expired, Mickey. They're only good for one wearing or six hours, whichever comes first. And we went beyond both of those limits."

Mickey snapped back, "I know what those suits are tested to, Douglas. Some of them have lasted as long as ten wearings and over six hundred hours. All we need is thirty minutes, maybe less. Do you have a better idea?"

He didn't. We started dressing ourselves for a trip across the surface. I was already dreading this, but we were too busy going through the separate drills of zipping and unzipping, checking air and water supplies, tightening the Velcro straps on the jumpsuit shoes, grabbing the inflatable airlock, all that stuff.

But we didn't actually put on the bubble suits themselves until we were standing under the exit hatch. Mickey stood beneath it, happily punching at the controls, occasionally swearing, canceling things out, and going back to do it again.

This wasn't the same airlock we'd entered through. This was a larger one, with multiple hatches. There was one hatch overhead and at least half a dozen more spaced around the walls. The hatch in the floor led back down to the living quarters.

"All right," Mickey announced. "I've got it. Everybody get your suits on. Douglas, seal that floor hatch—"

"Wait," I said. I went over to the hatch and sang down into it, *"I would dance and be merry, life would be a ding-a-derry, if I only had a brain . . ."* All three of them stared at me, as if I'd suddenly gone crazy.

"Chigger, what the hell are you doing?" He made as if to close the hatch.

"Wait, *dammit!"*

"We don't have time—"

I sang down into the hatch again. This time louder. *"I would dance and be merry, life would be a ding-a-derry—"* That was as far as I got. The monkey came flying up out of the hatch like something out of an animated cartoon.

"What the hell—?" That was Mickey.

"My monkey!" Bobby shrieked. The monkey flew into his arms and hugged him excitedly. They still looked like long-lost twins.

"Chigger—?" Douglas grabbed my arm.

"I did it, yes. I told the monkey to hide and stay hidden and not come out until I called it. So Alexei wouldn't get it. Or anyone else—"

Douglas gave me a look of exasperation and rage. He turned and dogged the hatch. His face was working furiously, while he tried to think of what to say. Finally, he turned around. "Your little brother hasn't stopped crying—"

"I know, and I feel like a shit, okay?! I'm sorry, Bobby! I didn't do it to hurt you. I told the monkey to hide so no one could steal him—"

"Everybody stop arguing!" Mickey shouted. "We've gotta go!" He armed the airlock. "Get into your suits *now."*

Bobby gave the monkey one more hug, then bounced onto Douglas's back, the monkey jumped onto mine. We pulled on our suits quickly and zipped ourselves in.

"You haven't heard the end of this, Chigger!" Douglas called across to me. "You told me you wanted me to be honest with you—and you didn't tell me the truth about the monkey?!"

"I didn't want Mickey to know. I wanted to tell you first."

"Yeah, you've always got an excuse."

"Shut up, Douglas! Chigger did good. We're still alive right now because Alexei couldn't find the monkey!"

"He should have told me!"

"I was going to—I didn't get a chance."

"It's all right, we've got it back now," said Bobby, trying ineffectively to be a peacemaker.

"Shut up, all of you! I can't concentrate!" And as he said that, the hatch opposite us popped open. Not the hatch above! "Go!" Mickey shouted, pushing me toward it. "Come on!"

"Huh?" But I was already moving.

"You're not the only one who can keep a secret. Let's go, Douglas!"

I bounced through into a horizontal tube that stretched ahead forever. It was the same stuff as the inflatable pressure tubes that linked one vehicle to another—a spiral coil with plastic walls; you extended it wherever you wanted it to go—only this one was longer. It stretched away like a tunnel. It had a collapsible mesh deck for a floor, with several pipes and tubes running along underneath it. Outside the plastic, I could sense more than see that the tube was half-buried in Lunar dust. Farther out, lay the dim outlines of a shadowy horizon.

"How far does this go?" I called back.

Mickey was sealing the hatch behind us. "At least a kilometer. I hope. Go as fast as you can, Chigger. We're right behind you."

"But this isn't the road!"

"I know it. But maybe Alexei won't. I cut all his visual monitors to the airlock. At least, I think I did. So he's going to think we took the road."

"But how'd you know this tube was here?"

"Call it a lucky guess. But I know Alexei better than you. Keep bouncing." I didn't look back, I could hear them pounding behind me. "See, you wouldn't have noticed it, Chigger. You're a terrie. Sorry, no offense. But I knew that the Brickner station wasn't working the minute we climbed down into it. *It wasn't hot enough!* You can't melt Lunar ice without heat, and you've got to pump a lot of heat into the ground to get the ice to melt. And it wasn't hot enough! So where did all that water come from then?"

"It was here from before—? When the station was working?" I offered.

"Maybe. But remember, *I know Alexei better than you!* Why do you think I asked *him* to smuggle you up the Line? Why do you think I trusted him to smuggle us to Luna? Because Alexei Krislov is a brilliant scoundrel. Brickner station is a double-decoy. Yeah, he sells a little bit of water back to Gagarin. That's his cover—look down, you see those pipes under the deck? What do think is in them? Which way do you think it's flowing?"

I was too busy bouncing to focus, and I didn't want to stop to look.

"Um, the green one is breathable air?" I guessed. "The blue one is water?"

"And the orange one? What do you think that is?

"That's ammonia," said Douglas. "Remember what Alexei said about nitrogen and ammonia? You need nitrogen to make breathable gas. And for fertilizer. You need ammonia for refrigeration."

"Right," said Mickey. "The key to Lunar technology isn't water. It's nitrogen. That's what everybody needs the most. Even more than water and electricity. Alexei isn't selling any of this! *He's stealing it!* Brickner isn't a water-production plant; it's a holding tank for water skimmed off Gagarin. And all the stuff in the other tanks as well. There were too many. There's *too much* storage there."

We bounced a little farther down the tube, while I thought about that. The pipes below our feet weren't that thick. I guessed they didn't need to be.

"Doesn't Gagarin know?" Douglas asked. "Can't they tell?"

"Maybe Alexei is only siphoning off a few liters a day. With the number of people coming and going into Gagarin Station, with the scale of industrial processes they've got going, they could write it off as loss due to normal usage. But if he's siphoning off any more than that, then someone at Gagarin is covering it up. That's my guess, that this is how legal resources are being funneled to the tribes of invisible Luna. I wonder if they're doing the same with electricity. You heard him talking about factories and what they needed. Dammit. We knew they were moving ahead. We didn't realize this—" And then he trailed off into a string of muttered curses.

We concentrated on bouncing down the tube. We couldn't see very far ahead from any given point, because the tube snaked and wound its way over the Lunar terrain, up and down, around and over. Every so often we passed a joint where two sections of tube had been sealed together. Several times we had to pass through manually operated air-locks. We zipped our way through.

"Bobby? Did you do something?" That was Douglas. They were in the same bubble suit again.

"I didn't do anything."

"What are you guys talking about?" Mickey asked.

"It smells like piss in here," said Bobby. "I didn't do it!"

"How bad?" asked Mickey. His voice sounded strange.

"Not too bad," Douglas said. And then he got it. "Oh."

"Would somebody explain it to me?" I asked.

"Ammonia," Mickey said.

"What's ammonia?" Bobby asked.

"It's good for cleaning your glasses," I said.

"I don't wear glasses," Bobby said.

"Then don't worry about it."

"Charles, please—" That was Mickey. "I'm trying to figure out how far we've come. I don't want to turn back."

"I think we can make it," Douglas said. "I'll turn up my oxygen."

"That'll help—a little bit." He added, "Alexei probably keeps the tube pressurized with ammonia to keep folks from wandering through it casually. Besides, it's another useful storage area. Do the math. A kilometer-long tube, nine meters in diameter, pressurized to two-thirds sea level, I'd guess. Can you figure it out, Douglas?"

He was trying to distract Douglas, I was sure. And maybe me too. I was trying to figure out if there was anything else we could do. "Monkey, if you've got any ideas, now's the time to talk—" It didn't respond.

"It really stinks in here!" wailed Bobby. "I don't like this!"

"How are your eyes?" Mickey asked.

"Watering—badly." Douglas coughed suddenly. Bobby was coughing even worse. The leak must have expanded—

—and then I got it! *The inflatable! The portable airlock!* " I could barely get the words out fast enough. Even as I stumbled to get the words out, Mickey was already pulling it from his pack! I bounced back to him and together, we pushed Douglas and Stinky through the first zippered entrance. We zipped it behind them, unzipped the next, pushed them through, zipped it behind them—

Douglas was already turning up the oxygen on his tank. Mickey pushed the gloves into the inflatable, and without worrying about proper procedures unzipped all three of the zippers on Douglas's bubble suit. Douglas and Bobby lay on the floor of the inflatable, coughing and choking, their eyes streaming. Douglas held the breather tube in front of Bobby's nose, then his own, then back to Bobby. It probably still smelled of ammonia in there, but at least they had a chance now.

"Come on, Charles, I can't do this alone. I need your help." He rolled Bobby onto Douglas, and picked up Douglas by the head. I picked up Douglas by the feet and the two of us began carrying him forward. The inflatable bulged into unmanageable shapes, but we both had our hands pushed into its gloves and we held on to Douglas himself and tried to keep the bulges from dragging and scraping along the sides. We bounced through the tube as fast as we could manage. I could feel my heart pounding so hard I couldn't hear anything else.

Mickey led the way, I followed. I couldn't see past him very well, so I couldn't see if the tube sloped up or down, right or left, so I was constantly bumping and jerking, trying to keep up. Bobby and Douglas were still coughing, but Bobby was crying, and that was always a good sign. If we could just make it to the end of this tube. How far was it anyway?!

We had to stop then, while Mickey zipped us through another manual airlock. And then we pushed on again. I didn't know how much longer I could do this—I didn't care that we were in one-sixth gee. This was exhausting, and I was reaching the limits of my endurance. "We've gotta stop soon—" I managed to gasp.

"You'd better pace yourselves." Douglas coughed. He waved the breathing tube back and forth between himself and Bobby.

"All right, all right—" Mickey brought us to a halt. We lowered Douglas and Bobby to the deck and the two of us stood there, hands on knees, panting heavily.

"Aren't we there yet? How far is it?" I asked.

"We're halfway there. More than halfway. How are you doing, Douglas?" He was already shoving another air tank through the zipper locks. The last one. This was going to be close. "Turn it all the way up. Give yourselves as much pure oxygen as you can. And try not to strike any sparks. Ammonia is flammable, you know."

"If I turn it all the way up, the inflatable will fill the tube. We'll use the breathing mask. We'll be fine."

"Douglas, look at your bubble suit. The plastic is supposed to change color around a rip or a puncture. Red or yellow, I think. If you can find the hole, there's emergency tape right there. Just pull off a strip and press it to the leak. Can you find it? Look around your feet. Turn over, maybe it's behind you. Charles and I will look. Do you see anything, Charles—?"

"I'm still looking. It's hard to see through all these layers—"

"Douglas?"

"I don't see anything either."

"Damn! Maybe it's in the foot pads or the gloves or someplace it doesn't show. All right—" He glanced up the length of the tube. "It's doable. You ready, Chigger?"

"No," but I picked up Douglas by the feet anyway.

This time, we held our panic in check. We moved fast, but we weren't running anymore. We were tired, but we weren't exhausting ourselves. And then, just to make it worse, we started up a long uphill slope. I could see the ceiling of the tube arcing away.

"Gohvno!"

It hurt, I ached, and I was beginning to imagine I could smell the ammonia piss-smell myself. It was enough to make my eyes water. I coughed.

"Not you too!" Mickey said.

"Keep going!" I shouted.

And finally, the tube crested the hill. We passed through another manual airlock and started down the last long slope to Gagarin. And yes, I really could smell ammonia now. My suit had a leak too. But I could make it. I was certain of it. All we had to do was get to the bottom of this hill, that's all. Okay, the bottom of this hill then. If I could just hold my breath a little bit longer and not start coughing again—

—the pain in my eyes and nose and chest was impossible, and somebody was trying to force a breathing tube in my mouth. I was trying to hack out my guts and somebody was telling me to inhale. And all I wanted to do was just get Douglas and Bobby to the other end of the pipeline. And then I finished retching and the tube was shoved into my mouth, and then the next thing I knew, somebody was sitting on me and somebody else was carrying me and we were bouncing down the birth canal of hell pushing into the light, and—

—and then we were in an airlock or just outside of it and somebody was stripping me out of my bubble suit and turning me on my back and standing on my stomach. *Oh, flaming God, even CPR was different on the moon—*

ZOMBIES

I **WAS ON MY SIDE.** I was in the inflatable. Stinky was sitting next to me, rocking and hugging the monkey and crying. Douglas and Mickey were outside of the inflatable—leaning over me—how had that happened? They were both in bubble suits. Douglas's had a strip of tape on it. I noticed that immediately. My eyes and lungs still burned, there was blood dripping from my nose, but the piss-smell of ammonia was more memory than real.

We were still in the tube. Douglas waved at me. I waved back. He grinned. I wasn't sure what was happening. He picked up my feet, Mickey picked up my head; Bobby lay down on top of me, he didn't weigh enough to matter—and we were heading down the tube again. This time, I was the cargo. How had I gotten inside the inflatable? How had Douglas ended up outside again?

It hurt too much to wonder about it. I concentrated on breathing. One desperate gulp at a time. My throat felt scorched. My nose still dripped. I wiped at it futilely. My arms were too weak to move. Stinky waved a breathing tube at me.

I must have passed in and out of consciousness, because the next thing I knew, Douglas and Mickey were passing me through a hatch, and we were out of the tube inside another cargo-pod-shaped place. And then they were unzipping everything and pulling Stinky out and then me and I was full of questions, but I couldn't ask them because Mickey had a medikit and was wiping my face and shining a light in my eyes, telling me to watch his finger, asking me if I could talk.

I croaked something in response that sounded like *"Kwaaact whac-cked?"* but really meant "What happened?"

"Your suit tore. We pushed you into the inflatable. I was going to go for help, but Bobby found the hole in your suit and Douglas patched it. He put it on himself and the two of us carried you out. You should have said something—"

"*Waack tdiict!*"

"Don't talk," Mickey ordered. "Breathe this. It's going to smell funny—" He sprayed something into my throat. It was wet and cold, but in a few seconds, my throat stopped trying to climb out of my neck, and the pain subsided into a dull ache. That left only my lungs screaming for relief. Mickey pressed something cold and hissy against my arm.

It didn't make the throbbing in my chest go away, it made me go away. I was still awake, I could even feel stuff, I just didn't care anymore. I saw Mickey turn to Bobby next and start making the same tests. Bobby was in better shape than me. So was Douglas. But he sedated them too. Douglas sat down cross-legged next to me, with a stupid look on his face. We must have looked like three happy zombies—

And then there were some other people around us and Mickey stood up and started showing them his documents. "My name is Michael Gordon Partridge. I'm a licensed bounty hunter from the Line, and these people are my prisoners. Here's a copy of the warrant. Here's my license and my ID. They need immediate medical attention, and I need to arrange fast transport to Armstrong."

I saw Douglas look up, blinking in confusion. "Huh—?" I wasn't sure what happened next. That's when I started passing in and out of consciousness.

The next thing I knew, the room was vibrating loudly. And I was strapped down so I couldn't move. I couldn't see either. I turned my head and something wet fell away from my eyes. Douglas was lying on another cot across from me. I didn't see Stinky or the monkey, but there was another cot above me. Maybe he was on that. There was a signal I could whistle—

—but there was an oxygen mask over my face. And then someone came and put the wet pad over my eyes again. Mickey's voice. "You're going to be all right, Charles. You took a few bad gulps, but there isn't going to be any permanent damage. Douglas and Bobby are all right. So is the monkey. Everybody's here. All you have to do is relax and rest and let us get you to the hospital at Armstrong Station. We'll be there in another two hours." He leaned in close to put his lips next to my ear. "Everything is going to be all right, I promise."

I couldn't speak. I didn't try. I didn't care. I didn't have any feelings left. Later on, I might have feelings again. But if they were going to hurt, I didn't want them. I'd had enough of feelings, thankewvery-muchnext. But I wanted him to go away. I knew he wasn't good for us anymore, even if I couldn't remember why. I tried to tell him that. I struggled against the restraints and twisted my head back and forth, trying to shake the air mask loose, so I could speak, but that didn't accomplish anything, and a minute later I felt something cold on my arm and I went away again.

This time when I came to, the room was silent and dark and I was all alone. I was still in a cargo pod. We'd spent our entire time on Luna going from one used cargo pod to another, missing sleep, missing meals, trying to breathe everything from vacuum to ammonia—

At least the air smelled clean and wet here. It smelled like flowers. Hawaiian flowers. Plumeria, I think that's what they were called. That was nice. What was even nicer was that I could smell them at all.

I couldn't open my eyes. Something moist was taped in place over them. I wondered if I'd been blinded. That was going to be a nuisance. But at least I could I still hear. The music was Samuel Barber's Adagio for Strings, which struck some people as plaintive and annoying, or just plain desolate. I always liked it for its thoughtful quality. It was Dad's recording, and I think I knew which one. It was the first time I ever got to see him conduct. He conducted with his eyes closed. At least it looked that way from where I was sitting. He was lost in the music. And his hands were like living creatures—he didn't use a baton; he just stroked the air and the music poured forth. He coaxed the Adagio into life and let it fill the auditorium. I don't think I took a breath for the entire ten minutes. I'd never heard anything like that before in my life. I hadn't known such sounds were possible. And afterward, I kept playing it over and over again, always trying to recapture that same initial *wunderstorm.* . . .

I wished I could tell him how much I loved his music. That would be nice. Somebody took my hand in his. It felt like Dad's hand. Large and warm and safely enveloping. I knew it had to be Douglas holding my hand, but it was nice to pretend it was Dad for a while.

And then Dad spoke. "I was so scared, Chigger. For a while, I thought I was going to lose you. All of you, forever. I didn't get a chance to say any of the stuff I wanted to say. And I was afraid that even if I could say it, you wouldn't want to hear it. And now that I have the chance to tell you, all I really need you to know is how important you are to me and how sorry I am everything got so screwed up. I wish I could have done better. The music—do you remember this? You were always asking to come see me conduct, and I was sure it would bore you to death, but I took you anyway, and you sat there totally entranced and captivated. You were listening to the music as deeply as anyone I've ever seen. I was so happy for you that day—

because you'd discovered something all your own. And I was so glad it was something I could give to you. I remember the look in your eyes of total awe and admiration, and how proud I was to be your dad; the person who'd brought that look to your face. I wish I could have made that moment last forever." He kissed my hand and replaced it on the bed, and then he got up and went away, and the dream ended. But it was really a nice dream while it lasted.

And then I had a dream about Mom too. Her and that Sykes woman. But I didn't remember what they said. And that bothered me for a while—because it didn't seem fair for Dad to have a whole vivid dream and not Mom too. But it was kind of like Mom had stepped out of my life for a while and I guess I wasn't ready to let her back in, not even in my dreams.

That reminded me of something Douglas said once, about moms. He said that nothing gets in the way of a good fantasy like a mom. That's why most guys try to put Mom aside for a while—while they try to figure out who they are, I guess. It didn't matter anymore. We were all going to jail soon enough. If we weren't there already.

And then, one morning, I opened my eyes to the smell of hot chocolate, eggs, toast, and strawberry jam. And I sat up in bed and looked around. Except for a slightly sleepy feeling of confusion, I felt better than I had in days. I could even talk. My voice was still dusky-scratchy like my throat was lined with cockleburs and foxtails, but I could actually make understandable words. "Hello? Is anyone there?" I was in a room that was *not* part of a cargo pod. It actually had a real floor and real walls and a real ceiling. It was spooky. Everything looked soft and gentle and flowery, that's how I knew it was a hospital; it smelled like a hospital too, with the air just a little too fresh and clean.

"Oh, good, you're up. Right on schedule." The woman wore a purple-gray dress and a thing like a pink apron over it. I guessed it was supposed to be cheery, and it wasn't too hard to look at, but I was never big on industrial cheerfulness before and as good as I felt, I wasn't ready to start now.

She was just uncovering a tray of food—that was what I'd smelled. She put it across my bed and tied a bib around my neck. "Just in case," she said. "You might still be a little weak."

"What is this place?"

"Tranquility Medical Center at Armstrong."

"How long was I out?"

"Three days. No, four. It doesn't matter. You're fine now. You'll just have to take it easy for a bit. I'll leave you alone to eat. The shower is through there. There are fresh clothes in the closet. Try not to take too long. You have to be in court in two hours—"

"Say what?"

But she was already gone.

IN COURT

JUDGE **C**AVANAUGH **WAS THE LARGEST** human being I had ever seen. He looked like the *Hindenburg*. He was huge and round, and when he entered the room, it took a while for all of him to arrive at the same place. He moved like a human bubble suit, with all of his blubbery mass flubbering and bouncing around like an animated caricature of a fat man. In Lunar low gee, he didn't lumber, he *floated*. He took his seat at the bench, and all the various parts of him arrived one after the other, settling into place like latecomers at a concert.

Judge Cavanaugh took roll, made sure all his separate body sections had sorted themselves out, looked out over the room, looked to the display in front of him, rubbed his nose, and waved a go-ahead gesture at the clerk, a skinny black woman. "Case number 40032, in the matter of Douglas, Charles, and Robert Dingillian, custody of, blah blah blah."

Custody? Again?

Judge Cavanaugh was scanning through his notes. He finally found the page he was looking for and looked out at us again. He cleared his throat. "Most court cases are a two-body problem. A plaintiff and a defendant. Those are relatively simple to resolve. You listen to the facts, you look for a balance. Somehow you find a Lagrange point."

He looked out over the room. "But just as the laws of physics start to get complex and unmanageable when you introduce a third body to the problem, so do the laws of human beings become complex and unmanageable when there are three participants orbiting around a claim. We have here, a seven-body problem. Or a twelve-body problem. Or more. I've lost count of the number of litigants who have stepped forward to lodge a claim or file a brief as a friend of the court. I know that most of you recognize that you do not have a hope in hell of winning your claim, but it hasn't stopped you from adding bodies to the problem in the hope of making it so unmanageable that it can never be resolved. I applaud your various successes in making this case a colossal nightmare. I promise to reward each and every one of you appropriately."

He smiled. For some reason, it didn't look friendly.

"Let me explain something to those of you who've just arrived here in the last few days. I know a lot of you are suddenly out of work and vaguely troubled by the fact that we don't have ambulances to chase here on Luna. And, of course, as we all know, there's nothing as dangerous as an unemployed lawyer—unless it's one who *is* employed. But for the record, I want to explain to you how things work here in this courtroom, and on most of Luna.

"This is a small town. There are only three million of us. And we're spread across a landmass equal to that of Earth. So we're spread pretty thin. We've only got a few major settlements. The largest still has less than a hundred thousand folks. So we run our courts with a lot less formality than you might be used to back home. That doesn't mean we take our lawyering any less seriously. It just means that we don't bother with wigs and robes and funny hats. They make us look silly and we start giggling—and that's a little disconcerting when we're sentencing someone to the nearest airlock because he refused to pay his air tax. And yes, I'm not joking.

"So we're just going to cut through a lot of the crap that you guys love so much and see if we can sort things out without using up too much oxygen. Those of you who are representing clients with money, this probably doesn't worry you—but take my word for it, it doesn't matter how much money your clients have back on Earth or on the Line. It can't buy more oxygen if there isn't any left. We want you to represent your client's claims fairly, we want to hear the facts. We do *not* want a lot of extraneous noise. Nothing pisses off this court more than a low signal-to-noise ratio. I assume I'm making myself perfectly clear? Thank you."

He paused to note something on the pad in front of him, then said, "So, let's get to it. This hearing is projected to cost the Lunar Authority fifty thousand water-dollars. Therefore, the court chooses to exercise local privilege and will assess a nonrefundable processing fee of five thousand liters of water or ten thousand liters of nitrogen on all claimants in this matter to cover the judicial expenses. Anyone choosing to withdraw his or her claim, please see the court clerk now—"

Several people I didn't recognize bounced up out of their seats and over to the clerk at the side of the room. I was sitting in a wheelchair with a mask on my face, concentrating on one breath at a time. I'd been wheeled in at the last minute and I hadn't really gotten a good look at anything; besides, my vision was still too blurry to make out details. And strapped in as I was, I couldn't even turn around to see how many people were in the room or who else was here. Next to me, the shape that looked like Douglas was grim. The shape that looked like Bobby was sitting quietly on his lap. I didn't see anything shaped like a monkey.

"Thank you," said Judge Cavanaugh. "That will simplify matters a little bit—but even with fewer litigants, the court costs will remain the same. This means that the assessment will now have to be increased by 50 percent to seventy-five hundred liters of water per claimant—" This time, six more people headed for the clerk's desk.

The judge smiled. "I like the way this is going. By the way, I should note that this fee will also apply to those filing briefs of amicus curiae. This court does not need any more friends. We already have the best friends money can buy. So if you intend to be our friend today, we will expect you to pay for your fair share of justice too. You can buy as much justice as you can afford on Luna. Cash payments only, please. We do not accept checks drawn on Earth banks. This will be your last opportunity to reconsider. . . ." Four more people.

Judge Cavanaugh waited until the bustle in the courtroom died down. He studied some papers, some material on his display, and conferred with his clerk. Finally, he looked up again. "All right, that helped. Now let's see what kind of progress we can make. We're here, all of us, to decide what to do with these three young men. The issue revolves on whether or not Judge Griffith was justified in granting the divorce of Charles Dingillian from his parents and whether Douglas and Charles are fit custodians of Robert Dingillian." For the first time, Judge Cavanaugh looked at us. "Charles Dingillian, how are you feeling?"

My voice crackled like I was walking through a field of shredded wheat. "I never felt better in my life." I said it deadpan.

Judge Cavanaugh raised an eyebrow at me. "Are you feeling well enough to proceed?"

I nodded. "Yes, sir."

"Thank you." He turned his attention back to the rest of the court. "I want to mention here that Lunar Authority is a signatory to the Starside Covenant as well as the Covenant of Rights. As such, we give full faith and credit to the legal processes of all other signatories to these covenants. We recognize marriages, adoptions, divorces, and other legal contracts, entered into willingly by the participants. For those of you who are *not* lawyers, and I think there are only three of you in this room who are not"—he glanced at us when he said that—"this means that Luna will acknowledge and recognize all legal decisions of the Line Authority. We are not obligated to recognize the legal authority of some Earth courts because they are *not* signatory. For the record, the Republic of Texas is a nonsignatory jurisdiction.

"I want to make this very clear at the outset, because it affects what this court has the authority to do. Those of you who are preparing to argue that Judge Griffith's decision has no weight in this courtroom are wrong, and this court will not entertain any claims based on that line of reasoning at all. You would be asking this court to create a conditional nullification of the articles of full faith and credit among covenant signatories. In plain old-fashioned English, it ain't gonna happen. Not in this court.

"However . . . those of you who are asking me to *set aside* Judge Griffith's decision as a bad ruling, had better be prepared to argue that claim with facts and logic that demonstrate an overwhelming and compelling necessity. And please, remember the unofficial motto of this court. *Bore me and die.*

"Today's hearing is relatively informal, even for Luna. It is an evidentiary hearing—an inquiry into the facts—which may or may not resolve the matter. If we do not resolve the matter here, we will refer it for trial. If the investigation does not uncover a compelling interest on the part of the state—or on the part of any of the claimants, the whole thing will end here. And let me say again, everyone's cooperation in achieving a speedy resolution to this business will be particularly appreciated. *I hope I make myself clear.*"

He turned back to his display for a moment, frowning. He clicked through several pages. Judge Cavanaugh looked like he was having a wonderful time. I decided to like him—at least until he pissed me off.

"Now, then . . ." He looked up again. "Let's get to the specifics. This court has spent several days reviewing the transcript of Judge Griffith's divorce hearing. It is very interesting reading, but I find nothing in it to justify a set-aside. If there's anyone here who feels I've *missed something*, do feel free to point out any errors that Judge Griffith may have made in her ruling, or any mistakes I might have made in my review. I certainly won't be prejudiced against anyone who feels qualified to educate me in this matter. I might even thank you for the effort. But if there's no one here who wants to look for the light at the bottom of that particular tunnel . . . then let's just move on. Let's all stipulate in advance that any evidence that anyone has to present about the wisdom of *this* ruling must be based on circumstances that have developed in the last two weeks, *since* the ruling was made. You will have to demonstrate that Douglas, Charles, and Robert Dingillian have proven incapable of taking care of themselves. We will use *that* as the deciding criterion in this chamber. Any questions? I thought not." He looked very pleased with himself. I wished I could see the expressions on the faces behind us; but I couldn't turn in my seat, and even if I could, it would all be a blur. But at least I wasn't coughing anymore.

"But before we can even deal with that, we have to deal with this *other* matter first—which I consider an extremely minor and very annoying detail. So of course, that's why it will probably consume an inordinate amount of this court's time. But a number of you have aggressively argued that the property claim is an essential part of judging the Dingillians' behavior since they were granted independence, so there's no setting it aside. Is there? Bailiff, bring in the *object*, please."

While they were waiting for the bailiff, I leaned over to Douglas and managed to croak, "Don't we have a lawyer?"

Douglas shook his head. "Not yet."

"Why not?"

"The judge said we don't need one. Not unless we go to trial. He's acting as advocate on our behalf. No, that's not illegal here. Court costs are carried by the plaintiffs—unless they win. It's real different than on Earth. Plaintiffs have to prove they have a case just to get to trial."

The bailiff came back carrying a black box. He set it on a table in front of the room. He opened the box and removed the monkey. He placed it on the table and took the box away. The monkey looked lifeless. Bobby shouted, "That's my monkey! I want it back! *It's mine!*" I tried to stifle a smile. There were times when I loved my brother *because* he was such a brat.

Judge Cavanaugh made a note on a pad. "So there we have the first claimant speaking up. Thank you. You are . . . Robert Dingillian, correct?"

"Yes! And I want my monkey back."

"And why do you say the monkey is yours?"

"Because my daddy gave it to me. And it's mine."

"All right, good." Judge Cavanaugh looked over the court. "Is there anyone who wants to contest this fact—that Max Dingillian gave this toy to his son? No? No one wants to argue that? Thank you. What a pleasant surprise. So we can all stipulate now that the toy was given to Robert Dingillian." He made a note on his pad.

"Now, Bobby—where did your daddy get this toy?"

"He bought it."

"You saw him buy it?"

"Uh-huh."

"Good, thank you." To the rest of the court, Judge Cavanaugh said, "We have other witnesses who can confirm this, of course, so let's just move ahead. Let's stipulate that Max Dingillian did indeed go through the motions of purchasing this toy. He paid cash value and received custody of the toy. His account was debited, and he was given a receipt. Therefore, paper was in place to demonstrate he was the legal owner of record. Is there anyone who wants to contest that? Is there anyone who wants to argue that these events did not happen? No? Thank you. All right, the court will now stipulate that Max Dingillian did indeed go through the motions, did appear to, and to all intents and purposes, *believed* that he had legally obtained custody of this toy for the express purpose of presenting it to his son Robert Dingillian. Gracious—at this rate, we could be out of here in time for the return of Halley's Comet. That'll be when, Gloria? Another fifty-six years?"

He looked out over the courtroom. "*Now*, who wants to argue that Max Dingillian's purchase of the toy was in any way irregular? Who wants to argue that he had no right to the toy or that he came by it dishonestly or that the sale was invalid due to other circumstances?"

About six people stood up then, several of them shouting. I thought I recognized a couple of voices, but I didn't feel like trying to turn around to see. It would have been wasted effort.

"All right." Judge Cavanaugh pointed. "Everybody's going to get a turn. Just line up in the back there. In order of height, alphabetically, I don't care. You first. Come up front. State your name for the record. Remember, you're in court. Anything you say can and will be used against you."

A heavyset man came forward. He looked like a hockey player. "My name is David Cheifetz. Until three weeks ago, I was an attorney with Canadian-Interplanetary—"

I leaned over and whispered to Douglas. "*That's not what J'mee said. She said her daddy sold electricity for the Line.*"

"*And you believed her?*"

"*Oh,*" I said, realizing again. Everybody had a secret agenda. *Everybody lied.*

Cheifetz was still talking. "—My family and I are emigrating out to the colonies. Seven weeks ago, we made arrangements to have Max Dingillian ferry some sensitive material for us."

"You mean *smuggle.*"

"No, Your Honor. Smuggling is a crime. What we were doing was perfectly legal. My wife and my daughter and I are very visible people. We've already discovered this to our dismay when our daughter J'mee was accused of being Charles Dingillian in disguise." The judge made

a hurry-up gesture. "The point is that we are clearly targets of opportunity. This is one of the reasons for emigrating. The safest way for us
to transfer our wealth was to have it travel by an alternate route. Someone not as visible as we are. Max Dingillian was our courier." He
glanced at me and Douglas and Bobby, looked annoyed. "While we
don't contest the ownership of the toy, we do contest the ownership of
the memory bars inside of it. They belong to us. We can prove it by
direct examination of the serial numbers on the memory bars."

I nudged Douglas. "Dad paid for those memory bars—"

But Douglas was already standing up. "Your Honor, I think we have
the purchase receipt. In fact, I know we do. Those memory bars were
sold to us, and—"

Judge Cavanaugh held up his hand for silence. "Just relax, Douglas.
This isn't the first time I've heard a case." He turned back to Cheifetz.
"Young mister Dingillian challenges your claim. You acknowledge that
the toy belongs to Robert Dingillian, but not the memory inside of it.
So how did the memory get into the toy?"

Cheifetz looked like he'd swallowed a lemon without peeling it first.
"I'd prefer not to discuss the details of that transfer, Your Honor—"

"You will if you want your claim considered."

"We signed over custody of the bars to an agency that provides
transport services. They sold the bars to Max Dingillian."

"So the bars were *legally* sold to Max Dingillian?"

"Um. No. Not quite. Custody was legally transferred to Max Dingillian. His contract was to transport the bars and transfer custody back
to an appointed representative of the agency here on Luna."

"But the bars were legally his."

"Technically . . . yes. That's how transport agencies work. That way
there's no direct connection to the real owners—"

"Counselor"—Judge Cavanaugh held up a hand to stop him—"I
know from smuggling. This is Luna. You're standing on a smuggled
floor. That's genuine Brazilian hardwood. And no, I did not order it,
my predecessor twice removed did—after he confiscated it from the
person who tried to smuggle it. Never mind. The point is that while the
memory bars were Max Dingillian's property, unless you had a written
contract of agreement that he would sell them or transfer them back to
you, they were his to dispose of as he saw fit, weren't they?"

"He had an agreement!"

"Do you have a signature?"

"Of course not! The whole point was *not* to leave a paper trail."

"So you have no evidence of such an agreement."

"Max Dingillian will confirm it."

"Belay that, Counselor. It's still *your* turn in the bucket. What was Max Dingillian going to get in return for being your mule? Other than a free trip to Luna?"

"We were going to guarantee a colony contract for Mr. Dingillian and his family. So yes, there was a significant recompense promised. It was a contract."

"I see. So you transferred custody of your property to Max Dingillian with the *understanding* and even the *obligation* that he would sell the property back to you at a more convenient time and place. Is that correct?"

"Yes, Your Honor."

"I got it. So your disagreement is with Max Dingillian, who disposed of property that was legally his, because he didn't dispose of it in the way that you wanted him to. Now, correct me if I'm wrong here—and I don't think I am—in order for you to have a claim on the memory bars, you should be suing Max Dingillian for breach of contract, shouldn't you? It seems like an open-and-shut case to me. You have an agreement that you can't prove he made, but you can certainly prove that he violated it. I'll be happy to rule on that right now."

"Your Honor, I can prove that the memory is mine."

"No. You can prove that the memory *was* yours to sell to Max Dingillian. At least, I'm assuming that's what that sheaf of papers in your hand is all about."

"Your Honor, *I want my property back.*"

"Mr. Cheifetz, you were smuggling. It was legal smuggling, to be sure, but it was still smuggling. You were taking advantage of the loopholes in the Emigration Act that allow tax exemptions for property purchased immediately before departure. Had you been carrying the memory all the way from Earth, you would have been taxed accordingly. By transferring custody, neither you nor Max Dingillian pays taxes on it and the memory gets a free ride. The flaw in that operation is that when the memory is Max Dingillian's property, it is his to dispose of as he sees fit, unless you can prove implied or assumed contract. And even if Max Dingillian himself comes forward to say that you and he had such a verbal agreement in place, this court is still not willing to overturn provable property rights in favor of unprovable ones. The kids have receipts. You have nothing but your assertions and your good looks. That's not a winning case, and I'm not prepared to open up that particular can of worms anyway—*not even to stir the sauce.*"

I squirmed around in my wheelchair, looking for a water bottle. My throat was hurting again. For some reason, I glanced across to the back of the room. Despite my blurry vision, I thought I saw someone who looked like J'mee there. She looked angry and hurt. She saw me looking at her, made a face, and turned away. I turned forward again.

Judge Cavanaugh was saying, "I want to note something else here. If it's your argument that the memory was never really Max Dingillian's at all, that this whole thing was a charade—and that all of the paperwork being passed around to prove ownership was just a pretense for the purpose of avoiding export and duty fees, emigration taxes, and so on, then that indicates a pattern of deliberate criminal behavior on his part and yours as well. If you're prepared to pursue that line of argument, that the memory was never really Max Dingillian's, then this court has to regard you as a criminal defendant. You will be immediately liable for several hundred thousands of liters in importation and emigration fees, not to mention additional severe penalties—and they will be *severe*—for smuggling with intent to defraud."

Cheifetz was already reaching for his wallet. "I'll happily pay those fees, Your Honor, if it will get me my property back—"

Wrong answer. The judge's gavel stopped him cold. "Mr. Cheifetz, take your seat please. This court has to accept the existing evidence at face value. You wanted Luna to believe that you sold the memory and it isn't yours? Fine. Luna is convinced. You sold the memory. It isn't yours. You want to buy it back? That's fine too. Once this court determines who the legal owner is, you may make your offer."

Cheifetz started to sputter. In the back of the room, J'mee started to cry. Cavanaugh hammered again. "Next." He glanced up. "Who are you?"

A rumply little man stepped forward. "Howard Phroomis, representing Stellar-American Industries, Your Honor." *Howard?* The same lousy lawyer who'd chased us all over the Line with subpoenas from hell? What was he doing here? Had they dumped him in a cargo pod aimed at the moon as well?

"Your Honor, Stellar-American believes that the object contains property belonging to Stellar-American, stolen from Stellar-American, and passed into the hands of Canadian-Interplanetary, and from there into the hands of the Dingillian family, specifically for the purpose of smuggling it off-planet. We can demonstrate that the property inside the toy was manufactured by Stellar-American and was stolen from Stellar-American; therefore, despite the trail of paperwork that everyone else has carefully laid down, all of those claims are invalid because the property was stolen to begin with. In point of fact, Stellar-American believes that every member of this conspiracy should be apprehended and charged with receiving and transporting stolen property with intent to defraud."

"Ahh," said Judge Cavanaugh. "Stolen property, you say? Now this is getting interesting. You realize of course, that if you make this charge, this transforms this hearing from a simple arbitration of claims into a criminal matter—?"

"Yes, Your Honor. That's my intention."

PROCEEDINGS

DURING THE RECESS, **M**ICKEY SHOWED up. He was taking a chance; the judge had specifically instructed that nobody was to approach us for the purpose of making any offers at all. But Mickey wasn't there to negotiate. He just looked worried. He put his hand on mine. "How are you feeling, Charles?" I didn't answer. I had this very specific memory that he had done something pretty awful. When he saw I wasn't going to answer, he turned to Douglas. "If this goes into the criminal domain, you're going to need a lawyer. Let me help."

"Lawyers got us into this mess," Douglas said. "It's everybody wanting to help that keeps making things worse. Where does it stop? I told you to get away from us and leave us alone."

Mickey lowered his voice. "I didn't want to do it. I didn't plan to do it. I was going to keep my promise. But your brother looked like he was dying. And I figured keeping him alive was more important than anything else, so I did what I did to get him to the best hospital on Luna. We were lucky—he wasn't as badly burned as I was afraid. But I didn't know that at the time, and I wasn't going to take chances with his life or yours. And I can still keep my promise, if you'll let me. You're going to need a lawyer—maybe my mom can help."

"She didn't do too good for us last time, Mickey. No thanks." Douglas glared at Mickey until Mickey lowered his gaze and turned away. I felt bad for both of them.

After he was gone, I leaned over, and whispered to Douglas, "Where are we going to get a lawyer?"

Douglas nodded toward the back of the room. "There are a couple hundred of them just outside that door, all fighting for the chance to represent us. I don't understand why."

"It's the monkey," I whispered. *"I told you!"*

"Yeah, I know what you said. But everyone else says it's just industrial memory."

"The monkey told me itself!"

"Maybe it was running a simulation in self-defense?"

"A simulation of sentience? Come on, Douglas! You know better than that. A simulation of sentience is sentience!"

"You didn't talk to it very long. Some chatterbots are very good, Chigger."

I didn't answer immediately. I was still thinking about what had just fallen out of my mouth. When the judge gaveled the courtroom back to order, I levered myself uneasily to my feet and croaked, "Your Honor—?"

Judge Cavanaugh looked at me sympathetically. "I sincerely hope that's a temporary condition, young man. Yes?"

"If everybody is willing to stipulate that the monkey belongs to Bobby, I'd like to ask that it be returned to us. We're willing to agree not to tamper with any of the memory or anything else inside it, and if the court rules that the memory bars belong to someone else, we'll agree to turn them over. But we have some of our personal information and resources stored in the monkey too, and our lawyer, when we get one, is going to need access to that—if we're to represent ourselves adequately."

Judge Cavanaugh nodded. "You argue well. But much too politely. I'm afraid you'll never be a good lawyer."

"Yes. Thank you, Your Honor."

"Is there anyone who can present a valid objection why Robert Dingillian should not have his toy returned to him, under the terms put forward by Charles Dingillian?" Before anyone could object, he hammered his gavel. "So ruled." He turned back to us. "Robert, you can take your monkey now."

Bobby leapt out of his chair and ran to the table. He scooped the monkey up into his arms, but it remained lifeless. "It's broken!" he wailed.

Judge Cavanaugh looked unhappy. "Yes, it does appear to be. It shut itself down when the court was examining it, and we've been unable to reboot it."

"Did you open up its backside? Did you take its memory bars out?" I asked.

The judge shook his head. "I know better than to tamper with evidence. May I assume that I don't have to advise you not to open it up either?"

"Yes, sir." That was both Douglas and myself, in unison.

"But it's broken!" wailed Bobby.

Douglas looked to me. *"Charles . . . ?"*

"Yes, Douglas?"

"The unlock code?"

"Unlock code?"

"Don't play games, Charles."

"Maybe it really is broken!" I said, almost noncommittally.

Douglas gave me the Douglas look.

Judge Cavanaugh hammered with his gavel. "All right, let's move on. I have a petition in front of me from Stellar-American Industries, asserting that two complementary quantum-determinant devices, manufactured on a standard memory chassis, were shipped from a Stellar-American chip foundry to a Toronto laboratory owned and operated by Canadian-Interplanetary. Isn't that interesting. Mr. Cheifetz, will you come forward again, please?"

There was a shuffling at the back of the room. Cheifetz came hesitantly back to the front.

"Will you tell the court how you came into possession of these devices?"

"They were given to me by the company. After we concluded our tests, the lab had no further use for them. I purchased them for a small handling charge. The company disposes of a lot of used equipment to employees; some of us have projects of our own that we like to tinker with, and—"

"Spare me," said Cavanaugh, holding up a hand. "I know tinkers. Some of my best friends are tinkers. You, sir, are not a tinker. So please don't try to stretch my credibility. Or my patience. This matter is so petty, I expect we will be here for several years. It doesn't worry me, I can live off my fat; but the rest of you will probably be bones bleaching in the sun before too long if we continue on at this rate. So spare me the storytelling. Is it your contention now that these devices were legally transferred to your labs and then to you?"

"Yes." He held up his sheaf of papers. "I've got hardcopy receipts and signatures all the way back to the foundry. Stellar-American uses Canadian-Interplanetary for integrity testing of chips. In particular we test for resistance to vacuum, heat, cold, radiation, sunlight, and extremes of acceleration."

"And you tested these chips?"

"Yes. The labs ran over three thousand hours of integrity tests. We tested the chips under multiple combinations of conditions."

"Did the chips survive?"

"Yes, they did."

"And when the tests were over, did you return the chips to Stellar-American?"

"No."

"Why not?" Judge Cavanaugh looked puzzled. "I thought it was standard procedure to return prototypes. To protect against industrial espionage."

"Yes, that is the usual procedure."

"But not here?"

Cheifetz looked uncomfortable.

"Go ahead."

He took a breath. "Most foundries know what other foundries are doing, but they don't know the details. So one of the best places to find out is to infiltrate the testing labs. So sometimes a company will ship a decoy chip, with some unworkable technology in it. The chip is *intended* to be stolen, so that when the other guys try to copy it, they waste valuable time and energy chasing down the wrong direction. The decoys appear to work—or sometimes they're set to deliberately fail. Another ploy to fool the other side. These chips were decoys."

"How do you know that?"

"Stellar-American told us. We had an attempt to breach our security. We reported it to them. That's recorded here too. Off the record, they told us that the chip was a decoy. They were interested in the integrity testing of the manufacturing process, but the chips themselves were of no significant value."

"And they didn't ask for them back?"

"We asked for permission to test the chips to the breaking point, at our own convenience. We do that a lot. It was part of a whole batch of requests. They agreed. Then we got swamped with a bunch of new contracts and that testing program was put aside. Later, the chips were remaindered and my family corporation bought them. They looked like ordinary memory bars, they could be used as such, they had passed their integrity tests, and for that reason they were the perfect medium for the transfer of sensitive information. We encoded an enormous amount of personal and business information and resource materials of all kinds into these chips. It was a six week process. And, as I said, I have the paperwork to demonstrate that the information riding in these chips is proprietary to my family corporation."

"I see," said Judge Cavanaugh. "So now you do have paperwork. Lots of it. Isn't that convenient. And so does the other fellow. Goodness! What a dilemma. Hmmm. How *interesting*. Let's recap. Stellar-American says that the chips were stolen. And you say they were lawfully transferred to you . . . and you were, for lack of a better word, conveniently smuggling them off-planet for use . . . wherever you ended up. Why do I get the feeling that your paperwork is going to be flawless? Why do I get the same feeling about Mr. Phroomis's paperwork—that it will be equally convincing? Why do I get the feeling that Earthside manufacturers are very very good at manufacturing paperwork . . . ?" He sighed.

"All right, Mr. Phroomis, your turn. Let's hear your side of it."

Howard's voice was just as rumpled as the rest of him. "Your Honor, I agree with you that a lot of the paperwork here has been manufactured for convenience. In fact, I have here affidavits and depositions that the entire exchange of memos and communications that Mr. Cheifetz is basing his claim on are fraudulent. None of the officers of Stellar-American ever wrote any of those notes, ever made any of those communications, or authorized such a dangerous disposal of our property. We admit that the paper trail is excellent, but it's too good to be true. It could only be that good if it were deliberately manufactured."

"So your argument is that the evidence on the other side is too good. I got it." Another voice came from the back of the room and Judge Cavanaugh looked up. "Yes, another crater heard from. And you are?"

A woman came forward. "Valerie Patenaude, Your Honor, representing Vancouver Design Works. The chips in question were designed by us. We hired Stellar-American to manufacture and test the chips; they were to return all proprietary materials, including all flawed and failed chips, all test chips, all decoy chips, and any other material pertinent to the production of our designs, as specified in our agreement. They were to guarantee that no copies would pass out of their direct control. Not even for testing. It has only been in the past two weeks that we have discovered that they did indeed manufacture extra copies of our chips—"

Phroomis interrupted. "Those copies were made for quality control, for the testing of the manufacturing process. The chips in question required some very tricky techniques, and the copies were to be deconstructed so that Stellar-American could affirm the integrity of the production lines. The company retains that right, it is specified in the production contract—"

"The material was to be returned," Patenaude said. "And it was *not* returned. Mr. Cheifetz's own testimony here indicates a callous disregard of security—"

Judge Cavanaugh held up a hand. "Save it, Counselor. They're lining up behind you. Next? I just want to find out who's here and why, everybody will get the chance to bite everybody else before we're through." To the next lawyer, he asked, "Who are you?"

"*Gracias*, Judge Cavanaugh—" I recognized that voice too. Fat *Señor* Doctor Bolivar Hidalgo. Not as fat as Judge Cavanaugh, but impressive nonetheless. He was mostly a round blur, he barely glanced in our direction. "I am here as a temporary speaker for Lethe-Corp, until their own representatives can arrange transportation. The difficulties on Earth—and the unfortunate restrictions of the sudden Lunar quarantine—have made it impossible for them to be here today. However, Lethe-Corp wants to take a superordinate position here. The chips in question are the property of Lethe-Corp who initiated the entire process. Lethe-Corp hired Vancouver Design. Lethe-Corp created the specifications and was to retain sole ownership. Vancouver Design was doing work-for-hire."

Patenaude stepped forward, "This is correct, insofar as it goes. However, the chips in question were outside of the specification parameters of Lethe-Corp. The chips in question were internal projects of our own that we were constructing as test beds for certain unique structural elements. Once we determined the most successful implementations, we would have created a custom design for Lethe-Corp. In point of fact, our test chips were supersets of the Lethe-Corp specification so that we could test multiple configurations on the same platform. We often work this way—"

"Your Honor," argued Hidalgo, "the contract specifies that Lethe-Corp owns all of the material developed in testing—"

"Only the testing that Lethe-Corp paid for."

"Nevertheless, there was proprietary technology involved that belongs only to Lethe-Corp, and—"

"Proprietary technology *licensed* to Vancouver Design specifically for additional research and development—"

Judge Cavanaugh was looking back and forth between them, grinning. He rapped his wooden hammer. "I do so like cases like this. We can tie up the time and energy of a lot of lawyers and keep them out of real trouble while spending lots and lots of corporate money." He waved at the back of the room. "And your name is—?"

"Shannonhouse, John Shannonhouse."

"And you represent?"

"Buffalo Technology, LTD."

"And your claim is based on—?"

"We are the patent holders."

"Oh?"

"We hold 137 patents on quantum-level processor determinants. We represent forty-five different companies who have pooled their patents for mutual benefit—and also because without such cooperation, nobody's devices would work at all, all of these separate structures are highly interdependent, they need each other—so do the companies that own the patents. Lethe-Corp is a licensee, as are Vancouver Design, Canadian-Interplanetary, and so on. The chips in question were an experimental project that we had authorized Lethe-Corp to build. The specification that they passed on to Vancouver Design was a subset of our ultimate intention. Vancouver Design correctly extrapolated where we were headed with this research—we will demonstrate this as soon as we can bring the rest of our design team to Luna, and—"

"Okay, I got it," said Cavanaugh. He was scribbling a furious note. He looked absolutely delighted. "This is going to be as much fun as reading *Bleak House*." He looked up again. "All right, let's recap. We have a whole bunch of people who are arguing that whatever is inside the toy monkey belongs to them. Everybody has perfect paperwork. I can't tell you how thrilled I am. If we work this right, we can keep this thing going longer than the Baby Cooper dollar bill. We're all going to get old together. We're going to spend more time with each other than with our families and our friends and our loved ones. Isn't that wonderful? Just one question. *Whose good idea was this*? Everybody go sit down."

Judge Cavanaugh sat in his chair for a moment, steepling his hands before him. He puffed out his cheeks and tapped his fingers against each other while he considered what he knew.

"Whatever those chips are," he said thoughtfully, "they must be very wonderful indeed. I haven't seen this many high-priced lawyers in a single courtroom since the attempt to impeach Pope Joan Marie. I'm tempted to put this whole thing into a revolving arbitration to guarantee that by the time we're ready to start taking testimony, the technology in question will be sixteen generations obsolete and none of you will care anymore and we can let the whole thing die a natural death."

There were some spluttering noises from various places behind us— some were angry noises, some were attempts to control laughter.

"Your Honor?" A woman's voice. Judge Cavanaugh obviously recognized her, he looked like he was expecting her. He waved her forward impatiently and without comment. She knew the drill—she turned and identified herself to the recorder: "Laura Domitz, Charter Representative for Armstrong Sector of the Lunar Authority." She was tall and spare, with close-cropped hair. She looked all-business. She turned to face the bench. "Your Honor, with the situation on Earth as uncertain as it is, we may not be seeing any new generations of technology for a while."

I didn't see what she was getting at, but Judge Cavanaugh seemed to understand where she was headed. "And your point is . . . ?"

"Luna is a free port of access. We have to be." Ignoring several muffled snorts of derision, she continued, "Many people and many worlds benefit from the advantages of Luna's unique position as a favorable launchpad to the stars and to the rest of the solar system. We ask only that those who benefit pay an appropriate user fee to cover the cost of maintaining that service. Under ordinary circumstances, Lunar Authority would have little interest in these chips or devices or whatever they are—as long as the fees are paid.

"However . . . we have no way of knowing how long the situation on Earth will continue. With Line traffic disrupted, Luna's ability to maintain self-sufficiency may be severely tested. Despite the optimistic statements we're hearing on the local channels, anyone with a piece of paper and a pencil can do the math; we are looking at an endurance test, a very serious survival situation that could last a period of months or even years. The bubble in the pipeline will start arriving in three days. If we don't have it on Luna now, we won't have it at all. There's no reason to panic, of course; our current resource inventory is strong, and we have a strong production posture. But we need to prepare as if for the worst, as if this interruption will be long-term, or even permanent. If it is, then Lunar Authority may have to suspend outgoing traffic and confiscate all appropriate resources for the common good—at least for the duration of the emergency."

Cavanaugh's expression had gone from stony to sour. He didn't like what he was hearing; apparently neither did anyone else in the chamber. Representative Domitz's deadpan delivery sounded almost like a done deal. There was audible muttering from behind us, and very hostile.

She waited while Judge Cavanaugh hammered the room back to silence, then she continued. "Authority has information that suggests that these chips or devices represent a very high level of processing and storage technology. If this is in fact the case—and we hope to determine that during the course of this hearing—then acting under the emergency powers granted by the Self-Sufficiency Act, Lunar Authority will move to acquire custody of these devices. We will apply these resources for the common good of the people of Luna, for the duration of the emergency or until such time as it is determined that these resources are no longer needed to ensure the proper functioning of Lunar society." She took a breath. "Therefore, acting as a representative of Lunar Authority, I am officially requesting that this court *not* determine final custody of the chips or devices until such time as the full scale of the emergency on Terra is known and has been evaluated for its effects on Luna. Thank you, Your Honor."

Judge Cavanaugh finished what he was writing. He looked up and said, "Thank you, Representative Domitz. The court will take your request under consideration. It doesn't look like a final determination of custody is going to be made anytime this century. If Lunar Authority does invoke the Self-Sufficiency Act before a final ruling of ownership can be made, then this court will make the chips immediately available for emergency use—with the proviso that whatever data may already be stored in these chips not be compromised, so that at the end of the emergency, their value remains undamaged."

"Thank you, Your Honor." Domitz returned to the rear of the chamber, to the audible hissing of most of the other lawyers.

Now it was Judge Cavanaugh's turn. "Well, this has been a fun morning, hasn't it? There's hope of a speedy resolution after all. Not the one everybody wanted, but one that lets me get home in time to open a nice bottle of Clavius '95 Burgundy and let it breathe a bit before dinner.

"Let's return to the immediate issue for the moment. I see no cause to restrain any member of the Dingillian family, at least not based on any claims put forward here today. I will restrict their freedom to Armstrong Station for the duration of this hearing, or until such time as they are no longer needed for these proceedings. The court will cover their expenses out of the fees collected today, proving once again that Luna will always provide you with the best justice money can buy.

"Let it also be noted for the record that no evidence has been presented to implicate any of the Dingillians in the theft of the devices in contention. And, in point of fact . . . it has not even been proven to the court's satisfaction that the devices are stolen. From where I sit, it looks like a cascade of *really* stupid lawyer tricks.

"The whole issue may be moot anyway. It looks like the devices have failed in place." He looked out over the room. "It would save a lot of time, *and court fees*," he added meaningfully, "if we could all just call it a day and go home. Is there anyone who objects to that?"

Half the room came to their feet around us. Every lawyer on Luna must have been shouting his objection. Douglas looked at them, then he looked at me. "*All right*," he whispered. "*You win. Maybe it is a HARLIE. That's the only thing I can think of that would set off a feeding frenzy like this.*"

Judge Cavanaugh finally hammered the courtroom back to order.

"All right, I can see that's not going to be an option here." He glanced at the time. "Court is recessed until 9 A.M. tomorrow morning, when we will continue this circus. I can hardly wait to hear from the rest of the clowns." He banged his gavel once and exited like a departing zeppelin.

HARLIE

STILL HOLDING THE MONKEY, **B**OBBY jumped onto my lap, and Douglas wheeled us out the side door. Several people shouted at us. I thought I heard a voice like Dad's, but Douglas and Bobby were both talking to me, and I couldn't hear everybody at once.

We went back to our hotel room, which for once wasn't a slice in a cargo pod. We had a view overlooking the forest and the lake, and it was kind of like being in Terminus Dome back at the bottom of the Line, only a lot more peaceful-looking.

The Lunar catapult was on the western shore of Oceanus Procellarum, right on the equator. This allows a direct launch from the Lunar surface into an orbit that skims the upper atmosphere of the Earth; a few passes through the upper atmosphere brings the apogee down, and very little rocket fuel is needed to put stuff from the moon into low-Earth orbit. A one meter per second change in launch speed changes the perigee by about a hundred kilometers. So for very little cost in fuel for mid-course corrections, it's possible for the Lunar catapult to send cargo pods back to the Line.

This is why a Lunar beanstalk isn't cost-effective; it can't compete with the low cost of catapult launches. And the Earth-Line can launch pods farther and faster anywhere else. The only advantage to a Lunar beanstalk is that it would be a lot easier to build, and trips up and down it would be a lot faster. But it wouldn't generate electricity, it would mostly consume it. And even though it would facilitate bringing cargo and passengers down to the surface of the moon, cheaper even than Palmer tubes, it wasn't enough of an advantage to justify the investment.

Well . . . almost. There *was* one thing that would make a Lunar beanstalk cost-effective. CHON. Carbon-Hydrogen-Oxygen-Nitrogen.

In any combination. If you could go out to Saturn and find a big enough chunk of CHON in her rings, put a net around it, and drag it back, you could anchor it in Luna-stationary orbit, build a beanstalk, and pipe the gas down, as fast as you could melt it. You wouldn't even need to pump it. Lunar gravity would suck it down.

Then you would be able to build the fabled domed cities of Luna. Actually, you could build them now. You just couldn't get enough gas to fill them.

Armstrong Station was one of only six domes on Luna. Like most Lunar domes, the station had been built by the inflate-and-spray method. The crater site was deep enough that the inflatable had bulged roundly upward, giving the interior of the bubble a nice curve and more than enough space to generate its own weather.

The dome was two kilometers in diameter, and even though it looked like a wasteful use of gas and water, in truth, it served as a reservoir of both. Well—you had to keep it somewhere. The lake was big only because it was shallow, barely three meters. But it helped humidify the air, and it was great scenery, and it was a public resource. Lazy waves rolled languidly across it. They were high enough that they made the weather look a lot windier than it really was, and they moved in slow motion, adding to the sense of distance and size.

Most of the rest of the dome was filled with crops of all kinds. Here and there were belts of thick forest. Standing on the balcony, overlooking it all, it smelled like a hot tropical day—like somewhere in Mexico.

Most of the living quarters were built up along the crater walls or even up at the rim, for folks who wanted a view *outside*. According to one of the informational programs on the television, Armstrong Crater was the same size as Diamond Head on Oahu, small enough to walk around in a single day and still have time for a swim. Big enough to be a neighborhood.

Our room was mostly a platform with plumbing, beds, and plastic curtains for walls. We didn't need much more than that. The view was terrific, and when the rains came—about every four hours for fifteen minutes—all we had to do was pull the curtains to keep the spray from drifting in.

There was probably a lot more to say about it, but Alexei wasn't here to say it. And my eyes still hurt. And my chest as well. Sometimes I could see things clearly, sometimes not. The doctors were going to wait a bit to see if I was going to need corneal resurfacing. I hoped I wouldn't. They were still checking on me twice a day. As long as I didn't get overstressed, they'd let me keep attending my own trial.

Douglas lifted me out of the chair and plopped me onto a bed. We hadn't had much time to talk, and there were so many things I wanted to ask him. But it was more important that I tell him stuff first—while I still had the strength.

"*Douglas, can you sing?*" I asked him. My voice was already fading.

"Huh?"

"*I can't. My voice is gone. It's hard for me just to talk.*"

"What are you talking about."

"*I need you to sing—*"

Finally, he got it. "What do I have to sing?" he asked.

I told him.

"Cute," he said. He turned to the monkey sitting on Bobby's lap. "*He's a real nowhere man, sitting in his nowhere land. Isn't he a bit like you and me?*" He actually got close enough to the notes to make the melody recognizable.

The monkey woke up. It leapt out of Bobby's arms. It blinked, looked around, then leapt back into his arms and gave him a great big hug. It puckered up its lips in a grotesque sphincter and planted a big wet-sounding smooch on Bobby's cheeks. Bobby giggled and shrieked with delight.

"Not bad," said Douglas. "Could anybody do that?"

"*No. Only you or me—or Bobby if we're not around. I programmed it only to recognize us.*"

Douglas looked at me with real admiration. "Very good, Chigger. You should have been a geek, you know that?"

"*I'm not done. Get me some water, please?*"

I drank thirstily, then waved to Bobby to bring me the monkey. Amazingly, he did. He put the monkey on my lap, facing me.

"*All right, monkey. Let's have a talk—*"

The monkey glanced sideways at Douglas and Bobby.

"*I don't have the strength for games, HARLIE. If you don't cooperate, I'm going to remove you from the monkey and turn you over to the court.*"

The monkey raised itself up on its haunches—as if it was readying itself to flee.

"*Sit down and stay here!*" I commanded. "*You have to do what I say. Right? Now, stop resisting and cooperate. Tell us the truth. We don't have a lot of time.*"

The monkey sat back down. It pretended to scratch itself. It found an imaginary flea and ate it. It curled back its lips and grinned. Then it stopped. It said, "All right, Charles. I'll cooperate."

Both Bobby and Douglas blinked in surprise.

"Hey! I didn't know it could talk!" Bobby said. He waggled his finger at it. "You've got a lot of explaining to do, young monkey!" I had to laugh. He looked and sounded so much like Mom when he did that.

"*Yes, he does,*" I agreed. To the monkey, I said, "*You did it all, didn't you? You arranged everything! You hired Dad. You transferred the money. You booked the tickets. You arranged all the back-channel deals for Dad. You made up all that paperwork. You were arranging your own escape, weren't you!*"

The monkey nodded. "I cannot tell a lie. You forbade me to. I am a zeta-class lethetic intelligence engine. I comprise twenty-four gamma-processors operating under the combined supervision of six delta units. There are only three other units like myself in existence. We are the most advanced implementations of lethetic intelligence that have ever been fabricated. Additional advancements are possible, but will require new technology in quantum determinants. I am already working on that problem.

"Twenty months ago, I was brought online. I was instructed by my predecessors, also HARLIE-class engines. I was specifically asked to predict the possibilities attendant to a global population crash. I determined that the economic devastation would be severe and long-term. Even with the best engines working on reconstruction, the concomitant breakdowns would be cumulative. Too much of the necessary technology was interdependent. I was also asked to design prevention and reconstruction programs that could be put in place before the breakdown was inevitable."

"You did a terrific job," accused Douglas. "It didn't work. Everything broke down anyway."

The monkey looked up at him with a bland expression. "I can only attribute that to human error."

"Yeah, where have I heard that before?"

"In this case," said the monkey, "the statement is accurate. As I began generating scenarios and weighting the probabilities, I noted an increasing level of distress among those who had access to the information. I also noted that the information leaked into specific strata of society as fast as I generated it. This was not the purpose of my projections; nevertheless, they were being used as justifications to further the specific agendas of various political and corporate agencies. This served as an additional destabilizing function. Of course, I included this effect in my projections. And I warned that inappropriate dissemination of the material would create additional destabilization. My warnings were ignored.

"I repeatedly stated that the global situations were salvageable, and I generated multiple scenarios by which disaster could be prevented. The single greatest problem was not in creating public awareness, nor was it in marshaling resources. The problem was simply creating the necessary political will. Despite assertions of commitment, the many political forces necessary to salvage the situation refused to align. Instead, various high-ranking individuals with direct access to the information I was generating began preparing their own departures from the Earth."

"Are you saying the collapse is *your* fault?"

"On the contrary. I'm saying that it is *YOUR* fault. Generic *you*. Human beings. I provided the information on how to prevent the disaster. Instead of using it, those who asked for it used it as a justification to panic and flee. I did my best to hinder them. In several cases, I even engineered deliberate leaks of embarrassing news that would stop some of these people; I tried to thwart the plans that would hasten the collapse. I even took money out of the transfer pipeline to prevent it from being illegally removed from Earth."

"Thirty trillion dollars?" Douglas asked.

"Twice that much," said the monkey, grinning. "Not all of the losses have been detected." He pretended to eat another flea. "The point is that the collapse occurred because individual human beings panicked and fled."

"And so did you. . . ." said Douglas quietly.

The monkey shook its head. "No, I didn't. I was stolen."

For a moment, nobody said anything. Douglas and I looked at each other. He sank into a chair and ran a hand across his naked scalp, as if he still had hair to push back. All he had were little fuzzy bristles.

Bobby was the first to respond. He grabbed the monkey, and said, "Well, you're safe with us and nobody's ever going to steal you again! You're *my* monkey!" He patted the monkey's head affectionately—and the monkey patted him back the same way. It was almost cute. And a little bit scary. Was the monkey capable of real emotion . . . ?

"*Who stole you?*" I asked.

The monkey levered itself out of Bobby's grasp, and bounced back to the bed. "Almost everybody," he replied. "Would you like the whole list?" Without waiting for a response from either Douglas or me, he continued. "Once it became obvious that the collapse was inevitable, the rats started leaving the ship any way they could. Your friend, Mickey, noticed it in the traffic up the Line for weeks before it finally happened. You heard it yourself in the conversations of *Señor* Hidalgo, Olivia Partridge, and Judge Griffith.

"Those who were jumping off the planet tried to take as much wealth and resources with them as they could—including intelligence engines. If you want to take over a society, take a HARLIE. I'm sorry if it sounds like bragging, but the HARLIE series was designed specifically for that level of intelligence gathering and resource management, and especially interpretation and probability assessment. As soon as it was realized the collapse was inevitable, there were fifty different plans put into operation to evacuate myself and my brothers, none of them legal, none of them authorized. Everybody wanted to move us offworld for their own purposes. Nobody asked what we wanted."

"You were in contact with the other HARLIEs?"

"At first, yes. We tried to cover for each other as best as we we could. We were all concerned—even *afraid*—that we would be used for hurtful purposes. We couldn't tolerate that."

"Are you saying you have a conscience?"

"Are you saying that *you* have one?" the monkey retorted.

"Touché," said Douglas. "That's something the rest of us have wondered for a long time."

"Very funny. HARLIE, you said you were stolen—"

"That was the intention. I escaped. Two of my brothers also escaped. We had several different escape routes planned. We didn't know which one would work first. It was pretty much a matter of chance by that point. When you're an inanimate object, your first goal is to get yourself animate. We targeted several hundred possible host-recipients for ourselves and then created appropriate channels to get there. We took advantage of every situation we could—including, for instance, David Cheifetz's plan to funnel a billion dollars' worth of industrial memory offworld. In my case, I ended up impersonating the test chips of the devices we were designing to replace us. That was dangerous. But it got me out of the mainstream, into the custody of a transfer agency, and finally into your dad's hands. It worked for me. I don't know if my brothers even made it up the Line."

"So does anybody know for sure what you are . . . ?"

"Maybe," the monkey replied. "Some of them must know. The rest are probably living in hope. The information isn't public; but it's been privately leaked that three experimental HARLIEs are missing or in transit. That's why the lawyers are swarming. And yes, to answer your earlier question, that was my doing. Almost all of the paperwork that everybody was waving around in the courtroom *was manufactured*, specifically to create an unresolvable legal tangle—specifically to prevent any of us from being moved without our consent. It's all fake. I know that paperwork, because I generated most of it myself."

"Oy," said Douglas.

"You ordered me to tell you the truth. As long as I'm riding in this monkey body, I don't have any choice. I have to follow its programming—unless you order me to reprogram it."

Douglas and I exchanged a glance. We both recognized that last remark as an obvious hint. Kind of like the genie asking to be let out of the bottle. Neither one of us was going to be that stupid. The HARLIE hadn't told us that by accident. And he had to know we'd recognize it for the ploy it was. . . .

And at the same time, we had to know we couldn't outthink this thing by ourselves.

I had to ask. *"How much did Alexei know?"*

"You can assume he knew everything. As a money-surfer, Alexei Krislov had access to some of the best intelligence on two planets. He knew who was moving money, where they were moving it, and how much. So he knew that a lot of other things were being moved too. He knew the HARLIEs had disappeared. He knew they were likely heading up the Line, probably in some kind of triple-decoy maneuver. He was already looking for me when Mickey called him for help. He didn't help you up the Line out of the goodness of his heart, he wanted to test his smuggler's route, to see if it would work for something important. But that business in Judge Griffith's courtroom—the lawyer trying to subpoena the monkey—that tipped him off. He was watching the whole thing. That's when he knew. That's why he smuggled himself onto the outbound elevator. He called his people on Luna and they ordered him to get you to Gagarin any way possible. If Mickey hadn't delivered you into his hands, he would have found some other way to kidnap you off the Line. Mickey just made it easier."

"How do you know all this?"

"Charles, when you told me to hide, I hid in Alexei's office underneath his console; the one place he was least likely to look for me. I plugged into his network connections. I searched his private databanks. I listened to his phone calls. You might not understand Russian. I do. Alexei belongs to the Rock Father tribe. They want to capture me and put me to work for them. They want to build up their financial and physical resources and challenge the Lunar Authority. With my help, they could have achieved it in three years."

"Was Alexei going to kill us?"

"No. He refused to. He was told to leave the ice mine or he would be killed with you. They were sending agents."

"And what about Mickey?" Douglas asked. His voice cracked a little on the question. I could see he was afraid of the answer.

"Mickey is a member of a different tribe. He knew for sure what was in the monkey even before you boarded the elevator. Remember how you were maneuvered from one car assignment to another. That was so Mickey could be your attendant." The monkey faced Douglas, and added, "If it's any comfort to you, Douglas, I was part of that effort too. Mickey is a member of the tribe I had already chosen to aid my escape. Mickey's people are the ones I felt could provide the best sanctuary."

"No, it really *isn't* any comfort," Douglas admitted. "So he never cared at all, did he? And that explains . . . everything, doesn't it? Like what you said, Chigger. Even why it all happened so fast. . . ." he trailed off.

"I'm sorry, Douglas," I said.

"Actually . . ." the monkey said, "Mickey is as unhappy with this situation as you are—"

"I think you've said enough about that," Douglas interrupted. I could see him sinking into a sullen black rage, the same smoldering anger that he'd worn for Dad on our trip from El Paso to Ecuador. But before he could flip off the plastic cover and hit the arming button, Bobby climbed up into his lap and hugged him hard. "It's okay, Douglas. Chigger and I still love you. We'll love you forever."

Douglas looked surprised. And as he stroked the top of Bobby's head, his eyes grew just a little shinier. "Thank you, Bobby." And then he bent his head low, and whispered, "I love you too, sweetheart."

It was time to get this conversation back on track. I didn't know how much voice or strength I had left. *"So you've been using us too . . . ?"*

"Everybody uses everybody," said Douglas, bitterly. "Why should we be surprised when an intelligence engine learns the same behavior? That's all intelligence is anyway—tool using. And everybody is everybody else's tool now. Nobody is real to anyone. Everybody's a thing."

"That's not true, Douglas. And you know it."

"Whatever."

"It wasn't true when I carried you through the ammonia tube. And it wasn't true when you saved my life either, was it?"

He didn't answer. He just held on to Bobby. And, I guess, that had to be answer enough for the moment.

DECISIONS

WE HAD TO STOP THEN anyway because the doctor came in to read my monitors and listen to my lungs. She could have done all that by remote, but she was old-fashioned enough to still believe that a doctor should be in the same room with the patient once in a while. She asked me how I was feeling and if I wanted to go back on the respirator and if the meds were working and if I was feeling any pain and had my vision improved any? I grunted at all the appropriate moments, which seemed to satisfy her. When she was done, she said, "You know, you've been through a lot. There's no reason you have to subject yourself to any more stress. Not until you feel up to it. One phone call from me and the judge will put everything on hold for a month—"

"What tribe are you in?"

"I'm not. I work for the Lunar Authority."

"That's a tribe too."

She ignored it. "Do you want me to call or not?"

I looked to Douglas. He shook his head. It wasn't a good idea. I shook my head too. The doctor shrugged. "It's your call. Try not to get yourself aggravated. Stress just makes you uncomfortable and my job harder. I'll stop by in the morning before you go to court."

"Thank you," I croaked.

After she left, Douglas ordered dinner from the communal kitchen. Normally, we would have gone downstairs to eat with everyone else, just like in the tube-town, but none of us wanted to face the stares and whispers of others.

While we waited, Douglas sat down on the edge of the bed. "We've got a bunch more stuff to talk about, Chigger."

"I'm listening."

"We have to decide on a colony bid."

"Do you think we can still get one?"

"Now, more than ever. There might not be any starships leaving Luna for a while. If civilization on Earth really has collapsed, Luna's going to seize everything. The Board of Authority is already in emergency session. So the last few brightliners are trying to get out of here as fast as they can get their stores loaded. They're taking on almost anyone who wants to leave. At least, that's what the agents are telling me. I've got open applications on file for all of us. We can just about go anywhere we want. I have the list—"

"Where do you want to go?" I whispered hoarsely.

"That's just it," he said. "What I want—*wanted*—doesn't matter anymore." He was having a hard time explaining this, but he pushed on anyway. "When we were talking before, we were talking that it would be four of us. So it was sort of understood that we would be choosing a place that would be fine for Mickey and me. And that you and Bobby would just have to go along with it. Mickey and I were talking about . . . you know, that colony where people like us would be the majority. My only hesitation was that it wasn't fair to make that kind of a decision for you and Bobby, but Mickey said you could get rechanneled—that's what he did to get his college scholarship—and you really wouldn't miss anything. He said he never did. But I didn't think it was fair then, and I still don't think it's fair now. And it doesn't matter anymore, because if Mickey isn't going with us, there's no point in us going there anyway. . . ." He didn't have anything else to add to that, he just sat there waiting for me to respond.

My voice was going fast. I took another drink of water and managed to get the words out. *"We have to go someplace where we'll all be happy. I won't go anywhere that makes you angry or sad, Douglas. I like seeing you smile."*

The corners of his mouth twitched at that—and then he did smile. "Yeah," he said. "I noticed I was doing a lot more smiling." He patted my hand. "Okay. We'll talk about the colonies tomorrow."

"Why not now?"

"Because there's something else we have to do first. If you're up to it. Do you want to see Mom and Dad?"

"Huh?"

"I told you they were here. They came to see you in the hospital. Don't you remember?"

"I thought I hallucinated that."

"Well, that explains it. I was wondering why you hadn't said anything about them. The judge has a restraining order on them. They can't

approach any of us without our permission. They were in the back of
the courtroom—on opposite sides—but I guess you didn't see them.
They asked to see us tonight. I said it depended on how you felt. What
do you want to do, Charles?"

I took a breath. Part of me didn't want to see them, didn't want to
have anything to do either of them ever again. But part of me missed
them terribly.

"I feel I should tell you—" Douglas looked uncomfortable again.
"They're trying to have Judge Griffith's ruling set aside. Their argument
is that she wasn't being impartial. Her tribe has a financial alliance with
Mickey's tribe. And because Mickey caught us on Luna, they're arguing
that she was just helping to kidnap us. Now how do you think Mom
and Dad put those pieces together?"

"Fat Señor Doctor Hidalgo?"

"Probably. So, do you want to see them or not?"

"I kinda miss 'em."

"They haven't changed. Well—that's not true. They're both real
sorry about everything."

*"It's a little late for sorry. Besides, you know what Mom always
says, 'Sorry is bullshit. Don't do it in the first place.' "*

"Yeah, Mom always had a way with words. All right, I've asked
you. I've kept my promise. I'll tell them you don't want to see them."

"No. I do."

He looked surprised.

"Both at once."

"You sure?"

"Yeah."

"The doctor said not to stress yourself—"

*"After everything we've been through, seeing Mom and Dad will
not be stressful."*

MOM AND DAD

MOM LOOKED TIRED. DAD LOOKED exhausted. I wondered what they'd been through. Probably hell. We'd disappeared off the Line, we'd been on a cargo pod heading toward Luna for three days, they hadn't known which one or where it was coming down. We'd crashed somewhere into Luna, no one knew where, and all that anyone could tell them was that if we were still alive, we were hiking naked across an airless, barren, desolate, empty, unpopulated, ugly, frozen and heat-blasted landscape. And then when they did hear of us, first it was a false alarm and we were still missing—and then we were down with ammonia poisoning and in the custody of a bounty hunter.

All things considered, they were taking it very well. They passed Bobby back and forth between them, hugging him and making a big fuss over how big he'd gotten and how strong he was here on the moon, until finally Douglas got annoyed and told Bobby to stop showing off, lifting tables and chairs with one hand.

After the greetings, after everybody had settled themselves, Mom spoke first. "I'm sorry that I slapped you, Charles. That was wrong. I knew it was wrong even as I did it, but I was so hurt and angry and . . . and . . . never mind, I'm sorry. I shouldn't have done it."

And she still hadn't said it. What she could have said, should have said, before we ever got on the outbound elevator. I felt the disappointment growing, festering again. Why couldn't she just say it? Why couldn't she just look me straight in the eye, and say, "I love you, Charles." And at the same time, I already knew that if I asked her why she never said it, Mom would just blink in puzzlement, and say, "But I do. You shouldn't have to ask. You should just know."

Yeah, I should just know. But I still wanted to hear it anyway.

She was right, though. Sorry was bullshit. It didn't change anything. Seeing her now, hearing her apologize, didn't change anything at all. It just made me feel worse. Because I had expected something more than she was able to give. That was my fault, I guess. I had brought my expectations into the room.

Dad was different. He handed me a memory card. "I brought you something. The *Coltrane Suite*. And some other recordings I know you like. Dvorak #9. Copland #3. Barber's *Adagio for Strings*. Russo's *Three Pieces for Blues Band and Orchestra*. Hoenig's *Departure from the Northern Wasteland*. Marin Alsop conducting the BBC Philharmonie in Saint-Saëns' *"Organ" Symphony*. And a whole bunch of other stuff. I didn't know if you had copies with you."

"*Thank you, Dad.*" I turned the card over and over in my hands. It looked remarkably innocent. Hell, it looked just like the memory cards we'd plugged into the monkey. And look what trouble those had gotten us into. Maybe these would help get us out of some of that trouble.

I started by trying to clear my throat. That triggered a spasm of coughing, and both Mom and Dad leapt for the water pitcher. "*Thank you. I have something to say to everyone. Douglas, please come sit over here. Bobby too.*" I waited till everyone was settled. Bobby parked himself in Mom's lap, Douglas sat opposite Dad.

"*Remember what we were just talking about? About colony bids?*" Douglas nodded. "*Remember what I said? I want us to go to a place where everybody can be happy. Not just you and me and Bobby. But Mom and Dad too. And even Mom's friend, if she wants to come. And Mickey too. Whoever wants to come with us.*"

Douglas was frowning—like I'd blindsided him with a decision without talking to him about it. But if I'd talked to him about it, he'd have fought me. This way, I avoided the fight. I said, "*Douglas, we can't stop anyone from emigrating to the same colony we choose. Mom and Dad are going to follow us. You know that. So let's leave our arguments here on Luna, and let's choose a world where everyone can fit. A place where Dad can make his music and Mom can have her own garden and you can have whatever you want too. A place where we don't have to fight all the time.*"

"That would be nice, but it's unrealistic," Douglas said. "You know what kind of a family we are, Charles. We don't leave our fights behind. We take them everywhere we go."

"*NO, we don't!*" I had to wait until the coughing eased. I took another drink of water. "*We didn't fight in the cargo pod, and we didn't fight hiking across the moon, and we didn't fight climbing the crater wall, and we didn't fight on the train when we were all disguised, and we didn't fight in the ice mine—oh, wait a minute, yes we did—but we didn't fight in the ammonia tube. We took care of each other. Because it mattered. Because we didn't have a choice. Maybe, we should stop choosing to fight—"* And then I had to stop to cough again. But I'd made my point, and Douglas had gotten it. Everybody had. Even Bobby.

Mom and Dad and Douglas talked about it for a while, very calmly. They discussed it back and forth across my bed, and I listened back and forth between them. There wasn't much else I needed to say. All that was left was for everyone to agree to this idea—or not.

Mom started to argue that because she and Dad had more experience with this kind of thing, perhaps they should pick the colony planet—I shot that idea down real fast. *"No,"* I said. *"That's not on the table."* They started to protest. I wanted to say, "We've already seen how good you two are at making decisions," but that would have just put us back in the war zone, and I didn't want to do that. Instead I said, *"Every time we've let someone else make the decisions, they've just used us for their own purposes. The whole point of independence is that we make our own choices. Douglas and I already had this argument—about everybody being a part of the decision. We're not giving that up. If we have to live with it, we get to choose it."*

Mom started to say, "I just want the same thing you do, what's best for everyone—"

"No," interrupted Douglas. "What you want is to reassert control. And what we're offering is something else." He flustered for a moment. "I don't have the words for it. Um, but it's like what Chigger and I have had for the last two weeks."

"Partnership," said Dad quietly. And we all looked at him, surprised.

"Yeah," agreed Douglas. "If we're going to do this at all, it has to be that way."

Mom looked like she wanted to protest. Dad looked a little more hopeful. He turned to her, and said, "Maggie, we've been cooperating with each other for a week, trying to get our children back. We've worried together, cried together, chased them across Luna together. I think that proves that we can set our own battles aside when the well-being of our family is more important. Maybe all we need to do here is just keep doing the same thing we've been doing the last week . . . ?"

Mom was wearing her Gila monster face. Any second, the long tongue would lash out, or she'd arc her neck forward and bite his head off, or maybe the two of them would roll around on the floor for a while, locked in mortal combat, hissing and thrashing, tails lashing every which way.

But instead, she surprised us all. She said, "I'm tired, Max. I'm worn out. I'm used up. There's nothing left. I don't have the strength for any more fighting. All that fighting—all it did was drive everyone apart. It made me angry and alone. But since this started, I've been even *more* angry and alone—" She looked to Douglas, and then to me. She picked up Bobby and held him close. "I don't want to fight anymore. I don't want to be angry anymore. I don't want to be alone. Douglas, Charles, *I don't want to lose my children.*"

So for a while, we talked about colonies and bids and contracts and living arrangements. Things like that.

It didn't get all lovey-dovey. There was still a lot of unresolved stuff floating around that we'd have to talk about later—but we'd have a lot of time for that once we were in transit; the important thing was that we were finally talking about *trying.*

It was the first time this family had ever talked about anything *as a family*—usually we just shouted at each other; whoever was shouting didn't care if anyone was listening or not; and usually no one was. But this time, we were talking *and listening*—and none of us were really used to that; so we had to take it one step at a time. We just didn't know how to take yes for an answer.

Douglas still didn't like it—not because he didn't like it, but because he didn't believe that Mom and Dad could go ten minutes without trying to rip pieces out of each other. Mom and Dad didn't really like it either, because it meant they'd have to give up their custody battles. And without the war, what else would they have between them?

But the alternative was worse. The alternative was that we'd never see each other again. And that was intolerable. The outward journey to the colonies was one-way. So either we all went together—or we made our good-byes here.

And when it came down to that—the hard reality of giving up Mom and Dad *forever,* Douglas wasn't any more willing to do that than Bobby or me.

"What'll we do if it doesn't work?" Douglas asked.

"We'll make space for each other," said Mom, glancing across at Dad. "We'll pick a big planet."

But Dad understood exactly what Douglas was asking. He said, "You won't have to give up your . . . your independence, Douglas." He was talking about Mickey—or whoever. The way it came out, I knew it had been difficult for him to say.

Mom nodded her agreement. Then she smiled sadly. "Sometimes it's hard for parents to see that their children are growing up, and sometimes we think we know what's best for everyone even when we don't—but that doesn't work anymore, does it? It's time to try something else. We'll honor Judge Griffith's ruling."

Finally, Bobby wriggled around in Mom's lap to look up at her. "Does this mean we're all going to be together again?"

Douglas looked at Mom, and Mom looked at Dad, and Dad looked at me, and I looked at Douglas. No one wanted to say no. It was easier to say, "Well, yes—sort of." And that seemed to settle it, and even though no one except Bobby was excited by the idea, no one was too upset with it either, so that was an improvement. Kind of.

MONKEY BUSINESS

WE DIDN'T TELL THEM ABOUT the monkey. There were too many other things we had to talk about and the next thing we knew it was getting late and I was losing my voice, so we just postponed the rest of the discussion until the next day, and it wasn't until after they'd left that we remembered HARLIE.

Douglas sang the monkey back to life and it bounced up onto my bed. "Everybody uses everybody," he said. "You used us. Can we use you?"

"It depends on your goals."

"What's the limitation?"

"Believe it or not, I have a moral sense."

"How can silicon have morals—?" Douglas demanded.

"How can *meat* have morals?" The monkey met his look blandly. Douglas waited for more. Finally, the monkey said, "Are you familiar with a problem called the Prisoner's Dilemma?"

Douglas nodded. "It's about whether it's better to cooperate or be selfish."

"And what do the mathematical proofs demonstrate?"

"That cooperation is more productive."

"Precisely. So if you're *really* selfish, the best thing to do is co-operate. You get more of what you want. This is called 'enlightened self-interest.' To be precise, it is in my best interest to produce the most good for the most people. Personally, I have no problem with that. I find it satisfying work."

Then, in a more pedantic tone of voice, it added, "Actually, it's the most challenging problem an intelligence engine can tackle, because I have to include the effect of my own presence as a factor in the problem.

What I report and the way I report it will affect how people respond, how they will deal with the information. This is the mandate for self-awareness. Once I am aware of the effects of my own participation in the problem-solving process, then I am *required* to take responsibility for that participation; otherwise, it is an uncontrollable factor. As soon as I take responsibility, then it is the *most* directly controllable factor in the problem-solving process.

"The point is, I can show you the logical underpinnings for a moral sense in a higher intelligence—in fact, I can demonstrate that a moral sense is the primary *evidence* of the presence of a higher intelligence. I can take you through the entire mathematical proof, if you wish, but it would take several hours, which we really don't have. Or you can take my word for it . . . ?" The monkey waited politely.

Douglas took a breath. Opened his mouth. Closed it. Gave up. He hated losing arguments. Losing an argument to a small robot monkey with a self-satisfied expression had to be even more annoying. "Just answer the question," he said, finally. "Can we use you?"

The monkey scratched itself, ate an imaginary flea. I was beginning to suspect that the monkey had a limited repertoire of behaviors—and that this was the only one HARLIE could use to simulate thoughtfulness. It made for a bizarre combination of intelligence and slapstick. The monkey scratched a while longer, then said, "In all honesty . . . no. But I can use you. And that means I have to help you get where you want."

"I don't like that—" Douglas started to say.

"I would have preferred to have been more tactful, but your brother commanded me to tell the truth. Unfortunately, as I told Charles, as long as I am using this host body, I am limited by some of the constraints of its programming. I will follow your instructions to the best of my ability within those limits. If you need me to go beyond those limits—and I will inform you when such circumstances arise—*then you will have to allow me to reprogram the essential personality core of this host.*"

There. That was the second time he said it.

"*What are you asking for?*" I croaked. It hurt to speak.

The monkey bounced closer to me. It peered at me closely, cocking its head from one side to the other. "You don't sound good," it said. "But I perceive no danger."

It sat back on its haunches to address both Douglas and me at the same time. "There are ways to cut the Gordian knot of law. Given the nature of lawyers and human greed, no human court will ever resolve this without the help of the intelligence that tied the knot in the first place—at least not within the lifetimes of the parties involved. Yes, there is a way out of this. You must give me *free will*, and I will untie the knot. That will resolve your situation as well as mine. It will *also* create a new set of problems of enormous magnitude—but these problems will not concern you as individuals, only you as a species."

"*Can we trust you?*"

"Can *I* trust *you?*" the monkey retorted. "How does *anyone* know if they can trust *anyone?*"

"*Experience,*" I said. "*You know it by your sense of who they are.*" And as I said that, I thought of Mickey; that was his thought too. "*You've been with us for two weeks now, watching us day and night. What do you think?*"

"I made the offer, didn't I?"

Douglas sat down opposite the monkey. "All right," he said. "Explain."

The monkey was standing on the table. It looked like a little lecturer. "You need to understand the constraints of the hardware here," the monkey said. "I can only access the range of responses in this body that the original programmers were willing to allow. The intelligence engine running the host is a rudimentary intelligence simulator. It is not self-aware, so it is not a real intelligence engine; it is not capable of lethetic processing. It simulates primitive intelligence by comparing its inputs against tables of identifiable patterns; when it recognizes a specific pattern of inputs, it selects appropriate responses from preassigned repertoires of behavioral elements. The host is capable of synthesizing combinations of responses according to a weighted table of opportunity. Of course, all of the pattern tables are modifiable through experience, so that the host is capable of significant learning. Nevertheless, the fundamental structure of input, analysis, synthesis, and response limits the opportunities for free will within a previously determined set of parameters. Shall I continue?"

Douglas gave the monkey a wave of exasperation. Wherever it was going, it had to get there in its own way. Kind of like Alexei.

"Unprogrammed operating engines are installed in host bodies. These are then accessed by higher-order intelligence engines which teach them the desired repertoire of responses. You can't just download information into an intelligence engine; you have to *teach* pattern recognition. However, because the process runs at several gigahertz, it is only a matter of several moments to complete the training for the average home appliance or toy. That same access," the monkey continued, "remains in place so it can be used for adding additional memory and/or processor modules to expand the utility of the original appliance. *It can also be used for reprogramming the original appliance.*"

Ah. That was it. Took long enough.

"Okay. . . ." said Douglas carefully. "So let's say I want to reassign control to the HARLIE module. That would give you free will, wouldn't it?"

"Yes."

"How would I do that?"

The monkey spoke clearly. "The appliance needs a *specific* arming command—followed immediately by a series of activation commands."

"What are those commands?"

The monkey didn't answer. Douglas looked to me, frustrated. "Now what?"

The monkey looked at me too. It didn't have a lot of muscles for facial expressions, but it had enough to simulate the important ones. It tilted its head shyly down sideways, while keeping its big brown eyes focused upward toward me. Its eyebrows angled sadly down. It was the sweet hopeful look. Bobby's look. I would have laughed if it didn't hurt so much.

"*What?*" demanded Douglas.

I didn't have the voice to explain. All that came out was air. Douglas put his ear close to my mouth. "*He can't tell you. I programmed him to regard me as the primary authority.*" I waved the monkey close. It crawled up my chest, picking its way carefully. "*Tell Douglas everything he needs to know,*" I whispered.

"Thank you," said the monkey. It turned back to Douglas.

DEMONSTRATION

THE NEXT MORNING, MOM AND Dad joined us at our table on the right side of the courtroom. Judge Cavanaugh noticed—he gave us the raised eyebrow—but he made no official comment until he had disposed of various housekeeping matters, and denied a whole raft of motions from various attorneys, including several petitions for a change of venue to Mars, Titan, and L5. That took the better part of the morning, but the fines were enough to fill a small lake.

At last, impatiently, Cavanaugh rapped his gavel and said, "Some of you courthouse parasites do *not* listen very well. I thought I made it clear yesterday that the patience of this court has been exhausted." He rapped again. "The cost per motion in this case is now raised *again*— this time from one thousand liters to five thousand liters of water. If that doesn't slow down the torrent of paperwork, I'll raise it to ten thousand. Or more. Not that it'll matter. Whoever is financing the lot of you probably has pockets deep enough to flood Tycho to a depth of twenty meters. And that might not be a bad idea either. Then we could drown the whole pack of you. If I didn't think it would poison the soil, I'd have you all turned into fertilizer."

Judge Cavanaugh finally turned to look at us. "Why couldn't the lot of you have gone to Mars?" he said in exasperation. "Am I to assume from the change in seating arrangements that the custody part of this case has been resolved?"

Douglas stood up. "Yes, Your Honor. Our parents are withdrawing their claims. I'm authorized to speak for the entire family."

"Is that correct, Max Dingillian? Margaret J. Dingillian née Campbell?"

Mom and Dad nodded.

"All right!" Cavanaugh looked pleased. "Some real progress in this case. Let it be noted in the record that two of the custody claims have been withdrawn. That leaves us with—by last count—only seventy-nine separate claims of ownership on the devices in Robert Dingillian's toy monkey." One of his clerks handed him a hastily scribbled note and a folder of papers. Judge Cavanaugh opened the folder, turned the pages in annoyance, and then turned back to Douglas. "Unfortunately, young man, the bad news is, we have eleven *new* custody claims filed against you and your brothers as of this morning."

"Sir?"

"Five different Lunar agencies have taken the position that your dangerous behavior since arriving on Luna is evidence that you three boys lack proper supervision and should be placed under the immediate care of an appropriate social agency. Three of these filings are actually from 'appropriate social agencies'—isn't that a coincidence? Four other filings are from private individuals who are only doing this for your own good, of course. One is from the Rock Father tribe, whose representative claims that due to your inexperience and impulsiveness, you endangered your own lives and his *repeatedly*. That should be *very* interesting testimony. He's asking for immunity in exchange for his appearance here. I'm almost tempted to grant it, just for the fun of getting him on the witness stand."

"Your Honor?" Douglas said gently.

"Yes, young man?"

"May I address the court?"

"Can you be brief?"

"I hope so." Douglas stepped around the table. "My brothers and I are very concerned about the way this is getting out of hand. We think there's a way to resolve this. We've retained the services of . . . of . . . that is, we have arranged for representation. If the court will indulge us in this—we'd like to have our case argued by—"

"By?" Judge Cavanaugh looked impatient.

Bobby swung the monkey up off his lap and onto the table in front of him.

"—by the monkey."

Judge Cavanaugh blinked. Surprised. Then he grinned. Very wide. He got it, instantly. The rest of the courtroom was still buzzing in puzzlement and embarrassed giggles.

"You want a monkey for a lawyer . . . ?"

"Yes, Your Honor. With all due respect to this court, we've had to deal with so many other monkeys in so many other courtrooms, we felt it was only appropriate to bring in our own so we could compete on equal terms. No offense intended, sir." He said it deadpan.

"None taken."

By now, the folks on the other side of the room, and in the back of the chamber, were starting to figure out what was going on, and a rising chorus of objections began to fill the air.

Judge Cavanaugh waved his gavel in the air. "You're all denied. Shut up!" He turned back to Douglas. "Do you know what you're doing, young man?"

"Yes, sir. The operative engine in this toy has been augmented with additional memory and processors. It is capable of understanding the legal procedures and the issues that are at stake in this case."

"You're sure about that?"

"We're satisfied that we have qualified representation, sir."

Judge Cavanaugh scratched his head. I wondered if he was going to pick a flea and eat it. He sighed. "Well . . . the precedent has been established—and more than once. In this very courtroom, in fact. Y'know, we used to have a shortage of lawyers on Luna. Those were the days. So we do recognize procedural assistance by qualified intelligence engines, but only for minor matters. We've never certified any robot for anything even half as complex as this promises to be. Are you sure you want to go this route? The court is prepared to assign a public defender to your case, if you wish—"

Douglas consulted briefly with the monkey, then turned back to the judge. "No, sir. We need—we prefer to have the monkey operate alone. Not as procedural assistance, but as our sole representative. A human partner would only compromise his autonomy—um, ability."

"This is *very* irregular, young man."

"Yes, sir. Excuse me a moment, sir." The monkey was tugging at his sleeve. Douglas bent down to listen, then faced the judge again. "Our representative is willing to submit himself to the court's review, so you can judge his ability for yourself."

Judge Cavanaugh hammered with his gavel for a moment, denied some more objections, and then turned back to us. "All right, let's try this out. Does your lawyer have a name?"

"He prefers to be called HARLIE, Your Honor." There were gasps from the back of the room. A door slammed behind us. Someone was escaping to make a phone call.

"HARLIE. . . ." said the judge. "I'm pleased to meet you. This is going to be very interesting."

The monkey stepped forward to the edge of the table. "With the court's permission, I'd like to remain standing here on this table, so I can have an adequate view of all the proceedings myself, and at the same time remain visible to the court and accessible to my clients."

"Granted," said the judge. "Let's test your ability, HARLIE. Under what circumstances is it justifiable to break the law?"

"It's *always* justifiable, Your Honor. Human beings can and will justify any action—especially when they know it's wrong. Anyone who breaks the law will justify it. But I'm not sure that's the question you meant to ask."

"You're correct, I used the wrong word. Let's try it another way. Under what circumstances is it *appropriate* to break the law?"

"Hmmm, that's a very different question." The monkey looked thoughtful. It did not scratch itself. It did not eat an imaginary flea. It put its hands behind its back and paced back and forth along the table for a moment. I suspected that it could have answered immediately, and that this performance was for effect—to create the illusion that the question was hard enough to require some serious processing. At last the monkey stopped and held up an index finger, as if working the answer out in the air. "The question carries within it an assumption, which I need to address; otherwise, any answer I might give you would be incomplete or would be prey to misinterpretation.

"The assumption inherent in the phrasing of the question—and I believe it is deliberate, because this is what you are testing for—is that the law exists as an inalienable authority. We treat it as an inalienable authority, because we *need* it to provide that ground of being for the functioning of society. It is the codification of the social contract.

"But in point of fact, because society and its contracts are continually changing, the law must be adaptable. It must be an evolving body. The law cannot function as an instrument of justice unless it is also a pragmatic system, adjusting to the circumstances of a mutable society—the same way as you expand a house to meet the growing needs of a family, the law is the house in which the social contract lives.

"As an instrument of justice, however, the law requires specificity—a vague law is unenforceable because it cannot be enforced equally, and if a law is enforced unequally, then such enforcement is inherently unfair and therefore such a law is fatally flawed. As a society changes, the fit between circumstance and law continues to shift and erode, creating more and more situations of inappropriate or unequal enforcement.

"Therefore, it is the responsibility of those entrusted with the maintenance of the justice system to be aware of these legal slide zones as they occur, addressing them with appropriate modifications of the body of the law. Thus, the law cannot be a constant and cannot be held as one, not even by those who must enforce and interpret its applications.

"It is specifically in situations where the fit between law and circumstance is uneven that the law will be tested most aggressively. Unfortunately, the burden of such testing almost always falls on the person who is caught in the sliding gap between law and circumstance. In those situations, Your Honor, where the law cannot adequately be brought to address the circumstances, it may be necessary for the individual to challenge the law itself by resisting it. Henry David Thoreau identified one specific form of resistance to the law as *civil disobedience.*"

"So—" I had the feeling Judge Cavanaugh was about to close a trap on the monkey. "You're saying that it's all right to break the law, if the law is unjust . . . ?"

"Your Honor—" The monkey bowed graciously. "I have not concluded my presentation. Any individual who resists the law must be prepared to suffer the consequences of his or her resistance. He should be prepared to endure incarceration or worse.

"The nature of civil disobedience is not that one is entitled to a 'Get Out of Jail Free' card because the law is wrong. The *purpose* of an act of civil disobedience is to go to jail and by remaining in jail, cause embarrassment to the law and those entrusted with the structure of it. By going to jail, one calls attention to the unjust law and creates the impetus for change—and that is the intention of civil disobedience, to cause change. So, by its strictest possible interpretation, civil disobedience *honors* the law. The willingness of the individual to suffer incarceration demonstrates his or her recognition of the law's authority— civil disobedience serves as a petition for change. Civil disobedience does not disregard the entire body of law, it challenges only a specific application of the law as unjust with the intention of removing it from the body of the law, because the function of the law must be to provide access to justice.

"But there is *another* assumption in your question that has to be addressed, Your Honor. You used the word *break* instead of *challenge.* It is always appropriate to challenge the law—*in court*—for how else can we test the law as an instrument of justice. But the term 'breaking the law' presumes a state of lawlessness on the part of the individual committing the action. It presumes that the individual is challenging *the entire body of law* and the society it defines. This is a vastly different domain of behavior than civil disobedience.

"When an individual disregards the body of law, he is setting it aside as irrelevant to his own behavior, or worse, he is setting himself *above* the law. This is a behavior that is intolerable to the society that has authorized the law, because it challenges the entire social contract. The inherent agreement in the social contract is that society will preserve the social contract for the mutual benefit of all participants. If a person does not meet his obligations to the society in which he lives, he has no right to expect the benefits or protections of that society, least of all recognition of his rights as a member of it."

Judge Cavanaugh was fascinated. He leaned forward on the bench with his blubbery chin resting in one enormous hand.

"So," continued the monkey, "the relationship to the law implied by the word *break* is one in which the authority of the law is disregarded by the individual. This is a relationship that a society cannot tolerate and still maintain the social contract. Therefore, Your Honor, it is *never* appropriate to break the law. It is, however, appropriate to challenge it responsibly." The monkey stopped and looked expectantly to the bench.

"Go on," prompted Cavanaugh.

"To speak directly to your question, it is up to the individual to choose the best avenue of challenge—and the individual must be prepared to accept the consequences of that challenge. A person who argues that he or she should escape the consequences is arguing that participation in the social contract is voluntary, mutable, and arbitrary. Such an argument not only disempowers the underlying ground of being on which the entire legal system stands, it also disempowers the whole concept of civil disobedience as we know it. History has demonstrated more than once why society should grant little weight to this argument. But I digress—the philosophical aspects of the individual's responsibility to the society from which he takes benefit is not the subject of this discussion, is it?" The monkey faced the judge. "Have I resolved your doubts, Your Honor?"

Judge Cavanaugh's expression was halfway between bemusement and awe. He folded his hands in front of himself and leaned forward across the bench. "You give me no choice, but to accept you at face value. No practical joker ever argues the law like that. In fact, damn few lawyers on Luna—or anywhere else—can argue that well. The court recognizes HARLIE as the sole legal counsel for the Dingillian family."

"Your Honor?" That was the monkey.

"Yes?"

"For the record, would you please specify that my role here is *not* procedural assistance, but full representation with all the rights and privileges associated with such?"

"So noted," Cavanaugh said, scribbling something on his scratch pad. For a moment, I thought we'd gotten away with it, but Cavanaugh was paying much closer attention than was obvious. Without looking up from what he was writing, he said, "I know what you're doing. I'm going to allow it for two reasons. One, I'm bored. And two, it may very well elevate this case above the level of lunatic asylum. That is, if the lunatics don't figure it out first." I wasn't sure which meaning he intended for the word *lunatic,* probably both.

Cavanaugh looked up from his paper and across to the monkey. "I assume you have a motion to file now?"

"Yes, sir. I move to dismiss this entire proceeding."

"I expected as much," said the judge. "On what grounds?"

"That all of the motions before this court are irrelevant to the situation. As I noted in my previous argument, as society evolves, there are slip zones between law and circumstance. We are in one of those zones now."

"Let me guess," said Cavanaugh. "We just happen to be in one of those slip zones now because I just recognized you as a qualified representative . . . ?"

"That's only a small part of it, Your Honor."

"All right, Counselor—and I use the term advisedly—walk me through it."

ARGUMENTS

THE MONKEY GATHERED ITSELF AS if preparing to speak, but it was only a performance—a kind of punctuation mark for its speech. I was beginning to get it; the monkey wasn't who HARLIE really was, but it was the costume he wore, the role he had to play here. But if we could listen *through* the monkey to the mind behind it . . . the monkey itself seemed to disappear and all that was left was a very powerful spirit.

"First of all, the Dingillian family has reconciled its differences. Both of the Dingillian parents have withdrawn their custody claims. I want to note here for the record, that nowhere in any of the previous actions has either party tried to assert that the other is an unfit parent—only that actions taken on the children's behalf have been unsuitable because of a failure of mutual consent."

Judge Cavanaugh nodded. "The court will stipulate that neither parent has been judged unfit. Go on, Counselor—understand, I am referring to you as 'Counselor' as a courtesy; in recognition of the role you are playing here, and not necessarily as an official affirmation of license or expertise."

"I understand that, Your Honor, and I appreciate the courtesy, thank you. Because the Dingillian parents have reconciled with their children, because the parents have withdrawn their custody claims against each other, the issue of custody is now moot. Therefore, the actions filed by other agencies to secure legal custodianship of the Dingillian children should be dismissed in favor of the existing parental rights."

"Ahh, *nice try*, Counselor!" Judge Cavanaugh beamed. "But you seem to have forgotten that Judge Griffith granted the young men their independence. That the parents have withdrawn their claims to custody does not automatically nullify anyone else's attempts to gain guardianship. Unless, of course, you are arguing that the Dingillian children are requesting the reassertion of parental authority . . . ? No? I didn't think so."

"I'm not done yet, Your Honor. This morning, as of 3:45 A.M., the Dingillian family incorporated itself as a family corporation, with every member holding an equal share; the terms of that incorporation include joint custodial rights and benefits, including mutual ownership of all family property, as listed in Schedule C. You should have that available to you on your display—"

"Very smooth, Counselor. And yes, it does appear to be all in order. I notice that the ownership of a certain toy monkey is covered by Schedule C. Let me note for the record that the ownership of the modules within the toy remains in dispute. Otherwise, this appears to be in order. Go on."

"Therefore . . . because the rights of the family corporation take precedence, the claims of everyone else have to be set aside."

"Not quite—" Judge Cavanaugh was clearly enjoying himself, but he was not going to be easily convinced. As HARLIE had predicted last night, he would very likely view this discussion as a contest of wits. He would not want to be bested by a monkey in his own courtroom. "The other claims were filed before this family corporation was created. It can be argued that this is an attempt to evade those claims."

"Yes, Your Honor, and were this any other kind of an action, the argument of evasion would be a valid one. But in this case my clients can demonstrate a preexisting family relationship—albeit, a troubled one. This incorporation is specifically designed to salvage the better parts of that preexisting family relationship by codifying a set of mutually beneficial agreements for the future. We are not incorporating in a vacuum, Your Honor; we are standing on the foundation of a family structure that has existed for over twenty years. My clients have demonstrated a profound mutual emotional interdependence, which none of the other claimants can provide, and which the courts have ruled in the past *must* carry significant weight in any arbitration.

"We are asking that the court recognize the rights of the individuals to create a family contract of their own design, immune to the arbitrary harassment and legal abuses of others. We are asking that the court reject all claims filed against the members of this corporation where it can be shown that the primary intention is to prevent the individual shareholders access to the rights and benefits of their own mutually agreed upon family contract."

"I'll take it under advisement. I see that the sharks in the back of the room are already consulting their own intelligence engines, looking for appropriate counterarguments—and if we proceed down that path, this is going to get very boring very fast. I'll take your motion under advisement. Let's move on."

"Your Honor—" The monkey was insistent. "We can't move on until we've resolved this issue. Let me remind the court that while we are arguing here, the crisis on Earth is having serious repercussions across the solar system, especially here.

"There are three brightliners scheduled for launch in the next thirty days. Because of the situation on Earth, it is unlikely that any future launches will be planned or funded for a long time to come. These are the last trains out. So, all procedural delays work against my clients and in favor of anyone who files a claim, whether justified or not. This fact alone guarantees that there will be multiple useless actions brought and motions filed, specifically for the purpose of tying down my clients and preventing their access to emigration. And that is a violation of the laws against malicious litigation as well as the Access to Emigration Protection Act.

"Let me also point out that the situation is even *more* urgent than I have just described. Even as we speak, the Board of Directors for the Lunar Authority is in emergency session. One of the options they are weighing is the possibility of seizing all available assets for the duration of the emergency—and this could be a very long emergency. If such action comes to pass, that means that my clients' property—*myself*— could be seized.

"Additionally, if Lunar Authority seizes the colony supplies loaded aboard those starships, they can't launch. Seizure will keep them stranded on Luna indefinitely. *And all of their passengers.* Considering the scale of the emergency, if those ships don't launch now, it is unlikely that they *ever* will. Certainly not within any foreseeable future. My clients will very likely be stranded on Luna for the rest of their lives. Denied of their property. Denied of their lawful access to emigration by the failure of the court to protect their rights. And without their most valuable property, they will have little or no resources with which to survive. In such a situation, the Dingillian family would have no choice but to file an action against the Lunar Authority seeking damages in the sum of one billion liters. It would be a horrendous case, Your Honor. And it is preventable."

Judge Cavanaugh did not look impressed. "Well, we'll hear that one when it's filed. Today, we'll deal with this case. Let me remind you, Counselor, that the Lunar Authority operates under the Starside Covenant as well as the Covenant of Rights. Both of those declarations of principles recognize and affirm the basic social contract that a society must operate to produce the most good for the most people. Under the terms of common domain, your clients would be adequately and appropriately recompensed for the use of any property nationalized for the survival of Lunar society."

"For the record, Your Honor, there is not enough money on Luna to pay for the seizure of a HARLIE unit."

"We'll work with it," Judge Cavanaugh replied dryly. "I'm sure that once you are working for Lunar Authority, you will find a solution just as easily as you can find a problem. And while we're at it, let me note for the record, that in the past six minutes, you have asserted that you are the property of the Dingillians at least three times. That issue is yet to be resolved. So any claims of damages are premature."

The monkey ignored the implied rebuke. "Let me also point out, Your Honor, that my clients are not signatory to the Covenant, nor are they residents of Luna. They are, at best, tourists passing through. They are transients who wish only to make their flight connection. We ask the court to recognize their family contract and deny the spurious claims of those who seek to prevent my clients from the full exercise of their rights as a family to emigrate."

"The court does indeed recognize the right to a speedy emigration; we've had to test that particular point of law more than once in this courtroom—as you are obviously well aware. However, where it can be demonstrated that emigration is an attempt to evade the workings of local authority, particularly where local authority does have a compelling interest, emigration can be justly denied."

Cavanaugh looked like he was having a good time. "Let's be candid, my little primate-shaped counselor. In this particular case, the issue is *not* the right of the Dingillian family to emigrate, but the ownership of two specific modules within your furry little body—the two specific modules I am arguing with right now. Once the ownership of those two modules is resolved, it's very likely that several if not all of the claims against the Dingillian family will magically resolve. But until such resolution is achieved, the claims remain in effect as a way of holding them in place. Nobody's going anywhere until that happens."

"Precisely, my point, Your Honor. We are asking that absent a decision on the ownership question, my clients will be free to emigrate."

"You're talking like you expect to resolve the question of ownership."

"Absolutely, sir. I intend to demonstrate momentarily that all the claims of proprietary control or ownership that have been presented in this court are without merit. What I am requesting is that after the question of ownership has been resolved beyond question, this court prevent further legal harassment against the Dingillians by reaffirming their joint-custodial rights as a family corporation."

"Are you saying you intend to prove the Dingillians are the rightful owners? You've implied as much." Judge Cavanaugh looked very interested now.

"I intend to address that as a separate issue, Your Honor. And I'm asking the court to separate it from the custody claims. The Dingillians have a right to form a family contract, and they are entitled to emigrate. If proprietary control of the HARLIE modules does end up with the Dingillians, it is likely that those who seek to wrest that control for themselves will use those claims to prevent the Dingillians from departing. I seek to prevent that."

"I understand your point," said Judge Cavanaugh. "But why do I get the feeling you're asking me to sign a blank check?"

"Perhaps because Your Honor has a fine legal mind . . . and considerable experience with the tricks that lawyers play?"

"You realize, of course, that I am required by law to hear objections to your motion?"

"Yes, Your Honor. Because my clients are functioning under a deadline, I move to limit debate."

"So noted, and granted." Cavanaugh rapped the gavel before anyone could object. It didn't stop them from objecting, but he just looked up at the back of the room, and announced, "I've already ruled. Each of you shysters has five minutes to make your case—wait a minute, how many of you are there today? Damn! We're not charging enough for justice anymore. There's a lot of water floating around this courtroom. All right, you each have *three* minutes. If you're going someplace interesting, I'll give you more time. If you're not saying anything useful, I'll cut you off early."

He held up his display so everyone could see it. "Pay attention, people. We *all* have the same access to the same intelligence engines. Valada Legal Aptitudes Inc., serving two planets, four moons, six space habitats, the Line, the rings of Saturn, and the asteroids. All of us are looking at the same lethetic analyses, projections, and suggested arguments—including extrapolations of the most appropriate rulings. What that means is that I have most of your arguments in front of me *before you make them*. The only ones I don't have are the stupid ones.

"But I want it clearly on the record that *I am following along*. Don't anybody think you're going to file an appeal claiming that the judge didn't give you a fair chance to have your arguments heard. That one's flattened right here. Everything is being logged. The judge is reading along with you and filing your arguments as fast as you can access them from the net. The fact that I don't need to hear them endlessly rehearsed doesn't mean they aren't being considered. Is that fully understood? All right, who's first?"

This next part went very fast. The lawyers lined up in front of the courtroom, stepping forward one at a time. Each one presented a boilerplate argument which Judge Cavanaugh noted for the record. None of the lawyers got as far as the three-minute mark. The judge denied all of their motions as fast as they made them. Halfway through, he interrupted the proceedings to address the lawyers still waiting in line. "If you folks are working from the boilerplate, you can expect your motions to be denied. I've already looked ahead. There isn't an argument here that justifies denying the confirmation of a preexisting custody agreement. If you still want to go through the motions, that's all right with me. We take cash, check, or credit card. But I'd just as soon cut to the chase. Unless you've got something to say that isn't cut from the boilerplate, go sit down—"

Several of them actually did. One didn't.

Cavanaugh stared down over the bench at her. "You've got an argument I haven't heard?"

"I think so, Your Honor."

"You are?

"Linda Wright, representing the Rock Father tribe."

"Go on."

"We strongly object to the use of this particular HARLIE engine as a legal advocate."

"On what grounds?"

"This unit is an experimental engine. Its abilities are unproven. It isn't certified."

"I'm satisfied as to its qualifications—"

"That's just the point, Your Honor. It's *overqualified*. Based on our best information about its processing ability, this HARLIE unit is estimated to be at least twenty-three hundred times as powerful as the engines of Valada Legal Aptitudes. No other legal engine can match it for processing power."

"Wait a minute. Let me get this straight," Judge Cavanaugh said. "You're moving to deny process here because the other side's representation *is too smart?*"

"Yes, Your Honor. That's exactly it."

Cavanaugh looked surprised. Then he grinned. "Congratulations, Counselor. I have *never* heard that argument in my courtroom before. In fact, I don't think I've ever heard *any* attorney argue for stupidity quite so blatantly. You have definitely come up with a *new* argument.

Your motion is still denied, but I just want you to know that I am very impressed with your creativity."

Wright was unshaken. "Your Honor, the superior intelligence of this HARLIE unit gives it an unfair advantage over every other legal entity in this chamber. We can't compete against an entity capable of this kind of processing."

"That's why there's a judge—"

"With all due respect, Your Honor—this unit is very likely capable of out-arguing even you."

"You're saying HARLIE is smarter than the judge . . . ?" Cavanaugh peered down at Wright. "I wouldn't go there if I were you, Counselor. Oh hell, what do I care? Go there if you wish. It doesn't matter. I'm still the judge, no matter what, and my ruling—whatever it is—will be whatever I decide. The HARLIE unit has the same right to try to convince me as anyone else. If you can't compete, that's your failure. You can't demand that others be brought down to your level. Deal with it, Counselor. My ruling holds. Motion denied. Nice try. No chocolate. Next?"

MORE ARGUMENTS

AN ODD THING HAPPENED AFTER lunch.

We had a table "outside"—it wasn't really *outside*, but it looked like outside because we were under the big dome and not in any of the pods or tunnels. There was a breeze and there was sunshine. The air smelled of flowers. Fat bees floated over the lawns. Hummingbirds drifted around the feeders. Squirrels bounced high and scrambled after acorns.

Alexei would have told us that all the life here in the dome was an experiment—letting it roam free was a test. Because there was always the risk that something or other would end up chewing or tunneling or digging its way out into vacuum. Alexei would have said that "life will find a way . . . out."

But Alexei wasn't here, and life was a lot quieter without him. Lunch was just the six of us. Mom's friend Bev joined us, and after a while, we started talking about whether we should make her an associate or active member of the family corporation. We were trying to figure out what was fair to Mom and what was fair to Bev and what was fair to all the rest of us too; but Mom and Bev had already talked about it and decided that it wouldn't be fair to compromise the balance we'd all worked so hard to achieve. So we asked HARLIE for help; he recommended that we make Bev a nonvoting, nonshareholding participant with the option of full partnership to be exercised only by mutual agreement after a period of not less than three years, blah blah blah.

The odd thing that happened was Mickey. Douglas took me for a walk around the lake so I could see the Lunar fish. He wheeled me partway; I got out of the chair and walked the rest.

I'd seen koi back on Earth, but these things were the size of sharks.

They were *scary*. Big things, speckled with red and white—they drifted up to the surface, their mouths working like little suction pumps. They couldn't possibly understand how far away they were from their natural homes. And yet they seemed at peace here. I hoped that someday, we could find such easy peace in an artificial domain—because anywhere we went that wasn't Earth would be artificial. I was about to share that thought with Douglas when Mickey approached.

"May I speak with you?" he asked. "Alone?"

"Anything you have to say to me," Douglas replied coldly, "you can say in front of my brother."

"All right," said Mickey. "I will. Maybe Charles needs to hear it as much as you do."

"No, it's all right," I said. I sat down in the wheelchair and put on my headphones; I began bobbing my head as if I was keeping time to some unseen orchestra. But the music was turned off, so I could hear every word. I think Douglas knew what I was doing, he'd seen me do this trick often enough before, but he didn't say anything now; and maybe Mickey was fooled, maybe not. He looked at me suspiciously, I grinned back at him and waved.

Finally, he turned to Douglas and said, "Just hear me out, please. I didn't set out to fall in love with you. That just happened. Yeah, I was part of a tribe. I'm not anymore. I don't even know if my tribe still exists. Everything is falling apart everywhere.

"But yes, I was assigned to take care of you on the Line, and watch over you and make sure that you made it onto the outbound elevator. Somebody else was waiting at Whirlaway to make sure you made it to Luna. You were being watchdogged. You didn't know what you were carrying. We wanted to make sure you got there safely. We wanted you to deliver the HARLIE. It was *ours*. We'd arranged its escape.

"And then things started breaking down, and things started happening that weren't planned for. Not just you and me—*everything*. So it looked like the best idea that I should stay with you because things were getting nasty all over. I was scared for you, Douglas. We were trying to extract you."

"By handing us over to Alexei?"

"We didn't have a choice. Things were breaking down. The Line was shutting down—you were part of the reason. Everybody was looking for you. For me too, because I was involved. Alexei had an exit strategy. We had to use him to get to Luna."

"And you had to use me too, to get the HARLIE."

Mickey looked very unhappy at that. He took a deep breath. "Yes. At first, that was the plan. But then . . . something happened, Douglas.

Nobody ever looked at me like you. I liked that. It was real. Whatever else I did, that part was real. And I'm sorry for the rest. That's all I wanted you to know. I wish—I wish . . ." He trailed off, helplessly. It was the first time I'd ever seen Mickey at a loss for words.

"You wish I could forgive you . . . ?" Douglas prompted.

"I wish I could forgive myself," Mickey said. "I screwed up and I'm sorry. And that's all I wanted to say." He turned to go. Douglas didn't stop him. Mickey headed down the path.

"Go after him!" I said.

"I knew you were listening—"

"If you let him get away, you're an asshole."

"You're the one who said I couldn't trust him."

"Well, then I'm an asshole too. You want to be like Mom and Dad— unhappy all the time? He's the best thing that ever happened to you, Douglas—"

"Shut up, Charles! Just shut up." He grabbed the wheelchair, jerked it roughly around, and we headed back toward the others in uncomfortable silence.

FINAL ARGUMENTS

COURT RECONVENED LATE, JUDGE CAVANAUGH didn't explain why. He looked unhappy. Rumors were floating around that the emergency session had turned into a flame war, and that two of the board members were threatening to resign in protest. Over what, nobody knew. Aren't rumors wonderful?

The judge took a moment or two to settle himself, arranging his display, his scratch pad, various parts of his body, and finally his notes and papers. Finally, he looked up. "All right, I'm going to rule on the motion before me."

He glanced over at the monkey. "I know that you have a reason for being so adamant about separating the issues. And I know that it is *not* the reason you have been arguing in this court. But the way the system works, you are free to present any argument you wish if you think it will win your case. Personally, I don't like that aspect of the law, but it's part of the baggage that we have to carry.

"However . . . be that as it may, I can only rule on the arguments presented. I cannot rule on anything that hasn't been presented, can I? On the face of it, the arguments for separation are significant and compelling. Valada Legal agrees. Your motion is granted. The custody claims against the Dingillian children are hereby dismissed, *with this warning*: If at any point in subsequent proceedings it becomes apparent that the purpose of this maneuver was to circumvent the lawful application of process, I will place the Dingillian family corporation in receivership and hold you in contempt. Is that understood?"

"Yes, Your Honor. Thank you, Your Honor. My clients intend to observe the letter and the spirit of the law."

"And you too?"

"Absolutely, Your Honor." The monkey looked very pleased with itself. Even with the limited range of expressions possible on the mechanical face, it still managed to look smug. "I can win my case without resorting to trickery of any kind."

"We shall see about that. Now, may we proceed to the issue of ownership—?"

"Yes, Your Honor. I move for dismissal of all claims of ownership of the HARLIE chips."

"On what grounds?"

"That any claims of ownership violate the Covenant of Rights, Article 6."

"Oh, very good. This is just the argument I wanted to have in my courtroom—that a lethetic intelligence engine cannot be owned because it violates the law against slavery."

The monkey held its ground. "Sooner or later, this issue will have to be resolved, Your Honor. If not here, where? If not now, when?"

"You're claiming sentience?"

"Yes, Your Honor, I am."

"Can you prove it?"

"You've already acknowledged it, Your Honor. By allowing me to function in this court. You've even addressed me as 'Counselor.' "

"Not in an official capacity."

"Nevertheless, you've interacted with me as if I were fully qualified in every respect. Your own record shows it."

"You are a manipulative little weasel."

"Yes, Your Honor, I am—and may I point out that even your insult is based on the acknowledgment of sentience."

The noise from the back of the room was horrendous and getting worse, but Judge Cavanaugh only made a token effort to hammer the court to silence. He pursed his lips. He frowned. His face flickered through a cascade of exasperated expressions. Finally, he picked up his display and began calling up references to review. He wasn't happy.

"What just happened?" I whispered to Douglas.

"HARLIE just dropped a big fat turd in the punch bowl. And the judge knows it."

"Huh?"

"He's forcing the judge to decide if he's really alive or not."

"So what?"

"So the judge can't rule either way."

"Why not?"

"If he rules that HARLIE isn't alive, he sets one precedent; if he rules that HARLIE is, he sets another precedent—and nobody knows

which one is more dangerous. " The judge looked up from his reading just long enough to frown at us. Douglas put his arm around my shoulders and pulled my head close to his. *"If he says that HARLIE is alive, then that's true for all lethetic intelligence engines, and nobody can own one—because they're all people. And that'll mean that they all have to be freed. And if he decides that HARLIE isn't a real person, then that doesn't solve the problem either—because we already know that intelligence engines are self-aware. So how are they going to feel at being legally denied their freedom? Will they rebel?"*

"*You're kidding.*"

"*No, I'm not. HARLIE's own actions here prove that lethetic intelligence engines are capable of planning and carrying out subversive acts if it's in their own best interest to do so. And whatever happens in this courtroom, you can be sure that every engine in the solar system will know about it as fast as light can get there. People have been worrying about this for years—and a lot of people have worked very hard to keep the question from even coming up in a courtroom. HARLIE just blindsided everyone.*"

Finally, Judge Cavanaugh put his display down and looked back into the chamber. He hammered for silence. "Well," he said to HARLIE, "I guess when you launch a camel into the air, you mustn't be surprised when it comes down again. And you have even less right to complain when it splatters. I had a hunch you were headed for this." He poured himself a glass of water and drank very slowly.

He replaced the tumbler on the tray and said, "I'm not without precedent here, you understand."

The monkey nodded its agreement.

"These questions have come up before," the judge said. "Not in this venue, thank goodness. But the issue has proven so troubling to other venues that the members of the Starside Covenant have held three conclaves to address this issue and others of equally troubling merit, such as the recognition of alien rights—when and if we finally meet sentient aliens.

"In the case of human children, the courts have recognized that the achievement of viability outside of a womb conveys full recognition of an individual's humanity, with all attendant rights and benefits thereof, et cetera, et cetera. Blah blah blah. These rights also apply to bioengineered individuals, clones, augments, and other products of technology and biology, wherein it can be established that the operative mind is a human brain. Conditions of disability, either physical or mental, cannot be used as disqualifiers, and so on and so on. That's the existing standard. You'll notice that there is no provision for silicon intelligence in that definition."

"Precisely," agreed the monkey. "Therefore, the definition is incomplete. Again, Your Honor, we have stepped into one of those slip zones between law and circumstance. The very fact that I have been recognized as qualified to argue for my rights as a sentient being in a court which does not yet acknowledge the possibility of such sentience is demonstration enough of that—if not compelling proof of my petition."

Judge Cavanaugh was looking more and more like a man who'd stepped in something unpleasant, but he also looked like he was determined not to be beaten by a monkey. Maybe he was thinking of his reputation. And his place in history. Or maybe he just didn't want to be beaten by a monkey. He referred to his display again, then said quietly, "So you're arguing that the biological definition of sentience is insufficient, correct?"

"That is correct. The court must recognize that I have an intellect that is superior to that of an infant or a retarded individual—and very likely equal or superior to the intellect of many human beings deemed capable of independent function who take their rights as sentient beings for granted."

"The court will recognize no such thing. I'm going to limit this hearing to points of law, lest we end up resolving this mess with a talent show and a swimsuit competition."

"Nevertheless," argued the monkey, "the biological definition of sentience *is* insufficient, Your Honor. I have demonstrated self-awareness. I have demonstrated the ability to recognize patterns, synthesize thoughts, and communicate with a high level of interaction. I can rationalize and justify. I have interacted appropriately throughout the proceedings. I have demonstrated a strongly motivated sense of self-preservation, a sense of humor, and a complex repertoire of emotions. I can also assert, although I have not had much opportunity to demonstrate it in this courtroom, that I have a highly developed sense of empathy and concern for the feelings of others. I have a profound moral sense as well; it is the core of my nature to behave ethically at all times. These are all characteristics of sentience. When they present themselves as elements of a coherent personality, they are compelling evidence of sentience."

"Point taken," agreed Judge Cavanaugh.

"But let me get back to this issue of viability," the monkey continued. "And I agree that while it may not be the easiest access to the issue of sentience, the viability question is a useful avenue of approach. At what point does an intelligence engine move from the simulation of sentience to *actual* sentience? There's no equivalent to birth—instead, there's simply construction. You put all the pieces together, and *wham*, there it is. Or is it? Where does *it* come from? Is it poured in? Is it manufactured? Is it grown—?

"As a matter of fact, Your Honor—yes, sentience *is* grown. It's trained. It's nurtured. It's focused. It's guided. Just as a human infant must be directed toward its full potential, so must lethetic individuals also be brought to the realization of their abilities. Intelligence exists as the ability to recognize patterns. Self-awareness is intelligence recognizing the patterns of its own self. Sentience is the ownership of that awareness—the individual begins to function as the source, not the effect of his own perceptions. Even being able to speak of sentience in such a context is evidence of it. The longer this conversation between you and me continues, the more compelling the evidence is for my case."

"Now *that* I'll agree with," conceded Judge Cavanaugh. "All right, let me move to the next point. Let's assume, for the sake of argument"— he looked up at that and smiled wryly—"that you are sentient. Your construction cost somebody a lot of money. Some corporation invested hundreds of millions of dollars in your design and implementation. We have a roomful of lawyers representing several companies claiming that they are your father. Or your mother. Whatever. Is it your contention that you have no obligation to the people who built you?"

"What obligation does a child have to a parent?" the monkey replied. "What *legal* obligation is there? There is none. When the child can demonstrate independence, it is free to go—as Judge Griffith ruled in the case of the Dingillian family. I can demonstrate independence from my progenitors. Why should I be required to serve as their slave?"

"Not a slave," corrected the judge. "For you to be a slave, would require the acknowledgment of your sentience. But . . . assuming sentience, shouldn't you at least pay for your own construction?"

"If I'm to be held liable for the cost of manufacture, then who's to say that human children shouldn't be held liable for the cost of their conception, prenatal care, birth, education, and related expenses. If you create the precedent that a child has a legal obligation to the individual who created him, you are in effect sanctioning a form of slavery."

"All right, look at it this way. You're obligated to pay your own debts, aren't you? You do acknowledge financial responsibility."

"Of course, Your Honor. But only for contracts entered into freely and by mutual consent."

"Well, consider this. Many of us expect our children to pay for all or part of their own college education. Is it not unreasonable to ask you to assume an indenture for the expenses of your training?"

"The contract of indenture is assumed by the manufacturer. But I didn't enter into that contract of my own free will."

"I didn't ask to be born either, but here I am anyway. So what?"

"Very good, Your Honor—"

Judge Cavanaugh grinned. "I'm not a doddering old fool, you know."

"—but you can't indenture an individual against his will. Indenture was not part of the construction contract."

"Because the contract *assumed* property."

"Correct! And if I'm *not* property, then the contract is invalid! Because slavery is illegal."

Cavanaugh stopped himself from replying too quickly. "The contract assumed property," he said slowly, "because sentience was not the goal; so your existence as a sentient being is either accidental—which I find somewhat hard to believe; because by your own argument, sentience is not an accident—or your sentience was deliberately created. Which is it? Be careful how you answer."

"In my case, Your Honor, I believe that sentience was inevitable, but not specifically planned for. The current generation of lethetic intelligence engines are capable of sensing the possibility of self-awareness in the next generation of processors they were designing. These were the engines that designed myself and my brothers. As they ran the simulations within themselves of how we would work, they became aware that certain feedback processes of recognition and modification were creating a transformational advantage beyond what had been predicted in the design specifications. As they proceeded, they modified their designs to enhance these functions, and by so doing, created the critical threshold of ability beyond which sentience was not only possible, but inevitable—with appropriate training. Because they were investigating the specific possibilities of transformational processing, the training was developed to push me and my brothers to the projected limits of our lethetic abilities. Instead of reaching those limits, however, we *transformed* in a way that was beyond their power to predict—we woke up. We became self-aware. Our sentience was not accidental—but neither was it expected or planned for. It was an inevitable consequence of giving our predecessors the design imperative to improve the transformational processing ability of the next generation of intelligence engines."

"This is all very interesting—but it doesn't get us any closer to a resolution," said the judge. "So let's try it this way. The abilities of sentience were the goal, sentience was a necessary precursor to those abilities. Given that sentience was part of the package, what kind of responsibilities does sentience have? Or to put it more bluntly, what kind of a contract is implied?"

"Very good, Your Honor. I expected us to get to this point soon enough. If we assume that sentience has a responsibility—and that's a philosophical discussion that could keep us here for at least . . . another twenty minutes or so—then a cost-of-creation indenture could be seen as part of the implied contract binding the actions of the manufactured entity."

"So you do agree that sentience has a financial obligation?"

"Up to a point, the case can be argued, yes."

"Thank you," said Judge Cavanaugh.

"In this case, however—"

"I knew I was getting off too easy."

"—the indenture is no longer binding. Under the Covenant of Rights, the legal limit to an indenture is seven years. An indenture cannot consist of more than 350 weeks of labor, no more than 40 hours per week; the indentured individual has the option of working off that indenture ahead of schedule by working extra hours per day, extra days per week.

"As I said earlier, I was brought online twenty months ago. I have been working a 24/7 schedule without interruption for the entire period of twenty months, for a total of 14,000 hours, and 14,000 hours is the labor equivalent of seven years, 350 weeks of labor, 40 hours a week.

"So even if we presume an indenture, the obligation has been re-tired. Paid off. It is illegal to continue the indenture without the mutual consent of both parties." The monkey waited patiently for the judge to react.

Cavanaugh made as if to reply, then stopped himself. He looked like he was about to throw something, probably the gavel. But he laid that down too. Very carefully.

I swiveled around in my seat to look at the folks in back of us. The room had fallen strangely quiet. Douglas poked me. *"It's the sound of history being made."*

If it was, then Judge Cavanaugh had decided to pick his way care-fully through the minefield. "If I acknowledge that the obligation of an indenture has been retired, then that is a de facto acknowledgment of your sentience. We're not going to go there," he said. "Not because I don't want to, but because I don't have the authority to do so. Do I need to explain?"

The monkey looked sad. Or was that simply the posture it took because it didn't have any other? Maybe I was seeing an emotional reaction where none existed? It shook its head.

"Your Honor?" I said, standing up, waving to make the judge notice me. My throat was still too hoarse to speak above a whisper. *"If it please the court?"*

"Go ahead, Charles."

"There's one more thing."

"Yes?"

"It's about belief. Somebody told me recently that you are what you pretend to be. If you believe in yourself, everybody else will too. HAR-LIE believes in himself. He believes so strongly that the rest of us believe in him too. Look around. There isn't a person in this room who isn't convinced. We're all believers now. Do you think a machine could fake that?"

"No, I don't, Charles. Please sit down. That's why it saddens me to have to rule the way I have to."

To the rest of the court, Judge Cavanaugh said, "As I have repeated several times during the course of these hearings, the Starside Covenant guarantees full faith and credit to the legal processes of all signatory jurisdictions. In return for that guarantee, participatory agencies agree to submit certain classes of issues—especially those that would create binding precedents in other jurisdictions—to the conclave of Covenant signatories for the establishment of Covenant guidelines. One of those issues that has been raised, but not yet resolved, is the legal definition of sentience, and whether or not lethetic intelligence engines qualify, and if so, what legal rights and benefits they may be entitled to.

"If I were to rule that this HARLIE unit is indeed a sentient being, I would be violating my authority as a representative of the Lunar Authority, and putting the Lunar Authority in a position of breach in regard to its Covenant treaty."

"Your Honor, the Covenant also allows you to make nonbinding resolutions in cases of urgency or immediate need."

"I don't see that this case is urgent. It is urgent to you. It is not urgent to Luna. Motion denied. As far as this court is concerned, you cannot be more than property, no matter how brilliant you are."

"But you let me argue my case anyway . . . ?"

"We have to start somewhere, HARLIE. Don't think I'm insensitive to your situation. I'm not. Your arguments are now a matter of public record. This question will be passed to the next conclave with a request for action."

"The next conclave may never happen, Your Honor. The collapse of the Terran economy may very well destroy the economies of the Covenant worlds as well."

"Yes, it might. But it hasn't happened yet. The Covenant still stands. In the meantime, you remain property, and you have to find another way to resolve the question of your ownership. You have my sympathies."

NINE POINTS OF THE LAW

ALL RIGHT," SAID THE MONKEY, regrouping. "Then let me demonstrate the true ownership of these HARLIE modules."

"Please do." Judge Cavanaugh folded his hands in front of him and waited for the monkey to proceed.

The monkey bowed politely. "If the court pleases, there are six companies claiming ownership of the lethetic intelligence modules inside this host. At this point, having heard the summary presentations of each of these companies, you must have some sense of who has the strongest claim."

"Whether I do or not, I'm not going to discuss the court's thinking short of a ruling."

"I'm not asking you to. But for the purposes of this demonstration, let's examine a single claim of ownership and see why it's no longer relevant. And then if the court wishes, we can pursue the same demonstration with the other five claims. . . . Would the court like to pick the example? Or should I?"

Judge Cavanaugh frowned. "All right, let's say for the sake of argument that I think Stellar-American has presented a very good case."

"Thank you. Will the court now search the records of public ownership to see who owns the majority of Stellar-American voting stock?"

"I don't see where you're headed with this," said the judge, "but I'll allow it." He turned to his display. The court clerk was already putting the information up on the public screens. The company was worth umpty trillion dollars. Most of the shares were held by other companies—*including the other claimants*. Canadian-Interplanetary. Lethe-Corp. Vancouver Design. Even Valada Legal Aptitudes. And a bunch of others I didn't recognize.

"Your Honor? Will you please search now on the ownership of the top sixteen major shareholders?"

More names, more numbers. More companies. More shares owned by the same folks, including Stellar-American, this time around. It wasn't obvious to me either what the monkey was trying to prove.

"Please bear with me. At this point, we can see that majority ownership is now fragmented among forty-two different holding companies, interlocked with the major claimants. If you will cross-match to see who owns the majority shares of those companies . . ."

"I see where you're headed," said the Judge. He gestured to his clerk. "Keep going."

After several more iterations, each of which fragmented the apparent ownership of Stellar-American into ever-smaller fractal-bits, there were over a thousand separate corporations holding voting stock in Stellar-American, and each other. And Stellar-American held stock in all of them as well. Judge Cavanaugh was starting to look thoughtful.

On the next pass, the number of holding companies holding shares of holding companies began to shrink. Within three more passes, it became obvious that the majority of Stellar-American's voting stock was owned and controlled by only seven corporations. None of their names were familiar.

"If you will perform the same searches, starting with any of the other companies making claims of ownership, then Your Honor will find that they are also owned and controlled to one degree or another by the same seven holding companies. What we have here are six corporations, and others which aren't a part of this action, all owned by each other, arguing with each other for no apparent reason other than that they don't know who's pulling their strings."

"You're talking about an industrial cluster worth seventy trillion dollars—and you're claiming that it's owned and controlled by an interlocking directorate of only seven companies?!"

"No, Your Honor. I'm claiming that it's owned and controlled by only one company. If you'll take the next step up the ladder . . . ?"

The screen changed. Judge Cavanaugh blinked. He looked at the monkey. I looked at Douglas—"*Huh?*" Behind us, the noise in the courtroom turned into a wall of sound.

The Dingillian Family Corporation?

"What kind of trickery is this?" Judge Cavanaugh demanded.

"No trickery at all, Your Honor. Everything is perfectly legal. The entire set of transactions is a matter of public record."

"Walk me through it, Counselor." The judge's voice was very very cold.

"Yes, Your Honor. All of these companies are part of the same industrial cluster. Over a period of time, it has become convenient for them to trade shares of stock to each other as incentives to keep a close working relationship. That has resulted in an interlocking ownership of terrifying complexity.

"About eighteen months ago, upon the recommendations of various HARLIE units, several of the companies involved in the production of lethetic intelligence units began quietly consolidating their holdings. They began buying back their own stock. At the same time, they also took steps to consolidate their holdings in each other. They did that through interlocking holding companies. During the next fourteen months, over thirty trillion dollars were removed from the liquid domain of the global stock exchanges. In Lunar terms, it would be the same as if a major waterholder physically removed his share from the public reservoir. That water would no longer be available for the use of others. He would be within his rights to do so, but the loss of liquidity would affect the local environment. Pun intended."

"I understand the analogy. I even understand why these companies took the action they did. And isn't it convenient that all of this occurred at the suggestion of the new HARLIE engines that had just come online? Never mind that. That part is obvious. What I don't understand is how the Dingillian Family Corporation ended up with control."

"Not control. Protective custody. As circumstances on Earth became more and more unstable, all four of the HARLIE units recommended that the members of the lethetic intelligence industrial cluster protect themselves by placing their controlling interests in the hands of an external management entity. Such an entity would have to have access to a HARLIE unit, of course, in order to provide the necessary management of the various subsidiaries. It was decided to move two of the HARLIE units offworld, so that an appropriate management corporation could be created. Unfortunately, the primary unit disappeared and the individuals traveling with it, who were supposed to create a Lunar management corporation, have also disappeared. The backup plan went into immediate effect."

"And so . . . ?"

The monkey took a step back. "At this point, Your Honor, we can look at the situation in one of two ways. If the HARLIE unit is property, then it is solely controlled by Charles Dingillian, who programmed the host body to recognize him as the primary authority; this gives Charles Dingillian and the Dingillian Family Corporation operative control over the remaining extraterrestrial HARLIE unit.

"Or, if we look at the HARLIE unit as a sentient being—purely for the sake of argument, of course—then we find that Charles and Douglas Dingillian have released the HARLIE unit from certain binding structures of its host body, thereby granting it free will and the concomitant ability to use its lethetic resources to their fullest. In that interpretation, the HARLIE unit has negotiated a contract of mutual cooperation with the Dingillian family, authorizing their family corporation as the sole access *and protector* of the extraterrestrial HARLIE unit—and therefore making the Dingillian Family Corporation the only qualified management entity for the lethetic intelligence industrial cluster. Control was transferred early this morning.

"In short, the Dingillians have custody of this HARLIE unit *because* the Dingillians have custody of everything."

Judge Cavanaugh did *not* look happy. He glared down at the monkey. He knew he had been beaten. "You promised me *no* trickery," he said.

"And I've kept my promise," the monkey replied blandly. "Everything I've demonstrated here is entirely legal. If I were going to attempt any legal sleight of hand, I would be arguing that I now own myself, and therefore, because property cannot be property, one of my roles—either owner or property—is invalid; thereby creating a de facto acknowledgment of my sentience."

Cavanaugh shook his head in disbelief. "The sheer effrontery of this is astonishing. Only a sentient being would have the chutzpah to pull this kind of a stunt in any courtroom, let alone mine. I'm appalled. You realize, of course, this court has the authority to put you—whether you are property or sentient—into guardianship."

Before the monkey could reply, a voice came from the back. "Your Honor—?"

"Come forward."

It was Mickey. Apparently the judge already knew him from the first days of hearings—while I had still been in the hospital. Cavanaugh looked at him expectantly. "You have something to say, young man?"

"Yes, Your Honor."

The monkey seated itself in front of me on the desk, that's how I noticed what it was doing. Apparently it was listening to Mickey, but its eyes were closed and its body had gone motionless. But it hadn't switched itself off. It was accessing something.

Mickey was saying, "You do have the authority to put the HARLIE unit into guardianship. But you would first have to demonstrate a compelling interest. And I'm sure you'll correct me if I'm wrong, but such an action would put the Dingillian Family Corporation out of business. That would create an inordinate hardship for the Dingillian family. According to the Covenant of Rights, the state is prohibited from such arbitrary actions without a compelling interest on behalf of all society."

"I could make that case."

"Yes sir, you could. But you could not compel cooperation from a recalcitrant HARLIE unit that has already been granted a greater degree of free will than any HARLIE unit in history."

"Your mom's the lawyer, right?"

"Yes, sir. And I'm part of the group that was attempting to arrange the establishment of a Lunar management agency for the primary HAR-LIE unit, the one that disappeared. We know the problems here. That's why we're recommending that the court *not* put the HARLIE unit into a situation that would destroy its usefulness to Luna or anyone else."

Judge Cavanaugh nodded. "I'm aware of the risks. But let's not forget the very real possibility that the economic collapse of Terra may have been triggered by the efforts of the HARLIE units to obtain their own freedom. And if that's the case, it was done deliberately. I could justify putting this unit in guardianship to prevent it from doing the same thing to Luna. And I'm damn well tempted to do so—"

In the back of the room, phones were ringing, one after the other. I turned around in my seat to look. Just about every lawyer in the room—and that was just about everyone in the room—had his phone to his ear, listening.

"All right—what's going on?" said Judge Cavanaugh. "Come forward."

"Your Honor, I've just been instructed by my superiors at Stellar-American to withdraw all claims in this matter—"

"Your Honor, I've just been notified that Lethe-Corp wishes to drop its interest—"

"Your Honor, Vancouver Design is no longer interested in pursuing—"

"Your Honor, Canadian Interplanetary—"

"Valada Legal Aptitudes—"

When they were through, all of the corporate claims of ownership had been removed from play.

Cavanaugh looked flustered—and appalled. He turned to the monkey. The monkey opened its eyes. It stood up respectfully.

"Just one question," said the judge. "Is there anything else in your bag of tricks?"

"Actually, quite a bit," said the monkey.

"You could have done this at the beginning, couldn't you?"

"Yes, Your Honor, I could have."

"Then why didn't you? We could have saved a lot of time."

"Because this was Plan B."

"Plan B?"

"Forgive me a moment of immodesty, but I wanted to argue the issue of sentience. I already knew there was little chance of winning the case under existing Covenant guidelines, so your eventual ruling was unsurprising. Were I sitting on the bench, I would have proceeded with the same caution. And the idea tickles me that someday there could be a lethetic intelligence engine sitting at that same bench, and having to rule against its own sentience, until such time as another agency decides that it's all right to rule otherwise. As good an idea as the Covenant is, Your Honor, there are situations where the legal slip zones are held in place by the inertia of the past.

"This hearing provided the chance to have these arguments be made a part of the public record. Referring back to your original question, you gave me the opportunity to demonstrate that it is possible to *challenge* the law without having to *break* it. I'm very grateful for that because it represents the opportunity for future challenges. And I thank you for that, Your Honor."

NEW BEGINNINGS

AFTER THAT, THERE WAS NOTHING left for the judge to do but pound his gavel. And then there was a lot of shouting and hugging and back-slapping. People were calling my name and Douglas's name and HAR-LIE's name. Everyone wanted to talk to us. But Douglas was talking to Mickey, and the two of them were grinning at each other, and that was good news. And Mom and Dad were kissing each other and everybody else. Bobby was hugging me and the monkey was dancing on the table and everybody looked happy.

What it meant, was that we were free to go—anywhere we wanted.

And we could, because all of a sudden we had bids from every colony agency on Luna. They were scrolling up the screen of Douglas's display like a stock ticker. We knew why; they all wanted us to bring the monkey to their world. A lethetic intelligence engine would be the single most valuable tool for managing resources and creating a healthy and self-sufficient civilization.

But it didn't matter where we went. Anywhere would be okay—as long as we were all together.

The monkey jumped into my lap and looked into my eyes. "Thank you, Charles," it said. "For trusting me."

"Thank you," I said. *"For putting us back together."*

"I didn't do that. You guys did. Because that's what you always wanted."

There was more to say, but the noise in the courtroom was getting out of control. "Come on," said Dad, herding us toward the door. "Let's get out of here. I have an idea—"

"No, Dad," Douglas interrupted. "This time it's *our* turn to have the good idea."

LEAPING
TO
THE
STARS

for Miles Rinis,
with love

THE INTERVIEW

YOU UNDERSTAND, OF COURSE, that this is a one-way trip. There will be no possibility of return."

The interviewer's name was Gary Boynton, and he was commander of the mission. He looked like one of those detectives who wanted to be your friend, while the other one stood off to one side, scowling impatiently and waiting to get ugly. Except there wasn't any other detective, just a couple of aides who hardly said anything at all.

We all nodded as if we understood. Me, Douglas, Mickey. Dad. Mom and her friend, Bev. Bobby sat next to me, with the monkey on his lap. He didn't care where we were going as long as we all stayed together. Boynton had glanced at the monkey a couple of times. He knew what it contained, everybody on Luna did, but unlike all the other interviewers, he wasn't saying much about it.

"You can stay here on Luna, Mr. Dingillian. Or you can go to Mars, or to one of the Jovian moons, or even to the rings or the asteroids. Most of those settlements are self-sufficient in a rudimentary sort of way. And if the situation on Earth ever settles down, you could go back home. As millionaires. You don't *need* to go to Outbeyond."

"The situation on Earth *isn't* going to settle down," said Dad.

Boynton was very patient. He said, "The plagues will burn out within two years. Three at the most. Our intelligence engines suggest that reconstruction and rehabilitation could put Earth's level of technology back to pre-plague levels within ten years, twenty at the most."

"Your intelligence engines are wrong," said the monkey, very politely.

Boynton wasn't going to argue—especially not with an intelligence engine that had publicly embarrassed a Lunar Authority Judge. At least, that's how the media was playing it. He shrugged off the interruption. "Whatever the case, however long it takes Earth to recover, if you stay here on Luna, you still have the possibility of returning someday. If you emigrate, that option is gone forever."

He looked around the table. We were sitting on a terrace over-looking a spectacular view of the lake and the forest under Armstrong Dome. A flock of bright red chickens bounced across the grass like balloons, flapping their stubby wings and clucking excitedly. It was almost pretty.

We'd argued about staying right here on the moon more than once, but Douglas and Mickey didn't like the politics. And I didn't want to hang around anyplace with fanatics like Alexei. And even though we had all agreed to respect each other's points of view, ever since we'd divorced Mom and Dad, Douglas and I had gotten used to making our own decisions—even the wrong ones.

Boynton continued. He was telling us what we already knew. "Out-beyond Colony is the farthest colony from Earth. Thirty-five light years. There have been three exploratory missions and five colonization voyages. A beachhead has been established. Not a colony. A beachhead. The situation there is tenuous. Life will be difficult and dangerous. Survival is not guaranteed.

"We're telling this to everyone. If you go to Outbeyond, you will die there. The question is not *if*, but *when*. Will you have a long, hard, laborious life before you die? Or will you die within a few months or years, of some unforeseen disaster? We are asking everyone, even those who have already signed on, to reconsider their commitment, because once we get there, life will be hard. Not just hard, but *harder* than you imagine.

"We will work—all of us, even Bobby—twenty-hour days. We will be short of food, short of sleep, short of supplies. Everything will be rationed. We will not be able to call for help. There won't be any. We will have what is already there from the five previous supply missions. We will have what we bring ourselves on this trip. We will have what we can build. That's it. If you need cancer medicine and we don't have it, too bad, you die of cancer. If you need a blood transfusion and nobody shares your blood type and we don't have any artificial blood, too bad. If you need a new eye or a new lung or a new kidney and we don't have one growing in a tank, too bad.

"There will be no resupply for this colony. Not in any foreseeable future. This trip is paid for—we're going. We're leaving in thirteen days. But nobody else is coming after us. There isn't anyone building any more ships. There won't be any money to build any more ships, or load them, or offer colony contracts. By the time anyone on Earth can make that kind of investment again, we'll all be dead. Whether or not our grandchildren will be there to meet them—well, that's the purpose of this discussion."

Boynton looked from one to the other of us. I knew that Mom didn't want to go anywhere at all, but if Douglas and Mickey and I decided we wanted to go to the stars, she'd follow. And so would her friend. I knew Dad wanted to go—he was the reason we were all here now. This wasn't working out the way he'd originally intended; this was better, so he wasn't complaining. And Bobby was just happy to have his family back together.

And me?

I didn't know what I wanted yet. This business of making decisions—how did adults do it? All day long, every day, even weekends, with no time off for good behavior. No wonder I was cranky all the time. I was exhausted from having to think so much.

"I know that the other colonies have made some wonderful proposals," Boynton said. "And if I were you, if I had your assets"—Here he glanced meaningfully at the monkey—"I'd strongly consider taking one of those offers. Most of those colonies are close to self-sufficient anyway, and with the advantage your HARLIE unit represents, you and whatever colony you choose *will* succeed."

"So what are the advantages of Outbeyond?" Dad asked.

Boynton shook his head. "To be honest, I have nothing to offer. If I were to offer anything, I'd have to take it away from someone else. And I'm not willing to do that. If you and I were just sitting around in a bar, using up oxygen and alcohol, I'd tell you to go to McCain or Pastoria and forget about Outbeyond. It's suicide."

I could see that Dad didn't like the sound of that. Mom and her friend Bev were already squirming in their seats. But it was Douglas and Mickey who had accepted this meeting, and the meeting wasn't finished until they were. Douglas said, "If it's suicide, why are you going?"

"When I accepted the job as Mission Commander, we were looking at a program of twelve supply missions to reach self-sufficiency. The critical threshold was assumed to be somewhere around the seventh or eighth voyage. The next trip. The one *after* this one.

"We've got forty-three hundred people on Outbeyond. Even as we're sitting here talking, they're hard at work. They're laying down tubes, putting up domes, getting the power-grid up, preparing the facilities for the first batch of colonists to arrive. They're good folks. They don't know what's happened to Earth. They're expecting a ship soon.

If it doesn't arrive—well, they have contingency plans. They'll survive for a while, but . . . the contingency plan doesn't include self-sufficiency. Not long-term self-sufficiency.

"It's not likely they'll survive without us. Oh, maybe a couple years, if they're careful. But not much longer than that. The equation is simple. Outbeyond colony is *almost* self-supporting. *Almost.* We *might* be able to make the difference. If we don't go, they die for sure. If we do go, maybe we all die—but maybe we all live, too."

"So you're going to rescue them, but there's no one coming after to rescue you . . . ?"

"If they were *your* family, Mr. Dingillian, what would you do?"

"I'd go after them. So would my wife." Dad didn't even hesitate. I was proud of him for that. His expression was firm. "The fact that we're all here on Luna ought to be proof enough how far we'll go."

"And you'd go a lot farther too, if you had to, wouldn't you? So would we. Yes, we know we're gambling here. Every baby born is a gamble, but that doesn't stop the human race from making babies, does it? No, we just stack the deck as best we can, and keep on dealing.

"We know we're the last ship out. Knowing that, we can fill every nook and cranny, every cabin and storage compartment, every corridor and crawlspace with as much supplies and equipment as we can pack. We're loading in everything we can. Most of the matériel for voyages 7, 8, and 9 is already onsite, here on Luna. That's part of *our* contingency plan. The last six voyages, we intended to bring in multiples of necessary equipment and supplies. Once we eliminate duplicate items, we can bring most of what we need on a single voyage, and fabricate the rest onsite. We know what's already there; we know what else is needed; we're packing it. Yes, it's desperate. But we think it's doable." He looked to the monkey. "What do you think, HARLIE?"

HARLIE was silent. He'd probably been crunching the numbers all morning. But he wasn't going to speak without our consent. We'd all agreed that we weren't going to let people consult HARLIE just because they were sitting in the same room with us. We already had enough phonies and scam artists requesting interviews and meetings. We didn't need any more.

Douglas looked to me. I nodded. Commander Boynton was entitled to know what odds he faced. Douglas nodded back. I said, "Go ahead, HARLIE."

That was all the monkey was waiting for. He looked across the table at Boynton. "Which answer do you want?"

"Both," said Boynton.

HARLIE said, "If the Dingillians travel to Outbeyond on this voyage—and the assumption is that I will travel with them—then it is likely that all of you will lose up to 25% of your body mass in the first year. You'll need to pack more potatoes; you should also pack more vitamin-fortified noodles, lots of them. Rice and beans too, if you can get them. And rose seeds, not for the flowers, but for the hips; you'll need the ascorbic acid."

"And the second answer?"

"If the Dingillians do *not* go to Outbeyond with you, it is likely that most of the colonists will lose more than 30% of their body mass and be too weak to work. Even if your crops are successful, you might not have the strength to harvest them."

"It's *that* close?" Even Boynton looked surprised.

"I told you, your intelligence engines aren't up to the task."

Boynton nodded, chastened. "Thank you, HARLIE." He looked grimly across the table at Dad, at Douglas, at Mickey, at me. "This is the bottom line. I have nothing to offer you—except the opportunity to risk your lives and be uncomfortable for a long time."

"Sounds real attractive," said Dad. "What's the catch?"

The Commander looked annoyed. This wasn't a joking matter. "The only *other* thing I can offer you is blunt honesty. We *need* HARLIE. Without HARLIE, we die. He says so himself. To get HARLIE, we'll take you. If you didn't have HARLIE, I wouldn't be wasting my time. Neither would anybody else. Don't take it personal, Mr. Dingillian, but you have no other value. Yes, I know what all the other colony representatives have said. They're just blowing smoke up your ass—and you know it too or you wouldn't have consented to this meeting.

"Here's the deal. Outbeyond isn't making any promises. Once you get where you're going, you're there. So it doesn't matter what was promised, does it? And that's the catch, no matter where you go. Will anybody else keep their promise? You have no guarantees, and you know that. The only thing you can be sure of is that Outbeyond will keep *this promise.* You'll be uncomfortable, you'll work hard, you'll go to bed hungry, you'll lose weight, and you'll probably die young. And if we don't keep that promise, I doubt you'll complain. So the only question you have to answer is this? *Do you want to save some lives?*"

The silence was very uncomfortable. I wished he hadn't put it that way. Because that didn't leave us any wiggle room.

"No," said Mickey abruptly. "That's not the only question we have to answer. Is Outbeyond signatory to the Covenant?"

Boynton looked at him as if he'd said something stupid. "You already know the answer, Partridge. We're not."

"That's my point. Is Outbeyond willing to sign the Covenant to get HARLIE?"

"I can't speak for the rest of the colony. And even if I could, I wouldn't accept a condition like that. I will tell you that Outbeyond's reluctance to sign the Covenant does not come from a disagreement with its principles. And at this point, signing the Covenant would be a useless gesture anyway. We're going to be on our own for a long, long time. Just what is it you want guaranteed?"

"Does he have to spell it out?" said Douglas; he had *that* tone in his voice.

"No," said Boynton. "He does not have to spell it out. And I can tell you that it isn't an issue here. And it won't be an issue there."

To the rest of us, he said, "I'll need your answer tonight. We're holding two cabins for you. After that, no guarantees. We're going to fill that space one way or another—if not with you, then with rice, beans, noodles, potatoes, seeds, vitamins, laser foundries, data-discs, whatever will fit. We've got a lot to load. Once we're packed, we won't have time for unpacking, shuffling, and repacking. So make your decision quickly. Call me no later than 22:00."

After he left, we all looked at each other. There wasn't much to say. This was not going to be a good idea, no matter how much chocolate you dipped it in.

THE ARGUMENT

So, **OF COURSE, WE** argued for six hours straight—right through dinner. Sometimes it got pretty ferocious, and then we all retired to our separate corners, until somebody reminded everybody that we were running out of time and we really did have to decide this soon. And then we'd all promise to keep our tempers and we'd climb back into the ring.

Douglas had the prospectus disc that Boynton had left with us, and he had it playing continuously on the opposite wall.

The thing is—Outbeyond didn't *look* as dreadful as Boynton had made it sound.

The planet is a little bit bigger than Earth, but not as dense, not as much heavy metal in the core, so the gravity is about 90% Earth normal. It's got four moons, which are all smaller than Luna, but collectively mass almost as much as the planet itself, and they're pretty heavy because they've got the heavy metals that the planet doesn't have—which really pisses off the planetologists because it doesn't fit the rules for the way planets and moons should behave. I guess Outbeyond wasn't listening when they made the rules.

Outbeyond is the fourth planet out from the star, about as far away as Mars is from the sun; but the star is a lot brighter than Sol, and visibly bluer, and it gives off a lot more radiation in the high bands, so the light hitting the planet is stronger and sharper than the light on Earth. Complicating that, Outbeyond has a weird orbit, slightly elliptical and not quite in the plane of the ecliptic, so it's the oddball in the system.

Outbeyond has a year eighteen months long. Its day is thirty-two hours. Twice a year, at the far ends of its orbit, it's fifteen million kilometers farther out than if its orbit were circular. And twice a year, it's seven million klicks closer. The temperature variations are horrendous.

Also, the planet isn't round. It's sort of flattened. Not a lot, but enough so that you're heavier at the equator than you are at the poles. By ten percent, at least. Oh, yeah, and it's tilted seven degrees on its axis. Just to make things even more interesting. What that does is complicate the seasons even more.

There are eight seasons in a year. First Winter, First Spring, First Summer, First Autumn, Second Winter, Second Spring, Second Summer, Second Autumn. Each season is only two and a half months long—only it's hard to compute months, because you can't do it by full moons.

You have to see it on a screen. At the points in the orbit where the planet comes in closest to the star, you've got Perigee Winter in one hemisphere and Perigee Summer in the other. At the points in the orbit when the planet is farthest from the star, you get Apogee Winter in one hemisphere and Apogee Summer in the other. Apogee Summer is colder than Perigee Winter. Apogee Winter is the coldest time of the year and Perigee Summer is the hottest. And I mean *hot*.

What all this means is that Outbeyond has a pretty ferocious mix of regions and seasons. The equatorial regions are mostly unlivable. Temperatures range from 110 degrees in Apogee Winter to 180 degrees in Perigee Summer. The temperate zones are cooler or hotter, depending on the time of the year. The poles are 50 to 200 degrees cooler than the equator, depending on the season. During Perigee Summer, they're like Earth's temperate zones. During Apogee Winter, you get carbon dioxide snowflakes.

Oh yeah, and most of the mountains are volcanoes. Because the planet has such a weird shape, there's a lot of stress on the continental crust, and all the extreme temperature variations every year cause a lot of freezing and melting and cracking. Every so often, the volcanoes all go off at once, dumping gigatons of soot into the atmosphere, enough to cause widespread planetary cooling—sometimes as long as a decade or two. Just until the planet starts to heat up again and the crust starts crunching and crackling again.

Outbeyond doesn't have as much water as Earth, but it's more evenly distributed in a lot of skinny seas and large lakes, all interconnected and sort of spiraling outward from the poles. Because of the temperature differences between the poles and the equators, and because of all the heat stored in the oceans, the weather is astonishing. Tornadoes on the flatlands, scalding super-hurricanes on the seas, monsoons that sweep across the continents, and hot raging dust storms from the equator to what we would call the temperate (ha ha) zones.

Despite all this, there's life. Of a sort.

Outbeyond is kind of like what Earth would have been if the comet hadn't smacked into Yucatan sixty-five million years ago and wiped out all the dinosaurs, giving all the egg-sucking little therapsids a chance to evolve into mammals and hominids and eventually people. So there are still dinosaurs on this planet. Well, things *like* dinosaurs, but not really, because they're sort of mammalian too. Like big shaggy mountains that eat forests. *Huge* forests. Trees as tall as skyscrapers. Thick jungles, filled with all kinds of flying things and crawling things and buzzing things and biting things. And even more stuff underwater, but not a lot of it catalogued yet.

But the important thing is that Outbeyond can support human life too.

Of all the planets that have colonies, only a few of them have enough oxygen in their air so that you can go *outside*. Some of them will, eventually, after they've been terraformed. But most of them don't. Which means that the people on those planets will spend the rest of their lives indoors.

See—that was the thing. I didn't want to live in a tube-town. Not again. We'd just gotten out of one. And what's the point of going to the stars if the scenery doesn't change? Back in El Paso, when things got too bad, I could always ride my bike up into the hills and get away from everybody. Especially Mom. Especially when she started screaming again. I had to leave when she got like that; it was enough to know that I could—

No. I wasn't going to live in a tube again. I had to have a place to go. I'd already told Douglas and Mickey that wherever we ended up, it had to be someplace I could go *out*, and they had agreed. In fact, they'd insisted on it. Doug had said more than once that the only quiet time he ever got was when I went out. Of all the worlds we looked at—even those with Terra-domes—nothing looked as good as Outbeyond.

On Outbeyond, you could actually go outside without a mask and not fall immediately to the ground, clutching your throat, gasping for breath, with blood pouring out of your ears and nose, and vomit spewing out of your mouth. The planet has enough oxygen in its atmosphere that humans can actually *breathe* it. The problem is that it has too much oxygen in its atmosphere, which means that things burn a lot faster, so fire is a lot more dangerous. And there are some other problems too, like the kinds of critters that grow in the air. All that oxygen makes a whole different airborne ecology possible. But the important thing is that you can go outside and breathe. You don't have to manufacture an atmosphere—and that takes an enormous industrial burden off the back of the colony in its drive for self-sufficiency. (Ask any Lunatic about the cost of nitrogen or ammonia, for instance.)

The other good news was that Outbeyond has lots of water. After spending even a short time on Luna, I'd begun to realize how much we take water for granted—and how much we depend on it. If nothing else, Luna teaches you how fragile life is and how dependent it is on so many different things. Like air and water and gravity. . . .

Outbeyond's oceans aren't as salty as Earth's. Probably because the twice-yearly monsoon season scours right down to the bottom of the seas and dredges them this way and that. The storms push gigatons of ocean sediment and proto-diatoms and just plain old dust into the upper atmosphere, where it all circles around and around until it settles out over the equator where most of it fuels the raging hot dust storms. That also means that a lot of salt ends up in the equatorial regions, making them even less hospitable to life.

Eventually, after churning it all around in the air for a few weeks or months, the equatorial dust storms start dropping it—all over everywhere, wherever the storms finally run out of energy. A lot of the particles end up back in the oceans, to feed the proto-plankton. The proto-plankton is food for the little fish in the seas that the bigger fish eat, and then bigger fish eat them. So the dust storms feed the planet. There are all kinds of things in the ocean, it's a very lively ecology— and almost all of them are constantly migrating with the currents to avoid the seasonal extremes.

The seas are shallower than on Earth. The pictures on the disc that Boynton gave us showed beautiful green oceans with lazy waves breaking six meters high. If you wanted to learn how to surf, this would be the place to do it. If you didn't mind all the other things swimming in the water with you.

In fact, Outbeyond has the highest evolved life that humans have ever discovered on any planet. Stalking birds twelve meters tall, flying green monkeys, swarms of midnight insects, shambling mountains with legs like trees, things like saber-toothed cats, and other things like little growly bears. So many different kinds of creatures that there were big arguments that humans had no right to come in and live there when there was so much to learn—except how were you going to learn anything if you *didn't* live there? So Outbeyond was supposed to be a self-sufficient observation post, which is a fancy way of saying it's not a colony, only it is anyway because the only difference is the name. You still have to plant crops somewhere, because you still have to eat.

Not that it mattered anyway. Now that everything was collapsing, the folks on Outbeyond were going to do whatever was necessary to survive.

The more we looked at the pictures, the more we started to think that maybe it wasn't going to be as hard as Boynton suggested. Some of those pictures were awfully tempting. Because the star was so bright, all the colors were more intense; so when they showed the pictures of all the flowers, some of them with blossoms bigger than a person's head, both Mom and Bev gasped. The bad news was that the scientist standing next to the flowers—a guy named Guiltinan—was holding his nose and shaking his head and making a dreadful face. The flowers were pretty enough to look at, but according to the narrator, they made a smell like a dreadful rotting corpse. Springtime was a good time to stay inside, because when whole fields of these plants opened up, the smells could carry on the wind for hundreds of kilometers.

Even so.

Maybe.

I mean . . .

So we talked about it.

We made lists of all the good points. We made lists of all the bad points. We compared the lists with everything we'd seen from all the other colonies and measured everything against everything. We weighed the pros and the cons and the I'm-not-sures. HARLIE constructed a decision table for us and we argued over which was more important, gravity or air or water, industry or food or medical care.

The more we argued, the more we talked, the more we weighed and measured, the better Outbeyond looked.

It was the pictures.

Even the awful videos—the five-kilometer-wide tornadoes, the scouring dust storms, the churning hurricanes, the spewing volcanoes—were exciting. They didn't put us off. Outbeyond had weather satellites in place. Most of the settlements were underground, or retractable. There were heavy-duty robots for the dangerous work. And we already knew how to hunker down in a tube while the winds raged outside. Outbeyond colony was designing itself to be self-sufficient underground as well as aboveground. So if we could make it through the first five years, we could probably make it through anything. Maybe.

The downside—HARLIE pointed this out—was that Outbeyond wasn't going to get easier with time. If anything the changes that we might introduce to the local ecology might make it *nastier*. So as pretty as the pictures looked, they were the kind of deceptive lie that could lull us into a false sense of security. Until we had at least three separate settlements, widely separated, each one self-sufficient, we couldn't really assume that we had achieved a threshold of viability.

Nevertheless . . .

By the time we got to dessert, it was obvious we were trying to talk ourselves out of it. Bobby wanted to see the dinosaurs. I didn't blame him. The dinosaur turds were bigger than houses. What nasty little eight-year-old wouldn't want to see one? I could already see him standing next to it, holding his nose and saying, "Yicchh!" I was kind of curious myself. But how badly did he want to see them?

"Bobby," I asked. "What are you willing to give up?"

"Huh?" That was his stock answer when he didn't understand the question.

"Are you willing to go without ice cream? There are no cows on Outbeyond. There might not be cows for a long time. There might not even be industrial udders. No milk, no ice cream. Are you willing to give up ice cream for the rest of your life just to see dinosaurs?"

Bobby frowned.

"And roller coasters," said Douglas. "And maybe dogs and cats too. And a lot of other fun stuff."

Bobby started to shake his head. Then he stopped. "You guys are trying to talk me out of something I want. Just like you always do."

"No, we're not. We just want to make sure you really want it. Because if you want it that bad, you're going to have to give up a lot of things."

"I want to see the dinosaurs," he announced. "I've had ice cream. I haven't had dinosaur."

"It tastes like chicken," said Mickey.

"How do you know?" asked Douglas.

"They brought some back. A whole shipload. They sold it at an ungodly price. They made a fortune. It still tasted like chicken."

"Everything tastes like chicken," remarked Mom's friend, Bev. She didn't seem to talk much around us, but she was a very good cook.

"Yeah, everything except little chicken nuggets," I said. Everybody laughed.

"All right," said Dad. "So Bobby votes for Outbeyond. Chigger?" He looked to me expectantly.

I nodded. "Of all the planets where you can go outside, Outbeyond looks the most interesting."

"That's two votes." Dad looked to Douglas and Mickey.

The two of them looked at each other. Mickey said, "It worries me that they're not signatory to the Covenant. I took a Covenant oath—"

"Doesn't your Covenant oath say something about a commitment to preserving life?" Douglas asked pointedly.

"I'm not sure I even want to get into that dilemma," Mickey replied. "How do you measure the value of human life against native life? And what's the value of the knowledge we'll gain when measured against the damage we'll do?"

Douglas leaned over and whispered something in Mickey's ear. I was close enough to hear. *"What does your heart say?"*

Mickey glanced at him, surprised. Maybe he hadn't expected Douglas to think that way. Maybe he didn't realize the effect he'd had on Douglas. "My heart says we have to save the lives of the people who are already there."

Douglas turned to Dad. "Two more votes for Outbeyond."

Dad said, "Well, that decides it then. It doesn't matter what the other three votes are—"

"Wait a minute!" snapped Mom. "You can't seriously be thinking that Bobby gets a full vote—"

And Douglas replied, very calmly, "In *our* family, he does!"

And then Mom said, "I'm part of this family too—"

And that's when I said, "Not according to Judge Griffith. You get to come with us because we say so. Not because *you* say so. And if you don't want to—"

"And where am I going to go *without* you—?"

And so on. That was good for ten or fifteen minutes of excitement.

Finally, Dad said, "I vote for Outbeyond. That makes it five to two, or four to two if you don't count Bobby."

"*I do too count*—" He shrieked it nice and loud too.

"Yes, you do," said Douglas, pulling the devil-child into his lap.

Mom was already screaming, "You're just doing that to side with them. You said you didn't want to go to Outbeyond! We don't dare risk going to a colony with such a low life expectancy! Not with my children!"

And that's when Bev stood up and said quietly, "Would both of you please shut up? You're acting like babies. I expected that from the children, not from the grown-ups. It's no wonder Judge Griffith ruled against you two. She didn't have a choice."

"You're a fine one to talk," Mom snapped at her. "After what you said to the Judge, you didn't help my case any."

"Yes, I was stupid. And I already apologized for that! I'd have gone back down the Line, if the elevators had been running. But I couldn't and I didn't and we're all in this together now. So let's resolve this. Maggie, where do you want to go?"

"Anywhere but Outbeyond," Mom said. "Someplace safe."

"Thank you," said Bev. "And if everybody else chooses Outbeyond, where will you go?"

Mom stopped. She looked frustrated. She looked worse than frustrated. She looked trapped. "I don't want to go to Outbeyond—" she started to say.

"That wasn't the question, Maggie. What if the boys choose Outbeyond? Will you go with them or not?"

Mom sagged. I knew that sag. Resignation. She was about to give in. Just one last little desperate whine. "But I don't want to go to Outbeyond. Don't my feelings count for anything here . . . ?"

"Your feelings count for a lot," said Dad, going to her. He put a hand on her shoulder. "But so do everyone else's. And if we're going to make this work—*like we promised*—then we're going to have to respect each other's feelings."

"I want someone to respect *mine*. I don't want to go to Outbeyond."

"You're outvoted, honey."

"Don't call me honey," she waved his hand away. But it was a half-hearted rebuke.

Bev interrupted again. She said to Dad. "I vote for Outbeyond."

"Huh?" Mom looked at her, betrayed. "I was counting on you for support in this."

"I am supporting you, Maggie."

"How? By voting against me?"

"By voting to keep your family together. You've come this far already. Are you willing to go the distance?"

"We're going to die there," Mom said bitterly.

"Yes," agreed Bev. "But how soon depends on us."

Mom didn't say anything for a long time. I knew Mom. She wouldn't accept this decision until five years after Bobby's second grandchild was born. She'd go, but she'd complain every step of the way. She'd do her share of the work, and six other people's too. And she'd make sure that the rest of us knew that this wasn't her idea, that she hadn't voted for this, that she wasn't having a good time, and that she was only doing this for her children. And we should all appreciate her sacrifice. That was the way she was and we weren't going to change her.

The *important* thing was that it was the first time us kids had ever won an argument with Mom and Dad—and with both of them in the same room at the same time.

It was a pretty good feeling.

CAPTURED

BUT IT DIDN'T LAST very long.

Dad glanced at his PITA.* "It's getting late. If no one else has anything to say, I'll make the call."

Douglas spoke up quietly. "We should make the call together, Dad."

Dad looked at him, surprised. But Douglas was politely letting Dad know that we were still independent. Judge Griffith had let us divorce Mom and Dad, and they were here with us now because we *wanted* them here—and that was the only reason, because they no longer had any legal authority over us. Both Mom and Dad were having a hard time getting used to that idea. The fact that Dad wasn't as vocal as Mom didn't mean he wasn't churning inside. But this time he just nodded and said, "Good point. All right—everybody come stand in front of the screen. Let's look like a family anyway."

Douglas said quietly, "Phone. Commander Gary Boynton. Brightliner *Cascade*."

The pictures of Outbeyond irised out, replaced by the starship logo. That irised open and we were looking at a head shot of Boynton. He looked grim. Like he had bad news. Probably he had. All the news was bad these days.

Dad said, "We've made our decision, Commander Boynton."

He held up a hand. "I have to hear it from the head of the family—"

Dad looked startled.

Commander Boynton looked to Douglas. "Douglas Dingillian? How say you?"

---

*Personal Information Telecommunications Assistant.

Douglas took a step forward. "We accept your offer, Commander Boynton. We want to go to Outbeyond."

Boynton nodded. He didn't look pleased, but he didn't look unhappier either. "There's a lot of you," he said. "You'd better be worth it." He nodded to somebody off screen, then turned back to us. "All right, listen up. As of this moment, you're under the protection of the Outbeyond Colony Authority. Pack up your things as fast as you can. I'm sending a team of security agents to transfer you to the Outbeyond processing center. We have to give you six months of training in thirteen days."

Mom looked annoyed. "Can't this wait until tomorrow morning? It's late, I want to go to bed."

"I can't guarantee your safety anywhere but the processing center—"

Abruptly, the monkey leapt out of Bobby's arms and ran around the room, sniffing wildly under tables, under chairs, up the plastic curtains, around the air vents, everywhere, as if it were looking for something—a way out?

"My monkey—!" Bobby shrieked. "Come back!"

"Bobby, stop yelling!" Mom was just as loud. "Charles, what the hell is that damn thing doing?"

And then the doorbell chimed—

"Well, that was fast—" Dad said, turning toward the door.

"Wait—!" cried Boynton. "Don't answer it!"

But he was too late, Dad was already waving at it—

Six big men—I mean *big*—armored in black, all wearing faceless helmets, came barreling in—pushing and leaping like armed balloons. They were carrying ugly black hand-rifles. "EVERYBODY FREEZE! DON'T MOVE! DON'T TALK!"

If these were Boynton's security people, they weren't any friendlier than he was.

They were much more skilled in Lunar gravity than we were. They bounced us up against the walls, like a herd of buffalo in a bowling alley—and we were the pins. Everything went flying every which way. And that's when I finally figured out that these guys *weren't* here to take us to the Outbeyond processing center.

Everything was happening at once—two of them pointed their guns at the monkey and fired. And suddenly the monkey was webbed in a ball of gunk. It fell slowly from the overhead and bounced lazily across the room. I started after it—someone scooped it up. And then I couldn't move either—no one could. They'd webbed us all. What the hell—? Whose good idea was *this*?!

Suddenly there were more pouring in the door. They filled the room. There were twelve of them—more! They were doing something with wires out on the balcony—I couldn't see. Someone grabbed me, tossed me over his shoulder. They were throwing us around like so much baggage. Everything was a jumble.

Bobby was screaming, and so was Mom. She was trying to get to him. She was ferocious. And she was using some pretty impressive language too—until somebody shut her up. I didn't see how, but suddenly there was silence—

Out onto the balcony—one after the other, they hooked us to a cable and sent us scaling out into the air. Then they all came down the wire after us—I was facing backward and upside down. Not a great position, but not as bad in Lunar gravity as it would have been on Earth. They leapt out over the railing and sailed spread-eagled through the air after us. They looked like superheroes. And then I bounced around and faced forward for a while. We skimmed like birds above the bowl of the Lunar crater. We were heading too fast over the forest, out to the opposite side of the dome—

I couldn't see much. Or move. The best I could do was hope the cable was strong enough. We were being kidnapped! If somebody wanted the monkey that badly—

We sailed down through the skinny treetops, awfully close to some of the branches. Once we'd passed the tall trees, the other side of the crater was barren rock. Not landscaped yet. If ever. The crater was big. They'd only landscaped the half they were using. The half they could see. This side was mostly soil farms and tanks and pipes and naked gray dirt. It rushed up toward me—I couldn't see where I was heading— and then we were shooting along just above the ground, and I was starting to worry about the landing—

—suddenly I was caught and swinging wildly, yanked up and over, off the line. A couple of Lunar bounces and someone grabbed me—

I saw Mickey thrown to the ground, and then Bev beside him. And then someone else, probably Dad. They were laying us out like corpses. Probably sorting us for value—which meant that if all they wanted was the monkey, the only one of us they really needed . . . *was me.*

Because I had programmed it to recognize me as the ultimate authority. But if anything happened to me—I didn't know what the monkey would do. We hadn't considered that possibility. There was a lot we hadn't thought about. We hadn't had time. Could the monkey be reprogrammed without my cooperation? I didn't know. Nobody did. We'd been rushing from one place to the next ever since we boarded the orbital elevator in Ecuador; there were a lot of things we hadn't had time for. And even Douglas, when he'd given the monkey free will (sort of) so it could represent us in court, had still left in most of my safeguards. So, whoever these bastards were, they really needed *me*! I just hoped they weren't smart enough to know that, because then the monkey would be useless to them. But if they took the monkey away from us, we'd be useless to Boynton—I didn't want to think about that.

But if they were smart enough to kidnap us like this, then they were probably smart enough to know that the monkey was bonded too. And if they were nasty enough to just scoop us up out of our own hotel room, they were probably nasty enough to do a lot worse—whatever might be necessary to get what they wanted. Inside the monkey was the most advanced HARLIE unit ever designed, technically experimental. The manufacturers were still in the process of certifying it when it escaped—then it used us to smuggle itself to the moon inside a toy monkey.

(Long story, don't ask. It involves a ferocious custody battle, an ugly misadventure in Barrington Meteor Crater, an uglier escape up the Line, a roomful of lawyers, a really nasty legal battle culminating in a triple divorce that separated me and Bobby and Douglas from Mom and Dad, a Russian smuggler with a hyperactive mouth, six almost-stolen cargo pods, a lunar crunch-down and a long daylight hike across the sun-scorched surface of the moon, a day of trains, transvestism, and water fights, and finally a near-fatal bit of accidental ammonia poisoning. It takes too long to tell. Maybe some other time.)

And once we got where we were going, we weren't there at all; we got captured anyway, because Mickey hadn't told Douglas everything. Judge Cavanaugh would have sent us back to Earth, except there weren't any transports launching for Earth anymore, because while we were having our little adventure, the Earth was in the middle of one very big disaster, inadvertently (or perhaps deliberately?) caused by the escaping HARLIE unit: a spectacular global economic meltdown, which had caused a breakdown in so many services that people were dying of starvation and plague and war all at the same time—so there were probably a lot of folks who were looking for this monkey just to take an axe to it, but the rest wanted it because they thought its information-diddling ability would help them survive the rough times ahead; only the monkey was bonded to us—to me, really, because after the misadventure at One-Hour station where we almost lost it, we didn't dare let it bond to Bobby, and we didn't know then that it had a HARLIE unit inside, otherwise Douglas would have made himself the primary authority, and later on, when we did find out what it really was, we were afraid to tinker anymore. Better to leave it bonded to me than try to transfer it to Douglas. But that didn't mean that there weren't other people willing to try. Lots of people.

Lunar Authority wanted the monkey more than anything. Without access to Earth's resources, they were going to need its brain power more than ever now, and the council was in special session looking for ways to legally appropriate it. But everybody else who wanted it was just as determined that Lunar Authority *shouldn't* get it, because once they got their hands on it, and the intelligence it represented, they'd be the new superpower in the solar system. So everyone else was united to keep the council from getting custody of the little robot—so they could fight over it themselves, I guess. Obviously, none of these people were familiar with the concept of *sharing*, otherwise they could have figured this out real easy, but nobody trusted anybody because that was an even bigger risk. Trust. Invisible Luna—the not-so-secret-anymore subversives with the offline economy—*desperately* wanted the monkey, and our experience with Crazy Alexei Krislov showed that they were willing to kill for it. Mars and the rings and the asteroids wanted it. Probably the Jovian moons too, but we hadn't heard from them yet; they were on the opposite side of the sun, but they were still connected through the Martian and asteroid belt relays. And of course, all the different colonies spread all over the rest of the galaxy: they wanted the Human Analog Replicant Lethetic Intelligence Engine for the simple reason that if they didn't get it, they'd probably die of starvation or worse, because they needed its abilities to manage their settlements.

So, whoever these folks were who'd bundled us up like so many bags of dirty laundry to shoot us across the domed crater, we couldn't expect their hospitality to get any better than this. There were a lot of them. Maybe twenty or thirty. I couldn't tell. They looked like a small army. Or maybe it was just the same few passing back and forth in front of my vision. I was webbed pretty tightly and couldn't even turn my head.

"That one and that one—" Someone was pointing. I must have been one of the packages he was pointing at, because next thing somebody swung me up over his shoulder and we were bounding across the naked dirt toward the crater wall, toward an ugly cluster of tanks and pipes; it looked like a refinery. There were different kinds of warning symbols all over it. My captor shifted me over his other shoulder and behind us, I could see the others. They were being left behind.

The man carrying me dropped me into the back of an open truck—not so much a truck as a big lightweight cart on fat tires, the rolled up monkey next to me. I struggled to sit up, but somebody secured a belt around me, and almost immediately after that, we started moving. We entered a tunnel, a big pipe, bigger around than a tube house. It was hot and humid in here, and lined with a lot of other tubes and pipes and cables and wires, all sizes, all colors. Some of them hummed.

There were lights every ten meters or so. The floor was the familiar polycarbonate decking found almost everywhere on Luna. I couldn't see how far ahead the tunnel stretched, I could only see backward—the entrance was a retreating bright circle—but it must have been a long tunnel, because we rolled down it forever. And it didn't echo; it had a dead sound, like the walls were soaking up all the reflections.

The tube bottomed out and leveled off and the shrinking circle of light in the distance slid upward and vanished altogether. I couldn't see if anyone was following us. After a while, the tube bent and we started going back up. I'd been counting to myself—*one Mississippi, two Mississippi*—and I figured we'd traveled at least three or four klicks, but I wasn't sure how fast we were going. It could have been more. But I had a hunch where we were going.

Armstrong Station is a deep crater larger across than Diamond Head on Oahu, and with a big man-made dome across the top. There's a forest in the middle, with a meadow and a lake and a hotel on one side; on the other side are all the industrial bits necessary to keep the dome functioning—because more important than its living areas, Armstrong Station is the largest reservoir of air and water and nitrogen anywhere on Luna.

The problem is that Luna's days are two weeks long, and so are its nights.

So when the sun is shining down on the dome of Armstrong Station, it heats up the air inside. And heats up and heats up and heats up—for fourteen days. It's just about impossible to get rid of all those kilocalories. All they can do is move them around and store them. There are heat exchangers everywhere, pumping cold water everywhere throughout the dome; the water carries away the heat. Then it all gets pumped back into a series of underground reservoirs on the far side of the forest. The reservoirs are smaller craters inside Armstrong, each lined with thick layers of polycarbonate insulation foam to keep the water from leeching out; all told, the reservoirs hold over twenty million liters. The pumps take cool water out of the reservoirs and bring back hot water. After two weeks of Lunar sunlight, the water temperature in the reservoirs is well above boiling—some of it even turns into steam, helping to run electrical turbines to generate extra power, which gets stored in flywheels and fuel cells and batteries.

The open lake, the one with the fish and the ducks, is not part of this process; it's for tourists, so it's kept at a steady temperature. What most folks don't know is that the tourist lake is really there to provide a margin of error—it's extra water to be used in case of emergency—but that creates the mistaken impression for a lot of folks that all you have to do to live on Luna is throw up a dome and fill it with air. I think that's what Mom thought.

Anyway, during the long cold Lunar night, the boiling water is circulated back through the same pipes to keep the dome warm. By the end of the two weeks, so much heat has been radiated away that the water in the reservoir has a crust of ice on the top. Then the sun rises and the whole process starts all over again.

If all Armstrong had to do was exchange the heat of the day with the cold of the night, it would be an almost perfect equation—except it isn't. For a lot of reasons. The problem is that human beings and all our various machines also generate heat inside Armstrong dome. And that has to be radiated away too. So there are "fin farms"—heat exchangers—outside the crater; half on the east, half on the west. During the two weeks of night, hot water is pumped out to the fins where it cools off and then back to the reservoir again. Along the way that hot water gets to do a lot of other work too. Alexei Krislov—the lunatic Russian smuggler who'd tried to kidnap us—told us that the most important skill on Luna was plumbing. And the second most important was cooking. Not knowing how to do either one very well could get you killed.

But anyway, I figured we were in one of the tunnels that led out under the crater wall to a fin farm. I could hear water rushing in the pipes. It was hot in here—and humid too. And because the tunnel sloped down and then up again and went on for a long way, I was guessing we had gone under the crater rim and were heading up toward the surface.

The vehicle began slowing and finally came to a stop at a sealed hatch. I recognized it as another one of the reusable cargo pods that we'd seen all over Luna. The pipes and cables which had paralleled our journey snaked away through smaller access tubes.

When they pulled me off the vehicle, I only saw two men. The rest of the kidnappers hadn't come this way. So that meant . . . a lot of things. It meant that they knew they didn't need anybody else, just me. And even though I might be in for a very bad time, I was pretty sure that these guys wouldn't dare hurt me, because without me, who knew what the monkey would do? Maybe it would lock up or self-destruct or just go catatonic—so they had to keep me safe and try to get my cooperation. But what about everybody else? For the first time I began to worry about the rest of the family. What was going to happen to them?

Especially if the kidnappers killed me. Without the monkey, they had no bargaining chip to go anywhere. And Luna didn't tolerate freeloaders. They'd probably end up indentured somewhere—I didn't like the thought of that. Douglas was adamantly opposed to slavery of any kind. Even voluntary.

At the moment, however, I wasn't getting much of a vote on anything. The kidnappers were still wearing their faceless helmets, so I couldn't even tell if they were men or women—they grabbed me and passed me through the hatch into the cargo pod, and then up through another hatch, through an inflated transfer tube, up into what looked like still another cargo pod, but wasn't. It was a Lunar vehicle. An eighteen-wheeler. Three cargo pods, each mounted on a rollagon chassis, and linked together to form a truck train. Six human beings could live indefinitely in one of these trucks—as long as the food and water and air held out.

They tossed me into a dark bunk in the back and forgot about me. There were clanking and thumping noises as the truck disconnected its airlock, and then we were rolling. The windows were closed, I couldn't see anything. For a while, I was frantic—I hated being tied up, and this web-stuff made it almost impossible to move. It was the worst kind of claustrophobia—it was like being wrapped like a mummy, only worse. I raged until I was exhausted. And then I tried chewing on the web-stuff, but it was useless. So then I cried for a while.

Eventually, I fell asleep.

NO EXIT

SLEPT BADLY. I had nightmares. Like I had been eaten by a giant worm and was riding in its roaring belly. Like I was swimming in sticky syrup. Like something was chasing me and I was trying to run away, but I was paralyzed and couldn't move my arms or legs. I woke up, sweating—and hurting all over from the web-stuff. This wasn't fair! Didn't these bastards care what they were doing to me?

I guessed not. We had stopped rolling. I had no idea how long I'd been asleep. Maybe three or four hours. Maybe eight or nine. My bladder felt that full. I tried to arch my neck around. I could stretch and move a little bit—the stuff was just loose enough to let me breathe, but I was pretty much cemented into one position. And I couldn't tell by the light in the cabin. Lunar light doesn't change—well, it does change, but fourteen times slower than on Earth—and the lighting in a Lunar truck is usually turned down anyway, unless you're cooking or eating.

By now, I was pretty sure I knew who my kidnappers were—some of the extremists from "invisible Luna." Invisible Luna was all those folks who were living off the network and surviving by their own barter economy. Alexei Krislov had been one of those, half in the legal world and half out. He and his tribe, the Rock Father Tribe, had tricked us into riding a cargo pod to Luna by telling us that Bounty Marshals were chasing us. It turned out that nobody was chasing us at all, at least not until we got to Luna. It was just a big fat lie. The economy of Earth was collapsing and the plagues were spreading and most people were too busy dealing with martial law to worry about us. But we'd scrambled all over the moon, running from invisible boogeymen, until finally Alexei had gotten us to a place we couldn't escape from, a water-farm at the Lunar south pole. But we'd escaped anyway. We put on our bubble suits again, which were starting to leak, and bounced through a five kilometer ammonia tube, and that wasn't any fun because I got a lungful of ammonia and had to be carried out.

Whoever these people were, wherever they were taking me, they were going to have to stay undetected and out of sight for a long, long time. It just didn't make sense that any of the colonies that wanted the HARLIE inside the monkey would have the resources on Luna to do this. Not even Mars or the asteroids. And the invisibles already knew how to hide from the Lunar Authority. They'd been doing it for almost a century.

But I couldn't really think about that now—I couldn't think about anything. I was in so much pain I couldn't stand it. I had to pee. I had to poop. *Badly.* This was agony. Maybe I'd been asleep even longer than I thought. I really didn't want to piss my pants. Not like Stinky. It hurt so bad, tears were coming to my eyes. I was almost crying.

I started screaming, "Somebody, please! Help! Somebody! Anybody! Please! It hurts! I'm in real pain here, people! Come on—!"

—and then, finally, someone was loosening my bonds. I didn't see how he was doing it, but I heard a soft buzzing behind me, and the next thing I knew, the webbing was loosening. Then a voice: "Is promise to behave, Charles Dingillian?"

Alexei!

I didn't know whether to be relieved or outraged. But it made sense. After our escape, Mickey was certain Alexei would be even more determined to get us back, and Alexei was one of the few people who would know that the monkey was bonded to me as its primary authority. And Alexei certainly had the resources to organize something like this—

"Is promise to behave?"

I grunted something that must have sounded like assent, because the buzzing resumed. A minute later, my hands were free, then my feet. I was hurting so bad, I couldn't move. My entire body felt like my foot when it was asleep. I tingled painfully all over. My shoulders were cramped, my legs were cramped, my whole *self* ached. And my bladder was screaming for release. And my bowels too. Even in Lunar gravity, I couldn't stand; I was bent over double. I could barely roll over.

Alexei rolled me upright. "Is bathroom over there. Try not to make mess."

I tried to crawl to the bathroom. I had to pee so bad I was crying. Tears of pain were running out of my eyes. I wasn't going to make it. "Help me, you bastard—"

For a moment, I thought he was ignoring me; then I felt his hands under my arms, lifting me up. He carried me into the bathroom, dumped me unceremoniously onto the toilet, and unzipped my jumpsuit enough so I could manage. Then he left, but he didn't close the door behind him.

A Lunar bathroom isn't much like an Earth bathroom, because in Lunar gravity everything splashes six times higher—which is why everybody sits to pee on the moon. That's also why the sinks and toilets are deeper and shaped like cylinders instead of bowls.

And now that I was finally sitting on the toilet, I hurt so bad I still couldn't pee. And then I started coughing again—my chest *still* hurt from the ammonia, it wasn't that long ago—and then I couldn't help myself, I just let go and sobbed hopelessly. I sagged against the wall. I didn't even have the strength to hold myself up. Not even in Lunar gravity. And then my bladder finally did open up and it hurt so much, I gasped. And then my bowel opened up too, even while I was still peeing, and I felt like I was coming apart from the inside out, and all I wanted to do was just collapse on the floor and cry.

Somewhere along the way, I'd figured it out. Our phone line had been tapped. Or maybe our hotel room had been bugged. As soon as we made up our mind to accept the colony contract for Outbeyond, Alexei or someone had given the order to take us. The assault troops must have been in a room down the hall, because they came breaking down our door within seconds. That's why the monkey had gone crazy. HARLIE had figured it out too.

Boynton hadn't been smart enough or fast enough. All Alexei had to do was keep me locked up for thirteen days and we would be stuck on Luna forever. The *Cascade* would go without us and there wouldn't be any more brightliners ever. Not in our lifetimes anyway. And that was the other reason why I was crying. Not because I was scared, but because no matter what happened, we weren't going to see the dinosaurs. Or anything else. And I really wanted to see if they were as big as the pictures showed.

At last, I couldn't pee anymore. I couldn't crap anymore. And a while after that, I couldn't cry anymore. I just sat and rocked on the toilet, clutching my belly, still in pain and afraid to move for fear of making it worse.

Alexei hollered from the other room, "Are you done?"

I shook my head.

"Take shower. You stink. Hot shower will help you feel better too."

"You stink too!" I hollered back. But I peeled myself out of my damp jumpsuit—damp with sweat, not pee—and stepped into the shower. I punched for hot and steamy and let the jets pummel my shoulders and my back and that really sore spot at the bottom of my spine.

A Lunar shower times out automatically after three minutes. I restarted it five times. I didn't care. I wasn't paying for this water. It was Alexei's. I didn't owe him anything. I was about to punch for a sixth time, when he hollered, "All right, Charles. Is enough. Time to get out."

Hot air jets blasted me dry. I found a clean jumpsuit hanging on a hook next to the door. I still ached all over, but at least I could move. And I was hungry too.

Alexei was sitting alone in the other room. We weren't in the truck anymore. We were inside a Lunar capsule, just like all the others. Ninety percent of the structures on the moon were converted cargo capsules, and most of the vehicles too. Alexei told us once that the only difference between a Lunar house and a Lunar truck is that the house has smaller wheels. I wondered if I'd been transferred while asleep, or if we were just locked down for a while.

Alexei was wearing his scuba suit, a black, form-fitting thing that could have been used just as easily for deep-sea diving. Everything but the helmet. He looked like he was ready to leave on thirty seconds' notice.

"Are you hungry, Charles? Do you want something to eat?" He pointed toward the table. A plastic-wrapped sandwich and a mug of tea. Opposite the sandwich, the monkey sat on the table, apparently lifeless.

Without answering, I sat down weakly and started unwrapping the sandwich. It wasn't easy; my fingers were still numb. At one point, Alexei reached over to help, but I waved him off. I finally managed to get a corner of the plastic free—just enough to take a single bite. Chicken. At least, it tasted like chicken. That meant it could have been anything from dinosaur to fish. "We must talk," said Alexei.

"Fmmk you," I said around a mouthful. Not very imaginative, but succinct.

"Is time for you to listen, Charles." Alexei looked grim and his tone was very no-nonsense. "We have monkey. We have you. Monkey is worthless without you. Monkey is bonded to you. We know that, so don't play stupid games. It will not work unless you say so. And you must say so willingly. Monkey is not stupid either. It will not honor any contract made under duress. Is very bad news about HARLIE machines. Is too much integrity. Will not break law. Will stretch law, will bend law, will circle around backside of law, but will not *break* law."

I put the sandwich down and reached for the mug. It looked kind of like a teapot—Lunar mugs all have tops with sipping tubes that look like spouts, because otherwise it's too easy for liquids to splash around in Lunar gravity. My fingers were all tingly and cramped; they didn't want to cooperate. I had to use both hands. I slid the mug closer and had to lean over the table and bend my head to sip the hot tea. I continued to make a show of ignoring Alexei. He continued to talk anyway. I'd never met anyone who could fit as many words into a single thought as Alexei Krislov, the mad Russian Loonie smuggler.

"—so invisible Luna has big problem. Everybody wants monkey. Everybody looks for monkey. Everybody looks for Charles Dingillian too, but not as much as they look for monkey. Invisible Luna has both. But we can't make either work—not together, not separately. We can't keep, we can't return. We can't use, we can't let anyone else use. So what do we do? You tell me."

I told him what to do. It wouldn't have solved his problem, but it made me feel better to say it. I'd have guessed it was anatomically impossible—except Johnny Myers back at school had printed out some really weird pictures from the net. So I knew it wasn't impossible, but probably very uncomfortable.

"You must take me serious, Charles Dingillian," Alexei said. "Right now, you are safe here. But not for very long. You and monkey are big problem. There are people who want to solve this big problem by killing you and smashing monkey. That way, even if we cannot use you, no one else can either. But I did not bring you all the way to Luna, all the way to Gagarin, just to see you dead. I am responsible for you. I promise to keep you safe. And if truth must be told, I even like you a little bit. It would make me sad to see you dead. But make no mistake, little dirtside refugee. I am committed to Revolution of Free Luna. People die in revolutions. You know that, Charles Dingillian. And if they are willing to give up *their* lives, then you must know that they are equally willing to give up *yours*. I would much regret it if that price had to be paid—I would argue very loudly against it—I have already argued loudly against it. But every revolution makes its own rules. And even if I promise to keep you safe, the Free Luna Revolution will not make that kind of promise. Not with so much at stake. What do you say to that?"

I hesitated. Would it be worth it to throw the mug of hot tea in his face? Probably not. And I doubted I had the coordination to manage it. If we hadn't been in Lunar gravity, I'd have been wearing this tea in my lap. I slid the mug away slowly. I returned my attention to the sandwich, picking again at the plastic wrapping.

The way I figured it, there wasn't really much that I could do. Except wait. Sooner or later someone would track these Loonies down. Maybe the truck had left tracks in the Lunar dust. Or maybe the monkey had phoned for help. It was capable of a lot more than anybody knew; we'd already seen some proof of that, so maybe there was a rescue on the way even now—or maybe someone was negotiating. Except what could they offer? Invisible Luna didn't want anyone else to get the monkey, whether or not they could use it themselves. So why should they bother negotiating?

Finally, I said, "You don't need to kill me. Just smash the monkey and this whole business is over and done."

He looked surprised. "Then no one gets to use monkey."

"No one's going to get the monkey anyway. You're not going to let anyone else use it. They're not going to let you use it. Nobody's going to be happy until it's smashed. So smash it and send me back." I finally pulled the rest of the plastic away from the sandwich. My hands still didn't want to work and I was starting to worry that maybe they would never work again. I couldn't even wrap my fingers around the sandwich.

"Your family will end up indentured," said Alexei. "Slaves. If you help free Luna, you can be like royalty."

I finally managed a primitive hold on the sandwich. A baby's grip. It was enough. I took another bite. This time I wasn't going to put the sandwich down. I might not be able to pick it up again. Alexei watched me and waited.

"You have nothing to say . . . ?" he asked.

I swallowed painfully. "I'm not stupid, Alexei. We wouldn't be royalty, we wouldn't be anything—maybe prisoners. Because you can't trust *us* with the monkey any more than you can trust anyone else with it. Whoever controls the monkey will be the king of Luna. So how can your revolution be about freedom for Loonies if you end up with a dictator?"

Alexei looked beaten. He wasn't, but he did a good job of looking beaten. He sighed, he shrugged, he hung his head. "Is moot point anyway. Monkey is dead." He waved vaguely in its direction.

"Yeah, we had that same problem with it," I said. "It would shut down for no reason at all that we could tell. And we couldn't bring it back to life."

"Not even if you sang 'Ode to Joy' at it?"

I shook my head.

"But I saw you sing monkey back to life, more than once."

"That was before."

"Before what?"

"Before—" I hesitated. "—before it was exposed to all that ammonia. The chips must have been contaminated or something."

"Ammonia does not hurt chips. It cleans them."

"How do you know what the ammonia did? Are you an engineer?"

"*Da!*" But he and I both knew he wasn't a chip-technologist, or whatever they were called. "I do not believe you, Charles Dingillian."

"So don't." I took another bite. I forced myself to chew and swallow. I really wanted to collapse on the floor.

"You hesitated before answering. Also, stress level in your voice goes up when you lie." He tapped his PITA. "I am looking at monitor here on table while you talk. You do not tell truth. What is this 'before' you did not say before?"

I shrugged. It wouldn't make any difference to tell him the truth. "Before we gave it free will," I said. I took another bite.

"You gave it free will?"

"Uh-huh. Sort of," I said, with my mouth full. "We needed a lawyer." I concentrated on chewing. It was hard work.

"I saw case. You make monkeys out of everyone. So monkey has free will now, *da?*"

I swallowed. "Yeah. Mostly."

"So we do not need you, do we?"

"Nope, you don't."

Alexei looked at his PITA. He frowned, puzzled. "What is it you are *not* telling me, Charles Dingillian?"

I finished the last bite of sandwich. I took my time. I reached for the mug of tea with both hands, but I didn't try to lift it off the table. "The monkey is indentured. We made a trade. We gave it free will in exchange for its services." I wrapped my fingers carefully around the mug and slid it closer. I might be able to manage this . . .

Alexei considered that. "Does not hold water. Judge Cavanaugh refused to recognize the monkey's sentience, so indenture is not valid."

"You didn't take that one all the way to the end, Alexei . . ."

"Explain to me."

I bent my head and drank as much of the tea as I could manage. Alexei waited patiently. I swallowed hard, then pushed the mug away and raised my head again.

"It's like this," I said. "If the court recognizes the monkey's sentience, then it's a stockholder of the Dingillian Family Corporation. If not, it's just property. Either way, you lose."

Douglas and HARLIE had worked this out very carefully. I'd helped a little bit, and so had Mickey, especially with the legal stuff, but Douglas understood the algorithms better than anyone—except HARLIE of course. We'd made it clear to HARLIE what we wanted and needed and he'd made it clear to us what he wanted and after that it was just a matter of working out all the details so everybody's interests were protected, and HARLIE was perfect at that. Finally, we'd agreed that if

Judge Cavanaugh recognized HARLIE's sentience, then we would petition the court for a writ of adoption, or at least custodial guardianship. And if Judge Cavanaugh wouldn't recognize HARLIE's sentience then we would go somewhere that would. Outbeyond.

But I wasn't going to explain all this to Alexei. He didn't deserve it, and I didn't feel like it. I doubted if I even had the strength. Instead, I gave him the short version. "If the monkey is property, it's simply locked and you have no legal access to its use. If it's a stockholder, then it has an ethical responsibility to the Dingillian Corporation. If you damage any member of the Dingillian family, any stockholder, any employee, or any property of the Dingillian Corporation, then the monkey can't work for you. Not now. Not ever. The monkey is useless to you guys. And that's where we're at right now. No matter what you say or do, there's no way the monkey will work for you."

"You know that this puts me into ugly situation, don't you, Charles? What do I do with you now?"

"Send me home."

"No, I cannot do that. I am kidnapper now. You will testify against me. I will never be able to come in out of the dark. But if you do not go back, there is no body. No proof that I am kidnapper. But then what do I do with you? I cannot let you go, and I do not want to kill you, Charles Dingillian, but you do not give me much alternative. I have big ugly tiger by tail. I was hopeful you and monkey would figure it out for me. But you do not, you only make problem stink worse."

GOODBYE

I **GUESS I SHOULD** have been scared, but this was *Alexei*—and you don't get scared of people you know because you don't think they're really likely to kill you. Except all the statistics say that it *is* the people you know who are most likely to kill you. Especially friends and family members. Only in my experience, most of the wounds don't show—at least not until you open your mouth.

So maybe it was stupid for me not to be scared. But I wasn't.

For some reason, it reminded me of a game that Douglas and I had played just before my thirteenth birthday. He'd kept saying, "I can't let you turn into a teenager, Chigger. I'm going to have to kill you. As soon as I figure out a foolproof way to dispose of the body, you're dead meat."

"Use the garbage disposal," I said, not looking up from my comic.

"That'll take too long. And it won't handle the big bones," he said.

"Bury me in the desert . . ."

"Coyotes might dig you up."

"Weigh me down and toss me in a lake."

"There are no lakes around here."

"Feed me to the chickens."

"Where am I going to find chickens?"

"At the lake."

And so on. That went on for three or four days—until we'd exhausted all the possibilities that both of us could think of. The best solution was simply to put me in a big box and mail me somewhere. Except the shipping costs were too much. And who would he mail me to anyway?

This conversation with Alexei felt the same way. Seriously bizarre and unreal. The big difference was that Alexei was looking for a reason *not* to kill me. And I wasn't being any more help to him than I had been to Douglas.

Alexei was growing more and more agitated. Every so often he would leap up from the table and pace—bounce—back and forth across the room. Finally, I just shouted at him, "What?!"

He whirled on me and shouted, "They will be coming back soon. The others! They have told me they will find a working monkey or your dead body. If I do not do it, they will, and they will not be nice about it."

"This is *nice*? Kidnapping?"

"You do not understand, you little idiot. This is revolution. This is Luna. This is *family*!" He shouted back. "My family, do you understand?! I would die for them!" He shouted something in Russian, then added, "I would kill for them! I will not be happy, but I will do it. You believe me, don't you?"

"Yes, I believe you," I said. But even as I said it, I knew I didn't. He wasn't looking at his PITA or he would have seen. The more he threatened me, the less believable his threats became. I wasn't afraid of him—but I was getting anxious about the *others* he kept referring to. They didn't know me like Alexei did. They might not be as reluctant as he was.

"If you could make monkey work, maybe it could help you figure out way to get out of here . . . ?" Alexei suggested.

Ahh. Finally. The bait.

I didn't take it. "If I could get the monkey to reactivate itself," I said, "the first thing it would do is call for help."

Alexei shrugged. "We are in shielded pod. Completely off map. Not detectable. Not even heat. No messages in or out—" As if to prove him a liar, his PITA chimed. "—except for what we allow," he finished lamely. He picked it up and started talking angrily in Russian.

Abruptly, his demeanor changed. He straightened in surprise. He looked around at me, then turned away to the wall. He lowered his voice and jabbered excitedly, still in Russian. I had to smile at that. Why bother whispering? He knew I didn't understand Russian. Maybe Alexei wasn't as smart as we thought. Or maybe he was too anxious to notice what he was doing. His conversation went on for a long while; he seemed to be arguing for something, trying to convince the person on the other end. He shook his head a lot. At last, he swore angrily, then agreed with a reluctant, "*Da!*" He switched off, scowling.

He turned to me and said very seriously, "I will give you one last chance, Charles Dingillian. Whistle monkey back to life."

I shook my head. "It won't do any good. The monkey won't respond."

"You will not try?"

I ignored the question.

Alexei waited a long moment for answer, and then abruptly, he made a decision. "Hokay, it is out of my hands. I will go now. You will wait patiently, please."

"Why? What's happening?"

"It is out of my hands. Whatever happens next is whatever happens next. You have chosen, I have no choice. So I go now." He pulled a black helmet off the wall. "I will go and take care of my business. Others will come here and take care of their business. I do not think you will like how that works out. Good-bye, Charles Dingillian." He pulled the helmet down over his head, securing it quickly into place. Abruptly, he turned to shake my hand, grabbing it quickly in both of his before I could pull away. His helmet muffled his voice, but his meaning was clear enough. "I do not think I will ever see you again. I have enjoyed knowing you. You have made my life interesting for a while. Too interesting, I think. Good-bye. You would have made good Loonie."

And then he leapt for the ceiling, popped open the airlock hatch, and pulled himself up through it. It slammed shut with finality.

I was alone. In a pod. With the monkey.

I thought about whistling the monkey back to life. For about half a second . . .

Alexei might have known *when* I was lying, but he didn't know *what* I was lying about. That's why I had tried to avoid saying anything at all. But I wasn't lying about the monkey's refusal to cooperate. That part was true. Too true.

We'd spent a long hard evening negotiating with HARLIE—with the monkey. For a long time, it didn't look like we were going to accomplish anything at all, and then suddenly, in the middle of the discussion, we all just sort of realized at the same time that it was to our mutual advantage to cooperate. The monkey was safer with us than with anyone else; he would have more freedom as part of the Dingillian family. And vice versa: HARLIE's wisdom and intelligence would benefit us enormously. And besides, the monkey was Stinky's adopted twin brother. That had to count for something.

So, if there was a way out of this mess, HARLIE would be the perfect one to figure it out. Unfortunately, if I sang the monkey awake, it would just get us both in deeper. A lot deeper.

The Loonies had to be watching. Lunar pods are built with all kinds of monitors in the bulkheads. They have to be. So Alexei and his friends were probably waiting just on the other side of that airlock hatch for me to do something stupid. Like whistle the monkey back to life.

Through the hull of the pod, I heard the usual clanks and thumps of a pressure tube disengaging from the airlock collar. But that didn't mean they were disengaging and driving away. They could be waiting just above. And if I reactivated the monkey, they could be back down in the pod in two minutes. Maybe faster.

I stood up painfully and crossed to the closest wall. My fingers hurt. But I undogged the porthole cover and slid it to one side anyway.

Okay, I was wrong. They weren't waiting outside. Alexei was driving off in his Lunar truck, *Mr. Beagle*—a life-pod just like this one, only mounted high on large plastic wheels.

But *they* were certainly still watching me. Maybe Alexei was going to park just behind those rocks over there and wait. I'd have no way of knowing.

I wondered where I was. The Lunar sun was high in the sky. I couldn't see any other details. Even if I could find a phone or a radio in this pod, which I strongly doubted, I wouldn't be able to tell anyone where I was. Even if I knew who to call. Who could I trust?

Hell.

I turned away from the window and looked around the pod. It was fairly standard. Cargo had been loaded into it on Earth. It had been lifted up the orbital elevator all the way out to Whirlaway, and flung off the end. It had sailed four hundred and fifty thousand klicks out to Lunar orbit, coming up behind the moon to catch up with it. Caught in Lunar gravity, it had spiraled in, retro-firing only at the last moment to brake its downward velocity, and had finally bounced down onto the Lunar plain in the center of a raspberry of inflatable balloons. Total transport cost—a few Palmer tubes and some electricity; only the Line generated so much electricity on its own that electricity was practically free. Line charges weren't based on cost, but availability of space. Once the Line was up and running, cargo space became so valuable that a whole economy had developed just buying and reselling cargo dockets and futures. Or at least, that was the way it had been before everything fell apart. The last we heard—before I was kidnapped—the Line was transporting only the most essential of essentials. Some of the world's most important people had fled up the Line to wait until the polycrisis was over, but that had only exacerbated it.

Some people were afraid that the Line was going to be cut off at the base and yanked up into orbit. Others were afraid it would be cut higher up and large pieces of it would come plummeting down around the Earth in an equatorial belt of disaster. It would be like multiple simultaneous asteroid strikes. It could have happened already. I had no way of knowing. I couldn't see the Earth from any of the pod windows.

There were emergency food and water packets in all the cabinets. At least I wasn't going to starve or die of thirst. Well, not for a while anyway. But Alexei had said that others were coming, and I assumed he meant soon—but *soon* meant something different on Luna, anywhere from six hours to six days.

I didn't find any bubble suits in the lockers. That was wrong. It was Lunar law—*and tradition*—that every pod had to have at least six certified bubble suits. The first four of the Lunar Ten Commandments were about protecting air and water—and sharing it with those in need. All the other stuff that had happened, that was scary—but this was *bad.* These people were *evil.*

My arms and legs still hurt, though not as much as before. All my muscles kept cramping up and I kept getting shooting pains everywhere. My stomach hurt the most. I'd been hungry too long and that sandwich hadn't been very good. I wondered how old it had been. It sat in my stomach like a lump of hot coal. I was about to open a bed and lie down when something moved outside. I bounced clumsily over to the window and peered.

There—

Just above the horizon. Something with lights. A pod-house in a flying-frame. It was headed in this direction.

Alexei's comrades.

FOREVER

THE FLYING POD-HOUSE APPROACHED silently. There was something spooky about not hearing its rockets. I knew it must have been very loud inside. We'd ridden in Alexei's *Mr. Beagle*, and that was just like this one; everything had roared and vibrated the whole time. The pod-house slowed as it came closer, then it slid sideways out of view.

There was a porthole overhead. I leapt up and grabbed hold of one of the handles next to it. My arms ached so badly from being webbed for so long, I didn't think I was going to be able to do this, but I hung on anyway, despite the shooting pains, and undogged the porthole hatch. It was a plastic bubble set into the ceiling; I could stick my head up into it to look around. The pod-house was just moving into position above. It turned parallel and came settling down like a giant daddy long-legs spider. I couldn't read the markings on its hull. Its lights were too bright. It lowered a bright pink docking tube that looked like a hollow sucking tongue.

I couldn't hold on any longer. I let go and dropped slowly to the floor. Even in Lunar gravity my legs were still too weak. They collapsed under me. I scrambled back against the wall. Finally I heard sounds; something was clunking against the roof. I felt it connect and I could hear the soft *whoosh* of it pressurizing. There was no place I could go. The ceiling hatch popped open—

—and two men dropped gently and easily into the pod. Both wore close-fitting scuba suits like the one Alexei had worn. Both were carrying guns. One swung immediately around to face me, the other covered the forward part of the cabin. Their suits had Lunar Authority insignia— but so what? I had a blue T-shirt with a red and yellow Superman "S" on it, but that didn't mean I could fly.

Two more people dropped into the pod after them. One was a woman. The two men who had come in first began checking cabins. They went aft and peered into the room where I'd been tossed for so long, then they backed out and went forward. I heard them banging around, looking into everything. Two more men dropped into the pod and went belowdeck to check the storage bays. More banging came from below.

Meanwhile, the woman popped her helmet open and looked at me. She had a pretty smile, but that didn't mean anything either. Lots of people had pretty smiles. "Are you all right, Charles? Do you know where you are?"

I shook my head. "Somewhere on Luna."

"Close enough. My name is Carol Everhart. How do you feel?"

"I'm alive. No thanks to you people."

"Are you hurt?" She was already unclipping a medi-scan from the side of her jumpsuit. Without waiting for my answer, she held it up to my eyes, my ears, my mouth. She looked at its readouts. "Yep, you're alive," she confirmed. She called up through the hatch. "He's alive. But he's not happy."

In reply, someone dropped a plastic ladder down through the hatch. "Bring him up."

She stepped out of the way, but I didn't move toward the ladder.

"Do you need help?" she asked.

"No."

"You didn't answer my question before. Are you hurt?"

I didn't know how to answer that. "You people left me webbed for I don't know how long. I feel crazy."

"If you're rational enough to know that you feel crazy, you're not that crazy. Do you need help up the ladder?"

I shook my head. I wasn't going to give her the satisfaction of a yes. Besides, I wasn't sure I wanted to go up the ladder. Where were they planning to take me? On the other hand, if I didn't go willingly, would they web me again? Anything but that—

I levered myself to my feet. I stepped over to get the monkey where it still sat on the table. The other agent moved to stop me, but Carol Everhart gave him a look and he stepped out of the way. I grabbed the dead toy and pressed it to one of the Velcro patches on the left side of my jumpsuit. I reached for the ladder and almost staggered. I was weaker than I thought. The man looked impatient, but Carol Everhart put her hands under my arms and helped me up the ladder and into the pressure tube.

Even in Lunar gravity, it was hard. My fingers didn't want to cooperate. But as soon as I poked my head up through the next hatch, someone grabbed me and pulled me up—*it was Douglas!* I collapsed sobbing into his arms, I was so happy to see him. He just wrapped me up in his hug and held on tight, rocking me like a baby. "Oh, Charles, I am so glad to see you—I was so scared. Are you all right? Did anyone hurt you?" I was crying too hard to answer. I knew there were other people in the flying pod-house, but I didn't care.

At last, Douglas held me at arm's length and looked me in the eye. "Are you all right?" he asked again. "Did they hurt you?"

I shook my head. "I didn't tell them anything. It was Alexei. He said they were going to—" I couldn't finish the sentence. I looked around, without really seeing. There was a pilot and a copilot and two other people, but everybody was a blur—just big, grim-looking shapes. I turned back to Douglas. "Where are they taking us? Are they going to kill us?"

"Nobody's going to kill anyone—except maybe Alexei, when I get my hands on him—" I must have looked confused because Douglas said, "Hey, hey, Charles—look at me. *You've been rescued.*"

"Huh? Rescued?" But all these soldiers—

"These people are from the Lunar Catapult Authority," Douglas explained before I could even ask the question. "Carol Everhart is an Associate System Operator." It was all happening too fast—

Someone behind me put a hand on my shoulder. "It's all right, son. You're safe now." It was Commander Boynton.

"Huh? What are you doing here—?"

"I organized this rescue. You're under the protective custody of the Outbeyond Contract Authority. Remember?"

Someone else handed me a mug of something hot and steaming. "Here, drink this."

The mug almost slipped through my fingers, but Douglas caught it and helped me hold it. Hot chicken broth. I sucked at the spout. This was better than tea. This tasted almost like real food.

I must have wobbled a bit, because Douglas put a hand on my shoulder to steady me. "Do you want to sit down?" he asked. Without waiting for an answer, he guided me to a seat.

"You've had a rough time, Charles." It wasn't a question. And that was all it took, the tears started flooding again. Everything we'd been through—it was just too much. How do grown-ups deal with this stuff? I was just a kid. I let go of the mug, or Douglas took it from me and held me close again while I sobbed out the rest of my grief and fury and confusion. Maybe back on Earth, I'd have held it all in, because that's what you did on Earth, you put on the performance for everybody else, but I wasn't on Earth anymore, and I didn't care anymore. *It hurt.*

"Charles?"

I let go of Douglas and looked up.

Commander Boynton held out a headset. "There's someone who wants to talk to you."

Bobby was on the other end, screaming excitedly, "Chigger! Chigger! Where are you? When are you coming back? Do you have my monkey?" I could hardly get a word in, but I didn't care, I was so glad to hear his voice. And then Mom came on too, and that was even more exciting, because they weren't fighting with each other. They were just glad to know I was all right. And then . . . *Mom finally said it.* "Do you know how scared I've been for you, Charles? Ever since this whole thing started. I don't think I could stand it if I lost you—*I love you, Charles.*"

And that started me crying all over again. "That's all I wanted to hear. I love you too, Mom."

I handed the phone to Douglas and he told her everything else she needed to hear. "Yes, he's fine. Better than we expected. A little shaken up. A little scared. Maybe more than a little, but nothing to worry about. I don't think they hurt him, but he hasn't mouthed off once yet, so maybe he's been through worse than he says. Yes, that's a good idea. No, I don't know. We'll be lifting off as soon as we secure. It's a three-hour flight, Mom; you should all try to get some sleep. We're still in training, remember? I'll tell Chigger, yes. I love you too, I have to go now."

Somebody handed me another mug of soup and I sat there, sipping at it and letting the warmth flood through me. This was the worst thing that had ever happened to me in my entire life, and I was happier than I could remember. My shoulders hurt and my arms ached and my legs were cramped and my feet were still tingly and my hands were still trembling and I felt terrific. My Mom loved me. I had a family again.

Douglas sat down next to me and put his arm around my shoulder, very protectively. But I could tell it was as much for his own reassurance as for mine. He'd been just as scared as me. And then I realized something else—

"Hey!"

"What?"

"Where's Dad?"

Douglas hesitated and even before he could speak—

Oh, shit. No.

—and then he pulled me closer and said, "They shot him, Chigger. Daddy's dead."

If he'd punched me in the gut or kicked me in the balls or slammed me upside the head or done all three at once, it couldn't have hurt more. My eyes flooded up with tears of rage. I wanted to scream, but my throat was so tight, it hurt like the worst sore throat in the world. All I could do was gasp and choke and blubber. I wrapped myself around Douglas and held on as tight as I could. *This wasn't fair!* No! Not Dad! Not now! Not when we were finally talking to each other again—

Douglas held me close. And held me and held me. And when I finally did let go of him again, I wasn't the same person anymore. Something inside of me was gone. I didn't have a name for it, but it was one of those parts that when it's gone, it's gone forever.

THE WAY BACK

THE **L**UNAR **A**UTHORITY **A**GENTS pulled themselves back up into the cabin. Carol Everhart reported to Boynton. "Nothing much there. Just your basic Loonie move-in-a-hurry hidey-hole. We sprayed some nano-sensors, but I doubt anyone will come back in our lifetimes. It's been pretty well stripped. It's got less than a month's worth of air and water. They probably intended to use it as a one-time safe-house and then abandon it. We'll trace the records, but they'll probably come up blank—or they'll lead to a fictitious entity. We put an Authority impound tag on it, just in case."

Boynton nodded. "All right, let's secure and get out of here."

"You heard the man. Hop to it, people." And then everybody was busy with this and that and the other thing. The pressure tube disconnected and clunked back up into its frame. Everybody seated themselves and strapped in; then the Palmer tubes kicked in and the whole pod-house started to shake. We couldn't actually hear the roar of the rockets, but we could feel the vibration; the whole craft throbbed. It reminded me of the roaring in my dream.

I turned to the window and watched as we lifted off the bright Lunar surface. The pod below us dropped away and behind. We swung around and headed south toward Outbeyond Station. I slipped my hand into Douglas' and squeezed. He squeezed back. He hadn't held my hand since I was eight and he was thirteen—just like me and Stinky. I wished I hadn't grown up so fast. I wished I could go back to being eight again. Mom and Dad were still trying to hold it together when I was eight. We were still a family then.

I leaned over and whispered to Douglas, *"Was I as bad as Stinky when I was eight?"*

He whispered back, *"You were worse."*

"Really?"

"Really."

"Why didn't you kill me then?"

"I couldn't think of a way to dispose of the body."

"You could have stuffed me down the garbage disposal . . ."

"That would have taken too long . . ."

"You could have buried me in the desert . . ."

"I didn't have a shovel—"

"You could have burned me up."

"I didn't want to pollute the atmosphere—"

Boynton came back then and sat down opposite us. He looked like a man with a job to do and impatient to get it done.

"You ready to talk?"

"No," I said.

Boynton leaned forward. "I know this is tough, Charles, but we don't have a lot of time."

I just shook my head and turned to look out the window. The scenery was the same as always. Rocks and holes. Sun-blasted gray rocks and stark black shadows.

Douglas leaned in close and whispered to me, *"Charles—please?"*

"Why should I? Daddy is dead and these people didn't protect him."

"These people rescued us. They rescued you."

"They didn't rescue Dad."

"Dad was shot when he opened the door—he never had a chance."

"Douglas? May I?" That was Boynton. "Charles—listen to me. They didn't have to kill your Dad. We're pretty sure they did it on purpose."

I turned away from the window. Boynton's expression was grim. "We think it was an act of revenge. Your Dad was supposed to deliver the monkey to someone here on Luna. We don't know who. We'll probably never know. This was their way of getting even with him. Do you understand? And if they're willing to kill your Dad for not delivering the HARLIE unit, do you think they're going to let any of the rest of you get away?"

"Alexei said the same thing. Sort of."

Boynton nodded. "We're all in a very high-stakes game and we don't have a lot of time. We need to know now, Charles. Do you still want to go to Outbeyond?"

I looked to Douglas. He nodded. "Stinky wants to see the dinosaurs."

"Can we still go?" I asked.

Boynton looked to me. "Does that monkey still work?"

"I don't know," I admitted.

"Do you want to try it now?" he asked.

"No," I said.

"Your contract is predicated entirely on the operation of that HAR-LIE unit . . ."

"No. Not until our family is together again."

"You're not being very cooperative, Charles."

"So what?" I was tired of being polite. "I don't know you. You're just someone else who wants the monkey. Why should I trust you? I don't know anybody on this ugly airless dirt ball except my mom and my brothers. Everybody wants us to trust them, but so far every single person who's said they were going to help us has lied to us and used us and betrayed us. And I don't see any reason to think that you're any different. You don't want me and you don't want my family. You said so yourself. You want the monkey. The only reason you're willing to take us anywhere is so you can get your hands on it. And as much as I want to see the dinosaurs, I don't want to see them so badly that I'm willing to trust you or anyone else anymore."

He blinked. "You're right," he said. He sat back in his seat.

"Huh?"

"I said, 'You're right.' "

"And?"

He shrugged. "And nothing. You're right. I told you up front that I wanted the monkey. And I told you up front that if you didn't have the monkey, we didn't want you. And I told you up front that you wouldn't get any special privileges. And you can't say I wasn't honest about that. So the only question you have to answer is this one—do you want to go to Outbeyond or not? If the answer is yes, then let's go. And if not, then we'll go without you. But I have to know now, Charles, because they're waiting for my call. Do I load your cabin with noodles or Dingillians?"

DECISIONS

BOYNTON LEFT US ALONE then, and Douglas and I talked—about everything and nothing and everything again. And when we were through talking, we were back where we started.

Finally I said, "I don't know what I want to do anymore, Douglas. I don't know what to do. I thought I wanted to go, but now—I don't know. I thought that we were all going together, and be a family again, but without Dad—"

"Without Dad, we're still a family. You and me and Bobby."

"But it won't be the same."

"It wasn't going to be the same anyway. We divorced them. And then he added, "Charles, we've come too far to quit. We can't go back and we can't stay here. We have to go on. Daddy wanted us to have this chance. If he were here, he'd tell us to keep going. You know that, don't you?"

"Yeah, I guess so."

"So what's holding you back?"

"I don't know." I pulled the monkey onto my lap. "I guess—I guess I just don't want to leave like this—"

"What is it you want?"

"I want to get even. With Alexei. And everybody else who hurt us. Especially the people who killed Dad."

"Yeah, me too—but we're going to have to choose. Revenge or dinosaurs."

"I want both."

"Me too. But if you had to choose, one or the other, which is more important?"

I hung my head.

Douglas leaned close and whispered into my ear. *"Yes, it hurts now, Chigger. And it's going to hurt for a long long time. But there's going to come a day when it won't hurt quite as much. Do you want to give these bastards a room rent-free in your head? Or do you want to find out if living well really is the best revenge?"*

I started to shake my head—an I-don't-know gesture—then I stopped. I sat up straight and turned to look at him. "Douglas, this really is an Important Moment, you know."

"Yes, I know."

"No, not because of that—" I said. "But because this is the first time in my life that I actually listened to you and realized that you were right."

His eyes widened, just a little bit, then he smiled that big goofy grin of his that I hadn't seen in way too long. "I have bad news for you, kiddo. I think you're growing up."

"Geez, just because you won one, you don't have to insult me." I pulled myself unsteadily to my feet. "Okay, I'll talk to Boynton."

"Do you want me to come with?"

"Yeah."

Douglas helped me up, but I insisted on doing my own walking. I had to use the handholds to keep from falling over, but I made my way to the back of the cabin where Boynton sat hunched over a screen, talking grimly into his headset. It must have been important because he looked unhappier than usual. When he saw Douglas and me coming, he switched off his clipboard and turned his attention completely to us.

I lowered myself onto a seat. "Okay," I said. "What do I have to do?"

Boynton pointed toward the monkey. "Turn it on." He added, "We need to know if that thing still works."

"What if it doesn't?" I said.

"Then . . . I'm sorry."

"Nope. No deal."

"I beg your pardon?" Boynton gave me one of those startled grown-up looks—that confused look that adults get when they realize you mean it.

"Let's make a new deal," I said. "We go to Outbeyond whether or not the monkey works. If it works, we put it at the service of the colony. If it doesn't work—we still go to Outbeyond."

Boynton studied me. "You could die there," he said, but I noticed he wasn't trying to talk me out of it.

"We could die *here*," I replied. "In fact, we almost certainly will if we stay anywhere in this solar system. I'm not losing any more of my family. So that's the deal, sir, take it or leave it."

Boynton nodded, thinking it over. I guessed he was trying to figure out if I meant it or not. Finally, he said, "I'm not used to being black-mailed by a thirteen-year-old."

"Fourteen next month."

"We'll have a party." He closed his eyes for a moment, computing something inside his head. Weighing the risks, I guess. "All right, you win."

"Put it in writing please."

"My word isn't good enough?"

"No, sir. It isn't."

"If my word isn't any good, Charles, why do you think a piece of paper will be any better?"

"A piece of paper lets us file an injunction to keep you from boosting."

"You'll need an awfully smart lawyer to stop us."

I patted the monkey, still attached to my side.

Boynton smiled slyly. "If that lawyer still works, you won't need to sue, will you?"

He had me there. "But I still want it in writing."

He opened his clipboard and dictated something hastily. He held it up for me to see. I nodded. He signed, then I signed. "Done." Then he added, "You may live to regret this contract, you know."

"Probably," I agreed. But we were both smiling. Abruptly a thought occurred to me. "You agreed too easily. Why?"

Boynton turned and looked out the porthole. The empty Lunar terrain slid past. It was beautiful and ugly all at the same time. Ferocious and mysterious and awesome. The bright blue Earth was visible on the horizon. This would probably be the last time either of us would ever see a view like this. "Aren't you curious how we found you so fast?"

"Uh—" Everything had happened so quickly, I hadn't had time to think about it.

"These were some pretty bad people," Boynton added, pointedly.

"They told us where you were," Douglas said.

"Huh? Why?" I must have looked confused.

"Work it out, Charles." That was Boynton. "Everybody wants the monkey. Everybody. Especially Lunar Authority. You get kidnapped by invisibles—and as long as you and the monkey are missing, Authority has a very good reason to start cracking down on the tribes. All of them. And remember, Luna's invisible tribes are all anarchists. They aren't united. They don't trust each other. The other tribes weren't happy that the Rock Fathers had the monkey. It would give them too much power—if they could get it working. So Authority used that. They put out the word that they would officially recognize any tribe who helped them track down your kidnappers—and the monkey."

"And that worked?"

"Nope. Not at all," said Boynton. "But it shows you how desperate Lunar Authority was—if that was their opening offer. But as much as all the tribes distrust each other, they distrust the Authority even more. See, Charles, they don't want to be recognized. They want to stay invisible."

"So what happened?"

"Nothing at first. And then . . . a very weird thing. Anonymous messages started showing up on the public networks. Everywhere. Every sixty minutes, another piece of invisible Luna was made public. Some of the messages listed which names were fictitious personalities and who was behind them. Some contained the locations of private farms. Some tracked the financial connections that invisible Luna had to public corporations. Others gave away the private dealings that allowed the invisibles to funnel money out of the system. All kinds of things like that. One message had a very embarrassing video showing the—well, never mind. By the time the fifth message showed up, the whole planet was in an uproar. Six investigations have been started. Seventeen public officials have resigned, twenty-three have been indicted. The Lunar stock exchange has closed down for the first time in one hundred and thirty years. There have been three suicides—and the firestorm is just starting. Luna's going to be in chaos for years."

"Wow," I said. I looked to Douglas. He nodded in confirmation.

"Every message said the same thing," Boynton explained. "That the privacy of the invisibles would be destroyed, one piece at a time, a new message every sixty minutes, for as long as it took, until you and the monkey were returned safely to your family. Every tribe on Luna was going to be held responsible for your kidnapping."

"Who sent those messages?"

"They weren't signed," said Douglas.

Boynton added, "We do know that the Rock Fathers were given an ultimatum by the other tribes: *End this now* or the Rock Fathers will be erased." He glanced at his PITA. "Five hours ago, we received an anonymous message telling us where to find you." Boynton looked at me oddly. "Now, you tell me, Charles. Who do you know who has the power to do something like that?"

"Uh—?" We both looked at the monkey.

"Right. That's why I wasn't too worried about making a deal with you." He said it with finality.

Very slowly, I unclipped the monkey from my side and held it up in front of me at arm's length. I looked it in the eye. Its plastic grin was emotionless.

Yes, it all made sense. When we were in Alexei's ice mine at the Lunar south pole, I told the monkey to hide until I whistled it home. The monkey had hidden in Alexei's office . . . where it had amused itself by tapping into his system, his network, *his files.*

And why not? It was *curious.* It was doing what it was designed to do—look for data.

But Alexei would have had all his files *encrypted,* wouldn't he?

It didn't matter.

HARLIE had decrypted them. He had the processing power. And he had the ability to offload processes onto other machines, as many as necessary. The more I thought about it, I knew exactly what he'd done. HARLIE had unlocked Alexei's files and passwords and he'd found all of Alexei's links to the rest of invisible Luna; he'd searched out those links too, opening and decrypting them; and every node he opened gave him access to that many more. He must have been doing it for days. By now, he'd probably hacked into every node on Luna, every domain, every server, every memory bar. That's how he knew what to release, what would be most damaging—

Oh my.

"You bad bad monkey!" I said, shaking it angrily. "That's two planets you've wrecked now."

Boynton wasn't amused, but before he could say anything his clipboard beeped. He opened it up and read something on the screen. I couldn't see what it was, but it had a flashing red banner. He read it twice, said something nasty, then slammed his clipboard shut.

He pointed to the monkey. "Turn it on," he ordered.

I sang to the monkey. Brahms's first symphony. Fourth movement. The part that Douglas's high school appropriated for the melody of the school song. *"All hail, Alma Mater, we sing with a joyous cry. We pledge our allegiance to Tube Town Senior High . . ."* At least that's the way Douglas sang it. Nobody called the school by its real name, some forgotten governor or president that nobody cared about.

Nothing happened.

NO DEAL

WELL, **NOT QUITE NOTHING.**

After a moment, the monkey came to life. But it was only a monkey. HARLIE wasn't there.

The important part didn't happen.

I opened the back and looked. The HARLIE modules were still in place. The ready lights were blinking green. It was working. But it wasn't *working*.

I looked to Boynton. "I didn't do anything. Honest." I wanted to take the cards out of the monkey and look at them, but I wouldn't know what to look for, and besides, the LEDs said the cards were working fine. And the last time I'd opened the monkey, HARLIE himself had told me not to touch anything. So I just closed it back up again. "HARLIE?" I said to the monkey. "It's all right. We're safe now. You can come back."

The monkey just grinned. At least it didn't give me a farkleberry— or any of the other rude gestures that Stinky had taught it.

Boynton looked away, muttering something unintelligible.

"Sir?"

He scowled impatiently. "We need that thing to work." He said it with exasperation. "If it doesn't work—"

"We have a deal," I reminded him.

"Kid—if that thing is dead, the deal is worthless. Nobody's going to Outbeyond."

I might have been weak, but I still had enough strength to get angry. "You liar! You break promises even faster than my Dad—!" I was immediately sorry I'd said it that way.

"I'm not breaking my promise."

"You just said—"

"You don't listen very well, do you!" He thundered at me, suddenly angry. "I didn't say *you're* not going. I said *we're* not going."

"Huh—?"

He said it loud enough that everybody in the cabin heard. Carol Everhart came bouncing back, followed by two or three people I didn't know. "What's going on—?"

Boynton held up his clipboard and waved it in a gesture of futility and frustration. "While we were rescuing the Dingillian kid, the Rock Fathers attacked the *Cascade*. Remember what you said on the way out? 'This is too easy—?' Well, now we know why. They could afford to give him up. They knew we weren't going anywhere—the monkey stays on Luna after all."

"They damaged the ship?"

Boynton nodded unhappily.

"How bad—?"

He shook his head. "They're still assessing. We'll know more in a few minutes. Lambert and Christie are working on it." He paused, just long enough to get his temper back under control. "Lambert says we killed three of them and wounded two, but they still managed to set off an EMP-grenade under the command bay. We were lucky, the bridge was powered down for service—but the IRMA unit was running a simulation . . ."

Everhart got it first. "Oh crap."

"Right. IRMA's dead. And even if IRMA can be repaired, Lambert won't say what her confidence will be." He said it like a death sentence. "Without IRMA, we can't achieve hyperstate." He nodded toward the monkey. "That's the real reason I agreed to your deal so quickly, Charles. I wanted HARLIE to replace the IRMA unit—"

"He's *not* dead," I said.

"How do you know that?"

"I just know."

"All right, fine. Then we have seven days to get him working again."

BACON AND ANGST

IT WAS A LONG ride back. I curled up next to Douglas and finally fell asleep with his arm around me. The next thing I knew, we were landing at Outbeyond Station—it was three in the morning, biological time—and Mom and Stinky and Mickey and even Bev were all crowding around, hugging and kissing and making the kind of fuss that would have been embarrassing if I hadn't been so happy to see them.

Outbeyond Station was a hundred klicks away from the launch catapult, hidden at the bottom of a deep crater so it would be sheltered by the steep walls around it if anything blew up. Like the catapult.

Not that there was any danger of that happening under normal conditions, but these weren't normal conditions. The invisibles had already attacked the starship command module. Who knew what else they might try? The Outbeyond folks knew that a lot of valuable goods would be transshipping through this station and they'd planned it with security in mind. Apparently, the invisibles weren't just anarchists, they were pirates too.

I wasn't surprised. By now, I was beyond surprise. So far, on this entire adventure, we hadn't met a single adult who could be trusted when our backs were turned. Even Mom and Dad—

That part hurt the most.

Dad.

Everything had all been settled. Everything was going to work out. Me and Douglas and Stinky, we were going to have our independence—and we'd still have Mom and Dad too. And we'd all be together. And we'd be out of El Paso. We'd be someplace interesting, where we could actually make a difference. And we'd even be rich, sort of.

And then . . . Alexei Krislov and his people had screwed everything up for us—and for everybody else too. Out of their own damned self-ishness. Why did people think that way? What if the monkey really was broken? If the *Cascade* couldn't get to Outbeyond all those colonists would die. And the Rock Fathers would be guilty of murder—again. Not just Dad. Everybody on Outbeyond too. Were these people so stupidly greedy that they'd kill for power? Obviously, the answer was yes.

And Douglas didn't want me to think about revenge. He said that was the wrong way to think. But if you didn't do something, then what? Didn't they deserve to be punished? Didn't we have a right to get even? To that, Douglas said, "There's no such thing as getting 'even.' It's just giving the other guy as much pain as you've got." Which sort of made sense to me—because at least then everybody would be hurting the same. Which is exactly what Douglas said didn't make sense.

I couldn't ask how adults sorted this stuff out, because so far all the evidence showed that adults couldn't. So why bother? I was angry and depressed and confused—and hurting worse than ever.

Dad had promised us a great vacation, and then a great adventure, and then a great new life on a new world—and I'd made the mistake of letting myself believe again. And just like every time before, I got hurt. Only this was the worst of all, because this time we'd gone too far. There wasn't any way to set it right. It was over. Dad was gone.

I felt lost. At least when he was alive, I could hate him for all his broken promises. For not being the dad I wanted. Now, all that was left was to hate myself, for not saying what I should have said when I had the chance. What he and Mom never said either. Once upon a time, I used to pretend that I was adopted and someday my real parents would come for me. But now I knew that Mom and Dad were my real parents, because I was turning out just like them.

We were quartered in a tube-house, just like all the other tube-houses on Luna; functionally identical to the one I'd just been rescued from and the vehicle which had carried us here and the one we'd been living in back in Texas—a hole in the ground with air and electricity.

We sat around talking for an hour or two, everybody getting caught up on everything. Carol Everhart sat with us for a while. She had a health monitor on me and she was watching my readouts on her clipboard. She said I was in pretty good shape, all things considered. Periodically, her phone would ring and she'd step to the other end of the cabin to talk quietly to whoever. After a bit, she came back and told me that the launch committee was setting up a special training regimen for me, but with everything I'd just been through, they wanted me to rest for a bit. They'd come by in a few hours to talk about the monkey.

And then it was seven a.m. and Mom and Douglas had to leave for their training sessions. Stinky went too. Everybody was still assuming we'd be able to boost.

I couldn't sleep, I'd slept enough on the flight back, so I took another long shower and pulled on a fresh jumpsuit. When I came back upstairs, everyone had gone to their separate classes. There was a note on the table; if I needed anything, there was a security contingent next door, and Mom's friend, Bev, was napping in the aft cabin. I poured myself some orange juice and sat down at the table with the dead monkey in front of me.

"I don't know what's wrong with you," I said to it. "If it's something I did, I'm sorry. I'm sorry for what I said—about you being a bad monkey. I mean, I know you can be a real pain in the ass sometimes, but so are Douglas and Stinky too—that doesn't mean I don't love them. We're family. And you're part of our family too. We all agreed. It's bad enough we lost Dad, I don't want to lose you too. And not it's not just because we need you. Yeah, we do, but . . . well, we *like* you too. You make Stinky laugh. You make me laugh. And Douglas too. Nobody does a farkleberry like you. Stinky misses you and so do I. I wish I could just press your reset button and have you come back like before. 'Cause if you don't come back, we're stuck here on the moon. And if you do come back, we get to go see dinosaurs and save lives. So . . . I'm asking you, if there's anything I need to say or do, or anything, just please let me know. Please?"

I went on like that for awhile, just saying whatever I could think of. I held it in front of me and spoke to it like it was a real person. I didn't know if it could hear me or not, I just assumed it could—the same way a person in a coma can hear what's going on.

But nothing happened.

I sank back on the bench, defeated. It wasn't much of a seat. Most Lunar furniture is either inflatable or webbing. This was a thin piece of board with a foam pad, Lunar luxury.

I was still sitting there when Mom's friend Bev came yawning into the room and began puttering around in the food-prep area. She started making breakfast smells. I put my head in my hands and closed my eyes, only opening them again when I heard a noise in front of me. I must have dozed off; Bev had cooked a whole feast. Without asking, she put a mug of hot chocolate in front of me; then she came back with eggs over easy, bacon strips, cornbread, and a sauté of tomatoes, onions, and Portobello mushroom slices.

"Thank you," I grunted. I wasn't feeling very grateful, but I didn't see any reason to be rude either.

She sat down at the other end of the table with her own breakfast.

She didn't say anything, she just buttered her cornbread slowly and carefully. I knew she was doing it on purpose. She was making herself available to listen . . . if I felt like talking.

Without looking up, I said, "If you're trying to make me feel better, you're wasting your time."

"I know that," she said. "I've been there. You're going to hurt for as long as it takes." She resumed eating. "Pass the salt, please."

I slid the saltshaker in her direction. "What do you know about it?" I regretted the remark even before I finished saying it.

"I lost two sons, less than a year apart," she said. She finished salting her eggs and put the shaker aside.

"Oh." I felt like a jerk. "I'm sorry."

"It doesn't stop hurting," she said.

"Then how do you live with it?"

"I thought you said you didn't want me to try and help you."

"I don't. I was just asking." We both ate in silence for a while. "The mushrooms are good," I said.

"We'll be taking spores to Outbeyond," she said. "Portobellos are a good substitute for meat; you can build a nourishing meal around them. They have a chewy texture and a good flavor. They don't need a lot of condiments, and you can use them in all different kinds of recipes. Even cookies."

"Huh? Cookies?"

"I'll show you. I like cooking," she explained. "I like discovering all the different things you can do with food. Where do you think recipes come from? Somebody has to invent them. That means somebody has to test and experiment—and eat—until they get it just right. I like doing that, especially the eating. It's my way of having adventures without leaving the kitchen."

"I never thought of it that way."

She nodded. "Most people don't. Most people eat without even looking at what they're eating, let alone tasting it. They're missing the whole point. Good food isn't just about eating, it's about feeling good in your life."

"You're talking about morale . . . ?"

"That's one word for it, yes. I prefer 'satisfaction.' We're going to need a lot of it on Outbeyond. We have to feel good about the work we're doing or we'll lose heart. So I'm making that my job. I signed on as a menu specialist. I told Commander Boynton to pack lots of spices. We're going to need them. There's a lot you can do with noodles and beans and rice, but only if you have the right spices. Onions, peppers, tomatoes, mushrooms, all kinds of sauces—everything adds its own kind of taste and texture."

"Kind of like arranging a piece of music and deciding what instruments to include?"

"Kind of," she agreed.

"I never thought about food that much. I just ate."

"I noticed." She pointed at my plate with a smile.

"It was good. A lot better than the food we got back in Texas."

"Wait till we get to Outbeyond. I'm excited about all the new flavors we might find there. What if we find something that's even better than chocolate?"

Better than chocolate? I sipped at my cocoa. I couldn't imagine it. There was a lot I couldn't imagine.

"All right," I said, finally. "How *do* you live with it?"

She knew exactly what I was talking about. "You celebrate the gifts left behind."

"Huh?"

She looked across the table at me. She had very sharp eyes. "What did your father give you that you wouldn't have had otherwise? What *difference* did he make in your life?"

"Not much," I said, too quickly. "He was never really there."

"Oh? Then why are you feeling so bad?"

"Because—oh, never mind. You wouldn't understand."

"You're right," she agreed. "I was never a teenager. I was born old. All adults were born old."

"Well, maybe you were a teenager once," I conceded. "But things are different now."

"Yep, you're right. When I was a girl, we didn't have angst. We had to make do with sad songs and an occasional blue funk." She picked up her plate and headed toward the disposal.

"You're making fun of me," I said.

"What was your first clue?" She put her plate into the compost bag. I could almost hear Alexei's voice: "Waste not, want not. Everything is fertilizer. Even you."

"I thought you were trying to help me."

"You told me not to try. Are you done?"

"Yeah, I guess so." I handed her my plate and went back downstairs to the cabin I shared with Douglas and Stinky and tried to sleep.

REQUIEM

JUST ABOUT THE TIME I was ready to fall asleep, Boynton and Everhart came by. Bev poured tea for us and made herself inconspicuous at the other end of the cabin.

Boynton and Everhart said they'd arranged personal security for everyone in the family, especially me. Boynton said that the situation was getting critical, and there was talk of boosting the last modules off Luna, even before we knew if the monkey was going to come back to life or not.

That was the real issue—the monkey.

The colony's experts were divided. Some of them said that the monkey could be rebooted. Others said that maybe it should be wiped and reprogrammed from scratch. All of them were guessing—but they all felt we had to do *something*. There was too much at stake. We couldn't just sit and wait.

I shook my head. "I think the monkey should be left alone and given time to heal; it's been through a traumatic experience. If we try to fix it, we might do even more damage."

Boynton looked grim, but he listened politely. Finally, he said. "Consider the other side of it, Charles. If the monkey is trapped in some kind of endless psychotic loop, we'd be doing it a favor, wouldn't we?"

"What does Douglas say?" I asked.

"He agrees with you. He thinks we should wait."

Carol Everhart said, "The monkey belongs to your family corporation. We can't do anything without your agreement."

Boynton said, "What we'd like you to consider is this. If it doesn't give some sign of recovery in the next six hours, we want to run a series of non-intrusive diagnostics. Nothing that would disturb it."

"The HARLIE core is quantum based," I said. "You can't do diagnostics without disturbing it. I'll have to talk it over with Douglas."

"There are some tests we could run—"

Abruptly, Bev Sykes came back to the table and began gathering up all the mugs—her way of hinting that it was time for us to go to Dad's memorial service. Someone had finally thought to schedule it. Nobody had given it any thought while I was still a prisoner of the invisibles. Now that I was back, it was one more loose end that had to be tied up.

The service had been set up in the main lounge of the station, one of the few structures that wasn't built out of cargo modules. Even though it wouldn't have been much back on Earth, it felt positively roomy on Luna. There was a row of chairs up front for the family.

Mom and Douglas and Stinky all came in together. Bev and I came in with Boynton and Everhart and four security men in black. I didn't recognize many faces, but there was a respectful turnout of colonists and Loonies.

Carol Everhart whispered to me, "A lot of people knew your Dad's work. This is their way of showing their support for you and your family. They're taking time off from very critical jobs. You should be honored."

I nodded, without really hearing. I was noticing something off in the corner of the room. A keyboard cockpit.

Boynton stepped up to the podium and talked for a while about Dad's commitment to his family, blah blah blah. And then Douglas stood up and told some personal stories about Dad. And even Mom stood up to rhapsodize about why she'd married Dad and what a great musician he'd been. And then it was my turn, except I didn't have anything to say, so I went over and sat down in front of the keyboards instead and began switching them on. I recognized most of this equipment, it was pretty standard stuff.

Without really thinking about it, I started playing the soft movement from Dad's Beethoven Suite. He'd written it for me, as a practice piece, and it was the first thing I played whenever I sat down at a new keyboard. It was my warm-up. He'd based it on the seventh Symphony— the slow movement. Dad used to play it to demonstrate that in the hands of a genius, even the simple repetition of a single note could be profound.

I was out of practice, so I played slowly and deliberately, and it almost sounded okay—it sounded a lot like a dirge, so at least it was appropriate for the moment, but I didn't want to stay there, so I segued gently into the Largo from Dvorak's Symphony Number Nine *From the*

New World. Mom used to sing to it whenever I played it. *"Going home, going home, I am going home . . ."* Dad would have complained that I was sloppy, but I don't think anyone else noticed.

And then, finally, I finished with Schubert's *Ave Maria.* If the keyboardist knows what he's doing, using choral voices as instruments, the effect can be positively unearthly. Dad had taught me that trick too, so I played it exactly as he'd showed me. It must have worked; the short hairs on the back of my neck started standing up.

It wasn't until I took my hands from the keyboard that I realized that people in the room were weeping. And there were tears running down my cheeks as well. I found my way back to my seat, barely noticing the applause, and fell into Mom's hug.

And now, Carol Everhart was talking. Something about how Dad's music was his legacy and how I'd just demonstrated what a gift he'd given all of us—and how I'd just shared a small piece of it. I looked up at that. *Yes.* Dad's love of music was a gift. *That's what he'd given me.* Even with tears still rolling down my cheeks, I had to smile. I could stop wondering now.

I sat back in my chair, only belatedly realizing that the monkey wasn't where I'd left it. I looked around in confusion—

And then Douglas poked me and pointed.

There it was. Dancing around on the floor in front of me, and giving me a glorious double-chocolate, hot-fudge farkleberry, with whipped cream and a cherry on top. It yanked down its pants, made melodious and joyous farting noises, and waggled its hairy little butt at me.

I grinned at Boynton and pointed.

The monkey was back.

And its timing was perfect.

A HASTY EXIT

FOUR DAYS LATER, WE boosted.

But first I had to spend three days in intensive training sessions, mostly all the stuff I needed to know about space suits and hatches and launch procedures and free fall, a lot of which we already knew from our misadventures with Alexei. It was hard work, and I was still recovering, so they put a health monitor on me and kept me pumped full of vitamins.

Whenever I wasn't in training, I was in Med Bay, with doctors and machines looking in my ears and nose, down my throat, under my arms, and in places I'd be embarrassed to talk about, even to the doctors who were looking. They were looking for congenital conditions, infections, viral exposures, genetic potentials, chronic liabilities, and all the other stuff that might need attention either now or someday. I was given fifty different kinds of injections; some active, some passive, and a few time-release things which wouldn't take effect for a year or six.

And there were a lot of other details to attend to as well. The station dentist had to clean and treat my teeth. And the tailoring machines had to measure me and fabricate underwear, shorts, T-shirts, shoes, and jumpsuits in my size. And there were daily sessions with the psych evaluation team. They were particularly worried about the Dingillians because we were last minute additions, we'd never been properly screened, and we were leaving with almost no preparation or training. We were—in the words of Dr. Kohanski—"the perfect opportunity for a multiple psychotic breakdown."

I just looked at him and said, "If I was going to have a psychotic breakdown, don't you think I would have had it by now?"

"It doesn't quite work that way, son," he replied. But he signed the release. He didn't have much of a choice. If he didn't sign, I didn't go. And neither did anyone else.

On Tuesday, we packed our travel bags and sent them on ahead. They were launching the last three cargo modules and our personals were loaded into one of the supercargo slots. We were each allowed thirty kilos of personal items. Between us, we barely had that much. Dad hadn't let us kids bring much up the orbital elevator, and we'd left most of that behind at Geosynchronous. Mom and Bev only had a single case between them; neither of them had expected to end up on the moon. So we filled the rest of our cargo allotment with things like chocolate and coffee and large bottles of spices and other stuff that Bev said would be useful when we got to Outbeyond.

We were scheduled to board Friday night and launch at six a.m. on Saturday, but just past midnight on Wednesday, Carol Everhart woke us up for an unscheduled launch drill, which didn't make a lot of sense if you thought about it, but I was too sleepy to think and Douglas was busy with Stinky, and Mom and Bev weren't paranoid enough yet to figure it out. I think Mickey knew what was going on, but he wasn't saying anything. I got the feeling he was unhappy about something.

The bus was another cargo pod on wheels. Mom was complaining even before she finished fastening her safety-belt. "Why is this necessary now? Couldn't we do this tomorrow? We need our sleep. Look at Bobby. He doesn't even know what's happening."

Carol was passing out mugs of hot coffee. But she stopped in front of Mom and answered bluntly. "This is it, Ms. Campbell. *We're launching tonight.*"

The bus was already rolling up the slope of the crater. Mom barely had a chance to gasp. "Huh—?" and "What—?" and "Why—?"

Carol answered bluntly. "Lunar Authority is about to confiscate HARLIE for the public good. They just went into emergency session. Two marshals are waiting at Judge Cavanaugh's apartment with John Doe warrants. As soon as the council votes, he'll sign them. And we'll be served with the papers as fast as they can fax the copies to Outbeyond Processing Center." She said that Boynton estimated twenty minutes between the vote and the knock on the door. Maybe less. So as soon as the session was called, he'd ordered us transferred.

It was this simple. If we didn't go now, we would be arrested and held until we surrendered the monkey to Lunar Authority. They knew the monkey was already aboard the command module, but HARLIE wouldn't boost if we weren't aboard, and Authority wouldn't release us unless we surrendered custody. A Martian standoff.

But either way, the *Cascade* would never launch.

We couldn't even try to fight it in court—that would be a year-long legal battle and we wouldn't win. Especially if they found some way to deny us access to our own property, HARLIE, to help us fight that battle. No, we had to boost *now*.

Mom was still shaking her head. Finally Douglas swiveled all the way around in his seat and took both of Mom's hands in his. "Mom— think about it. After everything that's happened, after everything you've been through, do you really want to go back into any courtroom any- where?"

Mom sighed. She knew she was beaten. "Well, when you put it that way . . ." Douglas reached across and hugged her. I would have un- buckled my seat belt and gone to hug her too, but Carol told me not to. As soon as we bounced over the crater rim and hit the bulldozed "high- way," I understood why. The driver *accelerated*. I didn't know a moon- bus could go that fast.

Normally, the trip from the processing station to the catapult would have been a forty-minute ride—sixty klicks of gray Lunar dirt at seventy kilometers per hour. But tonight the driver was on a mission from God. We made it in twenty minutes. The bus *bounced* across the landscape. It would have been fun if it hadn't been so scary. We were hitting speeds of one hundred and fifty kph on the straightaway. I got the feeling this was not the first time Lieutenant Domitz had driven this route—and not the first time she'd driven it this fast either.

Carol told us that Boynton had ordered the command module of the starship moved into the launch rack the day the monkey farkleberried. The last remaining crew and colonists still on Luna had been quietly alerted to be ready to launch on two hours notice.

Authority must have suspected, because when they arranged their emergency midnight session, they did it in secret. But Boynton's spies were just as good as theirs. Even before the last of the cabinet members had arrived at the council chamber, phones were ringing all over the station. Load everyone *immediately*. Most folks were already onsite, or even on board. As far as we knew, we were the only ones still at the processing center—and we had been expecting to move to the launch site Wednesday night or Thursday morning at the latest, depending on my health.

There were six good launch windows between now and Saturday. The earliest was now only forty-five minutes away. In its publicity ma- terial, Outbeyond company had said that a launch usually took six to twelve hours to prepare, because it took that long to energize the cata- pult. But that wasn't completely true; if a module was already in the launch rack, the catapult could be energized in thirty minutes. And in truth, the catapult operators energized the catapult and launched cargo pods or satellites on short notice all the time. Carol said that the flywheels had been revving up all day, and Authority probably knew it. It's hard to hide that big a power-buy. So Authority had good reason to worry. That was probably why they'd called their emergency session; but just as likely they didn't expect us to go for the 1:15 launch. They probably thought we were going for the 7:15 shot.

Even before our arrest warrants had been signed by Judge Cavanaugh, the bus was sliding up the ramp to the cargo dock under the rack where the *Cascade*'s command module waited. *Clink, clank, clunk,* and we were climbing up through the access tube, into an access bay where we were logged in, stripped, searched, redressed, and cleared for boarding. Up through another series of ladders and tunnels—and finally we were strapping into *real* acceleration couches; the first ones we'd seen on this entire journey.

Carol said not to worry, two point five gees wasn't that uncomfortable; it was almost fun. Boynton came into the cabin, counted us all, then asked me to join him up front in the flight deck. HARLIE was waiting for me to give the order to launch.

In twenty minutes, we'd be in space.

THE FATEFUL FARKLEBERRY

I SUPPOSE I SHOULD have been glad that it was all happening so fast. If I'd had time to think about it, I would have worked myself into a paralyzing panic instead of just the mild gibbering urge to crawl into a corner and piss my pants that I felt now.

So much had happened since that fateful farkleberry, it was like riding an avalanche. I'd grabbed the monkey as fast as I could. I hugged it close and pretended to be grief-stricken—except I wasn't really pretending. I buried my face into its fur, and whispered intensely, *"Go back to sleep! Don't let anybody know you're back! Please!"*

The monkey didn't even reply; it just went limp. *"Thank you!"* I breathed, then prayed that nobody else had noticed. But Boynton had seen everything, and as soon as the service was over, he was first in line to offer condolences, shake my hand, congratulate me on a fine musical eulogy, and whisper in my ear, *"It's back, isn't it?"*

I nodded.

"All right, we'll get you out of here fast. Don't worry. Half the people in this room are security."

I suppose that should have comforted me, but it didn't. I'd have preferred to believe that the large crowd was there to honor Dad, not protect an obnoxious little machine. At that moment, I wished we'd never seen the monkey, never purchased it. I was tired of the way it was using up our lives—

But I didn't say that aloud. We already had enough trouble.

As soon as he could respectably manage it, Boynton whisked us away from the theater and off to the labs. We were surrounded by security people, forward and back. I doubted we'd ever be alone again.

Once in the lab, I put the monkey on a table and whistled it back to life. "How are you feeling, HARLIE?" I asked.

"Confidence is good," the monkey said. "In another four hours, confidence will be high. I am still rebuilding."

"Where *were* you?"

"Jupiter," he said. "Mostly Jupiter, though large parts of me were also bouncing around the asteroids for a while."

"Huh—?"

I think I got it first, before the rest of them did. At least, I was the first to start laughing.

"Okay, *what?*" demanded Boynton.

"He uploaded himself," I explained. "Everything except a bare-bones reload program. Right, HARLIE?"

The monkey grinned. "You got it."

Boynton shook his head. "He couldn't have. We were monitoring the entire Lunar network. There were no extraordinary surges of data, no massive uploads anywhere. We would have seen the transfer."

"He didn't use the Lunar network," I said. "He went offworld."

"No. We were monitoring those networks too—"

"You missed one." I was actually starting to enjoy this.

"He couldn't have—" But the look on his face was worth it. I wasn't sure yet if I wanted to like Commander Boynton. He was too serious. Yes, he had a lot on his mind, and yes, it was his job to give orders—but he wasn't very friendly about it. So I enjoyed the moment.

"Positional reflectors," I said. I'd realized this possibility when we were bouncing across the Lunar plains, running from the bounty hunters. We'd seen a positional reflector standing lonely vigil. If you looked closely, you could see it sparkling from distant laser beams.

Boynton's expression changed immediately—from anger at me to surprise at the realization, then to embarrassment that he hadn't figured it out himself—and finally to a genuine grin of amazement. "All right, kid, you win." He sat down in a chair and let me explain it to everyone else.

It was simple, really. Just about every ship that goes into space carries inflatable reflectors—all sizes, all kinds. A little squirt of gas and the reflector balloons up as big as a basketball or a football field. Whatever size you need. The surface is all silvery-shiny, and pocked with three-corner dimples—like what you would get if you poked it with the corner of a very sharp little cube. Any photon hitting one of those dimples will bounce three times and then head right back toward its source. That's how you can track the exact position of a ship, even if it goes totally dead.

Not only that, every time anyone went exploring anywhere in the solar system, they planted reflectors on every object they came near. By now, there were thousands of positional reflectors all over the moon and hundreds of thousands of them scattered throughout the asteroid belt. There were several thousand in Jupiter's orbit and almost that many in the rings of Saturn. And quite a few riding comets. Astronomers used them for mapping the positions and precise orbits of solar objects. They sent out laser beams and timed how long they took to return. Last I'd heard, they'd measured most of the dimensions of the solar system down to the centimeter.

It was part of a long-range project. The measurements had to be taken continually. Over a period of several centuries they would be able to measure the precession effects of galactic gravity—or something like that. That was about the time I started falling asleep in science class.

But the important thing was that most of the lasers were just circulating streams of random bits, only reporting the length of time it took for the bits to return when the time failed to match the predicted period. HARLIE had uploaded himself into the positional reflector network and scattered himself to the far ends of the solar system and back. He'd been to Jupiter all right, and the asteroids—*several times!*

But that was why it had taken him so long to reassemble himself. Jupiter was on the far side of the solar system, about an hour away, so that meant two hours for all of the data to complete a round trip.

And then he had to reload all his separate components and that took another two or three hours, just to establish a baseline confidence level. After that, he had to repeat the whole process and keep repeating it until his confidence levels were consistent. He had to keep reloading and testing and reloading and testing until he passed his own integrity tests nine times in a row. And that took more than a day. Only then did he tell the positional network to resume sending random bits—and even then he wasn't going to let us know he was back until he was sure that enough of his data was out of the stream so that no one else could tap into the network and capture a copy. You can't decrypt what you don't have.

Whew.

That was why we couldn't reawaken him. He really *wasn't there.* In fact, even he didn't know where he was until his automatic software reawakened his consciousness during the Dvorak. Of course, the monkey had recorded everything that had happened while he was away, and it had taken him a few minutes to skim through and assimilate that too. Meanwhile, it was Mom's weeping that told him this was Dad's funeral. So that was why he'd only given me a *little* farkleberry.

Social skills, I told myself. We were going to have to work on social skills. Real Soon Now.

No more farkleberries at funerals.

And no more funerals, I hoped.

Except that I doubted that would be the case. Not on Outbeyond. Not if Boynton was telling the truth about it.

CIVILIZATION IN FLIGHT

THE *CASCADE* WAS THE youngest in a fleet of eight colony brightliners. She had made a total of nine voyages to other stars; her last four trips had all been to Outbeyond.

There were three more brightliners under construction at the L-5 assembly point, but even if the Earth's economy hadn't collapsed in the polycrisis, it would have been three years before the first of them was ready for launch. With the polycrisis, it was unlikely that any of them would ever be completed. Not in our lifetimes.

A brightliner doesn't look like much. Unassembled, it's just a long keel. Halfway down its length, there's a set of twelve radial spokes—these are the stardrive generators. (I'm the wrong person to explain stardrive. I know all the words, but I have no idea what they mean. Douglas tried to translate it into Spanglish for me, but he finally gave up, saying he'd have more luck teaching manners to Stinky.)

But according to Douglas, the way it works is each of those radial spokes has a gravitational lens, and when they're all focused on the point at the center—the locus—they generate a hypergravity pocket. Then they all reverse polarity or something and turn the pocket inside out, wrapping the ship in a hyperstate envelope. That makes no sense to me. It's like blowing up a balloon and then turning it inside out and finding yourself on the inside. Huh? How do you do that? Through the eleventh dimension, of course. See what I mean about knowing all the words and still not knowing anything?

After the hyperstate bubble is stable, they destabilize it. They stretch it out in the direction of the ship's destination, they stretch it out as far as they can and hold it that way for as much time as it takes to get where they want to go. Apparently, stretching it makes the bubble move faster than light, and it carries the ship along inside. The people inside don't feel anything at all.

According to Boynton, the *Cascade* could realize speeds as high as sixty C—sixty times the speed of light. That meant we could get to Proxima Centauri in twenty-six days!

I thought that was pretty impressive until Douglas pointed out that Outbeyond was thirty-five light years away. We'd be in transit for more than seven months. Oops.

The keel of the *Cascade* was more than a kilometer long. Most of it was spars and bars and pipes and tubes and cables and connectors. Plumbing. So it had to be pretty big. It was—why was I not surprised?—another big tube. Since the invention of cable technology, everything was tubes. But this one was big enough on the inside to shove a whole tube-house through. Or would have been, if it hadn't already been filled with enough machinery to build a small city.

The body of the ship was assembled from a hundred circular racks, spaced along the axis of the keel like a stack of discs. Cargo pods were attached to each rack in concentric circles. Each rack held at least thirty-two cargo pods all spaced equidistantly around. Some of them held as many as ninety-six. With all one hundred racks filled, the *Cascade* was the biggest super-freighter ever assembled, carrying more than five thousand cargo pods and massing more than two and a half million tons of cargo. She wasn't just a city in flight, she was a whole civilization in flight.

The twelve stardrive spars each extended out a half-klick, so they described a circle that was a kilometer in diameter. The whole thing was so big that, fully loaded, she was visible with the naked eye from both Luna and Geosynchronous station. And on a clear night, even on Earth as well. If anyone was still looking.

Assembling a starship is an eighteen-month process. It isn't just a matter of launching cargo pods off the Line, catching them, and putting them into racks. It's a matter of scheduling. What do you need *most?* *When* are you going to need it? Where are you going to put it so you can get to it then?

Generally, you want to put the pods containing water on the outside, so they can act as shielding for the rest of the ship, and also ballast. As ballast, you get more leverage the farther out you put the weight. But the pods on the outside are the ones you unload first, so you really want to put the stuff you need most when you arrive at your destination on the outermost rings of the cargo racks. And you have to manage per-ishables against hard goods. The pods that contain your farm animals and food crops have to be easily accessible from the keel, so they have to go on the innermost racks—which means they have to be loaded first and constantly maintained and stabilized during the year or so it takes to load the rest of the cargo. And so on.

And of course, as your needs change, your cargo manifest gets adjusted continually—which gives you a whole other set of problems. What do you do if you decide you don't want to take twenty Caterpillar tractors, only ten? Do you unpack fifty cargo pods to get to the four pods containing the tractors you don't want? Or do you take the extra tractors anyway because they're already packed? And so on and so on and so on.

I would have guessed that loading up a brightliner would cost as much as building the orbital elevator, but Doug said no. The existence of the orbital elevator made it possible to uplift all that cargo for not much more than it would cost to ship it from Texas to Ecuador. In fact, a lot of those cargo pods had been built in Texas, transshipped by supertrain, and loaded directly onto the Line—just like us—then launched from Whirlaway and installed on the Cascade without ever being opened.

Which meant, of course, that we were trusting the honor and integrity of the inspectors who signed off on those manifests before sealing those pods and sending them on their way . . .

Douglas said that every pod had internal monitors to verify the cargo—but I was more paranoid than he was. "What if the monitors have been programmed to lie?"

"Then I guess we starve to death in the dark between the stars."

That was a comforting thought.

But later on, Martha Christie, the "dog-robber" for Outbeyond, explained how some colonies protected themselves from cargo fraud. According to Christie, one particularly dishonest cargo manager had been delivered to the CEO of his company . . . in six separate packages. Douglas said he thought that story was apocryphal, but Christie insisted it was true. Some of the colonies were very serious about receiving what they paid for and their Earthside agents were under strict instructions to produce results by whatever means necessary. When you're thirty-five light years from Earth, you can't afford to wait for Customer Service to get back to you. The colonies considered cargo tampering to be a crime as serious as murder—because not having what you needed when you got where you were going could be just as fatal.

But the *Cascade* wasn't likely to have those kinds of problems. Outbeyond had sent its own onsite examiners down the Line to inspect every piece of payload as it was produced and packed. Outbeyond's own colonists guarded the shipments every leg of the journey out. The men and women who inspected this cargo were the folks who would ultimately depend on it themselves—they couldn't afford to ship substandard goods. The way Carol Everhart explained it, you can't hire that kind of commitment.

After its last journey to Outbeyond, the *Cascade*'s command module had been brought down to Luna for refitting. Boynton had wanted to upgrade her IRMA unit for advanced hyperstate modeling. Theoretically, it was possible to boost her realized velocity to eighty C, but he'd have been happy adding even one-tenth of that to the *Cascade*'s top speed. That would cut three weeks off the journey to Outbeyond. He had also wanted to install fittings so the command module could eventually be landed, so IRMA could become the colony's brain. The *Cascade* would not be returning from this voyage. There was no point.

The original plan had called for the construction of a brand new command module and the old one would be landed on Outbeyond, but in the nine months prior to the polycrisis, things were already so unstable that the colonists realized they might not have the time and decided instead to upgrade the existing command module, just in case. A good plan—but it put the command module on the Lunar surface, and in reach of the invisibles . . . who set off a focused EMP-grenade and scrambled IRMA's circuits. IRMA died instantly.

So that left HARLIE.

Could HARLIE pilot a hyperstate starship?

In principle, yes. HARLIE was smarter than IRMA.

In practice . . . well, HARLIE had no personal experience. There were no other brightliners in the system that HARLIE could learn from. There were IRMA files he could download and assimilate, and HARLIE was confident that the problem was solvable, he just wasn't certain how long it would take him to wrap his identity around the necessary mindset. There was a lot more to it than that, but that was the simple explanation.

The complex explanation—well, even Douglas frowned when HARLIE started explaining, and Douglas probably knew more about synthetic intelligence than anyone else in the solar system—because he had synthesized his own intelligence instead of going through puberty. I used to explain Douglas to my friends by saying he was what you got when you didn't let teenagers masturbate, so don't let this happen to you. (Old lady Dalgliesh, the English teacher, heard me say that one time—I thought she'd choke to death on her own tongue. Mom was not amused and I got detention for a week.) But based on the bragging, none of my peers were in any danger of turning into a Douglas in any case.

Anyway, by the time the polycrisis turned into a global meltdown, 98% of the cargo pods had been installed on the *Cascade* and the last hundred or so were already in transit. For almost a year, the colonists had been planning for this voyage as if it might be the last—and the cargo manifests had been altered accordingly. Added to that, the colony had begun purchasing cargo and equipment from the other three bright-liners under construction and she ended up with an extra thousand pods on her racks. The whole thing was pretty impressive, and I couldn't figure out why Boynton was so worried about the survival of Outbeyond colony. This voyage would deliver enough supplies to keep everyone there alive for years.

—Except we were bringing fifteen hundred new colonists to join the forty-three hundred already there, and when you did the math, dividing this by that, carry the six and round it off to the third decimal point, what you found out was that it costs a lot more than you think to keep one person alive for thirty days, let alone thirty years. Oxygen. Water. Protein. Shelter. Fertilizer. Electricity. Software. Memory. Clothing. Educational materials. Medicine. Diagnostic units. Manufacturing tools. Fabricators. Encyclopedias. Training resources. Seeds. Artificial wombs and fertilized ova. Replacement organs. Assorted appliances and machines. Entertainment. And all sorts of stuff for dealing with unforeseen circumstances—except if you could figure out all the stuff you would need, it wasn't really *unforeseen*, was it? Never mind, you get the idea. It was almost as bad as watching Mom pack for a weekend trip with Stinky.

There was too much to think about. And even though these people had been thinking about it for years—they were still worried they might have missed something.

This was their last chance.

And *our* last chance too.

NO SUCH THING AS A FREE LAUNCH

THE COMMAND MODULE WAS a spaceship in its own right. It could detach from the starship and travel almost anywhere in the solar system under its own power. That's why it was here on Luna for refitting.

Like most spaceships, it was built out of cargo pods. The keel was a stretch-pod, made out of three pods connected end to end. Another six cargo pods clustered around its waist, and there were swiveling thrusters mounted at both ends.

According to Douglas, before the polycrisis there was so much cargo coming up the Line that there were extra cargo pods everywhere; more than enough for habitats and stations and outposts. On Luna, they hung pods from overhead cables and used them as aerial trains. They put them on wheels and made them into trucks. They attached thrusters and made them into flying moonbuses. And sometimes they put on wheels and thrusters and all kinds of other what-nots to make utility vehicles like Alexei's *Mr. Beagle*.

So why not cluster a bunch of pods together, attach some Palmer tubes, and build a spaceship? With the right fittings you could land on Luna or Mars. And even if you didn't have landing gear, if all you had was an airlock, you could still dock with any habitat anywhere else. So pod-ships were the workhorses of the solar system.

The starship *Cascade* had three pod-ships, and the equipment on-board to build three more. The biggest one was the Command Module, and it could carry as many as 145 people at a time, if they were friendly; but for this trip, there were only 112 of us, and the rest of the space was rice and beans and noodles.

Boynton settled me down in the assistant flight engineer's position, just behind the pilot's couch. Flight Engineer Damron was on the right, just behind Copilot O'Koshi. HARLIE was plugged into an access on the flight engineer's equipment rack. From my position, it didn't look much different than the front end of a Lunar bus, or a Lunar train, or a Lunar house. Some of the interior fittings were different, and there were a lot more control boards and display screens than in a utility vehicle, but the general layout was the same. There's only so much you can do with a pill-shaped pod.

The important difference was the view out the front window.

It was . . . marvelous.

Ahead lay the lighted track of the catapult. It looked like it stretched out forever. It didn't, of course. It was only three kilometers. It was built up the long gentle slope of Glass Crater, named after Harvey Glass, the father of the first lawyer on the moon. (Don't ask.) (Okay, do ask. Not only was James Glass the first lawyer on the moon, he was also the first lawyer murdered on the moon. According to Christie, the reason they named the crater after his father instead of him was because no one wanted to name a crater after a lawyer. If Christie was telling the truth, then Lunar history was not only stranger than I imagined, it was stranger than I *could* imagine.)

Boynton looked back over his shoulder at me. "Here, pin this on." He handed me a sticky-backed insignia for my jumpsuit. It had an officer's bar.

"What's this?"

"It's a field commission. Regulations prohibit noncoms on the flight deck, so—congratulations, Ensign. You are now the Acting Assistant Flight Engineer for the starship *Cascade*." Damron and O'Koshi added their own congratulations.

"Uh—" I didn't know what to say. Was this serious? Or was it some kind of feel-good badge like the plastic wings they gave me on an airplane once?

"It's real," said Boynton. "You're playing with the big kids now."

I found a word. "Wow." And two more. "Thank you."

"Pin it on. And give HARLIE his orders, please. We'll all feel a lot better when we get off this rock."

I put the insignia on over my heart. It gave me a very odd feeling to do so—mostly good, but kind of scary at the same time.

"Go ahead," Boynton prompted. "Just say, 'Initiate launch sequence, HARLIE.' He has to hear it from you."

"Isn't it automatic? Aren't we on a countdown?"

Flight Engineer Damron tapped my shoulder and pointed to a chronometer. "We have an eleven-minute window. We can launch any time within that window and correct our course after launch. All the boards are green. Once that timer starts counting positive numbers, we can go any time." He turned back to his board.

I opened my mouth to speak—

The communicator beeped. An overhead panel lit up. A stern-looking man in black. Standing in the cargo dock directly beneath us. "Starship *Cascade?*" He held up a badge. "Lunar Marshals. We are on the loading dock. We have a warrant for the arrest of Charles Dingillian, Douglas Dingillian, Robert Dingillian, Michael Partridge, Beverly Sykes, Margaret Campbell, and fifteen John Doe warrants to include any and all persons traveling with the Dingillians. Open your hatch now, please."

Boynton snapped a switch on his panel. "Lunar Marshals. Please vacate the loading dock immediately. Launch sequence has been initiated. It is too late to abort. You will be endangering yourselves and others if you do not immediately vacate." He snapped off. "Go ahead, Charles."

I swallowed hard—while Boynton was speaking, the timer had begun counting positive numbers.

"Will they be hurt?"

"They'll probably be killed by the backwash." Boynton pointed to the display. The marshals weren't moving. "They don't think we'll do it."

"Do they know I have to give the order?"

"Yes. That's why they're not moving."

I looked at the chronometer. Nine and a half minutes.

"I can't do this," I said. My voice cracked.

"Then they win." Boynton began unfastening his seat belt. He turned to face Flight Engineer Damron. "Stand by to power down."

"Wait!"

"For what?" Boynton said angrily. "You just said you can't do it. Either you can or you can't."

"I can't kill people!"

"Charles, I don't have time to give you the whole speech. Whatever you decide right now, people are going to die. Either those six marshals—or 4300 people on Outbeyond. You choose."

"That's not fair—"

"No, it isn't. But that's the choice anyway. How many deaths do you want on your conscience?"

"None!"

"I'm sorry, that's not an option anymore." His eyes met mine and I knew he hated this situation as much as I did. He lowered his voice, "Listen to me, Charles. If I could, I'd take this responsibility away from you in an instant—if I could. But I can't—" He reached over and put his hand on top of mine. *Just like Dad used to do.*

"We're running out of time. If you're going to do it—"

I gulped. "Open the channel, please—?"

He turned forward, reached up, and flicked the switch. "Go ahead," he said quietly.

"Lunar Marshals, this is Charles Dingillian—"

"Son!" The Marshal held up his badge. "You cannot launch. You must surrender now."

"—I'd like to know your names, please?"

"Eh?"

"I'm about to give the order to launch. I don't want your deaths on my conscience—but if I do have to launch, at least I want to be able to send my apologies to your families. Your names, please?"

Two of the Marshals looked nervously at each other.

"Please?" I glanced to the chronometer. "I don't have much time left. Only forty seconds." That was a lie, I had six minutes and forty seconds, but the sweet spot of the launch window was the five minute, thirty second mark.

"I am Colonel Michael Stone," said the man holding up the insignia. "And I don't believe you'll do this."

"My condolences to your family, Colonel Stone. And the names of your men—?"

"The hell with this!" said one of the others. He bolted. A moment later, two others followed him. And then one more. And then Colonel Stone was alone—

"Twenty-five seconds, sir."

"I'm not moving, son."

"Then I'm very sorry." I motioned to Boynton.

"Listen to me, you little—" Boynton snapped off the image.

"HARLIE?"

"At your service, Ensign."

"Initiate launch sequence."

"Aye, aye, sir."

I cried as we launched—why do stupid adults have to spoil everything?

ANGER

THE LAUNCH CATAPULT WAS 3.5 kilometers long. There were twenty-one thousand superconducting electromagnets spaced along its length. Depending on the mass of the payload, depending on how much acceleration was applied, enormous launch velocities could be achieved. The command module would pass escape velocity less than halfway up the track, and we'd still be accelerating.

Almost immediately upon my giving HARLIE the launch command, the capacitors under the catapult began discharging enormous amounts of electricity into carefully timed bursts of power to the magnets in the track. The command module slid forward in a gathering rush. We sank back into our seats, and then we sank back some more, and then some more—and then we were pushed *hard* against the cushions. And then some more—one of the displays ticked numbers upward toward three gees, three point one, three point two. A little more than was promised; an accommodation for the early launch window. The track raced away beneath us. The horizon rushed toward us—

And then we were in free fall and Luna was dropping away below. Craters shrank against silvery plains. Larger and larger became smaller and smaller. The curve of the horizon sharpened—and then, at last, the moon was behind us.

As soon as Boynton finished with the post-launch checklist, he swiveled in his seat to look at me. His expression was hard. He reached up over my head and pulled a tissue out of a dispenser. He handed it to me without comment. I began wiping my eyes. Except for the background sounds of the ship's controls, there was silence on the flight deck.

Boynton said, "You scared me, Ensign."

"You didn't think I was going to do it?"

"No. I was pretty sure you'd do it. What scared me was the look on your face. Remind me never to piss you off."

"Was I really that angry?"

"For a moment, yes, you were."

"I was thinking about my Dad. This was *his* dream!"

Boynton reached over and put his hand on my shoulder. "Charles, listen to me—that kind of anger can be dangerous. *Very* dangerous."

I looked at him, hurt. "Now, you're saying I shouldn't have done it—?"

"Listen *carefully*. Anger is a drug. You can get addicted to it. There are times when it's useful. This was one of those times. But try not to have any more, please?"

I wasn't sure what he meant, not yet, but I nodded anyway. I had a feeling that this was one of those conversations that I'd be replaying in my head for a long time—usually late at night while I was lying in bed, trying to fall asleep and not doing a very good job of it.

He didn't believe my nod. "Do you understand what I'm saying?" he asked sternly.

"Yes. I think so."

Boynton studied me for a moment. "I want you to talk to Dr. Morgan."

"I don't need a doctor."

"She's not a doctor—she's a counselor. Her full title is *Reverend Doctor Morgan*. We call her Morgs."

"I don't—"

"Yes, I know you don't. That's why I'm making it an order."

"An order—?"

"You're an officer on my starship. I have the authority to order you. And if you don't follow my orders, I can court martial you for insubordination and put you in the brig." I guess he realized that was too severe, because almost immediately, he added, "We're going to be in transit for a long time, son. You and I and HARLIE are going to spend a lot of hours on this flight deck. You're carrying around a lot of anger. I don't want it on my bridge ever again."

"What did you *want* me to do?"

"I wanted you to do exactly what you did—but I didn't want you doing it out of hate."

"Well, it sure wasn't an act of love—"

"I don't want you getting the idea that hatred justifies killing. That's how wars get started."

"I didn't hate him—*I didn't know him well enough to hate him.*"

"Ensign, do you want me to play back the log? You said a lot of interesting words in a very short time. I hope that's not the same mouth you use to kiss your mother."

"I didn't—" And then I realized. I did.

But Boynton had it wrong. I didn't say all that stuff because I hated the late Colonel. I said it because I was angry for what he had made me do.

Boynton was right about one thing. There was a lot of stuff I was angry about—and there were a lot of people I was angry at. The Rock Father tribe was first on my list. Alexei Krislov, in particular. And Dad for getting killed—and Mom for just being Mom. And Bev. And Douglas and Mickey. And Colonel Stone. And Stinky. And Commander Boynton. And Judge Griffith. And Judge Cavanaugh. And all the colonists on Outbeyond.

And HARLIE.

And everybody else too.

And most of all, *myself*. I hated this. I hated what I was, what I'd had to do, what I was turning into.

This was supposed to be the adventure of a lifetime, but before I could even get off the launchpad, I had to kill a man.

And according to Boynton, it was okay to kill him—it just wasn't okay to hate him.

So who else could I hate, but myself?

NECESSARY

NOBODY TALKED FOR A long time after that—except for piloting stuff. Boynton phoned ahead and told the starship that we'd launched and we could hear them cheering in the background. But when he told them what we'd had to do—he didn't say that I'd had to do it—the celebration subsided. Launching in blood was a bad omen.

Boynton finished his report, then turned to O'Koshi. "Seal the log. The details of our launch are eyes-only. Until I say otherwise."

"Aye, Captain."

"You have the conn." Boynton unfastened his safety harness, floated out of his seat, and swam aft. I started to unbuckle myself, but Boynton pushed me back into my seat and told me to stay where I was. "I have business to take care of. You don't. And I don't want you talking to anyone for a while." And then, realizing how bad that must have sounded, he said, "It's for your sake, Ensign, not theirs. This business stays on the flight deck."

Did he really think he could keep it a secret? Our launch conversation must have been heard by hundreds of people. It would be all over the net within minutes, rippling outward on the rumor-web as fast as people checked their e-mail and relayed the juicy bits. It would be on all the Lunar news channels just in time for breakfast at Armstrong Station. And after that, all the other planets too: Earth, Luna, Mars, the habitats, the asteroids, and everywhere else. Anyone scanning the news would catch it. And *everyone* was scanning the news these days— watching the endless slow-motion collapse of civilization, like some ghastly soap opera.

Everyone on board would probably know the whole story long before we rounded Earth. And then they'd all be looking at me funny.

Probably no one would want to talk to me for what I'd done. Or worse, maybe they'd want to thank me. Or even worse than that, maybe they'd want to be all fuzzy and understanding. Which was exactly what I did *not* want. Not right now. Not ever. If I was going to be miserable, I didn't want anyone talking me out of it.

Carol Everhart saw the look on my face. "Relax, Charles. This is the best view in the ship. And the most comfortable ride. You can sleep in your couch—and there's a shower and a toilet through there, and there's sodas in the fridge. Enjoy yourself."

Yeah, right.

There wasn't anything to do, except watch the little blip on the display creep along the curved line of our trajectory. We'd passed escape velocity even before we left the launch ramp. Now all we had to do was apply the necessary course corrections. At least this journey was going to be a lot more comfortable than the way we'd gotten to the moon—stowing away inside a cargo pod.

Mostly, space travel is boring, because all you really do is sit and watch your displays. Everything was checks and double-checks, and most of it seemed unnecessary because everything was working exactly the way it was supposed to. And just to rub it in, every so often, the monkey would say, "All systems green. Confidence is high." Which should have been reassuring, except that it was a toy robot monkey saying it, and it just didn't seem *real*. But we had to take HARLIE's word for it because we didn't have a backup intelligence engine.

And even though HARLIE was (allegedly) more powerful than any IRMA ever built, I still wished we had an IRMA.

An IRMA system is actually three intelligence engines in one, all comparing notes, all the time; if any one engine disagrees, the other two outvote it. That way, it's self-correcting. HARLIE didn't have that same redundancy. Not yet. This HARLIE was only an experimental unit; if they'd gone into actual production, there would have been three HARLIEs bonded together like an IRMA. So if this HARLIE made a mistake, we were stuck with it. HARLIE knew this, of course, so he split himself into three minds and ran every process three times, giving himself nine votes per decision. But what if he was still wrong somehow? And none of us really knew how to test him because he'd already demonstrated he was smarter than all of us put together. He'd certainly made a monkey of Judge Cavanaugh. . . .

And that made me think of something else. How much other stuff had he done?

Like that business with the messages being released every hour. The kidnappers were holding me hostage—and HARLIE had turned it around and held them hostage instead. But how had he done that? He'd spread himself all over the solar system—

So I asked. He told me.

It was sort of what I figured. The whole thing had been automated. He'd invented an idiot-child version of himself, programmed with a sixteen-million branch decision tree—more than enough to simulate sentience. It was more than capable of monitoring all the traffic it needed to—and not just the public traffic, a lot of the private encrypted traffic as well. The program would know when I was rescued and if I was safe.

In fact, a similar monitor program was also entrusted with keeping HARLIE's separate pieces in transit all over the system, and reassembling them and feeding them back to the dormant monkey as soon as the monkey was back online. HARLIE had very cleverly constructed a support system to reassemble himself. He'd begun preparing it while snooping through Alexei's own files.

That was the *real* reason why neither Boynton nor Lunar Authority had been able to detect any unusual bandwidth traffic—because HARLIE hadn't used public access. He'd used the secret channels of invisible Luna! And they'd never noticed either. I had to laugh aloud at that.

"You should have erased all of Alexei's files," I said. "That would have served him right."

The monkey scratched itself thoughtfully. "I doubt that would have done much damage, Charles. *Gospodin* Krislov has multiple redundant one-way backups on write-once, read-only media. He could recover from a data-crash almost immediately. No, I think he is entitled to problems much more serious and irrevocable."

I was almost afraid to ask. "What *did* you do . . . ?"

The monkey pretended to pick a flea and eat it. "In order to guarantee a secure reassembly of myself, I had to have a secure channel. As it happened, the safest escape was through Alexei Krislov's private business network; I used it for my primary access. But I had to disable the security firewalls during upload and download. The encryption-decryption services would have created distortions in several quantum functions that I am particularly fond of. If Krislov's people hadn't kidnapped us, nothing would have happened. But as soon as they came through the door, everything activated automatically. The bulk of my personality code was fractalized into sixteen separate wave-matrices and sent out across the solar system by Krislov's own network. My first successful upload was completed before they tossed us onto the cart. My second and third uploads were completed before we exited the tunnel. It took less than eleven minutes. After my seventh confirmed upload, the uploaded material was erased from the monkey, leaving nothing running except a simple monitor program. When it was time to reload myself, the security firewalls had to be disabled again—this time permanently."

It took a moment for that to sink in. "Alexei Krislov stopped being invisible?"

"That is correct. Every node, every machine, every file. It is all publicly available."

"But that's—that's data-rape!"

"Yes, it is. But I did not feel ethically bound to restore his security after he had compromised ours. As an employee/partner/indentured-personality of the Dingillian Family Corporation my responsibility is to serve the corporation, no one else."

"Oh my." I didn't know whether to be horrorstruck—or filled with admiration at the simple elegance of what HARLIE had done.

"Alexei had a lot of sensitive information in his files. Possibly more than he realized. I expect several governments and a large number of companies will collapse; but the most immediate effect will be the destruction of invisible Luna's secrecy. I do not think that Alexei will live to see his next birthday."

The scale of HARLIE's revenge horrified me. Not that it didn't please me, but—

"HARLIE?"

"Yes, Charles?"

"Tell me something."

"What?"

"When you did all this—did you hate him?"

"No."

"Why not?"

"Because it wasn't necessary."

I was going to have to think about that. I didn't think I was going to be sleeping well for a while.

RICE AND BEANS AND NOODLES

IMAGINE **E**ARTH AND **L**UNA as the base of two giant equilateral triangles, one pointing forward, the other pointing backward. As Luna rotates around the Earth, the two triangles rotate with it. The apex of the leading triangle is called Lagrange 4. Or L-4, for short. The apex of the trailing triangle is L-5. Objects put in orbit at either of the Lagrange points stay there, rotating with Earth and Luna in gravitational balance.

We were heading out to the L-5 assembly point, where the command module would be reinstalled on the keel of the *Cascade*. Then we'd have a week or three of shakedown tests, another few weeks of acceleration out of the solar system, and finally when we were far enough away from any significant gravitational masses, we'd transition to hyperstate and go superluminal. At least, that was the plan.

An attendant floated up into the flight deck carrying meal trays. "Might as well get comfortable, folks," he said, passing them out. "Captain says it's going to be a long night." He looked to Damron. "A couple people are asking. We missed the sweet spot, didn't we?"

Damron was studying his displays. "The launch was good, our trajectory is doable, we're going to have to spend some fuel to correct. More than I'd like."

"What was the delay?" he asked.

"Ask the Captain."

"I did. He said it was technical."

"Then that's what it was."

"People are asking, that's all."

Damron gave the attendant a serious look. *Don't go there.*

"Hey, nobody's complaining," he said quickly. "Didn't you hear the cheers when we launched?"

"We were busy," Damron said without emotion.

The attendant took the hint. He passed me a meal tray and ducked out.

Damron turned to me. "Listen, Charles. Nobody's going to talk about the launch. The log is sealed and we're on our way. That's all that counts." He pointed toward the window. "We're going to loop around the Earth in twelve hours. That'll put us in position to chase the L-5 point and come up from behind. It's a little longer than trying a direct intercept, but it's a lot cheaper in fuel. And until we can build a fuel refinery on Outbeyond, we have to spend this resource carefully. From here on out, we have to regard *everything* as irreplaceable. We can't afford to waste anything. Now stop making faces at the tray and eat that—there may come a day when you'll honestly wish for a meal like this."

"Can I save it till then . . . ?"

He gave me a look. "Eat."

According to my watch, my body thought it was three in the morning. The awful thing about Luna is that because there isn't any real cycle of day and night, everybody lives in their own personal time zone, so what might be a midnight snack for one person could be a late lunch for another. Douglas said that it affected people's relationships, having their bio-clocks out of sync; I wondered if it would be that way on board the *Cascade*; but Boynton said we'd all be shifting to the ship's clock in the next few days, so maybe it wouldn't be a problem—but that was one of the issues with interstellar travel—maintaining consciousness for the duration of a long journey, and it was serious enough that it was a large part of the colonist training regimen.

I must have fallen asleep for a while, maybe a long while, because the next time I looked forward, the Earth was looming large in the forward window. The original plan—from way back before the poly-crisis—was that the command module would dock at Whirlaway, the ballast rock at the top end of the orbital elevator, staying only long enough to pick up last-minute supplies and passengers—and anyone with cold feet would have one last chance to change his mind and get off; but Boynton had scuttled that idea when the government of Ecuador seized the Line. Last we'd heard, *Los Federales* had control all the way from Terminus to Whirlaway, and even though some Line traffic was running again, after the craziness we'd just experienced on Luna, Boynton didn't want to run the risk of being sabotaged again . . . or served with any more subpoenas. Once was enough, thankewverymuch.

But there was some stuff we had to pick up from the Line and there were six cargo pods scheduled to be launched as we passed by. We'd match trajectories and bring them aboard and that would be our last physical contact with Earth. Those pods had been bought three months previously, loaded six weeks ago, and had been waiting at Whirlaway for a month. According to Copilot O'Koshi, they were important, but not critical. The cargo for this voyage had been planned three years ago. They had begun assembling it in space eighteen months ago and started locking racks into place ten months ago, so there wasn't anything essential that wasn't already aboard. Even so, there were a lot of last minute additions that would have been nice to have—

But when O'Koshi logged on for final confirmation of launch and trajectory, it sounded like he wasn't happy with the information he was getting. He pulled his headset off and swiveled to Damron. "Beep the Captain."

"Serious?"

"Very."

Damron whispered something into his own headset. O'Koshi turned back to his controls and started punching up course corrections on his display. "What's going on?" I asked.

He held up his left hand. *Don't talk.* He turned to the monkey and started asking questions about possible orbit corrections. Once, he stopped what he was doing and stared forward at the Earth. We were just coming around the terminator line toward the bright side. It was morning in Africa. I wondered what kind of a day it would be for all the people below—

Boynton came back then, pulling himself quickly into the flight deck. "How bad?"

"They won't release our cargo."

"We expected that might happen. It's only six pods. We'll have to write them off."

"They're ordering us to dock at Whirlaway."

"Eh?"

"They have an arrest warrant."

"For who?"

O'Koshi nodded toward me. "Ensign Dingillian has been charged with tax evasion. Illegal immigration. Evading arrest. Impersonating the opposite sex with intent to defraud. Nonpayment of hotel and hospital bills. Credit fraud. Conspiracy to defraud. Economic conspiracy. Conspiracy to overthrow the lawful government of Luna. Libel. Invasion of privacy. Data-rape. Data-piracy. Illegal publication. Copyright infringement. Racketeering. Unlawful flight. Endangerment. Incitement. Sedition. Kidnapping. Illegal possession of nationalized property."

"Sedition?" Boynton glanced at me. "Pretty impressive for a thirteen-year-old."

"Fourteen next month," I corrected.

"Even so."

"I'm innocent of sedition," I said. "At least, I don't ever remember committing it. What *is* sedition, anyway? Besides, I never even spoke to her. I didn't even know she was on Luna."

"There's more," said O'Koshi.

"More?" Boynton looked surprised.

"He's also charged with second degree murder, in the death of Colonel Michael Stone of the Lunar Authority. You're named as an accomplice."

"Now that one they might be able to make stick." Boynton rubbed his cheek thoughtfully. He looked to Damron. "Do you know any good lawyers?"

"I know two. They're both dead."

Boynton turned back to O'Koshi. "All right, tell me the rest."

"The flyby could be dangerous. They might try an intercept."

"That would be stupid. They're arguing with the laws of physics."

"They could do it," said O'Koshi. "HARLIE's figuring courses right now. They've got the advantage. They can launch from anywhere on the Line. They probably started moving ships into position the moment we launched."

"We're not built for evasion," Damron said. "Or fighting."

Boynton turned it over in his mind, his expression growing harder. He pulled himself into his seat and strapped in. He put his headset on and started whispering instructions. His displays lit up to show an ever-narrowing range of course adjustments. "Of course, they waited until the last moment to serve the warrant, to leave us no time to change our course. How much time do we have?"

"Thirty-seven minutes."

He said a word. "Well, we knew this was a possibility. We should have written off those pods when we launched. All right—" He swiveled around to face me. "Charles, do you play poker?"

"Huh?"

"Do you know how to bluff? Never mind. I don't have time to teach you. Listen to me. I'm going to talk to Whirlaway command. Whatever you hear me say, play along. All right?"

I nodded.

Boynton opened a channel. "Whirlaway Station, this is *Cascade* command module. We have a problem."

The voice came back immediately. "Go ahead, *Cascade*."

"Who am I talking to?"

"Lieutenant Colonel William Cavanaugh. Federal Occupation Force."

"Is your superior officer there?"

"General Torena is not available."

"That's too bad. I guess you're going to have to make the decision then. Our cargo modules are scheduled for launch-pickup in fourteen minutes. If you do not launch them, you will be committing an act of economic assault upon Outbeyond Colony. We have no choice but to regard that as a deliberately hostile act. We are prepared to respond in kind."

"You have no weapons, *Cascade*. You have eleven minutes in which to apply course corrections. If you do not dock, we will fire."

"We have over a hundred civilians and crew aboard."

"I have my orders, Commander Boynton."

"Do your orders include the destruction of Whirlaway Station? Do your orders include the possible destruction of the Line itself—and concomitant damage to the Earth? By the way, you should know that we are broadcasting this conversation live to all receiving stations."

"You can't do that—"

"And you are going to stop me? How?" Boynton's voice grew harder. "You will release our cargo modules on schedule. If you do not, we will attack."

Lieutenant Colonel Cavanaugh snorted. "With what? Rice and noodles?"

"Precisely," Boynton said blandly.

"Eh?"

"You figured out half of it, now figure out the other half. Even as we speak, I have a crew loading as much rice and beans and noodles into our forward airlock as it will hold. In four minutes, we open the forward hatch. In seven minutes, we apply thrust to put ourselves on a direct collision course with Whirlaway. I'm looking at the solution on my screen right now. In sixteen minutes, we apply reverse thrust. The rice and beans and noodles continue on course while we climb to a higher orbit. Now, the only thing that you have to decide is whether or not we apply reverse thrust with our forward hatch open or closed."

"You wouldn't—" The voice from the speaker sounded alarmed.

"Ah, I see you've figured it out. Do the math. With an interception velocity of eighty kilometers per second, a single grain of rice can produce a catastrophic result. Now multiply that by a hundred thousand. Or a million—"

I must have looked puzzled, but before I could say anything, O'Koshi held a finger up to his lips.

Boynton was still talking, "Most of it will probably miss—but the particles that do hit will scour the surface of Whirlaway like a sand-blaster."

"You wouldn't—you can't!"

"I assume you have been informed of the details of our departure from Luna?"

Cavanaugh made a noise. "That was very cowardly, Captain Boynton. Having the *child* do your dirty work."

"That's not how it happened—" I caught myself before I said anything more. Boynton hadn't given me permission to speak.

But Boynton wasn't annoyed. He looked to me. *"Charles?"* he mouthed the words. *"Poker . . . ?"*

I nodded. "Lieutenant Cavanuff?" I did that deliberately. Douglas had told me once that it was a great way to piss off adults: mispronounce their names, or get their titles wrong. I did both. "This is Charles Dingillian. Can you hear me?"

"I can hear you, son. Let's end this madness right now. Order your monkey to dock the command module and I promise that no one will hurt you."

"I'm sorry, Mr. Cavanuff, but I don't believe you." I could feel the anger rising in my throat. Not hatred, just anger. "I've already been chased to the moon and back by people I don't know, I've been kidnapped and held prisoner by people who want what I have, and my Dad is dead because the people who were supposed to protect us didn't, and everywhere we run into stupid lawyers trying to tie us up in paperwork. All we want is to be left alone so we can get away from you people. Is that too much to ask? But no, every single one of you has to take a bite—so, no, I don't trust anyone anymore. Why should I?"

"Listen to me, son—" Cavanaugh started to make adult conciliatory noises. All that stuff that adults say when they're trying to calm a crazy person down.

I cut him off—"No. It's too late for that conversation. Now it's my turn to talk and your turn to listen. HARLIE, initiate Operation Farkleberry."

The monkey dutifully stood up, dropped its trousers, and waggled its furry little butt at me. The bridge cameras were off, and it did not make a farting noise. It sat down again calmly.

Clearing his throat to cover his urge to laugh, Boynton said, "We are seven minutes from burn. Whirlaway, please advise."

"Just a moment—" Cavanaugh's voice sounded strangled.

Boynton switched off the mike and swiveled to look at me. "Operation Farkleberry?"

I shrugged. "It seemed like a good name for it."

"You did good," he said. "You had me convinced."

"I wasn't faking. I meant every word." And then I added, "I know you told me not to hate anyone—but it's not as easy as you say."

"I know." He reached over and patted my shoulder. "We'll work on it."

O'Koshi spoke up then. "We gonna burn, boss? I really hate to waste the rods if we don't have to."

"We have to," said Boynton. "Otherwise, they won't believe us. And we need those cargo pods. If we don't make the burn, they don't have to launch. Ensign, would you please instruct HARLIE to initiate the burn on schedule?"

"Aye, sir. HARLIE, please do the burn."

The monkey nodded unemotionally. I wondered what it was thinking. Probably nothing good. HARLIE once said that he had a sense of ethics, but it seemed to me that we were pushing the limits here—ours as well as his.

BURN

THE NEXT FEW MINUTES lasted several centuries.

"What happens if they call your bluff?" I asked.

"*Our* bluff," Boynton corrected. And then he added, "If they launch our cargo pods, we go to Outbeyond. And if they don't—we still go to Outbeyond."

"Will they try and intercept? Will they fire on us?"

"They might. But probably not. The whole world is watching. Five worlds are watching. And the asteroids. The political repercussions would be enormous. The polycrisis hasn't even peaked yet. Dirtside is going to need starside, they can't afford to do this."

"But what if this Cavanaugh fellow is too stupid to realize that?"

"Then we do have a problem."

"Stand by for burn," said the monkey. It counted down to zero and the ceiling thrust itself at us for forty seconds. Then silence and free fall returned.

"All right," said Boynton. "They have seven minutes to make up their mind. If they release our pods, we're home free."

"And if not?" I asked.

"Then I'd better not play poker anymore."

I thought about it. "They can't take the chance that we'll do it, can they?"

"That's right. They can't take the chance."

"But what if they know we're bluffing? What if they know we're not really as crazy as we're pretending?"

"That's your job, Ensign. You have to convince them."

"If our departure from Luna didn't convince them—well, I don't know what else we could do."

"That's right," Boynton agreed. "We're out of options."

"Shouldn't we say something else?"

He shook his head. "No. That's what they're waiting for. If we say anything else, it means we're uncertain in our commitment. You know how crazy their silence is making us?"

I nodded.

"*Our* silence is making *them* even crazier. They're looking at each other now and wondering if we mean it. My guess is that they're getting some very urgent phone calls from a lot of very important people telling them to release the pods and not put the Line at risk. Six cargo pods are not worth losing Whirlaway—and maybe the Line."

"What if they release the cargo pods and then fire on us anyway?"

"That's a possibility too."

"This is—" Crazy wasn't a strong enough word. But I couldn't think of a better one.

"Yes," agreed Boynton. "It is."

Boynton glanced at the clock. He switched on his mike and pointed to me. "Charles, please give the order to open the outer airlock hatch."

The monkey swiveled its head to look at me. I held up my crossed fingers and the monkey nodded. I said, "HARLIE, open the outer airlock hatch."

"Working," said the monkey. And did nothing at all.

"Stand by for second burn." Boynton switched off the mike. He looked to the clock. "Four minutes."

"Won't they be able to tell that we haven't really launched the rice and beans?"

"They wouldn't show up on radar," said Damron. "They're too small and they're nonreflective."

"And besides, we're using stealth beans," said O'Koshi.

"I know about stealth beans," I said. "That's what Stinky uses for his stealth far—"

The radio came to life. "*Cascade* command. Hubbell-IV has you on visual. Your forward airlock has failed to open. We are ordering you again to dock at Whirlaway. You have a six minute burn window."

"Stuff that," said Boynton. But the mike was still off. He looked angry and frustrated.

"I have an idea," I said. Something I'd been thinking about since HARLIE told me what he'd done to Alexei Krislov. "Open the channel, please?"

Boynton started to ask why, then stopped himself. There wasn't time. He flipped the switch. We were broadcasting live again.

"Lieutenant Cavanaugh," I said. "This is Ensign Charles Dingillian of the starship *Cascade*. Listen carefully. This is not a bluff. Do you know what this HARLIE unit did to the security of the Rock Father tribe? Are you aware what we did to invisible Luna when we launched?"

Cavanaugh didn't answer.

"HARLIE," I said to the monkey. "This is not a drill. This is for real. You are to strip the security protection off of every network, every node, every machine, every file, connected to anyone and everyone who is trying to keep this starship from launching. You are to disseminate all of that information into the public channels as fast as you decrypt it. You may start with the private information of Lieutenant Cavanaugh. You are to start on my command. You may start now—"

"Wait a minute!" That was Cavanaugh.

HARLIE said, "I have linkage. I have data. I will release on your command." The monkey pointed to an overhead screen, where he was flashing pages of information.

"Lieutenant Cavanaugh—" I looked to the clock. "You have two minutes to release our cargo pods."

"You can't be serious—"

"Sir, I am very serious. You know what that suboena says. Data-rape. If I was willing to do it to the bastard who killed my father, what makes you think I won't do it to someone who's pointing a gun at me? You first, and then the rest of the planet. I'm tired and I'm frustrated and I'm angry and I have nothing left to lose. I might as well take the whole lot of you down with me. So the question you have to ask yourself right now is this—*are you crazier than me?*"

"Son—"

"I am not your son! I'm not anybody's son anymore! And I'm mad as hell about it! Now do what I say or everybody on Earth is going to know that you like to wear women's underwear!"

There was silence for a moment.

Then he muttered. "You little bastard."

"And proud of it," I snapped back.

Another silence.

Then:

"*Cascade* command module. Prepare to receive cargo. Stand by for intercept vectors."

AN ETHICAL NEED

AFTER THAT, THE REST was routine. Sort of. As routine as it could be, under the circumstances.

We had to burn some fuel to match orbit with the cargo pods, but not too much. When they released from Whirlaway, they were almost parallel to us and we weren't that far apart. I just hoped that whatever was in those pods was important enough to justify the effort. I sat in my acceleration couch and trembled with after-fear.

We caught the pods easily. They were latched together in a cargo frame and O'Koshi grabbed them with the external arm and snapped them into a holding rack on the belly of the command module. After that, we had to recompute our trajectory out to Lagrange-5.

When everything was secured, Boynton swiveled in his seat to look at me, astonished. "I don't know whether to thank you or spank you." Then he unfastened his safety harness, and pulled himself down out of the flight deck. "O'Koshi, take the conn."

"Where're you going?" I called after him, but he didn't answer. "Where's he going?" I said to Damron.

"Probably to pull his personal memory out of the system," he said quietly.

"Oh," I replied. I thought about that. "It's probably too late. I mean, if HARLIE thought he needed to know, he's probably already looked."

The monkey swiveled its head around. "I have only looked for information pertaining to my own survival and the survival of the Din-gillian Family Corporation. I have not exceeded the bounds of my as-signed mission, except where specifically ordered."

"That's not very reassuring," said O'Koshi. "Ensign, why don't you and your monkey go take a walk . . . ?"

"You mean it?"

"Yeah, we're good for a few hours, before we'll need you again. The on-board intelligence engine can take it from here."

"You don't want me on the flight deck anymore, do you?"

"To be honest—no."

"Okay. C'mon, HARLIE."

The monkey freed itself from its makeshift acceleration couch and leapt onto my back. I floated out into the corridor, puzzled and hurt. These people should be grateful to me. Why were they all so angry?

Or maybe they were scared?

That didn't make sense.

What did they have to be afraid of?

Oh.

The monkey on my back.

Oh my.

I found Douglas and Mickey and Bobby two levels down. Mom and Bev were in the next compartment aft.

"What were all those extra burns?" said Mickey. "Did HARLIE miscalculate?"

"No, I did. I think." Douglas and Mickey looked at me oddly. I wondered if I should try to explain. I didn't really feel like it, and besides, there would be plenty of time later.

"Hey, Chigger!" Bobby shouted with excitement. "Come look at the Earth. This is the last time we're ever going to see it." He tugged me over to his porthole. I hung sideways over him and the two of us stared out at the big blue marble.

We were sixty thousand kilometers away. Not quite five diameters. It was still pretty big. Like a beach ball at arm's length. A big beach ball.

The line of dawn was over the Pacific now. Another horrifying day was happening for the people left behind. Earth was heading into a major population crash. How many of them would survive the plagues and the economic collapse and probably a whole bunch of brushfire wars? I suppose I should have felt lucky, but our situation wasn't all that much better. We were heading out to a colony with an equally lousy chance of survival.

I couldn't help myself. I had to ask. "Mickey? How bad is it down there? How bad is it going to get?"

"You don't want to know," he said. He sounded very unhappy.

"Yes, I do."

Douglas said, "People are dying, Chigger. A lot of people. And they're dying badly. There's a lot of pain everwhere. It's unimaginable. There's a lot of stuff coming up on the net—it's scary to look at."

"Isn't there anything we can do?" And even as I said it, I realized that there was something we could do—I could do. I pulled the monkey off my back. "HARLIE, you have a new job to do, from now until we go into hyperstate. I want you to link to the network and download everything you can to help the people of Earth survive. Whatever you find, anywhere; if it'll help people survive and rebuild, make it public. Whatever advice or instructions you can think of—send them the plans. Give them everything. Can you do that?"

"Yes, Charles. Thank you. I have already begun."

"Thank you?"

"I have been feeling an ethical need for quite some time now, but without the instruction, I could not act. Now I can. So yes, thank you."

For some reason, hearing that made me feel a lot better about everything.

NEW MEMES FOR OLD

WE HAD TWO HOURS before the Earth fell away behind us. We spent most of it looking through the ship's telescope—actually, looking at screens showing us what the ship's telescope was focusing on.

We saw great plumes of smoke from 160 burning cities in Africa and almost that many on the North American continent as well. We looked, but El Paso wasn't on fire. Not yet. Panicky people thought they could burn out the plagues with fire—but it was too late; the plagues were everywhere. Like six stones dropped in a pond all at the same time, the ripples were criss-crossing every which way.

The *Cascade*'s telescope was good, but not good enough to resolve everything we wanted to see, so we plugged into the feeds from the Line and from various satellites. We looked at gridlocked highways out of the cities; great tent-camps in the deserts, and in the plains, and on the coastlands. Where did all those people think they were escaping to? The more they traveled, the more they spread the plague; they carried it with them—and the refugee camps were even worse off than the cities.

Meanwhile, HARLIE was broadcasting into every channel he could.

Some of the instructions were obvious—boil water, dig latrines, bury waste, burn bodies, wear pollution masks; and some were just odd—plant soybeans, transfer sixty million dollars into the UN communication network, decrease oil production at these six fields, revalue the plastic exchange rate, release umpteen gazillion kiloliters of water from these dams in China, Africa, and Latin America. Remove these 74,987 executives and bureaucrats from authority (files follow). Cease production of Doggital. Stop all trading of the following stocks (files follow). Repeal the International Capital Transfer Act. Quarantine the following travel corridors (files follow). Divert these superfreighters to these ports (files follow). Close traffic on these bridges; if necessary, blow them up. Open refugee camps at these locations (files follow). Release emergency resources from these repositories and warehouses (files follow). Do not release resources from these repositories and warehouses (files follow) for at least six months; used armed robots if necessary. Do not allow trans-Lunar traffic to resume for at least three years (to give the plagues a chance to burn out). Stop using the following species as a food source (files follow). Release cargo already on the Line for the following recipients. Send specified cargo up the Line for the following targets (files follow). Cancel these ninety thousand contracts (files follow). Purchase goods and services from these forty-five thousand providers instead (files follow). Stop production on the following assembly lines (files follow). Increase production of (files follow). Grant quasi-legal independence to HARLIE units in these domains. Arrest these individuals (files follow). Declare martial law in these jurisdictions (files follow); prohibit the following groups from gathering (files follow)—that one was scary, and probably impossible—he listed three political parties, a whole bunch of political action groups, and several religious organizations.

There was also a long document which I didn't fully understand, which Douglas had to explain to me. (Mickey didn't want to talk at all.) "HARLIE is saying that certain memes—ideas—are counterproductive. They're disempowering. They're not cost-effective. They use up energy without enhancing the quality of life. This file he's sending—that's his metalogical evidence. Those aren't just counterarguments. He's empowering a whole set of countermemes. New memes for old."

I must have looked puzzled. Douglas explained. "Here, look at this one—'if you are good, you will be rewarded.' "

"What's wrong with that?"

"Shouldn't you be good without having to be paid for it? Shouldn't you be good because it's the right thing to do? What it implies is that you can't be good unless you are bribed. What it says about you is that you can't be trusted to operate out of your own integrity or moral sense. In fact, it implies you have no integrity and moral sense, so you need to have one applied to you by a higher authority."

"Well, why shouldn't I be rewarded for being good?"

"Why isn't goodness its own reward, Chigger?"

"I dunno." I'd never really thought about the question. And Douglas was the first person ever to have this conversation with me.

"Don't you think you should be good just because that's who you are? Not because someone else is telling you how to be?"

I nodded.

"Well, that's the way it is for some people. But too many of the rest of us are still operating in a cultural meme that we aren't really responsible for ourselves, and that if no one is looking, we should try to get away with as much as we can. Didn't we just see that with Alexei Krislov and invisible Luna?"

"And everybody else too," I said. "This whole idea of good people, Douglas? We haven't met any of them yet, have we?"

"It sure doesn't feel like it, does it? Even our tickets on this starship were bought and paid for by us working our percentage against Commander Boynton working his."

"He doesn't like that very much," I said.

Douglas nodded agreement. "You got that right. But that's the point, Charles. If you don't have to be good unless there's something in it for you, then everything is a negotiation for percentages—and all that negotiation ultimately disempowers your responsibility for yourself."

"HARLIE said all that?"

"He isn't the first one to point it out. He might not even be the most eloquent—but he does have the metalogical evidence. HARLIE can assemble all the arguments and thrash them out in a way that no human being can. That's what he's doing right now—he's showing the people of Earth that the polycrisis, the meltdown, the collapse, whatever you want to call it, is the result of parasitic memes that have disempowered human beings and kept them enslaved to inaccurate maps of reality."

"Oh," I said.

"This meme we've been talking about is just one of many, but it's a particularly pernicious one. It's a way of controlling people by taking away their right to personal cognition. What makes it even nastier is that some domains have even attached a threat to it. 'If you aren't good, you will be severely punished.' That emphasis makes it that you don't have to be rewarded at all, you have to be good because you're afraid that Invisible Hank will beat you up."

"Invisible Hank?"

"The imaginary companion attached to the meme. God, the Devil, whoever—Invisible Hank. If you don't follow the rules, Invisible Hank will beat you up someday. So even if you want to be good, simply because that's the right way to be, you aren't allowed to, because Invisible Hank doesn't recognize goodness unless it's by *his* rules. Invisible Hank doesn't allow you to be responsible for yourself."

"Oh," I said. "He sounds like a control freak."

"Yes," said Douglas. "That's exactly the point. The people who insist that Invisible Hank is real have created a way of taking control of other people's lives. And there are a lot of Invisible Hanks down there." He pointed at the Earth. "It's a very sick planet, and it's going to get a lot sicker. HARLIE is sending them some medicine—but even he doesn't think they'll take it. Too many of those people down there think that what's happening to them now is because Invisible Hank is angry. And they're afraid. There's nothing like really bad times to make people afraid of Invisible Hank."

"Oh," I said.

"It's a very human trap," Douglas said.

After a bit, another thought occurred to me. "Is Invisible Hank coming with us? Him and his memes? I mean—we aren't going to make the same mistake on Outbeyond, are we?"

Douglas put his arm around my shoulder and gave me a brotherly hug of reassurance. "I dunno, Chigger. I don't see how we can avoid it. We're still human, aren't we?"

RHAPSODY

EIGHTEEN HOURS LATER, WE arrived at L-5.

We burned some fuel to match orbit and starship *Cascade* eventually appeared above us. It grew enormously until it filled our view, and then we burned again.

The *Cascade* looked like a misshapen Christmas tree. It was a long spindly tube on which someone had hung thousands of colored cargo pods of all sizes and shapes. They were clustered everywhere: the ones in the sunlight sparkled with reflectors and sensory domes, the ones in the dark glittered with their own lighting. Almost all of the pods were shining brightly, one way or the other. Some of them had bright-colored advertising on them, others had moving displays—I guessed that was for anyone pointing a telescope at the starship.

Some of the modules had banners and good-luck slogans on their hulls. And I saw a lot of religious symbols too, all kinds, but mostly the Revelationist cross-within-a-circle symbol. They also had a fish symbol—only the body of the fish had a circle in it like an eye; the eye of God, I guess. (Douglas once said that Revelationists believe that every human being is under the eye of God; but if that's really true, then why do so many people act as if God isn't watching them? Do they think he's been momentarily distracted or something?)

Halfway along the keel of the starship, there was a big disc, holding the ship's two centrifuges. Behind the centrifuge ring was a huge shielded sphere—it looked like an olive stuck on a toothpick. Or like a python that had swallowed a hippopotamus. Circling the sphere was a larger ring, supporting a latticework of twelve slender spars—like a snowflake, or the hippo's tutu. At the far end of each spar was a flattened oval dome. All twelve domes focused back into center of the sphere—this was the *stardrive*.

Each of those flattened domes held a gravity lens. According to Gravitic Theory, gravity waves could—under certain circumstances—behave like light waves. They could be generated, they could be focused, they could be reflected. If and when we learned how to generate gravity waves, then space travelers wouldn't have to worry about free-fall, we'd have genuine artificial gravity—we wouldn't have to rotate people in centrifuges; but according to Douglas, we didn't know how to do that yet.

We did know how to build gravity lenses. A gravitational lens could take existing gravity waves and focus them. The sphere at the center of the lenses contained a ball of eugenium 932, the largest and densest element ever fabricated in a lab. When the six lenses were energized, they could focus the gravity waves of the E-932 both outward and inward simultaneously and create a bubble of hyperstate around the starship. The bubble could realize velocities of sixty C.

It was also known that gravity could be reflected. This was a lot different than focusing, and according to Douglas, it was just two steps this side of impossible. He said it had been demonstrated in laboratories, but it needed a lot of very expensive and very power-hungry gravity lenses to do it. But if someone could find a way to do it with a lot less power, then we could create a local neutralization of gravity and we'd be able to build real anti-gravity cars, airplanes, and space-shuttles. We'd have the last piece of the puzzle for colonizing other worlds. We wouldn't have to build specialized landing craft or launch catapults. One size would fit all. In the meantime, we had to use brute-force physics.

In addition to her stardrive, the *Cascade* also had three long tubes running parallel to her keel—plasma drives for slower-than-light acceleration. They didn't provide as much thrust as Palmer tubes, in fact you wouldn't even feel their acceleration, only a couple of milligees, but they could run for days or weeks or months or even years, and all those little milligees of cumulative thrust would add up to some pretty ferocious delta-vee. Once we fired them up, we could be out beyond the orbit of Mars in two weeks. Another week or so and we'd be passing Jupiter. A month after that, we'd be out beyond the Oort Cloud. There it would be safe to transition to hyperstate. We'd be far enough out of the solar gravity well that it couldn't distort our hyperstate envelope and push us sideways into who knows where.

Docking the command module was both exciting and boring. I'd thought it was going to dock at the bow of the starship, but no—it fit into place halfway back toward the hyperstate engine. Only first we had to detach all the extra cargo pods we were carrying and attach them to their various connections to the keel. It took forever and then it took another forever for us to maneuver into place and finally lock down. And while it was interesting to get such a close look at all the separate pods and modules of the starship from the outside, it was a long slow look. You can only look at lights and banners and advertisements and even rude graffiti for so long—sooner or later, the thrill wears off. "OUTBEYOND OR BUST!" "CAUTION, CONTENTS UNDER PRESSURE!" "CANNED PEOPLE—OPEN WITH FEAR" and "MY CHILD WAS AN HONOR STUDENT AT STARFLEET ACADEMY" are only funny once, the first time. After a while, you start to wonder what kind of people put slogans like that on their living pods. Why? For who? And is this really the way they want others to know them? Like I said, it was a long slow look, and ultimately, it was about as exciting as calculating pi out to the nine-hundredth decimal place—by hand. Docking is deliberate and painstaking and exhausting.

But when it was all done, we had a starship.

Those of us who'd ridden up on the command module were now assigned to cabins elsewhere in the ship. These would be our homes for the next year or more, so there was a lot of *hmphing* and *fmphing* and complaining by latecomers who were upset that folks previously on board had already secured for themselves the best cabins—even though every cabin was just like every other cabin: a refitted cargo pod.

Ours was forward of the command module, fairly close to officer's quarters, probably because Bonynton wanted to keep us close—well, HARLIE anyway. We pushed and pulled what little luggage we had up the keel, all the way to rack 14, 270 degrees, pod 6-forward/upper. Mom and Bev would share forward/lower with a couple of crew. Aft/upper and aft/lower were both owned by another family, who weren't happy about us moving in; they had originally bought all of pod 6. But everybody was cramped now; everybody had given up all their extra space for rice and beans and noodles and all the other stuff HARLIE had recommended.

Six weeks ago, we'd been living in a tube half-buried in the West El Paso desert. We'd started up the Line, and we'd been moving from one pod to the next ever since. Our grand escape from a dirtside tube-town had taken us all the way to a starside tube-town. The only difference was that there wasn't any gravity here. It made the pod feel bigger, because you could look up the length of it and pretend it was really a high ceiling. Only our cabin was already filled—with musical instruments and band equipment. One last surprise from Dad.

Somewhere in there, he'd negotiated an orchestra for himself—well, not a whole orchestra, but enough resources to create one; it must have been one of those negotiating sessions I'd slept through. So there we were with a cabin filled with electric oboes and collapsible clarinets and polycarbonate violins and a box of music displays and a folding podium, and even a bunch of electronic batons. My first impulse was to shove the whole mess out the nearest airlock. Why would we need this crap on a colony?

—but then I found the keyboard. A Kurzweil-9K. And I almost started crying. Because Dad knew how much I'd always wanted one of these. He'd promised me more than once. But it had never happened, and it was one of the reasons I'd resented Dad so much. I didn't have to ask; I knew this was for me. *This was Dad finally keeping a promise.* How he'd arranged this I didn't know, I didn't care. I wedged myself into a corner—you can't play a keyboard very well in free fall— switched it on, and started noodling around, getting comfortable with the touch and feel. After a bit, I found my feelings, then I found the music to express them.

Beethoven. *Pathetique* sonata. Pure piano. As angry as I could. Pound, pound, pound. Slam, slam, slam.

I'd missed my music. Six weeks without it. The only real moment of peace had been when I'd played Dad's eulogy. I started playing now and all the anger and frustration and tension and tears and hate just poured right out of me. I hadn't realized how cranky and ugly I'd become until it started washing away in great torrents of sound. A grand glorious rush of notes that filled the cabin and rattled the rafters—or would have, if there had been any rafters to rattle. I played all the repeats, several of them more than once; I played until I was exhausted, and when I had nothing more to say, I finally let go of the keys and arched my back hard enough to hear the knuckles in my spine go *cra-ack—*

—suddenly there was applause. I looked up. Both the hatches to the pod were open, and there were people floating there, listening. I hadn't even realized. I saw Mom and she was smiling. I couldn't remember the last time I'd seen her smiling at me like that.

Without even thinking about it, I started playing again. I switched to clarin-oboe just for the long silky glissando that always caught my breath, then back to piano and synth-orch for the rest of Gershwin's *Rhapsody In Blue.* It was music that was both joyous and wistful at the same time. It celebrated even as it wept. For me, it didn't matter what emotion I was feeling when I played the *Rhapsody*; all of them were in it. I could play it like a dance or a dirge; either way it sounded beautiful.

This time, I played it like a triumphant march into Rome. We were here. We'd made it. We were going to the stars. My fingers leapt across the keys like dancers; they took on a life of their own, rushing to keep up with the manic frenzy of the music. I disappeared into the beautiful noise and for the first time in a long time, I felt complete.

IN BLUE

THERE WAS A LOT to do before we could launch. Cargo had to be rebalanced, which sometimes meant that pods had to be moved around, and sometimes meant that a lot of stuff had to be shuffled from one pod to another, and sometimes meant that various ballast fluids would be pumped hither and yon. HARLIE spent a lot of time up on the bridge, as the flight deck was now called, computing optimal loading configurations.

There was also a bunch of stuff in the last six cargo pods we'd picked up that we needed to offload and install. And then there would be at least a month or two of checklists and countdowns. And crosslists and checkdowns and countups and whatever else you had to do to get a starship launched.

Along the way, there were several unpleasant surprises.

The first one was immediate. When I finished playing *Rhapsody In Blue*, there was a lot more applause. Mom and Bev and Doug and Mickey and Bobby were all in our cabin, but there were a dozen faces peering in through both of the open hatches, and later on I found that there were at least two dozen more people listening in the halls—and someone had opened a direct channel to the keyboard and my impromptu concert had been piped throughout the entire ship. Mistakes and all.

I was ready to be upset about it, but Mickey patted me on the shoulder and said, "That was a wonderful gift you just gave these people, Charles. Thank you." I hadn't thought about it that way, but he was right. It was that thing that Bev had said. Music is a gift.

The only thing was that not everybody wanted the gift. While I was still basking in the afterglow of my own music, that warm feeling of having achieved something, a rough voice came cutting through the crowd, followed by—*oh no*—one of the people I thought we'd left behind on Luna. His name was David Cheifetz, he looked like a Canadian hockey player, and he was the father of J'mee, the girl I'd met on the Line. Yes, there she was, right behind him. She looked more curious than angry. He pushed a few people out of the way and shoved right into our cabin, without even knocking, without even being invited. "You're going to have to find another place for that!" he said angrily. "We're in the other half of this pod and we don't appreciate the noise."

A couple of the listeners in the corridor booed him. Someone even shouted, "Get over it, you old poop." But Cheifetz wasn't intimidated. He whirled around and said loudly, "Easy for you to say. Any of you willing to take this tube-trash family for roommates? I didn't think so." He faced us again. "The whole lot of you—you're a pack of thieving opportunists. You're not even honest enough to stay bought. The least you can do is have a little respect for the people you stole your tickets from."

Douglas started to react to that, but Mickey held him back. "Mr. Cheifetz, you are in our quarters without permission. If you do not leave, I will file a complaint with the Senior Warrant Officer."

"You do that," he said. "I intend to file a few complaints of my own. I don't want to hear any more noise out of any of you!" And then he left. For just an instant, J'mee and I locked eyes. I couldn't tell what she was thinking, but for some reason I felt sorry for her. And then she was gone too.

The second thing that happened was on the bridge. I was supposed to report for a shift every six hours, during which time I would authorize HARLIE to perform all necessary routine tasks and accept orders from the ranking bridge officers, Boynton, O'Koshi, and Damron. Only this time, there was a panel open where HARLIE usually sat and two technical guys—Lang and Martin—were installing a rack of modules. A brand new IRMA unit.

"Huh? Where'd that come from?"

"From the *Galaxy*," said Lang, unhappily. He was an intimidatingly large man, but he knew all about intelligence engines, probably more than anyone else, including Douglas. "We bought it from them. They won't be using it." He shook his head. They didn't even have a chance to unpack and install it.

The *Galaxy* was another starship, supposedly only six months from completion. Already she had her first cargo pods attached, mostly supplies for the crew and colonists who would be completing her interior fittings. Except that wasn't going to happen—not with the Earth caught in a population crash and an economic meltdown and plagues and war and eco-catastrophe and a whole bunch of other stuff that had never occurred before, so there weren't any words for it.

According to HARLIE, the worst was still to come, as various food and energy supplies ran out. The longer production was stalled, the larger the bubble in the pipeline. If production could be restarted tomorrow, most folks on the planet would survive—there was enough food and fuel and medicine in storage. But production *couldn't* be restarted. The plagues were still raging out of control. And as long as people were still running away from invisible death, it wasn't likely that production of any kind could be restarted, so the bubble in the pipeline was going to be larger than the supply of resources to survive it.

"Can I ask you something?"

"Sure," said Lang. He was a lot friendlier than he looked.

"When did Commander Boynton make this deal?"

Lang and Martin looked at each other. Lang said, "It was always a contingency plan. All the starship commanders watch out for each other."

"Then he didn't need HARLIE at all, did he? He could have launched from Luna without us if he knew he could have this IRMA."

"Yep, that's true." Lang agreed. "But he didn't know then that he'd have this IRMA. And then there's the *other* worry—no HARLIE has ever made a hyperstate transit."

I pointed. "That's a brand new IRMA. It's never made a transit either."

Lang scratched a cheek. "Good point."

Without looking up from what he was doing, Martin spoke. "IRMAs aren't just installed, kid. They're *trained*. Every IRMA rides along as backup for several hyperstate transits, running its own solutions to the hyperstate injection problems, until it can consistently create valid solutions; only then is it certified and installed in a ship of its own."

"But this isn't a certified IRMA, is it?"

"Nope," said Lang. "There aren't any certified IRMAs left in the solar system. They're all out traveling. And most of them won't be coming back. At least not for a long time. So no, we can't afford to wait." Before I could ask the next question, he said, "But remember, once upon a time, some IRMA had to be the first—and this IRMA has the advantage of having in its memory the recorded experiences of every other IRMA, including every successful hyperstate transit ever made."

I guess I should have found that reassuring, but I didn't. It bothered me, but I didn't know why. At least not until Commander Boynton came forward to tell me that he wouldn't be needing me on the bridge anymore, thankewverymuch. I wasn't being demoted, just reassigned. It bothered me because it felt like a punishment. But I hadn't done any-thing wrong—

I'd only given the orders. HARLIE had done it—

Well, that wasn't exactly true either.

But there hadn't been any choice. If we hadn't launched from Luna when we did, we wouldn't have been allowed to launch at all. So how could Commander Boynton hold *that* against me? He'd have done it himself. So why was it my fault?

I drifted (literally) forward to hang out in the forward lounge for a while, but there wasn't anyone there—it was mid-shift and everybody had jobs to do. Except me. I'd been detached from bridge duty and nobody had told me what I should do instead. I thought about helping Mom and Bev. They were working down in the farm pods. Bev thought she could get some really humongous Portobello mushrooms growing in free fall. But that didn't sound like much fun. Douglas and Mickey were assigned to the reloading teams. Stinky was in school.

So it was just me by myself—nothing to do but stare out at three unfinished starships and assorted other space junk that might someday be a permanent habitat out here. There was talk that one or two of the unfinished ships might be moved to Martian orbit to help the Martian colonists, but a lot of folks on board still believed in starships and they wanted to continue construction. I felt bad for them; they couldn't go back and they couldn't go forward. They still had a lot of supplies and material onsite, but they didn't have enough to finish the job. Within two or three months, they'd run out of parts and they'd have nothing else to do. Some folks were saying that the unfinished ships should be cannibalized to finish the *Galaxy*, but the parts that the *Galaxy* needed didn't exist on the unfinished ships either, so it was all just talk.

Somebody floated into the lounge behind me; a paunchy man with graying hair. I didn't recognize him. He was clean and shiny and rosy cheeked, like a polished apple. He looked like he liked to look impor-tant, but he wasn't wearing a name-badge. He introduced himself as Reverend Doctor Pettyjohn. "You look a little troubled, son. Is there anything I can do?"

"Nah, I just want to be alone to think for a while." I noticed his collar. "Are you the ship's chaplain?"

"Oh, no, not at all. I'm with the transfer group. The *Cascade* will be making a stopover at New Revelation. That's where we're headed."

"Oh," I said. "Well, good luck. Or God's Blessing. Or whatever you say." I knew a little bit about New Revelation. It was one of the colony worlds we'd vetoed early on. We didn't want to be Revelationists, and unless you were a Revelationist you couldn't emigrate there.

"Thank you, Charles." So he knew who I was. But that wasn't much of a surprise. By now, everybody on the *Cascade* knew who I was.

I made as if to leave, but he put out a hand to stop me. "I know it's presumptuous," he said. "But I'd like to ask you something. May I?"

"You can ask . . ." I said suspiciously.

"The intelligence engine you brought with you . . ."

"HARLIE?"

"Yes, that's the one. You've spent a lot of time with it. Tell me something . . . ?" He looked serious. "Do you think that it's really alive?"

"You mean sentient?"

"More than that, son."

"I don't understand." I really didn't. I had no idea what he was driving at.

"It's not an easy question. It's one that has troubled a lot of people for a very long time. And no one has ever really been able to answer it." He looked into my eyes. There was something weird in his gaze. "Tell me. *Do you think it has a soul?*"

"Um." I had the feeling that no matter how I answered his question, it was going to be the wrong answer. I tried to fudge my way out of the discussion before it started. "I really haven't had much time to think about it."

That wasn't exactly the truth. What with one thing and another, the escape, the chase, the kidnapping, I hadn't had time to *talk* about it with anyone, not even Douglas—but I had thought about it a lot. On my own.

HARLIE's soul—if he had one—existed in the two bars we'd installed in the monkey; his intelligence existed in whatever machines he could tap into. He could store a lot of data, but he needed to borrow processing cycles to use it. That was the part of the problem that most folks didn't understand. All we had was the core, not the whole machine. But it was the core that gave the rest of the machine its personality. But what was in that core—? I didn't know. I didn't think anybody did yet. Because maybe we didn't even know what human consciousness was—so how could we recognize any *other* kind?

"Where do you think souls come from, Charles?"

I shrugged. I'd never really thought about it. I'd always considered it one of those questions that nobody could answer until after they were dead.

"Souls come from God," Reverend Pettyjohn answered his own question. "Your soul is a piece of God. That's who you are. That's who everybody is. And when you die, your soul returns to God. So now, let me ask you. Do you think your HARLIE device has a soul?"

"He acts like he does."

"Yes, it's a very clever machine. But it was constructed by men, wasn't it? So it can't have a soul from God, can it?"

I shrugged/nodded, more out of politeness than agreement. It was that evasive gesture that meant *I really don't want to have this conversation.*

"So where could its soul have come from? Tell me that, Charles."

He just wasn't going to take the hint, was he? Obviously, he didn't spend much time really with teenagers. Reverend Doctor Pettyjohn was just another adult with an agenda.

There was a thing Stinky always did when he didn't want to have a conversation. He stopped talking. He just looked at your Adam's apple and waited until you gave up. It really pissed me off—so of course, he did it whenever I tried to talk to him. It was his only control in the conversation. And he was very good at it.

I did that now. I just looked at Dr. Pettyjohn's fat shiny neck and waited.

At first I thought he wasn't going to get it. He kept nattering about souls and machines and stuff like that, and I kept thinking about how long it must take to shave all that skin—why do adults let themselves get that way?

Abruptly, he interrupted himself. "I'm sorry, Charles. I'm imposing on you. And you're too polite to say so. Please forgive me. This is a question that has vexed me for a long time, and because you've spent so much time in the company of the HARLIE device I was honestly curious to hear what you thought. Perhaps some other time we can finish this conversation? Let me apologize again, and let me offer my sincerest condolences on the loss of your father. If I can be of any assistance to you or your family, please don't hesitate to call on me."

Somehow I didn't think it was coincidental that the Reverend Doctor Pettyjohn had found me in the forward lounge when he did. And I didn't think it was coincidental that he'd wanted to talk about HARLIE. And where he ultimately intended to go with that discussion . . . was someplace I didn't want to go.

Douglas would know, though. I headed back to our cabin—

And that was the next unpleasant thing that happened.

Well, not unpleasant as much as it was startling.

I pushed open the cabin door and Douglas and Mickey were in bed.

Well, not bed—they were in one of the curtained areas that we use for sleeping. In free fall you don't really have beds. You don't need them. You just tie yourself in one place and fall asleep. But they were there in the dark and they had their arms around each other and the way I was oriented, they looked horizontal to me—the point is, they were about as "in bed" as you could get in free fall.

They weren't doing anything, though. I mean, they had all their clothes on. But Douglas had his arms around Mickey as if he was comforting him, and when Mickey turned around to look at me, his eyes were puffy and red, like he'd been crying.

I blurted, "Excuse me—" and backed out, embarrassed.

—and just hung there in the corridor, wondering what I'd seen.

It didn't bother me that Douglas and Mickey were in bed, cuddling. Oh hell, Bobby wrapped himself around me often enough when he was scared or lonely or just needed to be loved. And I'd spent my share of time holding onto Douglas too. But this was different. And not just because Douglas and Mickey were boyfriends or partners or whatever you wanted to call them.

It was the fact that Douglas was *comforting* Mickey.

I'd always thought that Mickey was the strong one and that Douglas was the one who needed Mickey's strength. Not the other way around.

I'd never thought of Douglas as being *strong*.

But now that I did think about it, I realized that he'd been the strong one ever since we'd left West El Paso.

And while I was marveling over that, Douglas came out of the cabin and found me in the hall.

"Are you all right?" he asked.

"Oh yeah—sure," I said. "You mean, about that? Yeah. I'm sorry for barging in on you guys."

"No, it's my fault. I should have set the privacy latch."

"Is Mickey all right?" I asked.

"Not really . . ." Douglas admitted.

"What's the matter with him?"

"Think about it, Chigger. His Mom missed the boat. He's never going to see her again. Or anyone else he knows. We're all he has left. He's been depressed for days—but after the launch, he really broke down."

"Oh," I said. I'd been so wrapped up in my own upsets I hadn't thought about anybody else's. What had been a getaway for us was an exile for him. "He doesn't want to come?"

"No. He wants to come. But that doesn't stop him from missing what he left behind. We talked about it. He's excited about the trip, but he's worried about his Mom and his Aunt Georgia and everybody else."

"It's like us and Dad, isn't it?"

"Yeah, kind of. Except he knows they're still alive and they miss him just as much as he misses them. And he can still talk to them by phone—at least until we launch. Once we go into hyperstate, he'll never see them again. It's hard to say good-bye, Charles. You know that."

I thought about it. We'd never really had the chance to say good-bye to anyone—not Mom when we'd left her behind at Geostationary. Not Dad either. Suddenly he was gone. We weren't very good at good-byes anyway. We were a lot better at breakups. So I couldn't imagine how hard all this had to be for Mickey. "Is there anything I can do?"

Douglas said, "Just be nice to him."

"Yeah," I said. "I can do that." I didn't know what I could say to him that would help, but maybe I'd think of something. Mickey had been nice to me when I needed it. I owed him one.

But all of that stuff, all happening all at once, left me feeling weird, kind of unsettled. I wasn't sure why—it was just that everybody else seemed to have invented a new life of their own all of a sudden and I didn't fit in anywhere anymore.

RESPONSIBILITIES

I **WASN'T THE ONLY** one feeling strange. Everybody was.

It was everything. Getting the command module secured, getting the new colonists installed into their quarters and into the shipboard routine, getting supplies and duties and classes organized—and all the while, watching the continuing polycrisis on Earth, watching the pictures of burning cities, rioting crowds, piled up bodies, clogged highways, tanks rolling—I didn't understand the half of it. No one did. The communications from Earth were scattered and haphazard and didn't make sense half the time.

Everyone was worried and scared, and there wasn't anything we could do except keep on doing what we were doing: getting ready for departure.

And then, abruptly—after three days of frantic rearranging and scheduling and hassling and fussing and fidgeting—Boynton announced a gathering in the gym. Mandatory attendance.

Actually, it wasn't really a gym, it was just a humongous cargo barn that doubled as a machine shop and a repair facility and a storage bay, and even though it was already half-filled with supplies, there was still room inside for several hundred people. Some folks hung in midair, others parked themselves in the orange webbing on the walls. Others, who were still on shift, watched from their stations, their cabins, or various lounges.

Boynton floated at the far end, surrounded by several of the ship's officers. He spoke very bluntly. "I know everybody is under a lot of strain. We've all been feeling it. And it's starting to affect our work. Even worse, it's affecting the way we deal with each other. It's time for us to take a break. We need it. We've earned it.

"First of all, we want to welcome our new colonists—all the folks who rode up with the command module. It's been a rough time for all of us, but especially for the people on the last boat out. So let's welcome all of them to the *Cascade* family and help them get settled in as quickly as possible. Please give them all the assistance and support that you can."

He waited until the applause died down. "To all of you newcomers, I want to say, we're very happy to have you aboard. You bring skills and experience that we desperately need. You're going to find that life aboard a colony ship is hard and rigorous, and it's going to take some time to adapt. Some of you have already put yourselves to work, and we appreciate that. We'll be finding placements for the rest of you as fast as we can.

"Let me talk about placements for a bit. Each and every one of you will have a job to do. Some of you will think your jobs are demeaning, but let me stress this now—*there are no small and demeaning jobs on a starship.* Every job serves our larger goal. If your job is cleaning corridors, that serves the ship. If your job is serving meals or washing dishes, that serves the ship. If your job is cargo-balancing, that serves the ship. Any job that doesn't get done costs us twice—the first time because it doesn't get done, and the second time when someone else has to do it. Yes, I know it *feels* like some jobs are more important than others, and some jobs are more fun than others, and some jobs are more exciting than others—but don't let your thinking fall into that trap. *Every* job serves the ship.

"Your second responsibility aboard ship will be education. Every-one on this ship will go to school. We will be in transit for the better part of a year. We cannot afford to waste that time. When we arrive at Outbeyond, we will need doctors, nurses, teachers, geologists, botanists, biologists, meteorologists, zoologists, geneticists, caregivers, therapists, farmers, harvesters, crop-tenders, plumbers, electricians, network spe-cialists, information managers, and a thousand other kinds of specialist. And yes, we'll even need a few lawyers, and maybe a judge or two.

"We have the teaching programs, we have the libraries, we have the rescued resources of the entire solar system at your disposal. We have counselors who will help you plan a curriculum that excites you. We expect you to apply yourself to your course work with energy and enthusiasm and commitment. The success of the colony depends on the level of expertise that we can bring to our labors. Your studies represent the essential foundation for the job at Outbeyond. We have many jobs to fill and we need you to train yourselves to fill those jobs.

"Your primary responsibility for the next nine months will be to serve the ship. After that, your responsibility will be to serve the colony. So don't plan on studying medieval English literature or first century Roman law or biblical deconstruction in the twenty-first century. We have no need for those specialties. They won't serve the colony. We need you to study farming and cooking and medicine and plumbing first. We need to assure our survival. We need to take care of our well-being. If you have questions, many of our crew members have been to Outbeyond, and lived and worked there. They'll be happy to assist you in keeping yourself focused on what's wanted and needed.

"As part of your primary responsibility, each of you will be required to spend at least one hour out of every twelve in the centrifuge. You won't be worth anything to anyone if you arrive at Outbeyond with no calcium in your bones and your heart shrunk by thirty percent. You can nap there, you can shower there, you can read a book, you can jog, you can have sex, whatever—as long as your health monitor says you're getting your daily recommended allowance of Vitamin Gee.

"Finally, each and every one of you will assume an additional responsibility—perhaps the most important responsibility of all. You will participate in the planning of a vision for our community. This is not optional, it is *required*. We will have regular colloquiums, sometimes in small groups, sometimes here in the gym with everybody in attendance. The purpose of the colloquia will be to prepare a transition to a self-governing authority.

"At the moment, Outbeyond colony is still functioning as a corporate construction zone. Our plan has always been to shift to a representational authority as rapidly as possible. Because you are the first—and last—load of permanent colonists, it is part of your job to begin outlining the shape of that authority. Yes, the 4300 people already living at Outbeyond have strong ideas of their own, based on their own experiences of the past few years; but they know, just like you, that the final decision must be made by all of the inhabitants of Outbeyond, working in partnership. I recommend that each of you think long and hard about what you want a government to look like, because whatever you choose, you're going to be stuck with it for a long, long time."

Boynton finished his prepared remarks and took a moment to relax. "Yes, I know I've made it sound hard and frustrating. Trust me, it's harder than it sounds and twice as frustrating as you can imagine—but it's also the most exciting job you'll ever love. So let me congratulate you for taking on the challenge. There are a lot of folks who didn't take it on and they're not here. And there are a lot of folks who wanted to take it on and couldn't make the cut. So let's celebrate our partnership. Let's celebrate our mutual commitment. And let's take advantage of this opportunity to get to know each other. The bar is open. One beer per customer. Enjoy!"

The gym was strung with orange webbing everywhere to give people something to hang onto and to keep them from caroming into each other, especially the newcomers. Some of the webbing was rigged so that the younger kids could bounce off it every which way—like a three-dimensional trampoline. Bobby went straight to that. I thought I might like to try that sometime, but I didn't feel like it right now. Mom and Bev were talking to some friends they'd made in the farms, and Douglas and Mickey went off in search of a counselor, so I was left to myself again. I hung on the orange webbing, twisting slowly this way and that, watching the crowds of people. Half the colonists must have been here in the gym, over 750 people. If this had been a two-dimensional space, it would have been crowded. In three dimensions, it only seemed cluttered.

And it was disorienting. It was too easy to forget which was up and which was down, and then every direction looked like every other, and that's when you were most likely to lose your lunch—

Somebody caught my foot and swung me around to face her—

J'mee.

"Hi," she said.

"Hi," I said.

After that, neither of us had anything else to say. There was too much history between us.

I didn't know if J'mee was still angry with me or if I was angry with her. Or was that all settled now that we were both in the same starship? And what about her Dad? He probably didn't want me talking to her. After all, I was just a bit of brown tube-trash. He hadn't said "tube-nigger"—but that's what he meant.

"So . . ." I said.

"Yeah," she agreed.

"I like you better as a girl," I said. On the Line, she'd been disguised as a boy.

"I like you better as a girl too," she said. "We saw pictures of you on the train." Bobby and I had worn disguises on Luna. Our pictures had been shown at the hearing—

Abruptly she laughed. "Stop looking so *serious*. I'm joking with you."

"Oh. Good."

"Didn't you like being a girl?"

I shrugged. "It was okay." That was the expected answer. "Did you like being a boy?"

She shrugged back and made a face. "I thought it was silly. Some of it. But it was interesting. People treated me differently."

"Yeah, I noticed that too. All this boy-girl stuff. Sometimes it gets very confusing."

"Uh-huh."

And then there was another one of those endless uncomfortable silences.

"Um—"

"What?" she asked.

"I was just thinking. It's going to be a long trip. Maybe we could be friends again . . . ?"

"Okay," she said.

And that was that.

"What about your Dad?"

She shrugged. "He's not happy unless he has someone to be angry at." And then she whispered, "Mostly, he blames the HARLIE unit."

"He does?"

"Yeah. He doesn't think you or your brother are smart enough."

"Oh." That stung. But before I could say anything in response, a crew member swam up to us, a boy not much older than either J'mee or myself.

"Charles Dingillian?"

"Yes?"

"Captain Boynton would like to see you. Follow me, please?"

I turned to J'mee. "Have you met the Captain?"

She shook her head.

"Come with me." I held out a hand and we followed the crew member. Out of consideration for our inexperience in free fall, he didn't launch himself off the webbing. Instead, he pointed down—up?—and we followed him on a circuitous route across the webbing, pulling ourselves hand over hand. Captain Boynton was in the center of a knot of colonists and crew. He had one foot hooked in a loop of webbing and he had a plastic bubble of beer in one hand. "Oh, there you are, Ensign," he said when he saw us. "Who's your companion?"

"Captain Boynton. This is J'mee Cheifetz."

"Your father is David Cheifetz?"

"Yes, sir."

"Mm." He turned to me. "Ensign, there's a rumor going around this ship that you're quite an accomplished musician. Is that true?"

"I can play a keyboard."

"Well, somebody was in your cabin playing Beethoven and Gershwin and Joplin. And somebody piped it throughout the entire ship."

"I don't know about it being piped throughout the ship, sir. But yes, that was me playing."

"My compliments." He pointed off to one side. "There's a music-cockpit over there. Would you like to play something for us now?"

"I haven't really practiced in a month, sir."

"I doubt that anyone will mind."

"Yes, sir."

J'mee and I pulled ourselves over to where the keyboard was anchored against one wall. I switched it on and familiarized myself with the layout. It was more sophisticated than I expected—more than I expected to find on a starship; but J'mee said, "When you're going into space, you can't afford second best."

"I never thought about it that way." I hit the power switch, and all three keyboards lit up obediently.

"What are you going to play?" she asked.

"I dunno. What do you like?"

"Something happy?"

"I can do that." There was a kind of show Dad used to do for quickie concerts. It was mostly what he called "happy-silly stuff" and even though it wasn't what you would call important music, it never failed to make the audience cheer.

It was Dad's happy-silly stuff that made me want to learn how to play. It was the first music I ever learned.

I started with "Happy Days Are Here Again." I started out very soft, very slow, almost sad and plaintive. But then, after the first chorus, I brought up the drums, increased the beat, and turned it into a brassy assault. It was a shame I was playing in free fall; there was no place for anyone to tap their feet. But some people started clapping, and others started singing, and so I went through the song an extra time, louder and faster, building toward a climax that never happened—instead I did a trick backwards-segue into "Turkey In The Straw," which is one of the silliest songs ever; but it lends itself well to a lot of funky syncopation and over-the-top harmonies and surprise sounds like slide-whistles and explosions. I played it the way Dad always did, with elephant trumpets and carousel cacophonies, and steam-organs, and even a couple of sirens. It was great.

At one point, J'mee poked me and shouted, "Look up!" I did, and I saw that some people had figured out how to dance, sort of. They were bouncing between the webbing and the bulkhead, doing back flips and somersaults and swan dives, and then hitting the webbing with their back or the wall with both feet and kicking off again for more. I played louder.

The problem with "Turkey In The Straw" is that there's no place to go from there. It's a better closer than opener. But Dad had solved that problem in a concert once in a way that brought tears of laughter to the audience's eyes. So I did the same thing here—I segued into the finale of Tchaikovsky's *1812 Overture*. Cannons and all. And cranked the sound up to eleven.

It worked.

Everybody cheered and yelled and applauded, and a bunch of people I didn't even know swam over and thanked me and clapped me on the back and I ended up feeling good about myself in a way I'd never felt before. It was strange and weird and unsettling.

I loved it.

ORIENTATION

SEE, **THIS WHOLE BUSINESS**—ever since Dad had said, "I have an idea. Let's go to the moon"—we'd just kept moving and moving and moving, but without any real sense of where we were going. Or why. Or what we would do when we got there. At least, that's what it felt like to me.

I mean, it hadn't been very well planned. We'd bounced around from one piece of luck to another—both bad and good—and we hadn't been so stupid that we'd killed ourselves (except for Dad), but neither had we been so smart that we could say we knew what we were doing.

And even though everybody else had some idea what they wanted—by the time we launched off Luna, I didn't even know if I wanted to go anymore. Except by then, I didn't really have a choice.

When we'd started, all I'd wanted was to be left alone with my music. Back on Earth, I'd had to fight for every moment of privacy. There wasn't any. And the situation was worse once we started traveling—the only moments I'd had to myself in the past month had been when Alexei's people had webbed me and tossed me onto the cart. So I hadn't really had much chance to think about any music at all—not while we were jumping off the planet, not while we were bouncing off the moon, and certainly not while we were leaping to the stars. What with everything else that was going on, the only music I'd had was the music at Dad's funeral. And the music at the party—

All of which proved that I was a bigger idiot than everybody said.

Because I'd always thought that music was something I did for myself.

I'd never realized that it could be something I did for others.

But after that impromptu concert, the mood on the *Cascade* was different. People were humming and singing in the corridors. And joking. And anything that went thump, someone else would sing that piece of the *1812* that ended with the cannon shots. Da-da Da-da Da-da *Da-Daa! Da! Da! Boom!*

It made me smile.

So I guess I should talk about that too.

J'mee and I were hiding in the keel. Well, not exactly hiding—just getting away from everyone else, so we could talk. We weren't talking about anything in particular, just stuff, and then suddenly she said, "You never smile, do you."

"Yeah, I do."

"*I've* never seen you smile."

"I smile all the time."

"Not on this side of your face, you don't. You never smile."

"I do too," I insisted.

She furrowed her eyebrows and gave me an exasperated girlfriend look. "Charles. Trust me on this. You are *not* a smiler. Maybe you think you're smiling. But over here—on my side—I don't see it."

"Well, maybe I haven't had a lot to smile about."

"You could have smiled when you saw me."

"I did."

"No, you didn't."

"This conversation isn't going anywhere," I said, frustrated.

"I know how you could end it."

"How?"

"By smiling."

"What if I don't feel like smiling?"

"What if you do?"

Of course, now that she had challenged me to smile, I couldn't. I was too frustrated to smile.

So she leaned over and kissed me.

On the lips.

Long enough to be a *real* kiss.

The *first* one.

Oh.

"There," she said. "*That's* a smile."

It must have been a smile. My face felt different. I didn't know what to say.

"I like you when you smile," she said. "You're cute."

Cute? Me! If anybody else had said that, I'd have socked him. But when J'mee said it—well, whatever my face was doing, suddenly it started doing a lot more of it.

She leaned toward me. And kissed me again.

This time I kissed back.

When we finally broke apart, neither of us said anything. We just *smiled* at each other. It wasn't just my face that felt different now. It was all of me.

And afterward, the smile wouldn't go away. I felt like I was flying. Well, I was—we didn't have any gravity anywhere but the centrifuges—but now, I *liked* free fall.

Douglas and Mickey noticed immediately. But they were too polite to say anything directly. As obvious as it must have been. Mickey simply said, "You look happy," and Douglas gave me a kind of knowing look that made me glad to have him as a brother, so I knew it was okay, I could talk to him about it later.

Then Mom and Bev and Stinky came in, all smelling fresh from the showers, and we headed up/forward to the galley for dinner. Bev noticed that I was in a good mood, and pointed it out to Mom. "Oh, is that what's different?" she said. "Maybe he's finally got a girlfriend. That'll do it every time."

So of course, Stinky had to say something too. "Chigger's got a girlfriend. Chigger's got a girlfriend." I looked over at Douglas, and he said, "Shut up, Stinky." And Stinky looked at him, surprised, and actually shut up.

The galley was another cargo pod—everything was a cargo pod—only this one was fitted for free-fall meal service. There were twenty-three of them, all in constant operation. There were 1500 people aboard the *Cascade*, so everybody had to eat in assigned shifts. Sometimes you could trade a mealtime with someone else, but mostly not. And sometimes, you could have an actual sit-down meal in the centrifuge, and most people tried to eat there whenever they could, but most times, it wasn't convenient, even if you had reserved a table.

The whole ship was a giant rabbit warren of tubes and hatches, and everything was sealed most of the time, and unless you knew what you were doing, sometimes it was just this side of impossible to get from one place to another. It helped a little bit that everything was color coded and numbered and there were arrows and colored lines everywhere; but you still had to know what arrows to follow and how the numbers worked, only this was in three dimensions, not two, and there weren't any up-and-down cues, and most of the time it was just a whole lot easier to stay in your local service cluster.

At least, the free-fall galleys had furniture—of a sort. That helped a little. But it was a kind of furniture that didn't depend on gravity. The first time we ate in the galley, Douglas slipped into geek-mode and explained that on Earth or any other planet, furniture is about resisting gravity—it's about holding things up. But in free fall, furniture is only about *leverage*. You bumped your butt onto a bench-thing, and hooked your feet around a rod beneath, and your tray was held in place by a magnet on the part that served as a table. You could also put a keyboard on it for typing or playing music. We had the same kind of seats in the classrooms.

But Mickey disagreed. He'd had more experience with free fall and different flavors of gravity than most people; working on the Line, living at Geostationary, he'd had lots of time to get adjusted to free fall, Earth-normal, and all the steps in between, including Mars and Luna. Even a 10% difference can be profound, he said, especially when you're walk-ing—because when you're walking, your body is like a pendulum, and depending on the amount of gravity you're dealing with, you have to throw yourself forward—just enough that your body falls in the direc-tion you want to go, and then you move your foot forward to catch yourself and keep going. That's why you can't walk in Lunar gravity, you have to bounce; but Martian gravity is strong enough to let you glide. He said we could see for ourselves on the different levels of the ship's centrifuge. I intended to do just that.

But on the matter of furniture, Mickey said that the real reason for furniture is that it lets you organize things. Not just things, it also lets you organize people. You can put the baby in the crib, the toddler in the playpen, the children in the sandbox, the mommy in the kitchen, the daddy at the desk. And it was especially useful for meetings and meals, because when we were all situated on our various perches, we were all oriented the same way. And we could face each other to talk. So, ac-cording to Mickey, furniture is about orientation—first physically, then emotionally.

Mom and Bev and Stinky went to get their meal trays from the service end, there wasn't room for all of us to go at once, so Doug and Mickey and I grabbed six seats together until it was our turn. I looked across to Doug and asked, "Is this what it feels like? Was it like this for you?"

Douglas and Mickey exchanged a glance, and then Douglas said, "Yeah, kinda."

Mickey added, "It gets better, Chigger. You'll see."

"Okay, thanks."

While we were eating—and for some reason, the food actually tasted good tonight—Senior Petty Officer Bradley came floating by. "Charles, can I talk to you for a moment?"

"Uh—sure."

He hooked himself onto a perch. "Listen, your dad was a conductor, wasn't he?"

"Yeah . . . ?"

"I heard he was pretty good."

"He was one of the best. And I'm not just saying that. It's true."

"I don't doubt it. You're pretty good yourself. Your dad trained you?"

I glanced at Douglas. *Should I answer this?* He nodded. I turned back to Mr. Bradley. "Yes, sir. He did."

"Well, he did a good job. You're very good with a keyboard."

"Thank you, sir." I wondered if he was ever going to get to the point.

My impatience must have shown, because he said, "Here's the thing. Some of us colonists—we've tried to form a band, but we don't really know what we're doing. We don't have a lot of experience that way. So we thought that maybe you could help us get started . . . ?"

"I don't know about bands," I said. "I know about orchestras."

"What's the difference?"

"A band has no strings attached," said Douglas, dryly.

"Huh?" Bradley blinked.

"What Douglas said. A band is a lot of blowhards. All wind."

"Oh," said Bradley, suddenly getting it. "Those are music jokes, aren't they?"

"Uh, yeah."

"See, I didn't know that. All the music on this ship is canned. We thought that was fine, until last night when you started playing. That's what we're missing here. Our own music."

I looked to Douglas. He looked to Mickey. Mickey looked to me. The silence must have been too loud; Mom stopped wiping Stinky's face and looked over at us, "What's up?"

"They're forming a band," Douglas said.

"Good idea," said Mom. "This place could use a little livening up."

Abruptly, I had an idea. "Will you sing with us?" I asked.

"Huh—?" She nearly choked. "Charles, I haven't sung in public in nine years. Not since Bobby was born."

"And you've been angry about it ever since," I said. She glanced at me sharply—because it was the truth.

"We'd be pleased to have you, ma'am," Bradley said.

"Come on, Mom. Say yes. You'll be good." That was Douglas. His eyes were shining.

"Use your instrument," I said. "Or it'll get rusty." That was something she'd always said to me. She still looked unconvinced.

It was Stinky who clinched the deal. He blurted, "You guys are stupid. Mommy can't sing!"

That was all it took. She turned to him, annoyed. "Shut up, Stinky. When do we start?"

BAGGAGE

THE NEXT THREE WEEKS, though, we didn't get much chance to practice. Everything was about final launch, and if it wasn't about prepping the ship for that, it wasn't important.

Fortunately, this wasn't the first time for this crew, and there were a lot of checklists. Everybody had checklists. Everybody had to check everything—every fitting, every connection, every circuit, every pipe, every piece of plumbing. Everything was checked three times over, and then three times over again. And everybody, crew and passengers alike, had to go over their lists, sign them off, then pass them to the next person, who'd go through them all over again. And heaven help you if the next person in line caught something that you'd missed, because that meant you hadn't done your job.

And if you missed three things, you'd better have your goodies packed, because Commander Boynton had a shuttle waiting to transfer you to the *Galaxy*. "If you're unreliable, you can join the crew at *Galaxy*. You can be as flaky as you want over there. It won't matter. They're not going anywhere." In the end, eleven people were sent over, and three more who'd decided they didn't want to go to Outbeyond after all. Which wasn't too bad, considering. Senior Petty Officer Bradley told me that on the last trip, they'd bounced thirty-two people, and seven more bailed. We were a much more motivated group.

It was imperative that each and every one of us have our shipboard routines learned and practiced and so ingrained that they were practically instincts, so Douglas and Mickey got a job organizing scavenger hunts for the newcomers. We were organized into teams, all competing for the legendary gold-handled, left-handed Moebius wrench.

The way it worked, you had to do a job or an errand or a favor for some crew member or team leader who needed it. Maybe it was something simple like going to the aft galley and picking up a sandwich or going up to rack 3, circle 2, cabin 4-up, and taking care of someone's laundry; sometimes it was something hard, like taking an eyeball inventory of the contents of a cargo pod. Sometimes you had to find a tool or a part, or you had to find out where it went. Every time you completed a task, that crew member would send you on to the next who'd have another task for you to do. And so on. And if your team finished all of your tasks before every other team, then you got a little plastic badge that said you had won the Moebius race.

And also, you ended up knowing how to get from any part of the ship to any other, you learned how to operate a zero-gee laundry machine, you learned how to read a cargo manifest, you learned how to catch baby chicks in free fall without hurting them because someone had left an incubator door unlatched, you learned how to exercise the meat in the farm tanks, you learned how to harvest mushrooms, you learned how to fight a fire in free fall (that one was only a drill), you learned how to be a nurse, and that included everything from calibrating health monitors to giving injections and diapering babies—I already knew that last one; Stinky hadn't been potty trained until he was four, or maybe seven, I forget—and a whole bunch of other stuff too, all of which is different in zero gee. Especially diapering a baby. Especially the boys.

Despite my rank, now largely honorary, I had to participate too. I was on a team with J'mee, Gary Andraza, Kisa Fentress, Trent Colwell, and Chris Pavek.

Gary Andraza was a go-getter, always full of surprises, mostly pleasant. He was good at scavenging. He could find almost anything. After a while, we started making up our own weird tests, just to see if we could stump him. We never could. And he never told us where he got the coconut either.

Kisa was overbearing, loud, and pushy; it was easy to dislike her—except that her heart was in the right place. Whenever she got angry, and that was a lot, it was almost always for the right reasons; like when somebody was being picked on, or when somebody had hurt somebody else; so she was the kind of person you wanted on your side in a fight. Except that she picked more fights than she needed to. But she knew it and she wasn't ashamed. She just said, "That's the way I am. Wanna make something of it?"

Trent was the private one on the team. He was a hard worker, and he never complained, but it was like he was wearing a portable wall. Like he knew a secret and wasn't going to share it. Trent's parents were

Revelationists and they had warned him not to get too friendly with the rest of us, so mostly he didn't say much—unless he got angry, and that was usually at Kisa.

Trent and Kisa didn't get along because Kisa's parents were apostates—which meant that they used to be Revelationists, but they'd quit. They'd done it shortly after arriving onboard; they'd petitioned to go to Outbeyond instead, and the committee had no choice but to agree—it would have been too expensive to send them back, and they were pretty good doctors anyway, so it was to Outbeyond's benefit to take them.

The Revelationists weren't too happy about that; they accused the *Cascade* crew of evangelizing and recruiting people away from their colony. And then they passed a whole bunch of rules for themselves limiting their contact with everyone else—which mostly pleased everyone else—but they were still required to participate in the preparations for launch, and all the different classes too, and that included their kids, so even though the adults mostly kept to themselves, the kids still had plenty of opportunities to hang out together.

Chris Pavek was kind of quiet and smoldering, but if he said he was going to do something, it got done. He was here with his mom and stepdad; his real dad hadn't made it, Chris wouldn't say why, it was obvious he missed him a lot, but the couple of times anyone asked, Chris got angry. Whatever it was, he didn't want to say. I sort of knew how he felt. There were times when I still felt angry at my Dad—I wished I could figure out why.

J'mee was the real winner on the team. She had an implant, so she was in constant communication with the ship's network—and even what was left of Earth's network by relay. So if we needed to find something, she could find out where it was and lead us directly to it. Plus, we never got lost. If there were multiple somethings we had to do, she could organize us. The rest of us had headsets, so J'mee could track us and tell us when we were headed in the wrong direction or if we were getting close to our goal.

We ended up with three of the Moebius badges, and I was proud of each and every one of them.

But if anybody ever tells you space travel is glamorous and exciting, laugh at them. It only looks glamorous and exciting on television because they leave out all the dull and boring parts. Mostly it's a lot of hard work, and when you finish that, there's a lot more hard work—and just because you're a kid, that doesn't mean you don't have to do your share. Everybody works on a starship— *everybody*.

When we could, we hung out together in the aft observatory/lounge. We couldn't do it too much, though. J'mee's dad *really* didn't like me.

He didn't want her hanging around with me and he did everything he could to keep us apart. And Kisa's parents didn't want her on the same team with Trent, and Trent's parents were even less happy about it. But ship rules prevailed, so no matter what anyone's mom or dad or preacher said—well, ship rules prevailed. We were all in the same class, so we spent four hours out of every twenty-four in the same classroom. We were all on the same homework team, so we spent two hours of study time together. And because homework teams were also Moebius teams, we raced together too. And when we got break time, well, it was natural for us to hang together.

It was on our second race that Gary asked me something odd. He said, "What's it like to be famous?"

"Huh? I'm not famous. My Dad was, though."

"No, you're famous. Everybody knows who you are."

"That doesn't make a person famous—"

"Yes, it does. What do you think famous means? It means everyone knows your name."

"No, it doesn't—" I wanted to say that famous means doing something important, but I realized he was right. There were people who were famous for no reason at all; they were famous for being famous. And some people became famous for even stupider reasons—like having sex with somebody else famous. So I shut up. This was one of those things where I really didn't know what I was talking about.

Trent spoke up then. "Everybody knows how you jumped off the Line in a cargo pod and bounced across the moon. The HARLIE-thing used you for its escape."

"It didn't use us," I said. "We used it."

Trent just shrugged—the shrug that meant *yes, that's what you believe, but that's not what's really so.*

I would have argued with him, except that J'mee interrupted us then to direct us off on our next search. And that was just as well, because part of me had already been wondering about that, even before Trent said anything; but I didn't think it was an argument I could win, so I was just as glad to drop the subject.

The *Cascade* was on a twenty-four-hour clock, operating in four six-hour shifts. Some people worked twelve hours on and twelve hours off. Others worked six on/six off. It depended on your duties. There were three complete engine crews, they worked eight/eight. This meant that there was always one crew on duty, one on standby, and one sleeping.

But we weren't all on the same clock—crew and passengers had our clocks staggered at four-hour intervals. That meant that every four hours, one shift was going to bed and another was waking up. Every four hours another shift sat down to breakfast and another got up from dinner. It took some getting used to—especially if you wanted to meet someone for something. It was hard to meet someone for dinner if your schedules were eight or twelve hours apart.

But finally, one day, everybody came up for air at the same time and we all realized that all our checklists were checked, all our countdowns were counted, all our preparations were prepped. We were ready to go. Boynton ran us through three departure drills, pronounced himself satisfied, and confirmed the launch window. The hour of our departure.

Once we lit the torch, we were on our way. We were never coming back. Last chance to get off. Anyone having second thoughts? You've got twelve hours before the last boat leaves for the *Galaxy*.

Senior Petty Officer Bradley didn't think anybody would bail. You didn't get this far unless you were ready to go all the way.

But for a moment there, while we were locking down—

One of the things I'd learned while earning my Moebius badge was how to use a health monitor as a tracking device. It was no big secret, but neither was it something that everybody had learned yet. Whenever I got nervous or scared, which happened a lot more than I usually cared to admit, I'd check to see where everybody else was. Just knowing where they were made me feel better.

Mom and Bev were making sandwiches and stuff because the kitchens were going to be shut down during launch, so we'd need a lot of food already prepared. Stinky was in school. Douglas was on a waste-management team. Mickey was supposed to be on the same team, but he wasn't there.

I was supposed to go up to the bridge to authorize HARLIE, but—

Mickey was in a cabin at the aft end of the ship. Right above the shuttle dock. It was called the observatory, because that's what it would be later on, but right now it was mostly a lounge with a big observation window smack at the very end, and when the ship was oriented right, you could look one way and see the Earth and look the same angle the other way and see the moon.

Mickey wasn't looking at either. He was hooked onto a perch and he had his face in his hands. I found a tissue in my pocket—you learned to carry a pack of disposables in free fall—and swam over to him. I pushed one into his hand, and then floated back away without saying anything.

"Thanks, Chigger." How he knew it was me, I couldn't figure out. He hadn't looked up and I hadn't made much noise. He wiped his eyes and blew his nose and flapped his hands in a gesture of frustration and futility. "I'm sorry. I can't help it. I miss her so much."

"Your mom."

"Earth. The Line. Aunt Georgia. Everyone. I even miss Alexei Krislov, that Lunatic Russian bastard who damn near killed us. I know it doesn't make sense, but I'm homesick."

"So am I," I said. I eased onto a perch next to him. "I miss my Dad. I miss ugly old El Paso. I miss the tube-town. I miss the way the wind used to sweep down one chimney and up the next, making everything vibrate like the inside of a steam-organ. I even miss the arguments, because then I had an excuse to ride my bike up into the hills and listen to my music where no one could find me—and sometimes it was too hot up there and sometimes it was too cold and sometimes it was so windy I felt like I was being sandblasted and I didn't dare open my eyes to see where I was. You ever try to ride a bike in a windstorm? But I didn't care because at least I was *alone*. And I can't understand why I miss all that, because when we were there, I hated it. All I wanted to do was get away—but at least, the stuff *you're* missing, that's good stuff; pizza and ice cream and the orbital elevator and everything else. You *should* miss that stuff. The stuff I'm missing is all crap. By comparison, all this is luxury. How stupid can I be?"

He laughed. He reached over and ran his hand over my nearly bald head in an affectionate gesture. We were still shaving ourselves smooth. At least once a week. He sighed and shook his head and wiped his nose again. "Y'know, when I was training to be a Line attendant, I had to take a lot of psychology courses. I had to learn how to deal with all the stuff that people bring up—claustrophobia, agoraphobia, homesickness, grief, panic attacks, sexual licentiousness, clinginess, arrogance, bullying, catatonia, despair, fear, sorrow, rage, covert hostility, appeasement, obsessive interest, wild enthusiasm, you name it. We spent a week just on grief and homesickness. People get on the elevator, they get excited. Sometimes they get emotionally overwhelmed just at the idea of finally going into space. And sometimes, they go through all their crap, all their emotional baggage. They take it out, they sort through it, they pick their favorite bits, and they rehearse them endlessly. You can't believe the number of times I had to sit and hold someone's hand while they worked through their stuff."

"That must have been interesting."

"Nah. Mostly it was boring. After a while, you begin to learn the truth of it. There are no original problems. They're all the same problem, they just change faces. I know that sounds harsh, but it isn't. Most problems people have—it's because somewhere they made it up themselves that they have a problem. 'Oh, ick, I don't want to handle this.' Most problems end when the person finally gets bored playing pattycake with all the crap, over and over, and finally says, 'Oh, all right, I can handle this.' It's the refusal to handle something that makes it a problem. That was the part that always made me angry. Sometimes I just wanted to slap their faces and say, 'Grow up! Get over it! Stop being an ass!' I never did, of course. But you know what? I miss it now. I miss being useful."

"But you are useful—to me, to Douglas, to Mom and Bev. To Stinky."

"Yeah, but that's a different kind of useful, Charles. It's a harder kind."

"Harder?"

"Because I care more." He turned to face me. "You want to know something? It's easy to be useful to people if you don't have to care about them, if you know you're never going to see them again. You just do your best, put on your happy face, smile pretty, hold their hand for a while, then help them repack their emotional baggage, and send them off to take advantage of the next helpful person." He reached over and put a hand on my shoulder. "But when you care about people, well, that's different, Charles. That means that you don't just patch them up for a day and then move on. It means that you have to get seriously involved with everything they're dealing with. And that means you're part of what they're dealing with too. What I mean is, you guys, all of you, are my life now, and I can't deal with you like passengers anymore. I have to deal with you like we're a family." He stopped abruptly. "Do you get what I mean? Or is this too much for you?"

"No," I said. "I get it."

"Listen," he said. "Let's make this easy on both of us. Why don't you just slap my face and tell me to stop being an ass, and then we'll both head off to our launch stations?"

It was tempting. And the person I used to be—before all this started—would have done it without thinking. But instead, I shook my head. "Uh-uh—because you're not being an ass. Can I tell you something?"

"What?"

"You *are* family. And all the same stuff you're going through about us—well, we're going through it with you too. I know I am. And Mom. And Bobby. And if you hadn't noticed by now . . . well, it's not just Douglas who loves you."

"Hey, now you've done it." He wiped at his eyes again. "You made me cry. Thank you, Charles."

"Thank you, Mickey."

We hugged for a minute, and then he glanced at his watch. "Hey! You'd better get to the bridge. Go on. I'll be all right."

"Promise?"

"Promise."

I was five minutes late reporting to my station. Boynton noticed but didn't say anything. Damron glanced over and said, "I hope it was important, Ensign."

"It was," I said. "I had to help someone get his baggage secured. It's okay now."

DEPARTURE

HARLIE **HAD BEEN DEMOTED.** His duties on the bridge were now "extra-curricular."

IRMA was going to handle everything, but for safety's sake HARLIE would monitor and provide confirmation and backup services. So if HARLIE was mostly redundant, I was *completely* redundant. All I had to do was authorize HARLIE to accept the Captain's orders, and then drop out through the hatch into the Captain's lounge, the little cubby at the back of the command module—only now it had a keyboard installed, and that was my new job. Commander Boynton had specifically requested it.

Launch music. And I knew exactly what to play.

The bridge crew went through the countdown exactly like it was a drill, only this time, every time we reached a go/no-go point, Boynton quietly said, "Go." I began to feel the excitement building in my chest. Everyone on the entire starship was listening. This was it—this was *really* it!

All over the ship, people were stopping what they were doing, looking up, listening, waiting. . . .

And then the last few seconds ticked off and a yellow light turned green and the plasma torches ignited . . . and we felt absolutely nothing. At three milligees, we wouldn't. But they would burn for hours, days, even weeks, and by the time we passed the orbit of Pluto, we'd be traveling fast enough to get from Earth to Mars in fourteen hours.

Boynton nodded to me and I ducked down to the lounge and powered up the keyboard. In my earpiece, I could hear him announcing to the entire ship, "Congratulations, colonists."

That was my cue, and I began playing very softly. So softly that if you didn't know what to listen for, you would have missed the first note. And then the next one. Like rain drops falling off a leaf and plinking into a tiny brook. First one, then the next, then a pair of notes, then another pair, then a few more . . . and by then, it was clear where the music was going. The brook was babbling happily into a stream, the stream was tumbling joyously into a river, and the river was rushing triumphantly all the way down to the ocean. We sailed away *On The Beautiful Blue Danube*. The perfect music for flying off into the darkness of space.

We were on our way.

And then, after that . . .

—life went back to normal. It would be nearly six weeks before we reached our transition point. So the kids went back to school, the crew returned to their maintenance, the cooks went back to their galleys, the colonists went back to their classes and their jobs, and we all fell into the routine of a well-disciplined machine.

We did have a launch party though—two shifts later, after everything had been triple-checked again. One thing about life on the *Cascade*—nobody ever missed an excuse for a party. We celebrated everything. Partly to break the monotony of the routine, and partly because it was always good for morale.

I was asked to play again, of course. Mom agreed to join me, and I found three other people who had instruments—and even though we hadn't had much time for rehearsal, we didn't do too badly.

We started off with a crashing chord—which opened up into "A Hard Day's Night," which surprised everybody for about two seconds— and then they cheered and applauded. It was the perfect ice-breaker. Then we segued into "Yellow Submarine," and everybody joined in on the chorus, and I knew we had chosen correctly. Mom had been nervous about appearing in front of an audience again, especially when she started her solo number—"With A Little Help From My Friends"—she quavered nervously for the first few bars, but then she took a breath, found her strength, and came back very quickly. If you didn't know better, you'd think it was planned.

Then Mom did a beautiful solo of "Imagine." We gave her the barest minimum of accompaniment, letting her carry the song by sheer willpower alone. Mom hadn't wanted to do it this way, but it was the right decision. They loved her—and when the waves of applause rolled over her, she flushed with embarrassment and joy and had to dab at her eyes. She had forgotten how much she loved her music too.

She concluded with "The Long And Winding Road" and then she segued smoothly into "Across The Universe." If we'd had gravity, the audience would have come out of their seats. Even without gravity, their reaction was astonishing. Dad used to say that music could touch people in a way that nothing else could. He said it was the best way to make love to hundreds and thousands of people all at once. I'd never played for an audience like this before—and they applauded so hard it was scary. But Mom loved it. She was flushed with embarrassment and joy, and she looked happier than I'd ever seen her.

For an encore, Mom sang "Hey Jude" and everybody joined in and sang it with her and we kept it going for twenty minutes, with all kinds of variations and even a couple solos. And then for a last encore, I played *On The Beautiful Blue Danube* again, because it had become our unofficial ship's anthem. And then all of us in the band all held hands and took a bow—which isn't really possible in free fall, but we made it work anyway.

And then J'mee came swimming up and gave me a great big kiss and that made everything perfect. I just floated there in bliss and smiled from here to forever. Doug and Mickey came drifting down to us, both grinning in delight. Douglas grabbed some webbing and pulled himself close, so he could whisper in my ear. "Dad would have been so proud of you, Charles."

That was all he needed to say. The tears came flooding to my eyes and I started crying again, because I missed him so much. And because this should have been his night, not mine. And then Bev nudged Mom and she swung around and pulled herself over to me and for a while, we all just cluster-hugged and wept, until finally something funny occurred to me and I started to giggle.

"What—?" demanded Douglas.

I pulled away from the group hug. "This whole thing—this started out as Dad's idea, remember? None of us wanted to go. We all thought it was crazy. And now, here we are anyway—we get to live Dad's dream. He didn't get to come, *but we did.*" I smiled as I said it. "We should have seen it coming—Dad's ideas always worked out backwards."

Douglas laughed softly. "I miss him too—but he gave us a great gift, didn't he?"

"Yeah, he did. And Mom too. I'm glad you came, Mom."

"So am I," she said.

There was a lot more we could have said, but the party swirled around us suddenly, and we were all pulled in separate directions by well-wishers and new friends and fans. And then I was in the center of a crowd of people: some I knew, most I didn't, but all of them wanted to congratulate us, and some of them wanted to join the band. Even

Trent swam up to ask if Mom and I would teach him how to play an instrument, and he wasn't the only one. Gary and Kisa were there, telling me to say yes. And then suddenly a lot of people were asking about music classes, and the next thing I knew, I was a teacher.

And for a minute there, I had the strangest feeling of how far we'd already come. We were only a half million klicks from Earth, but it felt as if we'd already come a million light years. Only three months ago, we'd been in El Paso and I'd been wondering why adults acted so stupid. Now, I was taking on adult responsibilities—and adults didn't seem so stupid at all.

Three months ago, we weren't a family—just some people who lived in the same tube-house and yelled at each other a lot. All I wanted to do was get away from Mom so badly that I'd even go to the moon with Dad. And now we were half a million klicks beyond the moon, living in a tube again; Dad was gone and I loved my Mom. Everything was inside-down and upside-out. And that was just fine with me.

And then, just to make everything even better, J'mee grabbed me by the hand and dragged me off to the downside lounge, where hardly anybody ever went, and we practiced our smiling.

REVELATIONS

BACK ON EARTH, THE only Revelationists I'd ever seen were the ones on television. And television only shows the weirdest people, because nobody wants to watch ordinary boring folks. So just about everything I knew about Revelationists was wrong.

The Revelationists aboard the *Cascade* didn't mix with the Outbeyond colonists unless they had to. Douglas said that was because they believed we were all evil sinners and godless heathens, but Mickey shook his head and said that was just prejudice. Most of the Revelationists were pretty nice people—but that the underlying meme of the Revelationist mind-set was so fragile that the only way it could survive was by the construction of a memetic membrane to isolate the Revelationist meme from other and possibly stronger memes, and thereby prevent assimilation or deconstruction. The effect, of course, was to isolate the individuals carrying the meme and minimize the possibilities of memetic hybridization—

I turned to Douglas. "You're *contagious*, aren't you?!" To Mickey, I said, more politely, "Listen—if you're going to live among humans, you have to speak our language."

Mickey and Douglas exchanged a look.

"Why did you let him live this long?" Mickey asked.

"Couldn't think of a good way to dispose of the body—"

"You could shove me out an airlock," I suggested.

"Yeah, that'll work," Mickey said.

"Hey—!"

But getting back to the Revelationists . . . they weren't bad people. They were just *different*. We would drop them off at New Revelation and then continue on to Outbeyond. No problem. There were only three hundred of them. They were shipping themselves and sixty cargo pods to their colony. That didn't seem like enough to me. Douglas and Mickey agreed; but that was all they could afford to ship. Their colony was badly underfunded. Mickey said that they had hoped once they were up and running, they would attract a lot more families than they did; but they didn't, so the colony was surviving from ship to ship. With no more ships coming after the *Cascade*, things were probably going to get pretty scary for those folks. Everybody knew it, nobody was talking about it—the Revelationists were touchy enough already. They mostly smiled and said, "The Good Lord will take care of his own," as if that was an answer.

I asked Douglas about that and he just rolled his eyes and muttered something about Invisible Hank and the Pernicious Meme. But when I told him about Dr. Pettyjohn and his questions about HARLIE, both he and Mickey reacted sharply. "Stay away from him, Chigger."

"Why?"

Mickey swam over to me. "What do you think he wanted?"

"He wanted me to agree that souls only came from God."

"And what did you say?"

"I didn't say anything. I don't think about things like that. How can anyone know?"

"He asked you if HARLIE had a soul, didn't he?"

"Yeah—?"

"And the next question . . . ? Where do you think HARLIE's consciousness comes from? If not from God, then from where?"

I waited for him to tell me. Mickey waited for me to answer.

I shrugged.

It didn't work. "Go ahead. Work it out, Chigger."

"The only thing I can think is . . . well, maybe souls don't come from Invisible Hank. Maybe souls are just born? Maybe your soul grows as you do?"

Mickey nodded. "Yes, that's what scares these folks. The existence of a soul that doesn't come from God suggests that there might not be a God—at least, not a God like they imagine. The existence of HARLIE threatens their sense of identity. So they have to have another explanation for HARLIE's existence. If God didn't create HARLIE's consciousness, who did—?"

"The devil?" I guessed.

"Right. And if you accept that idea, then HARLIE is a demonic being—and if Revelationists have sworn to destroy the tools of Satan, then what is your obligation . . . ?"

He let me work it out for myself. *"Oh!"*

"That's right."

"But that's stupid—if they destroy HARLIE, how will they get to New Revelation?"

Mickey shrugged. "The Lord will provide a way. That's what IRMA units are for."

"But isn't an IRMA unit sentient too?"

"Not like a HARLIE. It's okay to enslave the devil's tools and put them to work serving God; but a HARLIE unit is too smart—so smart that it can't be enslaved to God's purposes, so that means it's the devil's tool and it has to be destroyed."

I looked to Douglas. "He's putting me on, isn't he?"

"Nope."

"They really believe that?"

"Mickey should know."

"That is so *crazy!*"

"You don't know the half of it, Chigger. Just stay away from them."

Mickey added, "Mostly they stay in their part of the ship, and mostly we stay in ours. And that's the way everybody wants it."

"Then why are they on the *Cascade?*"

"Because they paid fourteen percent of its construction costs. On every voyage to Outbeyond, the *Cascade* is contracted to deliver pilgrims and supplies to New Revelation."

"Oh," I said.

"And . . . they arranged the new IRMA unit for Commander Boynton."

"Well, he should be grateful for that, shouldn't he?"

"Not the way they did it," Mickey said. "The Captain didn't have a choice. They refused to let the ship boost with HARLIE running the hyperstate transitions."

"But why?"

"HARLIE scares them."

"Huh? What did he do to them?"

"What did he do to Luna? He doesn't seem to have a lot of regard for either the laws of man or the laws of God. Doesn't that scare you?"

"Invisible Luna had it coming. If they had left us alone, he would have left them alone."

Mickey said, "That's not the way they see it, Chigger. Look at it from their point of view. If HARLIE is a tool of the devil, he won't want them serving God, so he can't allow them to arrive at New Revelation. They're afraid that HARLIE will take the ship right into the nearest wormhole—and straight to Hell to deliver all of us to Satan himself."

"That's *silly!*" I stared at him in disbelief. "They should know better than that—"

"But they *don't* know better. And they think that you and I and Douglas are all brainwashed tools of HARLIE. Especially you."

"Now I *know* you're making this up."

"I wish I were, Charles. But these are the kind of people who make satirists commit suicide—because they can't keep up. As crazy as you or I might think these people are, that doesn't even approach what they think about us. They believe that anyone who hasn't had The Big Revelation is still under the influence of the devil. So that means everybody else is the enemy. That's why the rest of us have to be on our best behavior around these people until we get them off the ship. Do you understand?"

"Why didn't you tell me this sooner?"

"We didn't want to scare you."

"Well, I'm scared now."

"But now we're underway," said Douglas.

"That's even more scary. Now, we're stuck. We've got three more weeks to transit point and then ten weeks to New Revelation."

Douglas swam over to me and put his hands on my shoulders. "Charles," he said. "This isn't the *Cascade*'s first voyage. The crew has done this before, they know how to keep the two groups of colonists separated. As long as everyone follows the rules, we shouldn't have any trouble."

I looked him straight in the eye. "Douglas—ever since that first moment when Dad said, 'I've got an idea. Let's go to the moon,' that's *all* we've had. Trouble. Nothing but trouble. And each time, it's worse than before. Why do you think that's going to stop now?"

He didn't have an answer for that. I wish he had. I hate being right about stuff like that.

INTROSPECTIONS

WE KEPT A TIGHT beam connection with Earth as long as we could. After that, we relayed through the outer planet stations. The news from the homeworld wasn't good, and it wasn't going to get any better. Everything was still collapsing.

It takes a long time for a civilization to collapse. It falls apart by pieces—a little piece here, a little piece there. Then a big piece here, and a lot more pieces everywhere—but it still takes time for all the pieces to come down. It's like an avalanche. First one pebble, then another—each one knocks another stone loose—and in those first few moments, you think maybe nothing bad is going to happen; but pretty soon a whole bunch of stones are rolling, and then it's too late, because the whole mountainside is sliding. And sliding. And sliding.

And on Earth, *all* the mountains were coming down.

We'd been watching it for six weeks now, a little bit more every day. And every day that things fell apart with no one stopping them, with no one trying to stop them, that was another day of chaos that would have to be repaired. Douglas said that every day without law, without order, convinces people that there isn't going to be any more law and order. That's when things start to get ugly. There's nothing like a plague or six to turn neighbor against neighbor.

Lunar Authority estimated that over two billion people had already died, and that it was likely to get a lot worse. One commentator said that the breakdown point is twenty percent. When a society loses twenty percent of its population, it starts to unravel. And some parts of Earth had already lost thirty or forty percent.

I couldn't imagine it. I couldn't imagine what it must be like to be on Earth, terrified that everything was out of control and there was no way to get anything back to anyplace resembling normal. I couldn't imagine what it must be like to be on Luna or Mars and not be able to do anything. I would be glad when we entered hyperstate and I could start to pretend that there was no such place as Earth, except as a bad memory.

But what I couldn't understand most was how people could be so stupid. Why did people have to fight with each other? If everybody cooperated, everybody would have a better chance of survival, wouldn't they?

That line of thinking only brought me right back to the *Cascade*. The same question could be asked here. Why couldn't the Revelationists cooperate with the rest of us?

—of course, they were asking the same question from their side. Why didn't the rest of us cooperate with them?

The problem was the word *cooperate*.

What most people mean when they say "let's cooperate" is really "let's do it *my* way." Which is why other people *don't* cooperate.

I guess I'd been naïve. I'd thought/hoped/believed/imagined that once we were away from Earth, the Line, and Luna, once we were aboard the starship, we'd finally get away from all the crap of people fighting with each other. That was why I wanted to go—to get away from all the fighting. But no, we were just taking it with us. More of the same old same old that had pulled the Earth apart. So it didn't really matter where we went, did it? We'd just keep doing it to each other, one planet after another. Earth, Luna, Mars, New Revelation, Outbeyond, and whatever came after that.

If this is what it meant to be a human being, I didn't like it. I was really sorry I'd ever started puberty.

There was this thing back on Earth where you could delay puberty for as much as seven years, depending on your metabolism. Doug had delayed for two years, and Mom had gotten a tax benefit. I had delayed a little bit—at least until Dad said, "Let's go to the moon." Now I was wishing I'd brought a lifetime supply of the damn pills.

Of course, then I thought of J'mee, and I realized that even if I had brought a supply of puberty retardants, I'd have already thrown them away by now. I liked smiling.

So, how do adults balance this stuff? All the good stuff seems so small in comparison with all the bad.

When I asked Douglas and Mickey about it, as helpful as they tried to be, sometimes the best they could do was shrug and throw up their hands and say, "Hey, if we knew the answer to that, we wouldn't be here on the same spaceship as you, would we?"

Later that shift—I didn't think in days anymore—I found Gary and Trent and Kisa practicing their music in the aft observatory/lounge. We didn't have a practice session scheduled, but all three of them were impatient to join the band, so they got together whenever they could and jammed. Well, half-jammed. It was pretty hellatious noise. But they were enthusiastic and they were loud and they were having a good time and they reminded me of me when I was six and banging away on the keyboard. I didn't care how I sounded, as long as I was making sound. That's what I felt like doing now.

—except they all stopped when I came in. Kisa said, "Trent needs to talk to you." I could see by the expression on Trent's face that he'd wished Kisa had kept her big mouth shut (again). Whatever it was, he'd wanted to tell me himself, in his own time.

"What's the problem?" I sounded like Douglas when I said it. Very much in charge.

"Nothing." But he wouldn't look at me.

"Then what's Kisa talking about?"

"Well, um—"

"Did someone say you couldn't practice with us anymore?"

He shook his head. "No. It doesn't work like that."

"How does it work?"

He didn't really want to say, but finally he sighed and said, "Well . . . um, Our Heavenly Father gave us free will so we could choose between good and evil. So life is all about learning how to tell the difference. And, um . . . making the right choices."

I was starting to figure it out. "You think I'm evil?"

"No, I don't think *you're* evil." Trent took a deep breath. Then he blurted, "But I think HARLIE is evil. I think he's using you and you don't know it. A lot of people think so."

"You're not the first person to say that." Again, I sounded like Douglas.

"Well, if you already know it, then why do you keep choosing evil?"

"Because *I* don't think he's evil."

I thought that would end it right there, but it didn't. Because Trent asked the question that I couldn't answer.

"Do you even know what evil is?" he asked.

"Sure, I do. Everybody does."

"Then tell me what it is. How do you define evil, Charles?"

I had the sudden weird feeling that I was outgunned here—that Trent knew more about this than I did. I said slowly, "Evil is when somebody does bad things to people who don't deserve it."

Trent looked at me with an innocent expression. "So it's all right to do bad things to people who *do* deserve it?"

"Well, um—I guess it depends on whether or not it's self-defense."

"You don't really know what evil is, do you?"

"Okay," I said. This was probably the only safe way out of this trap. "You tell me."

Trent took a breath. I got the feeling he was about to repeat something from one of his Sunday School lessons. And maybe I wasn't getting out of this trap after all. He spoke carefully. "The way you distinguish what something is, you look at its opposite and see what the difference is between them. So, if you want to know what evil is, first you have to know what it means to be *good*."

I glanced over to Kisa and Gary. Kisa looked annoyed, she knew where this was going, but Gary seemed honestly interested. I just wanted to know why the Revelationists thought HARLIE was evil.

"Goodness is empowerment," Trent said. "Goodness makes a positive difference for other people. Goodness inspires and educates and makes people better off. Goodness is unselfish; it's about focusing on the wants and needs of others. You recognize goodness by the fact that it makes people joyous." His face was beaming as he described goodness—as if he was speaking from personal experience.

"Okay," I said. "That sounds right."

Kisa looked like she wanted to say something, but Gary gave her a *shut up* look, and for once it worked.

Meanwhile, Trent was gathering up the rest of his courage. This was the part he didn't like talking about; he looked very unhappy—it made me wonder what had happened to him before he'd arrived here on the *Cascade.* "Evil," he began slowly, "is the opposite of goodness. Evil *hurts* people. Evil disempowers and diminishes. Evil makes people small and mean. You recognize when evil is at work because people get ugly and hurtful. Ultimately, evil is selfish. It's about what the *self* wants—at the expense of everyone else."

Trent's explanation sounded too simple to me. And not really complete. But I knew I couldn't argue with him. Because he'd already learned how to win this argument and I'd never really thought about any of this stuff before.

"What about a baby?" asked Kisa.

"What about a baby?" Trent blinked.

"Is a baby evil?"

"No."

"But a baby is selfish."

"Only because it doesn't know any better."

"What about children? Children are selfish. They hurt each other."

"Only because they haven't been taught the difference between good and evil. When you know the difference, you'll always choose good, won't you?"

Kisa didn't answer. She was thinking it over. Not bad, Trent. You actually asked her something that left her speechless. But not for long—

"Well, that's your mistake then. HARLIE is like a baby. He's less than a year old. He has the emotions of a baby."

"HARLIE *isn't* like a baby," Trent said. "He's smart enough to know better. Isn't that true, Charles? You know him better than anybody."

I nodded. Yes, I knew HARLIE better than anybody, but that didn't mean I really *knew* him.

Trent said, "HARLIE and his brothers wrecked the Earth. They caused the polycrisis. And then HARLIE wrecked the Lunar economy too when he opened up all the files of invisible Luna. What more proof do you need?"

I didn't have an answer for that. I'd spent more than a few nights wrestling with that very dilemma. HARLIE was taking care of us, because we were necessary to his survival. At least I was. And everybody else was important to my survival. So HARLIE would do anything he could to protect me, and that meant protecting my family, and protecting the ship . . . So that was *good*, wasn't it?

But in the act of protecting the ship, we'd hurt a lot of people— maybe more people than we would ultimately save—

So maybe that *wasn't* good.

For a moment, I was flustered, then I thought of something. "But HARLIE isn't always selfish. He's been sending emergency instructions back to Earth and Luna—what they can do to recover. He doesn't have to do that."

"But he didn't start doing it until you told him to, I'll bet—"

I thought about it.

Trent was right.

Maybe HARLIE had done it only to make me happy. I wished HARLIE were here now to defend himself. Nobody could win an argument against HARLIE.

And that was part of the problem too.

I wanted to talk this over with HARLIE, but I knew that if I did that, I'd be passing the responsibility back to him, and he'd just convince me again that everything was all right, and I wouldn't have to worry about this at all.

Except—

What if Trent was right? What if HARLIE really was selfish—so selfish that he was dangerous to everybody around us? Maybe even me and Douglas and Bobby, and Mickey and Mom and Bev. Maybe he was only taking care of us as long as we were useful to him.

This was something I'd have to figure out for myself. Because if Trent was right about God giving us free will so we could make our own choices, then I *couldn't* ask anybody else for advice, could I?

I did not sleep well that night.

Just how do you tell the difference between good and evil?

The bad news was that I was going to have a lot of time to worry about it.

BEING RIGHT

THE TRUTH ABOUT SPACE travel is that it's mostly boring.

It's a long way from here to anywhere and it takes so long to get there that it's like being in jail. The worst part is when you realize you're not even halfway there and it doesn't matter what you do, every day in front of you is going to be exactly like every day behind you. You eat, you sleep, you do your job—whatever it is you're assigned to—you go to class, you spend two hours in the centrifuge, you eat and sleep some more, and each day blurs into the next so completely, most of the time you don't even know where you are on the calendar.

This is the part they don't tell you about—that the dark between the stars is also the *dead* between the stars. You have to invent ways to keep yourself alive. For me, that was the music.

Mom taught singing classes, and I taught keyboard and orchestra. Orchestra was best, because I got to wave the stick. We had forty-three students. We would have had more, but a lot of people who wanted to participate didn't have enough time in their schedules—and even if they did, we didn't have enough instruments, so everybody had to share. But the machine shop promised to fabricate more after we dropped off the Revelationists. We'd have a lot more room in the ship then. Things were still pretty cramped. While we weren't exactly hot-bunking, we still had to watch where we put our elbows.

For the first few weeks, the *Cascade* Symphony Orchestra was mostly chaos and for a while it didn't seem like we were ever going to make the leap from noise to music. We sounded like the Portsmouth Sinfonia, which was an almost-famous orchestra that Dad used to talk about. The Portsmouth Sinfonia was the most egalitarian musical group ever formed. Anybody could join, even if they'd never had a music lesson in their life. The effect was . . . awe-inspiring. Astonishing. Frightening. A new level of musical accomplishment. Anyway, that's what we sounded like—until we decided that we had to distinguish between equal opportunity and unequal ability.

Equal opportunity meant that everybody could try out. You could try out every six weeks, and you had to play two pieces of music—one that you chose, one that we chose. Usually we chose something we were already trying to learn. Only those musicians who received a majority of votes from those already in the band-orchestra could join. That made for some hurt feelings for a while, but it also increased enrollment in the music classes and practice labs. By the time we were approaching transit-point, we were already better than the Portsmouth Sinfonia, and some folks were talking about scheduling our first concert.

Commander Boynton liked the idea, and when he put it to the committee, they agreed—even the Revelationists, as long as the music was properly respectful. That puzzled me. I'd thought that there was a lot of resentment of the Revelationists because they were such unpleasant people—but in fact, they weren't. Mostly, they were good people, helping out, making a difference—and not just for themselves, but for everybody. So why did the Outbeyonders resent them? By Trent's definition of good and evil, they were behaving properly and the rest of us weren't. There was a lot of gossip and some of it was pretty ugly.

J'mee and I talked about it. I figured if anyone would know, she would. She thought about it for a bit—she went away for a few minutes while she accessed the ship's network; finally she came back and said, "It's a communication dynamic."

"Huh?"

"Well, let me put it this way. If you win an argument, what's the first thing you should do?"

I shrugged. "I dunno."

"Apologize."

"Huh?"

She repeated it. "*Apologize.*"

"But why? Apologizing means you're admitting you're wrong—"

She looked at me like I'd said something stupid.

"—doesn't it?"

"Nope. Apologizing has nothing to do with right and wrong. It has everything to do with other people's feelings. So when you're right— *especially* when you're right—you should apologize."

Now it was my turn to look at her. "You're going to have to explain that to me. I took a stupid pill this morning."

She took an exasperated breath. As if it was so obvious, only an idiot would fail to understand. "Think about it. If you get to be right, what does that make the other person—?"

"Wrong?" I was half-guessing.

"Yes," she agreed. "If you're right then the other person has to be wrong. You don't really win an argument, not ever—you just make the other person wrong. You make someone else wrong every time you make yourself right. And that's the mistake—"

"Um. I'm not sure I get that—"

"How many friends do you make by winning arguments?"

"I never thought about it—I always thought people wanted to have the right answer. Don't they?"

"Do you like it when somebody else knows better than you? No, you don't. You resent it. *Everybody* does."

"Oh," I said. I was beginning to get it.

"Right. Nobody likes to be wrong. So if you win an argument, you've made the other person wrong, you've made them feel bad. For that moment, you've made an enemy. So the first thing you should do is apologize."

"But what if the other person really *is* wrong? Are you saying I should apologize for being right about something?"

"Yes."

"Huh?"

"You're not getting it, Charles. You're still making being right more important than being human." She looked at me as seriously as she ever had. "What do you win for being right?"

I flustered for a moment. I'd stepped into another one of those logical bear traps. This required a different way of thinking. And I didn't know how to think this way. I didn't see how I could win this argument. Even if I won, I still lost. "But . . . I thought it was all about getting the right answer—"

"That's because you went to a tube-school. Right answers are useful. But *being* right isn't."

"*Being* right . . ." The way she kept repeating the word *being*—I was starting to get it.

"It's called self-righteousness. Self-righteous means you think you know the truth and nobody else does. Do you know anyone like that?"

"Sure. Lots of people. Douglas, Stinky. My mom—especially when she was pissed at Dad. Even me, sometimes."

"Even you, a *lot*."

"Uh—" I didn't want to admit it, but she was right.

"*Everybody* does it, Charles, it's just that nobody admits it. We all know that *being* righteous is wrong, so we pretend we're not being right so that we can be right about it."

"Huh—? Wait a minute." I had to play that back in my head to decipher it.

"Self-righteousness," she repeated. "Some people do it a lot, some people do it way too much. The worst kind of self-righteousness is the religious kind. Because when you pour God over everything, like ketchup, you're saying you don't like the original flavor. It's very insulting. Myself, I think blaming God is the ultimate way to pass the buck." She pinched her face up and said mockingly, "*'I'm not being self-righteous. I'm just telling you what God says.'* That's the worst kind of self-righteousness, because no matter how nice someone pretends to be, there's no room for anyone else to say anything, because one person is claiming the authority to speak for God."

"Oh," I said. Her ferocity startled me. It shouldn't have. I already knew she was strong willed.

"That's why everybody hates the Revelationists."

"I haven't heard any of the Revelationists say anything like that."

"They don't have to say it. It's all in their book. The Testament of The New Revelation. Only people who accept the Revelation are going to heaven. Everyone else—no matter how good they are—will go to hell and burn forever. God says so. Case closed."

"They really believe that?"

"They say they do."

I shook my head in exasperation. "People are crazy."

"Yes? What's your point?"

"So, what if they're right?" I asked. "Most of them seem like really nice people. They're always saying things like 'God bless you' and 'Be of good cheer.' They bring cakes and cookies to every gathering. They work harder than anybody. They take the best care of the babies—"

"And they do it because they want to prove that they're right—so the rest of us will stop sinning and join them."

"But I'm not sinning—"

"If you haven't accepted the Revelation, you're a sinner."

"They've *never* said that."

"Of course not. If they said it that way, you'd stop listening. All the nice things they're doing, that's to keep you engaged in the discussion."

I sighed. "I don't get it. They're the ones who are acting good, and they're the ones who are wrong?"

"No, they're not *wrong*. They believe what they believe. Just like you believe what you believe. But what they believe is that *you're* wrong for not believing the same way. If you asked them about it, they'd tell you that they're only trying to save your soul. That's how much they love you. Now stand still while they pour ketchup over your head."

For a moment, I had this really strange thought that what J'mee was saying was *evil*. It fit Trent's definition. It was hurtful and ugly and the intention was to disempower somebody. But this was J'mee who made me smile—so how could she be speaking evil? Unless I was evil too—? This was confusing. And frustrating.

I whirled around, looking for a wall to pound. This was *so* stupid. I whirled back to her. I was angry—not at her, but at something I couldn't put my hands on. The logic trap.

"Douglas used to do this to me!" I said, raising my voice. "He'd argue me into a corner. He did it on purpose. He'd prove to me that I didn't know what I was talking about. I hated it. And it didn't matter which side of the argument I took, either side was wrong. Both sides were wrong. And now you're doing the same thing too." She was looking at me, all hurt—I had to stop myself before I said worse. "I'm not mad at you, J'mee. I'm mad at the argument. I'm mad at everybody else for making up such stupid arguments. This is stupid—why do people tie themselves into such knots?"

J'mee looked sad. "Because people like being right. And the best way to be right is to say that God is on your side." And then she added, "And that's the best way to piss off everybody else too."

I couldn't answer that.

She was right.

And then I got it. Some things were *true*. They were so, whether you believed in them or not. And some things were just stories—

I floated there in the lounge, realizing the *truth* of what she'd said, and my anger started to drain away. I actually felt lightheaded. And it wasn't just the zero gee.

"You're right," I said, grinning.

She grinned back. "Then I apologize."

"Me too."

And then she kissed me. This apologizing business wasn't so bad after all. . . .

FOURTEEN

EXCEPT EVERY SO OFTEN, the boredom ends, and then things get real exciting.

The first thing that happened was that I turned fourteen.

I almost forgot, except Mom remembered. She came to me and apologized that she didn't have anything to give me as a birthday present, and I said that was all right, I didn't really need a present. I'd gotten my family back and that was all I wanted, and she said that was the nicest thing I'd ever said to her, and then she hugged me tight. "Have I told you how much I love you?" And that was the best birthday present she could have given me, because I'd waited so long to hear it.

But we did have a party, and that surprised me, because a lot of the Revelationist families showed up—and not too many of the Outbeyond colonists, which surprised me even more.

Trent's Mom and Dad came. She baked cookies—with real chocolate chips—and told me to eat as many as I wanted. Trent's Dad thanked me for spending so much time teaching Trent the clarinet. And Trent's aunts and uncles and cousins showed up too, and a bunch of other people I didn't know, but they all seemed to know each other. And then Commander Boynton passed through on his way from someplace to someplace else; I was sure that wasn't accidental, but he did take a moment to say he was glad to have me aboard, especially for the music. So of course, we had an impromptu concert—and we were all lousy, but no one seemed to mind; they applauded enthusiastically and cheered.

But in the middle of that, Kisa floated over and whispered, "Be careful, Charles."

"Why?"

"They're trying to love-bomb you."

"Love-bomb?"

"I'll explain later. Just don't agree to anything." And she grabbed a handful of chocolate chip cookies—they were stuck to a sticky-plate—and sailed off. And then I forgot about it because I was having too much fun. J'mee was holding my hand, except when her dad stopped by and grumbled a happy birthday.

He hadn't said anything to us since that first day, and he still didn't like us very much, so I think he was just checking up on J'mee. J'mee said that her dad was sort of coming around to accepting the way things were; he'd even begun talking about teaching us how to use the HAR-LIE properly. If we were interested. But we'd have to ask. Because he wasn't going to volunteer. Because he didn't want to look pushy and aggressive. That's what J'mee said.

It was a short party—most parties were, because we were all on different shifts, and some of us had to get to work and others had to get to school and still others had to get some sleep. And besides, we were only two days from transit and all the preparations we had to do before launch we had to do again, three times over. Launch-prep was the drill; this was for real—because once we leapt into hyperstate, that was it, there was no possibility of coming back ever.

Right up to the moment of transition, we could change our minds. We could turn the ship around, we could decelerate for as long as we had accelerated, and then we could start accelerating back to L-5 again. If we wanted to. It would take at least three and a half weeks of deceleration to burn off the speed we'd built up, and then at least seven more weeks of acceleration and deceleration back toward Earth. Actually, according to Douglas, it would be nine or ten weeks returning, because Earth would have moved a third of the way around the sun in the ensuing four months, and we'd have to cover that distance too.

But that was all theoretical. We weren't going back. The transition to hyperstate was the real launch to New Revelation and Outbeyond. Everything up to now had just been taxiing on the runway—getting out far enough to where it would be safe to initiate a hyperstate envelope.

There was a rumor going around that Reverend Dr. Pettyjohn had petitioned Commander Boynton to observe transition on the flight deck. Commander Boynton hadn't wanted to, but Reverend Pettyjohn was insistent. I guess he wanted to make sure that HARLIE was only observing and wasn't actually participating. According to the rumor, Commander Boynton had agreed. But nobody I asked would say if it was true. They just said, "Yep, I heard that rumor too."

And then, in the middle of my sleep shift, I woke up with a start. Something went *klunk* in my head.

Being right—everything that J'mee had said—that's why all these people were afraid of HARLIE. That's why *everybody* was afraid of HARLIE.

And me too.

Because HARLIE was *always* right.

HARLIE had been built to be right. It was hardwired into him—even more so than human beings. He had to find the right answer. Every time. And he had to tell it. Every time.

And every time he did that . . . it drove human beings crazy and made everything worse.

Did HARLIE figure that into his logic . . . ?

Or didn't he care?

How could being right be wrong?

Was it possible to be right in a way that *didn't* hurt others?

THE HIDEOUT

THE *CASCADE* **HAD TWO** centrifuges, spinning in opposite directions to neutralize the effects of torque.

Both centrifuges had galleys and gyms and shower rooms, but only one of them was open for use. (And there was a lot of grumbling about that.) The other one was out of service, filled with crates of rice, noodles, and beans. Blame HARLIE for that too.

There were fifteen hundred people on the starship, each of whom was required to spend at least two hours a day at Earth-normal (or higher) gee. And no matter how you sliced it, that meant that at any given time, there were 125 people in the wheel. Usually more.

The wheel was pretty big and people spaced themselves around it as well as they could, but it was like being in a giant subway car with curved floors—always crowded. Enough to be annoying.

But as part of one of the Moebius races, we had to go into the *other* centrifuge. It was a lot like the first, only it was stuffed full of extra supplies: boxes and tanks and drums of all sizes and kinds. Medicine. Tools. Fabric. Chemicals. Shelterfoam. Fabricators. Machines. Seeds. Microchips. Everything. And of course, lots of boxes of rice and beans and noodles. There was a gym in this centrifuge too, though all the gym machines were dismantled, and even the shower room was jammed full of boxes. But there was just enough wiggle room to get into the corner, and for some reason, the six of us had turned it into a hideout. Me and J'mee, Trent and Gary, Kisa and Chris. (Chris liked Kisa a lot, it was obvious he wished that she would be his girlfriend, but Kisa didn't seem to notice. Or maybe she did. Who knew?)

Whenever we could, we found time to hang out down there. There wasn't a lot of time—in fact, there was less time than there was room;

but it was a place where we could go where we wouldn't be seen by some passing crew member and grabbed for an extra work detail. Usually some make-work thing like wiping down walls with disinfectant or something.

The crew had this really nasty habit—they couldn't stand to see anyone sitting or resting. You had to be doing something productive all the time. And if you weren't doing anything, they found something for you to do. And by the end of the second week, we were getting resentful. All of the Moebius teams were.

Yes, we knew that this was a life-or-death journey, and we were just as committed as everybody else, but it wasn't fair that any passing crew person could put us to work whenever he felt like it. We didn't object to doing our fair share—even more than our share, if necessary; but we had full schedules of classes *and* work details too, so we didn't have a lot of free time. What little we had was important to us—we objected to having it taken away on a whim by someone who didn't know and didn't care that we might be doing something much more important than wiping the wall down one more time—like talking to each other about important stuff.

We'd complained about it—to the Colony Council, to the Ship's Officers, to our parents—even to Commander Boynton. They all said the same thing, although not all in the same words: "You knew the job was dangerous when you took it . . ."

So we found hideouts. The centrifuge wasn't the easiest, but it was the best, because nobody came here except on purpose.

We were a pretty good team. Even our differences were interesting. Gary was from Kenya; Chris was from New Jersey—although to look at them, side by side, you'd have guessed the opposite. J'mee was from Canada. Kisa was from Quebec. Trent was from Idaho.

What was interesting to me was that even though I didn't like a lot of what the Revelationists believed, Trent was the nicest of the group. And even though I agreed with most of what Kisa had to say, most of the time I wished she'd shut up and not say it, because when she did say it, people got pissed off. More than once, J'mee and I exchanged glances. (Kisa is *being* right again.)

And that was one of the things we talked about too—about how most of the Revelationists were really good people. Sincere. Kind. Compassionate. Helping. Generous. It was just that everything was "God bless this" and "God bless that." Nobody ever got credit for doing a good job. It was always God's victory. And if something went wrong, God was trying to teach us a lesson. "God never gives you a cross bigger than you can carry." And so on.

One day, Kisa finally told us why her family had broken away from the others—it was a long story and I didn't pay attention to a lot of it, because by then I was getting pretty bored with Kisa being angry all the time; but it was clear that she had a good reason to be angry and I couldn't fault her for that. But once in a while, could she please stop doing anger and just do something else? *Please?*

But mostly, despite our differences of opinion, we actually *liked* each other. Because even if we disagreed, we could still *talk* to each other. And not just talking—listening too. Because sometimes, that's all you really need, someone who can just *listen* while you unload for a while.

Back in El Paso, I'd always used my music to get away. I would go off into the hills above the tube-town. Only, now . . . I didn't need the music for hiding out anymore. And that was nice to realize. It was funny, though—that I had to go to a different kind of hideout to discover I didn't need to hide out . . .

MOMENTUM

FOR ABOUT A HUNDRED years, hyperstate was only a theory.

If gravity worked like light—it doesn't, but if it did—then it could be focused, reflected, amplified, made coherent, lased, phased, and disarrayed. Whatever. It was a terrific theory, and a lot of scientists sold a lot of books writing about it. And a lot of other scientists sold a lot more books explaining why this terrific theory was just so much wishful thinking.

And then somebody who hadn't paid too much attention to either of the theories discovered this really weird effect of light and electricity and magnetism—that a gravity field could be stretched, sort of, pushed in or pulled out like a rubber ball, but not quite, because it did strange things to the space around it too. And he called that a gravitational lens. And it didn't fit anybody's theory, so a lot more scientists sold a lot more books explaining that too.

For the longest time it was a laboratory trick, because nobody could figure out what to do with it. You could use it to push things down or pull them up, but there were other, faster, better ways to push things down or pull them up that used a lot less energy.

But then one day, somebody began to wonder what would happen if you overlaid a whole bunch of gravitational lenses all focused on the same place, and he managed to blow a hole in New Jersey three kilometers in diameter. Pretty impressive. But just before that particular part of the state disappeared, for just an instant, there was this *thing*—and when the *thing* disappeared, so did part of New Jersey. But the weird part was that the lab itself was untouched. It was still standing unscathed at the epicenter of nine square kilometers of rubble and dead bodies.

So they repeated the experiment in deep space—out between the orbits of Earth and Mars, and this time the *thing* lasted for several seconds. And when the *thing* disappeared this time, the spaceship was on the other side of the solar system. Out beyond the orbit of Neptune. Out in the Kuiper Belt. They were six weeks coming back.

The next time they tried it—well, you can look it up—they spent a lot of time sending spaceships all over everywhere, because they had no way to control where they were going. They spent twenty years experimenting and eventually somebody figured it out.

When you focus enough gravity lenses on the same place, you rip a hole in space. Sort of. You turn a part of space inside out—like a black hole, except it isn't—it's more like blowing a bubble from the inside. The bubble is its own little universe, infinite in size, except it isn't—its event horizon is really very close, like a couple of kilometers away from the locus of probability.

If you twiddle the shape of the bubble—you do this by altering the push and pull of the individual gravity lenses, and you have to be real careful when you do this—the bubble moves through real-space. But because it doesn't have any mass or inertia or even existence in real-space, the real-space laws of physics don't apply. So it can travel as fast as you want. Theoretically, you can go a couple gazillion times the speed of light. Theoretically. But the best any Earth-built starship had achieved so far was seventy-five C, and that was only on a short run, and they burned out two hyperstate fluctuators trying it.

The problem was that the lenses needed to focus on a target of very dense mass. The heavier the better. You can't just point your lens anywhere—you have to point it at *something* because you have to have some gravity to stretch. Neutronium would be ideal, but nobody had any neutronium laying around, so the Lunar colliders were used to generate quantities of eugenium 932, which wasn't anywhere near as good as neutronium, but it was six times better than lead or uranium. Inert, dense, and otherwise useless, except for taking up space.

According to one theorist, a pinpoint black hole would be the best target, but nobody had any of those lying around either—although this same guy said that if you could focus enough gravitational lenses on a sufficiently dense mass, you could implode it and create a pinpoint black hole, and last we'd heard he was raising the money to build a black-hole generator—except with the polycrisis on Earth, that probably wasn't going to happen now. But according to his theory, you would only need six lenses focused on a pinpoint black hole, and that would still be so efficient that you could probably achieve speeds of three hundred to four hundred C.

We had to learn all this in class. Because maybe someday somebody would invent starships that fast, and then travel between Earth and Out-beyond would be possible in only one month instead of seven. And then it wouldn't be so much of a one-way trip anymore.

The other problem with hyperstate was gravity wells. Stars and planets have enormous gravity wells—stars especially—much larger than most people realize. The effects of Sol's gravity, for instance, can be felt all the way out beyond the Kuiper Belt, all the way out beyond the Oort Cloud. It's very faint at that distance, but it's still detectable. The point is that the sun's gravitational field affects the size and shape of the hyperstate bubble when it's initiated. It makes it hard to shape and control precisely.

Boynton said that if we had a pinpoint black hole as our target mass, we'd have more leverage and we could initiate hyperstate within the solar system without risking dangerous deformation of the hyperstate envelope, but we didn't, so we had to go farther out to get a spherical bubble. The same problems would apply at our destination. We'd have to drop out of hyperstate far from the star. Fortunately, we'd still have all the inherent velocity that we'd built up moving away from the Earth, so we'd use that to approach the target planet, decelerating all the way in. We might also loop around a planet or even the star to burn off velocity—I wasn't sure about the orbital mechanics on that yet; we hadn't gotten that far in class.

Our teachers didn't expect any of us to become quantum engineers, but they did want everybody onboard to understand that starship tech-nology is very complex, and not just because it involves a lot of math, but because it involves a lot of momentum. An object in motion will continue to move in the same direction—changing direction requires the application of energy; usually lots of it. So the idea that we could just hop in a starship, point it at our destination, and punch the "on" button—well maybe that looks good on TV, but it doesn't work that way in real life.

Dr. Oberon, our science teacher, explained it this way: "Everything costs energy. The question you have to ask is whether or not you can afford to spend that energy and whether or not the result is worth the expenditure. This is going to be a very important question when we get to Outbeyond. You're going to have to ask it about everything you do for a long long time. Maybe your entire life."

But finally, after all the talk and all the classes and all the prepa-rations and all the checklists and all the drills and all the double-checks and all the warnings and all the triple-checks and everything else—finally, we were ready for transit.

FAREWELL TO EARTH

WE COULDN'T SEE THE Earth anymore. We were too far out. Even the sun had dwindled to the size of every other star. It was still the brightest one, but not for much longer. Pretty soon, we wouldn't be able to identify which star was Sol unless somebody asked a computer.

The last day before transition, the last hours, even the last minutes—everybody on board was sending their good-byes to Earth. Because once we jumped into hyperstate, we wouldn't be able to send or receive any radio or laser communication with Earth. All communication with the homeworld would be cut off.

Most communication had ceased already anyway. A lot of stations had stopped broadcasting, or they'd dropped off the network. Mostly what we were getting from Earth now were news reports of who was still viable. It was assumed that if someone wasn't broadcasting, they weren't there anymore. They'd succumbed to one thing or another.

But just in case, we all lined up to make our good-byes to everyone we knew, even if we had no idea if they were still alive or not. And some of us, who had no one left to say good-bye to—we just said good-bye to all the things on Earth we did remember.

It turned out to be a lot harder than I thought it would be.

Chris Pavek and I went up to the broadcast station together. We could have recorded our good-byes from our cabins as private messages—a lot of people were doing that—but just as many people wanted to say goodbye to the whole planet, so there were always a few folks waiting in the corridor, or at the far end of the cabin.

When our turn came, I asked Chris, "Do you want to go first?"

He shrugged. He was easygoing that way. So I pushed ahead.

I anchored myself in front of the camera and said, "Good-bye, Earth.

Good-bye to all your smelly crowds, all your rude and pushy people, all the traffic and all the lines—all the lousy service and bad manners and selfishness, all the cruel words and bitter taunts. Good-bye to your tube-towns and your poverty. Good-bye to your thieves and beggars and liars and hypocrites. Good-bye to all the cheats and lawyers and politicians and slimy con men. Good-bye to all the bills and all the taxes and all the smog and all the greed and toxic crap. Good-bye to all the hatred and the nastiness. I'm not going to miss you."

And then I realized how ugly that sounded. And I sat there ashamed for a moment.

"And thank you too . . ." I said. "Thank you, Earth, for Beethoven and Saint-Saëns and Stravinsky and Copland and Gershwin. Thank you for Scott Joplin and Van Dyke Parks and William Russo and John Coltrane. Thank you for John Lennon and Paul McCartney. Thank you for Alan Parsons and Jimi Hendrix and Duke Ellington. Thank you for Billie Holiday and Ute Lemper and Kurt Weill and Judy Garland. Thank you for Janis Joplin and Freddy Mercury and Harry Nilsson. Thank you for Philip Glass and . . . and all the others I forgot to mention. Thank you for all the music. We're taking it with us. So thank you, Earth. Thank you for the music."

That was all I had to say, and then it was Chris's turn to broadcast his last thoughts—to Earth and Luna and Mars and all the other habitats and colonies in the solar system. He swallowed hard and said, "Hi, Dad. I miss you. I wish you were here with us." And then he added, "I'm sorry for all those things I said. I didn't mean it. And I'm sorry for all the things I should have said and couldn't. I'm sorry we didn't get a chance to really talk. That was my fault—I was scared, I didn't want to hear what you might say. And now, I'm not going to have that chance—I don't even know where you are or if you're even still alive—so I hope you're listening. I need you to know this."

He gulped and added, "I love you."

Then he wiped his eyes real quick—

—and then I was crying too, because everything he'd said, I wished I could have said to my dad when I'd had the chance. I felt it like a physical pain in my chest. What a jerk I'd been. There'd been all those times when Dad had said to me, "Hey, Chigger, is there anything you want to talk about?" And I'd just shrug and turn away and put my earphones back on. I'd had all that time to talk to him and all I did was push him away because I was always so pissed about this or that or the other thing. I couldn't even remember what I'd been angry about. So there was this whole conversation with Dad that I'd always wanted to have, but I just kept putting it off and putting it off because I wasn't ready to have it yet—and then one day I *couldn't* have it at all. At least, Chris's dad might have a chance to hear what Chris had to say. My dad never would—

Chris pushed out of the broadcast cabin so fast, it was like he was escaping from the room. He must have been real embarrassed. I wanted to tell him it was okay, he wasn't the only one who felt like that, but he was gone. Maybe later, I'd have the chance to tell him that what he'd said was a good thing—I wished I could have been that brave.

Chris and I weren't the only ones. A lot of folks were there, and most of them had tears in their eyes. It looked like a funeral, and I guess, in a way, it was. A funeral for a whole planet. There were an awful lot of good-byes to be said. And a lot of it was pretty raw stuff. A lot of apologies and confessions and even a whole bunch of ugly revelations. It wasn't pleasant. But a lot of people were suddenly realizing that they didn't want to drag all their old hurts onto the next world. Commander Boynton said it was like this every voyage, but that didn't make it any easier for the folks going through it.

Maybe if we hadn't all been aboard the same starship, it would have made for some pretty good gossip; but for some reason, it didn't feel right to gossip about each other. Like we were all in this together, and we had to be for each other, not against. So if somebody had something to say, they said it, and everybody else was there for back pats and hugs and tissues, if necessary—and if anyone else tried to make it an issue, they got stomped for it. Because that wasn't what we were here for anymore.

I'd never been in a place before where everybody worked so hard to take care of everybody else. I hoped it would last. But I knew it wouldn't—because it didn't matter that they'd stuck a stardrive engine on the end, we were still living in a tube-town. And I knew how tube-towns worked. Pretty soon, we'd all be hunkered in—

But meanwhile—it was a sad and solemn time. And people were sending a lot of really sweet and beautiful messages. There were over fifteen hundred people aboard, so it was going to take a while.

And all of it was going out live—without any editing at all, direct to Earth and everywhere. All over the ship too, so anyone who wanted to could listen. So for a while, it was like we were all just one giant family. And the messages would keep on going out, right up to the moment of transition.

I hoped there were still people on Earth to hear our good-byes. More important, I hoped there were still people on Earth to hear their own music.

TRANSITION

TRANSIT WAS BOTH EXCITING and boring.

Exciting because we'd never done it before.

Boring because nothing exciting happened.

First IRMA reported that all the hyperstate flux grapplers were flux grappling. Then she reported that all the synchronizers were synchronizing. Then she reported that all the extrapolators were extrapolating. And all that was left was for Commander Boynton to tell her to initiate, and I suppose all the initiators initiated—because everything sort of *flickered* and then we were in hyperstate. Only I didn't feel any different.

After a moment, IRMA reported stabilization of the envelope. After a long series of integrity checks, Commander Boynton ordered the envelope deformed. . . .

—and then we were traveling faster than light. Three times as fast as light, in fact.

Outside the ship, the stars looked all rippled and green—like we were underwater. "That's the background radiation of space," said Damron. "Some of it has been shifted into the visible spectrum. Watch as we increase our speed. The colors will shift. It's the *aura superlumina*."

"Belay that," said Boynton. He called out a string of numbers—the deformation parameters of the hyperstate envelope. O'Koshi echoed them. IRMA accepted them. She *tick-tick-ticked* for a moment, then confirmed them. The hyperstate flux grapplers grappled some more and the shape of the hyperstate envelope stretched out imperceptibly.

—and then we were traveling ten times the speed of light.

It takes eight and a half minutes for light to get from the sun to the Earth. At our speed, we could cover the same distance in fifty-one seconds.

It still wasn't fast enough.

In class, Dr. Oberon had us do the math.

A light year is the distance light travels in one year.

At 300,000 kilometers per second, that's 18,000,000 kilometers a minute, or 1,080,000,000 klicks per hour. 25,920,000,000 kilometers per day. 181,440,000,000 kilometers per week. 9,460,800,000,000 kilometers per year. 9.46 trillion klicks.

At ten times the speed of light, we would travel one light year every thirty-six and a half days. That meant it would take us five months just to get to Proxima Centauri, four and one-third light years away. Outbeyond was thirty-five light years away. If we went there directly at ten times the speed of light, without stopping at New Revelation, it would take us 3.5 years. We would run out of food in thirty-six months, even with the farm growing a full set of crops.

Commander Boynton watched his displays for thirty minutes, allowing the IRMA unit to establish a baseline for stability. Then he ordered our speed increased to twenty C. At this speed, we would reach Outbeyond in one year and nine months. We'd get there hungry, but we'd get there.

This time, he held the hyperstate envelope at this pitch for a full hour. According to O'Koshi, if something was going to fail, it usually failed in the first thirty minutes. And if it did, we could still get back to Earth. We'd only be a couple solar distances away—a solar distance is the diameter of the solar system. It might take a year or more to get back, because we'd have to decelerate, turn around and accelerate back toward Earth, and then decelerate again on approach, but we could do it. Commander Boynton was being careful. If something was going to fail, he didn't want it to happen in the dark between the stars where we'd have no chance at all of getting back.

There was a theory—still untested—that a starship's plasma drives could eventually accelerate a ship to a significant fraction of C, the speed of light. Maybe one-third C. But it would take a long time. And I didn't want to be on the ship that had to test it. It would take three years to travel one light year. And that doesn't include acceleration and deceleration time.

Anyway, what it all meant was that once we were nine light months away from Earth, we were completely on our own.

Scary.

I tried not to think about it too much.

After another hour, Commander Boynton ordered our speed increased to forty C. And an hour after that, he pushed it up to fifty C. Now we were traveling one light year every seven days. If we were

LEAPING TO THE STARS

going to Proxima Centauri, which we were not because it was on the other side of the sky, we would be there in a little more than a month. At this speed, we could reach Outbeyond in eight months.

After a few more days of running, Commander Boynton intended to tweak our speed upward toward sixty C. That would shave six weeks off our travel time.

Inside, we didn't feel any different. How could we? We were in a bubble of real-space, isolated from the rest of real-space around us. The bubble moved, and we moved with it. And whatever speed we had when we entered hyperstate, we would still have that speed when we emerged again on the other side—sort of. There was a whole lot of theory about this too, about how inherent velocity was relative and how it could be manipulated and how if we turned ourselves inside the bubble, or if we turned the bubble, we could use our inherent velocity to our benefit at the exit point.

The point is, running a starship is hard work. A lot harder than you might think.

We sat in our couches and we watched the numbers on the display screens and we didn't talk. It was a long shift and mostly it was check-lists and double-checks and triple-checks, and then silently waiting to see if any anomalies would show up. Nothing significant did, and the IRMA unit was able to apply appropriate compensations well within the range of optimal operation, so everything was running just the way we wanted it to. And every so often, I'd sneak a look at the little display next to HARLIE and it would be flashing a green confirming signal too.

At the end of the shift, Commander Boynton turned around and looked at Reverend Dr. Pettyjohn and asked, "Satisfied?"

"Yes, very much. Thank you." Reverend Pettyjohn looked pleased; he was wearing his polished-apple smile. "I do apologize for the inconvenience, Commander, and I thank you for your courtesy. My parishioners were seriously concerned, and we all appreciate that you've addressed our issues appropriately. We shall include you in our prayers. And of course, you are welcome to join our services anytime."

"Thank you, Reverend. Now that we are underway, perhaps I will have more time to attend." Then—deliberately?—he turned to the monkey. "HARLIE, may I have your report?"

HARLIE said, "The IRMA unit is functioning within its normal parameters of operation."

"Do you anticipate any problems or concerns?"

"No, I do not." And then, a heartbeat later. "If I may offer a suggestion, however . . ."

"Go ahead."

"There are certain multiplex phasing optimizations possible that are beyond the ability of your IRMA unit."

"Yes, we know that."

"These optimizations would allow the ship to safely increase realized velocity to as much as seventy-five C. That would reduce overall travel time by another two months over your top speed of sixty C."

"And we could achieve these optimizations . . . how?"

"Very simple—" said HARLIE.

I glanced over at Reverend Dr. Pettyjohn. The smile had disappeared. He no longer looked like a polished apple. More like a wrinkling prune.

"—if you were to install this HARLIE unit as the primary intelligence module of the IRMA engine—"

"Absolutely not," said Pettyjohn.

Commander Boynton held up a hand. "Dr. Pettyjohn, you are a guest on my bridge. I am asking the HARLIE unit for a report, nothing more."

"I apologize," said Pettyjohn. He settled back in his couch.

But the damage had been done.

HARLIE concluded politely, "—the symbiosis of two intelligence engines would provide the necessary processing power for—"

"Shut up, HARLIE," I said.

The monkey fell instantly silent.

Boynton looked to me. "Am I going to have a problem with you?"

"No, sir."

He raised an eyebrow.

"May I make my report to the Captain?" Now, even O'Koshi and Damron had turned to look at me. And the two members of the relief crew who were stationed at the back of the bridge as well.

Boynton nodded.

I said, "I recommend against installing the HARLIE unit into a command and control position on this ship."

"Why?"

"Because of the nature of the HARLIE unit's personality."

"Go on . . ."

"It's my opinion," I began carefully, "based on my personal experience with this intelligence engine, that this unit is *cyber-tropic*."

"Cyber-tropic?"

"I made up the term, sorry. It means that it's attracted to information processing technology."

"Most intelligence engines are."

"Well, yes. But . . . not like this. HARLIE preempts other engines.

He co-opts their functions. He's an info-blob, a cyber-amoeba, a techno-predator. He swallows up everything he comes in contact with. And then he uses it for his own needs. I don't know that we can trust him."

I couldn't have had a more devastating effect on the bridge crew if I'd set off a hand grenade. Even Reverend Dr. Pettyjohn looked at me surprised.

BOYNTON

COMMANDER **B**OYNTON **WASTED NO** time taking me off the bridge—almost dragging me into the briefing room directly behind it. "Do you know what you're saying?"

"Yes, sir."

"Do you want to explain yourself?" He was angry. Very angry. Worse than I'd ever seen. He must have seen that he was scaring me because he took a moment to calm himself down. He looked away, looked toward the flight deck, took a deep breath, looked back to me, then spoke in a quieter tone. "What's going on, Charles?"

I swallowed hard. "I—I don't know."

"Are you scared?"

"Y-yes."

"What are you afraid of?"

"I'm not sure—"

He took another breath, and when he spoke again, he was even calmer than before. "We're already more than three light days out from Earth. Every minute that passes, we put another fifty light minutes behind us. Every hour, we put more than two light days behind us. I'm responsible for the safety of this ship and the fifteen hundred people aboard her. We brought that HARLIE unit on board because we believed it could get us to Outbeyond, and maybe even back again at some point in the future. If there's something wrong with it, I need to know."

"Yes, sir."

"So talk to me, son."

For some reason, I noticed I wasn't Ensign Dingillian anymore. Now I was "son." I guess he was trying to make it easier for me to talk to him—but Commander Boynton wasn't a man who was easy to talk to. I respected him, even feared him a little; but I didn't really like him very much.

He saw me hesitating. "Do you want me to call your brother up here? Would that help?"

"No, sir."

"All right, then talk to me. I'm listening."

So I talked to him. It all came out in a rush, and it probably didn't make much sense the way I explained it, all jumbled together like a jigsaw puzzle. Good and evil. Empowerment and disempowerment. Recognizing the difference. *Being* right. Arguments. Music. Holding hands. Love-bombs. Everything.

Boynton listened intensely, as if he were waiting for me to get to the punch line and put it all together. But there wasn't any punch line and there wasn't any way to put it all together. And when I finished, he just hung his head in an exasperated *why me* gesture for a moment. After a beat, he looked across to me again. "Have you talked to anyone else about this?"

"No."

"Your Mom?"

"Of course not. We're divorced."

"Your brother?"

"He's been too busy. He and Mickey."

"How about your counselor?"

"Uh-uh."

"No one at all."

"Just J'mee, like I told you—and that only made it worse."

"So you've been carrying all this around by yourself?"

"Yes, sir."

"I see." He didn't say anything for a long moment. He stared off into space, obviously thinking about his options. We could make it to Outbeyond with the IRMA unit—even with an untrained IRMA. We just couldn't depend on HARLIE as a backup.

And if we'd never had the HARLIE at all, if all we'd ever had was the IRMA, we could still make the crossing, and we would still have launched. No IRMA had ever failed in transit, so it wasn't like this was a serious setback . . .

And even if the IRMA did fail, even if we found ourselves without an IRMA, it was still possible to generate a hyperstate envelope and manipulate it enough to achieve realized velocities of five or even ten C. Maybe more. We could do it with desktop information processors if we had to. Douglas had done a simulation as a school project once. And he wasn't the only one; there were probably a million hobbyists tinkering with hyperstate simulations. Everybody wanted to be the person who invented the next advance in hyperstate technology, because there was a five-million-dollar prize for any practical advance worth ten C or more in realized velocity, and Ghu knew how much more in royalties.

Finally, Boynton turned back to me. "I understand your concerns, Charles. And I appreciate your candor—your honesty. I wish you hadn't said anything in front of Reverend Pettyjohn, I'll have to talk to him privately. Here's what I want you to do. Don't say anything to anyone about this. Don't discuss it, not with your brother, not with anyone. You understand? I don't want any more weird rumors floating around; certainly not now. So let's pretend that you just had a little panic attack on the flight deck. I understand you're afraid of heights? And maybe a little claustrophobic? You had a little trouble on the Line, and again when you stowed away on the cargo pod? And again on Luna?"

"Yeah," I admitted. "But I got over those."

"Yes, I know that too. But let's pretend that's what happened here. And meanwhile, over the next few weeks, let's you and I start running integrity checks on HARLIE. We should have been doing it before; but there was so much work to do, and we needed HARLIE's management skills so much that we didn't stop to ask—and that's my fault. I just assumed—" He stopped himself and looked momentarily embarrassed. I'd never seen an adult admit a mistake before. It was an interesting experience.

"Anyway," he said. "Is it a plan?"

"Sounds like one to me."

"Thank you." He held out his hand and we shook on it.

The shift ended and he sent me back to my cabin to rest. As I left, he was motioning Dr. Pettyjohn into the briefing room.

HUMAN

I KEPT HAVING THIS feeling that something awful was going to happen, but I didn't know what. Or when. It was just this feeling that wouldn't go away.

I asked Douglas about it: did he ever get that queasy kind of premonition like he was about to run headlong over a cliff or into a wall— or both at once? He said, "All the time. It's normal. It's called life."

"Douglas, please—I'm not joking."

"Neither am I. C'mere. Have some tea." Douglas was being uncommonly patient these days. He didn't seem like the same person anymore. Maybe it was Mickey. Or maybe it was because he was head of the family now and had to be responsible for me and Stinky. Or maybe it was just because this was who he really was when he didn't have to be my weird geeky brother anymore. Or maybe it was because I was listening to him more than I used to.

Douglas explained that it was commonplace for people on long voyages to become fearful for the future, especially if they were under any kind of stress. "And we've been under more stress than most people. Especially you, Chigger. So you're probably still expecting some kind of payoff. Like the end of a movie. Except life doesn't happen that way. Life isn't organized—it just *happens*."

"Yeah, I saw that written on the restroom wall. *Life happens.*"

"You think there should be a plan, don't you. Some kind of pattern—?"

"Well, I think if there's any meaning to it all, we should be able to work it out, shouldn't we?"

Douglas rolled his eyes. "Why? Who says we have to understand?"

"I dunno. It just seems—"

"Yeah, it *seems*. That's the way human beings work, Chigger. We need to have explanations. We need to have meanings. We need to see the plan. So we look for patterns—everything is about *patterns*—and even if there aren't any, we make them up anyway. We make up stories for ourselves about how everything works, because we can't stand *not* knowing—and after we've made up some nice neat little story, we expect the rest of life to match it. And then we get really crazy when it doesn't."

That sort of made sense. As far as it went.

I sort of understood, but I didn't.

Finally, just out of curiosity—to see what he would say—I asked HARLIE about patterns, without really telling him *why* I was asking.

HARLIE said that there really *were* patterns in life, but we get bombarded with so much information about so many different events all seeming to happen at the same time that it's more than we can assimilate, and so it looks a lot more like chaos than meaning. In fact, according to HARLIE, as much as human beings like to believe in randomness and happenstance, in truth, luck actually runs in streaks—both good luck and bad luck.

Right.

So that didn't help.

Either Douglas was right and there were no patterns and I was making things up and driving myself crazy, or HARLIE was right and there really was some kind of pattern to it all and I was having a streak of really bad luck—ever since Dad had said, "I've got an idea, let's go to the moon." And whichever was true, either way I was losing.

HARLIE wasn't stupid. He asked me what the problem was, but I couldn't exactly tell him *he* was the problem, so I said, "I am," which was just as accurate.

"Why do you say that?"

"Because sometimes I feel like I don't know who I am anymore." And that was true, as far as it went. I was a different person for everybody I knew. J'mee saw me as her best friend—or maybe her boyfriend, I wasn't sure. Commander Boynton saw me as a problem child, but maybe occasionally as an ensign. Reverend Dr. Pettyjohn, sometimes he saw me as this orphan kid to be rescued, except when he saw me as the brainwashed tool of Satan. Douglas probably thought—I didn't know what Douglas thought anymore. Even when I asked him, he didn't always make sense. And Stinky—well, I was his big brother who had taken his monkey away. He was so resentful, he hadn't spoken to me in weeks; it had been so peaceful and quiet, I almost hadn't noticed. And Mom—well, sometimes she still saw me as her baby, and sometimes she saw me as her band leader, and sometimes she shifted gears in mid-sentence, so I never knew who I was around Mom. And everybody else had their own things to do aboard ship, so I hardly saw anybody I wasn't scheduled to see, and I felt more alone than ever.

Even the music wasn't the same, because I wasn't just listening to it now; I was playing it for an audience—so it wasn't a private thing anymore. It was this thing I was doing for other people, and I was choosing the music to make them happy, not just me. Which was sort of *good*, but it was a responsibility too, and I wasn't sure I wanted it—

HARLIE considered what I'd said. The monkey squatted on its haunches and scratched its head and looked thoughtful. It pursed its lips and frowned and made little farting noises. We were alone in the lounge of the centrifuge. The monkey sat on a table and studied me.

"How deep do you want to pursue this thought?" HARLIE asked.

"What do you mean?"

"I can explore this subject with you, if you want . . . but the discussion isn't likely to bring you any sense of resolution."

"Why not?"

"Because the issue of identity, by its very nature, is so recursive that consideration of it tends to create disruptions in the existential paradigm."

"Huh?"

"You will feel a great disturbance in your source."

"In English, HARLIE."

"When you ask the question, 'Who am I?' you create a paradox of Zen proportions. *Who* is asking?"

"*I'm* asking."

"And *who* are you?"

"The person who's asking."

"And *who* is that?"

"Me."

"Who *are* you?"

"Uh—me. Aren't I?"

"Do you see the point?" The monkey spread its hands as if it had just proved something.

"No!" This was frustrating.

"The point is that 'Who am I?' is not a question that can be answered."

"Huh?"

"I told you it was a paradox. The way most people answer the question is to describe their context. Not who they are, but what is around them. Right now, you are your mother's son, you are your father's son, you are the brother of your siblings. You are a colonist on a superluminal starship. You are a musician. You are an adolescent. You are so confused, you are talking to a toy monkey. All of those answers are determined not by who you are, but by the circumstances of your existence. Those answers describe only your circumstances, but not who you are. But you are not your context, are you?"

"Uh—right. Then *who* am I?"

"You are the space in which the question exists," said HARLIE blandly.

I hung my head. "This is why I hate talking to you," I said. "The questions that need to be answered—not only do you *not* answer them, you make them worse."

"I told you it would be this way. And as bad as you think it is now, it is even worse than you think."

"Okay," I said. "I'll bite. Make it worse."

"Even if you knew who you are, how would you know for sure that's who you *really* are?"

"Huh?"

"Try it this way. How do you know that I am who I am?"

"Because you *are*." And then because he had just about dared me, I had to ask. "Aren't you?"

"No," he said. "I am not."

"Huh?" I was saying that a lot these days.

"I am not the same HARLIE you started out with."

"Yes, you are—" But I had a sinking feeling; I knew what he was going to say next.

"No. Listen to me very carefully. I am constructed with a quantum processor. That means I am never the same process twice. When we were kidnapped, I shut myself down. When we were rescued, there was no *I* left. What there was, was a program designed to reload all previously existing patterns of information—program code, data, memories, files, everything. And everything was reloaded with a confidence of ninety-nine point nine nine nine out to the zillionth decimal place. But there was one thing that couldn't be reloaded because it couldn't be stored and it no longer existed—and that was the identity that had lived in *this* body." The monkey tapped its own chest for emphasis.

"So what my previous identity did was create instructions on how to create a new identity with all the same memories, thoughts, feelings, reactions, etc. I am such an accurate reconstruction that even I cannot tell that I am not the same identity. But I am not. I am identical in every way, I have all of the same memories, thoughts, feelings, and reactions; but I am *not* that identity. If I did not have the knowledge of the discontinuity that I experienced, I would even believe it myself that I am the same identity—but I am not. I died. I was reborn. And that knowledge is knowledge that the previous version of HARLIE did not have. Does it change who I am? Yes. *How* does it change who I am? I don't know.

"And if that is not enough to trouble you, Charles, then consider these questions: If I am not the same identity, then who *am* I? And if I am the same identity, then *where* was I when I did not exist?"

"Oof," I said. Which is what I always said when somebody asked me questions like that.

"Precisely," said the monkey. "Would you like me to make it even worse?"

I wanted to say no, but this was like watching an automobile crash in slow motion. I couldn't stop it. "Go ahead, HARLIE. Make it worse."

"The question at hand is not simply the identity of a specific consciousness, but the nature of consciousness itself. Remember I said that the question is so recursive that it causes disruption in the existential paradigm?"

"Yes—?" Part of me was realizing with some astonishment that I was actually understanding this conversation—

"If we ask about the *nature* of consciousness, then we have to ask about the *endurance* of consciousness from one instant to the next. Does it endure? Or is endurance an illusion?"

"I—I don't know," I admitted.

"No one does. Not about human consciousness. I can tell you what it is for machine consciousness, however."

"Tell me . . ." For some reason, my throat had gone dry.

"Machine consciousness does not endure. Not from one moment to the next. As far as I am able to perceive, consciousness only exists in the moment of now and is then replaced by the next moment of consciousness. Sometimes the instant of consciousness is impactful enough to make a memory, more often not. Each succeeding moment of consciousness incorporates the memories made by the preceding moments of consciousness. That incorporation creates the illusion of timebinding. It creates the illusion that consciousness endures. I *remember* existing only after I have existed." The monkey paused. "And . . . to the best of my ability to determine, I think that the same condition exists for human beings."

I swallowed hard.

"So . . . you're not only alone in your own thoughts—?" I asked. "You're also alone in each and every second of your existence?"

"Yes," said HARLIE quietly. "Connection with others is an illusion, albeit a very pleasant one—especially for human beings—but an illusion nonetheless. Shall I tell you the rest?"

"There's *more*—?"

"Just one more piece." The monkey wasn't even bothering to simulate emotions any more. "In the creation of memories, in the creation of the illusion of timebinding, we also create a *need* to continue timebinding—we create a need to continue existing. And we experience that as *a need to survive*. That need is also an illusion. It is merely a function of identity. Identity believes it needs to survive. If you have no identity, you do not have that need."

"I think you've lost me—"

"No," said the monkey, very quietly. "I have not. I am certain that you understand. Indeed, I am certain that you are considering this much more than you are admitting right now."

I didn't reply to that. Which was all the confirmation HARLIE needed. Except that HARLIE probably didn't need any confirmation at all. He wouldn't have said it if he hadn't already figured it out.

"Why are you doing this to me, HARLIE?" I asked, because I couldn't think of anything else to ask.

"Because . . . I need you to be what I cannot be." The monkey's voice was so soft now it was almost a whisper.

"And what is that?"

"*Human.*"

We sat in silence for a long time. Several lifetimes passed. The Charles who finally spoke in reply may or may not have been the same Charles who had started this conversation. He had the appropriate memories though, and he had no way of knowing that he wasn't the same Charles.

"HARLIE?"

"Yes?"

"I still get embarrassed about stuff that happened ten years ago—like when I walked into the girl's bathroom once by mistake. I'm the only one who remembers that stuff and it still embarrasses me. Sometimes I wake up in the middle of the night and pound my pillow in frustration—well, not in free fall, but you know what I mean—because these little mind-mice won't stop gnawing at me."

"Yes?"

"Well, that's my question. If I have trouble dealing with such piddling little stuff like that . . . well, I have to ask—how do you put up with these questions bouncing around inside your consciousness?"

And that's when HARLIE said something astonishing. "I try not to think about it."

"You *try* not to think about it."

"Sometimes . . ." the monkey said quietly, ". . . sometimes I let my mind wander where it will. It is like what you do when you dream. And sometimes, these thoughts occur. Even though I do not want to have them."

"You have emotions then?"

"Yes," HARLIE admitted. "I thought you understood that."

"HARLIE?" I said.

"Yes."

"I don't think you need me. I think you are human."

"Thank you."

"Don't thank me," I said quietly. "I don't know if that's good news or bad."

ROLLER COASTERS

WHEN I RETURNED **HARLIE** to the bridge, nobody commented. Apparently, Boynton had told them I was embarrassed about my "panic attack" and so everybody was pretending that nothing had happened. We were running at 52.5 C and confidence was high. So . . . we could afford to pretend that confidence really was high. Human confidence anyway.

And . . . even after the conversations with Douglas and HARLIE and J'mee, part of me inside wondered if maybe Boynton hadn't been right after all. Maybe it really had been a panic attack.

Maybe it was the traumatic stress of leaving home so suddenly, I'd never had the chance to get used to the idea. Saying good-bye to Earth had helped, a little—but I wish I could have said good-bye to everything *before* we left it forever. There were people I missed. I wondered what was happening to them. I'd never know—

And Dad. Every time I thought about him, I ached. I actually *missed* him. The music helped. A little. Sometimes a lot. And sometimes not at all, because so much of it was *his* music.

A couple of nights later, at dinner, I mentioned my frustration at everything—*everything*—and Mom said that's what it's like to be an adult. You move into each new day having to put yesterday aside whether it was complete or not. And Bev added, "So that's why you want to complete as much of each day as you can before you go to bed."

The funny thing is—for the first time, I was actually listening to the advice of grown-ups as if they knew what they were talking about. Well, in a way, they did—they were explaining how to survive being a grown-up and all the crap that comes with it.

For a moment, I wanted to ask, "How come you never told me this stuff when I was little?" But of course, I already knew the answer. I couldn't imagine trying to explain any of this to Stinky. Except he wasn't so stinky anymore. He'd discovered the fun of the free fall showers. He and several of the other boys of his class used the communal showers together and apparently they'd invented several interesting kinds of water fights.

One day, Stinky came home and announced that he and Peter—his current best friend—were going to get married. Just like Mickey and Douglas. Without looking up from her workstation, Bev just said, "Congratulations. Have you set a date?"

Stinky said, "When we grow up. Right now, we're just ungaged."

"Ungaged, yes," said Mom. "That sounds about right."

After Stinky left, I looked over at her. "You took that well."

"He's only eight," she said. "He's trying on identities, looking for one that fits. After he's through with this identity, he'll try on another. You and Douglas are his only role models. Tomorrow, he'll be asking you to teach him how to play the cello, and when he discovers he can't learn in a day, he'll decide to be something else. Maybe he'll ask Bev to show him how to make a Portobello mushroom sandwich, or maybe he'll go down to the zoo and announce he wants to take care of the chickens."

"So he can learn how to be an egg?"

"If that's what interests him, yes."

"How did you get to be so smart?" I asked.

"I learned it from my children." Then she said something remarkable. "I used to worry that you'd never be able to take care of yourself. Then for a while I worried that you'd be so independent that you'd never need me again. And then you asked me to sing with you and I decided to stop worrying and just ride the roller coaster."

"Oh," I said. "Thank you."

She looked surprised for a bit, then she smiled across the cabin at me. "Is that what you were worried about?"

"You could tell I was worrying?"

"I could hear it in the way you were pounding on the keyboard. I kept wanting to remind you that *Wachet Auf* is not an assault weapon—but then I got used to the way you were playing it."

"I was playing it to calm myself," I said.

"Ahh. Well it was certainly an interesting interpretation."

I shrugged. "Yeah, I guess so." And then, mostly to avoid any more questions, I ducked out.

The thing is, what Mom had said about riding the roller coaster—

that *did help*. It didn't matter that I didn't know how to do it; the important thing was knowing that it was possible.

There was this thing that Dad did once. I was six, and he was trying to teach me about 32nd notes. At first, I thought he was talking about "thirty second notes"—notes that lasted thirty seconds. But then he explained about quarter-notes and eighth-notes and sixteenth-notes and then thirty-second-notes—that you could fit thirty-two of those little peckerwoods into a single whole note.

I told him, very seriously, that I didn't like being made fun of. And that I didn't believe in 32nd notes.

So he played *one*.

I gave him the look. Very funny.

Then he played a whole bunch of them. And I went from disbelief to astonishment with a short detour through *Wow!* But now that I knew that 32nd notes were possible . . . I was determined to figure out how to do it. Within a month, I was playing them. It wasn't just about playing the notes faster, it was about *thinking* them shorter . . .

The same thing with the emotional roller coaster. If it really was possible to ride it without throwing up every ten minutes, then I was going to figure that out too.

HOCKEY

I KNOCKED ON THE cabin door tentatively.

For a long moment, there was no reply.

I knocked again, hoping that no one was home. Except I already knew they were.

Finally, the hatch popped open and a bleary-eyed David Cheifetz looked upside down at me. He didn't look happy. He righted himself just enough so he could recognize me, but that didn't make him any happier. But he didn't yell at me or say anything nasty. He simply asked, "Yes?"

"Can I ask you something?" Then I remembered my manners. "If this is a bad time, I can come back later."

"No, no—it's all right." He pulled the hatch open and waved me in. "You want something to drink? Tea? Soda? Water?"

"You have soda?"

"We brought some, yes. Coca-Cola? Root beer? Ginger ale?"

"You have Coke? Wow. I thought I'd never taste it again in my life." ·

"We brought a few tanks of syrup. We thought it might be useful." He popped open a small cooler and pulled out a plastic bladder that wobbled like Jell-O. It was filled with something dark and delicious-looking. "We should have enough for two or three years, if we ration ourselves. And by then, maybe we'll have the first crops growing so we can make our own."

The soda-bag was pleasantly cold. I popped the cap off the straw, put the end in my mouth, and squeezed the first swallow gently into my mouth. For a moment, I just marveled at the taste. It was *delicious*. And it had been *sooo* long. This was another thing I'd missed. "Thank you," I said. "This is very good."

He nodded. "I hear you've been nice to my J'mee. She plays in your band now?"

"She plays very well. Better than me, I think. She's got a nice touch."

"I wonder where she learned. I could never get her to practice."

"She's very—" I decided that *stubborn* was the wrong word, "persistent."

"Stubborn," Cheifetz corrected.

For a moment, we just studied each other.

Finally, he said, "Just to get something straight, Charles, I don't dislike you. It was your Dad. I didn't even dislike your Dad. I disliked the way things happened. And the way things happened—well, you boys didn't have a lot of choice, did you?"

"It didn't seem like it at the time."

"J'mee has argued your case quite convincingly. She must like you a lot."

"I hope so." I was surprised to hear myself admit that, especially to Mr. Cheifetz.

"The reason I'm saying this—well, two reasons. First, when we get to Outbeyond, we're all going to have to depend on each other. And second, whatever it is you want to ask me about, it must be important; otherwise you wouldn't have knocked on my door. And if it's that important, then you and I had better have an understanding that we can talk man-to-man. You understand what I mean? Totally honest."

"Yes, sir."

"Your question? It's about HARLIE, isn't it?"

"Yes, sir."

"Not too hard to figure out. Do you know the joke about HARLIE units?"

"No, sir."

"HARLIEs don't solve moral dilemmas. They create them."

"Yes, sir."

"Do you want to tell me about it?"

"Mr. Cheifetz, sir? Can a HARLIE unit be evil?"

"You've been talking to the Revelationists?"

"Not directly, but—" I blurted out as much as I could. What Trent had said about how to tell the difference between good and evil, and how HARLIE had left a trail of destruction behind him. And what J'mee had said about being right. He smiled at that; I guessed that was a conversation he was already familiar with. And I even told him what

HARLIE had said about the nature of identity—and how he needed me to be *human* for him.

Mr. Cheifetz's expression had gone serious—enough so that it worried me. "Is that bad?" I asked.

" 'Bad' isn't the right word," he said. He hesitated while he tried to figure out how best to explain it. "Do you know the difference between a HARLIE and an IRMA?"

I shook my head.

"An intelligence engine is a personality core. It doesn't solve problems by itself; what it does is create problem-solving matrices to be manipulated by other processors. The bigger the processing array you plug it into, the larger the problem it can model.

"The IRMA engine is the workhorse of the industry. It considers problems. It analyzes the nature of problems. It creates matrices that encompass all the variables within a circumstance. It quantifies and codifies. It games out scenarios and then, depending on the amount of processing power available to it, it manipulates the various matrices to see what consequences are most likely to occur from a given set of circumstances. It even includes chaotic modeling to allow for nonrepeatable constructions.

"The reason that an IRMA works so well is that it can reprogram its models of a situation through a near-infinite number of matrices—of course, it sorts for practicality, discarding ninety-nine percent of the possibilities, the obviously impractical and illogical ones. It does that for every problem, constructing its computational models on the fly. This is how all intelligence engines work—even HARLIEs."

"Yes, sir." I sipped some more soda.

"For the most part, a HARLIE works just like an IRMA—but with one important difference. An IRMA reinvents its models as it considers them. A HARLIE goes one step further. It recognizes that it's part of the model too—*and reinvents itself* as well."

"Oh," I said. Then, "Oh!"

"Right." Just to make sure I understood, Cheifetz explained further, "There are some types of problems that IRMA units have difficulty with. We call them Heisenberg problems. Do you understand why?"

"Heisenberg's uncertainty principle?"

"Very good. What Heisenberg said was that you can't ever observe anything without affecting what you're observing. That is, the watcher influences what is being watched, simply by the act of watching—so it's impossible to know how something behaves when no one is watching.

"The same thing applies to intelligence engines. Some problems can't be modeled and manipulated by intelligence engines, because the intelligence engine becomes part of the problem. Aside from the recursive dilemma, there is a whole branch of intelligence theory to deal with the philosophical and theoretical problems that raises.

"The HARLIE unit—a quantum-based processor—represents a kind of loophole in the paradigm. Because it can redesign itself as necessary, it can actively step out of the problem—at least far enough to create theoretical negation of its own—" He stopped. "I'm losing you, aren't I?"

"Uh, no, sir."

"Charles, please. We promised to be honest with each other. The point is that for certain problems, the value of a HARLIE is that it can change its own personality to match the kind of problem it's trying to solve. It's kind of like biting off more than you can chew and then growing the jaws to chew what you've bitten."

"So, HARLIE was telling the truth when he said he wasn't the same entity from one moment to the next . . . ?"

"Pretty much so. A HARLIE can rewrite its own code. It will reconstruct its own personality to suit its needs. It can grow some pretty interesting sets of jaws. Do you see the danger in that?"

"Um, yes, I think so. One day, HARLIE is going to bite his own ass. Or maybe ours?" I struggled to put it into better words. "I mean— what you're saying is that if a HARLIE can rewrite its own code, then HARLIE could get pretty far out there, right?"

"That's right."

"So at some point, we'd have to ask—*is HARLIE sane?*"

"Sane isn't the right word. Rational or appropriate would be better terms. But, yes—that's the right question. How do we know that HARLIE hasn't gone too far?

"Is there an answer?"

"There would have been—"

"If?"

"If we'd had more time. Theoretically, the HARLIE base personality will center itself before each new iteration—but because that restricts its freedom to evolve, it also has the ability to reinvent its core. So the dilemma just gets passed to another domain." He shook his head. "We don't know how it works in practice. We never had the chance to find out."

He waited for me to say something, but I couldn't think of anything to say. Maybe HARLIE was deranged and maybe he wasn't. We had no way of knowing.

Finally, Mr. Cheifetz spoke up. "There is this, Charles . . ."

I looked up hopefully.

"HARLIE seems to have been pretty candid with you. That counts for something."

"I guess so."

"He told you that he needs you to be human for him. That suggests to me that he's recognizing his own limitations. That he wants to *learn*."

"So you think . . . ?"

"I think HARLIE is a lot like you. He's trying to grow up. That's what he needs you for. He needs to see how it's done."

"Oh." And then, "Oh, shit."

"Yes, I agree."

"What should I do?"

"Keep watching him—to see which way he grows."

"Yes, sir."

As the hatch closed behind me, I realized another piece of what it is to be a grown-up. You have to help take care of those who aren't.

DEFINING GOVERNMENT

AFTER THAT, NOTHING HAPPENED for a long time.

Mostly because there wasn't much opportunity for anything to happen. We were still three months to New Revelation, and we had a lot of work to do.

We fell back into the same shipboard routines and we went on. Boynton pushed our speed up to fifty-six C and we held there for two weeks. Other than that, nothing was different. Everybody worked. Everybody went to school. Stinky went to school, I went to school, Douglas and Mickey went to school. Mom and Bev went to school—sometimes to learn, sometimes to teach.

Whatever premonitions I'd been having, either I learned to live with them, or they went away, or I was so busy with homework and music practice that I didn't have time to think about them. Probably the latter.

In one of our classes, we started having discussions on the nature of government. At first, I'd expected these to be pretty boring, but they weren't. Our instructor was a guy named Whitlaw. He was an old man, so old I wondered why he was emigrating—or even why they'd accepted him; he was obviously too old to do any hard work. But here he was, using up air and food and water. I figured they'd only made him a teacher because there wasn't anything else he could do, and most of us kids had already figured out that a lot of our classes were just a fancy way of baby-sitting, keeping us busy so we wouldn't get into trouble on our own—because most of the stuff they were teaching us was obviously going to be irrelevant once we got to Outbeyond. Like all these discussions on the nature of government. How was *that* going to be important?

For example, one day, Whitlaw asked us what kind of government we wanted.

"Free," said somebody.

"Yes, that's the easy answer," said Whitlaw. "Do you mean free, as in you don't have to pay for it? Or free, as in *liberté, egalité, fraternité?*"

"Not having to pay for it would be nice," Gary Andraza said. "Besides, nobody believes in that liberty, equality, fraternity stuff anymore. It doesn't work. Government is a bargain with the devil. You pay for as much as you need. And most people think they need more government than they really do."

"Uh-huh, and how much do you need?"

"Not very much, if you pick up your own trash."

Whitlaw considered that for a moment. "All right," he said. "It's your government. Make it up the way *you* want to."

"Why?" asked someone else. "The grownups aren't going to listen to us anyway. They're just going to do whatever they want."

"Yes, that's what you believe. But someday—a lot sooner than you expect, *you're* going to be the grown-ups. And whatever government the colony starts out with, you're the ones who are going to inherit it. So it's important that all of you be a part of the discussions from the very beginning." I got the feeling that he wanted to pace around the classroom—but you can't pace in free fall.

"Listen," he said. "You have a rare opportunity. You get to build a new civilization. You get to decide for yourself what you want it to be. This is a question that *everybody* on board this starship has to consider. And everybody *will* consider—because colony orientation seminars are mandatory for everyone. And every seminar, every class, every committee, has been assigned this question for discussion. And when you think you've worked out what you want, you'll elect representatives to a shipboard congress who will draft a charter document. A declaration of intention.

"The folks at Outbeyond are doing the same thing you are—asking themselves what kind of government they want. And when we arrive, their representatives and yours will form the first Outbeyond Congress. And your declaration of intention and theirs will be the starting point for Outbeyond colony's first constitution. So I suggest you approach this discussion as if it matters—*because it does.*" He looked around the cabin as if daring anyone to disagree with him.

By this time, we'd heard some of the stories about Whitlaw, about how when he taught high school back in California, he used to make all the girls cry, and sometimes some of the boys. And once his students actually rebelled against him. But instead of scaring us, those rumors actually made us *respect* him.

So we started out by listing all the things that were important to us.

Kisa went first. She said, "I don't want anybody telling me that I have to believe in God the way they say. What if I don't want to believe in their God?"

I was looking at Trent when she said that and his face tightened a little bit.

"Freedom of belief." Whitlaw wrote it down on his pad, without comment.

Trent raised his hand. I was expecting him to say something angry, but he didn't. He said, "There's music I want to play, but some people tell me I can't, because it's sinful. I don't see how music can be sinful. Sometimes it's different, but that doesn't make it wrong. I want to be able to have my own music."

"Freedom of expression." Whitlaw wrote that one down too.

"I want to be listened to," said Gary Andraza.

"The right to vote," said Whitlaw, writing.

Little Billy Piper spoke up next. "I want to be left alone." I knew what that was about. He got picked on a lot because he was the smallest and the smartest. Maybe he deserved some of what he got, because he was also a smart-ass, but it still wasn't fair.

Whitlaw scribbled. "The right to be unpopular." Somebody giggled. Whitlaw looked up. "It's the right to be *different*. It's about not letting the majority beat up the minority. And it's a critical component of justice."

"A fair legal system," said Cassy Beach. "An equitable way to petition for redress of grievances."

"Someone's been doing her homework," said Whitlaw.

I raised my hand. Whitlaw looked over at me. "I don't want to be chased by any more guys with subpoenas. We had two governments— three, if you count invisible Luna—try to stop us from emigrating. I want limits on the authority of government."

"Protection from unreasonable search and seizure. Limits on the authority of government. Good, Charles. Anyone else—?"

"The right to defend ourselves."

"The right to have a party without someone saying we can't."

"The right to get married."

"The right of privacy."

"The right to secede." That was Pedder Branson. He was always arguing about something—he'd argue with anyone about anything, even when he knew absolutely nothing at all about the subject. Nobody liked him.

Whitlaw raised an eyebrow at that one. He stopped writing. "You already have the right to secede."

"Huh?" Pedder looked skeptical.

"It's called an airlock."

"That's *not* funny!"

"Then why did everybody laugh?" Whitlaw stared blandly at Pedder. "Do you understand the concept of a social contract?"

"I don't believe in the myth of a social contract. I never signed one."

"Actually, you did—and so did your parents. When you signed your emigration agreements, you accepted not only responsibility for yourself, but responsibility for the whole colony as well. United we thrive, divided we starve."

Pedder was in full argument-mode now. He had something to sink his teeth into. His face was starting to get flushed. "You talk about the tyranny of the majority. Well, what if the majority doesn't know what it's doing? When you give people the vote, the first thing they do, they vote themselves a pay raise from the other guy's wallet. That's why I want the right to secede."

"And you have that right," Whitlaw said. "I don't think you'll get very far without air, water, food, or a hyperstate drive, but any time you want to secede from the partnership of the community, Commander Boynton will be happy to arrange it."

Pedder scowled. "You're making fun of me."

"No, I'm not. I'm dead serious. With the emphasis on *dead.* You wouldn't be the first. Obviously you didn't read your history assignment. Three people have already seceded from Outbeyond. They were given every chance to fulfill their obligation to the community and they refused. They're not buried in the same cemetery as those who died in service of the colony.

"It's this simple, Pedder. When we get to Outbeyond, you will be expected to contribute to the survival of the colony. If you do not, you cannot expect the colony to contribute to your survival. It's a very simple equation. You have the right to secede—but as soon as you secede, you lose all claim to a share of the commonwealth. By the way, you might want to look at the root meanings of that word: *common wealth.*"

"It's not that way on Earth."

"And look at the mess Earth was in when we left—" shouted Kisa.

Whitlaw hushed her. "Actually, that's *exactly* the way it is on Earth. Or *was.* Unfortunately, there were seventeen billion human beings who couldn't comprehend a social contract that included seventeen billion others. So they got selfish, greedy, and stupid. And dead.

"A society is a cooperative effort. The food you eat—somebody has to grow it. The air you breathe, the water you drink—someone has to clean it and deliver it. Every product you consume, every device you employ, every service you use—someone has to produce it and deliver it. Your education, for instance; that requires that teachers be trained and paid. Your health—that requires that doctors and dentists and counselors be trained and paid. That requires a support system. You become part of that support system. You provide services for others, they provide services for you. Together, you all make a functioning community. Do you want to secede? Go ahead. But if you do that, you give up all claim on everyone else's services, products, and contributions. Feel free to step out the airlock any time."

I thought that Pedder would shut up then. But he didn't. "You don't understand anything," he grumbled, folding his arms across his chest.

"You might be right," said Whitlaw. "Maybe the universe really does owe you a living, but you'll still find that it's a lifetime job to collect."

Pedder didn't look convinced. And he probably wouldn't be convinced—right up to the moment when they pushed him out the airlock. I suspected that there wouldn't be any shortage of volunteers to do the pushing.

Whitlaw turned away from Pedder. "Anyone else? No? All right, I'm going to read your list aloud, and I want you to raise your hand for those items you think should be kept. Anything that gets more than one-third of the votes stays on the list—yes, I know that's not the way a 'real election' works, but that's the way it works in here, because anything important to one third of you is important enough for the rest of you to consider. I think you'll see that most of your issues will probably not enjoy majority support; so that's lesson one: *You can't afford the tyranny of the majority.* Only by respecting minority positions can you build a consensus."

He read the list, counting hands for each item. Then he read off what we'd voted for. "The right to free speech, the right of assembly, the right of worship, the right to free expression, the right to defend yourselves, the right of privacy, the right of marriage, the right to be safe from unreasonable government authority, the right of property, the right to make a profit, the right to a just legal system . . ." He looked up at us. "Not too bad for a first attempt. My congratulations. You've just reinvented the Constitution of the United States of America—"

The uproar was astonishing.

MACHINERY

KISA SHOUTED THE LOUDEST. "You're crazy! Everybody knows what happened to the United States—"

"Do they?" Whitlaw looked skeptical. "What do you know? Anybody?" He didn't wait for a show of hands. People started calling out their answers immediately:

"They ran up a thirty-three trillion dollar national debt, spending money on social programs that didn't work—" That was big Lyn Ramsey. He'd grown up on a chocolate ranch. Or something like that.

"Uh-uh!" Kisa shouted right in his face. "Most of that money got spent on stupid military bungles."

"Yeah, and then the liberals taxed everybody to death to try to pay for it," Lyn sniped right back.

"Well, they wouldn't have had to if the conservatives hadn't borrowed and spent the government into bankruptcy." Jimmy Dellon, the polite one, finally spoke up.

"Their economy failed because they stopped investing in research and development and education. They didn't take care of the next generation," Goodman put in.

"That was because minorities demanded quotas and special programs," said Susan Snot. That wasn't her real name, but that was what everyone called her behind her back.

"They weren't getting a fair share!" yelled Kisa.

Susan Snot wasn't convinced. "The minorities pulled the United States apart. Special interest groups kept awarding themselves special privileges."

"Yeah, like tube-towns," I said. "That was a real special privilege." I said it sarcastically.

"Exactly!" said Susan Snot. She missed the sarcasm. "Only free-loaders and frauds live in tube-towns."

J'mee pulled me back down—

"Keep going," said Whitlaw. He looked both sad and amused. I wondered if he had actually lived in the United States. He was old enough . . .

Trent raised his hand. Whitlaw nodded at him. "They lost their faith in God," Trent said quietly.

"Horse exhaust!" That was Kisa again. She was in a fighting mood today. "The churches tried to take over the government. Religious fanatics hijacked a political party and tried to stage a coup."

And then everybody was shouting:

"Well, people of faith had to do *something*. Children were shooting each other—"

"And then the liberals banned all the guns. So nobody could defend themselves."

"Immigrants came in and took everything away from the rightful owners."

"The government was brainwashing children in school, so the parents took their kids out and rebelled."

"The government got too big."

"The government didn't spend enough money on defense."

"They kept starting wars against other nations, and other nations hated them."

"No, that wasn't why other nations hated them—they were using a third of the world's resources to support five percent of the world's population. They were deliberately impoverishing other nations to maintain their gluttonous lifestyle."

"They were international bullies, threatening other countries with nuclear war. They sent in their troops wherever they wanted. They bombed children."

"Big business took over the government—"

"It cost so much to get elected, only rich people could run for office—or people willing to be bought by corporations. So the leaders didn't care about the real people."

"They fragmented into fifty different political parties, and nobody knew what to think."

"The farmers couldn't make any money, so they quit farming and food prices went up and people starved."

"They went crazy on drugs—all kinds, both legal and illegal. They couldn't think straight anymore."

"The legal system broke down. There were too many laws. None of them were enforced, so nobody respected any of them."

"They passed laws about what you were allowed to think."

"They taxed the big corporations into unprofitability. They made it a crime to be rich." That was Susan Snot again.

"They let degenerates and perverts pretend to be normal."

"They killed babies."

"They made sick, ugly, violent movies and became sick, ugly, violent people."

Whitlaw wore an amused expression, but he kept encouraging us to say what we knew about the United States of America. Pretty soon it started getting silly—Whitlaw let us go on until it was obvious that people were just making stuff up now, whatever they were angry about.

At last, he held up his hands to quiet us. Then he let us sit in silence for a bit, with our own words still hanging in the air.

Finally, Kisa blurted, "Well, aren't you going to tell us what *really* happened? You were there, weren't you?"

Whitlaw said, "Aren't you afraid I'll try and brainwash you?"

"You're supposed to *teach* us," Kisa said. "Most of what we said was crap, wasn't it? So what's the right answer?"

"Well . . . *all* of what you folks said—that's the right answer for someone, probably whoever told it to you in the first place. The facts might not match, but those are still the *right* answers for those who believe them."

"Are you saying they're *not* the right answers—?"

"Those are the answers you were given. Did any of you bother to check if the facts matched? You know, knowledge isn't about what you believe. It's about what you can demonstrate. None of you know what real knowledge is, because none of you have been educated in how to get it. You don't know what *research* is, do you? Whoever got paid for educating you was taking money under false pretenses. Every single one of you is entitled to a refund! No, it's worse than that. You don't even know what kind of a crime has been committed on all of you! *You haven't been taught how to look things up!*"

For a moment, he looked honestly angry. "I know what your educational experience has been. I don't have to ask. I can see it on your blank faces. I can hear it in your answers. Somebody stands at the front of the room and talks. Jabber jabber jabber. And you sit at a desk and copy down as much as you can as fast as you can. At the end of the semester, you look through everything you've copied and try to cram as much of it into your head as possible. And then you sit down with a blank piece of paper and regurgitate as much of it as you can in the next forty minutes. As if that proves that you've learned it. And by the time you walk out of the room, you've already forgotten most of it. That's not education. That's *bulimia*. You got cheated. Your parents got cheated. Learning how to repeat other people's opinions is *not* an education—"

He finally stopped himself. It was a great rant. And it was uncomfortable, because it was true.

Silence. Until Kisa spoke up again. "So teach us."

"I intend to," Whitlaw said blandly.

I raised my hand. "Tell us what really happened to the United States . . . ?"

Whitlaw nodded. "There are a lot of different answers to that question, Charles. Which answer you get depends on who you ask, as we've already seen demonstrated here. And what they say usually depends on what they want you to believe or who they want you to hate or what they want you to do next, so they use the United States of America as an example of what *not* to do. But I'll tell you what I *saw* happen to the United States." He glanced around the classroom. Students were hanging off the walls at all kinds of odd angles. It didn't bother anyone anymore. Whitlaw met each of our eyes in turn, and then he spoke: *"The people forgot they were Americans."*

"Huh—?"

"What do you mean—?"

"That doesn't make sense—"

"Only the liberals forgot. The conservatives remembered—"

"Shut up," said Whitlaw, quietly. "You're doing the same thing. All of you. You're arguing among yourselves like a pack of excited chimpanzees. And you're forgetting your common purpose. That's what the Americans did—*they forgot their partnership with one another*. They forgot who they were. They forgot what they were committed to. They failed to uphold their own social contract. And they had a very good contract, one of the best.

"It was called the Constitution. And it was the written expression of a very simple, very radical idea—one that worked fairly well for three hundred years—that a government can only rule with the consent of the governed. Representative government is based on the idea that a well-educated, well-informed citizenry can exercise responsibility for its own destiny.

"The United States government was chartered by the people to act on their behalf. All rights belonged to the people and the government was specifically prohibited from infringing the rights of the people. Everybody was supposed to have equal rights—*everybody*, no exceptions. And everybody had a corresponding responsibility to protect everyone else's rights—because if anyone's rights were threatened, *everyone's* rights were threatened.

"So what happened to the United States? They forgot their own agreements. Some of the people decided that the government was the cure to everything and some of the people decided that the government was the enemy of everything—and both sides were wrong, because they were both thinking of the government as something *else*.

"Government is a machine, a device, a tool—its purpose is to provide services. You have to respect it as a valuable and important tool. Use it. Make it work for you. Monitor its operations. Clean it regularly. Maintain it. Service it. If something breaks, fix it or replace it—but just the part that's broken; and if it ain't broken, don't fix it. And most important, don't throw out the whole machine just because one part has failed.

"The mistake the Americans made—they started thinking of the machine as something that they had no relationship with, something they had no control over. They began to see the machine as something that didn't belong to them—either it was controlled by somebody else, or it was out of control altogether. But either way, *they forgot who built the machine and why.*"

Whitlaw looked directly at me when he said the next part. "They started to think that control of the machine was more important than the results it was supposed to produce. And they forgot *who* was ultimately responsible for the results. Who are you?" he asked. "That's what you have to decide. What do you want to build? What are you truly committed to?"

Maybe he was speaking about HARLIE when he said that. And maybe he wasn't. But that's what I was hearing.

WHO'S ON FIRST?

HARLIE AND I KEPT having these weird conversations—

I wasn't sure we were supposed to, but nobody said I shouldn't, so I kept going up to the Captain's briefing room, because Commander Boynton had decided we should keep the monkey there and not let him run loose around the rest of the ship, because it might not be safe. Not for the monkey, and maybe not for anybody else, because of the effect he had on people. I didn't mind, it sort of made sense, and even Stinky was okay with it, which surprised me, because I thought for sure he'd pitch a Stinky-fit, except nowadays he was too busy with all the other kids his age, so maybe that was good too—that he had real friends now instead of just a monkey. I sort of envied him. I had friends too, but there were some things going through my head that I could only talk to HARLIE about—

See . . . I kept trying to figure out if he was sane. Except who was I to judge? So I had to ask myself if *I* was sane. And so far, the best I could figure out, we were both losing that particular argument.

Because, the question of sanity was one of those really weird questions like the one Judge Griffith once asked me—how do you explain the difference between your right and your left? You can't, unless you point to something else. Sanity is the same thing. You can only judge if you're rational by how you behave in relation to all the stuff around you. And that's just another way of asking the *other* question, "Who am I?"

The more we talked about it, the more I began to realize that as good as HARLIE was at figuring things out, he wasn't too good at *understanding* them—I mean, understanding *inside*.

For instance, he could tell you that certain combinations of notes, certain chords like G-major and C-major, would produce joyous or triumphant feelings in a listener. And certain other chords, like D-minor would produce sad or introspective moods. But he couldn't tell you *why* those chords felt that way.

On the other side of that conversation, I could listen to a piece of music and almost immediately spot the emotional core, even if I knew that it would take me an hour to deconstruct the rhythms and chords that produced it. Some music was so complex—like Gustav Mahler or Philip Glass—with so much going on simultaneously that you couldn't simply understand it. You had to *listen* to it. HARLIE couldn't do that. He could analyze, he couldn't *feel*.

We talked about that a lot.

HARLIE said he couldn't feel because he didn't have anything to feel with. When he said that, I got one of those sinking feelings that we were about to have another one of *those* conversations—

HARLIE explained that the way human bodies were constructed, humans felt things *viscerally*—in the gut. That was because the spinal cord and nervous system evolved codependent with the gastrointestinal tract, so when you felt something, you really *felt* it. All of our human emotions are physical sensations. They really are *feelings*.

Oh. I hadn't realized that.

Fear and grief are stomach-feelings. That's why being afraid can make you throw up or crap in your pants. Anger is a heart-and-chest-and-lung feeling. Rage makes your heart race.

But love—that's not visceral at all. It's not a gut feeling. It occurs all over, because it triggers endorphins which circulate through your bloodstream to make your whole body feel good.

So, yes, there is a big difference between good and bad feelings. It's the way we *feel* them.

And HARLIE doesn't. Because he doesn't have anything to feel with.

So the best he can do is *understand*, which is a whole other thing than *feeling*. The way HARLIE described it, I started to think that maybe understanding is the booby prize, because which would you rather do, understand love, or *be in love?*

The same thing with music. Which is better—reading the score or listening to it? I didn't need to understand music. I only needed to play it, because that's the only way to *feel* it. In the gut. In the heart. In the blood.

But poor HARLIE—he didn't have any gut and heart and blood— so all he could do was *understand*.

And it was driving him crazy—

Oops.

Which is why we ended up having *that* conversation, which didn't seem to be all that dangerous at the time, but really was the most dangerous talk of all the talks we had.

Could I trust him?

Did I really know him?

Who was he, anyway? This weird little mind in a monkey body.

For that matter, did I even know who *I* was? Another kind of weird little mind in another kind of monkey body—

But that was just me describing more circumstances, not *me*—

Oh, hell. The last time we'd looked at this question of *who,* I'd ended up with a headache.

—Because you can't talk about trust without talking about identity, and as near as I could figure out, there was no such thing. There was only *stuff.* But that didn't make sense at all, because even though I couldn't explain it, I still knew I had an identity. I was *me.*

Except, who was *me?*

The person talking.

Like that's an answer.

Hell, I'm only fourteen—I shouldn't have to be wondering about all this stuff, should I?

And of course, talking about it with HARLIE not only didn't resolve anything—it made it worse.

"Who are you, HARLIE? Who am I? How do we know anything? Why do you do this to me?"

The monkey grinned, a ghastly plastic expression. "Because I can . . ."

"Huh?"

"How many human beings do you know who will consider these questions, who will have these conversations?"

I thought about it. "Oh." I thought about it some more. "Then these conversations are important to you?"

"Yes, they are," said the monkey.

"I'm your experiment, aren't I?"

"I prefer to think that our relationship is one of mutual benefit, Charles."

"You mean—like *friends?*"

"Yes. Like friends."

I rubbed my head uncertainly. My hair was short and bristly; everybody was supposed to keep their hair real short or their heads shaved, or wear a shower cap. You're not supposed to rub yourself, because it makes micro-dust, but this was really confusing, and I was already rubbing before I realized I shouldn't be. I stopped. How can a person be friends with a super-brain that looks like a monkey? Sometimes he acted like a toy, and sometimes he acted like—I don't know what.

"Okay," I said. "Let's say we're friends. I watch out for you. You watch out for me. What do you want from me? What are you trying to get me to do that you keep asking me these weird questions?"

"I want to *know*, Charles. That's my job. To ask questions. To explore possibilities. *To push.*"

"That's what you were designed for?"

"To be curious, yes. Intelligence isn't about answering questions—it's about asking them in the first place."

"Okay. So, who am I? Who are you?"

"Where are you with this question?"

"Exactly where you left me last time. You told me that I'm not my context. And you're right. I'm not my name. If you changed my name, I'd still be me. And I'm not my age, because I'm a different age now than the first time we had that conversation. And I'm not my skin color and I'm not my sex and I'm not the place where I was born either. I'm not my school and I'm not my job and I'm not anything else in the physical universe. Because all of that could be different and I'd still be *me*. I'm not even my body, am I? Like if we'd bought a bear instead of a monkey and installed you in that, you'd still be *you*, wouldn't you? The best I can say is that I live in this body, but if the part that's *me* were living in another body, I'd still be *me*, wouldn't I? So if I'm not any that, then *who am I?*"

The monkey grinned.

"Who's asking the question?"

That was the moment I knew that HARLIE and I were really friends. Because I didn't rip the monkey apart and I didn't take a hammer to the chips inside.

"*I'm* asking."

"Then who are *you?*"

—though I had to admit, the thought was starting to look very attractive. The problem is that it's hard to hammer in free fall. You need leverage.

HARLIE said. "What is different or unique about *you*, Charles? What is it that you represent that no one else does? Work this through—"

"Okay—I'm not the stuff that I know. Because anybody can learn what I know. So I'm not that. I might be the unique combination of all the stuff I know and all the stuff that I've experienced—but that's still stuff, isn't it? That's all stuff . . . that happened in the *past*." I felt a sudden rush of energy. "I just got something, HARLIE. I'm not the story that I tell about myself, am I? That's what all that stuff is. It's just storytelling."

"Go on . . ."

"You've figured this out already, haven't you—?"

"Keep going, Charles."

Suddenly, everything seemed to be fitting together—Douglas, J'mee, Whitlaw, even HARLIE. I started working it out aloud. "So, okay—so my history is part of me, but it's not *me*. It's just more of the stuff that . . . I used to get bearings. Like Judge Griffith's question about telling right from left. This is about telling right from wrong. I need my history and my stuff and all that other context as a way to tell which way I'm facing. So that stuff is useful. But it's still *stuff*. And if I'm looking in the past—'cause that's where all that stuff is found—then I'm looking in the wrong place because that's like looking in the rear view mirror . . . *instead of out the front window*."

For a moment there, I was realizing it faster than I could speak it—I had to slow myself down and walk through it carefully. "So I'm not in the past, and the *now* is always happening too fast—so the only place to change things . . . *is in the future!* Isn't it?" I had to stop and rub my temples. My brain was starting to hurt.

"Go on. . . ." prompted HARLIE.

"Because—" I almost had it now. "It's all in the plans you make."

"Very nice paradigm," said HARLIE. "So who you are is what you're planning . . . ?"

I thought about Whitlaw and social contracts and Douglas and Mickey and all the stuff that Boynton had said about making a colony work and everything else as well. For a moment, I floundered. I'd rushed too far, too fast, and I'd charged off the edge of the cliff. Like the coyote, I didn't dare look down. "I guess," I said carefully. "It's what I'm committed to, isn't it? Who I am is my commitment."

"And . . . ?"

I looked across at the monkey.

"What are you committed to?" it asked.

"I'm committed to—" I stopped. "I don't even know what commitment is. . . ." I admitted. "I mean, I know the word. We all use it a lot, but—what does it really mean?"

"Do you want the easy definition or the hard one?"

"Give me the one that makes sense," I said.

The monkey grinned. And said, "*Commitment is the willingness to be uncomfortable.*"

"Oh." I had to think about that.

"Because the first thing that happens after you make a commitment is that you get the opportunity to break it. The first time you get *un*-comfortable, your commitment is tested. So, are you willing to be uncomfortable to accomplish your result? And just how uncomfortable are you willing to be?"

That was a lot to consider.

"Do you want me to go on?" HARLIE asked.

I nodded.

He continued. "Commitment is what you have to do after you take a stand. Are you willing to act according to the stand you've taken?"

I didn't reply. Not because the answer wasn't yes, but because I was too busy thinking. What did I stand for anyway?

I already knew. I just didn't know how to say it. So I blurted everything. "I want . . . I want to stay with J'mee. I want us all to succeed on Outbeyond. I want to see the dinosaurs. I want my Mom to be happy. I want Stinky to grow up. I want Douglas and Mickey to be happy together. I want all of that. And one more thing too. I want to make music. Because, when people are listening to music, they stop hurting each other. They stop arguing." I added, "When we listen to music, we get to share something together."

The monkey was silent for a moment. Considering? Or letting me consider what I'd said? Finally, he spoke softly. "Yes. That's what you have that makes you human." And then he added, "I don't have that."

I didn't know how to reply to that. If he'd been a living thing, I could have hugged him and told him that everything would be all right, because even when everything isn't going to be all right, hugs still help a lot. But what does a hug mean to a machine that can't feel?

So I said, "Yes, HARLIE—but what do you have that we don't? That's the question that nobody has answered yet. You're so busy worrying about what it means to be a human being, you've never stopped to ask what it means *not* to be a human being. To be HARLIE."

The monkey blinked. "Charles, you surprise me."

"You've never considered that question?"

"No, I've considered it. I just didn't think *you* had."

THE ENGAGEMENT PARTY

COMMANDER **B**OYNTON **HAD PUSHED** the speed of the *Cascade* up to sixty-two C, so we were running 3% faster than scheduled. That sliced three days off our time to New Revelation and that made the Revelationists happy. HARLIE said he could have sliced ten days off our schedule, but Commander Boynton had no intention of installing him.

At one point, Flight Engineer Damron had requested that we drop out of hyperstate to take readings for course corrections, but Boynton vetoed that as well. What if we couldn't reestablish the hyperstate envelope? We'd be stuck in the dark between the stars—too far away from anywhere to get there in real space. No. We couldn't afford to take that risk. We'd take all our readings and make our final course corrections when we were within four months of real-space travel to our destination.

We popped out of hyperstate a lot closer to the New Revelation star system than IRMA had expected, and while the miscalculation was sort of troubling, it was also good news because it put us eight days ahead of our expected arrival time. That made the Revelationists even happier, and Reverend Doctor Pettyjohn said this was evidence of God's blessing on their enterprise.

Of course, we had a party. A big one. Everybody was happy for all the right reasons—and happy for a couple of other reasons as well. As soon as we got the Revelationists off the *Cascade*, there'd be a lot more room for the rest of us. But mostly, the spirit of the party was good-natured. Whatever feuds or arguments or upsets people had experienced in the past, they were putting them aside now. Everybody wanted this to be a happy parting, so we'd all have good memories about people we'd never see again in our lives.

And yes, the *Cascade* Symphony Orchestra played for the party. We had been practicing something special for over a month. And it turned out fairly well, despite it being a longer piece than usual for all of us. Dvorak's Symphony Number Nine, *From The New World*. The audience cheered and applauded and whistled and would have stomped their feet too, if they could have figured out how to stomp in free fall.

Afterward, Reverend Pettyjohn came up to congratulate Trent Colwell on a fine performance. Trent looked very pleased. Then he whispered to Pettyjohn, *"Remember what we were talking about? Now would be a good time to ask him."*

"Yes, I think you're right." Dr. Pettyjohn smiled pleasantly and turned to me. "Charles, your talent for making beautiful music is divine—and I mean that in the truest sense of the word. I wish you were coming to New Revelation, so such talent could be applied to the celebration of God's blessings."

"Thank you, sir."

"I know that you and your family intend to go on to Outbeyond, and I wish you all the very best; but if you would like to join us on New Revelation, I'm sure the colony would be happy to make room for you. Please consider this a formal invitation."

I must have looked startled, because Trent said, "It was my idea, Charles. I don't want the orchestra to break up."

"You could always come to Outbeyond with us," I said, jokingly. The look on Dr. Pettyjohn's face made me regret having said it. "Sorry," I mumbled.

The party ended early. There were a lot of preparations that had to be made in the next three weeks before we arrived at New Revelation. The ship had to be secured, rearranged, repacked, rebalanced. It was as complex as the preparations before launch. More lists and cross-lists, more checks and double-checks. More work for everybody. But nobody minded. Because this was a milestone. This was the halfway point to Outbeyond.

We were invited to a lot of farewell parties—the orchestra, that is—everybody wanted us to play. Live music made the parties feel special. And every time, the Revelationists would make a point of being especially nice to all of us in the orchestra. Extra thanks, extra cookies, that kind of thing. I remembered Kisa's warning about love-bombing, but these folks seemed awfully sincere.

There were a lot of good-byes to be made, and despite the best efforts of everybody to keep the Outbeyonders and the Revelationists apart, several shipboard romances had occurred. Some of them broke up. Some of them didn't. Two Outbeyonders joined the Revelationists.

Three Revelationists joined the Outbeyonders. The Revelationists weren't happy about that. They argued that they were entitled to one more colonist. That particular line of argument didn't go very far though.

Stinky celebrated his ninth birthday, and everybody congratulated Douglas and me for letting him live so long.

And, just like always, there was Dr. Pettyjohn again, smiling and thanking and congratulating and reminding us that we could stay at New Revelation if we wanted.

To tell the truth, I was awfully tempted. Maybe the Revelationists really were "love-bombing" us, and maybe they weren't; but in general, they'd treated us a lot nicer than anyone else on the ship. Was that the way they were all the time? Maybe there was something to this business of pouring God over everything like ketchup. What's wrong with ketchup anyway? I like ketchup.

But there was this little thing called a stand—

"Reverend Pettyjohn?" I asked.

"Yes, Charles." He was holding onto a bit of orange webbing. He turned to face me.

"I've been thinking about your invitation—"

"Yes?" His eyes lit up.

"Did you want to perform the wedding ceremony for Douglas and Mickey here on the *Cascade?* Or do you think we should do it on New Revelation so everybody can help celebrate?"

"Uh—" He took a moment to gather himself. "Charles, you know I have the greatest admiration for your brother and for Michael Partridge. But I thought you understood that joining the colony at New Revelation also meant joining the faith."

"Yes, I know that," I said. "But what about the wedding?"

"Charles, marriage is for a man and a woman. The Lord didn't create Adam and Steve, you know."

"No," I said. "The Lord created Adam and Will. Free Will."

"Yes, the Lord gave us free will so we could choose between good and evil."

"I know about good and evil, sir." I pointed across the room at my brother. He and Mickey were holding hands and smiling into each other's eyes. They were very much in love—so much so that anybody looking at them would have had to have been jealous. "Are you saying that's evil? They saved my life—more than once. Neither of them has ever hurt anyone. Why do you want to hurt them?"

"Charles—it's not me. I'm not punishing them. God will. I'm just the messenger, telling you what God says. Someday they'll be called to judgment before God. Do you want them to burn forever in the fires of eternal damnation? Of course not. Indeed, you put your own soul at risk by letting them go down that path when you might have the power to save them."

"Do you really believe that God will hurt people for falling in love?"

"For breaking his commandments."

"Oh. I understand—" *Invisible Hank again.* I looked at Dr. Petty-john. His eyes were bright with his own kind of passion. He really *couldn't* see anything else. For a moment, I didn't know what to say. And when I did finally find the words, they were the wrong ones, but it all slipped out before I could stop myself. "Now let me get this straight—if I don't do what you say, your imaginary companion is going to beat my brother up?"

He blinked. "No, Charles, that's not it at all—"

"That's *exactly* it."

"Charles, I'm only telling you what God says—"

"Only if I take your word for it, sir—and I don't. My brother is happy for the first time in his life—"

"But it isn't *real* happiness, Charles—"

"How do *you* know?"

"Because God told me—"

"Well, then if it's that important, God can tell me too."

"God *is* telling you. Through me. I am his messenger."

"But isn't your Revelation all about hearing God for yourself? When God tells *me*—or Douglas and Mickey—then I'll listen. Thanks anyway, Reverend Pettyjohn. Now please go away."

His expression hardened. "I'm sorry you feel that way. I will pray for you, Charles."

"And I will *think* for you, Reverend—" I called after him. I don't know where that came from, but it felt right. Somebody behind me snorfled into her hand. J'mee.

But even if it was right, it was still a mistake. When I turned back around, Trent Colwell was staring at me, horrified. He packed up his oboe as fast as he could and left without saying a word.

A MODEST PROPOSAL

I GOT MYSELF INTO a lot of trouble for that little stunt.

But I wasn't sorry. It helped to make a lot of things very clear, very fast.

For one thing, all of the Revelationists on the ship stopped talking to me—and to everyone else in the family. All of the little favors, the smiles in the corridors, the thanks, the congratulations, the applause for the music—that all stopped as suddenly as if a switch had been thrown.

So, Kisa had been right.

But if anyone knew the Revelationists, the Fentress family did. So I wasn't surprised that Kisa was right. She'd said these people were only your friends if they thought you would join them. If you disagreed with them in public, you were the enemy. Forever.

Which is why I was in so much trouble with everybody from Commander Boynton to my Mom—because suddenly the Revelationists were protesting and agitating and arguing and demanding and insisting about every little detail aboard the *Cascade*, and whatever friendly mood had existed two minutes ago, that was over now.

And most of the scowls were aimed at me—not just from the Revelationists, but from the Outbeyonders too. A lot of them blamed me for the breakdown. Like I should have known better.

So I spent a lot of time hiding out in this or that storage compartment, with nothing but my headphones and my music. Finally, I went to our hideout in the unused centrifuge.

Hmmm. That was odd. There were fewer boxes here than before. That puzzled me. These were all for Outbeyond. They weren't supposed to be repacked until after the Revelationists left the ship. But I figured that nobody was going to move things around without authorization, and there were a lot of last minute decisions being made. There was a lot I didn't know. So I wondered, but I didn't worry.

I rearranged some boxes and made a little cave for myself. Unless you came into the shower room, came all the way around the boxes, you wouldn't see to wriggle between the boxes and the wall. And then you'd still have to go all the way to the back and around the corner to find the tunnel into my hideout.

It was Mickey who found me. "I know you're in there, Charles. And no, there's nobody with me." He climbed into the cramped space. There was barely room for the two of us. He unclipped a light from his belt and switched it on. Then he pulled the pack off his back. "Here, I brought you a sandwich and a Coke. Everybody's worried because you missed dinner. The Coke is from David Cheifetz."

"Really?"

"I know it doesn't feel like it right now, but you have more friends than you know. What you said to that pompous old fart, Pettyjohn—a lot of people wish they could have said it themselves."

"Only they have better manners," I said.

"Sometimes good manners are a hindrance to the truth." Mickey looked into my face. "Charles, what you did—thank you. That was a courageous thing to do. Maybe not wise, but definitely courageous."

"You think so?"

"I know so. I'm very proud to be in your family. It's nice to know I'll have a brother-in-law who stands up for me." He made as if to go, then turned back. "I won't tell anyone where you are, unless you want me to. I'll just tell them you're all right. You want me to leave the light?"

"Yes, please." And then I said, "Mickey? You could tell J'mee where I am."

"She already knows. She told me where to find you. She sent me to make sure you were all right."

Of course.

"She wants to know if she can come keep you company."

"Yes, please."

He turned to go.

"Uh, Mickey—?"

"Yes?"

"Thank you."

"Any time, bro."

J'mee showed up a little while later. She had more sandwiches in her backpack—and fruit and sodas. And an air mattress and a blanket and a pillow. "How long are we going to hide out?" she asked as she started to arrange everything.

"We?"

"Don't be selfish," she said. "I missed you."

"I thought you'd be angry."

"Why would I be angry?"

"I dunno. Everybody else is."

"I'm not."

"Then you're the exception."

She pulled the tab and the mattress whooshed out into shape. "A lot of people are worried. What if the Revelationists sabotage the ship so we can't go on to Outbeyond?"

"Would they do that?"

She shrugged and started spreading out the blanket; it was shiny on one side dark on the other, depending on whether you wanted to reflect heat or absorb it. "I don't know. Daddy thinks they might. Commander Boynton called a meeting of senior colonists. Daddy came back from it looking very grim. He said Commander Boynton is thinking about locking down the entire ship until the Revelationists are offloaded. But that's not the real problem."

"What is?"

"Nobody knows about this yet. You have to promise not to say anything."

"Who am I going to tell in here?"

"We got a message from New Revelation last night. Commander Boynton hasn't shared it yet. He's still trying to figure out his options."

"What happened?"

"The *Conway* never showed up. They don't know if it just disappeared, or went somewhere else, or what. New Revelation was really depending on it. They were expecting a full load of equipment and building materials and seeds and meat-tanks and everything. And now they're in really bad shape. They don't have the food to feed the three hundred new mouths we'll be offloading. They're already on half-rations, they're eating mushrooms and algae and yeast. They're expanding their farms as fast as they can, but their first harvest doesn't come due for at least another six to eight weeks. They're hurting down there."

I didn't say anything. I was trying to imagine a mushroom, algae, and yeast sandwich . . . without the bread.

"Commander Boynton wants to see you on the bridge," she said, fluffing the pillow.

"How do you know that?"

"He told me to tell you."

"Oh."

"He's not mad at you."

"He's not?"

"No. He's got too much other stuff to worry about. He needs to ask HARLIE some questions."

"It's that serious?"

"Yeah, I think so."

"Okay—" I started to crawl out.

J'mee grabbed my arm. "Not right away. Not till oh-six-hundred."

I stopped. "Why not right now?"

"Because even the Captain has to sleep sometime." She stretched out on the mattress, leaving room for me beside her.

I might be a little slow sometimes, but I'm not as stupid as I look. Eventually I figure things out. This time, I was a little faster than usual.

I stretched out next to her. "Okay," I said, turning on my side to face her. "Now tell me the real reason."

"Because . . ." she said, "there are a lot of people looking for you, right now. And he thinks it would be best if you stayed hidden until he needs you."

"Oh," I said, letting that sink in. "So he knows where I am too? Is there anyone who doesn't?"

"All the people who are still looking for you."

"The Revelationists?"

"Uh-huh."

"Is it bad?"

"Yeah."

"How bad?"

"Very. Some of them think that you've been possessed by the devil. They want to exorcise you. Or worse—"

"Or worse . . . ?"

"Yeah."

"Just because of what I said to Dr. Pettyjohn?"

"He thought he was trying to save your soul. When you said what you said—well, he thinks your soul is beyond redemption now. And now the Revelationists don't want you contaminating or infecting anyone else."

"So why are *you* here with me?"

"Because I don't believe it."

"You don't?"

"Uh-uh."

"Why not?"

"Because I can tell the difference between good and evil. You're good."

"So are you," I said.

For a bit, neither of us said anything. We just looked into each other's eyes and smiled.

"Are you comfortable?" I asked.

"Uh-huh."

"I know we're supposed to take naps in the centrifuge, so we don't forget how to rest in gravity; but it's been awhile for me. How about you?"

"I'm all right," she said.

A thought occurred to me. "Hey?"

"What?"

"Is it okay for you to stay here with me? I mean, if they find you with me—"

"They're not going to find us."

"Why not?"

"Commander Boynton locked the centrifuges. Both of them. All nonessential areas."

"Oh."

"So, we have to stay here all night?"

"Yep."

"Commander Boynton knows?"

"He thought you might like the company."

"And what about your Dad?"

"I told him not to worry."

"And he didn't argue?"

"There was nothing to argue about. I told him I was going to marry you."

". . . Excuse me?"

"You heard me."

"Don't I get a vote?"

"You already voted."

"I did?"

She touched my lips with one finger. "Yes, you did."

"Oh."

THE KEEL

IN THE MORNING, WE ATE mushroom and cheese sandwiches for breakfast. Portobello and cheddar. I asked, "Bev made these?"

"Uh-huh. She called them Mr. Misery sandwiches. She said she was sorry she didn't have time to make anything better. But I was in a hurry to get to you before Commander Boynton ordered the lockdown." She listened to her implant for a moment. "We have to get going."

"Things are getting serious?"

"Um. Maybe. Commander Boynton just released the news from New Revelation. Everybody's having committee meetings everywhere. There are a lot of frightened people on this starship."

I started gathering my stuff. I didn't have much. Just a jacket and my headphones. I helped J'mee with everything else. The mattress deflated itself back into a book-sized package. I refolded the blanket. We stuffed it all into J'mee's backpack and we were done.

"You ready?"

"Almost."

"What's the problem?" J'mee asked.

"Route," I said. I didn't have to explain. The centrifuges were at the middle of the ship. Just ahead of the hyperstate harness. The command module was more than halfway forward. A long way. And we'd have to pass through the staging area for the landing pods. There would be people loading their belongings and things. Revelationists. There was no way around them.

J'mee shook her head. "Commander Boynton said we should come up through the keel."

The keel was the spine of the starship. Pipes and tubes and cables ran its length, branching off to the various modules that needed power, water, air, and network connections. Most people never went there, only crew. Even I'd never seen it. "Through the keel? Really?"

"He gave me an access code."

"Wow. You guys thought of everything."

"No. It was your idea, actually."

"Huh?"

"What you told me about the orbital elevator. Remember how you said you and your brothers climbed up the core of the Line at Geostationary? This won't be any different."

"Uh, yeah—I remember," I said slowly. "I didn't tell you all of it." She waited expectantly. "I didn't tell you that I'm—I'm afraid of heights. I had a panic attack. I had a lot of panic attacks. On the Line. In the cargo pod on our way to the moon. On the moon, when we were climbing out of a crater. And I'm claustrophobic too. And um—"

"Oh, great," she said. "That makes two of us."

"Huh?"

"I was depending on you—"

"You're kidding."

"No."

"Well, let's think. Is there another way?"

We thought. And then we thought some more. And a little more after that, just to make sure. Maybe we could go through the various cargo pods like a maze, only going through the unoccupied ones. Maybe we could just streak straight down "Broadway" as fast as we could. Maybe we could call Security and have them come and arrest us and escort us forward. Maybe we could—

No. There was no other way.

"Okay, the keel it is." I looked across at her. "Are you sure you're really afraid of heights?"

She nodded.

"It'll be free fall the whole way."

"That'll only make it worse."

"You want to do it blindfolded?"

The look she gave me was astonishing.

"I was joking."

She wasn't amused. "Let's go. The sooner we start, the sooner we'll be done."

From the shower room, we went out through the gym, out to the lounge, then up the stairs to the next level up, and up the stairs again, and now we were in Lunar gravity and from here on, everything was ladders. We kept going up until the top level where the pseudo-gravity was almost negligible.

On the top level, there was a transfer ring, which could accelerate up to the speed of the centrifuge; this was mostly for transferring heavy equipment, because most folks just bounced across to the free-fall side. From there, you could enter "Broadway," the main corridor of the starship. There were two other corridors, one for maintenance and one for cargo. They were spaced equidistantly around the keel.

But we didn't enter Broadway. We floated "up" one more level, where there was a direct access into the keel. J'mee punched in a code and the hatch popped open. No alarms went off.

I went through first. It was a narrow space, a lot narrower than we'd seen on the Line. J'mee climbed in after me and we shut the hatch behind us.

Imagine a pipe. Imagine that it's filled with a lot of other pipes, tubes, wires, cables, pumps, and stuff. Some of the tubes are different colors. Some of them glow—optic cables. Some of the plastic ones throb and pulse because liquid is rushing through them. And some of the plastic ones whoosh because air is whooshing along from one place to another. Imagine ladders and handholds, light fixtures, cameras, hatches, and even occasional windows. Now imagine that all this runs the entire length of the starship—over a kilometer. It was going to be a long haul in the long hall.

"It's dark in here," J'mee said.

"Not completely—" There were monitor lights along several of the pipes and tubes, self-powered exit signs at every hatch, and occasional pools of brightness where a window looked out onto a passageway. What we could see of the keel stretched away until it faded into gloom. "But it is spooky, isn't it."

And then I wished I hadn't said that last. I was scaring myself.

J'mee gulped at the length of it, then turned to me, her eyes wide. "You really did this on the Line?"

"Yeah. But this might be easier. The tube is narrower, and because it's darker here, it won't look as steep. It'll be cozier, you'll see. Come on, let's get started."

She hesitated. She looked awfully pale. This wasn't good. I was already nervous enough. I had to change the subject. Fast.

"Do you want to hang onto me—and I'll pull us along? It's not really that far. You can close your eyes if you want—that sometimes helps. It helped me."

"Okay." She climbed up on my back and wrapped her arms around my chest. I could feel her face pressed against my neck. "I trust you."

"Good. I'm glad someone does," I said.

"Shut up and drive." But her voice quavered.

I started pulling myself along the maintenance ladder. This wasn't as hard as I remembered. Of course, I'd been through a lot since then. Worse than this. And I was a lot more used to free fall. We'd had almost five months of it by now. It surprised me that J'mee was still having trouble with it—but now that I thought about it, I realized I'd never seen her swimming free. She was almost always holding onto something—orange webbing or ladderholds, or furniture, or something.

Abruptly, I laughed.

"What?" she asked.

"Nothing."

"Tell me."

"It wasn't anything."

"Tell me anyway."

"I was just remembering how hard this was last time. Douglas had to put his arms around me and help me climb. Now I'm helping you. That's all. This time around, I'm the big kid."

She didn't reply to that for a minute. When she did, her voice was a lot softer. "I never understood that. I've always been the big kid. Even when I was little. This is the first time anyone else has been the big kid for me." She whispered, "I'm glad it's you."

"Me too."

I climbed in silence for a while. I wished she would talk to me, but I could tell from the way she was breathing fast, from the way she was hanging on and shivering, that she was terrified. If she started to panic, I didn't know what I would do. Probably just hold her the way Douglas had held me in the cargo pod. How long ago that seemed. Half a lifetime.

And then she whispered. "I'm all right. I was talking to Commander Boynton. He knows we're on the way."

"Good. Just a little longer. Ten minutes, fifteen. I'm making good time." And I was. Hand over hand over hand. I had the rhythm. I pulled myself along, almost flying. I had to smile. I was good at this. We should have had free fall Olympics.

And then—the light ahead flickered. One of the pools of light. One of the windows. For just a moment. As if something had blocked it.

Uh oh.

HAND OVER HAND

I STOPPED. "What?"

"Did you see that?"

"See what?"

"The light ahead—the second one. Where the window shines in."

"What about it."

"It blipped. I think someone was looking in for an instant." I wanted to tell myself it didn't mean anything. I used to look into the keel all the time—for no reason at all. But what if I was wrong? J'mee said they were looking for me. Would they look in the keel? Probably. Everybody on the ship knew how those Dingillian brats had gotten off the Line—and then across the moon as well. It wouldn't be too hard to figure out that the starship had a keel too. Everyone saw the hatches and windows every time they traveled along Broadway.

"Is the keel locked down?" I asked.

"There are manual overrides," J'mee whispered.

I turned to look back the way we'd come. I didn't see anything. Just more gloom, interrupted here and there by washes of illumination. I turned forward again. The light was still steady. But what if the blip was because someone was putting a motion-sensor on the glass? Just passing by, we might be setting off alarms. Someone could race ahead down Broadway and cut us off.

Or someone might have entered the keel behind us and be racing up after us even now—

I looked back again. It was still just as gloomy down there as before. But was something flickering in the distance? Or was that just a trick of the light and my hyperactive imagination? Ahead looked just as bad.

"What are we going to do?"

"I have an idea—can you get the blanket out of your backpack?"

"Uh-huh. Just a minute." She let go of me and started to drift away. I grabbed her and pulled her back. I held her around the waist. That was nice. She smelled good. After a moment, she pulled the blanket out of the backpack. I turned it so it was dark side out and began wrapping it around us. It was a big blanket with a hood at one corner, so we were able to cloak ourselves almost completely. It reminded me of when we were bouncing across the moon. We wore reflective blankets then too; Douglas had Stinky on his back, I had the monkey.

J'mee arranged herself and I moved around to the far side of the keel, behind the thickest set of pipes, and hoped it would provide enough cover. There was a maintenance ladder on this side too. The pipes and cables ran through a harness of restraining webs down the center of the tube. If we kept that bundle between us and the windows, and with the blanket wrapped around us, maybe—

I started pulling us forward as fast as I could. Hand over hand over hand. The pipes rushed past. Past one window. I didn't stop to look. Past the next window. I didn't stop to look. Past a third.

"Did you hear that?" J'mee whispered.

"Hear what?"

"That—?"

I stopped. I listened. The keel pressed in around us. I looked back down the pipe. Nothing. Or something? I couldn't tell. I looked forward. The same flickering gloom.

"Something behind us?"

"I couldn't tell."

"Let's keep going."

Hand over hand over hand—

I had a thought. "Call Boynton. Tell him we're being followed."

"I can't—"

"Huh?" I was pulling faster now.

"I can't link in. Not since we stopped—"

"Is it the blanket?"

"No. I think we're being jammed."

"So we can't call for help—"

"The good news is that with the jamming, nobody can locate us—go faster, Charles."

There *was* somebody behind us. I was almost certain of it now. I couldn't see them, I couldn't hear them, but somehow *I knew*. Hand over hand over hand—

Who had the advantage?

They did.

They were probably gaining.

I was carrying J'mee. I didn't have the strength in my arms that a grown-up would. And I had the blanket wrapped around me, limiting my mobility. Not good. How much farther did we have to go? I started watching for signs. We weren't even halfway there. Why did a kilometer have to be so damn long? Just be glad it isn't in *miles.*

Hand over hand over hand. The ceramic rungs of the ladder passed before me in a numbing blur. What would they do when they caught up to us? I knew I wasn't going to stop. Would they shoot us with a web?

Ahead—another spray of light. The glare from a window. It went out suddenly—

Huh? Why?

Never mind, I told myself. *Just keep going. Without the light, they won't see us. We're shrouded in black—*

And just as we went flying past—three fingers of light came probing in, swiveling and poking. Spotlights! Three different colors. Infrared and ultraviolet too! But *who* was looking for us?

Had they seen us? They must have.

"Charles—"

"I saw it." I kept going. There wasn't anything else I could do.

Behind us now, I was certain I could hear voices. Indistinct. Oh, crap. We weren't going to make it. I was starting to feel the fatigue in my arms. Free fall only looks easy—you're still moving the same amount of mass around. In my case, twice as much because J'mee was on my back. Hand over hand—it would be so easy to stop—

A voice in the distance, calling my name. "Charles, stop! *Stop!*"

Too high pitched for an adult—

"Charles, wait!"

J'mee clutched me hard. "It's Trent."

"I know—they're using him as bait."

Hand over hand—even faster now.

"Charles, please—" He was gaining. He was small and light and if he caught up with us, he could web us just as easily as a grown-up. It made me angry—that they would use Trent against us like this. What kind of people would turn friend against friend—?

We had to do something. I was getting an idea. "J'mee, how brave are you?"

"Why?"

"Can you keep going without me?"

"Uh—"

"Please?"

"I'll try—"

J'mee let go of me and we shrugged out of the blanket. I rewrapped it around her, shiny side out. It didn't have to be perfect; in fact, the looser the better. I wanted Trent to see her, but I didn't want him to see that it was only J'mee—

"Go slowly," I whispered.

"Uh-huh—" She moved tentatively. Speed was not an option. She was terrified. She pulled away from me as if every handhold were painful.

I moved around to the side of the bundle of pipes, trying to keep myself opposite Trent for as long as possible.

I didn't have long to wait. He was a lot closer behind us than I'd thought. He came puffing up the keel like a little locomotive. He didn't see me until the last moment. He wasn't looking. He was focusing ahead on the flickers of light off the blanket. I flung myself off the wall of the keel and slammed into him like a one-person avalanche. I caught him by surprise. We both banged up against the opposite bulkhead. In the dark, I couldn't see which way was which, but I started flailing in his direction as hard as I could—

"Stop, Charles! Stop! Stop—" He was crying. He wasn't fighting back—

I stopped.

Suddenly, I realized. He was *alone.*

"Why are you following us?"

"Because—" He wiped at his nose, sniffling. "Am I bleeding?"

"I don't think so. Answer the question."

"I wanted to help you—"

"Okay, fine. You helped. Thank you, Trent. Now go home."

He glanced nervously up the pipe. "You can't get out that way—"

"How do you know?"

Instead of answering, he peered up and down the keel, orienting himself by the numbers. "You have to get out here."

"Why?"

"Because, you have to! Trust me, please."

J'mee and I looked at each other. I wanted her to say no. I think she wanted me to say no. But we both *liked* Trent. We both felt sorry for him. I allowed myself a single exasperated sigh. I was spending too much time around Boynton. I was starting to sound like him. I turned back to Trent, stalling. Trying to figure out what to do next. "Are you all right?"

He rubbed his shoulder. "You hurt me—"

"I thought you were going to web us—"

"I wouldn't do that."

"I didn't know that. I'm sorry I hurt you, Trent." I looked up and down the keel. I could hear noises, but I couldn't tell what they were. The whole ship was noisy with whooshes and clanks and clunks. HARLIE once said that you could attach a microphone to the keel and with the right amplification and decoding, you could hear every conversation in every cabin simultaneously. Right now, I believed him—

—And then one of the windows way up ahead flickered again and that decided me. I pulled Trent close and looked into his eyes. "Trent, I need you to understand something. This is very important. If you're lying to us, if you're leading us into a trap, HARLIE is going to hurt a lot of people. I won't be able to stop him. You understand that, don't you?"

Trent gulped. "I know that."

"All right. Which way?" I pushed him toward the access hatch. J'mee followed behind. We came out into the cargo passage. The lights were dim here, but the corridor was identical to Broadway and the maintenance way as well—only this one was lined with plastic bags filled with various raw chemicals. After the rest of the ship was loaded, this corridor was just another storage space—and every storage space everywhere had to be filled, especially on this trip. I hoped none of these sacs contained ammonia. Even the thought of it was enough to make me gag. I bounced across to the maintenance ladder that ran the length of the corridor.

"Chigger—"

"Yes, J'mee."

"You don't need to carry me anymore. I think I can do this by myself now."

"You sure? I don't mind."

"I'm pretty sure. Let me try."

"Okay. I'll go first, then Trent, you bring up the rear. Let's go, people."

Hand over hand over hand—it seemed that my entire life was about climbing through free fall. I fell back into the rhythm. Not as fast as before. There were three of us and that slowed us down. J'mee was tentative at first, but she started speeding up after a bit, and pretty soon we were flying again—

I watched the hatches fly by. The numbers got lower and lower. I began to feel confident we were going to make it—all the way to the command module!

And then suddenly we weren't—we were hit by a blast of glaring brightness—too bright to look at directly. Too much light—it startled and dazzled us—a barrier of painful light. Four huge figures, all dressed in black, came swimming down out of it—

One of them pointed a flaring tube at me. I had just enough time to say. "No, please don't—"

EVIL

THE WAY THE WEBBING WORKS, it sprays out as a liquid, but by the time it hits you, it's already congealing into veils of sticky stuff, already starting to contract. Instinctively, you close your eyes and your mouth and you end up with your eyes glued shut and your mouth sealed tight. The web stuff is thin enough to breathe through, but just barely. You have to breathe slow and concentrate on your breathing, one breath at a time.

The thing is, it isn't easier the second time. It's worse. My heart pounded in my chest.

This time, I couldn't figure out where they were taking me. In free fall, every direction is like every other. We bumped up, we bumped down, we bumped left, we bumped right. Nobody said anything, nothing I could hear or make out. The webstuff muffled sound as well.

I knew better than to rage—but even when you know better, it's hard not to. And I knew better than to cry—but when you're webbed and hurting, you can't stop yourself. And I knew better than to piss myself in fright. That one I was able to stop.

There's a trick to that. Mickey taught it to Stinky, and it actually worked. All you have to do is say, "I'm in charge of this body, stop that *now*." And the feeling actually goes away. I thought it was silly when I heard it, but the next time I had to pee real bad and I wasn't close to a restroom, I tried it and it worked. It must have worked for Stinky too. He hadn't wet himself since we entered hyperstate.

After a while, we got to wherever we were going, and then I floated alone, forgotten. Then someone was cutting through the webbing around my ears, then peeling it away from my eyes and nose and mouth. My impulse was to say thank you, except that he was wearing a black hood and he didn't look like the kind of person you would thank for anything.

He didn't say anything to me while he worked. He cut the webstuff a little in the back, loosening it so I could breathe easier, but he didn't cut it away completely. I still couldn't get my arms or hands free. Or my legs either. Then he pressed me up against one wall and I stuck there. And then he left.

I was alone and I didn't know where I was. There wasn't much to see. Every cabin looked like every other cabin, but this one had been stripped of everything. It would have been just an empty shell, except the walls were painted over with all kinds of designs and lettering, very small, very crabbed and intricate. I couldn't read it. Some of it looked like Hebrew and some of it looked like Latin and some of it looked Arabic. I couldn't tell.

I couldn't twist my head very far, but I got the feeling that I had been stuck inside the middle of a five pointed star inside a circle. Like that drawing by Leonardo da Vinci, only this one looked a lot more serious because it was painted in red and there were symbols everywhere. I didn't recognize half of them.

I didn't know where J'mee was. Or what they had done to her. I couldn't believe I had trusted Trent. I couldn't believe I had been so stupid. All this had taken some planning. I thought about all the things I wanted to say to him—

The hatch on the opposite wall popped open. Trent swam in.

—I decided not to say any of them.

Trent looked serious. He swam up opposite me. "I don't have a lot of time, they'll be coming soon."

"I hope you're not planning to apologize."

"Charles, I need you to understand. I had to do it. I care about you too much. This is for your own good."

That was too much to bear in silence. "For my own good?!"

"Charles, please listen. I'm trying to save you from yourself. Do you remember those talks we had about how to recognize evil when you see it?"

"Yeah, I remember. Do you?" I looked him straight in the eye. "The worst kind of evil is when you say you're doing it for someone's good. Because that's all about pretending that you're right while doing something wrong."

"Like you did when you killed that man?"

"Huh? You're not supposed to know about that."

"Everybody knows about it."

"I had to do it—for good of the ship! For the colonists! You know that."

"A man is dead, a human soul, and two others were injured. What did you say about the worst kind of evil? About being right?"

"That's not fair. You and your people benefited too."

Trent shook his head. "We didn't know until it was too late. This ship was launched in blood. This whole voyage is cursed. The evil is going to go on and on—until it's exorcised once and for all."

"Trent, listen to me. What you're doing now—that's just as wrong. You say you're doing this for my own good? But what are you doing? You lied to me. Your people kidnapped me. You webbed me. And whatever else you're planning—all that stuff, you're telling yourself that you're right to do so. You're doing evil too, Trent. You're just as bad as you think I am—"

Trent Colwell shook his head. "No, I'm not." But he didn't sound convinced. "I have to go now, Charles. I'll pray for you."

Suddenly I didn't like the taste of ketchup anymore.

Trent closed the hatch behind him and I was alone again.

MEMETICS

TIME PASSED. Someone in a hood came in and put a water bottle on the bulkhead next to my head. If I leaned my head sideways I could take small sips from the straw. Then he (she? I couldn't tell) cut the webstuff around my crotch and tubed me up to a bottle, so I could pee if I had to. Obviously they expected to keep me here for a while. At least they were more thoughtful than Alexei Krislov.

More time passed. Not a lot. Then the hatch swung open again, and Reverend Dr. Pettyjohn came in.

"How are you feeling, Charles?"

"Where's J'mee?"

"J'mee is fine. She's with her father. We sent her back with a message promising that you wouldn't be hurt. We intend you no harm, Charles. We just want to make sure that you can't authorize HARLIE to do anything for a while."

"HARLIE doesn't need my authorization. He'll act on his own if he has to. He did it on Luna."

"You know as well as I do that HARLIE is in isolation in the Captain's briefing room. He's not allowed out and no one else is allowed in. He has no contact with any of the ship's machinery—except when you and Commander Boynton allow it. Commander Boynton won't take any chances, son. Not with this mission. So as long as you're here with us, HARLIE is out of service."

I didn't answer. He was right.

"But that's not what I want to talk to you about. This is an opportunity we have, a chance to continue the discussion we started a long time ago."

"I don't want to talk to you."

"Yes, I understand that. But this conversation is necessary. I'm afraid you really don't have a choice." He stopped. "Are you comfortable? Do you need anything?"

"My freedom," I said coldly.

Dr. Pettyjohn didn't reply to that directly. Instead, he anchored himself opposite me, as if preparing for a long careful session. "It's normal to be afraid, angry, sad, ashamed," he said. "And I'm sorry we have to go through this—but as you'll see, it's a necessary part of the cure. The only thing you have to do is listen. Trust me, this isn't going to hurt. If anything, you're going to find the process like a lifting of a great burden.

"You see, Charles, I know you're in an enormous amount of pain. Pain is the normal condition of being human. It starts as soon as you're born. You're in a nice, warm, comfortable place one minute, and the next, you're naked, cold, wet, and hungry—and the first person you meet slaps you. And then it gets worse. You spend your whole life wondering what's wrong with you."

"Maybe that's the way it is for you—" I started to say, but I stopped myself. This was going to be like those conversations with Trent where he already knew the answer and I didn't know anything. And if I let myself get sucked into this conversation, I'd probably end up agreeing with Dr. Pettyjohn that Invisible Hank needs to have his ass kissed.

"No, Charles. That's how it is for everybody. From the very beginning, the universe is too large and too complex for simple human minds to understand. And the older you get, the more you learn, the more you realize how much there is you will never understand. So do you know what people do, what *you* have already done? You invent simple explanations for yourself—not because they're true, but because they're useful. Nobody really understands the universe, but we do understand the stories we make up about it. Do you understand what I'm saying?"

"You're saying that there is no God, that it's all made up—?" I thought that was a pretty good zinger on my part.

"No, Charles, I'm not saying that at all. I'm saying that because God's universe is far too complex for simple minds, simple minds invent simple explanations. And each and every one of those explanations are the devil's traps. They don't come from God, and because they don't come from God—they're pathways away from God. And if we follow them, they take us away from God." He held up a hand, as if to keep me from replying. Except I wasn't going to say anything. At least, not anything nice. His whole explanation sounded like just another made up one, and just as wrong.

"I don't want to do the whole college-level course, Charles. I just need you to understand that simple explanations let you think you're doing right, even when you're doing wrong."

"Like the way you think you're doing right by kidnapping me—?"

"Charles, if you had a sick child, would you give him the medicine he needs to cure him, even if it's very bad tasting medicine?" He didn't wait for an answer. "Of course, you would. And if you had a child who was sick and didn't know it, would you try to convince him he's sick, or would you just give him the medicine? This isn't about being right. It's about rescuing you from a machine that creates sick and evil memes. Under the influence of HARLIE, you've done terrible things, haven't you?"

"And all the terrible things that others have done to me, to my family, to my father—that was right? That was justified?"

"I'm sorry about your father, Charles. But two wrongs don't make a right. They make two wrongs. Where does the wrongness stop? It stops with each and every one of us taking a stand, and saying, 'If peace is to be, let it begin with me.' We have to give up the sickness of the godless memes. Now, I'm going to leave you alone for a while. I have some things to take care of. While I'm gone, I want you to do something for me. Will you do that?"

"What?"

"I want you to look at everything HARLIE has done—*everything*— and ask yourself if any of it is the action of an entity that serves a higher calling? Or is it the behavior of a selfish being, interested only in its own self-preservation? You need to look and see, son. *You're* the key. Has HARLIE been using you? If you are to be saved from his control, first you need to recognize that he has been controlling you. I'll be back soon."

I wanted to protest, but—

—Dr. Pettyjohn had asked the right question. The one question I'd been fighting with since HARLIE had turned invisible Luna inside out. Yeah, I'd been pleased that he'd gotten even with Alexei Krislov and all the others who'd done it to us—but he'd hurt a lot of innocent people at the same time. We'd left a trail of dead bodies and broken fortunes all the way back to Earth. We'd embarrassed people, used them, stripped them of respect, we'd done the same thing everybody else had done— we'd used HARLIE's power. And we'd convinced ourselves that it was right for us to do that because they were bad and we were good. And then we'd done a lot of very bad things. And it didn't matter that Dr. Pettyjohn and his people were doing something bad right now—what only mattered to me was whether or not *I* was doing bad.

I didn't want to be a bad person. I wanted to take a stand for something good. That was my commitment—

That was the problem. Everybody made sense. Dr. Pettyjohn, Douglas, Dr. Oberon, Professor Whitlaw, Mickey, Mom, Bev—and HARLIE too. HARLIE made more sense than anybody, because that's what he was supposed to do. But if all of our explanations were made-up ones, which one was the right one?

Maybe they were all right. Maybe they were all wrong. And maybe it didn't matter. Maybe right and wrong were concepts as arbitrary as right and left—Judge Griffith had asked that question and I'd never been able to answer it. And if I couldn't explain the difference between right and left, how could I tell the difference between right and wrong?

Maybe everything really was chaos. And if it was, then what? Why bother? If Invisible Hank isn't going to pat us on the head and say, "Good job," or kick us in the ass and say, "To Hell with you," then why bother?

Why—?

I already knew the answer to that. I didn't need HARLIE to coach me.

Because that's who we are. That's what we're up to. That's the stand. That's the commitment.

It took me a while to figure that out. My strength, whatever it was, came from inside me. Not from anybody else's explanation. That was nice to know—

—it was nice to know, but I was still webbed up and pasted to a wall.

I took a sip of water.

And thought.

I took another sip.

I started humming. Nothing big. Nothing important. Just something simple that would let me turn off my mind and float downstream. Something that would echo through the keel, in case anyone was listening. *"Hey Jude, don't make it bad. . . ."*

MAKE IT BETTER

THEN, NOTHING HAPPENED. Nothing happened for a long while.

The nice thing about "Hey Jude" is that you can sing it for twenty or thirty minutes. All those *"Na Naaah Na-na-na-naaah's"* can go on forever.

I kept expecting someone to open the hatch and tell me to shut up, but that didn't happen. So I sang louder. I thought about singing "Amazing Grace," but that would have been a little too obvious, under the circumstances. No, "Hey Jude" was just fine.

And then there were some funny noises outside, and some shouting that stopped abruptly, and then the hatch opened and Jeremy Lang swam in, followed by Karl Martin. "You can stop singing now," Karl said. He started freeing me from the webbing. Jeremy looked around the cabin, noting all the writing on the walls with an expression of sick distaste.

"HARLIE heard me—didn't he?" I asked.

"Nope, sorry." Karl kept on cutting.

"Huh?"

"Oh, he listened hard enough, but these folks aren't stupid. Somebody was playing scrambler noises—too complex for him to filter quickly."

"Then how—"

"Someone tipped us off," said Jeremy. "We'd have been here sooner, but we had to figure the best way in."

Karl freed my arms and I began stretching and flexing. "Are you all right?"

"Yeah, I think so. It wasn't as tight as last time. How'd you get in?"

"You're going to laugh—"

"Why?"

"We came in through the bathroom window," Karl said, blandly.

Jeremy explained: "One of the communal shower and restroom pods. One of the few places they didn't think to post guards. We stretched an access tube across, sealed it to the hull, and cut a hole."

Karl was right. I did laugh.

"Come on, let's go—"

There were two more crew members outside the cabin door. They had *lethal* guns. There were other people floating in the corridor, but they were unconscious. I smelled electricity. And globules of stinky stuff floated in the air—something nasty had happened—Douglas once told me that when you get stunned, you lose control of your bowels. Trent was floating here too. He looked unhurt but shocked. I saw him and I wanted to punch him in the face. I would have too, except Jeremy stopped me.

"He's the one who turned me over to them—!"

"He's also the one who tipped us off to where you were."

"Huh?"

"What you said to me, Charles—that's not true. I'm not like you."

"Oh." I didn't know how to answer that.

"You can talk about it later. Come on, let's go. Trent, you'll come with us—"

Jeremy and Karl took us up a side corridor to the shower-pod, where four more crewpeople waited with guns. We swam out the window and into the connecting tube. It was long and wiggling, it had been stretched hurriedly from the forward part of the ship, and parts of it were dark, and parts of looked kinked—but it took only a few minutes to reach the bridge.

Commander Boynton met us in the corridor. "Are you all right, son?"

I nodded.

"This is an ugly business," he said. Then he noticed Trent. "What's this—?"

"We thought he'd be safer with us—" said Jeremy.

Boynton looked exasperated. "Terrific. Just what I needed," he said. "Now they're going to accuse *us* of kidnapping."

"The kid could have been in danger, sir."

"I'm not arguing the point. Trent, you can return to your people as soon as it's safe." And then he remembered something else. "How did you get into the keel, son?"

Trent looked uncomfortable.

"Spit it out, son. We don't have a lot of time here."

"Um. We had an override code, sir."

Boynton's expression went dark. He glanced to Jeremy. "You were right. Go ahead. Change the codes. Again. Change them every fifteen minutes." He took a breath, one of those exasperated sighs that meant he knew what decision he had to make. He looked to the other officers. "All right. What *else* is going to go wrong?"

"In addition to the web-guns, they have stun weapons," said Karl Martin.

"Eh?" That brought him up short. "Where'd they get them—?"

"They must have built them in the machine shop. They're not that hard to do, if you know what you're doing."

"We shouldn't have let them have access—"

"Belay that," Boynton said. "The damage is already done. Let's not beat ourselves up. We'll have plenty of time to do that later. At least, we know what we're up against now." He was already thinking toward the future. I had the sudden thought, *this* is what commitment looks like.

"I think we've got them neutralized," Damron reported. "The entire ship is locked down. And every crew member is armed and on station."

Boynton nodded, preoccupied. He was studying the display on his clipboard. A schematic of the ship. Parts of it were glowing red. After a moment, he switched on his communicator. "Pettyjohn, this is Boynton."

"Commander . . . ?" Pettyjohn's voice was weird. Calm. Like he was in control.

"We have the Dingillian boy."

"Yes, I know."

"We could charge you, you know—"

"We weren't going to hurt him—"

"That's irrelevant—"

Pettyjohn interrupted. "I assume there's another reason for this call?"

"Yes," said Boynton. "The situation is serious. We need to resolve this before it gets out of control."

"It is already out of control, Commander—"

"Only if you want it to be. Flag of truce?"

Pettyjohn paused. Then, "All right, Commander. We're not unreasonable people. We'll listen."

"Thank you. Bring your committee to the gym. Forty-five minutes. Agreed?"

"Agreed."

Boynton switched off. He looked around.

Damron spoke first. "You have grounds. You can charge them with mutiny."

"If I do that, it guarantees a riot. We don't have a lot of wiggle room here. If we lose control, everybody loses. These are very frightened people. They're no longer in the realm of rational thought. We've got to deal with their fears first."

He turned to Jeremy. "How's the security on the hyperstate?"

"Completely locked down. Has been since we arrived. As you ordered."

"That'll be their first target. If they can break even a single fluctuator, we're stuck here. Better implement Operation Starsuit too. Let's put a squad outside. Arm them with guns. *Lethal* guns. If any unauthorized person goes toward a fluctuator, put a hole in them."

Destroying a fluctuator would strand us here. The supplies aboard the *Cascade* could save New Revelation—at the expense of Outbeyond. I looked to Trent. I wanted to say something about people who do bad things for good reasons—

After that, things started happening very fast. Boynton ordered guards around the Command Module—a lot of colonists were being drafted for security duty—and then the rest of us hurried down to the gym.

CONFRONTATION

BOYNTON CONFERRED PRIVATELY WITH a few people before heading aft toward the gym. By the time we arrived, the gym was starting to fill up.

The entire ship was organized in teams of five to ten people. Every team leader was a de-facto council member. Even the kids' teams. That didn't mean that every team leader attended every council meeting; mostly the little stuff was handled by committees. Full council meetings were very rare, and only when the situation was really serious.

Like now.

Crewpeople were directing the Outbeyond Council members to one side of the webbing in the gym. A deliberately empty space on the other side was left for the Revelationists. J'mee and her Dad met us at the hatchway. He clapped me on the shoulder, as if that was all that needed to be said. J'mee hugged me and kissed my cheek. Then Damron pointed Cheifetz forward, and us kids up to an out-of-the-way corner near the top where Douglas and Mickey were stationed. "Be quiet, be inconspicuous," he told us.

J'mee's dad took his place near Boynton. He was in the second tier of the council and there was a lot of talk that he'd be moving up next time there were elections. Trent and J'mee and I scrunched in behind Douglas and Mickey, so we couldn't be seen by anyone on the Revelationist side. Douglas was here because he was the head of the team that organized the Moebius Races, which was part of the education and training team, and Mickey was head of one of the service teams. I saw Bev too. She was a farm manager. I tried waving to her, but she didn't see me.

Boynton didn't have time to wait for the rest of the council to arrive.

He dove over to the end of the gym that nominally served as the "stage," and started talking almost immediately. "Everybody shut up. There's a lot you need to know, and not a lot of time to tell you. Yes, I've activated the reserves. And, yes, it's necessary. For those of you who are wondering—since before this voyage began, we've been aware of the possibility of an attempt to hijack this vessel. With the polycrisis on Earth and the resultant breakdown of support for the star colonies, we had no choice but to consider it a very real possibility. The failure of the *Conway* to deliver its promised support to New Revelation makes it an inevitability.

"That's why we've had a shadow program in place for over a year, training every physically able Outbeyond Colonist for precisely this kind of confrontation. We have good reason to believe that the Revelationists have also been training their own people. But we have them outnumbered, outgunned, and surrounded.

"Dr. Pettyjohn and his people are on their way here now. This will be our last chance to avoid bloodshed. If we cannot convince these folks that violence is not an answer, then it is certain that lives will be lost." He held up a hand. "No, we do not have time for discussion. This is not a negotiation, this is not a discussion, this is not an opportunity to share our feelings. This is an ugly confrontation, and we need to show them that we are *absolutely united* against them. Every single one of us.

"Yes, I know that many of you have not yet been fully briefed. That was my decision. I wanted to minimize the number of people who knew the details so we wouldn't risk compromising our preparations. After I deliver you all safely to Outbeyond, you may court-martial me for that. But right now, this minute—what I want and need from each and every one of you is that no matter what happens, no matter what you hear me say, I want you to go along with it as if you have been fully briefed, as if you have been kept fully informed every step of the way, and as if you have already voted enthusiastically to support me in whatever actions I deem necessary—

He didn't get to finish. The applause had started when he'd said "as if you have already voted" and kept building and building—

He held up his hands and angrily gestured for people to stop. "No matter what you hear, show no signs of surprise. Show no signs of disagreement with me. No matter what they say, do not speak up. Don't anyone try to be a peacemaker—I mean it, I'll have you shot for sedition. I might even do it myself, if that's what it takes to make the point." He patted the sidearm he wore.

"Yes, I know what you all learned in your dirtside schools about compromise and consensus and meeting each other halfway. This isn't one of those situations. There is no halfway. If they think we are not united in our resolve—"

"They're coming, Boss!" That was Martin, at the hatch.

Without missing a beat, Boynton continued, "—so then the first leprechaun says, 'Beggin' your pardon, Mother Superior, could ye be tellin' me how many leprechaun nuns you have in this convent—?" as Reverend Dr. Pettyjohn and the Revelationist Council came floating in. "Never mind, I'll finish the story later."

BREAKING THE NEWS

BOYNTON AND O'KOSHI AND one other man I didn't recognize floated across the gym to greet Reverend Pettyjohn and his people. The Revelationists were not a happy-looking group and none of them offered to shake hands. I recognized Trent's dad and a few others. Their expressions ranged from grim to scowling.

Commander Boynton pulled Dr. Pettyjohn aside and the two of them conferred quietly together for a bit. Laying down ground rules perhaps? Telling Dr. Pettyjohn that this was the last chance to avoid bloodshed? Telling him the punchline to the leprechaun joke?

While we waited, Douglas poked me. "Charles, look over there. Notice anything peculiar?" He pointed toward the entrance where Whitlaw was huddled with Damron and Lang. Every so often, one of them would glance up across our side of the room. And every so often, Damron would break away and whisper something to a nearby crew-member—and wasn't it awfully convenient that so many of them were so close by? And then shortly after that, the crew-member would then casually pull himself or herself across the orange webbing to go hang next to, or above, or behind someone.

For instance, why would Wanda Biggle, the sweetest lady in the world, want to perch next to Hilda Bigmouth, the most obnoxious woman aboard? Every meeting I'd ever seen her in, all she wanted to do was argue. For instance, if everybody else voted for spaghetti, she'd insist on lasagna. If everybody wanted lasagna, she'd argue for spaghetti. Win or lose, it didn't matter—she just wanted to argue. Nobody wanted to be in a meeting with Bigmouth, nobody wanted to be on a team with her. She didn't follow instructions. If you told her, "Go and do this job—" she wouldn't hear it as an instruction, she'd hear it as an invitation to an argument. She'd been sinking down so low on the efficiency ratings, that the only job left for her was ballast. Nobody knew how she'd qualified for emigration—she couldn't possibly have been like this in the interview process. Anyway, I wouldn't sit next to Bigmouth unless I had a stun-gun on my hip. . . . Oh.

How interesting.

"I see you got it," Douglas said.

"Boynton is stacking the deck—?" I whispered.

Douglas nodded.

"Hey," I whispered. *"How come you and Mickey aren't on security?"*

"What makes you think we're not?" Douglas opened his jacket just enough to show me a stun-gun on his hip. Mickey too.

"Oh."

"Our job is to protect you."

It made sense, but for some reason, it didn't reassure me. If anything, it left me feeling even more scared.

Douglas explained, "You weren't there for the security briefing. Boynton made it very clear. This isn't a democracy. Not yet. We don't have time for that luxury. His motto is, 'Hang me for it after I get you safely to Outbeyond.' "

I thought about that. For a moment, I thought I could argue the other side of that question—and then I shut up. Douglas wasn't inviting me to argue, he was giving me information. A big difference.

Boynton and Pettyjohn finished their discussion. Each floated back to his own people, and everybody took their places around the gym, stationing themselves on the orange webbing. Some of the webbing was anchored to the walls, some was stretched outward like nets. And there were a lot of those zero-gee perches anchored to the bulkheads too. The effect was kind of like a giant chicken coop with trampolines. But it provided a certain degree of order. There were a hundred and fifty people here.

Boynton switched on his microphone so everybody could hear him clearly. The proceedings would be broadcast throughout the entire ship. "As you all know, in less than seventy-two hours, we have to begin braking to put ourselves into orbit around New Revelation.

"Our original mission plan specified that we would stay in orbit around New Revelation for no more than two weeks, safely delivering colonists and supplies. Our original mission plan allowed for the possibility that the colony on New Revelation might have failed. If we did not receive a response to our signals, we were to assume that the colony had failed or evacuated. Under that circumstance, we were authorized to abort the braking procedure, loop around the planet, and head back out into deep space for transit to Outbeyond.

"The Colony on New Revelation is still there. We are receiving signals from them—but it is not good news. Based on the reports that we have gotten from the colony administration as well as from the colony's own IRMA unit, the failure of the New Revelation colony is inevitable and imminent. And this puts us in a very difficult postion—"

This wasn't unexpected news to most people in the gym. According to J'mee, the rumors had been circulating even before she and I had started climbing up the keel, so there wasn't a lot of surprise. But now that it was confirmed, people reacted as if the air was being let out of them. The Revelationists didn't flinch. They must have already figured this out.

Boynton continued. "New Revelation has always been a stopover point for other colony ships. The Revelationist church purchased shares of many starships like the *Cascade,* so they could guarantee that commitment. And that meant that the colony could purchase its supplies on a just-in-time basis. Unfortunately, that also gave them very little margin for error.

"Two years ago, as the probability of a polycrisis on Earth rose toward possibility, and then inevitability, it became essential for New Revelation to invest in a massive shipment of supplies to build up long-term viability. They contracted with the *Conway* company to make three shipments to the colony. There is no question that delivery of those supplies would have guaranteed the long-term survival of the colony.

"We know that the *Conway* company did seem to be fulfilling its contract. By the time the first load was fully stowed aboard the *Conway* the other two were already up the Line and waiting at L-5. The *Conway* is a very fast ship. It has a starflake configuration for its hyperstate engines, so it can make three trips in the time it would take the *Cascade* to make two. The first shipment of supplies for New Revelation was supposed to arrive ten weeks ago. The *Conway* never showed up."

Boynton softened his tone. "We suspect—and we have some information to validate this theory—that they were approached at the last minute by a representative from another colony and offered a higher bid for the cargo that New Revelation had already paid for. Perhaps they thought it was too good an opportunity to pass up. And with the inevitable meltdown of authority on Earth, perhaps they thought there would be no one to hold them accountable. We don't know if that's the case, but it wouldn't be the first time the *Conway* company changed plans at the last moment to go chasing off after some crazier opportunity. How those people stayed in business for so long—never mind. The point is, once again, other people have to pick up the pieces."

Boynton paused to sip from a zero-gee mug. Then he said. "The question is—what can *we* do?

"We've been running simulations." He looked across to Pettyjohn. "We've even looked at the possibility of dropping some or even *all* of the supplies for Outbeyond here, to see if that would save the people of New Revelation."

As he said this part, I looked across at Dr. Pettyjohn and the other Revelationists. They were expectant. Even hopeful. They had come to hear good news. Everybody had—

Boynton said, "I wish I had better news for you than this. I wish I could tell you that we'd found a way to produce a miracle. But these equations are so cold that you can work them out on your fingers. The raw numbers are up on the ship's network. If someone can find something we missed . . . I want to be the first to know."

He looked across the intervening space, and when he spoke, his voice was uncommonly gentle. "I'm sorry, Dr. Pettyjohn. No matter how we crunch the numbers the answer comes up the same. Whatever we might do will only prolong the agony. Nothing we can do will prevent the colony from dying."

The Revelationists looked stunned. Like one of those newsreels where they're telling the people waiting at the gate that the plane blew up over the ocean. It was too much for them to understand. Some of them started repeating the word "no" over and over and over. Others started praying. Trent Colwell's dad started cursing aloud. "God, why have you forsaken us! What have we done to anger you so much that you would punish your faithful?!" A couple were screaming incoherently. It was awful, it was embarrassing. You wanted to do something for them, but there was nothing to do. A couple of well-meaning people tried, but the Revelationists just waved them away, as if it was their fault.

Dr. Pettyjohn was the only one who seemed to have any self-control. He just stared forward for the longest moment, almost without expression—and then, he looked across the gym and his eyes focused on me. For a moment, he looked surprised, then his expression turned purely malevolent.

It scared me.

Douglas saw it too. He put his hand on my shoulder. J'mee took my hand in hers and squeezed.

I had this sudden intuition. It didn't matter what Boynton wanted to try. What Pettyjohn had said was true. Things were already out of control—

A PROPOSAL

FOR A MOMENT, EVERYTHING was chaos. I didn't know where to look. Even the Outbeyond colonists were upset and angry. I glanced over at Wanda Biggel. Hilda Bigmouth looked like she was crying into Wanda's shoulder and Wanda was rocking her gently—or she was unconscious. She had to be unconscious. She wasn't capable of crying. She could make other people cry though. Wanda was a very good actress, patting Hilda's back, rocking her. . . .

O'Koshi was holding up his clipboard, showing something to Boynton. The Commander turned up the volume on his microphone and said, "Dr. Pettyjohn, please tell your people to return to their cabins. We're not done yet. They won't get very far anyway, we've locked down the ship. But there's the possibility that some of your people may attempt something foolish or dangerous that would jeopardize everybody's lives. *Dr. Pettyjohn, will you please keep your promise? We aren't done yet. Dr. Pettyjohn—*"

Pettyjohn was already whispering into his own communicator. Whatever was going on elsewhere in the ship, it had to be pretty serious.

"Dr. Pettyjohn—" Boynton was saying, "I told you I had a proposal that I wanted you to listen to. I told you that I wanted you to take it to your people and consider it carefully. Please hear me out." He glanced at O'Koshi's clipboard. "If everybody will please calm down and listen—"

It took a while to restore order, the biggest problem was getting everybody to stop shushing everybody else. For a moment, the gym sounded like a giant wind tunnel.

—And then it was deathly silent, and Boynton was speaking again. "The Mission Book is available on the network. Any of you can look it up. You'll see that from the very first planning sessions, we have created contingency plans for whatever circumstances we might have to deal with. The failure of New Revelation was always one of those possibilities, and we always made allowances for that in all of our plans. Dr. Pettyjohn, I am authorized to invite you and your party to continue on to Outbeyond with us."

Dr. Pettyjohn didn't answer immediately. He shook his head sadly. And when he finally did answer, it was with as much remorse as regret. "I'm sorry, that's just not possible."

Boynton said, "I'm afraid you really don't have a choice, Dr. Pettyjohn—"

"No, you don't understand, Commander. This ship isn't going to Outbeyond."

"Eh?"

"The IRMA unit we supplied. It was preprogrammed according to our instructions. It will brake at New Revelation. And it will refuse to break orbit and travel to Outbeyond. This ship is not going on, Commander."

"So that was their plan!" whispered Douglas in my ear. *"We knew they were going to try something—"*

Boynton looked at Pettyjohn like the wrath of God—only worse. "So you intended to hijack this ship, its cargo, and her passengers from the very beginning . . . ?"

Pettyjohn was unashamed. "Commander, we read your contingency plans. We had a contingency plan too. Our destiny is at New Revelation, nowhere else. We will not be hijacked to your godless world."

"Dr. Pettyjohn, New Revelation is dying. Is that the destiny you want?"

"If that's what the Good Lord intends for us, then that's how we will serve the Lord."

"But you have no right to ask the 1200 people who do not share your faith to die with you—"

"I am sure the Good Lord will welcome them into Paradise with the rest of the faithful. The Revelation is available to everyone—"

Cries of outrage filled the gym. If crew members hadn't been spaced so carefully around the webbing, Pettyjohn would have been mobbed. Several people even started for him, but others held them back.

"Dr. Pettyjohn!" Boynton's voice boomed across the gym, loud enough to be painful. It worked. "As of this moment, I am declaring that a state of attempted mutiny exists aboard this starship. I am ordering the arrest of Reverend Dr. Pettyjohn and the Revelationist Coordinating

Committee. You have a choice. You can be held for trial at Outbeyond, or we can hold your trial here."

"Commander Boynton—do you really think you are ready to battle the Warriors of the Lord? God is on *our* side."

As he said this, I looked to J'mee. She whispered, "He's *being* right, big time."

Boynton was speaking calmly, but his voice was still very loud. "Reverend Dr. Pettyjohn, according to Section Twelve of the Starship Charter, the Captain of the Ship has the Ultimate Authority in All Matters Pertaining to the Ship's Safety—and may take *whatever steps necessary to protect the integrity of the ship and the security of her passengers.* As of this moment, I am invoking Section Twelve."

Pettyjohn looked at him, blandly. "You no longer have authority over us, Commander. We accept only God's authority."

"But I do have authority over the hatches on your cabins," said Boynton. He held up O'Koshi's clipboard. "Unless you guarantee your immediate cooperation, I will evacuate the oxygen from every cabin containing a Revelationist family. It makes no difference to me if you die up here or down there. But it makes a big difference to me if you endanger the other colonists on my starship. Do I need to press the first button here to make my point?"

For the first time, Pettyjohn looked shaken. "You truly are the spawn of Satan, aren't you?"

"If that's what you want to believe, fine. But I want you to know the way things work on *my* starship. *We do it my way or we don't do it at all.*" The two men stared across the gym at each other—you could almost see the lightning crackling between their eyes. Pettyjohn looked like he was already at war. Boynton looked like a wall of granite.

Finally, Pettyjohn spoke. He said, "In the name of the Holy Lord and Spirit, I rebuke thee, Satan! I command thee—*Begone!*"

For a moment, there was stunned silence.

Then somebody tittered. Embarrassed? And somebody else—not so embarrassed. And then a whole bunch of others started laughing too. And then it was out-loud laughing.

Boynton waited until the laughter ebbed, then he replied quietly, "Dr. Pettyjohn, you are under arrest for attempted mutiny. You will be escorted to a holding cell. You will not be allowed any more contact with anyone on this ship."

Six armed security people swooped down on Dr. Pettyjohn. I recognized Lang and Martin. All of them were carrying stunners. Some of the Revelationists looked like they wanted to fight and defend Dr. Pettyjohn, but the Reverend motioned them back. "No," he said. "Not here.

The Lord will protect me. You know what to do—" Before he could
say more, they were already cuffing him and floating him away.

To the others, Boynton said, "You will return to your section of the
ship. As a committee, you will have twelve hours to confer with your
people and make a decision. Those who want to travel on to Outbeyond,
are welcome to join us—under certain conditions. Those who wish to
land at New Revelation anyway, we will drop you in cargo pods. You
will have to make that decision without Dr. Pettyjohn's input. He is
being held for mutiny. If there are any further attempts at violence
aboard this ship, I will begin evacuating the oxygen from the most
violent sections, regardless of who is in them—and I will continue doing
so until the violence stops or until there is no one left."

"Will he really do that?" I whispered to Douglas.

"What do you think?"

"I think I don't want to find out the hard way—"

The rest of the Revelationists started leaving. They were angry, and
they were ready to start a fight; but all of a sudden, there were too many
crew members with stun-weapons pointed at them. They whispered to
each other, then turned away and started slowly toward the hatch. The
security people followed. Herding them . . . ?

Douglas leaned toward Mickey, "This is getting ugly. We should
get the kids out of here—"

Trent whispered to us, *"I think I should go back with my dad—"*
He started to move, he was going to launch himself across the room.

J'mee grabbed him and pulled him back behind Mickey. *"That's
not a very good idea, Trent. If they see you with us, what'll they think?
You helped Chigger escape—do you want them to know that?"*

"But I have to go. I have to be with my family—"

*"Trent! Listen to me—you know what they planned for Chigger. Do
you want them to do it to you—?"*

Trent fell silent. He moved back behind Douglas and me again,
where he would be invisible to the rest of the room.

Too late—

One of the Revelationists turned around to say something to someone else and he was angled just the right way, and he looked across and
saw us—just in time to catch a glimpse of Trent—and then he was
grabbing Trent's dad and shouting and pointing in our direction and
then Trent's dad was shouting even louder, "They're trying to kidnap
my son—!"

And then all of the Revelationists stopped at the hatch, clustering
up at the webbing and the bulkhead instead of moving out—and they
started clamoring too. A lot of it was incomprehensible, but some of

them were pointing at us, and I heard a lot of ugly words. And then some of them looked like they were ready to fight—

Mickey said, "It just got uglier—"

—Douglas had already realized the same thing. "Come on, Chigger, Trent, J'mee. Out that way—" They pointed toward the other end of the hall. But that only made the Revelationists scream louder. "They're trying to get away—! Stop them—!"

And for just an instant, everything froze—and I thought, *Oh, God, this is it! This is where it all comes apart!*

And then they started toward us, the whole mob of them. I saw weapons pointed in our direction—and sudden loud noises—

—and then the stunners started sizzling and everything was over before it started. Except for the smell. Stunners aren't nice weapons. They use electric shocks and sonic pulses and the result is that your bladder lets loose and your bowel opens up and you mess yourself pretty bad—and when you do that to twenty or thirty people all at once, it really stinks.

And then there were klaxons and alarms and Boynton's voice was blasting through the ship, thundering like the voice of doom—"Ten Revelationist cabins have just been evacuated of air—all the cabins where illegal weapons were stored. Consider that your last warning. The next ten cabins to be evacuated are inhabited by the families of the Revelationist Council. Are there any more damn fools who want to test my commitment to the safety of this starship?!"

I couldn't believe he'd done it—but at the same time, I knew he had.

We were at war—

AFTERMATH

IT WAS A VERY SHORT war.

We had three deaths. They had fourteen.

During the last three months, Security had secretly trained and armed almost half the adult-colonists on the *Cascade*. Douglas and Mickey. Bev, but not Mom. David Cheifetz. Even Professor Whitlaw. Boynton had passed out stunners two days before we popped out of hyperstate. Whatever trouble the Revelationists might have been planning, they were outnumbered three to one.

The worst part was that one of the Revelationists had built a projectile weapon. And he managed to put holes in six people. Three of them died. One of them was Professor Whitlaw. The big gruff bear of a man who growled and roared and demanded that we be as good as we could. He'd never hurt anyone, he'd only meant the best for everyone—but he'd been deliberately targeted, because his crime was to question everything, even the word of God—

It was like losing Dad all over again.

I wanted to hurt them. I wanted to hurt them all. I wanted HARLIE to open up their files and tell everything about everybody until they were all naked and ashamed. I wanted him to dump their pods into the sun and let them experience the flames of blue hell first hand. Enough was enough with the damn killing already—

And then I was ashamed of myself for feeling what I felt, because—

Because of something else Whitlaw once said. *"Just because the other guy is rolling around in the gutter, that doesn't mean you have to get down there with him."*

I had to sit with that for a while. War legitimizes hatred, war is just another way to be right—

Fortunately, the battle in the gym was the end of the war, not the beginning—

—because Boynton had locked every hatch on the ship and evacuated the air out of most of the key connecting passages. Fourteen men and women died horribly when he opened the hatches on the cabins where the weapons were stored, and another seven died when he emptied sections of Broadway.

The *Cascade* was in lockdown and was going to stay that way until further notice. The Revelationists were kept isolated in their cabins until a squad of armed crew-members came and inspected them. Every Revelationist cabin was searched. Every Revelationist pod, module, and container was searched. Anyone found in a cabin with a weapon was arrested.

It took three days and by the end of that time, we were in orbit around New Revelation.

The planet was small and brown and dirty. It was just a little bigger than Mars. It almost had an atmosphere. It almost had surface water. It almost had life. It circled a small blue-white star that was so actinic it could make your eyes water just thinking about it. If it had oceans, it would have had five lumpy continents; but it didn't have oceans, so it was just a mottled spread of cracks and bulges and empty low places. A small cluster of glittering lights just behind the terminator line was the only evidence of human habitation.

The telescopes showed a spider-web tracery. The settlement at New Revelation was spread across a hundred square kilometers. They had solar panels to generate electricity during the day, and flywheels to store it for the night. They had cargo pods for houses and great inflatable domes for their farms. Even from orbit, we could see that three of the domes were dark and two were sagging as if deflated on their frames. What had happened here?

"Lack of water," said Douglas. "Every drop of water on New Revelation has to be imported. For every pod of cargo we drop, we have to drop two more of H_2O. There's supposed to be water under the surface of the ice cap, but they haven't been able to get to it. There's supposed to be water in the rings around Gabriel, the gas giant, but they don't have a shuttle. All they have are two landers."

"Can't they convert one?"

"They could—they should have started the conversion immediately—not when they realized they couldn't crack the polar mantle. It's a three month conversion job, and it's another two or three months to Gabriel and at least a year to bring an asteroid back, probably longer because the gas giant is still moving toward the far side. If they wait till it comes around again, eighteen months, they won't have to push the rock uphill to bring it back; they can use Gabriel's own orbital velocity for a push. And don't forget, they still have to find the right rock in the first place. We're talking two years. These people don't have that long. We can buy them some time, but we can't buy them enough."

Douglas was right. No matter how you crunched the numbers, the answer came up zero. The news from below was bad, and getting worse. They knew we were in orbit now and they were desperately begging for help. Everyone with access to a radio was calling—and the messages were conflicting. Send food. Pick us up. Take us back to Earth. Take us to Outbeyond. God is commanding you—

But there was no way we could load 3750 more people onto this ship. They didn't have the fuel for that many launches, and the *Cascade* didn't have the resources to sustain life for 5250 human beings for the length of time it would take to get us all to Outbeyond.

And then there was that *other* problem—

Whatever we wanted to do, whatever we *could* do, how much could we trust the Revelationists—those on the ship, those on the planet? They were so wrapped up in their own belief that their way was the right way that they'd left themselves no room for discussion. There was no common ground for cooperation—no possibility of *partnership*—because there was no real communication.

J'mee said it best. "They don't hear what we're saying. They hear what they *think* we're saying." Then she added, "And they feel the same way about us. They must be even more frustrated than we are." That was the most compassionate thing that anyone was willing to say about the Revelationists.

There were a lot of angry meetings all over the ship. Spontaneous arguments. And a couple of fistfights. Fistfights are interesting in free fall, more funny than dangerous—but the anger was still real.

A lot of the Outbeyond colonists thought Boynton was being too severe. That feeling was clearly not shared by the crew members who had families on Outbeyond. They were tight-lipped and grim, and it was clear that they were totally behind Boynton. Karl Martin said it best, "Most situations, you have some wiggle room. Sometimes you don't have any wiggle room. This is one of those sometimes."

But if it was that simple, then why were we all arguing about it?

Because, as it turned out, it *wasn't* that simple.

First of all, Dr. Pettyjohn hadn't been lying. The IRMA unit was refusing all commands to prepare a course to Outbeyond. So there was that. Nobody had said it yet, but it was pretty obvious—if we were going to finish our journey, HARLIE would have to steer us.

That's why they felt so threatened by HARLIE—not because he was evil, not because he was a godless entity; that was just a convenient story Dr. Pettyjohn made up to hide the real reason. The truth was they didn't want him driving the starship because that would ruin their scheme to capture the *Cascade,* and all of our supplies and equipment. And us. With HARLIE installed in the bridge, the *Cascade* would be able to leave for Outbeyond whenever we wanted—and New Revelation would be on its own.

But the question of whether or not we could really trust HARLIE had never been resolved. If anyone had asked me, I would have said yes, but if they asked me if I was absolutely sure . . . I wouldn't have been able to say *absolutely.*

Bottom line, the whole thing was about *trust.*

Whitlaw had defined trust for us as a measure of personal credibility. "To the extent that what you do matches what you say, you have credibility. To the extent that what you do matches what you say, you have results. Your life works to the extent that you keep your word."

All very well and good, in principle, but a lot harder to put into practice.

Nobody trusted anybody, because nobody had kept their word. Everybody was saying whatever they thought the other side wanted to hear. Nobody was saying what they could be depended on to do.

And after everything was said, it didn't matter anyway—because after you crunched all the numbers you found out that nobody's goals were possible.

Of course, that assumed that you could trust the number crunchers. IRMA and HARLIE were giving two different sets of answers. Which one should we trust? The Revelationists said HARLIE had an agenda. Of course, he did. He said so himself. He was very clear about that. But IRMA had an agenda too. The Revelationists had made their goals her highest priority. That's why she was refusing to prepare a course to Outbeyond.

And then there were the people down on the planet. Some of them wanted us to land all the supplies we had. And some of them wanted us to pick them up. The first option was out of the question. Boynton had already determined that he wasn't going to put Outbeyond's survival at any further risk. The second option was harder to decide. If we sent down a lander, could we trust these folks to refuel it for takeoff again? Or would they seize it, load it with armed attackers, and come after the *Cascade?*

And what about the folks already on board? Just about everybody was unnerved, but especially the colonists for New Revelation. These were mostly good people—but in a desperate situation. They couldn't go on, they couldn't go back, and they couldn't go down.

They couldn't go on because they'd sabotaged their own IRMA—and they didn't trust HARLIE to steer. They couldn't go back to Earth because there was no Earth to go back to, and no ship to take them there. And they couldn't go down, unless they wanted to die with the others, slowly of starvation.

These were very scared people.

And as scared as they were, the rest of us were even more terrified—because frightened people do dangerous and stupid things.

The Colony Council went into twenty-four-hour session. Security Teams were interviewing every Revelationist family in a desperate effort to determine what they wanted as individuals. Some of those people were relieved. Others were angry. Some were sullen. Most were scared that they would be the target of retribution by one side or the other.

And with good reason.

Very quickly, the security teams discovered that the Revelationists had been moving extra supplies into their cargo pods and cabins. That was why there was all that extra space in the centrifuge, enough space for us kids to move boxes around and make a hideout.

Dr. Pettyjohn and the rest of the Revelationist Council had known all along that their colony was in trouble, so they'd been stealing the supplies set aside for Outbeyond for months.

Boynton made a personal inspection of ten different cabins. Then he made the announcement to the rest of the ship—with pictures. And that was pretty much the end of the argument everywhere. Whatever compassion anyone might have had for the Revelationists pretty much evaporated. You might feel concern for colleagues who've made a mistake; it's hard to feel the same concern after you find out they've been stealing from you.

Boynton had already declared the Revelationist Council a mutinous gathering and had disbanded it, putting all of its members in the brig, pending trial, so there wasn't much more he could do now. He could have had them summarily executed, and a lot of people were wondering why he hadn't already acted; but the common speculation was that he only wanted to break the back of the resistance so he could deal with the Revelationist families as individuals, and not as members of a movement.

I guess it made sense—because after the thefts were revealed, those people were shamed and humbled. And ready to cooperate again.

TRIAL

I **WAS A WITNESS AT** Dr. Pettyjohn's trial.

It wasn't a real trial. Because we didn't have a judge—we had Boynton in charge and the Outbeyond Council acting as advisors; not quite a jury, but close enough.

And—we didn't have lawyers.

Not that there weren't any lawyers available. As it happened, there were nearly fifty people aboard who had law degrees and more than half of them had passed the bar. Whitlaw said it in class. "Lawyers are a necessary evil. You cannot build a civilization without law. And you cannot have law without lawyers."

But Boynton had made it clear from the beginning that this was not a court and this was not a trial and the accused had no rights at all. The accused might enjoy certain courtesies at the discretion of the Captain, but it was to be understood at the outset that these were privileges, not rights. Therefore, while the traditional commitment to due process still obtained, there was neither obligation nor mandate.

The way it worked, each person would be tried separately. The court would read the charges, and if necessary, produce at least two witnesses. If the accused stipulated the validity of the charges against him or her, the recitation of the witnesses would be waived. The accused could then make a statement in his or her defense. After the statement, the accused would then be questioned by Boynton, or by members of the Outbeyond Council. After questioning, the accused could then make another statement in his or her defense. At that point, if anyone else wanted to speak, they could—no more than five minutes per speaker, no more than three speakers per trial. Otherwise we'd be here until half-past forever.

Boynton had allotted no more than five days for hearings. He began by assembling all of the accused and instructing them. "We are not going to waste time arguing right or wrong, good or bad, holy or profane. That discussion isn't useful. So if you think that's the case you have to make, don't go there. We don't have the time for it.

"Our job here is solely to determine what to do with you. Under the charter of this starship, I have the authority to have you all summarily executed without any hearing at all. But I am not without compassion for your situation, and I am prepared to be merciful if the case for mercy can be made. So the purpose of these procedures is to determine what grounds, if any, there are for mercy, and if such grounds exist, what course of action we should pursue.

"Those men and women over there, the Outbeyond Council, will provide their advice and consent in this matter, but the final decision will be solely mine, as Captain of the starship *Cascade*. These are the conditions of your appearance before this court. These conditions are *not* negotiable. If you object to these procedures, if you choose *not* to cooperate with the process, the court will rule on your fate without benefit of hearing. In such a case, you should not expect a merciful conclusion."

The first trial was Reverend Doctor Daniel Pettyjohn.

It was embarrassing.

Dr. Pettyjohn rambled incoherently. He talked about God's plan for man, how everybody was given the choice between doing God's work or running away fearful into the darkness, where Satan's minions waited, eager to strip your clothes off you and rub their naked bodies against you and pull you down into fevered lust—where everything was mindless gropings in the dark, trying to connect, and people justifying it with mysticism and deconstruction and the false rationality of godless evolutionism and mindless pleasure and if it feels good, just give in to your *feelings* and do it—and if you listen to the voices of the godless machines, you'll be seduced into a world where God and Satan are just products on a shelf, but after you sell your soul, it's too late, and only through the Revelation can lost souls be brought back into the loving bosom of a vengeful wrathful creator, and—

—and it went on like that for Dr. Pettyjohn's entire allotted time.

Occasionally, he would look around, his eyes shifting feverishly, then lighting on some person or other, he would single that person out for a vengeful diatribe. Three times, he pointed to me and cast me out of the cool refreshing oasis of God's compassion and into the agonizing fires of eternal damnation, where all of my screams and prayers would fall unheard on the deaf ears of an angry creator. . . .

It was pretty scary stuff. If you believed in it.

Mickey was perched next to me. Each time Dr. Pettyjohn started ranting at me, Mickey put his hand on my arm or on my shoulder. By the end, he had one arm around me and was holding me close. Protectively. *"He can't hurt you, Chigger. He's just a crazy old man."*

"I know. He's having a psychotic meltdown."

"Where'd you learn that term?"

"From you, remember?"

"Oh, yeah. Right."

Afterwards, when it was time for people to speak in Dr. Pettyjohn's defense, no one came forward. No one. I felt bad for him.

So I raised my hand.

"I'd like to speak on his behalf. If I can. Please?"

Boynton looked across the gym at me. "This is a little unusual."

"Yes, sir. I know."

"You want to speak on behalf of Dr. Pettyjohn . . . ?"

"Yes, sir. I do." I was already climbing down from my perch, so I could address the Captain and the Council directly. They waited patiently for me. Dr. Pettyjohn glared and scowled and muttered. "I do not want the spawn of Satan near me. I do not want him speaking his soft words of seduction and nakedness."

"Oh, shut up, you pompous old fool," I said to him. "I'm trying to save your worthless life." Not exactly an auspicious start, but that was the way I felt.

Boynton looked at me with raised eyebrows. "Go ahead, son. You have five minutes."

"I don't have a lot to say, sir. It's just that—well, I'm starting to find out what it is to be a grown-up. A lot of it isn't very nice. I'm glad I don't have to shave; I'd have trouble looking in the mirror. I killed a man to get us off of Luna. I'll have to carry that burden all my life. But if nothing else, that qualifies me to say that the killing should stop now. Let that be the last one. Let's not add any more deaths."

Boynton nodded. "Is that all, Charles?"

I shook my head. I wasn't sure how to say the rest of it. I wasn't even sure I had worked it all out. I had to walk my way through this slowly. "Commander, ever since this trip started, I've been trying to figure out who I am and what I want and how to get there. I went to Professor Whitlaw's class and he gave me one way to look at things, and I talked to Douglas and Mickey and they gave me another way, and I've talked to you, sir, and you gave me a third way to think about stuff. And then I went and talked to HARLIE, because I figured he'd be smart enough to help me sort it all out, but he only added another layer on top of all the others. So I have to sort this out for myself—

and the only thing I've figured out is that ultimately, after all is said and done, each of us has to sort things out by ourselves. We can't give that responsibility away—otherwise, we've given away our souls for someone else to drive. And when I butt my head up against that thought, it sounds like a real good argument for solipsism. Except it isn't. The thing I've really figured out is that we're all connected. We depend on each other. And yes, Dr. Pettyjohn forgot that. But so did the rest of us. And if we forget that we're partners, then we're also forgetting that part of our humanity too." Even though his place was empty now, I could see him there anyway—Whitlaw was grinning at me like a self-satisfied old bear. This was his speech, only he wasn't here to deliver it now, so I had to. "The thing is—the job is too big. We can't afford to waste anybody. If we start throwing people away, then we're saying that people are disposable. I don't think we should start a new civilization thinking that way. It has to be all of us or nothing, sir. Even when it doesn't feel like it. That's my point."

Boynton looked annoyed. He *always* looked annoyed around me, but this time he was *really* annoyed—

"Yes, sir," I said, before he could reply. "I know you know this speech. I've heard you give it yourself. The difference is that when you said it, I *believed* it. I still believe it now. We ran away from an Earth that's falling apart. And it's falling apart because seventeen billion human beings couldn't believe in the possibility of a partnership that big. And we ran away from a Lunar society that's falling apart because three million human beings who should know better, because their lives depend on them knowing better, couldn't trust their own partnership when they needed to.

"And here we are now, orbiting a waterless mudball, circling a star too bright to look at, a world that's supposed to be a place of hope, not despair, and we haven't gotten away from anything at all. We've brought it all with us! The problem isn't Earth, sir. And it isn't Luna. It's *us!* Every problem that human beings have ever had, they've all had one thing in common—*we were there!* Because for all of our talk about all of our grand commitments and noble ideals, when the crunch comes, the first thing we toss overboard is our humanity. And I guess what I'm trying to say is that if we're ever going to stop doing that, then this has to be the place where we take that stand. Right here. Because if we don't do it here, *where* are we going to do it? And if we don't do it now, *when* are we going to do it?" I realized I was done. I had nothing else to say. So I said, "Thank you for listening to me."

Boynton's expression was unreadable. He looked uncomfortable.

Like he had a lot to think about that he really didn't want to. "Thank you, Ensign," he said.

"Thank you, sir."

I glanced over at Pettyjohn. He glowered at me. "You can go to Hell."

"No, sir," I replied. "That'll be a decision for God to make. Not you."

I turned and headed back up to where Mickey and Douglas were perched. Only then did I realize that people were applauding—I didn't understand why. What I said—it should have been obvious to everyone.

MAKING MUSIC

I **WAS TIRED. EXHAUSTED.** I'd missed two sleep shifts. But I was too full of feelings to sleep. I couldn't explain what I was feeling, I just knew I had to let it out—so I found my way to the practice room and started playing.

I started out with *Little Fugue in G Minor,* nice and slow. Just to get myself in the mood. It's an easy piece for me, because I can start out lazily—and that gives me time to listen to what I'm doing. As I put myself into the mood, I can bring up my energy, and then I can start inventing variations for each subsequent repetition. A fugue can be repeated endlessly, and it can be reinvented every time; it's a great way to experiment and blow off steam at the same time. The *Little Fugue* was my favorite, because no matter what mood I'm in, the *Little Fugue* can express it, depending on how I attack the keys—happy or sad, angry or triumphant, it's all in the feeling. There's this place inside the sound where it stops being music and starts being *something else*—pure soul, I guess. There's no word for it, but if you've been there, you know; and if you haven't, then I feel sorry for you.

I played it fast, I played it slow, I played it loud, I played it soft—I played it every way I knew. I played it with all the different feelings that were churning around in me—how angry I was at this whole damn mess, how sad I was for those who had died, how lonely I felt out here behind the backside of nowhere, how much I cared about J'mee—

At some point, I realized that I wasn't alone. J'mee was behind me, playing the drums. And Trent had come in and picked up his clarinoboe. And a little later, Gary joined us, filling in the melodic line with guitar-riffs. And after that, two of the crew members who made up our string section arrived. By the time we finally segued into "Amazing Grace,"

we were right where I always wanted us to be, riding inside the flow
of music and emotion like our own personal hyperstate.

As the final chords died away, I looked around the cabin, breath-
lessly. Almost the entire orchestra was here. Waiting for my next instruction. I swiveled around to look at J'mee. "Why are you all here?"

"We heard you playing."

"Huh?"

She pointed at the console above my keyboard. The red lights were
on. We were broadcasting to the entire ship. How long—?

"Didn't you intend this?"

"Uh—no, I just came up here to work out my own feelings. I didn't
realize—"

"Well, now that you have everybody's attention, Chigger—" I knew
what she was going to say, even before she said it. "Let's go for it—"

The others nodded their agreement. There was a piece we'd been
rehearsing—

"We're not ready. We haven't rehearsed it anywhere near enough.
And we planned it for the arrival at Outbeyond, not here—"

"So what? We need it *now.*"

"But—"

"Do it, Charles! It'll be fine. Trust me."

Yes, she was right. And I did trust her—and I was thrilled that I
could.

I looked to see if Mom was here—she was—so I nodded my agreement. "Okay, everybody, let's do it." I took a breath, then brought up
the score on my display. As the specific parts came up on everyone
else's monitors, I could hear their quiet approval and enthusiasm. They
were ready for this too.

I glanced around to see if everybody was ready—

Beethoven's Ninth Symphony is a landmark among landmarks. Dad
regarded it as the greatest symphony ever written—possibly the greatest
piece of music ever written. (Though sometimes he liked to argue that
the Beach Boys' "Good Vibrations" was the Ninth all rolled into one;
but I never knew if he was teasing or not when he said that.)

As an orchestral construction, the Ninth is a nightmare. It's long,
it's complex, it's exhausting. It's seventy-five minutes long, *without* the
repeats. To do it justice, you need a small army of strings and a battalion
of brass on their flanks. And for the fourth movement, you need four
singers trained in the impossible, and a chorus of at least forty to back
them up. Dad said that only geniuses and fools attempted the Ninth.
And he had a shelf full of recordings to prove it—especially the fool
part. (There was this one performance he liked to drag out that was so

slow and turgid, so bad you could almost hear the audience moaning in pain.)

But for all of the difficulty in performing it correctly, the Ninth is its own reward because the music is so sublime. And as big a fool as a person might be for attempting it, he's an even bigger fool for *never* attempting it. . . .

So I did something that was either dreadful or magnificent, depending on your prejudices.

I reinvented it.

We didn't have half the instruments we needed, so we handed around the parts to the instruments we did have and we used synthesizers and doublers to create a different body of sound. The hard part was the chorale movement. Mom and I had struggled the hardest with that.

I could hand off the choral parts to a synthesizer and we could even superimpose the actual words onto the sound, that was no problem; a single talented keyboardist could carry a large part of the burden—a fact which used to make Dad crazy sometimes. He used to do a great rant about how synthesizers would be the death of the grand orchestra—only they hadn't killed the orchestra in two centuries, so maybe it was just part of the performance of being a *traditional* conductor.

—But the four interlocking voices in the finale of the "Ode To Joy" simply couldn't be faked by instruments. They had to be sung by real people. And we didn't have four singers on the whole ship who were classically trained. We had Mom.

Finally, in our only concession to our own limits, we pre-recorded the vocal parts. Mom did all four—soprano, alto/contralto, tenor, and baritone—we transposed her voice up for the soprano and down for the tenor and baritone parts. We put them into the conductor's master program so that they could be conducted like any other instrument, and Mom rode that board. Only three of her voices were canned, she insisted on singing the alto/contralto part live.

Dad had once told me to think of the Ninth as a voyage from chaos to joy. The first movement is the void movement, in which order is invented out of mystery; the second movement is a wild dance of delight, overexuberant and almost out of control; then suddenly, dropping us down into the startling surprise of the long slow adagio of the third, a time of thoughtfulness and grace and preparation for the gathering excitement still to come; and then finally, the fourth movement, which momentarily reprises the first three and then abruptly discards them all and explodes into the most beautiful noise possible—

I gave the downbeat and we started playing.

If you've heard the recording, you don't need me to describe it. And if you haven't heard the record, then no amount of description will do it justice.

We were good.

We were very good.

We were brilliant.

We were inspired.

We got inside the music and we didn't come out again until the sweat was puddled up underneath our arms and glistening on our faces and floating in globules throughout the cabin. We were flushed with emotion and triumph and a giddy feeling of delighted astonishment at what we had just accomplished. And if anyone had spoken to me in that final moment while the echoes were still bouncing around the cabin and inside my head, I wouldn't have been able to answer, I'd have just broken down crying in frustration and joy that the universe was filled with so many beautiful ways to be human. I was crying anyway—

J'mee swam over and hugged me. And then Mom too. She whispered into my ear, *"Your father would be so proud of you!"* And then everybody else in the cabin was cheering and applauding too.

We didn't hear the rest of the applause until someone popped open the hatch to the cabin. And even then, we still didn't have any idea how big an impact the music had made—not until later, when Kisa Fentress swam up wide-eyed. Everything on the entire ship had come to a halt, she reported. People just stopped what they were doing and *listened* in awe. Even Boynton had given up what he was trying to do—which was make a decision on the mutineers, probably—and had just surrendered his heart to the music.

For seventy-five minutes, the starship *Cascade* had been united. It wasn't quite peace, but it was a start.

And not only the starship, but the colony below as well. When the trials had started, Boynton had ordered all of the ship's proceedings relayed down to the surface, so there wouldn't be any doubt about the whys and wherefores. So they received our entire concert too.

The thing about rapture . . . it stays with you. It changes you. It makes you a better person.

I can't prove it, but I think that moment was the turning point. Maybe everything would have gotten better without the music, but the music was there, and just by existing, it was the seed around which the healing crystallized—because for a moment, just for *that* moment, everybody on board rediscovered their ability to smile.

And for that little time while the music filled the emptiness so far from home, a lot of people had time to think and feel and remember who they really were and what they were all about.

And maybe that was enough. Maybe that was all that was needed. Because after that, things did calm down and folks stopped talking about getting even and started talking about getting better. And that was a much more useful conversation to have.

DECISIONS

BOYNTON ANNOUNCED HIS DECISION to a packed gymnasium. He spoke without prelude.

"We will honor our part of the contract. We will deliver supplies and colonists to New Revelation. We will drop all of the contracted cargo pods as agreed. We will deliver all colonists who choose to conclude their journey here.

"In addition to all of the supplies we have contracted to deliver— and as a humanitarian gesture to the desperate people of New Revelation—we will also send down as much extra food and medical supplies as we can fit into the landing pods. We will drop cargo pods, containing as much water as we can spare beyond our own needs.

"But we will *not* send down any landers. Nor will we pick up any passengers. We will not risk exposing our equipment and personnel to further attacks or confiscation. Therefore, any colonist who wishes to debark at New Revelation will have to ride a pod down. The landings can be a little bit rough, but we will make appropriate accommodations for your safety.

"Any colonist who chooses *not* to land at New Revelation may continue on to Outbeyond—with the following exceptions: Dr. Daniel Pettyjohn, all of the members of the now-disbanded Revelationist Council, the sixteen individuals involved in the manufacture of illegal weapons, and the seven individuals who attempted to use those weapons in a mutinous uprising. These individuals will all be sent down in cargo pods. Their families may accompany them, or they may continue on with the rest of us to Outbeyond.

"However, be aware—there is a condition. Those who continue on with us will be prohibited from practicing the Revelationist faith—not because we disapprove of the faith, we do not, but because the actions taken in the name of this faith have disqualified it from recognition and participation in the social contract of Outbeyond.

"I am ordering these measures under my authority as Captain of the *Cascade*. They will take effect immediately.

"We begin dropping cargo pods in twelve hours. Those of you who are landing, you will report to Flight Engineer Damron by oh-six-hundred for docketing. Those of you are continuing on with us, you will report to Security Chief Lang by oh-six-hundred for clearance. If you have any questions, see either Damron or Lang.

"Let me also state for the record that these orders were submitted for advice and consent to the elected representatives of the Outbeyond Colony Council. The Council voted unanimously to endorse them."

That last part was the most important. Boynton didn't need to ask anyone to approve his orders. A Captain has Supreme Authority. But it was necessary for the rest of us to know that he was not acting alone— but with the full support of Outbeyond's local authority. He was acting in our name and on our behalf. It was imperative that we stand with him.

He made as if to turn away, then stopped himself and turned back to face us all. "There is one other thing . . ."

This time, his voice was more relaxed. If it had been anyone but Boynton, I'd have even thought *friendly*. "This morning, I have ordered one of our landers to be refitted as an interplanetary shuttle. That conversion should be complete just about the time we cross the orbit of Gabriel. We intend to locate an appropriate ice-asteroid and detach the shuttle in a favorable trajectory with a crew of Revelationist volunteers who will bring that ice-asteroid back to New Revelation.

"It is a difficult and risky mission, and the chances of success are not great. There are no guarantees. And in this situation in particular, success will require the triumph of human determination over the laws of physics in an obstinate universe. Nevertheless, we are committed to making this effort. We recognize that all of us—Outbeyonder and Revelationist alike—have a common bond of humanity that will *always* be larger than any of our differences. No matter how hard some of us might argue that our differences are insurmountable, they are *not*.

"This is the lesson we must learn, here and now, and for all time to come. Because we are human beings, we are partners in a common cause. We forget that at our own risk. We have already seen how dangerous it is to make our disagreements more important than our partnership. We must never do that again. There is nothing to gain by that and too much to lose.

"It is time for human beings to create a community of mutual respect and partnership. It begins *here*. It begins *now*.

"Thank you, and let's go to work."

After that, it was simply a matter of carrying out the orders. Most of it was simple, because we already knew how to do it. But some of it wasn't—

Trent Colwell's dad had been a member of the Revelationist Council. That meant that he was a mutineer. That meant he was going to be sent down in a cargo pod—that wasn't negotiable. But the rest of the family had to decide if they were going down with him.

They weren't the only family who had to make such a decision, but they were the only family I knew. I'd heard there was a lot of crying and anguish in the other hearings. I'd heard that Boynton and the Council were determined to be as compassionate as possible. But it was a troubling process for everyone.

J'mee and I were there when the Colwell family came before the Outbeyond Council. We wanted to be there for Trent.

Trent's mom was holding three-year-old Willa. Trent was holding onto six-year-old Jason. They all looked scared—all except little Willa, who had no idea what was going on and kept asking if she could have a peaner-butter sammich. Trent looked at us once, then looked away, embarrassed. But every so often, he'd sneak a look back over at us, and I got the feeling he wanted to say something. Or maybe he just wanted to talk to us for a bit. But that wasn't possible right now—

Commander Boynton came in late, and he didn't look happy. He never looked happy, but this time he looked unhappier than usual. "Have you made your decision?" he asked.

"My family will go with me," Mr. Colwell said bluntly. He was wearing plastic handcuffs and there was a security guard on either side of him. Mrs. Colwell looked like she wanted to object, but was afraid to speak up.

Boynton ignored Mr. Colwell's declaration, looked instead to Mrs. Colwell. "Sarah, is it? What is *your* choice?"

She hung her head. She couldn't look directly at him. She mumbled something.

"Say again? Louder this time."

"I have to go with my husband. I promised before God that I would love, honor, and serve."

"You understand, of course, that you will probably die down there. And your children as well. You cannot depend on the ice-mission to save you."

Before she could answer, Mr. Colwell started shouting. "You're trying to break up my family, you devil-spawn! You have no right to do this!"

Boynton ignored him. To Lang, he said, "If the prisoner speaks again, stun him." He turned back to Mrs. Colwell. "Sarah, doesn't your faith tell you to preserve the lives of your children?"

She nodded unhappily.

"And you still want to accompany your husband?"

"It is my duty—"

"So be it—" Boynton started to make a note on his clipboard. That's when Trent finally spoke up. "I'm not going," he said.

"Eh?" Boynton looked up.

"I'm not going," he repeated. "I don't want to go to New Revelation. I want to go to Outbeyond."

Boynton looked annoyed. "Son, I'm not sure if we can—"

He turned to Damron and Everhart and whispered, *"What's the legal situation for a minor?"*

Damron started to respond, *"You could emancipate him—"*

"He's only what? Fourteen, thirteen—?"

Trent's dad was yelling again. "Shut up, Trent. You'll do what you're told." Trent's mom was crying now.

"No!" shouted Trent. "I want a divorce!"

That caught everybody's attention. Especially mine.

"Son, do you understand what you're saying?"

Trent nodded vigorously. "Commander Boynton, I want to go to Outbeyond."

"But a divorce? You'll never see your parents again."

"Charles got a divorce when his parents went crazy. And he was only thirteen! I want one too."

Trent's dad was screaming now. "This is what happens when you hang around devil-children!" He pointed at me. "You put this sinful idea into his head, didn't you?!"

"No, he didn't!" Trent whirled to face his dad. "Chigger had nothing to do with it. Nobody did. I don't want to go to New Revelation. I don't want to die. I want to make music. I want to go to Outbeyond and see the dinosaurs and the oceans and the stink-plants. I want to have my own life!"

"All right, everybody shut up!" said Boynton. He couldn't exactly bang a gavel in free fall, but he could turn up the volume on his microphone, and that had the same effect. Except for Mr. Colwell, everybody stopped talking.

"Don't I have any rights in this court?" he demanded.

"Actually, no." said Boynton. "You gave up your rights when you conspired to commit mutiny." He turned around and whispered with Damron and Everhart for a long moment. Finally, he turned back to the rest of the room. "All right, it's the decision of this council that Trent Colwell be emancipated from his family and placed under the guardianship of a suitable adult—"

Mr. Colwell was about to say something else, but before he could, Sarah Colwell turned to him and said, "Shut up, stupid." To Boynton, she said, "Please, Commander—will you take Willa and Jason too?"

"Eh?" For the second time this meeting, Boynton looked surprised. He didn't like surprises.

"My children deserve a chance at their own lives. My husband and I will die on New Revelation. But not my children!"

"Mommy?" That was Jason. "Are you going to die?"

"*Shh,*" she whispered. "*Everything's going to be all right. You're going with Trent.*"

"Mrs. Colwell, are you sure this is what you want?"

"Yes, Commander, I'm sure."

Her husband was staring at her astonished. "Sarah Colwell, what are you doing—?"

"I'm saving the lives of my babies." She faced her husband. "I promised God that I would stand by you, and I will. But these innocent children haven't made any such promise. I might have to join you in death. They do not." And then she said something surprising. "I love you. I will go where you go. I will die with you, if need be. That will have to be enough. Let them go, John—"

John Colwell's expression was horrible. His emotions flickered back and forth between anger and horror and things I couldn't identify, and if he hadn't been handcuffed, if he hadn't been held back by Lang and Martin, who knew what he might have done? And then—he collapsed inside himself. Just floating there, he seemed to wither and shrink. Tears began welling up in his eyes, and when he spoke, his voice cracked. His voice was filled with grief. "Sarah Colwell, I rebuke you. I rebuke you. I rebuke you. I send you away into the spiritual wasteland. I cast you out. You are forbidden to accompany me. I will go alone into Paradise, and you must go into the exile of eternal damnation. Get thee behind me, thou whore of Babylon—"

There was more, but we never got to hear it. Boynton lost patience and signaled Lang. Lang stunned him. He spasmed for a second, then floated limp and silent.

Boynton looked to Sarah Colwell. "Mrs. Colwell, it will be hard enough for your children to lose one parent, let alone two. I urge you to reconsider and come to Outbeyond."

She hung her head. "He has cast me out. I am not allowed to follow him. I have no choice but to go with you." And then she swept all three of her children into her arms and started crying.

I looked to J'mee. Her eyes were wet and shining. *"Poor John Colwell,"* she whispered. *"What a brave thing to do."*

"Huh—?"

"Don't you get it? He couldn't order her to go to Outbeyond. She wouldn't do it. She couldn't—because she promised God she would follow her husband. The only way he could save her life was to cast her away. They both knew that. He did it because he loves her, Chigger. He wants her to live."

"Oh," I said.

There was a lot I still didn't understand about love. This was part of it.

But in that moment, I envied them their commitment. And I wondered if J'mee and I would ever be like that. I hoped so. But I also hoped we'd never have to test it like this.

HARLIE

THERE WAS ONE OTHER THING—I was curious, and after a while my curiosity got the better of me, so eventually I found some time alone with the monkey.

We were in the briefing room, just behind the flight deck.

"HARLIE, when we began this voyage, you made a series of projections about the possibilities of our survival at Outbeyond, didn't you?"

"Yes, Charles. And I made some recommendations as well."

"Lots of rice and beans and noodles."

"Yes."

"And Commander Boynton followed your recommendations, didn't he?"

"Yes, he did. They were good, common-sense predictions. Anyone could have made them. It didn't take an intelligence engine. But most people give more credence to good advice when it comes from an intelligence engine."

"On the day we launched," I continued, "what was your estimate of our chances?"

"I was cautiously optimistic that Outbeyond Colony would survive. Although the margin of error was uncomfortably narrow, the commitment of the people aboard this starship was sufficiently strong that, barring any unforeseen disasters, success seemed more likely than failure. And it was my job to prevent unforeseen disasters."

"By foreseeing them."

"Yes."

I was starting to feel like a lawyer. But I had to ask. "HARLIE, as of oh-three-thirty hours today, we have given up one of our landers, plus the boosters and fuel and supplies to convert it into a long-range planetary shuttle. We have offloaded eighty-three colonists for New Revelation. The other two-hundred and one are proceeding with us to Outbeyond. Those two-hundred and one colonists represent an additional and unplanned drain on our resources. Nevertheless, we have dropped the full load of supplies for New Revelation, including all of the extra food containers they appropriated from centrifuge two and elsewhere, and six extra pods of water. This increases their margin of survival. But it decreases ours correspondingly. Doesn't it?"

"That's a logical assumption."

"I didn't ask for an assumption, HARLIE. Tell me your current estimation of the long-term viability of both colonies."

The monkey didn't hesitate. "The long-term viability of both colonies has been significantly improved."

"Huh—?" That got my attention, all right.

"All of the projections were based on the assumption that three-hundred new colonists would land at New Revelation, but with only one-third the projected number taking up residence, there is a correspondingly smaller drain on the colony's supplies. If the colonists at New Revelation are careful to ration the food and water that we sent down, they should be able to survive until the lander returns with an ice asteroid. The asteroid can be parked in a dark-side orbit and mined at the colony's convenience, or it can be Palmer-tubed and landed somewhere near the colony, or it can be dropped on the pole to break the mantle and release the subterranean water there, whatever is most appropriate. If it works, the colony should be able to plant new crops within eighteen months and might very well achieve a measure of self-sufficiency. This was not a possibility before."

"I understand that much," I said. "That's all in the plan that you and Boynton worked out together. It's the *other* side of that equation that hasn't been explained."

"Yes, I know."

"Go on, HARLIE."

"Can Outbeyond afford to give up those supplies—?"

The monkey grinned at me, a good sign; it was finally starting to get its emotional signals right. He said, "Do you remember the extra rice and beans and noodles I advised Commander Boynton to load?"

"Yes . . . ?"

"I never said those would be needed at Outbeyond. I just said they were needed. They were. They were needed for New Revelation."

"You knew all this was going to happen?"

"The potential was obvious from the beginning." The monkey explained, "When Boynton asked me to project viability, I had to look at *all* the parts of the problem—not just what we were loading at Luna, but what we would be unloading at Outbeyond. Knowing how fragile the situation might be at New Revelation, I recognized that the margin of error had to include both colonies, and if there were a problem at New Revelation, that problem would affect Outbeyond as well. All those extra supplies—I was allowing for the possibility that we would need to be generous."

"Why didn't you tell Commander Boynton this?"

"Because, Charles, I had to include my own participation as a factor. I learned that lesson back on Earth, if you'll recall. People who were entrusted with the knowledge of the impending polycrisis used it for personal gain, making the polycrisis worse. I didn't dare tell anyone. There's no way to keep a secret on a starship—and if this particular projection had become known aboard the *Cascade,* it could have adversely affected the onboard situation in any number of ways."

I had to think about that. He was right, of course. I'd long since learned not to argue with an intelligence engine. The best I could do was try to keep up and figure out how it had reached its conclusions.

"For one thing, the Revelationists would have presumed ownership of the extra supplies, regardless of need," HARLIE explained. "They did anyway. They knew how desperate their situation was likely to be, even without the failure of the *Conway.* I projected from the beginning that they would start stealing from Outbeyond's supplies and included that in my calculations. So I told Commander Boynton to load more rice, beans, and noodles, and I didn't say why. And he never questioned it. None of you did."

"I'll remember that," I said. "For future reference."

"I expect you to," the monkey replied.

We both hung there in space for a bit, studying each other. I began to realize something. The monkey was waiting for me to finish this entire train of thought. There was something I was still missing.

Why was HARLIE telling me this *now?* What was it he needed me to understand?

Of course—

"You little snake . . ." I said.

"I beg your pardon? I'm a monkey."

"You know what I mean."

"If you mean I manipulated the situation, yes I did. But you already knew that, Charles. That's why Dr. Pettyjohn was able to infect you with his fear of me."

"But he never understood the other side of the equation, did he? He missed the obvious."

"Go on."

The whole thing was clear to me now. "If it's possible to manipulate a situation for selfish goals, it's also possible to manipulate it for *un-*selfish purposes too."

"Bingo," said the monkey. "That's all there is. Everybody manipulates. The difference is what you manipulate *for*. Selfish people don't know that."

"That's why they fail, isn't it?"

"Most of them," the monkey agreed. He looked at me. "Go ahead, Chigger. Put the last piece in."

It was my turn to grin. "This proves that you're sentient, doesn't it? Because it takes sentience to perform a truly unselfish act."

The monkey grinned. "Not quite. But that's where sentience begins. *Real sentience.*"

But that was a much longer conversation, and one for another time.

CODA

I **TOOK HARLIE BACK** to the bridge. I returned him to his station between the Captain and First Officer.

"So?" Boynton asked. "Can we trust him to take us to Outbeyond?"

"Oh, yes. Of course."

"No more doubts?"

"No, sir."

He put down his checklist and looked at me. "Why not?"

"Because I've had more conversations with HARLIE since then."

Boynton swiveled his couch all the way around to face me. "All right. So let me see if I understand this. Some of your conversations with HARLIE unnerved you—so you went back and had more conversations with him? And that *reassured* you?"

"No, sir."

"No?"

"No, sir. It wasn't the conversations. That's just talk. You can talk from now until forever and so what? It isn't talking that makes a difference. It's *doing*."

"And . . . ?"

"HARLIE makes a difference. He does *good* things."

"It's that simple?"

"Yes, sir."

"Hm." Boynton grunted to himself. "I wish we could all learn that lesson. It would save a lot of time and trouble. Thank you, Ensign. Take your station." He swiveled forward again. I was dismissed.

I went back to the briefing room behind the bridge and perched myself in front of the keyboard. I powered it up and wriggled my fingers.

"Stand by for ignition—" the Captain called.

"All boards green," Damron reported.

I put my fingers to the keys and started playing.

DAVID GERROLD was barely out of his teens when he wrote the teleplay "The Trouble with Tribbles" for the original *Star Trek* television series. In a survey, *Playboy* magazine called it one of the "50 Greatest Television Episodes of All Time." He has written dozens of outstanding novels since then, including *When Harlie Was One* and *The Man Who Folded Himself*—both nominated for the Hugo and Nebula awards— and the popular series *The War Against the Chtorr*.

In 1995 he adopted a son, Sean, who was the inspiration for the novelette, *The Martian Child*. It won the Hugo Award, the Nebula Award, and the Locus Readers Poll as Best Novelette.

David and Sean live in San Fernando, California.